VOYAGES

VOYAGES

A Maine Franco-American Reader

Nelson Madore & Barry Rodrigue
Editors

with
Corinna Miller & Chase Hébert

Normand Beaupré
French Language Editor

Tilbury House, Publishers
Gardiner, Maine

The Franco-American Collection
University of Southern Maine/Lewiston-Auburn
Lewiston, Maine

Tilbury House, Publishers
2 Mechanic Street
Gardiner, Maine 04345
800–582–1899 • www.tilburyhouse.com

The Franco-American Collection
University of Southern Maine/Lewiston-Auburn
51 Westminster Street
Lewiston, Maine 04240
207–753–6545 • www.usm.maine.edu/lac/franco

First paperback edition: October 2007
10 9 8 7 6 5 4 3 2 1

Library of Congress Cataloging-in-Publication Data

Voyages : a Maine Franco-American reader / Nelson Madore & Barry Rodrigue, editors ; with Corinna Miller and Chase Hébert. -- 1st pbk. ed.
p. cm.
Includes bibliographical references and index.
ISBN 978-0-88448-294-9 (pbk. : alk. paper)
1. French Americans--Maine--History. 2. French Americans--Maine--Social conditions. 3. French Americans--Maine--Literary collections. 4. French-Canadians--Maine--History. 5. French-Canadians--Maine--Social conditions. 6. Acadians--Maine--History. 7. Acadians--Maine--Social conditions. 8. Maine--Ethnic relations. 9. Maine--Literary collections. I. Madore, Nelson, 1943- II. Rodrigue, Barry H.
F30.F8V695 2007
974.1'00441--dc22

2007018129

Front Cover: Detail from Samuel de Champlain, "Carte Geographique de la Nouvelle Franse," 1612. Courtesy of the Osher Map Library and Smith Center for Cartographic Education at the University of Southern Maine.

Copyediting by Barbara Diamond, A Word to the Wise, Litchfield, Maine
Printed and bound by Maple Vail, Kirkwood, New York

Dedicated to

our descendents and neighbors,

who deserve to know about what has passed before

TABLE OF CONTENTS

LIST OF ILLUSTRATIONS

FOREWORD

At eighteen, when I left the protection of the St. John Valley, I began to learn that I was different. I felt like a cultural prisoner from then and throughout my young adulthood as I tried to make my way through the educational and professional systems of Maine. Not until then did I learn that I was Franco-American, as opposed to American, and that the contributions I would make would be restricted to certain acceptable accomplishments. Although I was proud of my heritage, I learned that it had to play a subordinate part in my life if I were to succeed beyond the role expectations of a native French speaker in Maine.

In my younger years, I attended a one-room school, grades K–8, taught in both English and French. I did not understand English in the first years, having come from an entirely French-speaking home. I believed the rest of the United States was like my Franco-American community in the St. John Valley. In 1957 I began riding the bus to Fort Kent High School, where all of a sudden, one day, French was banned. English was declared the only language to be used both in classes and outside of classes. French was out of bounds anywhere anytime on school grounds. This did not seem right to me, and I led a protest which succeeded in ending this rule.

From high school, I volunteered for the army, where my ability to speak French was highly valued and I felt no discrimination. After the service, however, returning to Orono, Maine, for college, I was once again a cultural prisoner. Professors and advisors tried to make me believe my culture was wrong and that I must assimilate into mainstream culture. They required me to take voice and diction in order to get rid of my French accent, as if I were second class from a second-class culture. This precipitated a crisis of identity for me. I felt un-American, not free to speak. Both speaking French and speaking English with a French accent were wrong. I did not want to assimilate, to be melted into a melting pot. Getting rid of my Frenchness was impossible, like having surgery to remove my brain or heart. And besides, I wondered, what is wrong with having a French accent? I was not rebelling against English language and culture. I was truly proud of both my French and American heritage.

On the social side, ethnic jokes and traditional putdowns like "Pardon my French" and "He must be French," represented public opinion that any mistake made was due to French influence or French heritage.

The trap grew more subtle as I pursued my master's and CAS degrees. Even my French was corrected, criticized because it was not Parisian. Neither St. John Valley French nor Québec French were accepted as languages then, and their native speakers came up against a "glass ceiling" effectively barring them from doctoral studies. Not only university work, but certain professions were considered closed to Franco-Americans; others, trades mostly, were encouraged as suitable employment. Everyone was telling me I couldn't speak correct French, couldn't speak correct English, and couldn't aspire to certain jobs. To help myself out of this plight, I should learn English well and forget French. Command of English made one upwardly mobile. All this talk about getting to the top, however, was not really truthful, because there was a professional plateau for Franco-Americans. Even those who spoke English well usually wound up doing drywall, plumbing, and other working-class jobs.

This has been a phenomenon of New England. Outside of Maine and the Northeast, this attitude toward French Americans is not existent. In Maine, however, the French were relegated to loyal working class but not considered intelligent enough to be supervisors. Many Franco-Americans changed their names to English equivalents in order to be accepted into management, the upper middle class, and for advanced university degrees. Others, like me, rejected for doctorates, went elsewhere for advanced study. Now the University of Maine has a different policy and more Franco-Americans are accepted into doctoral studies. The French Department has also expanded its boundaries to include Franco-American French and Québec French as acceptable languages.

Speaking for myself and, I believe, other Franco-Americans in Maine, I can say we did not mind learning English, but we did not want to have the language of our families and heritage blotted out. We want to preserve French language and be bilingual. We want to study French in school and become literate in French as well as English. We are proud to be French. Maine Franco-Americans have contributed much to the cultural heritage, economy, and political arena of New England. Current trends are encouraging a new appreciation and acceptance of ethnic cultures, including the Franco-American. Hopefully this attitude will grow and continue, putting an end to the days of marginality and low self-esteem, and ushering in a new century of cultural awareness, tolerance, and celebration.

Nelson Madore
Waterville, Maine

APPRECIATION

We would like to extend our sincere appreciation to the many people who assisted us in the production of this volume. From the start of this project ten years ago, historian C. Stewart Doty encouraged us, gave many good recommendations, and critiqued parts of the present volume. Nikelle Henderson, Susan Redner, and Brittany Oxley typed articles, made phone calls, sent letters, and did whatever was asked of them. Tracey Mousseau and Erika Jordan helped format early versions of the manuscript. Donat Boisvert of the University of Southern Maine's Franco-American Collection helped to select articles, find photographs, work on some translations, and even came up with a version of this book's title. The Advisory Board of the University of Southern Maine's Franco-American Collection provided the investment that allowed the book's production to move forward. Officers, faculty, and staff in the University of Maine System were instrumental in the administrative collaboration that made this book happen, including Chancellor Richard Pattenaude and—at the University of Southern Maine—President Joe Wood, Deans Zark Van Zandt and Marv Druker, and Pam Roy, as well as the Legal Affairs Office. Pénélope Markle provided invaluable editorial suggestions and Kenaï Rodrigue helped to transcribe material. We would like to thank the Osher Map Library at the University of Southern Maine in Portland for use of the cover map, as well as to express our appreciation to its curator, Yolanda Theunissen, for her kind help in facilitating its use. Ed Churchill at the Maine State Museum also assisted with providing illustrations from the state's rich collections. Robyn Holman, director of exhibitions at the Atrium Gallery of the University of Southern Maine's Lewiston-Auburn College, provided very helpful contacts in the use of graphic art. We would like to express our gratitude to the Maine Historic Preservation Commission, especially Earle G. Shettleworth, Jr., and Leon Cranmer, for their assistance with illustrations for this text. Yvon Labbé and Lisa Desjardins Michaud at the Franco-American Centre at the University of Maine (Orono) helped us with background material on the Ku Klux Klan and other important nuances of Franco-American history. Bob Michaud at the Maine State Law Library helped with answering obscure questions of constitutional law for us, and Jeanne Valois of Laval University assisted us in the recovery of lost data.

PREFACE

When I was asked to write the preface for *Voyages: A Maine Franco-American Reader,* I beamed with pride as my mind immediately raced through the past thinking of my own experiences growing up in Maine as a Franco-American. It is my hope that each of you reading this will reflect on your own diverse and unique memories in much the same way.

When I was a child a large part of my family life included regular attendance at Catholic mass. Involvement in church was not only an important aspect of our family life, but also, it was a central component of the local community. Like so many, I remember fondly attending suppers and family gatherings at our church. I have been a member of the Knights of Columbus for over twenty years.

Even to this day with the hectic schedule that comes with being a member of Congress, I still find time to attend mass each week at St. Peter's Church in Washington. In fact, I attend services at churches across the Second District and take the time to visit with parishioners since I rarely have the flexibility to attend my home church of Saint Peter's in East Millinocket.

In 1973, like so many young people throughout Maine regardless of cultural or ethnic background, I went to work at Great Northern Paper Company in East Millinocket directly after high school, following in the footsteps of both my father and grandfather. While they are not with me today in the flesh, they, along with my mother and other family members, formed a permanent part of my spirit and character. They taught me the values of hard work, honesty, and integrity. As it had for generations of Francos before me, the mill provided good wages with good benefits and an opportunity to share in the American dream, examples of which we see all across Maine in the mill towns that are throughout our state's beautiful geography.

Working at the mill, coupled with my family upbringing, provided the framework for a belief system: that everyone who works hard and plays by the rules should have an opportunity to succeed. Equally, they also have an important responsibility to give back to their community.

Not long after graduation I decided to run for a seat in the Maine House of Representatives out of a desire to clean up the polluted Penobscot River. I wanted to clean up the river to restore it to its natural beauty for generations to come, but I also knew that the cause of its degradation was from the very mill that provided thousands of families with a decent standard of living. There had to be a way to bring people together to find a common sense solution, and I was determined to find a way to do it.

Despite being the underdog, I won that race for the legislature and worked with industry leaders and environmentalists alike to find that very solution, and we succeeded. As I met other legislators in Augusta from similar Franco backgrounds, I came to realize that being the underdog was a way of life for Francos all across Maine; we simply had to work harder and be better to convince others to arrive at our point of view.

I served ten more terms in the legislature, and it was this incredible opportunity that allowed me to experience the vast richness of our state's population and diversity. I learned that no matter what socio-economic background, what language we spoke, or what religion we practiced, we all shared in a common desire to create a better tomorrow for our communities. But for that common purpose to thrive, we also needed to protect and preserve our own individual heritage and culture; this became a central force in my legislative priorities, not just for Francos but for all cultures.

During my twenty-two years in the legislature, I worked to support the Forum Francophone des Affaires, to help restore and preserve the St. Mary's Center in Lewiston, to provide funding for the 400th anniversary of Ste. Croix Celebration, and to establish Franco-American Day at the Maine State Legislature. I even remember asking the co-chairs of the Appropriations Committee if I could display a *Québécois* flag in the committee room. Certainly none of these tasks could have been accomplished without enlisting the support and hard work of so many others, Franco or not. And in this way more and more Mainers came to appreciate the vast contributions of so many Francos all across Maine and throughout time. You will no doubt enjoy the many essays that are included in this collection.

With my unprecedented election as the first recognized Franco-American ever to be elected from Maine to federal office, I externalized my Franco-American pride further and vowed to be a proud example for Francos all across Maine. In fact, my Washington, D.C., office is filled with reminders of our shared heritage: farming the fields, logging the forests, manufacturing in the mills, and our beginnings at Ste. Croix. Two items in my office are my fondest. One is the lunch bucket I carried to work for over twenty-eight years in the paper mill. It reminds me every day to never stop working as hard as the hard-working people of Maine. The other is a pink bunny rabbit given to me by a Franco woman in Lewiston, which she told me to

Mike Michaud (center), Nelson Madore (left), Barry Rodrigue (right)
At the Two Cent Bridge, Waterville, Maine, 2007.
Photograph by Rosemary Winslow

bring to Washington in order "to never forget the little guy."

Finally, you will no doubt read stories of discrimination in this book. Fortunately, I have never been the victim of discrimination. Sadly, it wasn't so long ago that members of my parent's generation did experience this. The stories of those who have experienced it are real. Discrimination remains an important part of the history of Francos in Maine. For me, this history has deepened my resolve to work for public policies that demand respect and civil justice, and to strive for an end to discrimination against Americans for any reason.

I hope that this book will serve not only as a tribute to those who have come before us, but also as a guidepost for the future. As the *Québécois* license plate reads: *Je me souviens*. May future generations of young people remember and continue to carry forth a strong spirit that is steeped in proud tradition, and may this book serve as a road map for discovering the past and charting the future.

Michael Michaud
Millinocket, Maine
Member of Congress
2006

Introduction

RENAISSANCE: FRANCO-MAINE IN A NEW MILLENIUM[1]

Barry Rodrigue
Bath, Maine
with Dean Louder
Québec, Québec

The State of Maine penetrates into the heart of French Canada like an arrow. This is evident by looking at a map and tracing out the 45th Parallel, which divides upstate New York and Vermont from Québec. If you extend that line eastwards, two-thirds of Maine falls north of it. Since much of the state lies "inside" of Canada and provides better access to the "mother country," Franco-American contacts with Canada have been better preserved in Maine than elsewhere in the United States.

Other factors also have helped to maintain this high degree of cross-border connection. Maine's territory is larger than the rest of New England combined, and its French population is more widely dispersed. This has tended to limit the influence of the urban Franco-American elite (in contrast to the situation in southern New England). Instead, a more diverse French heritage has been preserved in Maine—one that is more French Canadian or Acadian than "Franco-American." Indeed, the French people of Maine tend to act as a bridge between southern New England and Canada.

In the north and south of Maine, in the countryside and city, the French presence remains vitally important. In 2000 almost 23 percent of Maine's population claimed French, French-Canadian, or Acadian origins. Although an obvious underestimate, this was the first U.S. census in which the French outnumbered any other ethnic group—including the English.[2] Also, over 5 percent of the population spoke French at home, the largest percentage of any state in the Union.[3] Thus, Maine is arguably—in relative terms—the "most French" of the United States. This heritage is not new. Indeed, it extends back to the first European arrival on the coast of the "Mayne."

A brief presentation on a half-millennium of human geography in the borderlands of eastern North America presents a challenge. The members and names of many of the original groups of people have changed, as have their political boundaries.[4] For example, "Canada" was originally the name for the territory of one of the nations of the St. Lawrence Iroquoians and referred to the watershed of the lower St. Lawrence River. The French then expanded the term to embrace the whole of the St. Lawrence watershed, and the British expanded it further to include all of their northern colonies when they merged them into the Dominion of Canada.

In this same spirit, "Maine" was originally a French and English term that referred to a major waterbody. The French used the term for the principal stream in a watershed, even referring to the St. Lawrence as the "Mayne Rivier" in the early stages of exploration. The "Mayne" was similarly used by the English for the open sea and the area along the coast leading towards it.[5] So a reader must keep in mind that names are fluid and serve only as relative terms that change their meanings over time.

The first known European arrivals in the area that is presently known as Maine came from France as members of the Verrazzano Expedition in 1524. Their reception by the Indigenous people indicated that ships and crew such as King François I had provided were known to the Natives on the Gulf of Maine. Undoubtedly, European fishing people had been in the area earlier and would continue afterwards. Commercial fishing led to trade with the Native peoples and more complex interaction. The first European settlement in Maine took place with the French expedition of DeMonts and Champlain on Ste. Croix Island in 1604.

Despite Native American control of the region, the French incorporated most of today's Maine into New France as part of their administrative subdivision of Acadia. Important administrative links were also forged with New France's region of Canada, notably through Jesuit missionaries. English entry was largely confined to the southwest part of Maine, the lower Kennebec Valley, and a few coastal sites and islands. At first, the French and English tended to cooperate with each other and with the Indigenous people. However, the introduction of Eurasian diseases soon decimated the Native population of Maine.

Then, as the English turned from fishing and trade to possession of farms and timberland, conflict erupted. Almost a century of colonial warfare was fought in the Eastern Borderlands from the start of the War of the League of Augsburg (King William's War, 1688) to the end of the Seven Years War (the French and Indian War, 1763). Maine became a *glacis*, a field of conflict. In this period, England centralized its control in the British Isles to create the Kingdom of Great Britain (1707) and, with this new cohesion in its home country, slowly gained the upper hand in its overseas colonies. The British established a chain of fortifications along Maine's coast and rivers (1715), crushed Native communities like Norridgewock (1724), moved in new settlers loyal to the Crown (1752), and deported Acadians from Fundy Bay (1755).

After the British conquest of Canada in 1760, thousands of Yankee settlers abandoned their soil-exhausted farms in southern New England to establish new homesteads in recently "pacified" areas like Maine.[6] Some French families lived in Maine at this time, but were mostly scattered in remote locations, often living with or intermarried among the Indigenous peoples.[7] The French and Indian War never ended. It continues to this day, but in different forms than guerilla warfare. The territorial struggle in Maine continued after 1760, but was largely fought between the English-speakers during the Revolutionary War and the War of 1812. The Aroostook War (1834) and the resulting Webster–Ashburton Treaty (1842) established the present boundary between British North America and Maine, but divided French and Indigenous families on either side of the new border.

Just after the War of 1812 a new French movement from Québec and Acadia into Maine began. This was a result of several circumstances. Maine was undergoing depopulation as Yankee farmers again moved, this time to the richer farmlands of the Mississippi watershed. As Maine lost resident farmers, it regained its independence from Massachusetts in 1820 and the Industrial Revolution took hold in the 1830s. At this crucial time of needing workers to build a capitol, as well as dams and factories, there was a lack of resident laborers to do the work. As a result, French-Canadians and Acadians, along with newly arrived Irish immigrants, came south to Maine to fill the gap. Most came on a part-time basis, in order to supplement their own farm incomes in Canada. Some stayed.

French migrants continued to come during the U.S. Civil War (1861–65) to join the Maine regiments or to take jobs vacated by men in the military. After the war ended, French Canadians continued to arrive and find work in the booming mill and factory towns that were supplying the urban growth and westward expansion of the United States. Like others, they traveled throughout the region, back and forth across state and national borders.[8]

The popular Yankee image of this migration is that the French bred like rabbits, over-ran the Canadian countryside, and—under the malevolent guidance of their priests—invaded the northeastern United States, where they took jobs away from

These scenes are from Wings of the Border, *a film purportedly about the "plight" of Franco-Americans migrating down the Kennebec Valley into Maine. The film was made c. 1921 by Maine author Holman Day, who had formed a film production company in Augusta. Day and members of his crew subsequently went on to Hollywood and some of them achieved fame, including actress Mary Astor, who is seen kneeling above. This scene (and the movie as a whole) incorporates many Yankee stereotypes about Franco-Americans. Some were old images, like the oxcart laden with furniture and devout prayer at a roadside shrine (above). Others were "new" stereotypes, such as the hero's beret (below), a very un-Canadian* accoutrement *that doughboys returning from the trenches of World War I France came to associate with all Frenchmen. The photo below is in downtown Augusta, at Haymarket Square.*
From the Everett Foster Collection, Northeast Historic Film, Bucksport, Maine

god-fearing Yankees. Indeed, the movement of roughly a half-million French Canadians and Acadians to New England and New York in this period is frequently described as a "diaspora." This characterization is a biased overstatement that borders on racism. The French migration into the northern states was similar to the British migration to Canada or the Yankee migration to the Midwest. It was not exceptional.[9] In the case of Maine, the French came to an area that had always been part of "their" territory and in which there had always been a French presence. And, indeed, the increased French arrival during the Industrial Revolution benefited Yankee developers, who lacked a sufficient workforce in Maine.

Mill growth continued in the twentieth century as new migrants arrived from Europe. In this way, Franco-Americans became only one group of a new ethnic diversity that was developing in Maine. After World War I, the United States initiated a campaign to "Americanize" immigrants, including native-born French-speakers, and—with the start of the Great Depression in the 1930s—the United States began to restrict what had been an open border between Maine, Québec, and New Brunswick. Migration was allowed, but it was more closely controlled. At this time, manufacturing jobs also began to decline, so the new migration largely consisted of those involved in the contract timber industry.

World War II and Vatican II led to a new wave of Anglo assimilation in the United States and—by the 1960s—the economy changed again with the decline of the timber industry. This led to migration from Canada to Maine in order to be with relocated family members or to find job opportunities in new sectors, such as in expanding national retail enterprises. A newer tightening of border control began in the aftermath of the tragedy of 11 September 2001, as the U.S. Department of Homeland Security imposed even more stringent regulations.

Despite this concise synopsis, the history of Maine is complex. In general, one can distinguish four broad periods of French activity in our area:

1) Colonial period, 1500 to 1830

2) Early industrial period, 1830 to 1880

3) Late industrial period, 1880 to 1930

4) Modern period, 1930 to the present.

Rich though this tradition is, a problem has been that—since the "victors" write history—much French activity has been ignored, little researched, and seldom published.

Unlike most other immigrants, Franco-Americans (along with Indigenous

Americans and Hispanics) consider themselves to be "founder societies" who are at "home" in the United States—with as much right to speak their own language and live their own culture as the English. Since their lands and societies were carved up by Anglo-Americans to create the United States and Canada, these founder societies assert their cultural rights. Unlike other immigrant groups, these cultural rights are politically reinforced by the Spanish-speaking Mexican nation in the south and the French-speaking Québec nation in the north, as well as by the many Indigenous nations throughout the country and the multilingual Caribbean islands. This view of cultural and linguistic rights has not been shared by the dominant English-speaking society, except in the most token and superficial manner.[10]

As a result, there are many views of French society in Maine—even among Franco-Mainers themselves. The term "Franco-American" or, more simply, "Franco," is not universally accepted. It was coined in the late nineteenth century by elite, professional males in southern New England. Over the years, the expression has expanded in a haphazard fashion—adopted by some but not by others.[11] In this anthology, we guardedly use the term to describe those residents of North America whose mother tongue is French or those who are of French, French-Canadian, or Acadian origin.

Older English-language studies of Franco-Americans in Maine, as elsewhere in New England and Canada, were influenced by two major trends—either the French were ignored or they were caged in a web of stereotypes. When the French were discussed, they were often caught between clerical and anti-clerical conceptions of their past: If priests and their students celebrated a Catholic heritage, Yankee chroniclers denigrated its existence. As a result of such a polarized dialogue, French society in North America took on the image of a simplistic and monolithic entity with its great variety and rich heritage often ignored.

In addition, many scholars in the United States did not always keep abreast of newer studies published in Canada—usually in French—and had a tendency to present an outmoded, English-biased description of French-Canadian and Acadian society, as well as a simplified and prejudicial vision of their emigration to New England.[12] It also has to be said that the opposite has frequently been true: Canadian scholars have tended to ignore scholarly developments across the border in the United States. For a long time, studies of French society in Maine excited little interest except among a few specialists, as well as among the Franco-Americans themselves. Then, in the late-1950s, new efforts began.

The Soviet Union's launch of *Sputnik*, the first earth-orbiting satellite, forced the United States to deal with the fact that they had fallen behind the Warsaw Pact, at least in respect to science and technology. In response, Congress passed the 1958 National Defense Education Act, which provided federal assistance for education—not only for science and technology, but also for foreign language instruction. As a result, Franco-Americans were encouraged for the first time to pursue French language education, in order to strengthen the global position of the United States during the Cold War.

The 1960s was also a time for ethnic recognition and civil rights around the world. The movement for French rights in Québec was called *la révolution tranquille* (the Quiet Revolution) and spilled over to other Canadian provinces.[13] So it is not surprising that the French in Maine also sought new definitions, new empowerment, and new forms of expression at this time.[14] Franco-American studies also received unexpected encouragement from the administration of President Lyndon Johnson (1963–69).

As a result of the civil rights movement, the Johnson administration adopted the policy to create a "Great Society" for the United States. The goal was to merge marginalized populations into what political leaders considered "mainstream" society. One of the key elements of this policy was the 1965 Elementary and Secondary Education Act (ESEA). In 1968 a new provision (Title VII) was added to ESEA, one that focused on multicultural and bilingual education. Its goal was to better assimilate non-English-speakers. The focus of this act was primarily on Latino and Asian immigrants. However, the law was implemented in such a way as to also engage more widespread multiculturalism and—as a result—resident non-English speakers in the United States were also empowered, including Franco-Americans.

As part of ESEA Title VII implementation, the U.S. Department of Health, Education, and Welfare established National Assessment and Dissemination Centers for Bilingual Education (NADC) around the United States in 1975. They based the New England Center in Massachusetts, which—in turn—established a National Materials Development Center (NMDC) in New Hampshire. The job of the NMDC was to assemble bilingual and multicultural materials that were already available in French and Portuguese, as well as to generate new materials. Normand Dubé from the St. John Valley of Maine served as its very dynamic and creative director from 1977 to 1981. As a result, resource guides and seven anthologies of essays were produced about the French in the United States, in addition to a wide range of creative publications and activities, such as collections of plays and poetry, as well as conferences and workshops.[15] Although the materials in these volumes varied widely in quality, it was the first time such a broad range of material had been assembled.

In 1981 the NMDC published the two-volume *A Franco-American Overview: New England*, which made up Volumes 3 and 4 in the Franco-American series. These volumes were edited by Madeleine Giguère of the University of Southern Maine and consisted of essays by many of the people who would become participants in the new Franco-American renaissance in Maine. These Title VII projects and monies provided an important springboard for what was to happen next.

Two of the participants in these efforts were the geographers Ralph Vicero and James Allen who had begun to change the course of Maine Franco-American Studies in the late 1960s by tapping into wider contexts of ethnic identity with their Ph.D. research. Although Vicero's *Immigration of French Canadians to New England* (1968) and Allen's *Catholics in Maine* (1970) were never published, dog-eared copies of both dissertations have circulated widely as academic "classics."[16] Soon following them were four important regional histories about the French in New England:

Gérard Brault (1986), *The French Canadian Heritage in New England*
François Weil (1989), *Les Franco-Américains*
Yves Roby (1990), *Les Franco-Américains de la Nouvelle Angleterre, 1776–1930*
Armand Chartier (1991), *Histoire des Franco-Américains de la Nouvelle Angleterre*

While these four books did reach a wider audience, most took a long time in production and—when they finally did appear—often came out in French or in small print-runs. Only later were some of them made available in English or to a broader market. They also tended to focus on a generic "Franco-American" society—with southern New England serving as the basic model.[17] This was a problem, because many French Mainers did not easily fit into this definition, while the Acadians tended to disappear from view. Nonetheless, these works provided an important transition from an ignored or polarized stereotype into modern multi-dimensional studies.

As this new academic work on the French in New England began to take hold, new grassroots movements also developed. In older days, there had been a variety of social organizations that brought Franco-Americans together. These had included the Calumet Club in Augusta, French-language newspapers like *La Justice* in Biddeford, and large, annual, semi-religious festivals like St. Jean-Baptiste Day (June

24). However, new, more secular efforts began to develop. In Orono a dynamic group of young student-activists christened themselves the Franco-American Resource & Opportunity Group (FAROG), adopted a frog as their symbol, and began a free-wheeling, multimedia assault on the traditional establishment. New community festivals also evolved, as with Madawaska's *Festival Acadian* (1977), Lewiston's *Festival Franco-Américain*, (1978), Biddeford's *La Kermesse* (1982), and Waterville's *Franco-American Festival* (2002). At the same time, Franco-Americans began to join in a growing variety of non-ethnic events, as in spring 1992, when *Québécois* dance master Pierre Chartrand worked with Bates College students in a general course on "Dance as a Collaborative Art."[18]

Maine Franco-Americans had joined together into region-wide support groups since their arrival in New England during the late industrial period. One of the groups that not only survived, but transformed itself was the *Conseil de la vie française en Amérique* (Council for French Life in America, CVFA). Founded in Québec in 1937, it began as an organization to unite French Catholics throughout North America, but—over the decades—transformed itself into a secular federation that included representatives from Maine until disbanded in 2007.[19] *Action pour les Franco-Américains du Nord-Est* (Action for Franco-Americans of the Northeast, ActFANE) is one of the new groups that grew out of the Title VII activity in 1979. It sought to establish a political grassroots advocacy group for Franco-Americans in New England and New York, including activists from Maine.[20]

The interplay of community and academic activities supported and energized each other. Indeed, this dynamic is a recurring theme in the new Maine Franco-American life. In this case, they began to fuse together into new structures. Three such organizations stand out in Maine: 1) the Franco-American Collection in Lewiston; 2) the Franco-American Centre in Orono; and 3) the Acadian Archives in Fort Kent.

The first organization began in 1972, when students in Lewiston started to collect Franco-American material. It continued to be developed as *Le Centre d'Heritage Franco-Américain* (the Franco-American Heritage Centre). Today called *La Collection Franco-Américaine* (the Franco-American Collection), it houses artifacts and photos, as well as documents. As part of the University of Southern Maine's Lewiston-Auburn College, it regularly mounts exhibits, hosts colloques, and is the largest collection of its kind in the State of Maine—as well as one of the largest nationally.[21]

The second organization, *Le Centre Franco-Américain* (the Franco-American Centre) at the University of Maine in Orono, also was established in 1972. The Centre has organized activities for both public and academic audiences. These include conferences, art exhibits, theatrical productions, guest speakers, and many more. Most importantly, the centre's bilingual journal, *Le Forum*, has connected the Franco-American community in the State of Maine and beyond.[22]

The third organization started early but crystallized in 1989, when the *Archives acadiennes* (Acadian Archives) was created by the Maine State Legislature. It opened at the University of Maine at Fort Kent in 1991. The most important such collection in the state, its mission is to document, preserve, celebrate, and disseminate information about the culture, way of life, and history of the upper Saint John Valley.[23]

As these organizations were establishing themselves, new forms of Franco-American creativity developed throughout Maine. These included the poems and stories of Norman Dubé (Van Buren), the stage works of Greg Chabot (Waterville) and Michael Parent (Lewiston), the poetry of Susann Pelletier (Lewiston) and Jim Bishop (Old Town), the singing of Liliane Labbé (Madison) and Josée Vachon (Brownville Junction), the journalism of Paul Paré (Lewiston) and Yvon Labbé (Orono), the music compositions of Jean-Paul Poulain (Augusta) and Paul Caron (Lewiston), the artwork of Mercedes Gastonguay (Lewiston) and Don Cyr (Lille), and the creative writing of Normand Beaupré (Biddeford) and Rhea Côté Robbins (Waterville). The

Normand Dubé (foreground), at the Salon du livre, Québec, c 1982–83
Photograph from the Franco-American Centre, University of Maine, Orono

creative styles and geographic diversity of this effort was startling. However, it was still a difficult process to get this material before the public.

Traditionally, Yankee *concessionaires* had little interest in producing Franco-American material. So, these new artists produced when they could in existing journals, galleries, and auditoriums, but also began to search out new outlets. Besides resorting to private productions, two notable efforts sprang up to face the challenge of making Franco-American creativity accessible to the public. The *FAROG Forum* began to provide a print outlet for this creativity in 1972, under the direction of Yvon Labbé, and still is going strong. In 1988 author Denis Ledoux of Lisbon Falls created Soleil Press to publish Franco-American literature, but—while the press is still operating—the low economic margin for this private concern forced it to broaden its mission beyond Franco-American material.[24] In addition to this creative expression, scholars from a variety of academic disciplines also began to enter new areas of Franco-American research.

Reassessment of the rich documents of the industrial period and its aftermath (1860 to 1960) were the important initial focus of many scholars. Besides her groundbreaking text in 1981, sociologist Madeleine Giguère of the University of Southern Maine also constructed important databases from the U.S. Census on the Franco-American population of New England in general and on her native State of Maine in particular. At the same time, historian C. Stewart Doty of the University of Maine in Orono assembled two important works based on material from the Library of Congress and the National Archives in Washington, D.C., as well as many journal articles dealing with Franco-American subjects as varied as racism, fascism, and popular music.[25] While Giguère and Doty were senior scholars in their fields, a younger generation began breaking new ground in Franco-American studies. Historians Béatrice Craig and Yves Frenette of the University of Ottawa produced a plethora of essays on the formation of Maine's French communities; Craig parsed the Acadian and French-Canadian populations of northern Maine, while Frenette analyzed the French-Canadian migration into southern Maine.

As the creative artists had discovered, many of the new academics found somewhat limited venues for their works. So, efforts were mounted to expand the contents of older established journals, as new professional organizations and publications arose. One of the new efforts was the American Council for Québec Studies (ACQS), which formed in 1981. Besides hosting conferences, it publishes the journal *Québec Studies*, with Jane Moss of Colby College in Waterville (Maine) becoming its manag-

Alaric Faulkner (background), James Faulkner (left), and Kenaï Rodrigue (right), Canada Road Archeological Survey, Misery Gore, Maine, Summer 1995
Photograph by Barry Rodrigue

ing editor in 1994. They publish works on Maine Franco-Americans, notably in a special edition honoring Robert LeBlanc, the Franco-American geographer who died in 2001 at New York's World Trade Center tragedy.[26]

Meanwhile, focus on other periods and places was underway. Alaric Faulkner, director of the Laboratory of Historical Archeology at the University of Maine in Orono, has devoted over two decades to excavating sites on Maine's Acadian coast, most notably seventeenth-century Fort Pentagoet and Baron Saint Castin's

Habitation in the present-day town of Castine.[27] Similarly, Pamela Crane, one of Faulkner's crew chiefs and now a private research archeologist, reassessed National Park Service artifacts from the Abenaki village of Norridgewock on the Kennebec River, a site that had been heavily influenced by the French in the seventeenth and eighteenth centuries.[28] And, for a slightly later period, historian Jacques Ferland at the University of Maine at Orono not only researched French and Native interaction in early nineteenth-century Maine, but also trained students to continue this work.[29] One of both Faulkner's and Ferland's students, Barry Rodrigue, went to Québec to study with geographer Serge Courville and ended up dedicating over a decade of his life to searching out historic land routes between the Gulf of Maine and the Saint Lawrence River.[30] All in all, these pre-industrial studies illustrate that the French were in Maine long before the mills were built.

Much that has been produced in English by Anglo-American academics on the French in Maine—over the last three decades—has appeared within works about the wider region or on more general topics. Frequently, such coverage is uneven. For example, among the eighty-eight articles published in the journal of the Maine Historical Society between 1990 and 1999, only seven dealt with Franco-American subjects. This being said, almost an entire issue of this same journal was dedicated to Franco-American subjects, including two important historiographies by historians Yves Roby and Alice Stewart.[31] In 1990 amateur historian Neil Rolde made a significant effort to document the contributions of French Canadians and other ethnic groups in the State of Maine for his volume, *Maine: A Narrative History*. However, when professional historians produced a history of Maine eight-years later, *Maine: The Pine Tree State from Prehistory to the Present,* not a single chapter was devoted to Franco-Americans.[32] Certainly, the passage of time should not be confused with progress!

University students remain the primary researchers in Maine Franco-American Studies. Their efforts consist of senior theses, seminar papers, conference presentations, master's theses, and doctoral dissertations. For example, Jean Daigle's dissertation (1975), which is one of the best known, examined colonial exchange between Acadia and New England in the seventeenth and eighteenth centuries. Several of the newer works reinforce earlier studies, such as Michael Brown's 1992 thesis at the University of Maine at Orono on the development of that institution's Franco-American Centre, which updated and complemented the thesis done a decade earlier on the same subject by Yves Brousseau at Laval University.[33]

A major part of the challenge for Franco-American Studies is not the research and writing itself, but its hidden nature. Most of these works lie unpublished and forgotten in academic filing cabinets.[34] In order to try to improve this situation, the University of Southern Maine's Franco-American Collection at Lewiston-Auburn College has been building a collection of such unpublished documents from around the world, in order to allow scholars and the public access to this important material.

University work in language arts has followed a more troubled pathway than its counterparts in geography, history, archeology, and sociology. The French language as it was (and is) used in Maine by native *francophones* is a venerable dialect derived from *Québécois* and Acadian tongues. Often decried by state officials as an inferior *patois*, educators attempted to eradicate the Maine French vernacular language in favor of Parisian French throughout the twentieth century. Some encouragement was given to Parisian French and other languages during the Cold War (1945–91), as European philology was seen as a component in the battle against Soviet communism. However, the USSR's decline in the late twentieth century caused even this utilitarian study to decline, as language requirements began to be eliminated in public schools.[35] In reaction, private efforts were mounted to encourage language retention and revival.

In 1992 educator André Pied of Skowhegan began a cross-border French immersion program between residents of the adjoining counties of Somerset in Maine and Beauce in Québec. In 1995 a two-way French immersion program was begun with U.S. federal monies in elementary and middle schools in Madawaska and the surrounding areas of northern Maine. Efforts were also mounted to bring back mandated French language instruction in public schools.[36] More successfully, arguments have been made in several institutions to change the title of their "foreign" language program to "modern" languages, as French and Spanish are no more foreign than English. In addition, private schools also have developed, as a variety of conversational French language sessions have sprung up around the state, notably including *Les Bavards* of Waterville and *Le Rendez-vous* of Bangor.[37] Filmmaker Ben Levine made a celebrated documentary on this revival of the French language in Maine, *Réveil—Waking Up French*.[38] And, some of the older works from language departments have begun to be brought out of the shadows, as in 2006, when Professor Robert Rioux's study of the French language in Maine, *Enquête géolinguistique*, was re-edited and published.[39]

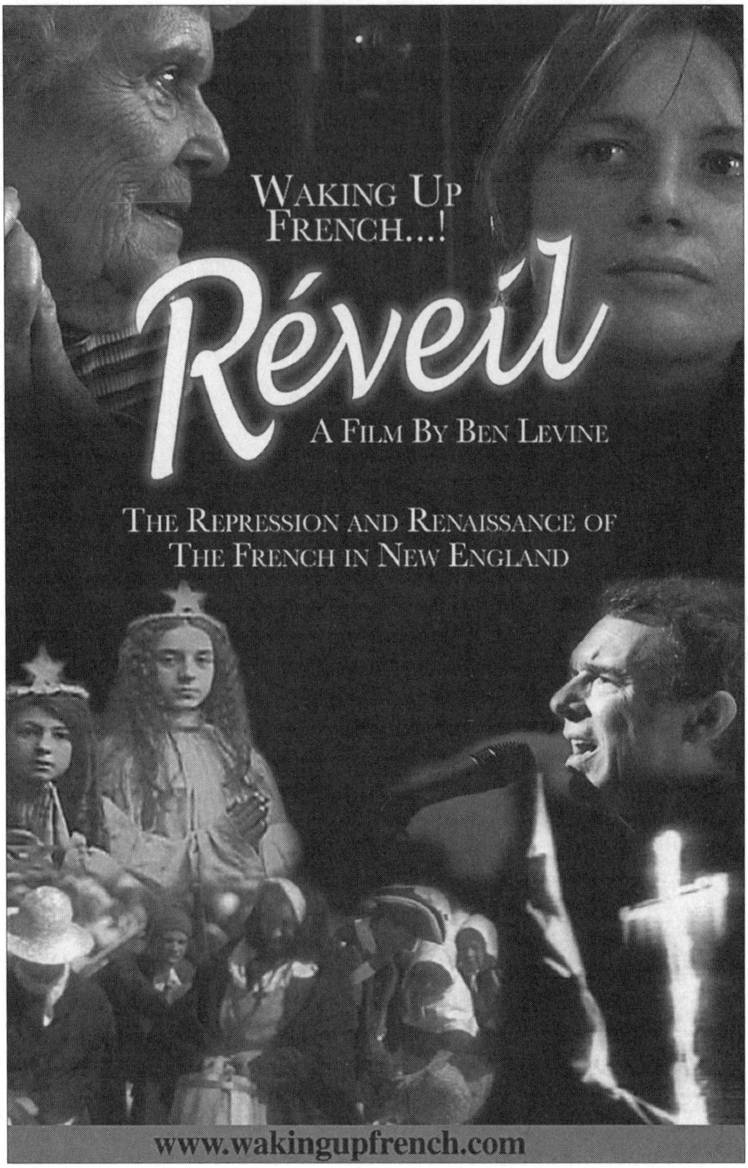

Poster for *Réveil—Waking Up French*, 2002
Ben Levine

Oral history and documentary photography have for some time formed important but somewhat neglected sources of Franco-American material. Such collections were anticipated by the social reform work of people like Lewis Hine, who documented Franco-American workers in Maine in the early twentieth century. Historian C. Stewart Doty pioneered the use of such resources with his *The First Franco-Americans* (1985) and *Acadian Hard Times* (1991), which were based on material from the Library of Congress and the National Archives in Washington, D.C.[40] Similarly, professionals from other fields—like photographer Jere DeWaters—have also documented Franco-American heritage in Maine. Nonetheless, Sandy Ives, the founder and guiding light of what has become the Maine Folklife Center at the University of Maine at Orono, lamented in the early 1990s that more scholars have not collected French materials in the region.[41]

In response to such concerns, starting in 1992, Jim Bishop, Amy Morin, and others began collecting oral histories and photos from residents of French Island, a small community in the Penobscot River that forms a Franco-American enclave in Old Town. Their research led to *Nos Histoires de l'Île*, a well-illustrated and exciting volume of the memories of residents, who were perhaps uncomfortable in writing their histories but perfectly at home in talking about them.[42]

Such documentary work has been an important component in the work of two ethnographers at the University of Southern Maine—Barry Rodrigue and Mark Silber, who regularly conduct documentary surveys as part of their research and train their students in this work. Their collaboration has resulted in their establishment of a Maine Ethnic Archives.[43] Likewise, at Bates College, French Professor Mary Rice-DeFosse has been engaged in the long-term collection of life stories from local French-speakers, while that institution's Harward Center is also gathering oral histories of workers from the Bates Mill in Lewiston. Shorter term projects centered on individual seminars have also been regularly made at these institutions and others.[44]

Most of these recordings, as well as transcripts, photos, and related background materials are stored at the University of Southern Maine's Franco-American Collection in Lewiston, the Acadian Archives of the University of Maine at Fort Kent, and the Maine Folklife Center of the University of Maine at Orono. These three repositories form the primary holdings of Franco-American documentary history in the State of Maine and reflect a close cooperation between community members and academic workers.

As an outgrowth of such community and university projects, as well as the cumulative effort of courses offered on Franco-American subjects, academic minors were established in 2000 in French North American Studies at the University of Southern Maine and in Franco-American Studies at the University of Maine at Orono, while the number of courses on Franco-America have multiplied in other institutions of higher education throughout the state. Also in 2000, a representative of each of these programs met with one from the Acadian Archives at the University of Maine at Fort

Yvon Labbé (left) and Andrew Redmond (right)
Oral History Interview, Madison, Maine, Spring 2003
Photograph by Barry Rodrigue

Kent to found the Maine Franco-American Studies Alliance (MFASA).[45] Its mission is to foster cooperation between their respective institutions and to assure community participation in Franco-American Studies throughout the state's public universities.

Increased focus on Franco-American Studies in the state universities was again mirrored in Maine communities. In the 1990s the *Forum francophone des affaires* (French Business Forum, FFA)—a global network of governments and businesses from thirty-seven French-speaking nations—established their U.S. headquarters in Maine with Attorney Sévérin Béliveau as their president (Béliveau also serves as the French consul in Maine).[46] The Father Leo E. Bégin Chapter of the American-Canadian Genealogical Society opened in Auburn in 1980 and, by 2001, became the Maine Franco-American Genealogical Society, an independent organization devoted to helping Franco-Americans track their ancestry. In 2000 the Franco-American

Sévérin Béliveau, at the University of Southern Maine, Lewiston-Auburn College, Lewiston, Maine, 17 October 2000
Photograph by Barry Rodrigue

Heritage Centre at St. Mary's opened in Lewiston as an important meeting center and performance space for Franco-Americans.[47]

The celebrating of French heritage has spilled over into more generally "public" events, including sport and cinema. Sport has always been a Franco-American passion. It gained a new impetus in the 1980s and 1990s with marathon runner Joan Benoit of Freeport and boxer Joey Gamache of Lewiston becoming celebrated national champions in their fields. Maine's links with Québec became even closer in 2003 when Lewiston's "MAINEiacs" Hockey Club, a largely French-Canadian team, began playing in the Québec Major Junior Hockey League.[48] In 1998 the Maine International Film Festival began in Waterville at the Railroad Square Cinema. It has shown French films from Maine and from around the world, and a Maine Franco-American Film Festival grew out of its success.[49]

All this activity has been tied to Franco-American political life, which has been exceptionally dynamic in Maine, although more on a local level until recent years. Unlike southern New England, Maine Franco-Americans historically tended to more often join labor unions and the Democratic party. This trend, however, went against Maine's Yankee and rural conservatism, as well as Republican-party dominance. So, until recent years, only local government in Franco-American industrial cities tended to be progressive and French. The ethnic and political divide was noticeable on a national level when Maine's celebrated Republican senator, Margaret Chase Smith (1897–1995), concealed her Franco-American background, it not being considered an asset, and perhaps even a liability, for election.[50] However, Maine state government became more equally balanced between the two dominant parties with the liberalization of national politics in the 1960s. As a result, the French began to exercise more political influence around Maine and more Franco-American opportunities resulted.

One of these new directions for Franco-Americans was in the area of education. Although the second largest metropolitan area in the state, Lewiston was also a stronghold of the Democratic party and, in the old days, Republican legislators had refused to establish a public university there. Backing up this punishment of the political opposition was an old ethnic and class stereotype: "Why would people who are French and blue collar need an institution of higher learning? All they are going to do is work in the mills!" However, more pressure began to be exerted and, among other successes, led to the establishment of the University of Southern Maine's Lewiston-Auburn College in 1988. Similarly, in 2002 Michael Michaud became the first self-acknowledged Franco-American from Maine to be elected to Congress, and his successful campaign was, in part, built on his heritage.

With the change in the ethno-political landscape, cultural reality has been grounded in physical space elsewhere in the state. Based on archeologist Barry Rodrigue's studies of the Canada Road—and in response to his 1993 proposal—the governments of Québec and Maine created the Kennebec-Chaudière Corridor to revive the common heritage of the border region, while the U.S. government followed suit with the establishment of the Old Canada Road Scenic Byway. This route is now highlighted on the State of Maine's roadway signs and highway maps.[51] Further south, the City of Lewiston developed a self-guided tour brochure on Franco-American sites in its *centre-ville*, and industrial exhibits from the Bates Mill in Lewiston were brought together to form Museum L-A. Biddeford and Waterville

Evan Haynes's Sculpture, Comunique: "To Hold in One's Arms,"
State House, Augusta, Maine, 2007
Photograph by Barry Rodrigue

inaugurated their *Musée dans la rue* (Museum in the Streets): A series of public and bilingual plaques that commemorate Franco-American contributions to these cities.[52] Evan Haynes's sculpture, *Comunique* (2001), was incorporated into the walls of the underground corridor of the State House in Augusta. It merges texts in French and the Eastern Algonquian languages (with English translations), recalling the tenacious link between the French and Indigenous worlds that have existed in Maine. The sculpture stands in strong testimony to the non-English origins of Maine's history. Even state agencies such as the Maine State Museum have begun to produce French-language brochures.[53]

In the past, researchers interested in Franco-Americans have frequently worked in isolation and have not known each other. This has changed. With the growth of the Internet there has been a proliferation of websites devoted to Franco-Americans in the State of Maine and elsewhere. In 1998 Rhéa Côté Robbins founded the Franco-American Women's Institute (FAWI), which encourages the production of women's studies in order to underscore and celebrate the role, too often neglected, of Franco-American women. She made it a very effective Internet organization (www.fawi.net).

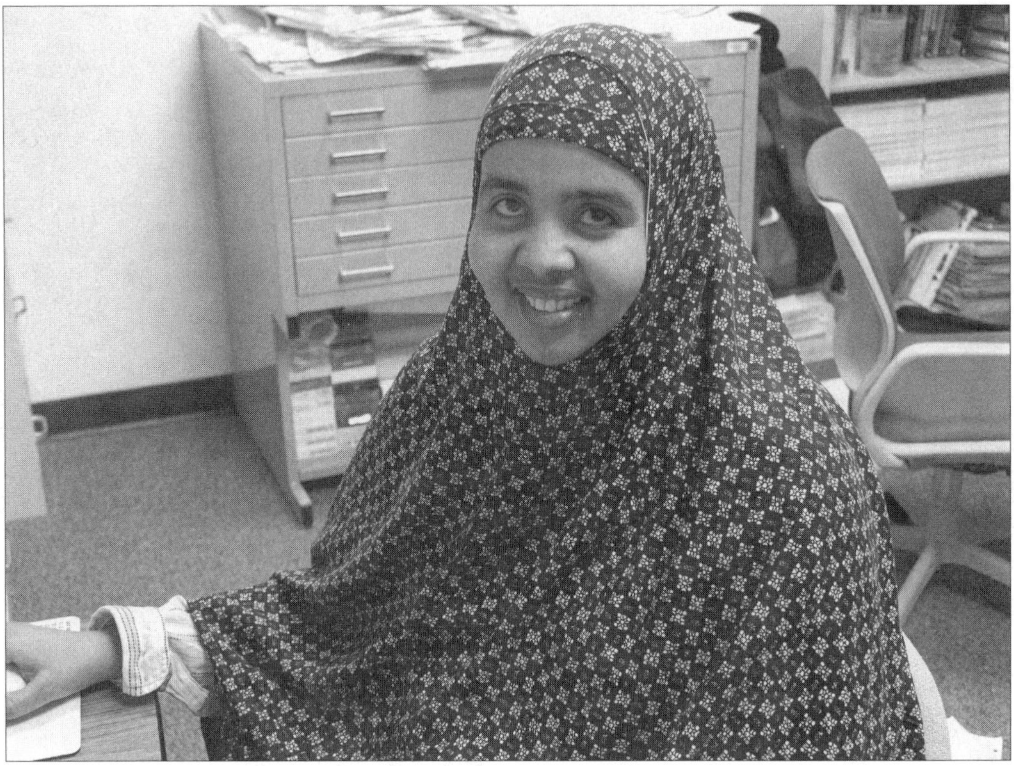

Hibo M. Omer, francophone of Somalia, now living in Auburn, Maine, 2005
Photograph by Dan Philbrick, University of Southern Maine at Lewiston-Auburn

Similarly, *Le fait français du maine* / Maine's French Communities (francomaine.org) was inaugurated in 2000 as a partnership project between Laval University, the University of Maine, and the University of Southern Maine.[54]

One of the strengths of French activity in Maine since the 1960s has been the diverse framework of its sources—not driven by just one university, newspaper, or powerbroker. Within Maine there has been a lot of healthy overlapping between people. In addition to *métissage*, which often has taken place between ethnic groups in the region, strong ties also have been forged between academic researchers and the Franco-American community; indeed, many scholars themselves are Franco-Americans.

So, we felt it was time to bring together some of this material. There are many caveats to creating such an anthology.[55] This collection is neither complete nor exhaustive, but it is our hope that by bringing together over fifty modern-day contributors it will serve as a guide to some of the new directions of Franco-American society. Unlike many earlier endeavors, we have purposely sought to include a wide variety of perspectives in order to illustrate the fascinating diversity of Franco-American life in Maine. We also have created a master bibliography at the back of this volume to help readers appreciate and access Franco-American materials.

A new addition to Franco-American society in Maine has been French-speakers from other parts of the world. The arrival of *francophones* from Togo, Haïti, Martinique, Chad, Cambodia, Djubuti, Tahiti, Congo, and many other points of the compass has made the fabric of Franco-Maine very exciting. All this contributes to a rich blend of cultures, which lately has taken on the image of a "French Renaissance."[56] This beautiful *mélange* is particularly relevant today, given the ever-widening spread of global enterprise and trans-border populations, as well as the need of a multicultural consciousness to comprehend them. Suddenly, Franco-Maine is central to the needs of a new world!

1 Part of this introduction is derived from an article that was published in a festschrift celebrating the career of Professor Yves Roby, who retired from Laval University in 1999 and was one of the primary scholars of Franco-American and French-Canadian history. Jeanne Valois of the Culture d'expression française en Amerique du Nord (CEFAN) at Laval University (Quebec City) assisted with recovery of the original bibliography for this essay. Mary Rice-DeFosse translated the original article into English and Barry Rodrigue reworked it into this introduction. Dean Louder and Barry Rodrigue, "Recherche sur les Franco-Américains du Maine, 1970–2000," in *Les parcours de l'histoire*, Yves Frenette, Martin Pâquet, and Jean Lamarre, editors, (Québec: Laval University Press, 2002), pp. 207–29.

2 The census numbers for those having French ancestry in Maine are low, as many people of mixed heritage frequently list themselves as being "American" or "English." This is a general problem for calculating ethnic figures in the United States census. A more frequently cited number for the portion of the Maine population having French heritage is around 40 percent.

3 According to the 2000 U.S. Census, 5.3 percent of Maine residents spoke French home, exceeding any other state. The three highest ranked states behind Maine are Louisiana (4.7 percent), New Hampshire (3.4 percent), and Vermont (2.5 percent).

4 Even the identity of and area for the French and the British in Europe have changed considerably in the last 500 years. At the end of the Middle Ages, neither existed as well defined national groups. Both were more strongly divided by ethnicity or religion, as well as by geography. Today's "French" would have been better identified as Parisian, Basque, Breton, or Huguenot when New France was established. Likewise, many of the English at the time of the settlement of New England would have been seen more as Anglicans, Londoners, or Welsh.

5 Long before their arrival in North America, the French and English both had used the term "mayne," in its various spellings, for the main or principal part of waterbodies. For example, the French had used it for the Mayenne River and its associated Province of Maine in France, while the English used it in reference to the "Spanish Mayne" for the Caribbean Basin. Many hypotheses have tried to establish a more definitive pedigree for the naming of the State of Maine, but it seems to have been just a colloquial expression. Interestingly, geographer Pierre Poulin of Laval University (Québec)

has noted that the relative orientation of Orléans, Beauce, and Maine in France is coincidentally reproduced in a reverse image (negative) to the layout of Orleans Island, Beauce County, and the State of Maine in the New World. Pierre Poulin, Personal Communication.

6 Besides moving to Maine after 1760, Yankee settlers also moved from their "dust bowl" farms in southern New England to New Hampshire, Vermont, the Eastern Townships of Québec, and the Maritimes, as well as to the "West." Eves.

7 Historian Neil Rolde has documented some of the French presence among the Native-American communities of Maine, such as that of Jean-Baptiste La Cote among the Passamaquoddy in 1794 and an unidentified Frenchman buried at the Penobscot's Indian Island in 1847. Similarly, Historian Jacques Ferland has documented Franco-Indigenous connections before the mill migration period; the Rancourt family being one of the important French families to intermarry with the Penobscots. Rolde, *Unsettled Past*, pp. 15, 207–08. Ferland, personal communication.

8 The French and Irish migration to Maine for work was a logical outcome of industrial development in North America. While there was similar industrial work available in Canada in the nineteenth century, the smaller scale of Canadian industry required fewer workers and the large number of immigrants from the British Isles—along with resulting lower wages—made these jobs less attractive. Thus, French Canadians and Acadians who lived near to the border tended to seek higher paid work in the larger-scale U.S. industry.

9 Geographer Serge Courville rejects the popular use of the term "diaspora" to describe the French-Canadian migration to the United States in the late nineteenth and early twentieth centuries. His study of colonization projects supplies a global context for such ethnic relocations, projects that primarily benefitted developers, not migrants. Courville, *Immigration, colonisation et propagande*; personal communication.

10 See the *Manifesto of Franco-America* at (http://usm.maine.edu/lac/francoamericanstudies/cfa.html).

11 In its most restrictive use, "Franco-Americans" are considered to be the descendents of French-Canadian factory workers in the cities of the northeastern United States who are Roman Catholic and French-speaking. In its widest application, Franco-Americans are any people of French heritage in the Americas—from the Arctic Archipelago to Tierra del Fuego.

12 The issue of Anglo-American bias continues, as was highlighted in the referendum campaigns of the Parti Québécois and the Bloc Québécois for Québec soverignty rights in the late twentieth century, when U.S. journalists would seek information from their English-speaking counterparts in Canada (often Toronto) and would, of course, receive a federalist interpretation, which was then reported as "impartial" news in the United States.

13 The struggle for French rights in Canada in the 1960s gave new life to a long overdue reassessment of French-Canadian history and culture. There had always been criticism of the biased and inaccurate fashion in which French-Canadian history had been presented by both the English and French Catholic elites, but the critics had often been dismissed as eccentric or fringe intellectuals. At the time of the Quiet Revolution in Quebec, these dissident views began to be reconsidered and amplified. Some of the more modern works that have set the trend in rigorous new studies about French Canada include the work of historian Jean-Pierre Wallot and economist Gilles Paquet, who in turn inspired researchers associated with the Centre interuniversitaire d'études québécoises (www.cieq.ulaval.ca) and the Institut interuniversitaire de recherche sur les populations (www.irep.umontreal.ca). Notable in these "New Quebec Studies" are geographers Serge Courville and Gérard Bouchard, and historians Normand Séguin, Jean-Claude Robert, and René Hardy.

14 The "Quiet Revolution" in Canada was not always so quiet. In the 1960s and 1970s, as the revolutionary Front de Libération du Québec (Liberation Front of Quebec, FLQ) carried on underground

activities in Canada aimed at securing sovereignty for Québec, the U.S. Federal Bureau of Investigation (FBI) went so far as to tap the phone of the mainstream Franco-American politician, John Martin of Maine, fearing a spill-over effect of covert operations along the U.S./Canada border. The implied message was that anyone who was French in this region was a potential enemy of the state.

15 In 1976 the National Materials Development Center produced *A Resource Guide for New England Libraries* on Franco-American Studies by Phyllis Hagel, followed by Pierre Anctil's more complete *A Franco-American Bibliography: New England* in 1979. The seven volumes of the *Franco-American Overview* were published between 1979 and 1982 and consisted of an introductory volume by Renaud Albert, André Martin's volume on the Midwest and West, Madeleine Giguère's two volumes on New England, and Mathé Allain and Carl Brasseaux's three volumes on Louisiana.

16 While being innovative geographies for their time, Vicero's and Allen's dissertations still used outdated interpretations of Québec society, as well as simplistic reasons for the French-Canadian and Acadian migration to New England.

17 By the beginning of the twentieth century, strong ethnic organizations like Woonsocket's Union Saint-Jean-Baptiste (USJB) and Manchester's Association Canado-Américain (ACA) spread throughout southern New England, in response to the concentration of French Canadians in the region's industrial cities. Although begun as mutual aid societies (insurance companies) for French Catholics, they also created large libraries and active cultural centers. Since it has been easy for researchers to use such concentrated archival holdings to study "Franco-American" society, the resulting scholarship has tended to follow the USJB and ACA vision of "their" people. Exceptions to their norm just "did not exist" or were under-reported—such as people like Ted Roderick (Rodrigue), the Socialist party's Franco-American candidate for mayor of Lewiston in 1932. Studies that have exclusively used these collections have been "source driven" works that lump the Maine experience with the very different but well documented experiences of southern New England. Indeed, when historian Barry Rodrigue's work on the life of Franco-American entrepreneur Thomas G. Plant came out in 1994, readers questioned multimillionaire Plant's Franco-American heritage because Plant did not fit the stereotypical image of a poor millworker. Rodrigue, *Tom Plant*; "The Cultural Trigonometry of Franco-American Stereotypes;" and "Tom Plant, la route du Canada et les stéréotypes sur les Franco-Américains." A file on Ted Roderick is in the Franco-American Collection at the University of Southern Maine's Lewiston-Auburn College, Lewiston, Maine.

18 In the course "Dance as a Collaborative Art," Pierre Chartrand taught Bates students traditional French-Canadian dances, including *contre danses* and *quadrilles*, some of which featured stepdancing. The students then toured elementary schools presenting an interactive program entitled "Swing la Baquaise," which involved dance participation as well as demonstrations. Larock. This participation of Franco-Americans in non-ethnic venues also occurred with the National Folk Festival that ran in Bangor from 2002 to 2004, as well as its successors, the American Folk Festival and the Bangor Folk Festival.

19 For the *CVFA* website, see (http://www.cvfa.ca/).

20 ActFANE was established in 1979 in Manchester, New Hampshire, but moved to Lowell, Massachusetts. It was somewhat inspired by the Council for the Development of French in Louisiana (CODOFIL), which was formed in 1968. See Waddell, "French Lousiana," pp. 229–51. Editor Yvon Labbé of the *FAROG Forum* and geographer Dean Louder ran afoul of some of the gangster elements in Louisiana when they began working with *métis* critics of the high-stakes backers of CODOFIL. Yvon Labbé and Dean Louder, Interview.

21 Madeleine Giguère, Madeleine Roy, and Donat Boisvert have served as coordinators of the Franco-American Collection at USM. Barry Rodrigue became its first university-appointed scholar, succeed-

ing Professor Madeleine Giguère, who had staffed the collection as a retired scholar. Franco-American Collection (www.usm.maine.edu/lac/franco/).

22 Directed by Yvon Labbé, the Franco-American Centre and its journal have been staffed by many, including Josée Vachon, Jim Bishop, Rhea Côté Robbins, and Lisa Desjardins Michaud.

23 Lisa Ornstein served as the director of the Acadian Archives until 2007. In pursuing its mandate of cultural conservation and affirmation, the archives focuses particular attention on the Acadian and French-Canadian presence in the St. John Valley. Its director serves as the University of Maine System delegate to the Maine Acadian Heritage Council, a regional non-profit organization which partners with the National Park Service to implement the Maine Acadian Culture Preservation Act, a federal act passed in 1990. United States, Public Law 101–543, 8 November 1990, 104 Statute 2389; Department of the Interior, National Park Service, North Atlantic Region, Implementing the Maine Acadian Culture Preservation Act; Acadian Culture in Maine. Acadian Culture in Maine (http://acim.umfk.maine.edu/index.html). The Maine Acadian Heritage Council replaced the Maine Acadian Culture Preservation Commission in the late 1990s.

24 Soleil Press evolved into the more inclusive Soleil Lifestory Network, an organization focused on the creation of personal memoirs. Their website is at (http://www.turningmemories.com/index.html).

25 Although C. Stewart Doty is of Yankee heritage, he is usually spoken of as a Franco-American scholar. This is not only in tribute to his scholarly dedication, but also a result of the affection and esteem of colleagues, students, and the community. Doty, "Franco-American History Projects in the State of Maine"; "Rudy Vallée"; "The American Identity of Louis Dantin"; "M. Maurras est ici"; "The Intellectual of the Quebec Diaspora: The Case of Henri d'Arles"; "The Future of the Franco-American Past." Two of his senior seminar students published articles on Franco-Americans in Dexter, Maine, and on the International Paper Company strike of 1910 in *The Maine Historical Quarterly*, 33, 1 (Summer, 1993).

26 The Northeast Council for Québec Studies formed in 1981, but soon changed its name to the American Council for Québec Studies (ACQS). *Québec Studies* 33, Spring/Summer 2002. In 1991 the University of Ottawa began publishing the journal, *Francophonies d'Amérique*, which also includes material concerning Franco-Americans and Maine.

27 In 1992 *Spells of Moonwitch*, a ballet based on the seventeenth-century life of Maine's Baron Jean-Vincent d'Abbadie de Saint-Castin, premiered in Bangor. The music for the ballet was composed by Heinrich Snyder and the dance choreographed by a person only known as Holyoake. It was based in part on the research of Alaric Faulkner and Gretchen Fearon Faulkner.

28 Pamela Crane and her husband, Peter Morison, have also been engaged in a study of the historical archeology of Waterville, including its Franco-American traditions. Crane and Morrison.

29 Notable among Jacques Ferland's students are Kraig Schwartz, who wrote on the development of class consciousness among workers at the asbestos mines in south-central Quebec in the late nineteenth and early twentieth centuries, and Micah Pawling, who wrote on Indigenous and Euramerican relations in the late eighteenth and early nineteenth centuries. Schwartz, *Empowerment and Class Struggle*; Pawling, *Wabanaki Homeland and the New State of Maine.*

30 Rodrigue and Faulkner have identified over 300 archeological sites in the Kennebec watershed alone, many with a French connection. Faulkner and Rodrigue, Canada Road Archaeological Survey. When Rodrigue attended Laval University, he reactivated an old Franco-American tradition. Laval (1852) had grown out of the earlier Jesuit College (1635) and the Seminary of Quebec (1663), which makes it the oldest institution of higher learning north of Mexco. It is also the largest French university in the Americas, having 40,000 students in 2007 (compared to 10,000 students at the University of Maine in Orono). In the nineteenth and twentieth centuries, Franco-Americans seeking baccalaureate

or professional degrees frequently attended Laval. This custom declined in later years, as Franco-Americans learned English and gained access to Catholic institutions of higher learning in New England—such as Boston College (Chestnut Hill, Massachusetts) and St. Michael's College (Winooski, Vermont)—and then were allowed into other public and private schools in the States. So, it was with this old Laval tradition of treating Franco-Americans from the United States as "their own" that Dean Louder, chair of the Geography Department, and Professor Serge Courville obtained in-province tuition and other special provisions for Rodrigue. Other students from Maine have followed Rodrigue to Laval.

31 In addition, the *Maine Historical Society Quarterly* began carrying material reappraising earlier, inadequate studies. One example is Béatrice Craig's devastating book review of Dyke Hendrickson's *Quiet Presence*. Stewart, "The Franco-Americans of Maine." Roby, "Québec in the United States." As an example of a complete issue related to Franco-American subjects, see the *Maine Historical Society Quarterly* (33) 1, Summer 1993. Craig, Book Review.

32 Some contributors to *The Pine Tree State* claimed that the book's lack of major sections dealing with French activities in Maine was an intentional strategy to integrate Franco-Americans into the state's history as a whole, in order not to "ghettoize" them in separate chapters. In reality, there was a lack of qualified historians participating in the project who could write on Franco-American history. This resulted in the volume diminishing the role played by Franco-Americans in favor of that of the English and Yankees. In this way, a traditional and long-standing bias was perpetuated by an historiographic deficiency. Judd, Eastman, and Churchill.

33 Newer theses on Franco-American subjects include Gerard Forgue's analysis (1994) of the arrival of French-Canadian workers in Jackman and Matthew Laflamme's study (1995) of the development of a French-Canadian workforce in Waterville. Mark Richard's thesis (1994) on linguistic assimilation in a Lewiston parish complemented Yves Frenette's dissertation on Franco-American industrial settlement in Lewiston, which Frenette had defended at Laval University six years before, followed by Richard's dissertation (2001) on the acculturation of French-Canadians in Lewiston, Maine.

34 Besides theses and dissertations, smaller research papers frequently disappear forever or occasionally end up in the files of retired professors. The unpublished work of professors often suffers the same fate of obsucity. Fortunately, the many student papers submitted to sociologist Madeleine Giguère and historian C. Stewart Doty ended up in their retirement files. Those from the students of Giguère are in her files at the Franco-American Collection at the University of Southern Maine's Lewiston-Auburn College. Those of Doty's students are in his files at the Fogler Library's Special Collection at the University of Maine in Orono.

35 Belluck.

36 In January 2002, the National Science Foundation (Washington, D.C.) gave $301,000 over three years to two researchers in linguistics, Cynthia Fox of the University of Albany (New York) and Jane Smith of the University of Maine, to study the Franco-American language in eight localities in New England, three of which are in Maine—Van Buren, Waterville, and Biddeford.

37 The Penobscot School in Rockland began in 2001 and caters to French and other language instruction for adults. *L'école française du Maine* (the French School of Maine) in South Freeport began as a French-immersion pre-school in 2001 and has added primary grades to its program.

38 *Réveil—Waking Up French* (http://wakingupfrench.com/).

39 There is a debate whether the new interest in the French language in Maine reflects a renewed interest in Franco-American history and culture or actual revival of the French language.

40 Doty's sources for *The First Franco-Americans* and *Acadian Hard Times* were documents and photographs that had been buried for over fifty years in the files of the U.S. Works Progress

Administration and the Farm Security Administration.
41 Ives.
42 Morin and others, 1999.
43 Between 1991 and 1993, Rodrigue collected oral histories, photographs, and other materials in order to compile biographies on industrialist Thomas Plant, judge Albert Béliveau, and entrepreneur Andrew Redmond. Collection of oral histories and other materials related to his Canada Road work continued from 1993 to 1999. Most of the Thomas Plant material is housed at the Sagadahoc History and Genealogy Room of the Patten Free Library in Bath, Maine. The Albert Béliveau and Andrew Redmond collections, the Canada Road Collection, and the student collections are housed at the University of Southern Maine's Franco-American Collection in Lewiston, as well as at Maine Folklife Center at the University of Maine at Orono.
44 Rice-DeFosse is engaged in the long-term *Franco-American Oral History Project: Documenting the Transmission of Franco-American Culture*. Similar to the project in Old Town, it involves collecting life stories in French from local French-speakers. The aim is to preserve these voices on video for future reference and exhibits. The *Franco-American Oral History Project* was in part funded by Bates Colleges' Harward Center in Lewiston, Maine and is a thesis option for French majors there. In 2003 the French majors in one of Professor Arthur Greenspan's senior seminars at Colby College made a collection of interviews with Franco-Americans in central Maine. From these, they produced a CD the folowing year, *Francos of Waterville—Les Francos de Waterville racontent*. Similarly, in 2004, French majors in Alexandre Dauge-Roth's senior seminar at Bowdoin College also collected Franco-American oral histories, and then students either made a documentary or produced a stage dramatization based on their work. Lisa Peterson.
45 The Maine Franco-American Studies Alliance (MFASA) was formed in 2000 at the Common Ground Fair in Unity, Maine, when Susan Pinette and Rhea Côté Robbins from the University of Maine and Barry Rodrigue from the University of Southern Maine met with Lisa Ornstein from the Acadian Archives at the University of Maine at Fort Kent.
46 In 1997 delgates from Maine attended an international trade mission to Vietnam that was sponsored by the *Forum francophone des affaires* (FFA). The FFA also works with the Maine International Trade Center. Maine, Legislature, Commission to Study the Development of Maine's Franco-American Resources.
47 The websites of these organizations are as follow: Forum Francophone des Affaires (http://www.ffa-usa.com/4436.html), the Maine Franco-American Genealogical Society (www.avcnet.org/begin/), and the Franco-American Heritage Center at St. Mary's (http://www.francoamericanheritage.org/).
48 Joan Benoit of Freeport raced in both the Boston and Chicago marathons and won a gold medal for the women's marathon at the 1984 Summer Olympic Games in Los Angeles. Franco-American boxer Joey Gamache of Lewiston became the Featherweight World Champion in 1991 and the Lightweight Champion in 1992, the only world contender from Maine.
49 One of the founders of these film festivals was Maine filmmaker Ben Levine, who had examined the thoughts and feelings of the inhabitants of the borderlands world of Québec and Maine in a documentary film during the 1980 referendum campaign for sovereignty in Québec, *Si je comprends bien* (If I Really Understand). Twenty years later, Levine produced a documentary on the revival of the French language in Maine, *Réveil—Waking Up French*. In the 1990s Francis Gagnon of Lewiston produced "Franco Festivities," a documentary about Maine's Franco-American festivals. Additionally, some attention has been directed from across the border into Maine from Québec. This included the production of *L'Arbre de la mémoire* (The Memory Tree), a sixty-minute documentary film that focused on Franco-American society in Maine and northern New England. Produced by a consortium of

French-speaking filmmakers, in collaboration with TFO (TV-Ontario) and the Institut national de la recherche scientifique—Culture et société (Quebec's National Institute for Scientific Research—Culture and Society), the film was developed, in part, by author Denis LeDoux of Lisbon (Maine) and scholar Yves Frenette of Ottawa (Ontario).

50 Chenard, *Margaret Chase Smith's Franco-American Heritage*. More recently, national Republicans attacked Maine's Republican Senator Olympia Snowe and other Republicans opposed to President George Bush's 2003 tax bill as "Franco-Republicans," in reference to France's opposition to the U.S. organized War in Iraq. This confused and amused many voters in the region who were used to thinking of "Francos" more locally in ethnic terms.

51 Besides the Kennebec–Chaudière Corridor Commission, Rodrigue also founded the Canada Road Historical Society, which was made up of local historians in the villages of northwest Maine and south-central Québec. His vision was to establish an international park and trail system to benefit the local trans-border economies of Somerset and Beauce counties, which are among the poorest in the region. However, the Corridor Commission and the Historical Society were taken over by urban managers from the private and public sectors, who commercialized them into tourism projects. Such expropriation of local initiative is not an unusual phenomenom. For example, the *Maine Ethnic Atlas*—developed by Franco-American activists Yvon Labbé and Barry Rodrigue c. 1996—was taken over by administrators and scholars at the University of Maine atOrono and turned into the *Historical Atlas of Maine*. Rodrigue made a conference presentation on these situations at the 11th International Conference of Historical Geographers in Québec in 2001—"Harmonizing Agendas: Public Geography, Government Policy, and Private Goals." More about this controversial process can be found in files at the Franco-American Collection at the University of Southern Maine's Lewiston-Auburn College.

52 The concept of a Museum in the Streets for Maine was, in part, derived from a similar program in France. Wack.

53 Maine, State Museum.

54 The website, *Maine's French Communities/Le fait français au Maine* (francomaine.org), was founded by the Department of Geography of Laval University and the Franco-American Centre of the University of Maine (Orono). The primary organizers were Yvon Labbé of the University of Maine and Dean Louder and Barry Rodrigue from Laval University. The University of Southern Maine subsequently joined the project, when Rodrigue began working there, and the website was officially inaugurated at USM's Lewiston-Auburn College in Lewiston on 17 October 2000. During a workshop about this website at Fort Kent on 26 September 2000, the participants, all *francophones* from the region, expressed their joy at "finally being on the map" ("enfin sur la *mappe*").

55 Attempting to assemble more than fifty different items into an anthology is a major task, not the least from a stylistic point of view. For example, we have tried to make the style of citation and punctuation conform to eachother as much as is possible. Nonetheless, a reader will see a lot of variability.

56 A humorous incident, reflecting this new surge in Franco-American Studies happened in 2001 when an officer of a historical society in Brunswick, upon hearing that a graduate student proposed to do a study of local French musical traditions, remarked: "Oh, no, not another Franco-American project!" This reaction highlights the recent activism surrounding Franco-Americans in Maine, as well as the dismay of some traditional authorities to this resurgence. Mckeen.

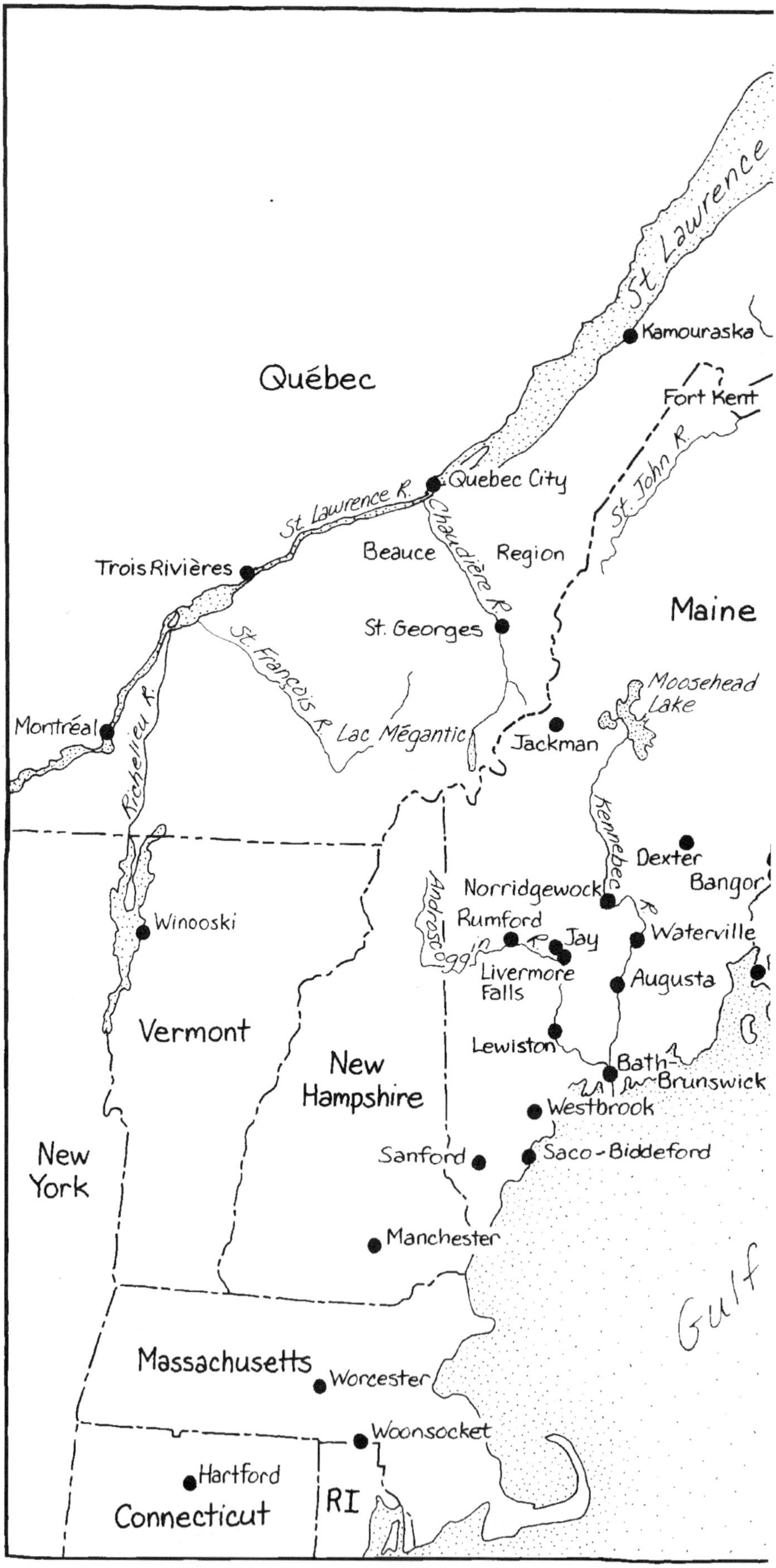

St Lawrence
Kamouraska
Québec
Fort Kent
St. John R.
Quebec City
St. Lawrence R.
Chaudière R.
Beauce
Region
Trois Rivières
Maine
St. Georges
St. François R.
Moosehead Lake
Montréal
Richelieu R.
Lac Mégantic
Jackman
Kennebec
Dexter
Androscoggin R.
Norridgewock
Bangor
Winooski
Rumford
Jay
Waterville
Livermore Falls
Augusta
Vermont
Lewiston
Bath-Brunswick
New Hampshire
Westbrook
New York
Sanford
Saco-Biddeford
Manchester
Gulf
Massachusetts
Worcester
Woonsocket
Hartford
RI
Connecticut

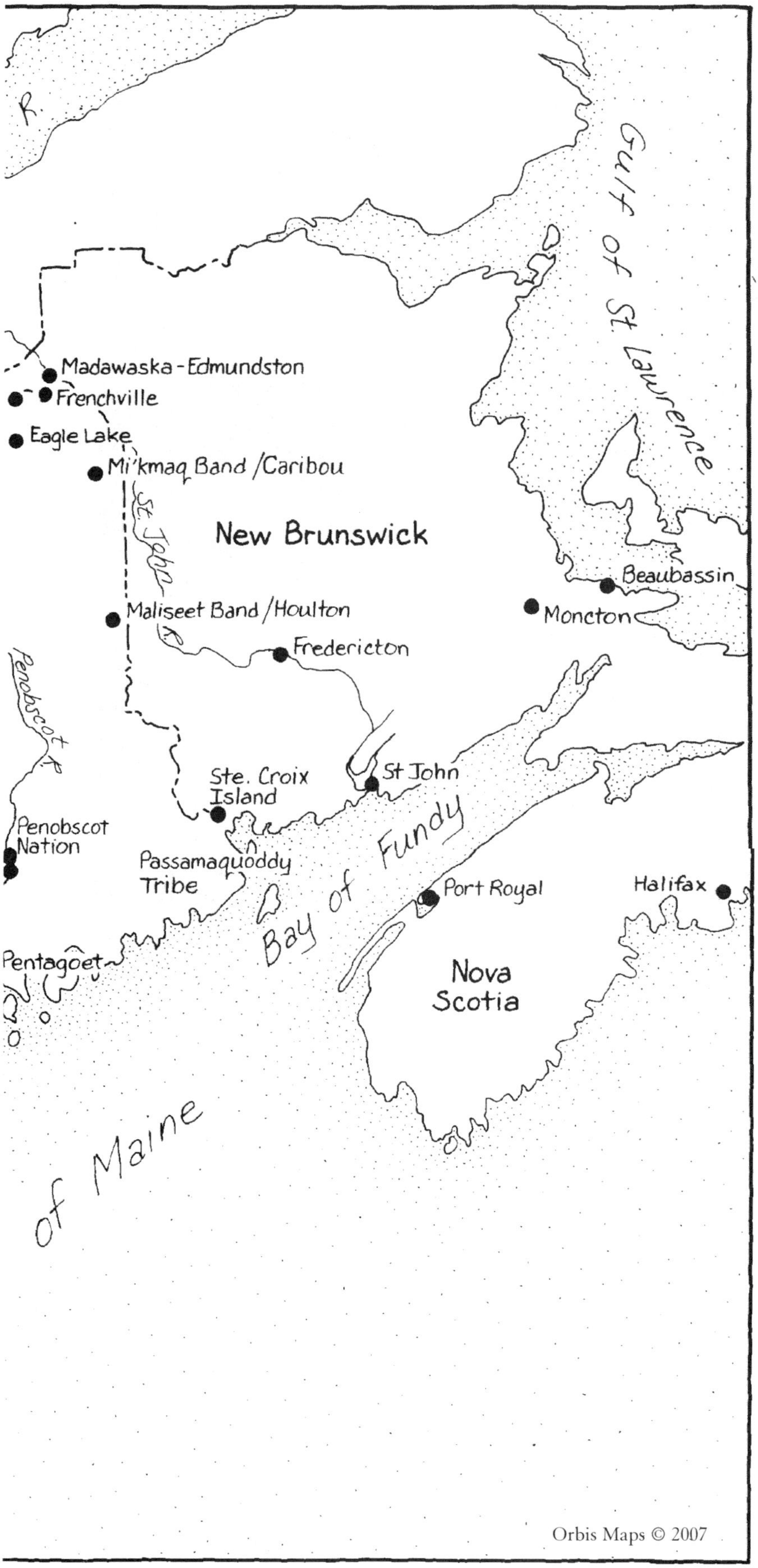
Gulf of St Lawrence
R.
Madawaska - Edmundston
Frenchville
Eagle Lake
Mi'kmaq Band /Caribou
St John R.
New Brunswick
Beaubassin
Moncton
Maliseet Band /Houlton
Fredericton
Penobscot R.
Ste. Croix Island
St John
Penobscot Nation
Passamaquoddy Tribe
Bay of Fundy
Port Royal
Halifax
Pentagoet
Nova Scotia
of Maine
Orbis Maps © 2007

The oldest-known, continuously occupied French community in Maine lay along the Kennebec River in what is now the town of Dresden. Although the French had certainly been in Maine much earlier, their communities had disincorporated as their settlers moved or merged with Indigenous bands. These settlers in Dresden were French Protestants who had been recruited by the Kennebec Proprietors to purchase lands contested by the Abenaki. About twenty families arrived on this fertile floodplain in 1752, just before the outbreak of the Seven Years War, and helped to build Fort Shirley and the Pownalborough Courthouse. One of them, Charles Houdlette, had been an educated lace-weaver in Picardie (France). He moved first to Baden-Württemberg (Germany) in the 1730s, and then sailed with his wife Susanne Macret and their extended family aboard the ship Priscilla *from Rotterdam to Boston in 1751. Their descendents still live in Dresden. Above is a photograph of the Houdlette Burial Ground, which lies in the woods of West Dresden. Corinna Miller, a student at the University of Southern Maine's Lewiston-Auburn College, and geographer/archeologist Barry Rodrigue, are presently engaged in locating the original site remains associated with this settlement and reassessing its history.*

Caption by Barry Rodrigue and Corinna Miller; photograph by Barry Rodrigue

GENTILITY ON THE FRONTIERS OF ACADIA, 1635–1674: AN ARCHAEOLOGICAL PERSPECTIVE[1]

Alaric Faulkner
Orono, Maine

Unlike the open agricultural villages of New England, the coasts of Acadia in the middle seventeenth century were dotted with small fortified outposts dedicated to specialized extractive industries, among them fishing, lumbering, and the fur trade. The rival French entrepreneurs who controlled these enclaves attempted to establish in them New World versions of the traditional aristocratic life to which they aspired. Archaeological excavations of early Acadian sites in Maine, New Brunswick, and Nova Scotia have turned up unusually high proportions of artifacts which, while they were not all luxury goods, speak of pretensions towards a noble lifestyle. Corroborated by documentary research, this image of gentility on the harsh seventeenth-century Acadian frontier seems incongruous and begs for an explanation.

The essential features of Acadian gentility are reflected in an inventory of personal possessions of Isaac de Razilly, one of the progenitors of Acadian settlement. A veteran naval officer and lieutenant general of New France, Razilly organized a major expedition in 1632 bringing three hundred *hommes d'élite* to settle in Acadia to offset the growing strength of New England. These elite included, in addition to members of the Catholic Capuchins, some noblemen, a few of whom became his lieutenants. Together they expanded French settlement through much of the territory newly regained from the English by the Treaty of Saint-Germain-en-Laye, and by 1635 the French were re-established as far as the Penobscot River in Maine.

In December of that same year Razilly died, and his personal property in Acadia was inventoried by the Capuchins. This inventory survives in Tours, France, and has been published in English in a revealing article by Joan Dawson.[2] No monetary appraisal is given, but the sheer number and character of the items listed testify to Razilly's commitment to maintain himself in style. Fully 758 separate items can be identified, falling into the categories: wardrobe, foodways, household furnishings, arms, and miscellaneous.

Some 440 items, or 58.5 percent of the total, were wardrobe items, comprising 421 items of clothing and nineteen grooming articles such as toiletries and dressing table accessories. Colors ranged from subdued black, grey, and olive to green, bright scarlet, and royal blue, while materials varied from common woolens to taffeta, satin, velvet, and silk. Nearly half the items are described by ornament—as tasseled, fringed, with braid, with aglets, with silver wire buttons, embroidered in gold or silver thread, trimmed with lace, or lined with velvet or satin. Such ornamentation is found on nearly every clothing type from suits, gloves, garters, and nightcaps to sword slings and dressing table cloths. With his thirteen suits of clothes, eight cloaks, eight riding coats, and fourteen nightcaps, Razilly was surely prepared to look his best at all occasions.

While most of Razilly's possessions were dedicated to maintaining his physical appearance, items related to foodways were nearly as important, comprising 360 items or 34 percent of the total. These were not mundane items used in the procurement, storage, and preparation of food, but rather were stylish utensils intended for its presentation at the table and consumption. In addition to three dozen pewter dishes for everyday use, a dozen plates, a dozen knives, five drinking cups, and a ewer were included, all of silver or gilt. Razilly was prepared to entertain and dine in style, although the absence of forks and the inclusion of 121 napkins indicate that he was prepared to eat much of his food with his fingers, as was fashionable in the French court.

It is understandable that Razilly, as a formal naval officer, would have household furnishings that were few and portable; just 46 or 6 percent of the items fit into this category, including a half-dozen folding chairs. Nevertheless, at home in a canopy bed with its featherbed and red damask curtains and surrounded by fine furniture draped with various sets of tapestries, Razilly must have cut a genteel figure.

Altogether, items related to dress, dining, and household comforts make up 98.5 percent of the personal inventory. Most of these are clearly formal items, which were as important for their social symbolism as for their utilitarian uses. This could be said of the remaining items as well. The arms category, which includes two arquebuses, a pair of wheelock pistols, a rapier, and a cavalry sword probably functioned as much as essential costume accessories as they did as weapons. Even the four remaining miscellaneous items—two astrolabes, a gold cross, and a brazilwood checkerboard—proclaim the rank or social position of their owner.

While the personal goods of the Acadian governor can hardly be construed as typical of the possessions of the early Acadians, they do establish a pattern held in com-

Young French gentlemen playing a game of "Tric Trac," a board game similar to backgammon, popular in the seventeenth century. French artist Mathieu Le Nain, 1650

mon with other Acadian leaders and those who emulated them. Razilly's death in 1635 left a number of rival entrepreneurs struggling for control of the colony: Charles d'Aulnay, Charles La Tour, Nicolas Denys, and others who were either Razilly's lieutenants or had shared control of Acadia with him. These new leaders were all minor impecunious aristocrats or gentlemen with pretensions to nobility who came to be addressed as "Chevalier."

Unlike English and Dutch leaders, many of whom were merchants with urban backgrounds, these French nobles came from a country with a rural-based economy which offered them very limited opportunities for financial improvement. They sought to augment their fortunes by engaging in the few commercial activities which were considered "respectable." While this excluded most forms of manufacturing, pursuits which involved the management of natural resources were permissible, including the fur trade, lumbering, mining, and management of the fisheries in Acadia.

Competition between these rival factions rapidly evolved into outright warfare. The ensuing conflicts make up a complex plot worthy of the most intricate soap opera. For the next decade, these entrepreneurs launched continual raids against each other, often soliciting the involvement of the New Englanders. The latter were placed in the awkward position of alternately choosing sides and mediating between the factions in order to avoid all-out war between New England and Acadia.

The resulting confusion of alliances helped bring about the collapse of the Massachusetts government of John Winthrop and fueled a growing animosity towards the Acadians. Subsequently, New Englanders took advantage of European power struggles to abet the efforts of England and the Netherlands in wresting Acadia from France. Acadia fell temporarily under English control from 1654 to 1670; in 1674 it was ravaged by Dutch pirates; and in 1713 the major portion of the colony came permanently under British rule.

The tastes and aspirations of the early entrepreneurs are recorded in archaeological collections from three fortified trading posts operated respectively by Charles d'Aulnay, Charles La Tour, and Nicolas Denys.

Fort Pentagoet was located at the mouth of the Penobscot River near modern-day Castine, Maine. Formerly the location of a Plymouth Colony post, it was taken over and completely rebuilt by Charles d'Aulnay in 1635 to control the fur trade along the Penobscot. Pentagoet was a formidable construction built largely of stone, having four bastions and a waterfront battery which defended a compound of five major

The site of Fort Pentagoet, on the lawn of Our Lady of Holy Hope Church, 1982. The excavation of the Dwelling, Structure 1, marks the southwest corner of the curtain. Backfill is piled immediately to the right. The northwest corner of the fort is indicated by a single test pit located between the excavation and the storage tent. The large stain on the grass has nothing to do with subsurface features, but is located near the northeast corner of the fort.
Alaric Faulkner

buildings. After a period of English control from 1654–70 it became the headquarters for the military governorship of Acadia. Destroyed by the Dutch four years later in 1674, it informs on the lifeways of d'Aulnay and his employees, as well as on the later Acadian governors.

Charles La Tour's outpost at the mouth of the St. John River in modern Saint John, New Brunswick, provides corroborative data. Fort La Tour was constructed in 1631 to control the fur trade on the St. John. Enlarged c 1640, it also housed a small mission of Récollet priests until its destruction by d'Aulnay in 1645.

Nicolas Denys' trading post, Fort St. Pierre, located at modern St. Peter's on the southeastern coast of Cape Breton, Nova Scotia, has only been tested. Although built perhaps as early as 1636 by French merchants from La Rochelle, Denys operated it from c. 1650 until its burning in the winter of 1668/1669.

These small fortifications epitomize the distinction between English and French establishments noted by Plymouth's Governor Bradford when he observed: "To the Great danger of the English, who lye open and unfortified, living upon husbandrie...[the French lie] closed up in their forts, well fortified, and live upon trade in good security."

Although construction materials and organization varied, these forts were originally all about the same size, with compounds measuring less than twenty-five meters square. Consequently, they each probably garrisoned a comparable nearly all-male

Reconstruction of the inner compound of d'Aulnay's original Fort Pentagoet as it might have appeared in aerial view looking south, c. 1650
Alaric Faulkner

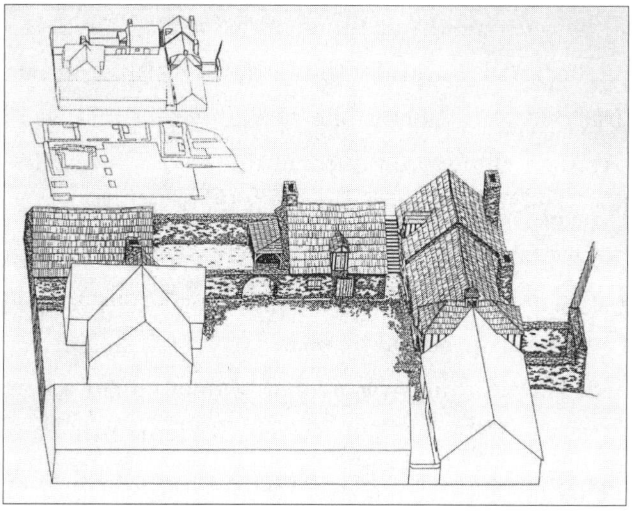

complement of soldier employees, which in the case of Pentagoet never numbered more than twenty-five individuals.

Constructed to offer security for the private investments of their founders, they defended as much against rival Frenchmen as against Indigenous, English, and Dutch enemies. Pentagoet was a prime target for La Tour; Fort La Tour was destroyed by d'Aulnay; and Denys' Fort St. Pierre was assaulted first by d'Aulnay's widow and later by La Rochelle merchant Emmanuel LeBorgne. Yet these miniscule outposts were very effective, allowing the leaders not only to control the resources of huge regions with very few men, but also to maintain small islands of civility in the wilderness.

The artifact assemblages from these three sites are remarkably similar and distinct from Dutch and English colonial sites in the northeast. Affinities are strongest among the numerous ceramic utensils but also can be recognized in metal objects, glass bottles, clay tobacco pipes, and other durable goods. This is due partly to their arrival via a common supply source in France: La Rochelle. But the high proportion of similar status symbols reflects the common backgrounds, aspirations, and demands of the Acadian leaders themselves.

As a general rule, the leaders of all nascent European colonies brought with them the more portable status symbols as reminders of the social order. But for the French, perhaps more so than for other Europeans, it was especially important to act one's station in life, and these frontier Acadians took extreme measures to keep up appearances.

High fashions of dress are indicated at all three sites: at Pentagoet by bits of fabric, gold galloons, braided buttons, a metal sword sling and spur buckles, and other ornaments and accoutrements all found in association with a brass badge bearing d'Aulnay's crest; at Fort La Tour by similar fancy clasps and buckles; and at Fort St. Pierre by a purported glass "slick stone" used for pressing lace. Dressing the part of cavaliers, the Acadian elite wore rapiers at their sides and spurs at their heels. They kept up this incongruous show even though there is little evidence in the extensive refuse from the workshops at Pentagoet that the swords saw regular use as weapons, and there is no evidence for the use of horses; transportation along the jagged coast of western Acadia was only practical by boat.

This taste for fine clothing was evidently maintained among later seventeenth-century Acadians as well. La Rochelle merchant Henri Brunet, who cruised the coast of Acadia in the 1670s and traded at Pentagoet, composed in 1675 a requisition for

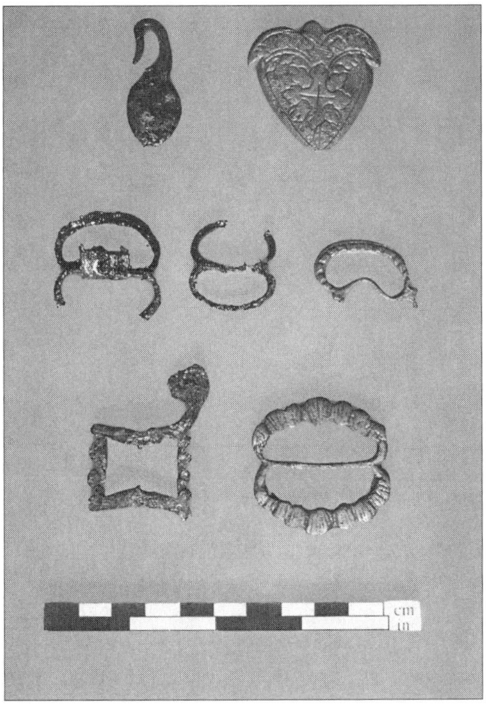

Left: Clothing accessories related to noble status: upper right, cast brass badge with staple fastening on the back, bearing the cross and oak leaf motif of the Aulnay crest; lower left, fragmentary "butterfly" spur buckle; remaining items, hook and buckles from sword slings. Right: "Foppish" French dress of the middle seventeenth century including high-crowned beaver hats and ribbons layered in rows, was apparently no less popular on the Acadian frontier than in France itself. French gentleman 1646, unidentified artist

goods for trade in Acadia which shows clearly this continuity. The item of greatest value was salt for the fisheries in Placentia, followed by brandy and other alcoholic beverages. But the remaining goods, which comprised fully 80 percent of the listings, were items of clothing and personal grooming resembling in type and quality the items on Razilly's inventory. As these were not all finished goods, they were supplemented with appropriate tailoring supplies. Indeed, with silk galloons and wire braided buttons in many colors, Brunet's cargo comprised a veritable floating emporium of sewing notions.

As for his personal wardrobe, Brunet was intent on impressing his frontier clientele, ordering "a black beaver hat with a rather fine black plume and a wig...of beautiful, life-like hair," along with other personal articles worthy of Razilly's wardrobe. But a practical attitude to frontier fashion is revealed in his request for two new doublets:

> ...one of brocade, the other of floral cloth or watered mohair. It doesn't matter whether this material is in fashion—they don't care if it is in these parts—but the whole has to be proper and well garnished with lace: one gold and the other silver—it matters not whether it be sham or genuine.[3]

Clearly Brunet was marketing discount goods which, although out of fashion in Europe, affected the highest standards of grandeur.

Ribbons, a fragmentary example of which was actually recovered at Pentagoet, seem to have become especially popular with the early French Acadians. Brunet intended to do more business in ribbons from St. Étienne than in any other item of clothing, ordering 250 livres worth. A letter written in 1662 by an anonymous New Englander records the Puritan reaction to this French taste and also indicates just how these ribbons were worn. Apparently, Boston merchant Thomas Breedon adopted the French style of dress to excess while he was managing the Acadian interests of Sir Thomas Temple during the 1654–70 period of English control:

> He appeared in Boston in a strange habit with a 4 Cornerd Cap instead of a hat, and his Breeches hung with Ribbons from the Wast downw a grt depth, one row over another like shingles on a house: The Boyes when he came made an outcry, from one end of the streete to the other calling him a Devill, which was so greate, that people woundering came out of there houses to see whatt the matter was.[4]

Ribbons and other ornaments were even used by the English to identify French involvement in Maine's manifestation of King Philip's War in 1676. A report to Governor Leverett includes the following account of surveillance of the enemy:

> There are two or three Frenchmen with them, one who leads being brave [i.e., smartly dressed] with blue, black & yellow ribbons on his knee, a hat buckled with a silver buckle, brave [i.e., stylish] belt &c. & heard him inquire in French...of the [English] captives whether it were difficult to take Richmond Island & Blackpoint.[5]

Feasting and elegant presentation were important to the French long before the rise of *haute cuisine*, as is shown in Denys' description of a picnic feast he provided for Governor Razilly, c. 1633:

> I had him enter a hall which I had built, covered with branches, where he found a table very well furnished, with pigeon soup, with Wild Geese and Brant; with these all his retinue enjoyed themselves as well as he, for they all had good appetites. To this course there followed another of Brant and Teal, and to that a third of large and small Snipe, and Plover in pyramids.... Raspberries and Strawberries in abundance served for dessert...White wine and claret were not wanting for this little feast, so that Monsieur de Razilly and all his retinue were very well pleased.... Game never failed me—they had it every day.[6]

Nearly all these wild species are represented in the faunal remains found near the d'Aulnay period house at Pentagoet, showing the marked preference of the French for wild fowl. Indeed, these kitchen middens indicate that a wide variety of wild fowl, fish, and mammals was consumed regularly, often with elegant preparation. Wild birds were prepared in deep pastry shells and served as casseroles or pies.

On special occasions they feasted on bear, a meat praised as being "very delicate and white as that of veal." The bear's head was commonly cut lengthwise and served in profile on a platter as was the customary presentation for veal. Gradually, as in all the northeastern colonies, domestic mammals displaced wild mammals in the diet, but the basic French love for wild fowl and fish continued.

The common vessels used for food preparation and storage were predominantly coarse green- or yellow-glazed earthenwares manufactured near La Rochelle in the Saintonge region of western France. But other ceramics, although not expensive by themselves, tell of refined traditions in dining. A variant of the Saintonge ware is gaudily painted in polychrome with distinctive relief-molded masks of humans and animals executed in the fashionable style of the renowned sixteenth-century French potter-artist Bernard Palissy. Forms include chafing dishes which held boiling water to keep food warm at the table, miniature barrel costrels for serving brandy, and various fonts and serving dishes. Plain white tin-glazed serving vessels were also common, often ornamented with elaborate knobs or finials and with handles in zoömorphic forms. Both wares imitate shapes which were originally executed in silver and gold.

Although these ceramic types went out of fashion by 1650, the later Acadians

Principal forms of utilitarian, buff-bodied earthenware found at Fort Pentagoet and imported from western and southwestern France. At left is a typical green-glazed Saintonge storage jar with a single strap handle. At right is a yellow-glazed "marmite" or cooking pot with two rod handles. Both specimens are glazed only on the interior of the rim to keep their lids from sticking.
Alaric Faulkner

Reconstruction of a relief-molded polychrome chafing dish from Fort Pentagoet I, 1635–54, used to keep food warm at the table. Gaudy to our eyes, this style followed that of the popular craftsman Bernard Palissy, and was imported from the Saintonge area of west central France.
Alaric Faulkner

Charles de Menou d'Aulnay (c. 1605–50),
governor and lieutenant-general of Acadia and founder of
Fort Pentagoet, at age thirty-seven, 1642.
New Brunswick Museum

were no less committed to fine dining. At Pentagoet they brought with them matching sets of knives with handsomely carved bone handles. But perhaps the most elegant items to grace the table were matching stemmed wine glasses blown eggshell thin in the Venetian style.

Gentility was expressed not only in symbols and habits, but also in the most ephemeral of artifacts: words. When Charles d'Aulnay took possession of the Pilgrim truck house in Penobscot in 1635 and sent their agent packing, he did so with the civility of a noble. Enraged as he was by the takeover, Governor Bradford of Plymouth still could not help but comment on his enemy's manners:

> Partly by threatening and other wise, [he] made, Mr. Willet, their agent there, to approve of the sale of the goods there unto him.... So thus turning them out of all, with a great deal of compliment and many fine words, he let them have their shallop and some victuals to bring them home.[7]

John Winthrop (1588–1649), first governor of Massachusetts Bay. School of Sir Anthony Van Dyck, c. 1625–49. American Antiquarian Society, Worcester, Massachusetts

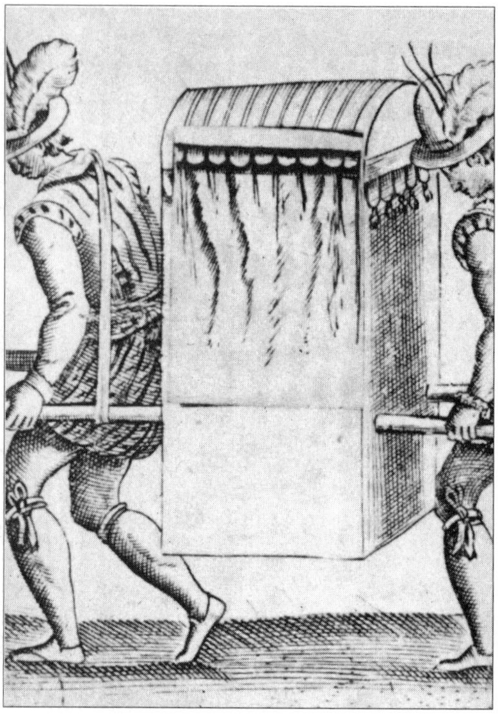

Servants bearing a nobleman in a sedan chair, similar to that presented to d'Aulnay by Governor Winthrop

According to Governor Winthrop of Massachusetts Bay, communications from La Tour in 1642 soliciting Massachusetts's assistance in fighting d'Aulnay were similarly "full of compliments."[8] This perception of French extravagance probably affected his diplomatic gestures towards them. In 1646, when Winthrop wanted to make amends to d'Aulnay after many years of siding with La Tour, he presented him with a "very fair" sedan chair, which "could not be less worth than 50 lbs." Originally intended as a gift from the viceroy of Mexico to his sister, the sedan had been seized by an English privateer who presented it to the Massachusetts governor. Having no use for the sedan, Winthrop passed it on to the horseless French noblemen, presumably so that he might be carried about in style by his employees.[9]

Archaeology also provides evidence which tempers this image of frontier French gentility. The lack of spoons and forks and the pattern of butchering revealed in the

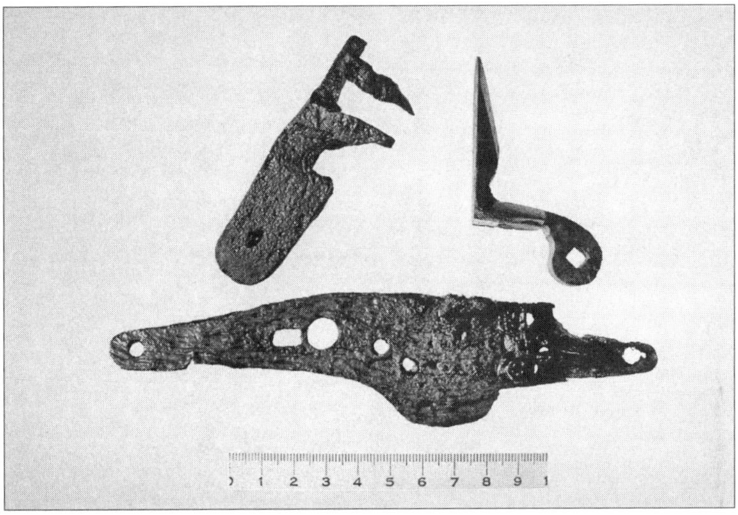

Representative sample of finished, worn out, and unfinished gunlock parts recovered from the Armorer's workshop at Fort Pentagoet. Top: unfinished replacement guncock with finished upper jaw; complete replacement early "frizzen" or battery/pan cover. Bottom: worn-out bellied lock plate from an early snaphaunce of Dutch or English design.
Alaric Faulkner

food remains seem to confirm that they treated their meat stews and bird pies as finger food. Moreover they apparently threw their food wastes on the floor, in the alley, in the cellar, or wherever else was immediately convenient.

Throughout their existence the outposts of Acadia were at the end of an infrequent and chronically unreliable line of supply. Though they kept their own livestock at Pentagoet, the garrison also depended on barreled meats which may have come from New England; even Brunet brought along empty barrels to buy such provisions in Boston rather than ship them from France. Yet the New England supply was no more reliable than the French. Famine struck the Pentagoet garrison during the winter of 1671/1672, and is reflected by hawk and domestic cat bones and other "starvation foods."

Judging from the refuse from Pentagoet's smithy/workshop, d'Aulnay came well prepared to cope with shortfalls in durable goods through the manufacture, repair, and recycling of those items which saw the heaviest everyday use or were essential to the conduct of the fur trade. Gunflints were made on site as needed, as were cast lead musketballs and shot. All manner of firearms were repaired and replacement parts for them were fabricated from scratch as needed. Various fittings and structural hard-

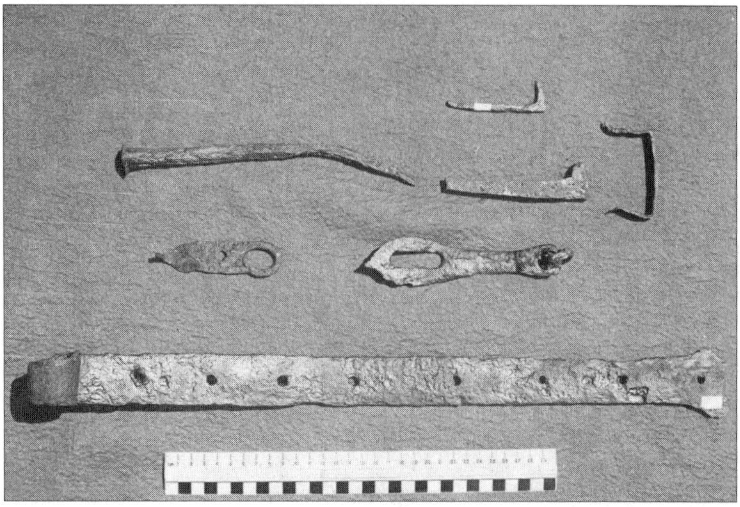

Sample of hardware from Fort Pentagoet, some of which was surely fabricated locally at the forge. Top: spike, two masonry anchors, and a drop bar guide for a latch. Middle: gudgeon of a strap hinge for a strong box and a hasp. Bottom: Strap hinge from the cellar door of the Dwelling, Structure 1, recovered in place.
Alaric Faulkner

ware were formed and repaired at the forge. Tools were also manufactured or remanufactured, particularly cutting implements such as saws, files, and axes. Very little was discarded until every bit of usefulness was extracted from it. Sheet copper and brass salvaged from worn-out kettles was reworked to make everything from candle holders, hinges for small boxes, and small tools to rivets and patches for repairing other copper kettles.We also see a few tools made in this fashion: a thread gauge, a saw pattern, and an awl. We also find decorative items for both Europeans and their Abenaki trading partners: lace tips, tinkling cones, a perforated cruciform disk, and a hair tube. The French employed sheet copper for ornamentation much in the same way as did their Indigenous trading partners, forming makeshift aglets and "tinkling cones" to adorn the fringes of their clothing.

A sewing kit found at Pentagoet comprising a fancy braided button stuffed into a thimble symbolizes the paradox of gentility and deprivation in seventeenth-century Acadia. The button was surely intended for a stylish garment, but the thimble was actually a makeshift item produced by cutting the ears off a pewter cartridge cap such as was worn on the bandoliers of seventeenth-century musketeers.

In assessing this evidence, it is difficult to weigh the differences between cultures which are fully three and a half centuries removed from our own. Distinguishing the unusual from the normative, the outlandish from the fashionable, the practical from the superfluous, and the necessary from the extravagant is a formidable task, demanding the pursuit of many lines of evidence. Most of the artifacts mentioned are distinctively French and would be considered anomalous on seventeenth-century English sites. Some reflect an unusually comfortable, even luxurious standard of living, considering the circumstances, while others merely seem to be superfluous or out of place. But taken together with primary documents which make explicit the reactions of English and French contemporaries to the behavior of the Acadian frontiersmen, these artifacts form an inescapable image of gentility on the frontiers of Acadia.

The early Acadian elite dressed, ate, and spoke in manners which seem foppish and thoroughly incongruous, considering the hardships of the frontier. Yet to forsake the requisite customs and symbols of rank was totally unacceptable to them. One of the fixed costs of living, even for the minor, impecunious nobles of early Acadia, was the maintenance of one's image, an obligation as important and inescapable as the maintenance of one's tools or one's firearms.

1 This article initially appeared in the 1989 *Proceedings of the Dublin Seminar for New England Folklife*. We express our thanks to Director and Editor Peter Benes for permission to reproduce it. Alaric Faulkner, "Gentility on the Frontiers of Acadia, 1635–1674: An Archaeological Perspective," in *New England/New France, 1600–1850*, Peter Benes (editor), *Annual Proceedings of the Dublin Seminar for New England Folklife* 14, 1989, (Boston: Boston University Press, 1992), pp. 82–100.

2 Dawson, pp. 99–112.

3 Henri Brunet.

4 Unidentified correspondent, to John Davenport.

5 Scottow and Josselyn, to Governor Leverett.

6 Denys.

7 William Bradford, pp. 275–76.

8 Winthrop, p. 85.

9 Winthrop, pp. 273, 285.

EASTERN ABENAKI AUTONOMY AND FRENCH FRUSTRATIONS, 1745–1760[1]

David Ghere
Stillwater, Minnesota

As the English–French struggle for the continent approached its conclusion in February 1759, a group from the Penobscot Nation appeared at Fort St. Georges (near Thomaston, Maine) seeking to re-establish peace and trade relations with Massachusetts. They carried with them a letter indicating a growing French frustration over their unwillingness to renew hostilities against the English. This situation, which contrasted so sharply with the earlier expectations of French Governor La Jonquière, that the Abenaki would be the "most faithful allies [of France], and will never forget what [he had] done for them," illustrates an important feature of Abenaki diplomacy during the later colonial wars.[2]

Abenaki warriors accompanied almost every French military operation during the mid-1700s from the Ohio Valley to Cape Breton Island. Yet the strongest support for France came from the Western Abenakis, in present-day Vermont, New Hampshire, and Quebec, who, in previous wars, had enjoyed more direct French support and had repeatedly conducted successful frontier raids from relatively secure villages at St. François, Bécancour, and Missiquoi. The Eastern Abenaki, those tribes located between the Saco River and the Machias River, were more vulnerable to English militia attacks and had been frustrated by limited French support in the past. During the Five-Year War (Dummer's War, 1722–27), they had suffered several significant military defeats, including the destruction of their two principal villages, Penobscot (at Old Town) and Norridgewock (on the Kennebec).[3] For the Eastern Abenaki, the matter of French or English alliances was much less certain.

All of the major Abenaki villages consisted in whole or part of refugees driven from their traditional homes further south by a half-century of warfare and the expansion of English settlements. Many chose to migrate to the Canadian missions at St. François and Bécancour, aware that this placed them under the protection and influence of the French. The Eastern Abenaki, both refugees and original inhabitants, largely rejected the safety of Canada, thereby retaining a greater degree of autonomy.

U.S. eight-cent postage stamp memorializing the English massacre of the Abenaki at Norridgewock in 1724.
Franco-American Collection, University of Southern Maine/Lewiston-Auburn[4]

The Eastern Abenaki were politically divided during the eighteenth century. Factionalism resulted primarily from internal disputes over diplomatic relations with the English. The English government claimed sovereignty over the Eastern Abenaki and sought to force them to act like subjects of the king. The militia posed a threat to the safety of their villages, and the expansion of English settlements into Abenaki territory ultimately jeopardized their subsistence and culture. Consequently, while relations with the French might be confused or troublesome, the focus of Abenaki political dissension was with the English.[5]

Members of the conciliatory factions believed that trade and peaceful co-existence with the English would preserve their land and culture. They sought to avoid becoming involved in disputes between the French and English, repeatedly professed their desire for peace, and warned English settlers when raids were imminent. Members of the confrontational faction thought that English domination could only be prevented through repeated, unswerving resistance to every English settlement expansion or encroachment on Abenaki hunting and fishing areas. When an English–French conflict erupted, these Abenaki migrated to the Canadian missions, welcomed French support for their raids on the Maine frontier, and participated in French campaigns.

French and English diplomatic rivalry intensified during the two decades of peace (1725–45) that followed the Five-Year War. French officials sought alliances by issuing officer commissions with pay, awarding medals, and distributing shares of the fur-trade revenue to the Eastern Abenaki. They hoped to gain influence over the conciliatory faction by reducing the prices of their trade goods and by presenting ever larger quantities of gifts. The French even considered a proposal to send Abenaki leaders to visit Paris.[6]

French policy-makers faced a confusing dilemma regarding those Abenaki who remained on the Maine frontier. Large numbers of the Abenaki would oppose English land claims, retard English settlement expansion, and block the Kennebec River invasion route to Quebec, but French officials feared that close proximity would expose the Abenaki to English influence. Following the Five-Year War, Father Laverjat was directed to continue serving at the Penobscot mission, and another Jesuit missionary was appointed to the Norridgewock mission on the Kennebec River in 1728. However, in the early 1730s French officials, attempting to reduce the number of Natives moving to Norridgewock where they could be subverted by English trade, intimidation and presents, removed the missionaries from the frontier.[7]

Despite these various French efforts, the conciliatory faction dominated Eastern Abenaki relations with the English in the early decades of the eighteenth century. There were occasional raids on settlers' livestock, angry moments at conferences, and strong reactions when English settlements expanded near the St. Georges River, but friendly relations predominated.[8] Deteriorating Anglo–French relations in Europe in 1743 prompted concern over the loyalty of the Eastern Abenaki in a colonial war between the two powers. France declared war on England in March 1744, and—when this news arrived in the Colonies—nine canoes of confrontational Penobscot warriors immediately set out for Canada, as did a smaller group of Norridgewock. Conciliatory Penobscot and Norridgewock professed a desire for peace, in 1744, and provided Massachusetts with information on Mi'kmaq and Maliseet raids in Nova Scotia.[9]

Both French and English officials were disappointed in this minimal support for their respective countries and vigorously sought to win the allegiance of the Eastern Abenaki. Canadian Governor Beauharnois offered them military protection and supplies if they relocated to Canada and pledged the support of the Western Abenaki. He recruited the confrontational Norridgewock and Penobscot visiting Canada to join in the attacks on English settlements in Nova Scotia, offering presents and supplies as incentives. Massachusetts Governor Shirley sought to maintain peace with the Eastern Abenaki through a combination of incentives (continued trade and generous presents) and intimidation (threats of retaliation). Massachusetts demanded that they join in an alliance against the Mi'kmaq and Maliseet.[10]

The Eastern Abenaki who remained in Maine refused the alliance with Massachusetts but continued to profess their desire for peace. Then, in October 1744, a group of English scalp-hunters killed one Penobscot and wounded several others along the Penobscot River—over 160 kilometers (100 miles) from the nearest established area for bounties. The murderers were never identified, but Massachusetts officials, following the advice of conciliatory Penobscot, gave the widow presents to compensate for the loss of her husband, as was Abenaki custom. Despite this atrocity, Massachusetts renewed its demand for an alliance on November 14, and was quickly turned down. This refusal and reports of Penobscot involvement in attacks in Nova Scotia increased the distrust of Massachusetts officials, but open trade was maintained.[11]

French Governor Beauharnois, also disappointed by the Abenaki reaction to these events, remained determined to turn the Eastern Abenaki against the New England settlements. The growing tensions between the Abenaki and the English offered an opportunity, and in April 1745 the French king directed the governor to promote Abenaki raids in an effort to force a break in Anglo–Abenaki relations. In July a war party from Canada attacked Fort St. Georges, and the confrontational factions of the Norridgewock and Penobscot assaulted Pemaquid. These were the first significant attacks on the Maine frontier in sixteen months of war, and they prompted Massachusetts to declare war against the Eastern Abenaki on August 23.[12]

The declaration of war prompted more Eastern Abenaki to migrate. French officials promised supplies to Eastern Abenaki allies along the St. John River, but these proved inadequate, resulting in an additional influx of Eastern Abenaki to Quebec in November.[13] During the next two years, in 1746 and 1747, these Abenaki engaged in various raids on the Maine frontier and participated in French military expeditions to Beaubassin (on the Nova Scotia border) and the Lake Champlain Valley.[14]

A group of conciliatory Penobscot remained in the Penobscot River Valley, but shortages of food and supplies worsened, and the prospect of French provisions in the refugee villages near Quebec loomed as a powerful inducement for them. French records indicate that there were at least five villages of Indigenous peoples from Acadia in the Quebec area during the early winter of 1747—with two, totaling 600 people, containing the "greater portion of the village of Pannaouamske [Penobscot]." This significant increase in the number of Eastern Abenaki in Quebec suggests widespread hunger in Maine.[15] Surviving records of the last year of the war—1748—provide few details, but most of the migrants from the previous fall seem to have remained near Quebec, while other Eastern Abenaki migrants (probably Norridgewock) were living at Bécancour.[16]

The English–French conflict was resolved with the treaty of Aix-la-Chapelle in October 1748. French colonial officials had already canceled scalp bounties and prisoner ransoms and had ordered attacks on the English to cease. However, many of the confrontational Abenaki ignored these proclamations and continued to launch sporadic raids until the summer of 1749. Meanwhile, the conciliatory Penobscot and Norridgewock sent a delegation to Boston to arrange a peace conference for late September. Early that month a letter from confrontational Penobscot urged the postponement of the conference, and the late arrival of the Penobscot delegation ultimately delayed the meeting until mid-October. The Treaty of Falmouth marked the official end of hostilities on 16 October 1749, but none of the Penobscot confrontational leaders signed the treaty and there is no indication of their presence at the conference.[17]

The friendly relations that followed this treaty were extremely brief. A small group of Abenakis returning from the peace conference was attacked near Wiscasset on 2 December 1749. One was killed and several others wounded.[18] The Western Abenaki favored immediate revenge upon Wiscasset settlers, while conciliatory factions among the Norridgewock and Penobscot urged Massachusetts to "cover the blood" with compensatory presents. The confrontational factions of the Eastern Abenaki demanded swift and severe punishment for the men responsible, but did not yet propose attacks on settlers to avenge the atrocity.[19]

Massachusetts officials sought to soothe the anger of the Natives with condolences and compensatory presents, and by assuring them of justice against the murderers. However, angry mobs thwarted the initial arrests and, after numerous delays, the trial ended, in June 1750, in an acquittal.[20] Confrontational Abenaki responded to this and other incidents by killing cattle near St. Georges in early June. Massachusetts sent another set of presents to the victim's relatives and hoped that the annual distribution of presents in early October would further appease the Abenaki.[21]

French officials were disappointed with the Eastern Abenaki reaction to the Wiscasset incident. The French foreign minister informed Governor La Jonquière that nothing was of greater importance than maintaining the support of their Indigenous allies and authorized him to distribute the gifts necessary to accomplish that goal. Intendant Bigot complained that the conciliatory factions were "so connected with the English, that they did not wish to insist on justice." He and Governor La Jonquière used their influence to convince the Abenaki that it would disgrace their people if the crimes went unpunished. They also promised to provision retaliatory raids against the Maine frontier.[22]

These efforts were only partially successful. In late August a large number of Western Abenaki arrived at the Penobscot and Norridgewock villages urging retaliation for the murder. On 11 September 1750, thirty Penobscot warriors, along with eighty Western Abenaki, attacked Fort Richmond on the lower Kennebec River.[23] When Western Abenaki continued the raids through the spring and summer of 1751, conciliatory Penobscot and Norridgewock leaders professed their desire for peace and warned English settlers whenever assaults were imminent.[24] These events placed the Norridgewock in a very precarious position. Shortly after the assault on Fort Richmond, twenty-one warriors migrated to the Canadian missions where they resided for about eighteen months. Many families of the Norridgewock conciliatory faction journeyed to the Penobscot village, and a third group stayed at Norridgewock, professing a desire for peace and facing down the threat of retaliation from the militia or angry settlers.[25]

Penobscot peace efforts resulted in a preliminary conference in late August 1751, but frontier tensions continued. A month after the conference, a Penobscot letter warned Governor Shirley of French efforts to incite the Norridgewock migrants and Western Abenaki to renewed hostilities. The Penobscot sent emissaries to Canada to dissuade the other Abenaki from attacking the frontier. After a year without incidents, a treaty was finally signed in October 1752 with representatives from the Norridgewock, Penobscot, Maliseet, and Western Abenaki.[26]

Peace enabled the Norridgewock migrants to return to their village, but a new source of tension quickly surfaced. In 1751 a new settlement was established north of Fort Richmond and, at the 1753 conference, for the first time, Massachusetts revealed that English land claims extended 89 kilometers (55 miles) above Fort Richmond to within almost 10 kilometers (6 miles) of the Norridgewock village.[27] This caused a dramatic shift in Norridgewock attitudes, as indicated by hostile interactions with settlers. The Penobscot confrontational faction likewise expressed its displeasure.[28] French officials also grew concerned, since new settlements would open the Kennebec River as an invasion route to Québec. Governor Duquesne urged the Norridgewock to resist the settlements, promised forts and troops to protect them, and dispatched Fathers Audran and Gaunon along with numerous Western Abenaki to the Maine frontier to lend their support.[29]

Anglo–Abenaki tensions increased dramatically in the months following the 1753 conference. Late in the year two St. François Natives were murdered on the New Hampshire frontier, and in March 1754 two Penobscot were murdered on an island near St. Georges.[30] In January some Norridgewock informed Captain Lithgow, commander of Fort Richmond, of a new French fortress and settlement at the head of the Kennebec River.[31]

The report, although verified by other parties, was false, but it may have been the result of confusion over Duquesne's promise to provide forts or a Norridgewock tactic for intimidating settlers. In any case, Governor Shirley proposed a military expedition to eliminate any French installations on the Kennebec River and to construct an English fortress at Taconic Falls, 60 kilometers (37 miles) above Fort Richmond. Before the expedition was launched, the English scheduled a conference with the Eastern Abenaki, largely to intimidate them with a large militia force.[32]

Despite Abenaki protests and repeated assurances that no French fort existed, Shirley's expedition began moving up the Kennebec River on July 6. Construction of the fort at Taconic began on July 25, while the main body of the expedition (500 men) ascended to the headwaters to attack the rumored French fort. After a thorough search, the militia determined that no French installations existed. By October 17, Fort Halifax was completed, and all the contractors and non-garrison militiamen dismissed.[33] The expedition presented a crisis for the Norridgewock, resulting in divisions and migrations similar to those following the Wiscasset incident three years earlier. A small group remained at the village and informed Colonel Winslow at Fort Halifax of their desire to live in peace.[34]

Predictably, the French were upset by the events of 1754. The strategic implications of Fort Halifax were of particular concern, and Governor Duquesne was incensed that the Eastern Abenaki had not resisted its construction more vigorously. Fathers Audran and Gaunon had failed in their efforts to influence Eastern Abenaki diplomacy, and even the Western Abenaki had violated Duquesne's orders in some ways. Recognizing Norridgewock vulnerability, he encouraged their emigration to Canada and caused the recall of Father Audran to facilitate this action. The French provided supplies for an Abenaki attack on Fort Halifax, and officials began urging all the Abenaki, Maliseet, and Mi'kmaq to engage in a united war against the English.[35] Many Abenaki needed little encouragement. A large war party of 110 Western Abenaki and Norridgewock emigrants departed from the Canadian missions hoping to surprise and overpower Fort Halifax. On October 30 they encountered a six-man logging detachment near the fort and killed or captured all but one member. The subsequent attack was unsuccessful and the raiders returned to Canada.[36]

Although Governor Shirley's expedition and the subsequent hostilities prompted some Penobscot to migrate to Canada, others sought to resume normal trade relations. Conciliatory Penobscot sent three letters to Shirley professing their desire for peace and pledging to warn the settlers of future raids. They also sought to reduce the chance of frontier incidents by moving their village upriver and requesting that a supply ship be sent to trade with them at their village.[37] Massachusetts responded by lifting trade restrictions and distributing annual presents. However, the movement upriver was interpreted as a possible preparation for assaults on the English frontier, so the request for a supply ship was denied.[38]

Abenaki raids resumed in April and May 1755 in western Maine, prompting Massachusetts to declare war on all the Abenaki except the Penobscot. Then, in June, Abenaki warriors from the Canadian missions (accompanied most likely by migrant Penobscot) conducted a series of attacks in the St. Georges area, causing many settlers and colonial leaders to assume the Penobscot were responsible.[39] The resulting tensions prompted Massachusetts to propose that the Penobscot move their village to the "protection" of Fort St. Georges and that their warriors join the English in attacking hostile Natives. After these proposals were read on 27 June 1755, the local militia refused to allow the Penobscot leaders to leave Fort St. Georges without accepting the demands and leaving hostages. The Penobscot reluctantly agreed, but five days later English scalp-hunters attacked them and their families at nearby Owls Head, killing fourteen. These events prompted another group of Penobscot to migrate to the Canadian missions.[40] Massachusetts officials sought to soothe the anger of the Penobscot with condolences, promises of justice, and compensatory presents. The summer was spent in an exchange of letters between angry Penobscot and consoling Englishmen. By September it appeared that Anglo–Penobscot peace would be preserved.[41] Then, on 24 September 1755, Abenaki warriors from Canada bypassed Fort Halifax to attack the St. Georges area again. Massachusetts, suspecting Penobscot involvement, renewed its demands for an alliance. Fearing scalp-hunters or militia attacks, the Penobscot failed to return to Fort St. Georges. The deteriorating situation finally resulted in a Massachusetts declaration of war, on 1 November 1755, against the Penobscot.[42]

Even though the Penobscot and Norridgewock were officially at war with the English, many refused to ally with the French. These tensions prompted some Penobscot (probably including the conciliatory Norridgewock) to migrate to the relative safety of the Maliseet villages in Acadia. Others retreated up the Penobscot River and generally avoided contact with the English, except for occasional attempts to sell their furs.[43] For the next two years, these conciliatory Penobscot and Norridgewock remained inactive in the Anglo–French dispute; those still on the Penobscot River even attempted to initiate peace negotiations.[44]

The confrontational factions of the Eastern Abenaki remained near Quebec, during 1756 and 1757, and participated in raids on the Maine frontier.[45] Abenaki warriors were praised for their scouting and fighting capabilities during successful French military operations near Lake Champlain, but the Penobscot were criticized by General Montcalm for attacking the English after their surrender at Fort William Henry. Widespread famine in 1757 and 1758 ultimately forced some conciliatory Eastern Abenaki to become French auxiliaries. In 1758 the Penobscot in Acadia joined several hundred Maliseet warriors and French militia in operations east of the St. John River and conciliatory Norridgewock joined their kinsmen at Quebec.[46]

The largest French and Native expedition in the history of the Maine frontier occurred in late August 1758. The French wanted the Penobscot, Maliseet, and French militia operating in Acadia to move to Cape Breton Island to help defend Louisbourg. The Natives rejected the request in favor of a surprise attack on Fort St. Georges. As a result, an expedition of 50 French militia and over 250 Penobscot and Maliseet made their way into eastern Maine and, on 26 August 1758, attacked Fort St. Georges. They were unsuccessful, since the fort and nearby settlements had received prior warning. After several days of siege, the warriors broke into small bands and roamed the area throughout the following month.[47] The Franco–Native attempt on Fort St. Georges and subsequent raids were the last attacks of the war on the Maine frontier. For the remaining years of the war, the Abenaki avoided contacts with the English, except to trade occasionally. A French official lamented that their Native allies were "unwilling to go fight unless we feed their women and children." Then, in February 1759, Penobscot representatives sought to initiate peace talks and indicated French anger at their decision.[48]

Throughout this stormy period of diplomacy with the French and English, the Eastern Abenakis maintained their autonomy. Several very fluid political factions made decisions concerning war and migration in their own best interest, often frustrating the French by their restrained reaction to Anglo–French warfare, to the murder of their kinsmen, or to the expansion of English forts and settlements. Those who chose to become French allies often acted against French orders and refused to serve unless their families were well-supplied. Religion was of minimal importance in determining Eastern Abenaki allegiances during this period. No missionary lived in the Eastern Abenaki villages during the 1730s and 1740s, and the occasional visiting priests had little impact on tribal factionalism. When Fathers Audran and Gounon were dispatched to Maine, from 1753–54, they failed to have any influence on the crisis there.

The limited nature of French influence is further indicated by the lack of correlation between periods of Anglo–French war and Anglo–Abenaki hostilities. No significant Native attacks occurred on the Maine frontier during the first sixteen months of the War of the Austrian Succession (King George's War), but Abenaki raids continued for seven months after the Anglo–French treaty. During the next conflict, the Seven Years' War (the French and Indian War), Massachusetts's declaration of war on the Penobscot came a year and a half after the first French-supported Western Abenaki raids, while attacks on the Maine frontier ceased two years before the conquest of Canada was completed. The need in both wars for a declaration of war and a peace treaty with the Eastern Abenaki indicates their autonomy from the French.

Most Eastern Abenaki eventually became French allies during these wars, but not all by choice. The outbreak of hostilities in both wars prompted many confrontational members to journey to Canada, while a second migration generally occurred whenever Massachusetts declared war on the Eastern Abenaki. Then during the two conflicts, subsistence needs eventually forced some conciliatory members to migrate and become French allies to secure supplies. Clearly, French diplomatic efforts failed to win over the conciliatory factions, but the delay in migration of the second confrontational groups indicates limited success in cementing the loyalty of that faction as well. Ultimately, English actions drove the Eastern Abenaki into supporting the French, despite their efforts to remain neutral in these imperial wars between the European occupants of their homelands.

1 An early version of this article appeared in *Maine History*. David Ghere, "French Frustrations and Abenaki Autonomy, 1750–1760," (in *Maine History* 34, Summer 1994), pp. 2–21.
2 La Jonquière to Pouille, 16 July 1750, (10: 209); in O'Callaghan. McKechnie to Pownall, 12 February 1759, (13: 151–52); in Baxter.
3 Vaudreuil au ministre, 25 October 1724, (3: 109); in Canada, Public Archives, *Collection de documents*. Westbrook to Dummer, 23 March 1722, 22 June 1725, (10: 146–47, 289); in Baxter. Calloway, pp. 113–31.
4 Franco-American Collection: Maine History, Box 2, Native Americans.
5 Ghere, "Abenaki Factionalism, Emigration and Social Continuity."
6 Louis XV to Beauharnois and Dupuy, 14 May 1728, (9: 1002–04); Abstract of Beauharnois and Hocquart Dispatches, 25 October 1729, (9: 1014–15); in O'Callaghan. Beauharnois and Hocquart au ministre, 15 October 1730, 1 October 1731, 1 October 1732, 12 October 1736, (52: 33, 54: 14, 57: 5, 65: 28); Beauharnois au ministre, 10 October 1731, 22 September 1741, 26 September 1742, 23 September 1743, (54: 410, 75: 163, 77: 115, 79: 148); in Canada, Public Archives, AC, C11A.
7 Louis XV to Beauharnois and Dupuy, 14 May 1728, (9: 1002); Canada, Abstract of Dispatches, 20 October 1727, (9: 994); in O'Callaghan. Beauharnois and Hocquart au ministre, 15 October 1730, 1 October 1731, 1 October 1732, (52: 33, 54: 14, 57: 5); Beauharnois au ministre, 10 October 1731, (54: 410); Canada, Public Archives, AC, C11A. Byrne and others, 1: 487–488. Mulvey, pp. 18–20.
8 Massachusetts, *A Conference at Falmouth*, p. 3; Testimony concerning livestock losses, 6 August 1742, (23: 283–85); Assorted petitions by Waldo, 5–27 July 1736, (11: 156–72); Indian Conference at Boston, 25 June 1736, (23: 236–38); in Baxter. Proclamation of Governor, 28 October 1734, (295: 35); in Massachusetts, Archive*s*. Belcher to Gyles, 28 February 1735, (4: 505–06); in Massachusetts Historical Society. Massachusetts, House of Representatives, *Journal of the House*, 25 June 1736, 2 July 1736, 3 July 1736. Massachusetts, *Records of the Council*, 17 May 1736, 25 June 1736, 2 July 1736.
9 Shirley. to Bradbury, 9 December 1743, (23: 289–90); Shirley to Colonels (Fall 1743), (11: 290); Cols. Pepperell, Moulton, and Waldo to Shirley, 9 December 1743, (11: 291–92); Bradbury to Governor, 18 June 1744, (23: 290–91); Oulton to Shirley, 8 August 1744, (11: 298–300); in Baxter. Shirley to the Lords of Trade, 10 August 1744; in Lincoln, 1: 138–39. Beauharnois au ministre, 23 September 1743, (79: 148); in Canada, Public Archives, AC, A11A. Beauharnois to Maurepas, 8 October 1744, (9: 1107); in O'Callaghan.
10 Beauharnois to Maurepas, 8 October 1744, (9: 1106–09); in O'Callaghan. Beauharnois au ministre, 23 September 1743, 8 October 1744, (79: 148, 81: 140); in Canada, Public Archives, AC, C11A. Bradbury to Governor, 18 June 1744, (23: 291); Governor's Instructions to Commissioners, 7 July 1744, (23: 293–95); Declaration of War, 19 October 1744, (23: 296–98); in Baxter.
11 Declaration of War, 19 October 1744, (23: 296–98); Proclamation on Bounties, 19 October 1749, (23: 298); Shirley to Bradbury, 25 January 1744 [1745], (23: 298–99); Letter to Bradbury, 25 January 1744 [1745], (23: 298–99); Bradbury to Shirley, 18 June 1744, (23: 290–91); in Baxter. Willis, p. 116; Williamson, 2: 218.
12 Beauharnois to Maurepas, 8 October 1744, (9: 1106–07); in O'Callaghan. Shirley to Bradbury, 22 July 1745, (1: 253–54); Bradbury to Shirley, 29 July 1745, (1: 261); in Lincoln. Massachusetts, House of Representatives, *Journal of the House*, 23 August 1745.
13 Rapport de Beauharnois and Hocquart, 2 November 1745, (3: 265); in Canada, Public Archives, *Collection de documents*. Willis, p. 121. Beauharnois and Hocquart to Maurepas, 12 September 1745, (83: 3); Canada, Public Archives, AC, C11A. Beauharnois and Hocquart to Maurepas, 27 October 1745, (10: 17–18); in O'Callaghan.

14 Military and other operations in Canada during the years 1745–1746, 8 May 1746, 30 May 1746, 12 June 1746, 17 June 1746, 17 July 1746, 1 August 1746, and 24 September 1746, (10: 42, 45, 48, 51, 54–55, 67); in O'Callaghan. Beauharnois au ministre, 1 October 1746, 13 November 1746, (85: 197, 248); Bishop de Quebec au ministre, 10 November 1746, (86: 260); Journal of Occurrences in Canada, 1746–1747, 19 November 1746, 24 May 1747, 14 June 1747, 21 August 1747, 20 September 1747, 3 October 1747, (10: 89, 99, 107, 121, 126–27); Expedition against Fort Clinton, (10: 79–80); in Canada, Public Archives, AC, C11A.

15 Journal of Occurrences in Canada, 1746–1747, 17 September 1747, 20 September 1747, 7 October 1747, (10: 126, 128); Journal of Occurrences in Canada during the year 1747–1748, 7 December 1747, 14 June 1748, (10: 146–47, 166); in O'Callaghan. Galissonière au ministre, 28 January 1748, (91: 114); in Canada, Public Archives, AC, C11A.

16 Journal of Occurences in Canada during the year 1747–1748, (10: 153–54, 158, 160, 163–66, 172–74); in O'Callaghan. Waldo to Powell, 5 September 1748, 1 October 1748; Jeremiah Powell Papers, Collection 7, Box 1/3; Portland: Maine Historical Society. Raymond au Rouille, 19 November 1751, (31: 63), C11B; M. Bigot au ministre, 7 November 1748, (92: 195), C11A; Canada, Public Archives, AC.

17 Journal of Occurrences in Canada during the year 1747–48, (10: 174–78) in O'Callaghan. Journal Extract, 18 May 1748, 29 May 1748, 19 July 1748, (3: 405, 408); Canada, Public Archives, *Collection des documents*. Indian Conference, 23–27 June 1749, (23: 306–15) Governor's Letter About Indians, 3 June 1749, (23: 319); Indian Letters, 4 September 1749, 7 September 1749, (23: 320–21); Bradbury Letters, 5 September 1749, 9 September 1749, (23: 319–20, 322); in Baxter. Massachusetts, Bay Province, *A Journal of the Proceedings...of the Peace...at Falmouth*.

18 Denny to Phipps, 9 December 1749 (31: 666–67); in Massachusetts, Archives. Willard to Shirley, 19 December 1749; in Lincoln, 1: 493. Thayer, pp. 81–86.

19 Lithgow to Phipps, 2 February 1750 (31: 688); in Massachusetts, Archives. Indians to Massachusetts, 17 April 1750, (23: 328); Indian Letter, 9 June 1750, (23: 328–29); in Baxter. La Jonquière au ministre, 18 October 1750 (3: 493–94); in Canada, Public Archives, *Collection des documents*.

20 *Records of the Council*, 13 December 1749, 28–30 December 1749; Lithgow to Phipps, 2 February 1750 (31: 688–89); in Massachusetts, Archives. Moulton to Willard, 24 February 1750, (23: 325); in Baxter. Bigot to Rouille, 6 August 1750 (10: 218); in O'Callaghan. Thayer, pp. 81–103.

21 Bradbury to Phipps, 9 April 1750, (23: 327–28); Indians to Massachusetts, 9 June 1750, (23: 329); Indian Conference, 6 August 1750, (23: 365–66); in Baxter. Complaint of Davis, 9 July 1750 (32: 49); in Massachusetts, Archives. Thayer, p. 99.

22 Bigot to Rouille, 6 August 1750, (10: 218–19); in O'Callaghan. Minister to La Jonquiere, 11 September 1750; in Nish, *French Regime*, p. 145. Bigot au ministre, 18 October 1750 (96: 51), AC, C11A; La Jonquiere au ministre, 18 October 1750 (3: 493–94) *Collection des documents*; in Canada, Public Archives. Lithgow to Shirley, 15 May 1751 (32: 136–38); Penobscot letter, 12–25 September 1751 (32: 199–200); in Massachusetts, Archives.

23 Rapport de Bigot, 6 August 1750 (3: 490); La Jonquière au ministre, 18 October 1750 (3: 493–94); in Canada, Public Archives, *Collection des documents*. Lithgow to Phipps, 4 March 1751, (23: 377); Assorted letters, 7–12 September 1750 (12: 80–87); Lithgow to Phipps, 6 October 1750 (12: 101); in Baxter.

24 Penobscot letters, 10 October 1750, 30 October 1750, 1 March 1750 [1751], (23: 373–74); St. Castin to Phipps, [25] January 1750 [1751], (12: 121–22); Report of Committee, 25–30 January 1750 [1751], (12: 122–23); Lithgow to Shirley, 13 May 1755, (12: 395); Bradbury to Wheelwright, 22 April 1751, (23: 379); in Baxter. Gaunon to Phipps, 22 July 1751, (32: 161–65); Penobscots to Phipps, 3 August 1751, 13

August 1751, 12 September 1751, (32: 177, 182, 199–200); Bradbury to Phipps, 15 May 1751, 19 July 1751, (32: 136–38, 155); in Massachusetts, Archives. Phipps's speech, *Boston Gazette,* 15 January 1751.

25 Lithgow to Phipps, 6 October 1750, (12: 101); Lithgow to Phipps, 4 March 1751, 15 May 1751, (23: 375, 381–83); Letter of Denny, 25 April 1751, (23: 380); Memorial of Whitney, 4 December 1751, (23: 396); in Baxter. La Jonquière au ministre, 13 October 1751, (3: 505–06); in Canada, Public Archives, *Collection des documents*. Sevigny, p. 197.

26 Report of Conference, 19–24 August 1751, (23: 412–23); Instructions to Treaty Commissioners, 15 August 1751, (23: 411); Squadook's letter, 12 September 1751, (23: 425–27); Loron's letter, 25 September 1751, (23: 427); Bradbury to Shirley, 10 October 1751, 25 November 1751, (23: 428–30); Lithgow to Phipps, 9 March 1752, 12 June 1752, 1 September 1752, (12: 201–02, 23: 432–36); Phipps to Bradbury, 5 June 1752, (12: 179–80); Bradbury to Phipps, 31 August 1752, (23: 433–34); in Baxter.

27 Massachusetts, Bay Province, *A Conference Held at St. Georges*, pp. 3–21. On English land claims above Fort Richmond, see Ghere, "Mistranslations and Misinformation."

28 Shirley to Eastern Tribes, 1 March 1754, (32: 467–469); in Massachusetts, Archives. The Penobscot letter has not survived but is referred to in Shirley's letter to them.

29 Shirley's speech, 28 March 1754, (12: 247); in Baxter. Duquesne au ministre, 1 October 1753, (99: 249); in Canada, Public Archives, AC, C11A. Duquesne au ministre, 10 October 1754, (3: 515); in Canada, Public Archives, *Collections des documents*.

30 Massachusetts, Bay Province, *A Journal of the Proceedings at Two Conferences*. Shirley's speech, 28 March 1754, (12: 247); Gardiner letter, 26 December 1753, (12: 235–36); in Baxter. Shirley to Robinson, 19 August 1754, Lincoln, (2: 74, 82). Duquense au ministre, 10 October 1754, (3: 515); in Canada, Publc Archives, *Collections des documents*.

31 Massachusetts, *Records of the Council*, 8 February 1754. Massachusetts, *Journal of the House*, 12 April 1754. Shirley to North, 25 April 1754, (54: 298); Shirley to Bane, 11 April 1754, (74: 291); Goodwin to Shirley, 15 May 1754, (32: 519–20); in Massachusetts, Archives. Shirley to Lords Commissioners, 23 May 1754; in Lincoln, (2: 69).

32 Massachusetts, *Records of the Council*, 8 February 1754. Shirley to Eastern Tribes, 1 March 1754, (32: 467–69); Shirley to Legislature, 18 October 1754, (108: 635); in Massachusetts, *Archives*. Shirley to General Court, 28 March 1754, (2: 36–37); Shirley to Lords Commissioners, 23 May 1754, (2: 69); Robinson to Shirley, 21 June 1754, (2: 70–71); Shirley to Robinson, 19 August 1754, (2: 74–75, 82); Shirley to General Court, 28 March 1754, (2: 36–37); House of Representatives to Shirley, 10 April 1754, (2: 49–50); in Lincoln.

33 Goold, pp. 226–38; Account of expedition, *Boston Gazette*, 8 September 1754.

34 Shirley's speech, 18 October 1754, (12: 320–22); Shirley to Willard, 3 September 1754, (12: 309); Howard to Phipps, 11 October 1754, (12: 312–13); in Baxter.

35 Duquesne au ministre, 10 October 1754, (3: 515–16); in Canada, Publc Archives, *Collections des documents*. Massachusetts, Bay Province, *Journal of Two Conferences*, pp. 3–6.

36 Massachusetts, Bay Province, *Journal of Two Conferences*, pp. 3–6. Account of the expedition, *Boston Gazette*, 8 September 1754. Massachusetts, *Records of the Council*, 7 November 1754. Massachusetts, *Journal of the House*, 6 November 1754. Massachusetts, House and Council Resolution, 12 November 1754, (32: 560, 565–66); in Massachusetts, Archives.

37 Kehoorit's letter, 11 November 1754, (24: 21); Penobscots to Shirley, 9 December 1754, 8 January 1755, (24: 22–25); Shirley to Council, 17 February 1755, (24: 25); Robert Monckton to Shirley, 3 July 1755, (12: 443); Memorial of William Ross, 30 December 1757, (24: 86–87); in James Baxter, *Documentary History of the State of Maine*.

38 Shirley to Council, 17 February 1755, (24: 25); Legislative Committee Report, 24 February 1755, (24: 25–26); in Baxter.
39 Declaration of War, 9 June 1755, (24: 30–32); Fletcher to Shirley, 9 May 1755, (12: 391); Lithgow to Shirley, 11 May 1755, (12: 391–92); Burton to Proctor, 6 June 1755, (12: 402); Memorial of Ross, 30 December 1757, (12: 86–87); in Baxter. Burton to Shirley, 6 June 1755, (54: 453); Killpatrick to Shirley, 14 June 1755, (54: 465); in Massachusetts, Archives. Duquesne au ministre, 12 June 1755, 12 July 1755, (100: 7, 24); in Canada, Public Archives, AC, C11A.
40 Shirley to Penobscots, 17 June 1755, (24: 33–34); Phipps to Bradbury, 16 August 1755, (24: 50–51); in Baxter. Penobscots to Shirley, 27 June 1755, (32: 647); Bradbury to Shirley, 27 June 1755, 3 July 1755, (32: 648, 77: 382); Cargill's Journal, 1–4 July 1755, (38: 167); Bradbury to Phipps, 17 July 1755, (32: 659); in Massachusetts, Archives.
41 Bradbury to Shirley, 3 July 1755, (77: 382); Penobscots to Phipps, 16 July 1755, 25 July 1755, 6 September 1755, (32: 661, 674); Phipps to Penobscots, 10 July 1755, 12 July 1755, 18 August 1755, (32: 650, 652, 670–71); Bradbury to Phipps, 17 July 1755, 25 July 1755, (32: 659–60); Phipps to Bradbury, 16 August 1755, (32: 668–69, 672–73); in Massachusetts, Archives.
42 Lithgow to Phipps, 26 September 1755, (24: 54–55); Memorial of Bradbury, 26 September 1755, (24: 56–57); Legislative proposals, 27 September to 3 October 1755, (24: 57–58); Phipps to Bradbury, 3 October 1755, (24: 59); Phipps to Penobscots (3 October 1755, (24: 60–61); Bradbury to Phipps, 24 October 1755, (24: 61); Declaration of War, 1 November 1755, (24: 62); in Baxter.
43 Bradbury to Phipps, 24 October 1755, (24: 61); in Baxter. Vaudreuil to minister, 30 October 1755, (100: 130); Abbe de l'Isle Dieu to minister, 29 November 1755, (100: 239); Canada, Public Archives, AC, C11A. Willis, p. 165. Eaton, p. 97.
44 Franquet au ministre, 18 June 1757, (37: 289–91) AC, C11B; Memoire concernant les Sauvages, (76: 41–42); Archives de la Marine, B4; in Canada, Public Archives. Bougainville to Paulmy, 19 August 1757, (10: 607, 611, 616); Montcalm to Webb, 14 August 1757, (10: 618–19); in O'Callaghan.
45 Vaudreuil au ministre, 1 August 1756, 6 November 1756, AC, A11A, (101: 72, 148); Memoire concernant les Sauvages, Archives de la Marine, B4, (76: 41–42); in Canada, Public Archives. Willis, pp. 165, 168–69. Eaton, p. 97. Coleman, 2: 275–77. Montcalm to Loudon, 14 August 1757 (10: 619–20); in O'Callaghan.
46 Montcalm au ministre, 10 April 1758 (4: 154–155); Vaudreuil au ministre, 28 July 1758 (4: 174); in Canada, Public Archives, *Collection des documents.* Vaudreuil au ministre, 18 April 1758, 3 August 1758, (103: 84, 140–141); in Canada, Public Archives, AC, C11A. Coleman, 2: 281–84. Williamson, 2: 333.
47 Vaudreuil au ministre, 5 November 1758; in Canada, Public Archives, AC, C11C (9: 199). Pownall to Monkton, 30 August 1758; Pownall to Lords of Trade, 12 September 1758, in Pownall, pp. 112, 113.
48 "Memoir on Canada," winter 1758–1759, (10: 933); in O'Callaghan. McKechnie to Pownall, 12 February 1759 (13: 151–52); in Baxter.

AN ALBUM IN THE ATTIC: THE FORGOTTEN FRONTIER OF THE QUEBÉC–MAINE BORDERLANDS DURING THE REVOLUTIONARY WAR[1]

Barry Rodrigue
Bath, Maine

For the Revolutionary War period, historians and the public generally focus their attention on the Thirteen Colonies and dramatic events like the Battle of Bunker Hill or the winter at Valley Forge. Such a focus has overshadowed the fact that this war actually involved seventeen colonies of British North America and that important activity also took place in the northeast boundary area of today's Canada and the United States.[2] This disinterest in the frontier campaigns of the Revolutionary War is understandable. Although the northeastern borderlands were a strategically important area, they remained a relatively minor theater of operations for both sides.

However, for the United States, such a lack of drama was compounded by embarrassing failures that historians have often thought best forgotten. This was certainly the case of the ill-fated Penobscot Expedition that tried to drive the British out of eastern Maine in 1779. It ended not only in what has been called the United States' worst naval disaster before the World War II attack on Pearl Harbor, but courts martial for erstwhile heroes like Paul Revere. Therefore, it is no surprise that little attention was paid to the Penobscot Expedition in the decades immediately following the Revolutionary War. A similar problem of history has also plagued the Arnold Expedition, which passed through western Maine and attempted to dislodge the British from Québec in 1775.

One of two expeditionary forces that attacked the British in the Province of Quebec at the start of the war, this two-pronged invasion of the St. Lawrence Valley attempted to "close the back door" for the colonies in rebellion. The Montgomery Expedition came through the Lake Champlain and Richelieu Valley corridor to Montréal. The Arnold Expedition crossed the Kennebec and Chaudière corridor to attack Quebec City. It was hoped that by liberating the province, the British then would not be able to use the St. Lawrence Valley as a staging ground from which to attack the Thirteen Colonies from the northwest. The invasion was less than successful. Their combined attack on Quebec City in December 1775 failed, only 100–200 Québec men were induced to join the Continental Army, and the rebels were forced out of the province in June 1776 with the arrival of British reinforcements. The "back door" remained open.

As the revolution intensified, it largely bypassed the Québec–Maine frontier, being fought further south in places like Savannah and Yorktown. After the war ended in 1781, the memory of the Arnold Expedition quickly faded—although it was locally cherished in the areas through which it had passed. Antiquarian interest in the expedition somewhat increased soon after Maine separated from Massachusetts in 1820 and sought to stake out a Revolutionary War history of its own. In 1824 one of the Maine Historical Society's founding members, William Allen of Norridgewock, retraced portions of the expedition's route. In 1831 Vice President Aaron Burr, who had been an expedition member himself, donated a collection of Arnold's papers to the Maine Historical Society. These two events prompted publication of Allen's account of the expedition in the first volume of the society's collections in 1831. Nonetheless, the Arnold Expedition remained largely ignored by national historians and their audiences in the United States and British North America for more than a century.[3] When the Québec campaign was celebrated, it generally focused on the Montgomery Expedition—as when General Richard Montgomery's body was brought back from Quebec City and reburied in New York in 1818. The first major writer about the expedition, John Codman II, explained the reasons for this neglect of the Arnold Expedition:

> The rank and file who returned to tell the tale were few in number, weak in influence and widely scattered. Many of them reenlisted and perished during the war. Most of the surviving officers gained a wider reputation by brilliant exploits in more conspicuous fields, and continued to live the active lives, which make history but afford little time to write it. Moreover, this was one of the first military movements of importance in the war, and records at that time were not preserved with much care, so that a great deal of valuable information has only recently become accessible, while perhaps still more has been destroyed or lost forever. The young nation was not likely to dwell with pride on the failure of the invasion of Canada, and gladly allowed everything connected with it to fall into oblivion. Doubtless, also, a campaign which was so closely associated with the name of the

traitor Arnold, the truthful account of which could not fail to reflect credit on that evil genius, was willingly slighted.[4]

Codman's book, *Arnold's Expedition to Quebec*, came out in 1901. It was followed by Justin Smith's "The Prologue of the American Revolution" and *Arnold's March from Cambridge to Quebec* two years later. These works helped stimulate other efforts. Between 1912 and 1935, the Maine Daughters of the American Revolution commemorated the Arnold Expedition by placing twelve markers along the expedition's route through the state. In Québec various publications concerning the invasion occasionally came out, such as the 1913 reprint of one of Arnold's commissary accounts and Philippe Angers' coverage of the expedition in a 1924 local history.[5]

The first big turning point of national interest in the history of the Québec–Maine frontier during the Revolutionary War took place in the 1930s, when Maine author Kenneth Roberts published his historical novel *Arundel*, the storyline of which centered on the Arnold Expedition. This book helped advance Roberts's career to where he became one of the United States' most popular historical novelists by the mid-twentieth century. As his literary star rose, so did interest in the Arnold Expedition. A second spurt of attention began as part of the United States' bicentennial events.

"Working against the flood on Dead River"
Sydney Adamson, artist; H. Davidson, engraver[6]

The Arnold Expedition Historical Society was formed in 1967 and organized a historical re-enactment, in which about a thousand people retraced the route from Massachusetts, through Maine, to Québec in celebration of the expedition's two-hundredth anniversary.[7] Enthusiasm for historical re-enactment continued to blossom after the Bicentennial, combined with growing enjoyment of local history and genealogy, and revived appreciation of Roberts's novels. In this way, these two nodes of attention (in the 1930s and the 1970s) cooperated to heighten popular regard for the Arnold Expedition.

The Arnold Expedition Historical Society still publishes a newsletter, sponsors events, and helps designate the route. Since 1994 the Norridgewock Historical Society has held an annual "Arnold Days" event in Maine with speakers, a barbecue, river races, and tours. The "Ancient Ones," a re-enactment society based in Canton, Maine, recreates pre-1840 living history, including that of the Arnold Expedition. In 1994 author Barry Rodrigue began a process that led to the creation of the Chaudière–Kennebec International Corridor Commission, which sought to develop historical and cultural ties between Québec and Maine, including those surrounding the Arnold Expedition. In 1998 the Société Historique du Québec and Parcs Canada sponsored a Revolutionary War re-enactment on the Plains of Abraham in Quebec City that was largely based on interest in the Arnold Expedition. Individuals continue to want to retrace the route, pot-hunters search for artifacts, and the desire to make a documentary film has been expressed.[8] So it seems that fascination with the Arnold Expedition is here to stay, at least in the region of the northeastern borderlands.

Local historians generally have done an excellent job of placing the expedition in a proper perspective. However, a caution needs to be given about the more focused celebration of the Arnold Expedition by regional and national groups. Although laudable, these efforts tend to be a somewhat self-congratulatory exercise in United States' patriotism and re-enactment enthusiasm—out of proportion to the expedition's actual historical significance and overlooking important aspects of the historical events themselves.

A big blind spot in these celebrations is the Revolutionary War history of Québec. While this is a major deficiency, it is understandable. Most of the commemorations have occurred on the Maine side of the border and have emphasized the United States' role in the invasion of Canada, much of the Québec material has not been easily available in the United States, and many of the publications have been in French, which has made the information largely inaccessible to many English-speakers.

Additionally, prevalent anti-French attitudes in Maine, where the French have been seen as just the followers of Yankee ingenuity, have compounded this problem.[9]

There is strong irony in how Maine antiquarians struggled to gain recognition for the Arnold Expedition, but once they achieved their goal they virtually ignored the history of the expedition's allies in Québec who had saved the Continental Army. It is as though a photograph had been taken out of an album and treasured, while the album with all its other mementos had been cast into the attic and forgotten. The treasured image is of brave Yankees advancing into enemy territory to liberate a continent, while the discarded album is that of the French-Canadian and Abenaki struggle in south-central Québec for their own liberty.

The following discussion of events in the Chaudiere Valley during the Revolutionary War shows how casting a wider net can bring some interesting perspectives to borderlands studies. The focus of this essay is not so much about the editorial process by which the Arnold Expedition has become an historical icon in Maine, but on the larger context of this frontier during the Revolutionary War period—on the rest of the album left in the attic.

The Frontier Between Wars, 1760–1775

It is important to remember that the Arnold Expedition was merely a small event in the last of a series of seven colonial wars in North America.[10] The first six wars had involved the French, British, and Native Americans in antagonistic relations from 1675 to 1760 and had greatly influenced the settlement pattern in the frontier area of Québec and Maine. The primary avenue of attack on this frontier had lain along the Chaudière and Kennebec valleys, which had been for the most part employed by French and Native forces against the British in southern Maine.

A counter-strategy for both sides during these wars had been to establish barriers in their respective river valleys—in the form of fortifications and settlements. In the 1670s and 1680s, French fur traders and a Jesuit mission for the Abenaki had been established in the lower Chaudiere Valley, followed by agricultural concessions in the middle Chaudiere Valley in the 1730s that were called Nouvelle Beauce (New Beauce), after a fertile province in France.[11] In this way, the French-Canadian militia and its Native allies guarded the south-central approach to Quebec City. For their part, the British had been driven out of the lower Kennebec Valley in the early colonial wars, but moved into the middle Kennebec Valley with the establishment of a series of military garrisons in the 1750s. Both buffer zones worked, as the North

American campaigns of the Seven Years' War (1754–60) were not fought along the Chaudière–Kennebec rivers systems, as they had been in previous conflicts.

After the British seizure of the St. Lawrence Valley in 1760, French Canada was made part of British North America and was administered as a Crown colony like Massachusetts, in which Maine was a district. Several population streams then began to move inland, with the Chaudiere Valley in Québec and the Kennebec Valley in Maine continuing to provide pathways into the northern Appalachian Highlands. Wabenaki peoples still traveled between the St. Lawrence Valley and the Gulf of Maine lowlands along portages over the *haute terre*. Acadian refugees and Anglo-Irish migrants settled in the Chaudiere Valley, while the earlier French-Canadian settlers began to move further upriver to join Abenaki encampments at Sartigan (St. Georges). Yankee and Anglo-Irish *émigrés* moved towards the upland areas of the middle Kennebec Valley—beyond the garrisons at Fort Western (Augusta) and Fort Halifax (Winslow). By 1775 the frontier settlements of Sartigan in Québec and Norridgewock in Maine lay on either side of the Appalachian Highlands with about 160 kilometers (100 miles) of mountainous forest between them. Each frontier settlement eked out a subsistence lifestyle and was connected by a primitive road system to their respective cultural hearths and commercial centers in Quebec City and Boston.

Two landholding systems took root on either side of the frontier: The "seigneurial system" in the Chaudiere Valley and the "freehold system" in the Kennebec Valley. In both cases, the crown granted a large block of land to a proprietor (*seigneur*/patentee), who would then concede smaller grants to farmers (*censitaires* or *habitants*/yeomen) and receive rents from them. Farmers on both sides of the border received similar-sized lots (about 40 hectares or 100 acres). A system of laws governed the relations between proprietors and farmers (*Côtume de Paris*/English Common Law). Proprietors provided mills, roads, and other infrastructures, which were maintained by farmers' in-kind labor. While both landholding systems have been portrayed as being extremely different, they were actually quite similar in practice.[12]

Although settlers in this border region enjoyed freedom, they also endured privation. Hugh Finlay, surveyor of post roads for British North America, wrote about the settlement he found at Sartigan in 1773:

> We launch'd our canoes again into the water and continued setting against a strong current seven miles to the river called La Famine; at the mouth of this river we found two huts inhabit'd by two families employ'd in clearing lands; the soil

> is rich here, and the wheat it produces is plump and heavy. These Canadians regal'd us with green ears of Indian corn roasted, and bak'd [champignons] & milk; we pass'd the night on straw spread on the ground....[13]

Even in 1788 the Norridgewock town selectman used grim humor to request abatement on their state taxes:

> It is found, on strictest inquiry, that there is not seven dollars in money, comprehending every farthing in the town of Norridgewock, neither do the inhabitants of this place, considered at large, eat bread in their families more than three-quarters of the year. It is not uncommon to find a whole neighborhood without a cow, and there never was a piece of fulled cloth made in Norridgewock.[14]

Passage between the new British Province of Quebec and the old British colonies in New England became more frequently reported after the surrender of New France in 1760. The British sponsored several surveys for post roads between the St. Lawrence River and the Maine coast, such as those made by John Montresor and John Howard in 1761, John Preble and Joseph Chadwick in 1764, and Hugh Finlay in 1773. However, these plans were not implemented because of financial and political problems stemming from the Seven Years' War. Indeed, it was these problems that would soon embroil the frontier in yet another conflict.

A Road to the American Revolution

The expenses incurred by the Seven Years' War, administrative needs in the new territories, and development of an enlarged imperial infrastructure unleashed a series of conflicts between the North American colonies and the British government. The Seven Years' War had doubled British territory in North America, but the Proclamation of 1763 prohibited colonial settlement west of the Appalachian Mountains in the southern colonies. British attempts to rationalize their control in North America and force the colonists to pay for their share of the Empire's debt succeeded in collecting ten times as much revenue as the British had collected before 1763, but the resentment it caused brought about further problems. British success led to their downfall.[15]

The Quebec Act of 1774 and related regulations also contributed to growing discontent in British North America. These legislations created the Province of Quebec;

established rule by a governor and an appointed legislative council; extended the new province's boundaries to include the old French-Canadian settlements along the Great Lakes, in the Mississippi and Ohio valleys, and along the Labrador coast; and they recognized French civil law, the seigneurial system, and the Roman Catholic Church. Its passage antagonized colonial Protestants in the old British colonies who still harbored fears about Roman Catholic domination and who saw French Canadians as a privileged enemy who were now allowed entry to western lands that was denied the other colonies under the Proclamation of 1763. Indeed, objection to the Quebec Act is even enshrined in the United States' Declaration of Independence:

> For abolishing the free System of English Laws in a neighbouring Province, establishing therein an Arbitrary government, and enlarging its Boundaries so as to render it at once an example and fit instrument for introducing the same absolute rule into these Colonies.

Armed revolts broke out in Pennsylvania in 1763, in North Carolina in 1771, and in Boston in 1770 and 1773. Boycotts developed, and committees of correspondence were organized throughout the colonies to coordinate resistance. The British passed the Coercive Acts of 1774 to suppress revolt, but when they dissolved the provincial assemblies, the colonists organized their own assemblies and called for intra-colonial co-operation. In September 1774 the Continental Congress was convened in Philadelphia. In need of allies, they unsuccessfully tried to undo the damage done by their earlier protests against the Quebec Act. Congress composed a public letter to the French-Canadian people the next month, but by then events were rapidly unfolding and it proved ineffective.[16] In April 1775 fighting between the British and rebels took place at Lexington and Concord, Massachusetts.

British authorities in Québec watched the turmoil in the more southern colonies with apprehension. After conflict broke out in Boston, they began to react. One of their programs was to organize the French Canadians into militia units, which were an indication of the degree of British alarm, as they had kept their erstwhile enemies purposely disarmed for fifteen years. The concern of the military authorities was not groundless. Three "spies" had entered the province from the more southern colonies by way of the St. John River and gathered information before returning up the Chaudiere Valley to Maine.[17] It would seem that these agents were reconnoitering the northern colonies in the aftermath of the fighting at Concord and Lexington.

In June 1775 the Continental Congress ordered a 1,200-man army that came under the command of General Richard Montgomery to invade the Province of Quebec along the Lake Champlain and Richelieu River corridor. The overall hope was for Montgomery to capture the province and deny the British its use as a staging ground for a reconquest of the rebellious colonies. It was a plan that was largely based on overly optimistic reports of both French and English disaffection with the colonial administration in the Province of Quebec. Later in the summer, General George Washington ordered Benedict Arnold to lead a second invasion along the Kennebec–Chaudière route. Washington's strategy was to use the Arnold Expedition as a diversionary maneuver to pin down British troops in Quebec City and prevent them from opposing Montgomery's force or, if the British did leave the city, it was hoped that the Arnold Expedition could indeed capture it.

Arnold's 1,100 soldiers departed from Cambridge, Massachusetts, on 15 September 1775. He carried detailed orders from George Washington, a specific outline of the route, and printed copies of a manifesto to the Canadian people in French and English. Washington's orders stressed the need to encourage the Canadians and Natives as allies or, short of that, not to alienate them. In the first week, the men walked to Newburyport, from where they sailed across the Gulf of Maine and up the Kennebec River to Gardiner. They then spent a week in the vicinity of Fort Western (Augusta), preparing for their trek through the wilderness and recruiting Abenaki guides.[18]

Arnold dispatched scouts to reconnoiter the countryside between the Kennebec River and Lake Megantic in the Appalachian Highlands, as well as to speak with Natives hunting in the area. A surveyor and crew went ahead to lay out the route along the Great Carrying Place, across the bow of the Kennebec and Dead rivers, followed by three companies of men to cut a road so that they could better transport their bateaux and supplies. As the other companies were outfitted, they departed north. Arnold noted that the country between Fort Western and Norridgewock was "thickly inhabited." Local people helped the expedition's passage around fast water with their sleds and oxen, but no white settlers were found above Norridgewock.[19]

On October 13 Arnold dispatched three men over the Appalachian Highlands to contact the French and Abenaki settlers at Sartigan. Three days later, the expedition entered the Dead River. On October 20 and 21 the edge of a hurricane passed over the area, raising the river eight feet (2.5 meters) in nine hours. The river's main channel disappeared in the high water, men lost their way, boats were overturned, and the already damaged provisions became further waterlogged. With no news from his couriers to Québec and his situation getting desperate, Arnold sent an advance party of fifty men to Sartigan three days later. Then snow began to fall. The expedition struggled out of the Dead River, through the Chain of Ponds, over the Height-of-Land, and finally to Lake Megantic on October 27, leaving a trail of lost, dead, and dying men.[20]

Arnold and his forward detachment proceeded down the Chaudiere River and arrived at Sartigan on October 30. It was at this point that French-Canadian and Abenaki settlers were alerted to the presence of the main body of the Continental Army in their territory. They rushed to the Yankees' aid, bringing cattle and supplies for the men struggling over the highlands. As clusters of troops stumbled into Sartigan, they proceeded down-river over the next week to Arnold's headquarters at first Ste. Marie and then at Lévis. The Beauce settlers took care of the sick and injured men in their homes.[21] A soldier from Pennsylvania described their march from Sartigan to Ste. Marie in very complimentary terms:

> On the morning of the 6th Nov. we marched in straggling parties, through a flat and rich country, sprinkled, it might be said, decorated by many low houses, all white washed, which appeared to be the warm abodes of a contented people. Every now and then a chapel came in sight; but more frequently the rude, yet pious imitations of the sufferings of our Savior, and the image of the virgin. These things created surprise, at least, in my mind, for where I expected there could be little other than barbarity, we found civilized men, in a comfortable state, enjoying all the benefits arising from the institutions of civil society.[22]

The expedition arrived at the St. Lawrence River in the second week of November 1775. The entire trip from Cambridge to Quebec City had taken them six to seven weeks. Arnold's troops were joined by 300 soldiers of Montgomery's army that had marched down the St. Lawrence Valley from Montréal, the rest of them occupied with holding the southern portion of the province and maintaining lines of communication with New England and New York. The Continentals' joint attack of Quebec City on the night of December 30 to 31 failed. They managed to occupy Canada until June 1776, when British reinforcements and a lack of local support forced them to evacuate Canada over the Richelieu and Lake Champlain route.[23] Although this was the end of the Arnold Expedition, it was not the end of rebellion in the Chaudiere Valley.

The Chaudière "Mutiny"

Despite the departure of the rebels, the British authorities found their situation extremely tenuous. They had insufficient troops, dilapidated fortifications, and were surrounded by armed and disaffected French Canadians and Native warriors—their late enemies. Even Governor-General Haldimand thought that a second serious attempt at invasion could overwhelm the Province of Quebec.[24] However, the British would have little about which to worry. As in the previous colonial wars, topography was the great ally of the residents in the St. Lawrence Valley. It had been said that the major British problem during the Seven Years' War had been less about how to fight the French and Natives—being more about how to just get at them behind their wilderness barrier of the northern Appalachian Mountains. The same situation existed for the Revolutionary War, as the Arnold Expedition had so recently demonstrated.

Many of the political problems faced by the residents in the Chaudiere Valley during the Revolutionary War illustrate the difficulties of rebellion in a *cul-de-sac*, where a main road connected the *habitants* to the British garrison in the St. Lawrence Valley but only a poor trail linked them to the rebels in New England. Nonetheless, rebellion did take place there, as elsewhere in British North America. Although the population of Nouvelle Beauce was somewhat diverse and therefore not very cohesive, few of its Native, French-Canadian, Acadian, and Anglo-Irish settlers were well disposed to the British authorities. These frontier settlers had voted with their feet by moving towards the highlands, which reflected a disinclination to accept authority. Their rebellion was a *mélange* of factors, including resentment against the British rulers and their elite French allies. Rebellion actually had begun before the invasion by the Continental Army, which helps to explain why the Beauce settlers helped the Arnold Expedition.

For example, some farmers on the Beauce frontier had found opportunity in the removal of French authority in 1760. After the conquest the British allowed continuation of the existing French seigneurial system of landholding in those areas where it had been established, but the property owners who returned to France had only eighteen months to sell their possessions in Canada. It became a buyer's market. In this climate of wheeling and dealing, two farmers from St. François obtained land that would have been normally available to only the elite. In 1764 Jean Rodrigue bought the *seigneurie* of Ste-Barbe-de-la-Famine and Charles Doyon that of St-Charles-de-la-Belle-Alliance. Both were undeveloped concessions in the Appalachian

Highlands—towards the agricultural limits of the Chaudiere Valley in Sartigan. With these purchases, both farmers stepped onto the lowest rung of the nobility. However, it seems that they were unable to maintain their financial commitments. Rodrigue lost his land about 1773, when it was sold to a rich French ally of the British. Doyen became indebted to Québec merchants, which resulted in the sheriff selling off his land eight years later. Although a direct cause-and-effect relationship is difficult to prove at such a distance in time, circumstantial evidence indicates that this kind of bitter experience contributed to a rebellious mood in the middle Chaudiere Valley.[25]

The first cracks in the province's armor started to appear in the spring of 1775. In response to the troubles that had broken out in the southern colonies, Governor-General Carleton had organized a French-Canadian militia and declared martial law. However, the *habitants* declared that the *seigneurs* had no right to demand military service from them and the *seigneur* of Ste. Marie, Gabriel-Elzéar Taschereau, imprisoned one of the *habitants* who resisted the order to march.[26]

A Monsieur Launière also had passed on orders from the government to the captain of the militia to arrest rebel spies in the area, but it was claimed that the militia had not done their job. Rebel manifestos had been brought to Nouvelle Beauce in advance of Arnold's expedition. In Ste. Marie, they were read on the Day of the Dead (October 31), before and after mass, in houses near the church where groups of settlers had been gathered by the captain of the militia, Etienne Parent, and a gentleman-writer by the name of Demergue. Word of the rebel army, just then straggling into Sartigan, undoubtedly raised the level of excitement. Rebellious sentiments were contagious and officials trying to do their jobs were harassed. Philippe Valière, the bailiff, was insulted by *habitants* while trying to make a public announcement from the doorway of the church about marking roadways in the winter. Jean Bilodeau, Jr., spoke to him with *"termes indécents,"* asked where his "king" (the *seigneur*) was, and answered his own question by saying that he was in the city hiding behind a cannon.[27]

One of the most significant indications of the rebellious sentiment in Nouvelle Beauce was the aid the *habitants* gave to the Arnold Expedition. If the French and Abenaki settlers had wanted to destroy the Yankees, they could have easily done so. They were a tough frontier people, veterans of the colonial wars and used to guerilla fighting. The wretched state of the Arnold Expedition would have made such a task easy. However, the Beauce families rushed to help the Continental Army.

The primary provider of livestock for the Arnold Expedition as it passed through the valley was Pierre Rodrigue of Sartigan, a member of the family that had lost its *seigneurial* concession to a *functionaire* of the British two years before. Arnold paid him thirty-three pounds for oxen, sheep, and other items, in addition to four shillings for powder and another four shillings for a day's work of driving cattle. His brother, Charles Rodrigue, was paid twelve shillings for driving cattle for three days. All in all, Arnold's accounts showed that he distributed just over a hudnred pounds during the expedition's week-long passage through Nouvelle Beauce.[28] At a time when one pound would buy five days' work, this was no small income for the residents along the Chaudière.

Even after the Yankees departed from the Beauce to lay siege to Quebec City, they continued to purchase supplies from the Chaudiere Valley. In February 1776 a man by the name of John Mack came to Ste. Marie in the company of a bailiff named Claude Patry and the gentleman-writer Demergue. Mack claimed to have orders from Benedict Arnold to confiscate and sell *seigneur* Taschereau's goods. Although subsequent accounts have presented this act as pillaging, it seems to have been done in a rather organized manner. Farming equipment and household goods were gathered from Taschereau's estate and sold at auction. Pierre Rodrigue bought a pig and mattress. Even militia officers were present at the sale and bought items. Just over fifty pounds was raised at this event. François Nadeau, the miller for both the parish of St. Joseph and the family of *seigneur* Fleury de la Gorgendière, gave Mack and his associates wheat and money that belonged to Taschereau. Likewise, the militia captain, François Lessard, gave Mack's party monies he held for both Taschereau and the Fleury de la Gorgendière families.[29]

In June 1776, after the departure of the rebel forces, Québec merchant François Baby, *seigneur* Gabriel-Elzéar Taschereau, and lawyer Jenkin Williams made a seven-week tour of the parishes in the District of Quebec under orders of Governor-General Carleton. Their job was to re-establish the militia system and to inquire as to the rebellious situation that had prevailed. They collected information from the priest, assembled the militia, replaced officers who had worked with the rebels, publicly burned rebel commissions, and hectored the people about their duty to the Crown. However, the sentiment of rebellion was so prevalent that little could be done to punish the offenders. British commissions were withdrawn from militia officers in thirty-seven out of fifty parishes in the district and the local militia captain was only absolved of guilt in two parishes. About all that could be accomplished was to put new, more trusted people into positions of authority, rather than those towards whom the people had shown a preference in the previous year when the British militia system was first organized.[30]

On June 26 two officers, five sergeants, and a hundred and fifteen men were reorganized into the militia at Ste. Marie. The six major supporters of the rebels were forced to ask forgiveness in front of the militia and loyal subjects. Since Taschereau was the *seigneur* in Ste. Marie, it was important that he made a show of authority there. It was the only place in Nouvelle Beauce that punishment was meted out, albeit in a benign fashion, and much of the problem was blamed on outside agents—rebels from the southern colonies or troublemakers from nearby parishes. Thus, Taschereau somewhat saved face to the British authorities by blaming others and retained some dignity by being lenient in the eyes of his *censitaires*. On June 27 two officers, four sergeants, and eighty-three men were reorganized into the militia at St. Joseph. It was noted that "...this parish unanimously revolted and would not recognize the authority of the king." The sentiment of rebellion was evidently so strong in St. Joseph that no attempt at punishment was made, as had been done in Ste. Marie. St. François and Sartigan were unorganized frontier communities of French and Abenaki settlers in which the inquiry was only able to hold a review of twenty-two men. Since none of the old militia officers or bailiffs even showed up, the officials could not continue their inquiry.[31] Since the weak British government could barely maintain order in the large cities, they could do little on the margins. Regulation of the Chaudiere Valley would come by the imposition of external power.

Military Occupation of Nouvelle Beauce

In October 1776 the governor-general ordered the 62nd Regiment to take its winter quarters in Nouvelle Beauce and "other mutinous parishes" on the south shore of the St. Lawrence River. In December Launière, who knew the Chaudière area and its people, was dispatched to the commanding officer on the Chaudière in order to serve as an advisor. Although the regiment's primary responsibility was to intercept "treasonable correspondence" between New England rebels and "disaffected subjects" in the Province of Quebec, the soldiers were also warned to be vigilant against attack. A special concern was indicated for Sartigan and the routes to Temiscouata Lake. All "suspicious persons" were to be seized, especially those caught coming into the country or trying to leave it, as well as those who "stir up sedition." Those arrested were to be sent to headquarters in Québec. The detachments posted on the upper Chaudière and towards the headwaters of the St. John River were ordered to make every effort to contact the Native Americans in the area and solicit their help.[32]

The man referred to as serving as a military advisor in the Chaudiere Valley at this time, and who is just called "Launière," was likely the Joseph Launière whom Hugh Findlay described as having the last house (as opposed to cabin) on the Chaudière in 1773 at St. François. During the Revolutionary War, he provided valuable service to the British in maintaining their control of the Chaudiere Valley, served with the Department of Indian Affairs, and participated in a raid on Machias, Maine, in 1780. In 1796 his family was shown still living in St. François as farmers.[33] His is a good example of how a historically important individual can be made obscure by fragmentary records and by historical attention focused elsewhere.

The military presence was reduced in the Chaudiere Valley after the British campaign in the spring of 1777 into New York began. Apparently, British alarm about invasion and internal revolt in the Province of Quebec had somewhat diminished. The officer of the detachment at Nouvelle Beauce was told that it was not necessary to express post all his reports to headquarters. Although French Canadians and Native Americans were being employed as scouts, they were still under suspicion. It was ordered that a proportionate number of the scouts on patrols be from the garrison of British soldiers.[34]

Maine, which adjoined south-central Québec, was a conflicted buffer zone. The British took control of the regions east of the Penobscot River and maintained their hold on the territory northwest of the Kennebec River. After their expected victory against the rebels, British plans called for two roads to be built through Maine in order to connect Boston to Quebec City and Halifax. In the meantime, proposals were made in 1779 to create lines of communication between Quebec City and the territories still under British control. It was planned to use the Chaudière-Kennebec and the Chaudière-Penobscot trail systems to ice-free Nova Scotia and eastern Maine ports, which could then transmit messages by vessels to British garrisons, such as that in New York City. Despite their victory at the Battle for Penobscot Bay in 1779, these attempts seem not to have been particularly successful. Part of the problem was that the British had no "establishment" on the Kennebec River. Nonetheless, scouts were to be sent in the direction of the Kennebec, as well as to other frontier regions, to destroy rebel harvests in their barns.[35]

Although the rebels were in control of southwestern Maine and the lower Kennebec Valley, guarding the frontier was also a concern on the New England side of the border. In August 1777 a scouting party of five men was sent from

PAR SON EXCELLENCE

GEORGE WASHINGTON,

Commandant en Chef des Armees Des Provinces unies de L'Amerique Septentrionale.

AUX PEUPLES DE CANADA.

AMIS & FRERES,

LA Contesse denaturè entre les Colonies Ameriquaines, et Grande Bretagne est arrivè au point, que les Armes seules peuvent la decider. Les Colonies, se fiant a la Justice de leur Cause, & la puretè de leurs Intentions, sont obligè avec Repugnance, de [illegible] à cêt Etre qui regle tous les Evenements humains. Jusqu'ici il a Beni leurs vertueux Efforts; La Main de la Tyrannie est arretè dans le Cours de ses Ravages, & les Armes Brittaniques, qui ont Brillee avec tant de Eclat dans tous les Parties du Monde, se sont [illegible], disgraciès et frustrees. Des Generaux de la plus haute Experience, et qui se sont vantez de subjuguer ce grand Continent, se trouvent resserrez entre les Murailles d'un seul Ville & de ses Fauxbourgs, souffrants toute la Honte & la [illegible] d'un Siege.—Tandis que les Enfants de l'Amerique animes par l'Amour de la Patrié et le principe de la Libertè generale, s'unissent de plus en plus, chaque Jour se perfectionnent en Discipline, repoussent avec Courage toutes les Attaques & meprisent touts les Dangers. Nous, nous rejouissons sur tout que nos Enemis sont trompez a votre Egard. Ils se sont flattès, ils ont osè dire que le Peuple de Canada ne furent nullement capables de distinguer entre les Douceurs de la Liberte, et la Misere de Servitude; qu'on n'avoit qu'a flatter la Vanitè d'un petit Nombre de votre Noblesse, pour eblouir les yeaux des Canadians. Ils ont crû par cette Artifice vous rendre faciles a toutes leur Vues. Mais ils se sont heureusement trompèz, au Lieu de trouver en vous, cette Bassesse d'Ame, & pauvretè d'Esprit, ils voient avec un Chagrin egal a notre joie que vous etes Hommes eclarès, genereux, et vertueux, que vous ne voulez ne renencer a vos propres Droits, ni servir en Instruments pour en priver les autres.

Venez donc, nos chers Confreres, unissons nous dans un [illegible] indessoluble, courons ensemble au meme But. Nous avons pris les Armes en Defense de nos Biens, de Notre Liberté, de nos Femmes & nos Enfans—Nous sommes determinès de les conservir, ou de mourir. Nous regardons avec Plaisir ce Jour, peu eloigné (comme nous esperons) quand touts les Habitans de L'Amerique auront le meme Sentiment et [illegible] les Douceurs [illegible] Gouvernement.

Incitè par ces Motifs, et encouragè par l'Avis de plusieurs Amis de la Libertè chez vous, le Grand Congress Ameriquain a fait entrer dans votre Province un Corps de Troupes sous les Ordres du General Schuyler, non a piller, mais a proteger, pour animer et mettre en Action les Sentiments liberaux que vous avez fait voir; et que les Agents du Despotism s'efforcent d'eteindre par tout le Monde. Pur aider ce Dessein, & pour renverser le Projet horrible d'ensanglanter nos Frontieres par le Carnage des Femmes & des Enfants, J'ai fait marcher le Sieur Arnold Colonel avec un Corps de l'Armeè sous mes Ordres pour la Canada. Il est enjoint, et je suis certain qu'il se conformera a ses Instructions de se considerer et d'agir en tout, comme dans le Pais de ses Patrons & meilleurs Amis—Les Necessaires et Munition de toute Sorte que vous lui fournirez, il recevra avec Reconnoissance, et en payera la plein Valeur. Je vous supplie donc comme Amis et Freres de pourvoir a touts ses Besoins, et Je vous garantis ma Foi et mon Honneur pour un bonne et ample Recompense aussi bien que votre Suretè et Repos. Que Personne abandonne sa Maison a son Approche—Que Personne s'enfuit—La Cause de l'Amerique et de la Libertè est la Cause de tout vertueux Citoyen Ameriquain, quelle soit sa Religion, quelque que soit le Sang dont il tire son Origine. Les Colonies unies ignorent ce que c'est la Distinction hors celle que la Corruption et l'esclavage peuvent produire——Allons donc, chers & generaux Citoyens, rangez vous sous l'Etendard de la Libertè generale que toute la Force et l Artifice de la Tyrannie ne sera jamais capable d'ebranler.

G. Washington.

BY HIS EXCELLENCY

GEORGE WASHINGTON, Esquire,

Commander in Chief of the Army of the United Colonies of North-America.

To the INHABITANTS of CANADA.

FRIENDS and BRETHREN,

THE unnatural Contest between the English Colonies and Great-Britain, has now risen to such a Heighth, that Arms alone must decide it. The Colonies, confiding in the Justice of their Cause, and the Purity of their Intentions, have reluctantly appealed to that Being, in whose Hands are all human Events. He has hitherto smiled upon their virtuous Efforts—The Hand of Tyranny has been arrested in its Ravages, and the British Arms which have shone with so much Splendor in every Part of the Globe, are now tarnished with Disgrace and Disappointment.——Generals of approved Experience, who boasted of subduing this great Continent, find themselves circumscribed within the Limits of a single City and its Suburbs, suffering all the Shame and Distress of a Siege. While the freeborn Sons of America, animated by the genuine Principles of Liberty and Love of their Country, with increasing Union, Firmness and Discipline repel every Attack, and despise every Danger.

Above all, we rejoice, that our Enemies have been deceived with Regard to you—They have perswaded themselves, they have even dared to say, that the Canadians were not capable of distinguishing between the Blessings of Liberty, and the Wretchedness of Slavery; that gratifying the Vanity of a little Circle of Nobility—would blind the Eyes of the People of Canada.—By such Artifices they hoped to bend you to their Views, but they have been deceived, instead of finding in you that Poverty of Soul, and Baseness of Spirit, they see with a Chagrin equal to our Joy, that you are enlightned, generous, and virtuous—that you will not renounce your own Rights, or serve as Instruments to deprive your Fellow Subjects of theirs.—Come then, my Brethren, unite with us in an indissoluble Union, let us run together to the same Goal.—We have taken up Arms in Defence of our Liberty, our Property, our Wives, and our Children, we are determined to preserve them, or die. We look forward with Pleasure to that Day not far remote (we hope) when the Inhabitants of America shall have one Sentiment, and the full Enjoyment of the Blessings of a free Government.

Incited by these Motives, and encouraged by the Advice of many Friends of Liberty among you, the Grand American Congress have sent an Army into your Province, under the Command of General SCHUYLER; not to plunder, but to protect you; to animate, and bring forth into Action those Sentiments of Freedom you have disclosed, and which the Tools of Despotism would extinguish through the whole Creation.——To co-operate with this Design, and to frustrate those cruel and perfidious Schemes, which would deluge our Frontiers with the Blood of Women and Children; I have detached Colonel Arnold into your Country, with a Part of the Army under my Command—I have enjoined upon him, and I am certain that he will consider himself, and act as in the Country of his Patrons, and best Friends. Necessaries and Accommodations of every Kind which you may furnish, he will thankfully receive, and render the full Value.—I invite you therefore as Friends and Brethren, to porvide him with such Supplies as your Country affords; and I pledge myself not only for your Safety and Security, but for ample Compensation. Let no Man desert his Habitation—Let no one flee as before an Enemy. The Cause of America, and of Liberty, is the Cause of every virtuous American Citizen; whatever may be his Religion or his Descent, the United Colonies know no Distinction but such as Slavery, Corruption and arbitrary Domination may create. Come then, ye generous Citizens, range yourselves under the Standard of general Liberty—against which all the Force and Artifice of Tyranny will never be able to prevail.

G. Washington.

Broadside Proclamation
Aux Peuples des Canada / To the Inhabitants of Canada
from George Washington, 1775
Library of Congress (USA)

Norridgewock to investigate enemy activity north of the Great Carrying Place—in the area between Moosehead Lake, the Dead River, and the Appalachian Highlands. The men divided into two parties and were ordered not to fire their guns unless Natives were encountered. However, one of the men shot a bear, which caused the other party to retreat to Norridgewock and alert their headquarters in Hallowell. A detachment of troops was sent to reinforce Norridgewock before the truth of the "attack" was learned. Nonetheless, the scouting party did find the tracks of three Natives and two Whites in the Dead River area. It was later learned that two Yankee hunters had been captured near the Dead River and taken back to Canada, where they were given to the British for a bounty. One of the men, Roger Chase, escaped from a prison frigate in the St. Lawrence River in December 1777, swam to shore, and escaped up the Chaudiere Valley with the help of French-Canadian settlers. It took him nine days to travel from Sartigan to Norridgewock, with a rotten bear's paw being his only nourishment along the way.[36]

In August 1778 two Abenaki hunters from St. François told the captain of the militia there that they had encountered three Native hunters who had been sent through the woods by the Bostonians. These messengers had been told to "warn" all those they met on their hunt to come over to the New England side because the English were said to be ready to hang all the Natives remaining on the Canadian side and that seven had already been hanged at St. François. They added that thirty French vessels had entered Boston Harbor and that a merchant had brought a great deal of merchandise to Pannaouarsket (Old Town, Maine), which was being sold cheaply, and that fur had a good price. The lieutenant governor thought that this misinformation campaign was just the work of a New England trader trying to get more furs. Nonetheless, the following month he reported that only a few Natives had come to the Beauce area that year and it was supposed that they had remained on the New England side. This made the soldiers in Nouvelle Beauce apprehensive for members of their scattered detachments being carried off in any attacks.[37]

Indeed, Wabenaki on the Maine side had become allied to the rebel cause, dissent in the Chaudière had continued, and the threat of another rebel invasion of the Province of Quebec was very real. In 1778 rebel military forces planned a feint over the Kennebec-Chaudière portage, as a diversion to a main invasion up Lake Champlain and the Richelieu River, as had been done three years before. Such proposals for the invasion of Québec would continue until the war's end and were a special passion of the Marquis Motier de La Fayette. In response, the British established a system of fortifications, detachments, and patrols along the south shore watersheds of the St. Lawrence River in order to protect the province from overland attack from the rebel colonies.[38]

Ironically, more British regulation came to the Chaudiere Valley from the rebel colonies themselves as about fifty thousand Loyalists migrated into Québec and Nova Scotia. These *émigrés* had lost their farms and enterprises to the rebels because of their loyalty to the British Crown, so the British authorities were forced to accommodate them. In these times, when it took an average of three years to start to make a farm productive, accommodation of the Loyalists became a major project. The government provided housing and rations to the families, while organizing the men into military units.[39]

As a part of the plan to resist another invasion, Loyalist Captain Daniel McAlpin of the 60th Regiment became the leader of a mixed command in Nouvelle Beauce. In August 1778 a company of the 34th Regiment was merged into his contingent of Loyalists and newly arrived German troops were dispatched to the lower Chaudière with the ominous warning to "behave" themselves and a reminder that they were not "in an Enemy's country." Nonetheless, the quartering of troops in *habitant* houses in the Province of Quebec created bad feelings. In order to relieve this tension, as well as to provide better protection for the troops, the construction of barracks was added to the development of fortifications.[40]

Construction of a picketed fort and barracks was begun at St. François in the autumn of 1778 at an estimated cost of forty-five pounds. Local labor was supplied under the direction of the ubiquitous Launière and was organized through the militia at St. Joseph. Pierre Poulin, the militia captain at St. Joseph, reported that his men had contributed about 160 worker days, with their own equipment and at their own expense. It was completed in November 1778. The barracks was a "strong log house," two stories high, 32 feet (10.5 meters) long and 20 feet (6.5 meters) wide, with a central chimney of stone and lime. It was meant to house twenty-five men. The upper story overlooked the pickets and grounds around the fort. Captain McAlpin thought that it could not be taken without artillery, "providing the troops within do their Duty."[41]

The French-Canadian militia units were then ordered to supply the troops in the blockhouses in the Chaudiere Valley with firewood. Although there is some ambiguity in the orders for troop placements at St. François, it appears that—in December 1778—its blockhouse was taken over by a detachment of twenty-eight "invalids," who came under the command of the fort's sergeant. In May 1779 Captain McAlpin was relocated to Sorel, where he took command of the Loyalist military units.[42]

By the summer of 1779 almost a thousand Loyalists had been established at St. John's, Chambly, Montréal, Sorel, Machish, and Nouvelle Beauce. Their accommodations were rough and they were placed on half-rations. The twenty-nine Loyalists in Nouvelle Beauce made up the smallest of these settlements and consisted of eleven men, seven women, and eleven children. The family of Captain McAlpin was there, as well as members of six other families, who were mostly refugees from Albany County, New York. As the authorities began to organize the Loyalists, their placements also changed. In July 1779, the military garrison in Nouvelle Beauce consisted of an ensign, a surgeon, a sergeant, and twelve privates. Four months later, only a sergeant and twelve privates were left on duty, and—a year after that—there were no Loyalists being listed in Nouvelle Beauce.[43]

Throughout the rest of the war the mission of the frontier detachments remained essentially the same: To intercept travelers from the rebel colonies, quash dissent, and watch for enemy attack. Despite the network of detachments and blockhouses, rebel activities continued. Spies and agents continued to infiltrate the region. In the autumn of 1781 a spy by the name of Bowman entered the Province of Quebec. An alert was sent to all militia captains, priests, and post commanders. An intense search was gotten underway. The commander at Sorel doubted that Bowman could escape through the territory between the Bécancour, St. François, and Sorel rivers, because of the many hunting parties of loyal Natives from St. François in the area. However, he was advised that "there is a very convenient Road for any Person who wants to escape out of this Province by the Parish of St. Egan (Sartigan) on the Chaudiere." Reportedly, four spies sent from Maine into the Province of Quebec were captured and condemned to hang. They were saved by the intervention of Robert Forbes, an Irish resident and ex-soldier in Québec.[44]

The Loyalists were increasingly replaced by German troops in the Chaudiere Valley. Sometime during the winter of 1779–80, a detachment of the Anhalt Zerbst Regiment, consisting of a low-ranking officer and six men, was assigned to the blockhouse at St. François. In January 1781 the Prince Frederick Regiment was sent into winter quarters at Ste. Marie, St. Joseph, and St. François. Thirty of their men were to relieve the Anhalt Zerbst detachment at the St. François blockhouse and were to come under the command of Captain Launière and his son. In September 1781 most of the Prince Frederick Regiment was ordered to Québec, except for the woodcutters along the Chaudiere Valley. Evidently the garrison at the St. François blockhouse was again given to a detachment of the Anhalt Zerbst Regiment. The defeat of the British forces at the Battle of Yorktown in Virginia ended the Revolutionary War on 17 October 1781. Peace treaties were concluded over the next two years. When the orders to send the German regiments back to Europe came in June 1783, the non-commissioned officer and fifteen men of the Anhalt Zerbst Regiment were withdrawn.[45] This ended the British military occupation of the Chaudiere Valley.

Conclusion

The Arnold Expedition did not have much physical impact on the area through which it passed. It did not found any villages or build any lasting structures. It used a trail already in use for hundreds, if not thousands, of years, and the tote road it did construct was quickly overgrown by the forest. Although its passage through Nouvelle Beauce encouraged insurrection, the expedition did not cause the mutiny in the Chaudiere Valley. While the Beauce rebellion is often cynically dismissed as farmers just trying to make a fast buck, the historical record indicates otherwise. Discontent had existed before and continued after the Arnold Expedition passed through Nouvelle Beauce—just as it did in Maine. Nonetheless, we have to give the Arnold Expedition and its historians credit for their contributions. The soldiers brought better knowledge of the northeastern borderlands to people's attention in the late eighteenth century, as indicated on maps and in reports. Likewise, several expedition members later settled on the Québec–Maine frontier and pioneered cross-border exchange based on their hard-won knowledge of the area. More recently, the Arnold Expedition has inspired histories, novels, articles, re-enactments, festivals, and societies. Therefore, it is fair to say that both the expedition's and its later commentators' primary significance lie in the realm of Intellectual History—the history of ideas.

However, by looking at the wider context of the Québec/Maine frontier during the Revolutionary War (the "album in the attic") we can begin to see that there was more to this region's history than just that of the Arnold Expedition. A view long expressed by local historians and historical societies, it has tended to go unheeded by regional and national promoters of Arnold Expedition history. Indeed, antiquarian focus on the expedition as a symbol of events in the northeastern borderlands has actually served to retard historical investigations for other periods—even that of the much more significant agricultural and forestry development of the following two centuries. The *raison d'être* of this essay has been to throw some light in one of the dark corners overshadowed by images of the Arnold Expedition–Revolutionary War events in south-central Québec.

The British occupation of Nouvelle Beauce after the passage of the Arnold Expedition had been to protect its vital garrison in the St. Lawrence Valley, establish an "early warning system" to detect invasion, and to suppress "mutiny." But what had the Chaudière mutiny been about? Briefly, the Beauce rebels sought many of the same liberties that others in British North America had sought—freedom from arbitrary rule by elites. A difference was that they developed their own idea of freedom, one motivated by the ideal of regional French self-determination. This rebellion would not go away, but would continue and expand after the Revolutionary War—as one can see in the present-day sovereignty issues of Québec.

However, despite rebellious sentiments within the Chaudiere Valley, the Beauce settlers remained prisoners of geographic and economic conditions in the late 1700s. The failure of the Arnold Expedition, itself, as well as earlier—more successful—use of the Chaudière–Kennebec portage by French and Native forces, highlighted the impracticality of this wilderness passage for all but small groups of experienced travelers or very lightly armed and well-trained military personnel. Difficult terrain and poor transportation routes hindered southern connections during the Revolutionary War: Because no major routes existed, economic links between Québec and Maine remained weak. At the same time, a more benign situation promoted northern connections. Nouvelle Beauce remained a part of British North America during the Revolutionary War because its connection to Quebec City was being strengthened by roads, as well as by systems of economic and social exchange, at the same time that the St. Lawrence Valley's connection with the rest of the British Empire was being expanded. This linking of the Beauce frontier, through the St. Lawrence Valley, into the British Empire was successful. It allowed the British to garrison and fortify Nouvelle Beauce, hold the rebels and dissenters in check, and encourage trade. Thus, these carrot-and-stick maneuvers by the British overcame even local sentiment in favor of revolution.

Nouvelle Beauce would continue as a strong sub-region of Québec in the decades immediately after the Revolutionary War. Overseas trade with the British Empire would increase as British North America came to serve as Britain's woodlot during the Napoleonic Wars and as a dumping ground for population made redundant by agricultural and industrial revolutions in the British Isles. This orientation would only start to change in 1819 with the construction of the Canada Road, between the public road networks of the Chaudière and Kennebec valleys, which would then allow for a more efficient exchange network to finally develop between Québec and Maine. We then find many of the family names of the Revolutionary War participants from Nouvelle Beauce among the first to migrate to Maine—Rodrigue, Poulin, Labbé, Doyon, and others.[46] In this way, the rebellion would be fulfilled, but by the descendants of the Beauce rebels—who would then serve as mediators of cultural exchange in a new climate of cross-border amity.

1 A version of this essay was first published as "An Album in the Attic: The Forgotten Frontier of the Quebec–Maine Borderlands during the Revolutionary War," (in *The Journal of the Historical Society* 3, # 1, 2003), pp. 45–73. Madeleine Paré Roy of Lewiston translated this article into French with the assistance of her sister, Sister Sylvie Paré (O.P.) of Phoenix, Arizona. This French translation is in the University of Southern Maine's Franco-American Collection at Lewiston-Auburn College.

2 The four North American colonies that did not successfully rebel during the Revolutionary War were Québec, Nova Scotia, Prince Edward Island, and Newfoundland. Despite disinterest in the history of their "loyalty" by many United States' scholars, some specialists have focused attention on the frontier area during this period. They include Justin Smith; John Brebner; and George Rawlyk.

3 William Allen's field research on the Arnold Expedition in 1824 was greatly assisted by the newly constructed Canada Road, which had just been located along portions of the expedition's route in northwest Maine and for which project Allen had worked. The blackout of popular interest in the Arnold Expedition and the invasion of Canada in the nineteenth century was not complete, as there was reportedly a railroad outing to Quebec City in 1875 as a part of the United States' centennial celebrations. William Allen. Rodrigue, *The Making of the St. Lawrence–Maine System*, p. 251. Cunningham, Communication, 20 November 2000.

4 Codman, p. 1. Several very brave and talented members of the Arnold Expedition later became "notorious" in United States history, which contributed to a decline of interest in the invasion of Canada. The expedition leader, Benedict Arnold, is better known as a traitor who went over to the British in 1780. A young officer, Aaron Burr, became vice president of the United States in 1800, killed ex-Secretary of the Treasury Alexander Hamilton in a duel in 1804, and was accused of treason when implicated in a scheme to carve out a Mississippi Valley kingdom in 1806. Although Henry Dearborn would rise to become commander of the United States' northern army during the War of 1812, his failure in the field subsequently led to a major restructuring of the army along French models. Such individual disrepute gave the larger Arnold Expedition an undeserved poor image in the nineteenth century.

5 Codman. Justin Smith, "The Prologue of the American Revolution;" *Arnold's March from Cambridge to Quebec*. Coburn. Jellison, *Commemorative Markings on the Arnold Expedition Trail. Expense Book of John Halsted*. Angers, "La Beauce en 1775," unidentified author.

6 From Justin Smith, "The Prologue of the American Revolution," p. 532.

7 In 1938 Kenneth Roberts also published a collection of diaries and journals of members of the Arnold Expedition in his *March to Quebec*. His historical romance *Northwest Passage* was made into a classic

Hollywood film with actor Spencer Tracy in 1940, which enhanced Roberts's popularity. Québec local histories continued to celebrate the Arnold Expedition, as when Madeleine Ferron and Robert Cliche included an account about the Arnold Expedition in their survey of rebellious Beauce traditions in 1972. Roberts, *Arundel*; *March to Quebec*; *Northwest Passage*. Metro-Goldwyn-Mayer, *Northwest Passage*. Ferron and Cliche, *Les Beaucerons ces insoumis*, pp. 81–124. Jellison, Communication. Forgue, Communication. Lucille Greer, Communication. Cunningham, Communication.

8 This regional interest in the Arnold Expedition translated somewhat to a national level, as when the *Smithsonian Magazine* published an article about the expedition in 1987. Although it has become popular to refer to the route that the Arnold Expedition used as the "Arnold Trail," this is a misnomer. The route was actually part of an older Native American system of portages, had been developed by the French in the seventeenth and eighteenth centuries, was employed by English surveyors in the 1760s, and was even described in Yankee almanacs in the early 1770s—all before the Arnold Expedition. The route is more properly called the Kennebec–Mégantic Trail. Winter. Park. Rodrigue, "Canada Road / La route du Canada." Forgue, Communication. Jellison, Communication.

9 C. Stewart Doty's article on anti-French racism in New England is applicable to how many French activities have been minimized or erased from Maine history. Several references to local histories that include material relative to the Revolutionary War period and the Arnold Expedition follow: Bélanger and others. Garant. Mathieu. Jackman Bicentennial Book Committee. History Committee of the Bingham Sesquicentennial. History Committee of the Solon Sesquicentennial. Doty, "How Many Frenchmen Does It Take to...?"

10 The earlier colonial wars were as follows: The War of the League of Augsburg (1688–97), also known as King William's War (1688–99); the War of the Spanish Succession (1701–13), also known as Queen Anne's War (1703–13); the Five-Year War (1721–26), also known as the Three-Year War, Dummer's War, Rale's War, and Lovewell's War; the War of the Austrian Succession (1744–48), also known as King George's War (1745–49); and the Seven Years' War (1754–63), also known as the French and Indian War (1754–60). The Five-Year War is the Barry Rodrigue's name for the conflict of 1721–26. It is inappropriate to name wars after individuals since the causes of conflicts are never so easily pinpointed. The dates of this conflict can be variously described, but this war was of five years duration from the time of its first to last battles.

11 Nouvelle Beauce was named after the agriculturally rich Province of Beauce in France, southwest of Paris in the Eure and Loir valleys. Various toponyms have changed in the Chaudiere Valley in the last 200 years. Those most noticeable for someone trying to find locations from this essay on a modern map is that St. François is now known as Beauceville and Sartigan is within the bounds of St-Georges. Since it is easy to confuse communities, as there were several parishes known as St. François in Québec, it was customary to add a descriptive, such as St-François-de-Beauce or St-François-du-Lac. However, in this paper, all parish names refer to those in Nouvelle Beauce, unless otherwise stated. For a regional overview of the Beauce area, see the following references: Poulin, *Paysages, territorialités et représentations*. Bélanger.

12 Although the word "peasant" has been commonly used by English writers to refer to farmers under the seigneurial system in Québec, the settlers themselves had discarded the term *paysan* in the seventeenth century in favor of *habitant*. Similarly, *censitaire* was a technical term defining their relationship to a *seigneur*. These word-uses are part of a much larger debate about the relative modernity of nineteenth-century Québec agriculture. The following references discuss some of these issues. D'Arce, Letter, p. 264. Choquette, p. 282. Allan Greer, pp. 23–35, 192. Harris. Courville, "La crise agricole du Bas Canada." Rodrigue, *The Making of the St. Lawrence–Maine System*, pp. 11–13.

13 The settlers that Finlay found at the Famine River were probably members of the Rodrigue family, who had held the seigneurial concession of Ste-Barbe-de-la-Famine (see text, above). Finlay, p. 50.
14 Norridgewock, Town Meeting, Petition.
15 The French foreign minister, the Duc de Choiseul, had concluded that strong British colonies would lead to independence, which was a major reason that the French Crown decided not to attempt to recover Canada after the fall of Québec. Eccles, p. 232.
16 United States, Continental Congress, Letter.
17 Baby and others, p. 470.
18 Washington, Letter, pp. 50–60; Manifesto. Arnold, Journal, Part A, pp. 1058–60.
19 Arnold, Journal, Part B, pp. 45–49.
20 Arnold, Journal, Part B, pp. 50–61.
21 Arnold, Journal, Part B, pp. 58–61.
22 John Henry (1759–1811) served as a soldier in the Arnold Expedition to Québec. John Henry, p. 346. Roberts, *March to Quebec*, p. 297.
23 Although the French Canadians failed to rise *en masse* to support the rebels, some served with United States forces throughout the war and, after the Treaty of Paris in 1783, many of their families settled in upstate New York.
24 Haldimand, Letter, to Germain, 15 October 1778.
25 After losing their *seigneurie*, the Rodrigue family assisted the Yankee rebels, became involved in a church dispute with Catholic hierarchy and local *seigneur* George Pozer, and some emigrated to Maine when the Canada Road was built in 1819. There is a personal element in this story, as the author is a descendant of this pioneer Rodrigue family from Sartigan. I began my research as a "simple" exercise in family history, but became surprized by how English-language accounts of the Arnold Expedition quickly brushed over the local settlers as if they were mere props in a theatrical production. Pierre-Georges Roy, 5: 20, 22–26.
26 Martial law was declared in the Province of Quebec in June 1775. Unidentified officer.
27 Baby and others, pp. 469–71.
28 Arnold, "Arnold's Account Sheets," pp. 717–24.
29 On 19 March 1776 Arnold's commissary paid Pierre-Jacques Guay 39 livres (£1 12s 6p) for going to "St. Egan" (Sartigan) to buy beef for the Continental Army. *Expense Book of John Halsted*, p. 10, UNIDENTIFIED AUTHOR. Arnold, "Arnold's Account Sheets." Baby and others, pp. 471, 472. LeMoine, pp. 69–70.
30 Baby and others.
31 The above quote was translated by the author and originally read: "...cette paroisse se revolta unanimement & ne voulut point recônaitre l'authorité du Roy." Baby and others.
32 Carleton, to Cramahé; to Powell; to Anstruther or Officer Commanding; to the Officer Commanding upon the Chaudière; to the Commanding Officer at Nouvelle Beauce.
33 Finlay, p. 55. Buerger, p. 988. Roman Catholic Church, *Dixmes de la paroisse St. François*.
34 Carleton, to Commanding Officer at Nouvelle Beauce.
35 Joseph Williamson. Haldimand, to Germain, 13 September 1779, N/23, and N/32, p. 47.
36 Chase's friend eventually escaped from the frigate in Boston Harbor. Howard, pp. 257–60.
37 Cramahé, to Haldimand, 17 August 1778, p. 10, and 17 September 1778, p. 42.
38 Military posts upriver from Lac St. Pierre were considered extremely vulnerable to rebel attack in 1778, so the primary southern garrison was established at Sorel. Smaller military sites and patrols were extended to the Chaudière, Bécancour, St-François, Yamaska, Sorel, Richelieu, St-Jean and other rivers. Trudel, pp. 137–48, 186–233. Haldimand, to Germain, 15 October 1778, and 14 September 1779,

p. 55. Everest.

39 I would like to thank Barbara Snyder of the Geography Department at Queens University (Ontario) for directing me to documents on the Loyalist settlement in the Chaudiere Valley. Haldimand, to Germain, 15 October 1778, pp. 14–15, and 14 September 1779, p. 56. LeMaistre, Letter, to McAlpin, 10 January 1780.

40 There are two possible origins of this warning for the German troops to behave themselves. German troops had been accustomed to fighting the French in European wars, so it might have been normal for them to view the French Canadians with some suspicion. The bad reputation of German troops during the Revolutionary War era was a popular stereotype that has been disputed by scholars. Carleton, to von Riedesel, 20 December 1776. Haldimand, to St. Leger; to McAlpin; to Germain, 15 October 1778, p. 14. (Von) Eelking and Rosengarten, pp. 7–9, 87–98.

41 The work done by the Beaucerons on the barracks at St-François could have been normally expected *corvée* labor, but because of the emphasis given by Captain Poulin on their effort, it could also have been viewed as a form of punishment and/or redemption for the Chaudière "mutiny." Haldimand, to Germain, 15 October 1778, p. 14. Poulin, to Haldimand. Daniel McAlpin, to Haldimand, 24 October 1778. Cramahé, to Haldimand, 17 September 1778, p. 42, and 21 September 1778.

42 Haldimand, to Johnson. Le Maistre, to McAlpin, 14 November 1778, 18 December 1778, 2 January 1779, 5 January 1779; to Militia Officers at Nouvelle Beauce, 14 November 1778, p. 30. Daniel McAlpin, to Haldimand, 26 July 1779. Mary McAlpin, to Haldimand.

43 In the summer of 1779 Nouvelle Beauce was evidently considered adjunct to the garrison at Sorel and in the District of Montreal, as shown by Loyalist returns combining the two settlements and by correspondence about the Nouvelle Beauce settlements coming from the officers at Sorel. By October 1779, Nouvelle Beauce was being associated with the District of Quebec City. The detailed listing of Loyalists receiving provisions in the District of Montreal from 25 July to 24 August 1779 does not list Nouvelle Beauce, which is cited only in the recapitulation at the document's end. After November 1780 the number of Loyalist settlements increased and were largely located south of Trois Rivières, in the eastern and western townships, and towards Lake Ontario. This makes sense, as these Loyalists were largely from New York and this was the sector through which a rebel invasion was expected to enter. In the summer of 1779 all but one of the Loyalist families in Nouvelle Beauce were from Albany County (the exception was from Charlotte County). Daniel McAlpin, "An Effective List"; "Monthly Return"; "Return of Loyalists"; "Return of Royalists & Their Families"; "The State of the Loyalists"; Nairne, "Return of Families of Loyalists"; "Return of the Loyalists"; "General Return."

44 "Loyal Natives" probably refers to those at St-François-du-Lac, a Native reserve on the St. François River that is also called Odanak. Von Riedesel, to Haldimand, 19 October 1781, 19 December 1781. Everest. True, to Rodrigue, January 1997: Stinchfield genealogy, (published manuscript), p. 8.

45 Sernoult, to Praetorius; to von Riedesel and von Speth; to von Loos. Le Maistre, to Praetorius, 1 September 1781, 3 September 1781.

46 About 1.5 million people migrated from the British Isles between 1815 and 1846, before the major British migrations began. Rodrigue, *The Making of the St. Lawrence-Maine System.*

LIFE ON THE FARM AND RECIPES[1]

Luella and Eva Ashland Roderick
Augusta, Maine

Our father lost his mother when he was very young.[2] He and his step-mother didn't get along too well, so he left home in St. George, in Beauce, Québec, when he was a young lad of about seventeen years. He arrived in Maine at haying time in 1876 with other men from Canada and worked at haying and other jobs. He returned to Canada to help his father on the farm, but left again later. This time, he went to Augusta.

He met our mother and got married.[3] They had seven children and lived in different cities here in Maine. They landed in Livermore Falls, where my father worked as a machinist in the paper mill. He would be called out all hours of the night to go to the mill to fix some machine that was out of order. He would no more than get back to bed when someone would come after him to go back to fix some other machine. He didn't have much rest. He had built a new home, but he got tired of working like that.

So, he bought a farm in Belgrade. He had only a driving horse and a wagon to start with, no farming tools, and he had to do everything by hand. Both our mother and father worked hard. They planted a large garden. Mother canned a lot of different kinds of vegetables and fruit. Us kids picked berries, so my mother made jam and jellies.

In the summer, our father would get up at 3:00 A.M. to mow hay by hand before the sun would get hot. Then, when the hay was ready, it was loaded on the hayrack. Us kids had to sit on the load or walk with it so the hay wouldn't fall off. So we all helped, the whole family. It took about two to three weeks before it was finished.

Then, it was harvest time. Us three kids stayed out of school about three days to help pick potatoes. We also had lots of cows. Mother made sometimes twenty-four to twenty-five pounds of butter a week, which you could buy for twenty-five cents a pound. We had hens and sold eggs at ten cents a dozen.

Asselin–LeClair Farm, Belgrade, Maine, c. 1920
Mary Adeline LeClair Ashland (sitting on the step), Luella Ashland Roderick and Richard Roderick (standing), Henry Roderick, Jr. (in the car).
Barry Rodrigue

Haying at the Asselin–LeClair Farm, Belgrade, Maine, c. 1920
Lawrence Roderick (foreground), Henry Roderick, Sr., and Henry Roderick, Jr. (atop the hay), Joseph Ashland (with the horses).
Barry Rodrigue

Mother's Gingerbread[4]

Into the mixing bowl put 1 cup sugar.
Add 2 tablespoons molasses, 4 tablespoons melted butter,
1 teaspoon salt, and 1 teaspoon cloves or allspice.
Stir and rub well together.
Then add 1 egg beaten and 1 cup sour milk.
Sift 1 teaspoon soda with 2 cups flour.
Then sift with the other mixture.
Bake in a moderate oven.
Sprinkle sugar on top.

Our mother used to do a lot of cooking in those days. She made her own bread, doughnuts, cookies, and pies. When she made the doughnuts, we used to eat about a half-dozen of them when they were hot!

Old Fashioned Molasses Doughnuts

(This recipe was used more than fifty years ago)[5]

1 cup molasses
1 teaspoon cinnamon
4 teaspoons melted lard
1/4 teaspoon salt
1 cup cold water
1 teaspoon soda
1 teaspoon ginger
4 cups flour

In the fall, our dad used to go and thresh grain for other people. He also had a cider mill and made sweet cider. In the spring, he made maple syrup and maple sugar. He also sawed wood for himself and for other people. This saw ran with horses; it was some kind of thing that horses would get on and keep on walking and go nowhere, only make the saw run.

In the winter months, he cut wood for the house, which was about twenty cord. He also cut wood to sell, about twenty cord of hardwood fitted for the stove. He did this the old way; he didn't have machines to work with like they have today! This wood had to be dry, so it would stay under cover until the next winter. He then would

Asselin–LeClair family, at the farm, Belgrade, Maine, c. 1927. Left to right: Eva Ashland Roderick, Doris Libby Ashland, Frank Ashland, Albert Ashland, Joseph Ashland, Mary-Adeline LeClair Ashland, Luella Ashland Roderick. Barry Rodrigue Collection

take it to market, where he got eight dollars a cord. It would take him about three hours to get to town (Augusta) with a cord of wood; the horses had to walk all the way, it was ten miles. Sometimes after he was gone, we would have a bad storm, so when he got home, his eyelashes and moustache were frozen with ice, also the horses. It was a hard trip!

1 This selection is a composite of writings and interviews of two Franco-American sisters, Eva Ashland Roderick and Luella Ashland Roderick. The narrative comes from a letter Lou wrote to her grand-nephew, Barry Rodrigue *dit* Roderick in 1977, and an oral history interview she made at about the same time. The recipes come from Eva's cookbook. These materials have been edited somewhat. The original materials, as well as other materials pertaining to their family, are held at the University of Southern Maine's Franco-American Collection at Lewiston-Auburn College.

2 Their father was Joseph Asselin (1859–1948). A Maine postmaster changed his family name to Ashland.

3 Their mother, Mary Adeline LeClair (Marie-Adeline Houde-Clair), was born in L'Avenir (Durham) in the Eastern Townships of Québec c. 1862. Moving with her family to Maine, she married Joseph Asselin (Joe Ashland) c. 1880.

4 Mary Adeline LeClair.

5 The notation, "more than fifty years ago," probably meant before Eva Ashland Roderick was born—prior to 1892.

IMMIGRANTS IN A FRONTIER COMMUNITY: MADAWASKA, 1785–1850[1]

Béatrice Craig
Ottawa, Ontario

> The Acadian French, who are settled in numbers in the upper part of this valley, are described as fine industrious men; but the Lower Canadians who came across from the shores of the St. Lawrence, are represented by the English settlers as a "miserable set." This probably arises from the fact that, as the Irish do with us, the poor Lower Canadians come into and through the country as beggars in great numbers.[2]
>
> J. F. W. Johnston, 1851

J. F. W. Johnston, a British agronomist, had been invited by the New Brunswick government to investigate the farming potential of the Province. He traveled widely, and his travels took him to the upper St. John Valley, also known as the "Madawaska Territory" or the "Madawaska Settlement." Johnston's own opinion of the French Canadians did not contradict the one of the valley's few English-speaking settlers: The French Canadians were, in his eyes, squatters and "both needy and indifferent farmers."

Johnston's distinction between "Acadians" and "French Canadians" among Madawaska residents was a recent, but increasingly frequent, phenomenon among visitors. Earlier accounts of the settlement did not distinguish between two groups, especially two groups of unequal worthiness. Insiders, however, had begun to make distinctions between recent immigrants and the rest of the community a generation earlier. In 1829 the French-Canadian priest of the district sent an unhappy letter to the bishop of Quebec, reporting that the "scum" of the lower St. Lawrence parishes was invading the settlement and leading some of his flock astray. His reaction was not unique, as even local priests repeatedly described French-Canadian immigrants as undesirable rowdies. On the other hand, they tended to describe the old established families in glowing terms.[3]

How the latter felt about the newcomers is harder to ascertain. They were almost all illiterate and left no written trace of their feelings. However, we can observe their behavior, and it suggests they viewed the French-Canadian immigrants less and less as equal. As the years went by, established families became increasingly endogamous (more and more prone to marry each other). Charter-family endogamy paralleled the increasing poverty of the newcomers, who were excluded from local credit networks and from access to the best land and the most productive farms.

The charter families were the descendants of Acadians from New Brunswick and French-Canadians from the lower St. Lawrence Valley, who had opened the upper St. John River region to Euramerican colonization in 1785. In 1800 sixty-nine families were permanently established on the banks of the St. John; despite its mixed origins, this settlement was tightly bound together by extensive kinship ties. Everybody was related to several other persons in the community and, in 90 percent of the cases, family connections pre-dated resettlement on the St. John. Thirty-two families were headed by a mixed Acadian-Canadian couple.[4] Only six additional Acadians came afterwards, but French Canadians kept on arriving in increasingly large numbers.

For instance, French-Canadian immigration accounted for 19 percent of the population increase on both sides of the river between 1840 and 1850 (see Table 1). The district, which had been part of the territory disputed by Great Britain and the United States, was divided between the two powers by the Webster-Ashburton Treaty of 1842. The southern bank of the river became part of the United States, but the change in sovereignty had absolutely no impact on French-Canadian immigration. By 1850, Madawaska society, still unaffected by the international boundary supposed to divide it, was stratified along socio-economic and kinship lines, and segmented by language and religion. A small group of Anglo-Protestants (from the United States and New Brunswick) worked in the forest industry, did business with the French, but—as a rule—did not marry them. Religious differences precluded such unions. French-Canadian migrants crowded the bottom rungs of the social latter. Descendants of the sixty-nine charter families were, on the other hand, over-represented in the well-to-do and politically active strata.

Stratification stemmed from one underlying phenomenon: The population was growing rapidly, but economic resources failed to expand accordingly. The charter families and their descendants, in their attempts to maintain their social and economic status, incidentally as well as consciously, curtailed the newcomers' opportunities to achieve an equal level of wealth and security. Madawaska was not the only settlement in the Northeast in which population eventually outstripped resources. This suggests that the difficulties encountered by the French-Canadian migrants into

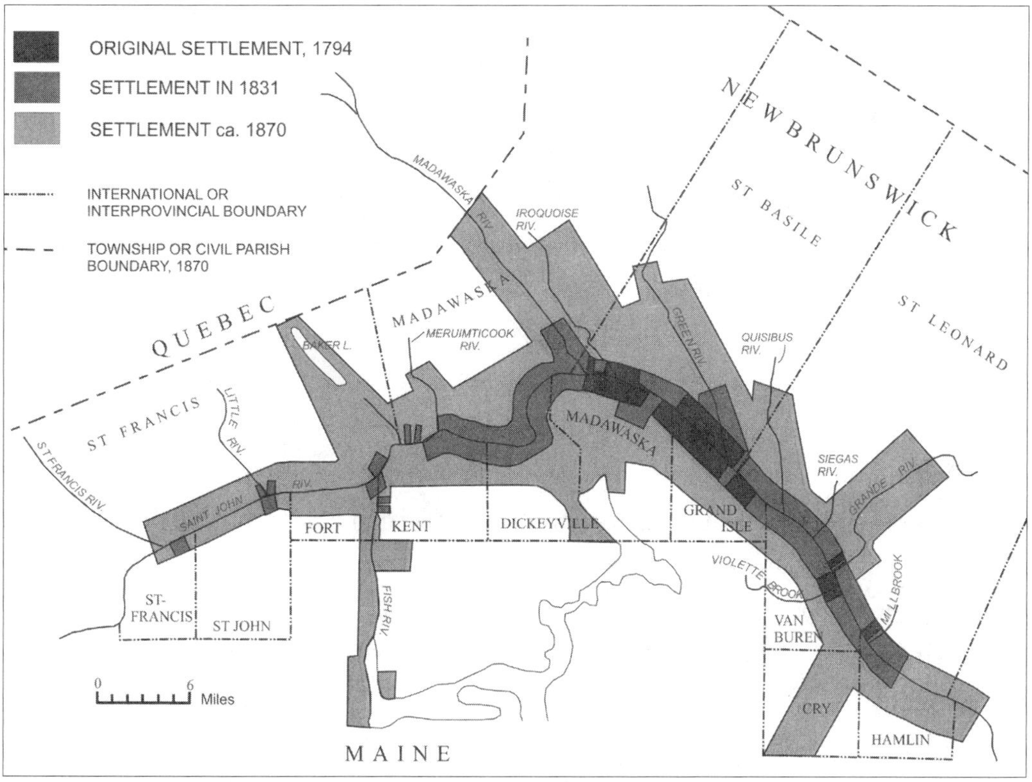

Figure 1: Map of the Upper St. John River Valley, Maine and New Brunswick, 1794–1870.
Béatrice Craig, with Sam Herald, artist

this area could have plagued similarly other groups of immigrants in other localities. The St. John Valley thus constitutes an interesting case study in the fate of geographically mobile people.

Quantitative and qualitative changes characterized the Madawaska Settlement between its foundation and the middle of the nineteenth century. The population grew rapidly. A head count sent to the bishop of Quebec in 1799 listed 331 persons. The 1,000 mark was reached by 1820, and—in 1850—the population exceeded 6,000 people distributed in about 850 households.[5]

The non-Catholic population was insignificant until the 1820s. A dozen New Englanders interested in lumbering arrived around 1817–18. The numbers of non-Catholics gradually increased, and were almost 600 in 1850. This sub-population was characterized by a high proportion of males, as well as a high degree of celibacy and a high turnover rate. Most came after the boundary was settled. Those latecomers were mostly merchants, lumber-camps operators, or officials like postmasters or telegraph operators. English-speaking Catholics were even scarcer. They normally married locally and assimilated, like Thomas Kennedy, who was listed as "French" in the census and was called "Canada" by some of the priests, or Joseph Fraser, said to be "French of Scot origins" in the 1851 census.[6]

The number of farms increased with the population. The New Brunswick government had granted 74 pieces of land averaging 220 acres (89 hectares) each in 1790 and 1794. No more grants were issued until 1842; immigrants occupied land without title. After the Webster-Ashburton Treaty in 1842, Maine and New Brunswick legalized the situation of the squatters and issued deeds for 563 and 505 lots respectively.[7] The growing population spread along the banks of the St. John, as the river was lined with intervales, and dotted with islands providing natural meadows. Virtually all this preferred riparian land was occupied by the mid-1840s (see Figure 1). A second tier of farms began to appear in the central part of the settlement. Those back settlements were still very small in the 1850s, as the settlers preferred to take land along the tributaries of the St. John River, which at least gave them access to the water.[8]

By then, it was very likely the local population had come to the conclusion that the supply of farm land was limited and rapidly diminishing. The settling of the international boundary and—a few years later—of the boundary between Lower Canada/Canada East (Québec) and New Brunswick compounded the problem.[9] Land, which had been free for the taking, now had to be purchased from the state or the province. In Maine the terms were generous, as one could acquire 100 acres (40.5 hectares) of public land in exchange for road labour. New Brunswick waited till 1849 to pass a similar law. Securing a piece of the dwindling supply of good land became more difficult after the treaty.

Despite this considerable territorial expansion, nodes of population in any given area had not yet appeared. Mills, stores, and blacksmith shops, although more numerous in the central area, had not yet led to the formation of a nucleated village. In 1850 Madawaska was still a settlement strung out along waterways. Until 1842 it lacked clearly defined boundaries, as well as a clearly defined focus. Remoteness and the uncertain international situation meant civil authorities did not attempt to organize it into any form until 1833, when New Brunswick created the civil parish of Madawaska. This unit did not have a defined territory, only an eastern boundary. Until the signing of the Webster-Ashburton Treaty, the term "Madawaska Settlement" labeled an aggregate of people rather than a defined space.[10] Ecclesiastical organization followed the same pattern; the parish of St. Basil, created in 1792, expanded territorially with the population until it finally was divided into three sections—an eastern division in 1838 and, in 1842, a western division.[11]

Economic growth and limited development paralleled population increase. Before 1825, the settlers made a living from farming, as well as some fur trading, and possibly from the manufacture of maple sugar, which they were selling out of the region in large quantities in 1831.[12] Shortly after the close of the War of 1812, Madawaska emerged as an important wheat growing region. In 1825 Peter Fisher, the first historian of the province, noted that:

> ...wheat, oats, grains, etc...flourish there in great perfection. The inhabitants are all farmers, and generally raise more than they can consume, having a surplus of grain to sell to traders in the settlement or to take to Fredericton.[13]

Two local Yankee loggers, John Baker and John Bacon, similarly reported that the Madawaska settlers were exporting their surplus, which was very large; however, they claimed the destination was the St. Lawrence Valley:

> Great crops have been raised in Madawaska for several years past—latterly sufficient for their own consumption and the support of emigrants thither, besides exporting four or five thousand bushels to Canada.[14]

The sales of flour in Fredericton and of grain on the St. Lawrence were, of course, not mutually exclusive. But although the riparian land was good, agriculture, especially wheat-growing was a precarious venture. The climate was often uncooperative and ruined the crops in 1816–17, 1828, 1833, 1840, 1855, and possibly in 1827 and 1832 as well.[15]

In the winter of 1824 lumber camps operated by New Brunswick lumber dealers opened in the area. They provided the local population with a source of wage labor and a market for some of their products. The timber trade reaching the upper St. John Valley also meant that farmers could sell the timber that was a by-product of clearing their own land. Some of the French also organized their own logging parties.[16] Cutting took place in the area disputed by the United States and Great Britain, and—owing to U.S. protests—the British decided not to renew the timber licenses, which had been issued for five years. The moratorium on the issuance of timber licenses lasted till the signing of the Webster-Ashburton Treaty, but illegal cutting continued nonetheless. Soon after legal lumbering resumed, a slump in the timber trade—in 1848—brought local operations almost to a standstill.[17] Road building, which had been carried out both by the United States and the British in the 1830s, provided the local population with an additional source of income, but agriculture and forestry remained the mainstay of the local economy well beyond 1850.[18]

Before 1825 immigrants to the St. John Valley encountered a small and close-knit community of interrelated farmers. Land was plentiful and for all to grab. After 1825 newcomers faced a numerically larger community more closely articulated to the wider Atlantic economy. Opportunities for non-farm employment had appeared, but on the other hand, land was becoming scarce. Post-1825 immigrants themselves were quite different from their predecessors. They were, firstly, more numerous.

Estimating the number of immigrants who came to the St. John Valley is—at best—a tentative endeavor. The precise number shall never be known. Nonetheless, one method is to compare the natural increase (excess of birth over death) with the population increase during a given period of time.[19] These figures suggest that immigration was not numerically very important in the St. John Valley between 1800 and 1820. After 1820, on the other hand, immigrants kept coming in increasing numbers—except between 1830 and 1834, when people were leaving the settlement in large numbers (see Table 1). The period of 1833–34 was an especially bad period, when the population of the settlement actually decreased.

Net migration figures are also a rather crude estimate. They do not take into account those who came and left between two population counts, nor the locally-born who out-migrated. Nor do they take into account the contribution of the migrants to natural increase. Those figures therefore hide as much as they reveal. Nonetheless, these net migration figures are worth keeping in mind, because they corroborate the ones derived from a more finely tuned approach—using parish registers.

Table 1: Estimated Net Migration to Madawaska, 1803–1850

Dates	Total population	Corrected population[a]	Natural increase[b]	Net migration	Net yearly immigration
1803	456	456			
1820	1,171	1,160	481	223	13.1
1830	2,474	2,249	638	451	45.1
1833	2,518	2,403	336	-182	-60.7
1834	2,272	2,170	98	-331	-331.0
1840	3,460	3,227	869	188	31.3
1850[c]	6,167	5,580	1,910	457	45.7

[a] These people are identified through the linkage of family reconstruction cards of the 1820, 1830, and 1850 population schedules, as well as the 1833 Maclauchlan return. The 1834 provincial census and the 1840 U.S. census provide only aggregate population figures. These figures exclude non-Catholics. I assumed the proportion of non-Catholics was the same in 1834 as in 1833 and estimate the 1840 proportion of non-Catholics by interpolation between the 1833 and 1850 figures.
[b] Natural increase = Number of births less number of deaths.
[c] The United States took a census of the right bank of the river in 1850, and New Brunswick counted its portion of the population in 1851. Fortunately, the New Brunswick census also indicates the number of births which took place in the preceding year and indicates the year of arrival of immigrants in the province. French-speaking immigrants all came from Lower Canada/Canada East (what has been called "Québec" since 1867). One can therefore estimate with relative accuracy the population of the left bank in the year preceding the census.[20]

With the exception of the small group of easily identifiable Anglo-Protestants, virtually all immigrants were Catholics from Lower Canada/Canada East. They were married and buried in the church, and their children were baptized at birth. Local priests recorded these marriages, burials, and baptisms in the parish registers. The priests were quite conscientious, and—after 1806—there are virtually no gaps in their records (parts of the parish registers are missing for the 1800–05 period). Immigrant couples were usually young and in their reproductive years, having a new baby on the average every twenty-two months.[21] Consequently, if families have been reconstituted, one can time the immigration of couples with a relatively narrow margin of error. The first time they are mentioned in the parish register, less one year, can be taken as a substitute for the year of arrival. Similarly, the last time a couple is mentioned, plus one year, can be used as an estimate of the year of departure.[22]

Figure 2 shows the amplitude and fluctuations in migratory movements starting in 1806. The numbers reported are the total number of couples identified as arriving or leaving in a given year, and—with a few very rare exceptions—they are all French Canadians. Family immigration was limited before 1825 (an average of two a year). The second quarter of the nineteenth century, on the other hand, witnessed the arrival of two large waves of immigrant families: One in 1825–27 and another in 1837–39. Family out-migration was generally low but peaked in 1832–34 and again in 1846.

There is no contradiction between these figures and the ones presented in Table 1. Both data sets point towards a low level of immigration before 1820, increasing afterwards, and heavy population losses between 1830 and 1834. The second

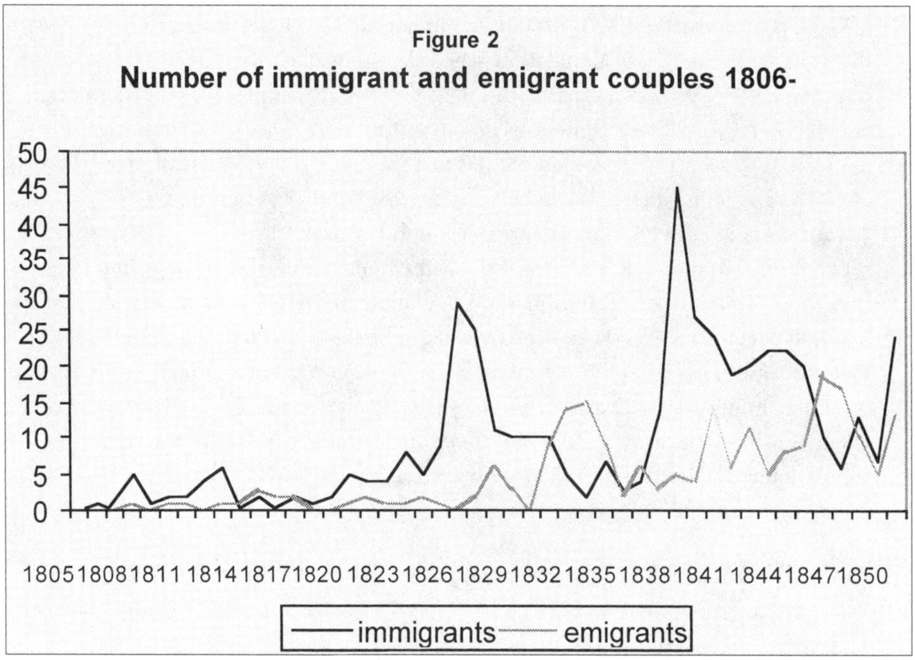

Figure 2: Number of Immigrant and Emigrant Couples, 1805–1850

method, on the other hand, reveals some sharp intercensus fluctuations that were smoothed out by the first approach. These fluctuations closely echoed existing local economic conditions. The arrival of the first wave of immigrants coincided with the opening of lumber camps on the upper St. John in the winter of 1824. U.S. protests and occasional seizures of cut wood, coupled with the moratorium put by the British on issuing timber licenses, restricted the activities of the lumber operators. This slowdown coincided with at least two, and perhaps three, successive failures of the wheat crop in 1828 and 1829 and possibly in 1827.[23] As the food and job supplies constricted, immigration started declining.

The decline continued until 1833, when immigration reached its lowest points since 1819, and out-migration its highest. This population loss coincided with an unusually severe failure of the crops in the fall of 1833, which affected the entire province. The summer of 1833 had been unusually wet, and the first frost came to the upper St. John as early as September 2, a whole month ahead of schedule. It also seems that the preceding year's harvest had not been sufficient either, as reports mentioned people who had been obliged to go into debt to obtain seeds in the spring of 1833.[24] Between 1836 and 1839, crops were again adequate, and illegal logging was at its peak, creating job opportunities. The St. John Valley was once more an attractive place, but not for long. In 1840 the crops failed again, and—again—this failure was followed by a decrease in immigration.[25]

Immigrants who arrived in the 1840s were confronted with greater difficulties in securing good farmland. There was less and less of it, and it had to be purchased. Non-farm employment in the neighboring lumber camps was also very scarce, due to the severe recession that affected the New Brunswick lumber trade at the end of the decade.

At the beginning of 1844, immigration declined precipitously. Out-migration increased again sharply, and—for the first time—it included a large proportion of newlyweds; half of the 1843–45 out-migrant couples were young people who had married at Madawaska, but left before the birth of their first child. Previously, hardly any locally married couples had left permanently. There is no qualitative evidence positively linking migration movements with the short-term cycles of the local economy. Nonetheless, the fluctuations of the former echo the fluctuations of the latter closely enough to suggest one was a response to the other.

Demographically active couples were not the only people to move in: Single people of both sexes came as well. A comparison of Table 1 and Figure 2 shows that family immigration could not have been entirely responsible for the sharp population loss of 1831–34, nor could it account for the relatively high level of net-migration in 1820–30 and 1841–50. Information about these unmarried immigrants is nonexistent. Some married at Madawaska, and their marriage records tell us where their parents resided at the time. This helps us locate the origin of migrants who came alone, but we do not know when they came into the valley, how long they resided there before marriage, how many there were, nor what proportion left while they were still single. One aspect of the migrant experience therefore escapes us almost entirely.

More than absolute numbers differentiated the various phases of immigration; the kin ties and persistence rates of the two groups of immigrants were different as well. Before 1830 immigrant families were more likely to have a relative at Madawaska prior to moving there. Kinship and persistence also were linked: Unrelated immigrants were less likely to persist in the area. After 1830 the proportion of unrelated immigrants' families kept increasing and was above 50 percent by 1837. After 1839, the link between the existence of kin ties and residential persistence also weakened (see Table 2).

Nonetheless, one should not draw the conclusion that immigrants could more easily integrate into the community in the 1830s and 1840s than they had previously.

Table 2: Kinship and Persistence Among Immigrant Couples, 1800–1850[a]

	Immigrant couples With kin at Madawaska					Without any known kin					Grand total
	Persisted		Didn't persist		Total	Persisted		Didn't persist		Total	
Dates	# (N)	%	# (N)	%		# (N)	%	# (N)	%		
1800–24	28	90.3	3	9.7	31	9	33.3	18	66.7	27	58
1825–29	32	80.0	8	20.0	40	18	43.9	23	56.1	41	81
1830–36	16	84.2	3	15.8	19	10	34.5	19	65.5	29	48
1837–42	35	92.1	3	7.9	38	58	65.9	30	34.1	88	126
1843–50	19	70.4	8	29.6	27	88	64.7	48	35.3	136	163

[a] Couples were classified as persistent or non persistent according to the following criteria: 1) if either head died at Madawaska, a couple was considered persistent; 2) if no death was reported for either head, a couple was counted as nonpersistent if the couple was not mentioned in the 1850 U.S. or the 1851 New Brunswick census and the couple ceased to be mentioned in the parish register for at least five years before the date of the census; 3) all couples formed or arrived before 1845 and mentioned in either census were counted as persistent; 4) all couples formed or arrived after 1845 were excluded from either category, as well as all couples not in the census, but mentioned in the parish registers between 1845 and the census dates.[26]

The ability to persist did not automatically entail the removal of any social or economic distance that could have existed between newcomers and old residents. On the contrary, other evidence points towards the widening of the gap between the two groups. One symptom of this widening gap was the increased tendency towards endogamy that was displayed by the descendants of the founders after 1825. Endogamy is not a result of factors beyond human control; selecting a marriage partner is a matter of individual or familial choice. Members of the charter families, that is the founders and their descendants, did not marry outsiders because they either viewed native-born Madawaskayans as more desirable marriage partners or because they believed outsiders were not so desirable additions to society in general. Increased endogamy would have far-reaching consequences, preventing the two groups (charter and immigrants) from blending into a single population. This facilitated the emergence of a society stratified along kinship as well as socio-economic lines.

Pre-1825 immigrants were readily accepted as marriage partners by the local population, because most of them were not unknown quantities. Between 1800 and 1825 fifty male immigrants and fifty-five immigrant females married at Madawaska. The majority of them (thirty-four women and twenty-nine men) married a member of a charter family. Although those marriages were exogamous, involving locally

Table 3: Endogamy and Exogamy of Successive Generations of Locally Born People Who Married at Madawaska 1825-1850[a]

	Females Marrying a locally born # (N)	%	Not marrying a locally born N	%	Total	Males Marrying a locally born N	%	Not marrying a locally born N	%	Total
•Locally born children of immigrants	33	50.8	32	49.2	65	37	78.7	10	21.3	47
•Second-generation charter family	37	53.6	32	46.4	69	34	49.3	35	50.7	69
•Third-generation charter family	122	57.3	9	42.7	213	126	70.4	53	29.6	179
•Fourth-generation charter family	47	61.8	29	38.2	76	42	85.7	7	14.3	49
TOTAL	239	56.5	184	43.5	423	239	69.5	95	27.6	344

[a] 174 marriages were celebrated at Madawaska between 1800 and 1825, involving 119 locally born brides and 124 locally born grooms. Between 1825 and 1850, there were 797 marriages: 239 were endogamous, 289 were exogamous, and 268 were immigrant intermarriages. The number of Catholics marrying outside the church and local people marrying in a different parish was insignificant.[27]

born and outsiders, the non-native spouses were not really strangers. Half of the "outsiders" who married within the charter population had a relative at Madawaska prior to their marriage. More than one in ten were closely enough related to their spouses to need a dispensation for consanguinity before the marriage could take place. On the other hand, most of them were unlikely to have spent most of their lives at Madawaska. Two-thirds of the males and half of the females were children of people still living in Lower Canada when they married, and one can presume they were already adult when they arrived in the St. John Valley.

After 1825, when immigrants became more and more numerous, different patterns of exogamy and endogamy appeared. The percentage of exogamous marriages remained relatively constant over the period, shifting from 37 percent of all marriages before 1825 to 36 percent afterwards. At the same time, the proportion of outside spouses having relatives at Madawaska prior to marriage dropped from 49 percent to 23 percent. Does this mean the two populations were more inclined to intermarry?

Migrants were also subject to new cultural influences. This often-reproduced photograph shows two houses along the Madawaska River near the "Petit Sault," around 1870. The house parallel to the river follows Canadian practices. Its neighbor, perpendicular to the river, is laid out "American Style."
Université de Moncton-Edmundston, CDEM PB1–12

Not really. First of all, the composition of the marriage market had changed dramatically: Before 1825 immigrants represented a little less than one-third of all brides and grooms; after 1825 their population rose to 47 percent of the brides and 57 percent of the grooms. Outsiders now slightly outnumbered native-born among people contracting marriage. The proportion of migrant intermarriage increased from 12 percent to 35 percent. Charter family members were slightly more likely to marry strangers, but immigrants were three times less likely to marry locally born people than they had previously. The two populations were not blending as freely as previously.

In addition, people whose family had been established at Madawaska for several generations were less likely to marry outside the core population than sons and daughters of the founders (see Table 3). The 1800–25 charter-family brides and grooms had almost all been second-generation residents, and 73 percent of them married another member of a charter family—by choice or necessity, as marriageable

Table 4: Origins of Male and Female Heads of Household in 1850–1851

	Both heads born in Lower Canada	Male head born in Lower Canada; female head born in Madawaska	Female head born Canada; male head born in Madawaska	Both heads born in Madawaska	Total
N.B. Madawaska, 1851	146	188	24	155	513
U.S. Madawaska, 1850	115	128	45	157	445
TOTAL	261	316	69	312	958
Percentage of total	27.2	33.0	7.2	32.6	100.0

immigrants were not in large supply. The second generation members of the founding families who married after 1825 took advantage of the enlarged marriage market. Their descendants, on the other hand, did not follow their example. Each successive generation was more endogamous than the preceding one, and grooms were far more endogamous than brides. Locally born women were at a disadvantage on the marriage market. Before 1825, an almost equal number of locally born males and females married at Madawaska. This was no longer the case afterwards, and there were 20 percent more locally born brides than grooms. There is no evidence of an imbalanced sex ratio at birth favoring girls or of excessive male mortality in childhood. On the contrary, there seems to have been a shortage of little girls.[28] Slightly more boys than girls should therefore have reached marriage age, as before 1825. This was not the case, suggesting that locally born males were beginning to emigrate while still single. Some of the locally born women had to marry "outsiders," whether they liked it or not, or remain single, a prospect socially and economically undesirable. They found themselves marrying outsiders more frequently than did their brothers. The mid-century censuses corroborate the conclusions drawn from parish register data: Locally born females were much more likely to marry men born in Lower Canada than the reverse (see Table 4).

Economic factors could probably explain much of the locally born men's preference; locally born women could have come from better-off families than outsiders. This hypothesis is difficult to prove, because the evidence is sparse. There are no existing tax records for the period and no marriage contracts. The reports of the U.S. and British land agents, nonetheless, allow us a glimpse into inheritance patterns. They list daughters as co-heirs of their recently deceased fathers. Daughters could also receive gifts of land upon marriage; some were even given a whole farm lot.[29] Property transmission data suggests that daughters normally received moveable property upon marriage; the minimum appears to have been a milk cow. In addition, they could receive ewes, fowl, a bed with bedding, a spinning wheel, some household equipment, and some clothing.[30] If charter families were better off, their daughters were probably better endowed.

The relative level of wealth of charter and immigrant families before 1850 can be derived from a document pertaining to the 1833 crop disaster. In November of that year the inhabitants petitioned officials in Fredericton, New Brunswick, for relief. The governor requested a report from the commissioner of the disputed territory, James Maclauchlan. Maclauchlan sent an extremely detailed account of the situation of the 403 families in the territory, including a detailed inventory of their livestock, crops (past and present), and any other piece of information he deemed relevant.[31]

All families had land, except twenty-seven tenants, of whom only two were locally born. Thirty-two family heads were listed as laborers, 85 percent of them immigrants. There were altogether 168 families headed by an immigrant male, and 52 percent were listed as destitute and in need of immediate assistance, compared to only 23 percent of the others. Immigrants had less livestock, fewer crops, and often had no crops listed for the preceding years. They were probably still clearing land. Their land also was unlikely to be as good as that of the charter families. Old residents had taken the habit of marking lots for their children very early in their tenure, which they gave to their children when they came of age or married. The selected lots were normally the best sites for farming or milling.[32] Immigrants took the leftovers. Newcomers would therefore have been hard pressed to provide as much for the establishment of a newlywed child as old residents could.

Locally born males looking for a spouse were in an advantageous position on the marriage market. They were in a position to be selective and apparently made economically wise choices: They chose dowries to match their portions of land. As blood ties were numerous among the various charter families, this led them to marry their cousins. The proportion of consanguineous marriages declined in the population at large from one in four before 1825 to one in ten afterwards. Among the core population on the other hand, consanguineous marriages increased from one in three to one in two. These marriages were disapproved by the church, but official discouragements, red tape, fines to be paid, and increased opportunities to marry out of the family were to no avail. By mid-century, locally born males even preferred brides who belonged to charter families to locally born daughters of migrants. All women belonging to the latter category who married before 1842 married a non-migrant.

Only 32 percent of them did so after 1842; their chances of marrying in the local population were then only three percentage points higher than one of the non-native females. Locally born sons of migrants on the other hand did not suffer from this form of discrimination.

Two contradictory factors therefore affected the evolution of endogamy and exogamy. The composition of the marriage market favored increased exogamy, and—consequently—the integration of newcomers into the existing kin networks. This happened, but not at all to the extent one could have expected, because economic factors encouraged members of the charter families to marry each other, rather than the less-well-off immigrants and their children.

The tendency towards endogamy among the charter families reflected, as well as aggravated, the economic distance between the two groups. Endogamy was not the only symptom of the gap separating newcomers from old residents. Immigrants had greater difficulties entering the local trading networks: In the 1840s they were not given credit at the Dufour store, which belonged to two wealthy brothers who were members of a charter family. The ledger of their general store depicts a population buying a great variety of articles on credit and settling the account in trickles and dribbles with products of any kind: cash, man power, woman power, child power, and animal power, or credit on someone else's account. This pattern was not unusual and could be found throughout the Northeast; a shortage of specie was the cause of it. But the names of the newcomers are conspicuously absent from the store credit book. The names that do appear are those of the founding families. This form of economic organization, resting on acquaintance, worked to the disadvantage of strangers—they did not have a credit rating. When newcomers needed store goods—nails, tools, salt, and anything else from patent medicine to tobacco—they had to pay for them immediately or do without.

Newcomers may also have generated hostility at one point. It is quite plausible that the charter families came to view the later generation of newcomers as undesirable interlopers. The Madawaska Settlement was not a juxtaposition of unconnected individuals. Because of the coincidence of settlement and kin networks before 1825, a strong sense of communalism could have developed among the founders and their descendants. Immigrants, who were related, would not have been perceived as strangers, but as members of the community who had happened to have been born elsewhere.

Immigrants who were not members of the kin network, however, simply would not "belong." Before 1825 they tended to leave; afterwards, they persisted, accelerating the demographic growth of the valley and threatening the future livelihood of the charter families. Local residents had numerous children to provide for: Completed families averaged ten children and infant mortality was low.[34] Before 1825, when land was abundant, it had been easy to establish them on a farm. In the 1830s and especially in the 1840s it was obvious the immigrants were competing for space with the children and grandchildren of the old residents and were taking land the latter probably had mentally earmarked for their not-yet-born descendants. This situation was hardly conducive of good will.

The attitude of the priests was consistently negative, despite their being themselves of French-Canadian extraction. One described the newcomers as undesirable elements trying to escape the controls of more organized parishes in order to indulge in lawlessness and ribaldry.[35] In the eyes of another priest, the migrants were potential freeloaders: During the food shortage of 1840 he warned the government against giving relief in cash or in kind, as this would encourage outsiders to come. Instead, he advocated some form of public work for the destitute.[36]

It is hard to know whether the priests' opinions reflected reality, their own prejudices against geographically mobile people, or whether they echoed the opinions of the local inhabitants. Nonetheless, the evidence drawn from the behavior of the charter families and some members of the local economic elite parallels that derived from the statements of the spiritual leaders of the community. They all convey the impression of the division of the community into two clearly distinct groups, with a possible undercurrent of resentment and unfriendliness towards the newcomers. And, as we have seen at the beginning of this text, the division was palpable enough to be noticed by visitors.

The position of immigrants *vis à vis* the core population changed markedly over time. Before 1825 immigrants often had relatives at Madawaska. The related immigrant couples' chances of persisting were fairly high, and related single immigrants were likely to marry a member of the community. Immigrant couples who did not have relatives found themselves at a noticeable disadvantage, reflected by their low persistence rates. After 1825 immigrants were more likely to be complete strangers. This had a less adverse effect upon their persistence, but persistence no longer equated integration into the local family network through marriage. Gender became an additional factor, with female immigrants less likely to marry into the core group than male immigrants. Persistence did not automatically provide admission into the local commercial networks, including credit in the general store. Kinship networks and local population had been almost conterminous before 1825. This was no longer the case afterwards. Then, a core population bound together by innumerable alliances lived side by side with an almost as large population of newly arrived strangers. Those strangers were kept at a distance in many aspects of the social and economic life.

Changes in the volume and composition of the migratory cohorts took place within the broader context of regional demographic growth and economic development. The wheat trade out of the St. John Valley found its stride at about the time the lumbering industry began. Local farmers had access to profitable outlets. But the repeated failure of the wheat crops in the 1830s and 1840s prompted a large-scale change in local agricultural production. By 1850 wheat was no longer king, but a marginal crop; its place was taken by potatoes, buckwheat, and oats.[37] Buckwheat pancakes replaced bread in the local diet; oats, hay, and potatoes were grown for the lumbering market as well as for local consumption.

Lumber camps provided more than a market for already productive farms. They provided employment for surplus sons, as well as for farm families until their land could support them. It took seven to ten years, on the average, to make a farm productive; pioneers needed a means of support in the meantime. The forest industry provided them with wage work and bought the wood resulting from their clearing their claim. Nearby lumbering was well suited to the needs of the local population, as it occupied the men during the winter, when farm work was greatly reduced. This pattern of combining winter lumbering with summer clearing and farming, using the wages earned to support one's family and farm, was not uncommon in areas where agricultural land coexisted with forested territories.[38]

The availability of wage labor was critical to immigrant families, especially for immigrants without relatives or close friends in the area. Locally born people clearing new land could always rely on their parents for temporary support; related immigrants could call on kin solidarity for help or relief. Unrelated immigrants, on the other hand, did not have access to those forms of help and were therefore more vulnerable. If they did not manage to produce enough to satisfy their basic needs, they could not turn to better-off next of kin for assistance. Even when such help was not needed, the functioning of the local economy could work against the immigrants, as credit for weekly purchases was not available to them. Nonrelated immigrants were more dependent on cash income than the remainder of the population. If they did not have enough, they might have been forced to leave.

Before lumber camps opened, nonrelated immigrants had a low rate of persistence, which reflected their precarious standing in the community. After the lumbercamps opened, unrelated migrants had a higher rate of persistence; they were less dependent on their not yet fully productive farm for their subsistence. Their winter wages could tie them over until the next harvest. Their economic security had improved. Nonetheless, the economic situation of the related migrants and of the locally born remained better, as those two latter categories were protected by two safety nets instead of one—nonfarm employment and their kin network. In times of crisis, newcomers suffered most, had fewer alternatives, and were the first ones to leave. The persistence rate of unrelated migrants who arrived, between 1830 and 1836 when agriculture faltered, was lower than for the preceding five-year period and subsequent five-year period. Unrelated migrants also provided the bulk of the couples who moved out between 1830 and 1834. Another crop failure occurred in 1840, and the priest reported the most destitute were Canadian migrants who had arrived in the preceding two years. When the food was in short supply, there was none to spare and sell to those less able to grow sufficient quantities.[39]

Local economic changes originally facilitated the settlement of migrants unconnected with the already existing community in the St. John Valley, but the increased ability of unrelated migrants to persist accelerated population growth in the valley, growth which harmed them in the long run and forced their descendants to leave. The Madawaska Settlement was in the process of repeating the pattern of population growth already occurring in the lower St. Lawrence Valley. There, the old parishes from which the migrants originated were filling up rapidly. By the late eighteenth and early nineteenth centuries, their population was spilling eastward into the Rivière du Loup and Rimouski area.[40] By 1830, the arable land in the lower St. Lawrence was almost entirely occupied, and population surplus had to find nonagricultural outlets or migrate a great distance. Some joined the lumbering teams of New Brunswick and Lower Canada. Others, in Gaspé, turned towards the sea and engaged in fishing, and large numbers of families tried to open farms in peripheral areas, starting with the Saguenay in the late 1840s.[41]

A similar situation prevailed in the St. John Valley in the 1840s. Land was filling up, newcomers and old residents scrambled for whatever land was still available. The charter families had to devise new strategies to provide for their children. Their options were limited. They could divide the land among several children. This was not a solution they favored, unless they had a larger-than-average amount of property. Land division took place before all the valley had filled up, not after. Lot sizes in the old part of the settlement dropped from an average of 220 acres (89 hectares) in 1790–94 to 165 acres (67 hectares) in 1831 and 150 (61 hectares) in 1846. They remained stable afterwards. Farm lots in the newly opened western section dropped from 170 acres (69 hectares) in 1831 to 130 acres (53 hectares) in 1846 and also remained stable in size afterwards.[42] Lot boundaries also remained very stable.[43] Longtime residential families resorted to other means to take care of their offspring: One would get the family farm, others would purchase land from people who were leaving, and some simply left the area to find their fortune elsewhere—in mill towns, in the lumbering industry, or out West.[44] This explains the deficit in locally born males. Single locally born women did not leave; instead they married immigrants. The locally born young men who stayed, married the daughters of other landed families in order to consolidate their economic position. As most of the landowners were members of charter families and were related to each other several times over, this meant they married their cousins. There is no evidence that marrying a cousin was a deliberate move to keep the patrimony in the family and protect some members of the lineage against erosion of their economic status.

The integration of immigrants depended on the interplay of several sets of factors. One set was structural: In the absence of opportunities for wage labor, as before 1825, nonrelated immigrants were less likely to succeed in opening a farm than those individuals and families who could rely on the help of kin already established at Madawaska. Such a situation minimized the problem of integrating immigrants, as those who persisted were already linked to the community through blood ties. The existence of opportunities for wage labor, on the other hand, increased everyone's chances of becoming a farmer, as long as land was accessible. It would lead to the appearance of a larger number of strangers in the midst of the old community. When land ceased to be abundant, established families tried to prevent property from leaving their hands, and one strategy available to them was a high rate of endogamy. Landowners' sons married landowners' daughters.

Another set of factors resulted from economic and demographic changes. The better opportunities for local employment offered by lumber camps accentuated a pattern of rapid demographic growth, which reduced the chances later-coming migrants had to find land suitable for farming. The last factor stemmed from attitude. Strangers represented a threat to the livelihood of the community's descendants, and therefore one could not expect them to have been welcomed.

The locally based population benefited from the compounded advantages of lengthier residence, well-established farms on the best land, and pre-emption of the best unoccupied sites (intervales and mill sites). This, combined with a high level of endogamy, helps to explain why members of the locally born families were found in disproportionate numbers in the wealthier socio-economic group. Economic and social capital reinforced each other.

The immigrants, on the other hand, consistently crowded the bottom rung of the socio-economic ladder. This was true as early as 1831. That year, the State of Maine sent two land agents to the St. John Valley to assess people's titles to their land. The agents' report reveals that seventeen of the twenty "better-off" residents belonged to founding families.[45] In 1850, the date at which the first census giving the value of real estate held was taken, a similar picture emerged. Forty-three properties were valued at $1,000 or more (10 percent of all the farm lots). Six belonged to Anglo-Saxon lumbermen. Thirty-three belonged to a member of one of the founding families or to their descendants or to a migrant who had married in the community.[46] The proportion of nonlocal landowners increased as the value of the land diminished, as shown in Table 5.

One was more likely to own valuable real estate if one had been born in the St. John Valley than if one had moved there in adulthood, unless one had capital to invest, as was the case of the lumber-operators. This does not necessarily imply that social mobility was out of the reach of the migrants, but it certainly does mean that it was not easy to achieve. In addition, public offices and other status-conferring positions were bestowed by the British upon the local "elite." Immigrants were seldom justices of the peace, registers of deeds, or even pound-keepers, and so on.[47] After the partition of 1842 U.S. institutions were introduced on the southern bank of the river. Immigrants, being Canadians, could not vote legally, nor could they be elected. This gave an added advantage to the founding families, who elected their own as representatives to the State House.[48]

Immigrants who had assets other than a good name, a strong back, and a local relative could be very successful too. They were as visible as they were statistically insignificant. One was Louis Bellefleur, son of a Québec officer. The priest referred to him as "sieur" and to his wife as "demoiselle" in the parish register, a unique privilege. He was a merchant, apparently quite wealthy. In 1831 he invested $2,000 in a grist and saw mill.[50] His four sons and daughters married into the best local families,

Table 5: Farm Value by Social Group, U.S. Madawaska, 1850[a]

	Farm value $200-399[b] # (N)	%	$400-499 # (N)	%	$500-799 # (N)	%	$800-999 # (N)	%	$1,000+ # (N)	%	Total # (N)	%
Owners: Charter families and immigrant kin	3	27.3	6	27.3	26	45.6	22	51.2	33	76.7	90	51.1
Owners: Other immigrants	8	72.7	16	72.7	31	54.4	21	48.8	10	23.3	86	48.9
TOTAL	11		22		57		43		43		176	

[a]Similar calculations cannot be done for the New Brunswick side, as the census schedules for the region do not report farm value.

[b]The census taker reported a value for farms assessed at $300 and more only, with the exception of one piece of property valued at $200. All heads of families for whom no land was reported were listed as "laborers." Hardly any of these were landless, though, as a comparison between the 1843 land survey and the census schedule reveals. Their holdings included a large number of farms opened within the previous ten years. The low value of the land could therefore be attributed to two distinct factors. Either the farm was really worth very little (small size, poor land) or it was not yet cleared. It is impossible to sort out one group from the other.[49]

owned an abundance of real estate, including grist and saw mills, and the best general store in the area (next to the parish church). The men also became officers of the militia or justices of the peace.[51]

The other success story is that of Francis Rice, an Irishman who began his career as a schoolmaster. He became the first Catholic justice of the peace in the St. John Valley and the first local member of the Provincial Parliament. Rice capitalized on a locally very rare combination of skills: Literacy and bilingualism. He married into one of the charter families and, because of his official position and language abilities, cooperated closely with Commissioner Maclauchlan.[52] Such stories are few and far between, though. Neither Bellefleur nor Rice were ordinary immigrants. The normal immigrant's experience involved struggling and—as the years went by—greater and greater difficulties escaping initial poverty. Partly through deliberate action and partly through circumstances, the founding families and their descendants succeeded in preserving the socio-economic status of a large number of their own—at the expense of most newcomers.

Cultural consequences resulted from this dominance. The local oral tradition claims the Madawaska people are descendants of "Acadians," the group which constituted most of the original families.[53] This is obviously inaccurate. It seems that the dominant families, who were able to impose their visions of the past upon the rest of the community, chose to define themselves as Acadians. They chose to ignore their French-Canadian ancestry, and they chose to obliterate the contribution of the latter-arriving French Canadian from the collective memory. Boasting about their blue blood may have been a convenient way to disassociate themselves from the newcomers and their children, and to perpetuate their social dominance. There was an additional reason to define oneself as "Acadian" on the U.S. side of the valley: The Yankees had a positive image of "Acadians," thanks to Maine's celebrated poet Henry Wadsworth Longfellow and his poem "Evangeline," about the Acadian diaspora, but the Yankees had a negative view of the French Canadians.[54]

Madawaska was a pioneer settlement that became a stratified society in less than three generations. Strangers were kept at bay by the socio-economic process underway in the settlement, as well as by the deliberate actions of the charter families. Many members of the founding families—who perceived the entire St. John Valley as their territory—had strong advantages over the newcomers: Better land, longer residence, membership in close-knit kinship networks. They were the economic, political, and cultural elite of the settlement from the beginning. They controlled its present, recreated its past, and were in a better position to shape its future than the French-Canadian migrants who came to make a living among them after 1825. And they strove to preserve their position by all means at their disposal.

Was Madawaska an idiosyncratic settlement or was it unexceptional? The non-integration of migrants seems to have been the result of rapidly increasing population pressure on not very elastic resources. A similar process characterized many North American pioneer settlements in the seventeenth, eighteenth, and nineteenth centuries. An article by Darrett Rutman describes the process of social and economic evolution underway in Anglo-colonial communities exactly in those terms. Those "little societies" shifted first from an early favorable ratio of resources per settler to a later period of scarcity, leading to out-migration, unless the community could expand its resources by moving away from an exclusively agricultural base. Secondly, economic growth and diversification brought a marked sharpening of social stratification.

Finally, colonial settlements were gradually integrated into the larger society partly through the actions of their small, more cosmopolitan-oriented elite.[55] This description of Anglo-colonial settlements applies very well to the St. John Valley.

Demographic growth would inevitably lead to a shortage of land, however. Even the older families could not provide all their sons with land to preserve the standard of living of their members; those families passed their property to only a limited number of offspring. The others took up trades or left altogether.

Herbert Mays, in his study of the Toronto Gore Township, found that such a strategy quickly led to a close link between persistence, kinship, landownership, and early entry by the mid-nineteenth century.[56] The most common way to acquire land in this area was through inheritance: People with local kin or descendants of the earliest settlers were therefore in a favored position. This strategy was also detrimental to immigrants, who—for all practical purposes—were barred from acquiring land and left, as no other forms of local employment were available. The behavior of the Toronto Gore farmers paralleled closely that of the St. John Valley charter families, who were mostly farming families. An article by Timothy Lewis describes a similar situation in Sunbury County, New Brunswick: Increased out-migration was accompanied by increased geographic stability of a core group of families.[57] Sinking deeper and deeper roots into the community was only one of the available strategies, though; in some cases, an entire family pulled up stakes and moved away to some less populated area where all members could enjoy their customary lifestyle and social status.[58]

Those who stayed behind intermarried and kept land in their hands. In at least one eighteenth-century New England town, cousins were favored marriage partners—for economic reasons.[59] The Toronto Gore permanent residents also married each other, rather than outsiders, and probably for the same reasons. Out-migration, if it prevented the fragmentation of holdings, could prevent the pauperization of the landed descendants of the earlier settlers. As for poor migrants, they stood a limited chance of acquiring good land, either through purchase or marriage. It was difficult for them to achieve economic equality with the old residents or integration into existing kin networks. Those impoverished newcomers were viewed with suspicion, since they could become a financial burden on the community.[60] New England, for instance, continued the practice of "warning out" poor strangers until the American Revolution.[61]

Migrations were not individual ventures; instead, they were carried under family auspices—family and kin networks provided help and assistance to their members on the move. This characteristic was neither cultural, time, nor place specific; it was shared by social groups as different as those in seventeenth- and eighteenth-century New France, eighteenth-century New England, or the Saguenay in the late-nineteenth century. In New France, there seems to have been a positive link between the existence of kin ties and successful relocation.[62] Two factors common to most agricultural areas can help explain this phenomenon. One was the characteristic of the local economic organization. Regional subsistence, associated with the interdependence of various producers, depended on complex networks of debits and credits. This type of economic organization works to the disadvantage of outsiders, who are "unknown quantities." Migrants, who have the greatest need for the help of their neighbors, are in the least position to secure it.

The other factor is the need for the alternative sources of subsistence in the first few years of pioneer farming. There are basically three means to satisfy this need: Possession of enough provisions on arrival to last for a year or two; help from others (kin, or a credit-giving local merchant); or access to jobs. The existence of wage labor was particularly critical for the success of socially isolated migrants. In frontier areas, wage labor was usually associated with lumbering—a complementary activity, but any seasonal activity could do. On the other side of the continent, in Oregon for instance, a similar situation prevailed, but unrelated migrants supported themselves by working for the Hudson Bay Company.[63]

Madawaska may not have been the archetype of all agrarian Northeastern pioneer communities, yet it shares a sufficient number of structural and attitudinal characteristics—with New England colonial communities, French- and English-Canadian pioneer settlements, and even the Oregon frontier—to be placed within the norm, not considered an exception.

1 This is a revised and updated version of "Migrant Integration in a Frontier Society: The Madawaska Settlement, 1800–1850," *Histoire sociale-Social History* 38, November 1986, pp. 277–98.

2 Johnston, *Notes on North America*, 70.

3 Roman Catholic Church, Archdiocese of Québec, Lettres des prêtres missionnaires: 4 April 1829, 11 September 1822, 8 November 1834.

4 Roman Catholic Church, Parish of St. Basile (New Brunswick), Register; Parish of St. Bruno (Maine), Register; Parish of Ste. Luce (Maine), Register. Langlois, *Dictionnaire généalogique du Madawaska*. Arsenault, *Histoire et généalogie des Acadiens*. Tanguay, *Dictionnaire Généalogique*; *Dictionnaire national des Canadiens Français*.

5 Roman Catholic Church, Archdiocese of Québec, Lettres des prêtres missionnaires: 1803. New Brunswick, Provincial Census, 1851.

6 New Brunswick, Provincial Census, 1851.

7 New Brunswick, Crown Land Office, Survey map of the Mazzerolle Grant; Survey map of the Soucy Grant; "Maps of the Madawaska Survey." Maine, Commissioners, "Report of the Commissioners Appointed under the Resolve of February 21, 1843." Some farmers were single, and boarded with other families. Some household heads possessed more than one farm, or a farm consisting of scattered holdings. This accounts for the constant excess of farm lots over households.

8 New Brunswick, Crown Land Office, Survey map, Mazzerolle Grant; Survey map, Soucy Grant; "Maps of the Madawaska Survey." Maine, Commissioners, "Report of the Commissioners Appointed under the Resolve of February 21, 1843."

9 Until 1867, what is now Canada was known as British North America. "Canada" referred to Upper Canada (Ontario) and Lower Canada (Québec) until 1841, and to Canada West (Ontario) and Canada east (Québec) between 1841 and 1867.

10 Ganong, pp. 137–49. Wynn, "New Brunswick Parish Boundaries."

11 Thomas Albert.

12 Hudon. Massé. Fisher, p. 53. Roman Catholic Church, Archdiocese of Québec, Lettres des prêtres missionnaires: 22 January 1802, 18 December 1804. Deane and Kavanagh, p. 455; Ward, p. 86.

13 Fisher, p. 53.

14 Committee of American Citizens of Madawaska.

15 *Bangor Register*, 10 October 1827. *Republican Journal*, 12 August 1829. New Brunswick, House of Assembly, Journal: 13 February 1834, 20 February 1834, 1 March 1834, 11 March 1834, 14 March 1834, 1840, pp. 159–60; Legislative Assembly, Papers relating to the settlement of Madawaska, 1834, Report of the Commissioner of Affairs at Madawaska, 1834.

16 Roman Catholic Church, Archdiocese of Québec, Lettres des prêtres missionnaires: 27 March 1824: "Les effets ont assez bon cours à présent parce que des faiseurs de bois de tonnes ont ouvert cet hiver des chantiers dans nos endroits." On the other hand, as late as November 1821, the priest was complaining he could not sell the products collected as tithes.

17 Wynn, *Timber Colony,* pp. 33–53.

18 Ward, p. 88. Wynn*, Timber Colony,* p. 37. *New Brunswick Courier*, 18 February 1826.

19 Henry, *Manuel de démographie historique*, pp. 56–57.

20 Roman Catholic Church, Parish of St. Basile (New Brunswick), Register; Parish of St. Bruno (Maine), Register; Parish of Ste. Luce (Maine), Register; Archdiocese of Québec, Lettres des prêtres missionnaires: 1803. United States, Treasury Department, Bureau of the Census, Census of the United States, Maine: 1820, 1830, 1840, 1850. New Brunswick, Provincial Census: 1834, 1851; Legislative Assembly, Papers relating to the settlement of Madawaska, return showing the number of inhabitants in the settlement with their stock (this is a household census taken by J. Maclauchlan, New Brunswick Warden of the disputed territory).

21 Intergenesic intervals were calculated using the family reconstitution cards.

22 Gérard Bouchard used this approach to time out-migration in "Family, Structure and Geographic Mobility at Laterrière," p. 36, footnote 19. The existence of a local genealogical dictionary ensures that locally born people marrying outside the parish and coming back will not be confused with true immigrants.

23 See footnote 15 above.

24 New Brunswick, Legislative Assembly, papers relating to the settlement of Madawaska: Letter from R. Mercier, Priest, 14 November 1833; Certificate of Commissioners Rice and Maclauchlan, 16 November 1833.

25 New Brunswick, House of Assembly, Journal, 1840, pp. 159–60.
26 Roman Catholic Church, Parish Registers: St. Basile, St. Bruno, and St. Luce.
27 Roman Catholic Church, Parish Registers: St. Basile, St. Bruno, and St. Luce.
28 In 1820, there were 87 girls under the age of ten for every 100 boys of the same age in the district; in 1830, the ratio was 88 to 100. United States, Treasury Department, Bureau of the Census, Maine Census: 1820, 1830.
29 Deane and Kavanagh. New Brunswick, "Maps of the Madawaska Survey"; Legislative Assembly, "Report of the Commissioners."
30 Craig, "La femme face à la transmission des patrimoines au XIXe siècle."
31 New Brunswick, Legislative Assembly, papers relating to the settlement of Madawaska, Report of the Commissioner of Affairs at Madawaska, "Return showing the number of Inhabitants in the settlement of Madawaska with their Stock," 1833.
32 Deane and Kavanagh.
33 Madawaska Historical Society, Ledger of the Dufour General Store, 1844–1848. Clark. Hobbs-Pruytt. McCalla, "Retailing in the Countryside"; "Rural Credit and Rural Development"; Craig, "Solder les comptes."
34 Completed family size was calculated using the family reconstitution cards. See Craig and Sorg.
35 Roman Catholic Church, Archdiocese of Quebec, Lettres des prêtres missionnaires: 25 May 1825.
36 New Brunswick, House of Assembly, Journal, 1840, pp. 159–60.
37 Craig, "Agriculture in a pioneer region;" "Le développement agricole dans la haute vallée du St Jean en 1860;" "Agriculture et marché au Madawaska, 1799–1850;" *Backwood Consumers and Homespun Capitalists*.
38 Wynn, *Timber Colony*, pp. 79–84. Bowen. Bouchard, "Family Structure and Geographic Mobility at Laterrière." Séguin. The agro-forestry system is usually described in negative terms, as farming activities often were subordinated to the needs of the lumber industry and forced to take place in the vicinity of the cuttings, whether the soil was fit for agriculture or not. When the camps departed, the farmers—unable to subsist without their winter wages—had to abandon their farms, follow the lumber operators, and start all over again. In areas like the St. John Valley, on the other hand, where the soil was good enough for farming, agriculture was able to develop alongside and even independently of the lumber industry, even though some members of the community engaged in both activities. The Madawaska settlers survived on their farms for forty years before the lumber camps opened in their vicinity and farming is still a viable activity for a significant proportion of the population. See Craig, "Agriculture and the Lumberman's Frontier."
39 New Brunswick, House of Assembly, Journal, 1840, pp. 159–60.
40 Canada, *Censuses of Canada, 1665 to 1871*, pp. 64–80.
41 Biaya, pp. 247–300.
42 Deane and Kavanagh. Maine, Commissioners, "Report of the Commissioners Appointed under the Resolve of February 21, 1843." New Brunswick, Crown Land Office, "Maps of the Madawaska Survey."
43 The stability of the lots' boundaries is evident when one compares the mid-nineteenth-century maps with later ones, such as the ones contained in Roe.
44 Craig, "La transmission des patrimoines fonciers dans le Haut St-Jean au XIXe siècle." For migrations to the western United States see Langellier, "Tickling the Past."
45 Deane and Kavanagh.
46 United States, Treasury Department, Bureau of the Census, Census of the United States, Maine:

1850, Hancock, Madawaska, and Van Buren Plantations.

47 Craig, *Backwoods Consumers and Homespun Capitalists.*

48 Albert, *Histoire du Madawaska,* Appendix. The representatives sent to the State House of Maine between 1842 and 1860 were Joseph and Paul Cyr, two brothers; their second cousin François Thibodeau, whose sister was married to Paul Cyr; Firmin Cyr, first cousin to the four above mentioned; and Joseph Nadeau, a more remote relative. The five men were sons or grandsons of founders. They were well-to-do; the poorest owned $800 worth of real estate. Nadeau was a merchant worth $1,700 in property; Paul Cyr and Thibodeau were among the richest landowners on the U.S. side of the river, boasting $4,000 and $3,000 worth of property respectively. In addition, the Cyrs and the Thibodeaus were all married to their cousins, and the women were closely related to each other. Two of these men also had sons elected as state representatives in the following fifteen years. The justices of the peace on the New Brunswick side of the border were equally interrelated and had close connections with the U.S. political elite. New Brunswick Justice of the Peace Joseph Cyr was a brother to State Representative Firmin Cyr. Justice of the Peace Firmin Thibodeau, who owned land equivalent to eight average farm lots before giving it away to his children, was uncle to two New Brunswick justices of the peace, first cousin to wives of two others, and second cousin to a fifth. He was also State Representative François Thibodeau's father, and father-in-law to State Representative Paul Cyr. Two of the New Brunswick justices of the peace also had a son returned to the Provincial Parliament later in the century.

49 United States, Treasury Department, Bureau of the Census, Census of the United States: 1850, Maine, Van Buren, Madawaska and Hancock Plantations.

50 Deane and Kavanagh.

51 Roman Catholic Church, St. Basile, Parish Register. New Brunswick, Provincial Census, 1851; Victoria County, General Sessions, Minutes, 1851–56.

52 Roman Catholic Church, St. Basile, Parish Register. New Brunswick, Provincial Census, 1851; Victoria County, General Sessions, Minutes, 1851–56.

53 This is especially striking when one glances through the innumerable centennial and commemorative brochures that were published at the end of the twentieth century. Earlier local histories displayed the same bias; Albert's *Histoire du Madawaska*, which relies on much greater archival material than most publications of its kind, was not different. An even earlier history, written by an Anglo-Saxon, also depicted the Madawaska French as essentially Acadians (see Charles Collins).

54 Craig, "Before Borderlands: Yankees, British, and the St. John Valley French."

55 Rutman.

56 May.

57 Lewis.

58 Bouchard, "Geographic Mobility at Laterrière." Henretta, "Family and Farms."

59 Waters, p. 66.

60 Barron. Bouchard, *Quelques arpents d'Amérique.* Bruegel.

61 Gross, p. 90.

62 Beauregard. Greven, pp. 162–71. Gross, pp. 79–80, 82, 88.

63 Bowen, pp. 65, 68, 69–70.

AN ACADIAN ODYSSEY

Don Cyr
Lille, Maine

The Cyr family is from Acadia, which was settled in 1604 by the French—before the Jamestown settlement in Virginia and the Pilgrim settlement in Massachusetts Bay. Many of the family now reside in the Saint John Valley, on the northern border of Maine, and have been there since that area's settlement in 1785—a generation before Yankee settlers arrived from southern Maine. The Cyrs and other Acadians took refuge there from a series of wars with the English that had been nearly continuous since 1613. Their odyssey was one of strife and hardship, and their search for peace and isolation would always elude them.

The founder of the Cyr family in Acadia called himself Pierre "Sire." He could write, and that is how he signed his name. There are actually many ways to spell the name, because there was no standardized spelling at that time. Whoever wrote the name then did so by sound and by what was familiar—both versions of name are pronounced the same way. Pierre was born in 1644, but where in France he actually came from is not certain, although two spellings of the name (Cyr and Sire) are common in the old province of Touraine, on the Loire River, southwest of Paris. Pierre arrived in Acadia in about 1668 and is found in the 1671 census, where he is listed as a twenty-seven-year-old gunsmith married to eighteen-year-old Marie Bourgeois. Married in 1669 at Port Royale, they had a three-month-old son, Jehan (Jean). They owned eleven head of cattle and six sheep, but none of their land was yet under cultivation.

Pierre had married into a network of families that had been in Acadia since 1636. Marie was the daughter of Jacques Bourgeois, surgeon, and Jeanne Trahan of Beaubassin—near the present-day border between Nova Scotia and New Brunswick. Beaubassin was a new settlement in Acadia, at that time, and had been created by Jacques Bourgeois and his extended family. Its topography is that of a huge diked plain, known for agriculture. However, King Louis XIV granted Beaubassin to the Sieur de la Vallière as a *seigneurie*, probably to the disappointment of Jacques Bourgeois, who had hoped to be the *seigneur*.

When the French resettlement of Acadia began in the 1630s, they began to reclaim tidal marshlands, where the tide was held back with huge dikes built with communal labor. This gave the Acadians access to fabulously rich land, which was cultivated in grain. Some of these diked lands consisted of thousands of acres: up to 11,000 at the settlement of Grand Pré alone. Their grain was often illegally traded with merchant ships from New England.

Acadia had been renamed "Nova Scotia" by Sir William Alexander, from Scotland, when he attempted a settlement at the abandoned site of Port Royale in 1628. The Treaty of Saint-Germaine-en-Laye put an end to that effort, but the name would be remembered and used each time the English won Acadia. This happened in 1654, and again in 1710. Beaubassin was burned twice, once in 1696 and again in 1704, by expeditions led by Benjamin Church from New England. The Treaty of Utrecht in 1713 saw Acadia again in British hands. From the point of view of the Acadians, this was a temporary situation. They had experienced British rule before, only to be returned to French administration later. This time would be different.

The British were in a peculiar spot. The Acadians were French-speaking and Catholic, but the British had to convince them to stay, otherwise, who would provision the troops? Protestant, English-speaking people were not interested in settling in contested territory, especially in a territory that had Natives allied with the French. Possible settlers from New England saw the colony as hostile territory.

For their part, the Acadians also had a problem. The British demanded an oath of loyalty to the Crown. How could they swear an irrevocable oath, to an entity from which they expected to be delivered? An oath was honor-bound, sacred, and was not taken lightly. Pledging loyalty also meant the probability of serving in the army and marching against their compatriots in Canada. The Acadians negotiated an oath of neutrality and that oath seemed to work until 1749, when Governor Cornwallis pushed for an unqualified oath.

Change had come about over the course of forty years. Halifax had been founded, more troops had come to the colony, and German Protestants were being directed to set up settlements. The British garrison no longer depended on Acadian supplies, and Britain was preparing for another war with France. Nova Scotia needed loyal subjects, not a possible enemy within its borders. Despite ongoing Acadian problems with English translation, as well as their stubbornness and independent spirit, the situation had not changed much from a local Acadian point of view. However, in the larger world the situation had changed dramatically.

The British saw new dynamics pulling at the Acadians with greater intensity. The Acadians had a long tradition of kinship, trade, and religion with the Mi'kmaq.

The British saw this link as a severe threat, because the Mi'kmaq were a part of a much wider confederacy allied to the French, one that was encouraged by the French garrison at the nearby Fortress of Louisbourg. The Acadians also were influenced by priests and missionaries appointed by the bishop of Québec and paid by the French Crown. So, when Colonel Charles Lawrence became acting governor of Nova Scotia, because of the mental illness of Governor Hopson, he was able to implement a plan to settle the issue of Acadian loyalty once and for all. War between the British and French had broken out in the Ohio Country, and the French, with their Native allies, were considered a strong threat. Lawrence did not want to have to defend British settlers from an "enemy" majority within the colony.

As the war in the Ohio Country spread, events quickly unraveled in Nova Scotia in 1754 and 1755. Some 300 Acadians sought refuge in the nearby French post of Fort Beauséjour, because Father LaLoutre, a partisan missionary, and his Mi'kmaq warriors had burned their settlements in retaliation for their neutrality (most of them were Cyrs or related to the Cyr family). Lawrence saw this "reinforcing" of the fort as an insurrection and called for troops. The commandant of the fort surrendered because most of the Acadians refused to take up arms against the British.

The resulting deportation proved to be a formidable task for the British. About 50 percent of the Acadians escaped to French territories in Isle Royale (Cape Breton), Isle Saint Jean (Prince Edward Island), and what is now New Brunswick. Many eventually reached Canada. The Cyrs were among these people. They did what Lawrence feared—went to the aid of the enemy. Seven thousand Acadians were captured and sent to British colonies over the next seven years. Lawrence hoped to assimilate them by spreading them all over the British-American colonies. However, many Acadians died in transit, as they had not experienced epidemics and were vulnerable to diseases such as smallpox.

The deportation was not just a one-year event but continued until the Treaty of Paris in 1763. Many refugees who had escaped the initial wave of deportation were rounded up later. In one of these operations Moses Hazen and his men attacked Acadian refugees on the lower St. John River. Some were killed but most escaped into the woods. From this, the idea of finding a more isolated place to settle probably developed in the minds of the beleaguered Acadians.

After fleeing into the forests of New Brunswick, many Acadian refugees initially assembled in the Kamouraska region of Québec, on the lower St. Lawrence River. In 1758, they were joined by other Acadians escaping from Prince Edward Island when it was cleared by the British on their way to Quebec City. Thus, the implications of the capture of Québec by the British must have been devastating to the Acadian refugees. The Treaty of Paris, which ended the Seven Years' War in 1763, meant that the French Empire in North America had all but disappeared. The treaty did allow the French the freedom to move wherever they wanted. What most of them wanted was to return to Nova Scotia, but their fabulous diked farmlands had been confiscated by British subjects.

At the end of the Seven Years War (1763) the Cyr family members were listed as British "prisoners" at Crock's Point, on the lower St. John River near Fredericton, New Brunswick. Named were Jean-Baptiste Cyr, born in 1710; his wife, Marguerite Cormier, a sixteen year old whom he had married in 1734 in Beaubassin; and their nine sons born between 1737 and 1768. Many of the sons married women from Kamouraska. When or if they moved to Kamouraska is unknown, but they—and others—would move back and forth between Kamouraska and Crock's Point, along with families from Beaubassin. Why? One answer might lie with the Ayotte family.

The Ayottes had originally moved from Kamouraska to Beaubassin shortly before the troubles began in the 1750s, and then moved again to Crock's Point, where they lived for sixteen years. Their familiarity and connections with Kamouraska and Beaubassin may have attracted other families to Crock's Point. In any case, there was much intermarriage between families from these three areas, but not much of a paper trail as to their comings and goings.

The large extended family of Cyrs settled at Crock's Point before 1763, where they were joined by many other families from Kamouraska and Beaubassin. One reason was that the Kamouraska area was running out of good farmland, while the Saint John River offered many fertile islands—perfect for grazing—that were unoccupied. When the Acadians first settled in this area it was considered "French territory," because the British didn't have the manpower to hold it. This settlement at Crock's Point, however, was only a brief interlude in the violence.

A Malecite village also lay close by, so they had the services of a missionary priest from time to time. Priests were scarcer than today, so church services were intermittent ceremonies where the settlers would "catch up on the sacraments." An elder man in a community would perform baptisms, marriages, graveside rituals, and prayer services when a priest was not available. Locating near an Indigenous village assured that the priest would come at least once a year. The British regime did not allow new priests in the Maritimes, because they saw them as subversive elements. In this period there was only one Catholic missionary in what is now the Maritime Provinces.

The American Revolution, from an Acadian and French-Canadian point of view, was a somewhat confusing event. Many of the Acadian deportees from 1755 were scattered throughout the thirteen colonies that would become the United States. While the Revolution was a popular cause in New England and the South, it was not popular in New York. Nova Scotia, which included what is today New Brunswick, was essentially a military camp with few permanent residents. American colonists who remained loyal to the British moved to the Maritimes and Canada. These Loyalists were a sizeable number. The Crown awarded them with land grants in strategic places to stop rebel incursions into British territory.

The St. John River was one of those strategic places, and the Acadians on the lower St. John were "in the way" again. It seemed that a cloud of injustice was following them wherever they went. They had cleared farms over the past decade and now the area was being claimed by the Loyalist newcomers. Land tenure in old Acadia had been very loose, so the Acadians had the attitude that one could settle anywhere without being molested. This was not so with the British, for whom paper deeds showing ownership meant everything. There was some compensation for improvements that had been made to the land, but the Acadians lost again. Jean Baptiste Cyr, the father of nine sons, most of whom were future Madawaskans, cried out: "My God, can it be that you no longer create land for the Cayens?"

Twice fooled, they got the message! They knew that French sovereignty in North America was gone, not to return. Now was the time to give in to the British system. They petitioned the king for land in the northern part of New Brunswick. Their purpose was isolation. They petitioned for land above Grand Falls, on the middle St. John River, where there was a settlement of Malecites and intervales of rich, low land. The authorities approved the petition for the Madawaska Territory, as well as the northeastern part of New Brunswick near Caraquet, splitting the petitioners into two groups. The British knew that the Madawaska Territory was a contested area with the United States and saw an Acadian settlement as providing a buffer zone in case of a territorial dispute. Thus, the tribulations of the Acadians were guaranteed to continue.

The settlement of the Madawaska Territory began in 1785. It was necessary to carve farms out of the forest before the land grants would be finalized. When the first settlers arrived, they found a trading post run by two half-brothers, Pierre Lizotte and Pierre Duperé. It lay near the mouth of the Madawaska River, close by the

Malecite village, where the commercial center of Edmundston, New Brunswick, is today. Most of the Acadian settlers settled on the south bank, or United States side of the river, away from the Malecites. The Malecites were probably not thrilled with their presence.[1] The initial Acadian settlement area spread from present-day St. David Flats to the flats in Grand Isle. By 1789 settlements had expanded onto all of the flats to Grand Falls. The deeds were finalized in 1790 and 1792. In 1789 the Violette family, along with the Cyrs and Soucys, started clearing land in the Grande Rivière Settlement where Van Buren-Saint Léonard is today.[2]

The settlers laid out their farms in long thin lots that allowed all to have good bottomland, access to the river for transportation, and uplands with good timber. This arrangement also allowed homesteads to be in close proximity for mutual support. The settlers were mostly kin, so long-held and familiar patterns of communal life were continued. Shared projects such as dike-building, house-raisings, or church-building were the custom. Large families were the custom, and all of the early settlers were connected by the Cyr brothers who had a total of eighty-seven children by 1814. The children and their numerous offspring married into all of the other families of the region.

In 1797 a famine (*la misère noire*) provided Marguerite Blanche Thibodeau Cyr, known as "Tante-Blanche," the opportunity to show her leadership and strength of character. Tante-Blanche was the granddaughter of Réné LeBlanc, a legal notary from Grand Pré and the only real person mentioned in Longfellow's poem *Evangeline*, an epic poem about the misery caused by the Acadian deportation. She lived in the Grand Rivière Settlement, along with the families of her two sisters and a brother. Tante-Blanche rose to the occasion when the settlement was in famine. Food was running out and the men had gone hunting, only to be caught up in an eight-day snowstorm. Tante-Blanche went from house to house and gathered up and redistributed all of the remaining food, thus saving many lives. She was a strong, respected woman who had to have had the complete trust of everyone to have been able to take food away from the needy in starvation times. She became the stuff of legend, was venerated as a living saint, and was eventually buried inside the church at St. Basile. There were many heroines among the Acadians, who were rough, resolute survivors. To this day, when some of the old people ask you how you are, they ask: "How are you surviving?"

It seemed to the Acadians that they had found a permanent home. But there was one more storm to weather. The British had erred in describing the borders between their colonies after the first Treaty of Paris in 1763, an unimportant matter at the time, because it was "only" settled by the French and Indigenous people, and was all British territory, anyway. The problem came with the second Treaty of Paris in 1783, when the language from the previous treaty was copied without thinking of its future implications. The border was based upon the supposition that the watersheds between the St. John and St. Lawrence Rivers were divided by highlands, but actually the whole region is a low plateau. The highest land lies in central Maine, where Katahdin and the mountains west of it divide the rivers that flow into the Gulf of Maine from those that empty into the St. John River, which empties into the Bay of Fundy. The result was a growing dispute between Britain and the United States over the unclear language of an unknown geography.

The inhabitants of the Madawaska Settlement, in the midst of this uncertainty, came to experience a kind of "cold war" between the British and the United States. New Brunswick had been carved out of Nova Scotia in 1784 and Maine broke away from Massachusetts in 1820. Both these new polities needed start-up cash, and timber was the resource that provided it. The area witnessed arrests on both sides for incursions on each other's claims. The Northeastern Boundary Dispute was about British claims in order to have easy access to the St. Lawrence. The Aroostook War was about timber rights. They are actually two separate issues, but were "fought" at the same time in the 1830s.

The Acadian settlers were used by each side to anchor their claims to the region. Maine had little leverage in the area. The Acadians, British subjects of French ancestry, outnumbered the Yankees dramatically and had been there since 1785, whereas only a pitiful number of Yankees began to arrive after 1817. These Yankees were, however, in the lumber business and had U.S. financial backing. The Acadians, armed with British deeds, were all farmers and had no backing. Maine tried to incorporate Madawaska as a town in 1831, and then elected a reluctant Pierre Lizotte as a legislator. Lizotte refused to go to the State House in Augusta because he said he was a British subject.

In actuality, neither London nor Washington wanted war. They were both of the opinion that the land in dispute was valueless, except for trees, which seemed to be plentiful everywhere. Negotiations resulted in the Treaty of Washington in 1842, also known as the Webster-Ashburton Treaty. The St. John River was declared the northern border between Maine, Québec, and New Brunswick. War had been averted. Although spared bloodshed and removal, there was a price for the Acadians.

Notre-Dame-du-Mont-Carmel, Parish of Lille, Grand Isle, Maine, from New Brunswick, looking across the St. John River, 1995
Photograph by Barry Rodrigue

The price was that the Madawaska Settlement was divided in half—stranded in different nations—on either bank of the river. Canadians condemned Britain for negotiating away 2,000 "loyal" and "British" subjects on the south bank of the river. Maine felt shortchanged, losing trees but getting 2,000 French settlers without their consent. If the settlers had been asked, they certainly would have declined their assignment to Maine, as the deeds to their land were from the British. Nonetheless, Maine honored the deeds by transferring them to the Maine registry.

Learning the U.S. way of government took some time. James Madigan, from Houlton, French-speaking and Catholic, came to the St. John Valley to help with the transition. The parishes were really the power structure in the region, but now town governments had to be set up and Maine law had to be abided. One of those laws, passed in 1851, was prohibition. This law interfered with local custom and was not respected. Wine was used in the Catholic mass, and liquor could be manufactured and bought across the river from the British colonies. Prohibition, which lasted until

1934, created a publically sanctioned illicit trade and a tradition of smuggling in the valley.

The U.S. side of the St. John Valley would be, and still is, a backwater of little significance to the rest of the country. The Canadian side, however, contains a main transportation corridor for Canada. The railroads and the Trans-Canada Highway pass parallel to U.S. Route 1 about a mile apart for forty miles. Mainers south of the St. John Valley believe that the world ends with the border. Valley people see the border as a beginning.

These days, most of the investment in northern Maine is coming from New Brunswick, with the McCain family in farmland and potato processing, and the Irving family buying farmland and woodland, and engaged in oil refining. These families are creating jobs in northern Maine as they take over the economy of the region. Lord Ashburton may have given northern Maine away, but the Canadians are buying it back.

1 The Indigenous peoples of New Brunswick were wards of the colony and had no rights in the eyes of the government. Any encroachment by Europeans on their grounds would have been seen as an undesirable development, yet they were powerless to stop it.

2 The only families in the Madawaska Settlement that had been deported aboard Colonel Lawrence's ships in 1755 were the Mazzerolle and Thibodeau families.

SOLDIERS, SPUDS, AND SPRUCE: MAINE'S MILITARY ROADS TO THE MARITIMES*

Barry Rodrigue
Bath, Maine

The Aroostook River is a rather small water body, originating in the low wetlands of north-central Maine. It develops an S-shape in its eastward course as it waters the communities of Presque Isle, Caribou, and Fort Fairfield. It then flows across the border of New Brunswick into the St. John River, south of Grand Falls. Mainers expanded the toponym of "Aroostook" to encompass the whole region, because this river was the location of their major communities at the time of the Northeast Boundary Dispute.[1] Today, the administrative district of "Aroostook County" makes up the northern quarter of the State of Maine, a geographic polygon bounded on the east by New Brunswick, on the west by Quebec, and on the north by the St. John River.

This region was the traditional territory of the aboriginal Mi'kmaq and Maliseet nations. The primary seventeenth- and eighteenth-century portages between Canada (Québec) and Acadia (the Maritimes) followed the Chaudière-Penobscot and the Temiscouata–St. John river systems. In the late-seventeenth century, the French-Canadian merchant Charles-Aubert de la Chesnaye of Rivière du Loup (Québec) extended his trading and trapping empire into the northern Aroostook Territory. The first topographic survey of the area was made in 1794, but was largely restricted to the area's river banks. Maps from even forty years later showed a blank space for much of the Aroostook Territory. Surveyors were forced to resort to maps cut into birch bark by their Indigenous informants and described the area as "one mass of dark and gloomy forest to the utmost limit of sight."[2]

An idea of the Aroostook Territory's landscape can be had from the routes of entry used by the four groups of Euramericans who settled here in the late-eighteenth and early nineteenth centuries.

French Canadians and Acadians Around 1785 French Canadians from the lower St. Lawrence River Valley came over the Temiscouata Portage to the northernmost bend of the St. John River. At about the same time Acadians were being crowded off the lower St. John by Loyalists and settled between Grand Falls and the mouth of the Fish River. The merger of these two French societies became the celebrated Madawaska Settlement. By 1808 this French population numbered about 600 people. Of the 1,500 or so settlers in the Aroostook Territory in 1820, approximately 1,200 of them were French Canadians and Acadians.[3]

Yankees Massachusetts had huge war debts as a result of the American Revolution. The state had exploited much of its own lands and was undergoing an environmental crisis. In the 1790s it began paying many of its debts by issuing lands from its District of Maine to soldiers *en lieu* of pensions and selling other lands in bulk. Parts of the eastern Aroostook Territory had good soil. In 1799 the Massachusetts town of New Salem bought a land grant on the Menduxnekeag River, a tributary of the St. John. Surveyed in 1805, Joseph Houlton and a group of others moved there from New Salem. Their dispersed farms coalesced to form the community of Houlton, the region's first English-speaking town. Yankees from other parts of Maine also filtered into the region and took-up residence in the existing settlements.[4]

British Maritimers Nova Scotia had harvested mast timber along the St. John River in the 1770s. After New Brunswick was set-off from Nova Scotia in 1784, the colony's Loyalist settlers busily developed a lumber infrastructure in response to Britain's needs for wood products during the Napoleonic blockade of the early nineteenth century. This staple trade laid the basis of New Brunswick's entry into the upper St. John Valley. The arrival of British, Irish, and Loyalist lumbering families up the St. John River, beginning around 1810, established provincial centers like Woodstock, New Brunswick.[5]

In this way, a handful of dispersed, ethnically distinct settlements began to pursue small-scale agriculture and logging along waterways flowing out of a largely uncharted wilderness. By 1831 British surveyors reported that the Aroostook area was inhabited by only "a few settlers, wandering Indians, and occasional lumbermen." In fact, however, over 3,000 settlers lived there and helped themselves to logs, largely unconcerned with who they belonged to.[6]

Although logging had been underway since the first decade of the nineteenth century, most of the operations had remained small. A family would squat on land in a rough cabin and harvest nearby trees, which could be easily hauled with block and tackle to a stream, then sent downriver to mills in Fredericton or St. John in New Brunswick. Many combined small-scale agricultural production with work in the woods industries.[7] These local operators successfully cooperated in a profitable international timber trade, but industrial and political events began to disrupt this apparent harmony.

Conflict in the Aroostook Territory had been virtually preordained by the geographically inaccurate language in the Treaty of Versailles (1783). After the American Revolution, this ambiguity and ignorance was compounded by diplomatic posturing and cartographic distortion. The border of Maine and Nova Scotia (New Brunswick) was to follow the Ste. Croix River, from which a "monument line" was supposed to run north to a height of land. This highland was thought to separate those rivers that emptied into the St. Lawrence River from those which emptied into the Atlantic Ocean. The boundary was to then follow this height of land between western New Brunswick, northern Maine, and eastern Québec. However, the discrepancy between diplomatic assumptions and geographic realities caused major problems. For example, the Ste. Croix had three outlets. Predictably, the U.S. claimed the eastern stream and Britain the western one. And no continuous chain of hills ran through the northern area.[8]

Small border arrangements were made, as with treaties in 1794 and 1798, but no consensus was reached for the northeastern frontier. The boundary question was submitted to the king of the Netherlands for arbitration, but Maine rejected his decision in 1831. There were several reasons why the U.S. government allowed Maine's rejection to stand. States' rights were still honored at this time, and it was considered poor form to force a federal decision on a state of the Union (the Civil War would later do away with such political niceties). It also served the U.S. government to have a scapegoat for not accepting less land. More importantly, since Maine was a Democratic party stronghold at this time, Democratic presidents did not want to offend Maine voters by conceding land to the British and run the risk of losing Maine to the Whigs.[9]

Although Maine separated from Massachusetts in 1820, the Bay State's presence was still strongly felt in the region, since it retained ownership of half of Maine's public lands—to sell and compensate itself for its prior "investment" in the state. Both states issued cutting permits on what they assumed to be their lands, but since they overlapped British claims, New Brunswick also issued cutting permits in the same areas. Starting in the 1820s Maine and Massachusetts sent agents to put New Brunswick-licensed "timber pirates" out of operation. New Brunswick was not so active in prosecuting the New England pirates, since their mills were getting the wood downriver on the St. John, no matter who cut it.[10]

Although the 1830s do not command as much popular attention as, say, the period of the Civil War, there was no lack of drama in this decade. The Oregon Territory was held in conflicted division between Great Britain and the United States. A balance between senators from "Slave" and "Free" states had been maintained in the U.S. Congress, but the admittance of new territories as states had stalled so as not to give either side more votes. The ironic result of this situation was that the Republic of Texas received support from Great Britain, while senators from Free States blocked its admittance to the Union. There was also more overt conflict as the U.S. went to war against the Seminoles in Florida, and the Canadas went into rebellion in 1837 and 1838. The last thing either Britain or the U.S. wanted was additional problems in the Aroostook Territory.

Nonetheless, preparations were made for war. The United States developed both offensive and defensive strategies against British North America. A secret U.S. War Department plan detailed invasion routes for the U.S. seizure of British North America. Likewise, the Maine delegation to Congress requested construction of a major fortification at the foot of Moosehead Lake, which would allow rapid troop deployment either west to Lower Canada or east to New Brunswick.[11]

The British believed that although the Treaty of Versailles (1783) was vague in its details, it was clear in its intent. By the 1820s, they realized that they had neglected this issue for too long. These forty years, during which the boundary had remained unresolved, had allowed a new generation of militant Maine politicians to expand their claims to within 32 kilometers (20 miles) of the St. Lawrence River.[12]

The strategic importance of the Aroostook Territory to Britain lay in the direct overland communication it allowed between the St. Lawrence River and the Maritimes. Modern roadways had been built along older portage routes. Opened in 1783, the Temiscouata Portage Road ran for 1010 kilometers (627 miles) from the St. Lawrence River to Halifax, Nova Scotia. By 1831 the Kempt Road connected the south shore of the St. Lawrence River to the Ristigouche Road and Baie des Chaleurs. Post roads were later extended to Fredericton and St. John.[13]

Except for these overland routes, the Aroostook controversy's only major significance for the British Empire was a potential loss of timber. But even this was not a major concern by the 1820s. The end of Anglo-French conflict after the Battle of Waterloo (1815) had ended Napoleon's embargo on the importation of Baltic timber to Britain. Also, the opening of timberlands in the Ottawa Valley began to provide new sources of timber for shipment downriver to Quebec City and then over the Atlantic to British ports.[14] However, regional economics began to further disrupt a situation that had found a *laissez faire* equilibrium.

From 1832 to 1855 Maine lumber mills on the Penobscot River processed three billion feet of lumber, while up to three-quarters of New Brunswick's export revenue came from wood products. An economy of scale became an economy of contention as large concerns from Bangor (Maine) and St. John (New Brunswick) entered the rich western Aroostook timberlands, which contained one of the last stands of virgin white pine in the region, as well as white cedar, spruce, yellow birch, tamarack, and hemlock.[15]

However, supplies for logging operations were expensive. They were either produced by the six hundred dispersed farms in the area, brought up the St. John River from the New Brunswick coast, carried over the Temiscouata Portage route from the St. Lawrence River, or transported from central Maine over prohibitively difficult land and water routes. Since the major rivers of the Aroostook Territory flow southeast, Maine farmers and lumbermen found it cheapest to bring supplies through New Brunswick. There was a good deal of amicable cross-border trade, but this caused settlers to run afoul of the U.S. revenue agents and promoted rampant, small-scale smuggling.[16]

The rivers' flow to the southeast also favored the New Brunswick timber merchants; their mills got most of the Aroostook logs, regardless of who cut them. The first steam mill opened in St. John, New Brunswick, in 1822. In contrast, mill owners in Bangor had a difficult job moving logs from the Aroostook Territory's St. John watershed into the Penobscot drainage, being forced to rely on a complex system of dams to change water flow.[17]

Starting in the 1820s, Maine had begun to promote settlement of the Aroostook Territory aggressively. The state had lost a lot of residents to "Ohio Fever" and the better agricultural lands of the Midwest. Although Whigs and Democrats in the Maine Legislature had been divided on land policies, the boundary dispute forced both parties to dust off deadlocked laws and reform them into a liberal system of land distribution. And, because of such geographic adversity, Maine entrepreneurs and politicians also demanded that roads be built into the Aroostook Territory. The roads, they reasoned, would open the north to further Yankee settlement and connect them to markets in Maine.[18]

The economic situation was also compounded by local politics. In 1825 a Yankee mill man raised the U.S. flag in the Madawaska Settlement and proclaimed the region's annexation to the United States. He was arrested by British authorities. Other events followed. In order to avoid more extreme incidents and to retain a hold on the territory, the United States government established a garrison of 200 men in a lightly fortified structure near Houlton in 1828. Besides keeping the peace, the federal troops at Hancock Barracks produced a newspaper called *The Meltless Icicle* and assisted in the construction of the 87-kilometre (54-mile) "Military Road" between Bangor and Houlton, which was finished in 1832. The War Department estimated a savings of about eighty dollars per ton for supplies shipped on this road, and military spending bolstered the local economy.[19]

U.S. residents in the northern Aroostook Territory saw that the Military Road had helped their neighbors to the south and also wanted a road to connect them to the Penobscot River and southern markets. Although first proposed in the 1820s, the Aroostook Road had been delayed, like land reform, by the political standoff between Maine's Whig and Democrat parties. However, the increasing tension between Maine and New Brunswick forced the state into action.[20]

Maine built the 93-kilometre (58-mile) Aroostook Road from the village of Molunkus to that of Masardis on the Aroostook River in 1832, followed by a 74-kilometre (46-mile) Madawaska Road north to the Fish River in 1836. Bridges and causeways were constructed, bumps were leveled, stumps were cut down to fifteen-centimeters (six inches), and all was made into a three-meter- (ten-foot-) wide trail. In 1836 the state began to turn the Aroostook Road into a turnpike, a job that took four years.[21] Thus, by 1840 a traveler could leave the relatively comfortable road network of central Maine and journey to the frontier communities of Houlton and Madawaska on something that could be loosely called "roads."

Accounts described how these "few wretched roads" were strewn with mud-filled potholes or "honey pots" (a graphic euphemism for chamber pots or toilet receptacles). An early traveler on the route was the renowned ornithologist and artist, John James Audubon. In 1833 he optimistically described the Military Road as the "best" turnpike in the United States, but reported how unfinished sections became a "complete bed of mud" during storms and how his horses had to be rescued from the muck by a team of oxen.[22]

Roads became weapons in the war for the Aroostook Territory. These routes, as well as progressive land distribution policies, had their desired effect. Many small, backwoods farms were linked by them to both Bangor and the Aroostook Territory's lumber camps, which set up an important infrastructure as agriculture developed in tandem with the timber industry. Several families and millwrights almost immediately settled along the Aroostook Road, traffic with Bangor was said to be "brisk," and—by 1841—about 1,500 new people had settled along it. However, this migration tended to overwhelm some of the older French settlements and made war almost inevitable.[23]

Having made such a huge investment in roads and then overextended itself in commitments to new settlers, the State of Maine needed greatly enhanced revenues. Politicians had expected this money to have come from timber sales. However, the international boundary question was no closer to resolution, as the state watched what it considered to be its timber vanishing down the St. John River into New Brunswick.

In 1837 a Maine census enumerator had been seized by New Brunswick officials. The governor and Executive Council convened a special session in Augusta, and there was barroom talk of seizing a British army captain staying at the capital's Mansion House. A man building a flat-bottomed boat by the Kennebec River advocated "driving the British into hell's kitchen," a sentiment that the Irish immigrants, French Canadians, and Yankees could equally share. In 1838 Governor Fairfield embarked on a state timber and land survey. New Brunswick newspapers ridiculed his aggressiveness. Maine demanded federal troops, but President Van Buren hoped the situation would blow over and did nothing.[24] Maine then decided to act unilaterally.

In 1839 the governor denounced federal foot-dragging, and the Penobscot County sheriff was ordered north with an armed posse of two hundred men to put a stop to "timber piracy." They reached Marsardis, at the end of the Aroostook Road, when the Maine land agent was captured by an armed group of New Brunswickers and hauled into Fredericton. The posse retreated into fortifications. The governor insisted on his land agent's release, but his New Brunswick counterpart, Sir John Harvey, refused. Governor Fairfield dispatched 3,000 members of the Maine militia to the frontier and called for 10,000 more. The New Brunswick warden was seized.

Lieutenant Governor Harvey sent provincial militia and British regulars into Madawaska, Tobique, and Temiscouata Lake. Finally, President Van Buren delegated General Winfield Scott to assess the situation.[25]

Although the Maine militia was largely composed of unruly lumbermen ready to march on Fredericton, and General Scott even had to threaten to join U.S. forces with the British 69th Regulars to drive the Maine volunteers from contested land, New Brunswick had little fear. The Maine militia mutinied under military discipline, the powder they were given had been surplus from the War of 1812, and the cannon balls were too large for the small weapons they dragged behind them.[26]

General Scott did get an agreement for a joint boundary commission. Between 1839 and 1842 Senator Daniel Webster and Lord Ashburton managed to negotiate what became the Treaty of Washington, which prepared the way for resolution of the northeastern frontier of the United States and British North America. The resulting boundary in the Aroostook Territory lay roughly between the troop positions and dismembered the French Madawaska Settlement between the United States, Québec, and New Brunswick.[27] Today, all that is left of the Aroostook War in Maine are a few rotting blockhouses in the forest and packing crates of musty claims for compensation from teamsters who have been dead for 150 years.

Stability came to the Aroostook territory. The soldiers departed. The agroforestry *mélange* grew into a major international industry. Although farmers and loggers would go their separate ways later in the century, spruce and spuds would become mainstays of the Aroostook economy.[28] However, as the idea of a rigid border became established in people's minds, the complex regional dynamics which had created the Northeast Boundary Dispute in the first place began to degenerate into simplified stereotypes. Indeed, three myths about the Aroostook French are still prevalent outside of northern Maine.

1) Many assume that the French moved "into" northern Maine, when in fact the boundary agreement of 1842 merely allowed the U.S. to absorb half of an already existing French community.

2) Many consider that these French settlers had come mostly from only New Brunswick. However, when a 1994 federal (U.S.) study referred to their descendants as "Acadians," it drew a strong response from individuals in these Aroostook communities with Québec origins.[29]

3) A view is that the Northeast Boundary Dispute took place only on the

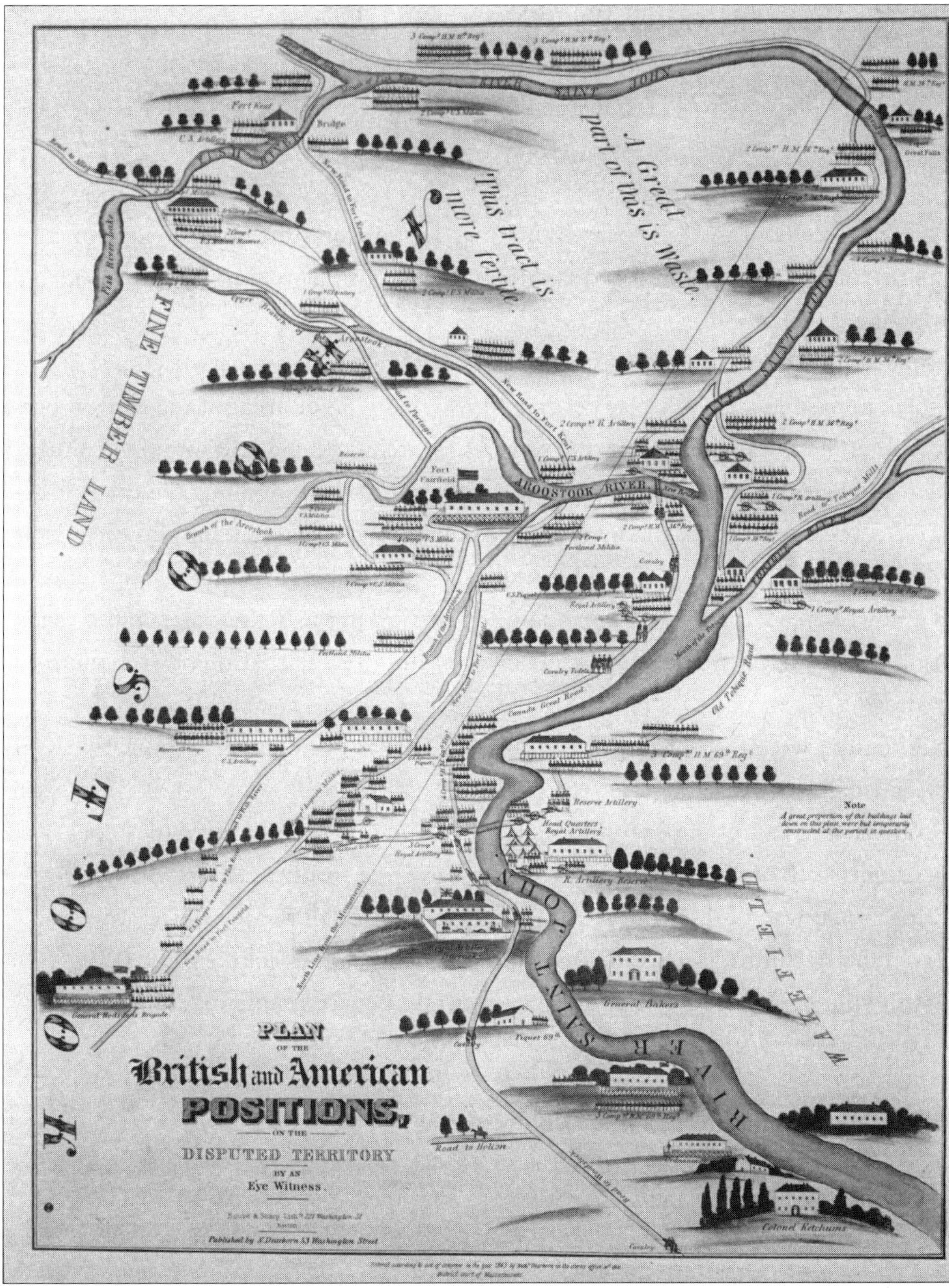

Plan of the British and American Positions on the Disputed Territory by an Eye Witness, Boston: Bouvé & Sharp, Lithographers, Nathaniel Dearborn, Publisher, c. 1843
Maine State Museum

Maine–New Brunswick border. While many of the more dramatic incidents of the Aroostook War were acted out there, a review of the records shows that the whole border region of Lower Canada with northern New England was included in the area of contention.[30]

However, a study of the Northeast Boundary Dispute and the Aroostook War does more than illustrate a need to better differentiate cultural streams and to broaden a geo-political context.

Later in the nineteenth century, the Aroostook Territory experienced a shortage of good, accessible farm land, as occurred in so many other areas of the eastern borderlands at that time. Residents were forced to search farther afield for opportunities. Whereas single men might have traveled through the woods or along the rivers looking for work before 1828, the new roads of the Aroostook Territory allowed whole families relatively easy access to the previously inaccessible industrial centers of central Maine. Indeed, the initial French families arrived in the Bangor area in the 1830s, during the road work, and approximately one hundred settled there over the next two decades.[31]

Although we are accustomed to think of roads as avenues for colonization, our view is usually in one direction—as a grandiose expression of Manifest Destiny. Such an outlook is apparent in the traditional Yankee presentation of the Aroostook War, when the United States used roads to seize control of a frontier region. However, this unidirectional way of thinking is a simplistic expression of the territorial imperative by a dominant culture. Agriculturists also used these roads to colonize both new rural areas and industrial centers. In short, the French settlers made the roads into two-way streets.

* A version of this article appeared in *Le Forum* in 1998. Barry Rodrigue, "Soldiers, Spuds, and Spruce: Maine's Military Roads to the Maritimes, 1810–1824," Le Forum 26 (2), April 1988.

1 Some of the names for parts of the greater Aroostook Territory include Temiscouata, the Madawaska Settlement, Haute Beauce, etc.

2 Judd, Aroostook, ix–x, 2. Moses Greenleaf, *Map, c. 1829.*

3 Many of the Québec settlers came from near Rivière Ouelle; many of the Acadians came from around the area of Fredericton. Leo Cyr, pp. 224–25. Pelletier & Ferretti, pp. 26, 93, 107. Judd, *Aroostook,* 7. Hamlin, Letter to Noyes. Béatrice Craig, "Immigrants in a Frontier Community," pp. 277–97; "Agriculture and the Lumberman's Frontier in the upper St. John Valley," pp. 125–37.

4 Judd, *Aroostook,* pp. 1–2, 7–9, 43. Eves, *Yankee Immigrants*, pp. 1, 3–4, 55–70, 92. Burnham, "The

Military Road." Kiernan & Whitaker, pp. 1–5. Irene Foster, Interview. Béatrice Craig, "Immigrants in a Frontier Community." Maine State Archives, The Maine Historical Records Survey Project, *Counties, Cities, Towns, and Plantations of Maine,* pp. 117–24.

5 Judd, *Aroostook*, p. 7.

6 Judd, *Aroostook*, pp. 2, 8–9.

7 Hamlin to Noyes. Judd, *Aroostook*, pp. 8–9. Wynn, *Timber Colony,* pp. 72–73, 43. Béatrice Craig, "Agriculture and the Lumberman's Frontier," p. 127.

8 Yule, pp. 9, 16. Judd, *Aroostook*, p. 23.

9 Yule, pp. 9, 16. Judd, *Aroostook*, p. 23.

10 Courts in Bangor would return verdicts of "Not Guilty" against timber pirates since their sympathies favored loggers over the state. Judd, *Aroostook,* pp. 24, 30–31.

11 U.S. War Department, Memorandum on the Attack of Canada by the U.S., Ruel Williams, et al.

12 Yule. Hamlin to Joseph Noyes.

13 Bouchette, *A Topographical Dictionary*, "Roads, Temiscouata Portage Road and Kempt Road."

14 My description of the Northeast Boundary Dispute is very simplified. Both Britain and the U.S. wanted to get as much land as they could, and both nations used militant factions in Maine and New Brunswick as excuses for not settling the boundary. Yule, pp. 8–13, 15, 18, 19, 25–27. Bouchette, *A Topographical Dictionary*, "Roads, Temiscouata Portage Road and Kempt Road."

15 Wynn, *Timber Colony*, p. 43. Judd, *Aroostook*, pp. 2, 7–9, 13.

16 The following two citations are only a sample of perhaps a dozen surviving letters regarding the seizure of local goods by U.S. Treasury agents in this era. Pearce to Ingham. Gooch to Ingham. Hamlin to Noyes. Judd, *Aroostook,* pp. 1, 5, 27–28, 59–61. Caron, Hebert, & Michaud. Bouchette, *A Topographical Dictionary*, "Roads."

17 Judd, *Aroostook*, pp. 43, 62–71.

18 Judd, *Aroostook*, pp. 24, 29–31.

19 The Military Road actually began just north of the confluence of the Penobscot and Mattawamkeag rivers. An apocryphal story had persisted about how Robert E. Lee and Jefferson Davis, soon to become famous for their part in the U.S. Civil War, worked on the Military Road. Correspondence between the federal and state governments show that they did not have any part in the construction. U.S. Congress, 20th Congress, Session I, *An Act to Provide for Opening and Making a Military Road in the State of Maine*. John Burnham, "The Military Road." Davis to Dunnack. U.S. Adjutant General's Office, *Order No. 39, Hancock Barracks*. Judd, *Aroostook*, pp. 26–27.

20 Judd, *Aroostook*, pp. 29–30.

21 Weber & Gilmore. Moses True. Isaac Small. Judd, *Aroostook*, pp. 29–30.

22 Audubon, p. 220. Judd, *Aroostook*, p. 2.

23 As an example of how local French settlements were somewhat marginalized, the Acadian community around Violette's grist mill, which had been established in 1791, was absorbed by the town of Van Buren. The town was named for the U.S. president at the time of the Aroostook War. Pelletier & Ferretti, pp. 26, 93, 107. Judd, *Aroostook*, pp. x–xi, 29–31.

24 Yule, pp. 3–4. Hawthorne, pp. 58, 68. Judd, *Aroostook*, p. 31.

25 Judd, *Aroostook*, pp. 32–33.

26 Judd, *Aroostook*, pp. 34, 38.

27 U.S. surveyors had seen the poor land north of the St. John River and were willing to concede that area. Lord Ashburton's family owned much timberland in Maine and expected to profit no matter the outcome. Webster played both ends against the middle. He bullied the aggressive Maine commission-

ers with an old map showing British rights to territory near the Penobscot River and used Maine's intransigence as a tool to get Ashburton's compliance. Britain's primary concern was satisfied by their retention of the Temiscouata Portage, which connected the St. Lawrence River to the Maritimes. Judd, *Aroostook*, pp. 33, 37.

28 Judd, *Aroostook*, pp. 97–101.

29 Genealogist Robert Chenard estimates that up to 80–85 percent of present-day French residents in Aroostook County are actually descended from Lower-Canadian settlers. Historian Béatrice Craig has documented the eighteenth- and early nineteenth-century migration of French settlers from Québec and New Brunswick, and demonstrates how the Acadian migration soon stopped, while the French-Canadian migration continued. Chenard, Letter to *Bangor Daily News*, p. 1. Craig, "Immigrants in a Frontier Community."

30 For example, the watershed of Metjarmette Stream, which flows into the Chaudiere River, received almost as much attention as the St. Croix River in Captain Yule's booklet. Yule, pp. 25, 28, the key to his sketch.

31 Historian Béatrice Craig has demonstrated how the first families of the Madawaska Settlement tended to be endogamous, and how unrelated later arrivals from Québec were often forced to move to either less valuable lands in the Aroostook Territory or out of the region. Later in the century, such internal migration became necessary for even the descendants of the more privileged first families, as the better lands filled. For examples of internal migration, the progenitor of the Thibadeau family migrated to Houlton (1861) and the True Road in Limestone, Maine (1877), became known as the Cote Road or the "French Road" as settlers from the north moved in. This pattern was similar to that of the Old Canada Road (today's Route 201) between Québec and Maine. Chenard, *Marriages of St. Joseph's Catholic Church*, pp. 7, 296. Thibadeau, pp. 70–71. Linda Page. Map of Limestone, Maine. Côté Family Tree. Béatrice Craig, "Immigrants in a Frontier Community: Madawaska." Rodrigue, "Tom Plant, la route du Canada et les stéréotypes sur les Franco-Américains."

UNDERSTANDING THE FRENCH CANADIANS OF LEWISTON, 1860–1900[1]

Yves Frenette
Ottawa, Ontario

Maine's distinctive rural landscape has given the state much of its character. To some, the "Pine Tree State" invokes images of sand beaches, austere granite cliffs, lobster fishermen, and lighthouses. To others, it means a wilderness of uninhabited forests and turbulent rivers. A few might think of potatoes growing in the northern part of the state, where farmers speak the Acadian language and cling to old traditions. But rare is the individual who thinks of Maine in terms of industrial cities such as Biddeford, Waterville, and Lewiston. These centers and others like them, nonetheless, did as much to shape today's Maine as did the better-known rural landscapes.

Industrial cities are synonymous with another poorly understood facet of Maine's past. During the nineteenth century, thousands of French Canadians were attracted to Maine's mills and mill towns. At the turn of the twenty-first century, 23 percent of the state's population was "French" in origin, a demographic mix typical of New England, which received approximately half a million French Canadians between 1840 and 1930. Numbers alone indicate that an examination of the French-Canadian presence is a crucial step in understanding the history of New England and Maine.[2]

Until the 1960s most of New England's French-Canadian history was written by the same pro-clerical elite who sought to fashion cultural norms for the French-speaking community.[3] Preoccupied with cultural identity, these historians voiced a common concern for *survivance*, the protection of the group's language, values, and traditions from U.S. influences. In the last forty years, a broader interest in the French-Canadian past has been generated by the rise of the "new" social history, which attempts to recreate the past "from the bottom up," and by the popular quest for ethnic "roots." Although written from somewhat different perspectives, these new works, too, betray a preoccupation with cultural change and persistence.[4]

Although the importance of culture cannot be denied, it is clear that other forces helped shape the lives of these Canadian migrants. The need for a broader perspective on the shaping of Franco-American history can be clearly illustrated by looking at a single community: Lewiston, Maine. Here the interplay between the evolving urban and industrial environment, the increasing stability of the French-Canadian population itself, and the rise of class distinctions within the ethnic neighborhoods clearly indicates the diversity of factors that gave form to the community in the years before the turn of the century.

The timing of the arrival of the first French Canadians to Lewiston in the 1860s and 1870s was significant, for Lewiston was undergoing rapid transformation into a prospering industrial center highly dependent on an immigrant workforce. The context into which the French Canadians migrated is critical to comprehending the transformation of the ethnic community's identity. Lewiston, originally settled by Massachusetts residents at the time of the American Revolution, remained at the beginning of the nineteenth century "a struggling self-sufficient agricultural community" of slightly more than 1,000 inhabitants. Under the leadership of local businessmen, the economy gradually diversified. By 1842 two small textile factories and several saw mills and grist mills had been drawn to the town's cheap source of abundant power, Lewiston Falls. Despite this economic potential, entrepreneurs were hampered by a lack of locally available capital.[5]

In 1845 Lewiston businessmen organized the Lewiston Water Power Company. Two years later, a group of Boston capitalists acquired a major portion of their stock. Among these new investors was Benjamin Bates, who soon came to be the most prominent figure in Lewiston's growth. Obtaining ownership of most of the land and waterpower rights in Lewiston, Bates and his associates began constructing mills in 1852. In 1857 they formed the Franklin Company. All land and water rights would be bought or leased from this new concern, a strategy that permitted Lewiston industrialists to profit from real estate as well as textile production. Lewiston prospered under the new regime. The arrival of the railroad in 1849 ended the town's isolation, and—unlike other mill towns in New England—Lewiston thrived during the Civil War. Gambling on a long war, capitalists there acquired large stocks of raw cotton and expanded the town's mill capacity. By 1871 seventeen corporations were in operation with an invested capital of $7 million. More than 220,000 spindles ran in the town's nine cotton mills.[6]

As Lewiston industrialized, its demographic character changed. Its population nearly doubled between 1850 and 1870, and a growing proportion was foreign-born (22 percent by 1870)—mostly Irish. The Irish made their first appearance in the late 1840s, arriving from Boston, Québec, and the Maritimes to build the railroads and

Postcard of the Grand Trunk Railroad Depot, Lewiston, Maine, 1911
Maine Historic Preservation Commission

canals and work in the mills. In 1850 95 percent of Lewiston's Irish males held unskilled jobs, while most females appear to have been unemployed.[7] As elsewhere in New England, rural Yankee girls from Lewiston's surrounding area and from far-away places in the Maine hinterland constituted the first labor pool for the mills;[8] in 1871, 58 percent of the Lewiston millworkers were female, the majority born in the U.S. Thirty years later, 60 percent of the foreign-born Irish were still laborers. It was only the second-generation Irish who were able to find semi-skilled jobs in the mills.[9]

Lewiston's expanding population created housing problems of major proportions. Living in disease-ridden quarters, the Irish exemplified Lewiston's deteriorating urban conditions. Without resources upon their arrival, they built shanties on the land of the Lewiston Water Power Company. Despite the occasional ability of immigrants to move into tenements built by their compatriots, by 1870 very few Irish owned any real estate. Catholic and poor, Irish immigrants faced prejudice that sometimes turned violent. In 1855 a mob burned an Irish chapel on Lincoln Street. It was only with difficulty that the Irish obtained land from the Franklin Company to build a new parish church.[10]

As this growth spurt in industry and immigration radically transformed the city in the two decades following the railroad's arrival in 1849, Lewiston's municipal structure necessarily adapted. Lewiston was incorporated as a city on 5 March 1861, and two years later a charter was adopted. The new mayor-aldermen-common council government, however, was still quite ineffectual in the face of problems created by urban growth.[11] More streets were being laid out yearly, so that by 1873 most of what is today downtown Lewiston had been built. Although construction was proceeding at a fast pace, lodging was scarce, unsanitary conditions and disease plagued the city for the rest of the nineteenth century, and schools were unable to accommodate the growing number of students or to deal adequately with their diverse origins.[12]

This rapid, sometimes seemingly uncontrolled growth of Lewiston was a result of the Industrial Revolution, during which 37 million immigrants such as the Irish came to this country between 1820 and 1930. In that context, special attention must be paid to the similarities and differences between the French-Canadian immigration experience and that of other ethnic groups. In essence, the French-Canadian migration was a regional movement, largely of family units, by a traditionally transient populace. Of all the immigrant groups, only the Canadians and Mexicans crossed no ocean and completed their relocation in a matter of only a few days. In the minds of French-Canadian migrants, the border barely existed, and the proximity of the mother country had far-reaching effects on the evolution of the ethnic group.

This French-Canadian migration arose out of several economic problems in Québec. In some regions overpopulation was coupled with agricultural downturns. Elsewhere, a developing market-oriented economy encroached on traditional farming patterns. In all cases, the result was the same: A surplus population with few prospects for employment in other sectors. The fur trade was simply a memory, Great Britain's abandonment of preferential tariffs in 1846 had depressed the lumber industry, and Québec industry was unable to absorb the excess workforce, especially in a context of job competition.[13] To this general economic uprooting must be added another, more subtle factor, often overlooked by most scholars—since the founding of New France, French Canadians, like other North Americans, had been on the move. Structural geographic mobility, exemplified in the fur trade, in the settlement of new land, and in the timber trade, was an essential characteristic of the *Québécois* experience.[14]

Often lengthy itineraries from places of origin to places of destination marked the mass migration of French Canadians to the United States. The French-Canadian immigrants to Lewiston often arrived after a stay in another U.S. city. Some made

Lewiston their permanent home; others made it a base from which they traveled in search of better opportunities; some stopped in the city for only short periods of time, continuing farther south or returning to Québec.[15]

Georges Carignan, in 1860, was the first identified French Canadian in Lewiston. Ten years later, only 720 of his compatriots were in the city, but—by 1873—the busy cotton mills had attracted 2,300 French Canadians to Lewiston. In 1880 the census listed 4,475 French Canadians in Lewiston. By 1900 10,000 French Canadians lived in the city.[16]

Aside from its rapid growth, the French-Canadian population of Lewiston bore two striking characteristics. First, it was composed mostly of families. A 1915 biographical listing of locally prominent Franco-Americans reads like a litany: "one of (seven, eight, nine, ten children)" or "came to Lewiston with his parents and brothers and sisters." Only sporadically does one encounter an orphaned or adventurous individual who came to the "Spindle City" by his or her self. This is confirmed by census data. At any point in time, between 1860 and 1900, more than 90 percent of Lewiston's migrants were members of households in which they had at least one relative.[17] There would be no influx of French-Canadian males in Lewiston, as was the case among other immigrant groups and among earlier French-Canadian migrants elsewhere in Maine and New England. In fact, females dominated numerically.[18]

More importantly, this population displayed a low rate of persistence. Much like Europeans who came to America, the majority of French Canadians who chose Lewiston as a destination—before 1880—were not immigrants but migrants who had no intention to settle permanently.[19] Indeed, only one-third of Lewiston's French Canadians enumerated in 1870 can be found ten years later. The remainder expected to live in Lewiston temporarily and then go back to their native country. But after 1880 the French-Canadian population of Lewiston became more stable. The persistence rate was 61.5 percent in the 1880s and 66.2 percent the following decade, a remarkable rate considering that an economic depression struck the city between 1893 and 1897. Many migrants were becoming immigrants.[20]

Evidence indicates that the stereotype of going "from farm to factory" insufficiently defines the background of French-Canadian immigrants to Lewiston. Many had previous contact with urban-industrial life in Canada or elsewhere in the United States.[21] Moreover, the fact that most French-Canadian immigrants were born in the countryside is not necessarily proof that they had been farmers. And even if they had tilled the land, there is also a good chance that they had been woodsmen at the same time.[22]

These complex migration patterns shaped the experiences of Lewiston's immigrants, not only as individuals but also as an ethnic community. Indeed, the slow growth of social, political, and institutional organizations among the French Canadians—prior to 1880—is largely attributable to the group's extremely high rate of transience. With the expansion and greater stability of the French-Canadian population during the last two decades of the nineteenth century, the community grew in strength and ethnic institutions flourished.[23] Therefore, the history of the French Canadians of Lewiston in the nineteenth century falls into two periods: 1860–80 and 1880–1900.

The first of these two periods was characterized by demographic flux, instability, and poverty. Of the 392 persons listed in the city's valuation book in 1880: 354 had to pay only a poll tax; 21 had property valued below $899; 5 between $900 and $1,499; 7 between $1,500 and $1,999; 3 between $2,000 and $4,999; and 2 between $5,000 and $9,999. This property was mostly real estate.[24]

The manuscript censuses of 1870 and 1880 show that more than 40 percent of Lewiston's heads of household, especially those older than forty, were listed as laborers or as working in saw mills or other small-scale enterprises.[25] During this earlier period, the factory labor force was still made up mostly of Yankees. Moreover, as in other mill towns, textile managers might have found middle-aged men too old for work in their mills.[26] As a result, many French Canadians found work as laborers, working for low pay and uncertain lengths of time and sometimes at some distance from Lewiston.

Housing was critical. Partly because of the French Canadians' meager monetary resources during the 1860–80 period and partly because of a scarcity of lodging in Lewiston following the city's transformation into an industrial center, immigrants from Canada lived wherever they could find space, several families often temporarily sharing an apartment. They moved often, looking for a better place to stay. For the most part, they were crowded into poorly ventilated tenements where inadequate sewerage encouraged disease.[27]

With the "invasion" of the Irish and French Canadians, Yankees moved north of Lewiston's commercial artery, Lisbon Street. In 1880 up to 76 percent of French Canadians concentrated between Lisbon Street and the river, living in the shadow of the mills, on streets and in back alleys. Thus, in 1880 French Canadians were concentrated in the industrial heart of Lewiston, south of Lisbon Street. But French-Canadian concentration was even greater: 61 percent of households—amounting to about 2,750 individuals—lived in a quadrangle between the railroad tracks and Oxford, Cedar, and Ash streets—on a territory of about 0.06 square kilometers (0.02 square miles). Human density was high; for example, on Hines Alley, which was not more than 244 meters long (800 feet), 570 persons could be found![28]

In bad times French Canadians relied on each other for survival. Their familial economic strategy was such that it was very rare that all members of a family would be unemployed at the same time. And even if this did happen, they had the support of relatives or friends. The annual statistics of the city's Overseer of the Poor bear witness to the French Canadians' reluctance to rely on public charity, contrary to the tendency among the Irish.[29]

However, a petty bourgeoisie of businessmen, professionals, and religious leaders with roots in the French-Canadian neighborhoods arose rapidly, laying the foundation for the social stability that developed between 1880 and 1900. The businessmen apparently came to the United States without capital and seized upon the economic opportunities offered by their new milieu. Alphonse Auger, for example, migrated to Biddeford with his parents and siblings in 1860. After working in the mills there and in Brunswick, he moved to Lewiston in 1866 to work at the Lewiston Bleachery. One year later he became a mule spinner at the Hill Mill. In 1870, acquiring provisions from a wholesale merchant in Portland, he and a co-worker opened a small grocery store. It was an immediate success, and Auger was able to establish a good credit rating. In 1876, with a brother, he opened a larger store near the Grand Trunk railroad station. By 1880 his business was worth $5,000.[30]

Auger's financial rise was more dramatic than most, but he was not alone in achieving success. In 1881 the French-Canadian community boasted of nine grocers, two cloth merchants, two shoe retail stores, two pharmacists, two saloonkeepers, one furniture dealer, one stationery-book store and a few contractors.[31] The story of these entrepreneurs is similar. Born in the Québec countryside, these businessmen were rarely more than forty years old when they started their businesses. Quite likely they came to Lewiston with social capital, including some English-speaking ability. As part of the first wave of French-Canadian immigrants to New England cities, these businessmen found opportunities in "helping" the large numbers of their compatriots whose English language skills were poor.[32] It was not by chance that the Augers and several other merchants located their store near the railroad station. There, they could welcome immigrants, help them find places to stay and jobs, and provide them with necessities until their first pay. And they guaranteed the newcomers would meet their obligations by having their wages assigned to the store.[33] Timing of arrival seems to have favored social mobility among this immigrant petty bourgeoisie.[34]

On the same rung of the social ladder was a group of French-Canadian professionals who, faced with dim opportunities in their homeland, also had migrated to the United States. These doctors and lawyers found opportunities for social leadership in the French-Canadian communities of New England. Often more interested in public life than the businessmen, they made *survivance* their cause. In Lewiston,

First St. Peter's and Paul's Church,
Corner of Bartlett Street and Ash Street, Lewiston, Maine, 1872–1905.
Franco-American Collection, University of Southern Maine,
Lewiston-Auburn College[37]

Louis-Joseph Martel typified such men. Born in Saint-Hyacinthe, Québec, in 1851, he came to Lewiston fresh from medical school in 1873. Martel quickly became the leader of the French-Canadian community, founding and participating in several national societies. In the 1880s this sort of activity led him to politics.[35]

A third group of leaders emerged out of the immigrants' religious activities. French Canadians brought to Lewiston distinctive religious traditions and practices. Unsatisfied with the different language and traditions that they found in the existing Irish-dominated Catholic church, the French Canadians demanded a priest of their own. Because of their growing numbers, they obtained a partial separation from the Irish in 1869. The French Canadians were given the basement of Saint Joseph's Church for their services. Moreover, the Flemish pastor was able to preach the homily in French. One year later they were granted their own parish with a resident pastor. They used an old chapel on Lincoln Street as their house of worship until 1873, when St. Peter's Church was built by Father Pierre Hévey, an enterprising pastor who had arrived two years earlier. Having friends and relatives in Lewiston, the priest easily gained the confidence of his parishioners. A leader and builder, he persuaded them that, poor though they were, they had the resources to build a church. They accomplished this by lending money to the parish, the project taking the form of a savings bank. Hévey laid a solid foundation for the French-Canadian parish of Lewiston.[36]

In 1872 Hévey became the principal advocate of a local chapter of the Société Saint-Jean-Baptiste, a fraternal organization "whose financial goal would be mutual aid in difficult time, and the moral and religious goals, the preservation of national character and faith." The society was also organized to help elevate the French-Canadian image in the United States. Like other ethnic institutions, the new organization was to play a dual role, preserving traditional values on one hand and easing the adaptation of immigrants to their new surroundings on the other. Under the leadership of Dr. Martel the Institut Jacques-Cartier, another fraternal society, began meeting in 1873. There was rivalry between the two societies, the Saint-Jean-Baptiste being foremost a mutual society; it was very disorganized while the Institut Jacques-Cartier was more ideological in outlook. In 1875 the Institut absorbed the Société Saint-Jean-Baptiste, and it became a leader in fostering cultural and "national" activities, such as the annual Saint-Jean-Baptiste parades to celebrate the patron saint of French Canadians.[38]

Around Saint-Jean-Baptiste Day in 1879, thirty-nine men got together to create a local chapter of the Union Saint-Joseph, another mutual society that had seen the light of day in the Montréal of the mid-nineteenth century. The preamble and the goals of the new society resembled those of the Société Saint-Jean-Baptiste seven years before. Evidence points to this organization being created in reaction to the Institut Jacques-Cartier. It is notable, that except for one person, there was no exchange of leaders between the two societies, as was the case in medium-sized cities in the nineteenth century. However, the Union's leaders came from the same social strata as the Institut's. Thus, by 1880, Lewiston's French-Canadian community had two national societies that each boasted 150 members. The Union Saint-Joseph put emphasis on mutuality while the Institut Jacques-Cartier was a tool of the militant *petite-bourgeoisie* led by Dr. Martel.[39]

While fraternal organizations secured the needs of adult French Canadians, schools were built in the 1870s to help foster French-Canadian nationality, of which the Catholic faith was an essential component. Earlier, the education of children had greatly concerned Yankee civic leaders of Lewiston, for education was synonymous with progress and mobility, and these civic leaders worried about the thousands of illiterate immigrants pouring into the city.[40] The city schools, on one hand, were not equipped to meet this demand. But more important, a large proportion of children worked in the mills rather than attended school. In 1871 Lewiston schools listed 4,316 registered pupils, but the average daily attendance was 1,496. Maine state laws prescribed three to four months of schooling before a child could enter the mills, but these regulations were neither respected nor enforced.[41]

Just as critical to Hévey and other ethnic leaders was the lack of religious instruction in public schools. Catholic faith and Catholic education were essential components of French-Canadian nationality. In 1878, when three Gray Nuns arrived from Saint-Hyacinthe, a parochial school was founded. It was bilingual and bicultural: During the half-day in French, pupils learned "French-Canadian subjects," such as religion and Canadian history, while in the English half-day they were taught the history of the United States and arithmetic. Hévey also asked the sisters to offer evening courses in order to teach young men and women English and to acquaint them with U.S. institutions. As a result, French-Canadian enrollment in public schools declined (although it did not disappear).[42]

The growth of the French-Canadian community did not leave Yankees indifferent. They no doubt looked with suspicion on the growing ranks of unskilled laborers who professed a different religion and spoke a different language. In 1871 Hévey was unable to find convenient lodging when he arrived in town: No one would rent to a disciple of the pope. However, the Yankees displayed no overt violence. In marked contrast to the burning of the Irish chapel a few decades earlier, the *Lewiston Evening Journal*, in 1873, saluted the completion of Saint Peter's Church.[43] Undoubtedly, Yankee civic leaders and business interests, whose views the *Journal* expressed, were aware of the importance of a ready and docile workforce and appreciated the stabilizing role played by the Catholic church.[44]

Yet, the period between 1860 and 1880 was characterized by population instability. The constant shift between Lewiston, Canada, and other U.S. towns discouraged naturalization. For French-Canadian migrants, Lewiston was only one of various places where they would spend some time. By 1881, only 4,000 French-Canadian immigrants had been naturalized in the entire United States, and Lewiston counted only a few hundred of these. It is not surprising, therefore, that no French Canadian held public office. In 1879, for the first time, Charles Sabourin, the son of a French-Canadian man and an Irish woman, ran as municipal councilman. He was not elected.[45]

In this early period, from 1860 to 1880, a few French Canadians, nonetheless, established roots in the city, founded a parish, recruited a permanent pastor, and began to establish control over an unstable population. The ethnic community remained weak, but a foundation had been laid.

After 1880 the French-Canadian community would flourish. As the City of Lewiston continued its transformation and expansion, French Canadians became more persistent despite continued poverty. They founded their own hospital and French-language newspaper, helped develop their "Little Canada," and became more politically active. A major factor in the stabilization of the immigrant community was the arrival of the Dominican Fathers from France, who tried to minimize the allegiance to Canada, supporting Americanization over *survivance*. During this period the Yankees, wishing to flee from the immigrants and their "vices," moved to the outskirts of the growing and modernizing Lewiston. The almost-doubled French-Canadian community helped the steady but slower increase in overall city population from 19,083 in 1880 to 23,761 in 1900. The 10,000 French Canadians represented 42 percent of Lewiston's population in 1900.[46]

In many ways, however, the character of the French-Canadian neighborhoods remained as they had been in the earlier period, and many changes came from forces external to the community itself. Rooted in the neighborhood below Lisbon Street, the immigrant community expanded outward to the north and into Auburn.

Tenements remained the normal form of accommodation; 86 percent of the French-Canadian population still owned no real estate in 1900 and French Canadians held less than 5 percent of the total value of Lewiston's property. Among the most important proprietors were the Dominican Fathers, the ethnic associations, businessmen, and companies. For the majority of small proprietors, real estate consisted of a piece of land and buildings in the rural parts of Lewiston, which may indicate the persistence of farm life as a goal for some immigrants or a complementary means of subsistence.[47]

The Franklin Company, through both sales and rentals, continued to exert strong influence on the geography of Lewiston's neighborhoods. People often owned their houses but paid a land rent to the company. As land rose in value, the company developed aggressive policies to capitalize on its holdings. Around 1879 it began renting parcels on the "island," a swampy piece of land between the canal and the Androscoggin River, to budding French-Canadian entrepreneurs who built tenements. The area became known as "Little Canada." In 1889 the company began selling the land outright and used prominent "Frenchmen" like Pierre-Xavier Angers to promote sales. Finding the market sluggish, the company resorted to the threat of raising rents.[48]

To Yankees, Little Canada represented the evils of immigrant life. In 1888 the municipal board of health declared the neighborhood to be the "worst and most dangerous place in the city." Newspapers reported such incidents as babies "drinking whiskey."[49] Having internalized such negative attitudes, later generations of Franco-Americans would be torn between seeing New England's Little Canadas in terms of closeness and family life, and symbols of their low status. Few realized that such neighborhoods were in fact created in part by a group of their own people who used real estate as a means of social mobility.[50]

The industrial milieu, in which the neighborhoods developed, shaped the community in general. Most French Canadians remained poor: By 1900 80 percent of the ethnic group still had no personal or real estate. But there were French Canadians in all occupational categories. A study done at Bates College in Lewiston in 1942 established a sample of the occupations listed in the 1896 city directory: Of 909 French Canadians—33 percent were laborers, 28 percent worked in the mills, 12 percent were employed in shoe factories, 20 percent were clerks or worked in other skilled occupations, and the remaining 7 percent were businessmen or professionals.[51]

As immigrant numbers grew and an economic depression settled upon the city in the 1890s, poverty increased, and the city became more involved in charitable operations. Necessities were distributed by the Overseers of the Poor, who also paid rents and found work for the impoverished. Sometimes the city provided train fare to send destitute immigrants back to Canada. The city's police matron, in addition to helping the police department, visited "lost" women and the needy, as well as distributed clothes and food donated by charitable organizations. In September 1899, the police matron and Bates College founded the College Social Settlement for the children of the poor. Impressed by the connection between disease and poverty, the city government also inaugurated a formal board of health in 1887. The board's attempts to promote sanitary conditions were frustrated, however, by inadequate funding and widespread public apathy or outright opposition. Entire sections of Lewiston remained dirty and were a continuous source of disease.[52]

The years after 1880, however, brought greater coordination of efforts within the French-Canadian community itself, in large part a reflection of the growing stability of the population. Concern for health was an important example. French-Canadian leaders, especially doctors, felt that a hospital was needed to serve the Catholic population. By 1888 they encouraged the Gray Nuns to open such an institution, which would also strengthen Catholic influence in Lewiston. The campaign for a Catholic hospital provoked an immediate reaction in the non-French population. Most of the Yankee doctors, along with some Irish doctors, founded their own Central Maine General Hospital and obtained a subsidy from the Maine State Legislature. They characterized the "French Hospital" as deficient in medical care. Nevertheless, the Catholic institution progressed and, in 1894, obtained a state subsidy, which permitted more efficient medical organization.[53]

To the French Canadians, spiritual health was as important as physical. One important factor in the stabilization of the French-Canadian community was the arrival of the Dominican Fathers in September 1881. Seeking asylum from anti-clericism in France, they signed a convention with the bishop of Portland that gave them—in perpetuity—St. Peter's parish—in exchange for an annual pension of $500 for Father Hévey and the obligation to carry out all religious services and provide parochial schools. Hévey had laid solid foundations for his parish, but it was now time for him to leave. Between 1878 and 1881 parishioners had doubled in numbers. It was too much for a man with fragile health. More importantly, the priest was in conflict with some of his parishioners. In January 1881 the launching of another subscription for St. Peter's Church was a failure, as parishioners preferred putting their meager savings in a real bank. Also, a mass movement to retire the money from his savings bank took him by surprise. Unable to reimburse all the subscribers, while still owing $22,000 for the church's debt, Hévey became neurasthenic and he accepted to leave St. Peter's. Consisting of only four priests at the outset, the Dominican Fathers soon doubled in number and were helped by four or five brothers.[54]

In Lewiston and Auburn the Dominicans found 6,000 parishioners whose devotion was profound. On Sundays they were busy from dawn to dusk. In addition to local duties, they were often asked to preach elsewhere in New England. Under their control, a number of religious confraternities and societies were established, the most important being the Association Saint-Dominique, founded in 1886 to protect young men from the dangers of the world and to prepare them to be better Christians and citizens. Although its membership was limited, the association undoubtedly exerted a strong influence upon the community. The Dominicans built schools and persuaded two other European religious orders to help teach in Lewiston: the Marist Brothers (1886–94) and the Dames of Sion (1892–1904). The Canadian Gray Nuns continued their teaching activities until 1893, when they left this field to turn their efforts to the care of the needy, the true vocation of their order. In addition to their involvement in the new hospital, the Gray Nuns established an asylum for orphans and for children of working parents.[55]

The arrival of the European religious orders opened a breach within the French-Canadian community. For the thousands of French-Canadian children who attended Lewiston's parochial schools, the Dominicans created distinctions between the spoken language of the French-Canadian milieu and the Parisian French, which students were taught at school. The Dominicans also developed different attitudes toward the larger U.S. society. Grateful to the United States, which had welcomed them, the Dominicans were enthusiastic advocates of naturalization and "Americanization."[56] In a history of Saint Peter's parish that they wrote in 1899, the Dominicans' frequent references to the virtues of U.S. life and institutions and their pro-U.S. attitudes conflicted with those of the militant faction of the French-Canadian *petite-bourgeoisie.* From the beginning, conflicts existed between the French Dominicans, especially the vigorous Father Mothon, and the provincial headquarters in Saint-Hyacinthe. Behind personality conflicts and questions of procedure were two different views of the Dominican mission. The Canadians believed that the preservation of French-Canadian culture, especially the language, was essential to the preservation of the faith. Mothon, on the other hand, accepted U.S. society with its religious pluralism while agreeing to Irish domination of the U.S. Catholic church at the expense of more recent immigrants such as the French Canadians.[57]

In addition, as typical elsewhere in Canada and New England, territorial divisions threatened Saint Peter's parish. When, in 1889, the Dominicans publicized their project of enlarging the church, which was too small for the increasing population, Auburn French Canadians organized a subscription campaign to build their own house of worship. Although unsuccessful, the movement nonetheless stirred the waters of religious unity. The following year the residents of Lewiston's Little Canada, in turn, asked for their own church, again without success.[58]

By the end of the century, Lewiston's ethnic leaders had gained regional as well as local authority. Under the leadership of Dr. Martel, Lewiston figured prominently in the French-Canadian movement. Martel, one of the most important French-Canadians in New England, was very active in conventions on both sides of the border.[59] His creation, the Institut Jacques-Cartier, had risen to 575 members in 1899. By then, five or six other ethnic associations were also active in the city. In addition, the French-Canadian elite was involved in a broad range of theatrical and musical activities, and it congratulated itself for having made Lewiston "the Athens of French America."[60]

As a voice for the cause, Martel and his associates founded a newspaper, *Le Messager,* in March 1880. In the pages of this French-language bi-weekly, the ideology of *la survivance* was expounded, and French-Canadian events throughout New England and Canada were reported. The newspaper also covered local affairs and, taking up the Democratic cause, soon had enemies, among them the *Lewiston Evening Journal*. However, Martel and his friends lacked business skills and faced growing financial difficulties. Around 1893 Jean-Baptiste Couture acquired *Le Messager,* changed the orientation, and transformed the paper into a profitable enterprise. The readers found more articles on United States politics and on national sports. Issues in 1897–98 were devoted almost exclusively to the Spanish-American War. Illustrations, caricatures, and advertising for local and national products appeared. Increasingly, the newspaper played an acculturative function. By 1900 *Le Messager* had a circulation of 3,000 and had become one of the most important French-language newspapers in the United States.[62]

Historians have never given satisfactory treatment to the question of the political allegiance of French Canadians in the United States.[63] It is too soon to assess the political choices of Lewiston's French Canadians. But one thing is certain: The seeds of the

Dr. Louis Martel. Announcement of a banquet in his honor at the Dewitt House, Lewiston, Maine, 26 October 1893
Franco-American Collection, University of Southern Maine
Lewiston-Auburn College[61]

Democratic domination of the city in the twentieth century were planted in the French-Canadian community of the nineteenth century.[64] In this respect, the role of the elite was crucial. The Democratic party was the choice of a group of leaders who exerted great control over the life of the immigrant community. In trying to understand this choice of a political party, a few factors must be taken into consideration.

Young French-Canadian professionals—like Martel—held the Canadian Conservative party responsible for the difficult economic situation that had forced them to emigrate (the Tories had been in power in Canada at both the federal and provincial levels for most of the 1880s). Moreover, the French-Canadian intelligentsia believed that "Orange" activists controlled the Conservative Party (the Orange movement wished to see the destruction of French Catholicism in North America). Correspondence between Martel and J. D. Montmarquet, the first editor of *Le Messager,* indicate that they equated the Conservative party of Canada with the Republican party.[65] The official voice of French Canadians in Washington, Major

Edmond Mallet, a staunch Democrat, surely influenced local and regional leaders through his correspondence.[66] In addition, Republican Yankees locally labeled the French Canadians and Irish "rumsellers" during the prohibition crusades. Continuing political attacks such as these drove many ethnic leaders into the arms of the Democrat party.[67]

Eventually, willingly or not, Yankees learned to accept French Canadians as a permanent element of the New England social landscape. Although still disparaged in private, French Canadians were given increasing consideration in public.[68] Despite one of the lowest rates of naturalization among U.S. ethnic groups, they were a political force to be reckoned with. By 1900 French Canadians in Lewiston constituted 23 percent of city voters.[69] In 1880 they had elected their first councilman, and thereafter they were always present both on the Common Council and the City Council. As a result, they received their share of patronage. At the state level, Martel was elected to the House of Representatives in Augusta in 1884 and was followed by others. In 1894 he was chosen as the Democratic candidate in the mayoral race. Martel was beaten, however, in part due to numerous French Canadians voting against him, if we are to believe *Le Messager*.[70]

The beginning of the twentieth century found a French-Canadian community in Lewiston much changed since the arrival of the first Québec migrants in the 1860s. The first twenty years were characterized by a highly transient population, which slowed down the formation of a cohesive community. It was only after the development of such social institutions as a parish, schools, and fraternal organizations that the migrants put down roots. A concomitant factor was a moderate degree of occupational mobility and the emergence of a *petite-bourgeoisie* composed of businessmen, professionals, and clerics. Yet the key to social and cultural stability in Lewiston's French-speaking population was demographic stability. This, more than anything else, laid the foundations for the French-Canadian community in the city.

1 The initial version of this essay was Yves Frenette's first foray into Maine Franco-American history. It led to his Ph.D. dissertation and several publications, as well as the James Phinney Baxter Award for the best article published in the *Maine Historical Society Quarterly* in 1985–1986. Yves Frenette, "Understanding the French Canadians of Lewiston, 1860–1900: An Alternate Framework," (*Maine Historical Society Quarterly* 25, 4, Spring 1986, pp. 198–229).

2 Maine's Franco-American population figures consist of the number of persons who declared themselves to be totally or partially of "French" descent in the 2000 U.S. Census. For works on French-Canadian immigration, see Lavoie, *L'émigration des Québécois*; *L'émigration des Canadien*; "Les mouvements migratoires des Canadiens entre leur pays et les Etats-Unis au XIXe siècle," pp. 73–88. Vicero, "Immigration of French Canadians." Paquet, "L'émigration des Canadiens français vers la

Nouvelle-Angleterre," pp. 319–70.
3 The term "Franco-American" appeared only at the turn of the twentieth century. Since my work deals with the nineteenth century, I generally use the term "French Canadian," in respect for the self-perceptions of the group I am studying: See Frenette, "French Canadians," pp. 538–86.
4 For a thorough review of the literature on Franco-Americans, see Roby, "Quebec in the United States," pp. 126–59. A work that adheres largely to the *survivance* model is Guignard, *La Foi–La Langue–La Culture*. Typical of the literature that sees Franco-Americans as an ethnic group undergoing the effects of the melting pot is Haebler.
5 Leamon, *Historic Lewiston*, pp. 1, 6–8. Lewiston Public Library, scrapbooks on Lewiston history.
6 Leamon, *Historic Lewiston*. Dingley, pp. 10, 21–23.
7 Lewiston, City of, *First Annual Report of the Receipts and Expenditures...February 29, 1864*, p. 145. Myhrman, "The Second Colonization Process," p. 17.
8 We get a glimpse of these young women's lives in Bethel Historical Society papers. The best study on this group is Dublin, *Women at Work*.
9 Buker, pp. 6–10, 17. See also Morrissey.
10 Franklin Company Papers, "Shanties Accounts." Buker, pp. 17–18, 19–20.
11 For an introduction to Lewiston's government, see Kirk, pp. 1–3.
12 On streets, see Lewiston, *Map of Lewiston and Auburn*, 1873; City Clerk's Office, *Record of Streets* 1 (November 2, 1840–August 4, 1919). On construction and neighborhood conditions, see Lewiston annual reports. By 1872 the number of pupils in Lewiston's schools was increasing by an average of 300 to 500 a year. See Lewiston, School Committee, *Ninth Annual Report*, p. 127.
13 For an overview of the causes of French-Canadian emigration, see Roby, *Les Franco-Américains*, pp. 33–60.
14 Frenette, "French Canadians," pp. 538–86.
15 United States, Treasury Department, Bureau of the Census, Manuscript Census of Population, Lewiston, Maine, 1870, 1880, 1900. Frenette, Data Bank on Lewiston's French Canadians, 1860–1900.
16 The most reliable sources for Lewiston's French-Canadian population are the figures given annually by the parish priest to his parishioners. They surely include a few families of other origins, but also miss an unknown number of families, as the Dominican Fathers were aware. Unfortunately, they do not cover all the years. The next reliable source is the parochial report sent annually to the Bishop in Portland, although the numbers are rounded up and may have been a bit inflated for showing off parochial progress.
17 United States, Treasury Department, Bureau of the Census, Manuscript Census of Population, Lewiston, Maine, 1870, 1880, 1900. Lawton. On this question, see also Ramirez, p. 137.
18 For sex-ratio statistics in the immigrant population, see Archdeacon, pp. 135–39. For early French-Canadian migration to another Maine town, see Fecteau.
19 European immigrants' repatriation rates varied between 25 and 60 percent: Bodnar, p. 53. Authors, including Vicero, who have seen the ongoing back-and-forth movement of French Canadians as specific to the group, have therefore been mistaken. However, it was easier to return to Québec than Europe and French Canadians probably visited back more frequently.
20 The basic sources for this study of mobility and persistence are the manuscript censuses of 1870 and 1880, the municipal evaluation book of 1880, and the 1890 and 1900 Lewiston and Auburn city directories. It is more difficult to follow women who do not appear in the latter source and who change their name at marriage. I have considered those individuals absent at the end of the ten-year period but who died in Lewiston after this date as persisters: Labonté.
21 Others have noticed this phenomenon. See Hareven, pp. 122–23.

22 Because of space limits, I have barely touched upon the complexity of French Canadians' migratory patterns to Lewiston. A more detailed analysis can be found in Frenette, "Macroscopie et microscopie," pp. 221–32.
23 For contemporary accounts of stabilization, see Hamon, *Les Canadiens-Français de la Nouvelle-Angleterre*; Macdonald, pp. 245–79.
24 Lewiston, *Evaluation Book*, 1880. In this respect, French Canadians were not different from the laborers of Newburyport studied by Thernstrom.
25 United States, Treasury Department, Bureau of the Census, Manuscript Census of Population, Lewiston, Maine, 1870, 1880.
26 Blazon found only 25 percent of heads of households working in the textile mills in the 1870s and 1880s. Blazon, p. 140
27 Boisvert, "Place Ste-Marie," p. 6; Lewiston, Annual Reports.
28 The manuscript census of 1880 indicates the electoral district and the street of residence of 531 of the 650 French-Canadian households. Since we know the limits of the districts, it is possible to approximately locate the migrants. On general residential patterns in Lewiston, see Oliver, pp. 13–14.
29 Lewiston, Annual Reports. For a comparison with the City of Lowell in Massachusetts, see Early, "The Settling-In Process," p. 28.
30 Auger, pp. 10–12; Lewiston, *Evaluation Book*, 1880.
31 Wright, pp. 49–50.
32 United States, Treasury Department, Bureau of the Census, Manuscript Census of Population, Lewiston, Maine, 1880. Frenette, Data Bank.
33 Although it is impossible to quantify this phenomenon, the Franklin Company Papers bear witness to its existence.
34 On this question, see Bodnar; Kessner; Blazon, pp. 110–14; Early, "Mobility Potential," p. 221.
35 For a succinct biography of Martel, see Roman Catholic Church, St. Pierre, no page numbers.
36 The best religious history of Lewiston's French Canadians is provided by Plourde, "Les dominicains à Lewiston," pp. 3–70. French-Canadian and Irish hostility in New England is described in Roby, *Les Franco-Américains de la Nouvelle-Angleterre*.
37 Franco-American Collection: 19-K, Dominicans, Catholic Church, Box 4, Parish History, File A-Buildings/Architecture General. Photograph donated by Madeleine Giguère.
38 *Album Souvenir*, pp. 3–8 (quote on p. 5: free translation), unidentified author; *Programme-Souvenir*. For similar patterns in the Midwest, see Lamarre, pp. 88–89. For a comparison with other immigrant groups, see Bodnar, pp. 124–30.
39 Frenette, Personal Data Bank. *Programme-Souvenir*; Wright, *The Canadian French*, pp. 49–50; Donat Boisvert, "1879: rapatriement ou naturalisation," pp. 10–11.
40 On the attitudes of Yankee elites toward education, see Thernstrom, pp. 76–77.
41 City of Lewiston, *Eighth Annual Report* (Lewiston, Journal Steam Press, 1871), p. 8.
42 Plourde, "Les dominicains," pp. 15, 40; City of Lewiston, *Seventeenth Annual Report* (Lewiston: Lewiston Journal, 1880), pp. 11, 18–19. On Franco-American parochial schools, see Brault, *The French-Canadian Heritage in New England*, pp. 74–75.
43 *Lewiston Evening Journal*, 5 May 1873. On Yankee attitudes toward Franco-Americans, see Roby, *Les Franco-Américains de la Nouvelle-Angleterre*, pp. 185–89; Early, "The Settling-In Process," pp. 27–32.
44 For a similar viewpoint, see Thernstrom, p. 172; Blazon, pp. 39, 73.
45 Chaput, p. 405. *Album Souvenir*, p. 27, UNIDENTIFIED AUTHOR. Lewiston, City Clerk's Office, *Record 3*, p. 542; Annual Reports, 1874–1879.

46 Lewiston, Annual Reports.
47 Burnap, p. 22; Lewiston Public Library, Scrapbook 3, "Auburn in Its Earlier and Later Days." Lewiston, *Evaluation Book,* 1900.
48 Franklin Company, Letterbooks, especially 1889–91. Boisvert, "Place Ste-Marie," p. 11.
49 Lewiston, *Twenty-Fifth Annual Report*, p. 112. Howe-Kendrick, p. 16.
50 On real estate activities among French-Canadian petits-bourgeois, see Linteau.
51 Lewiston, *Evaluation Book*, 1900. Kendrick, "Americans in Process," p. 54. Kendrick's findings must be used with caution.
52 Lewiston, Annual Reports, especially mayor's address for 1898, p. 16; City Clerk's Office, *Records of the Overseers of the Poor* (1879–1900); *Record* 6 (22 March 1886–22 April 1890), p. 138.
53 *Pères Dominicains,* pp. 59–61. Roman Catholic Church, St. Peter and St. Paul Parish, *Album souvenir du 75e anniversaire*, p. 50.
54 Roman Catholic Church, Dominican Order, Convent of Lewiston Records, "Prônes," 12 June and 28 August 1881; *Paroisse canadienne-française*, p. 39. Plourde, "Les dominicains," pp. 15–22; *Dominicains au Canada,* p. 124. Michaud, p. 14. On the emigration of religious orders from France, see Laperrière.
55 Plourde, "Les Dominicains," pp. 24, 53. Roman Catholic Church, Dominican Order, *Paroisse canadienne-française*, pp. 53–58, 84–94. *Cinquantième anniversaire*, p. 13, UNIDENTIFIED AUTHOR. For a more in-depth study of the Dominicans in Lewiston, see Frenette, "Vie paroissiale et antagonismes culturels," pp. 25–35.
56 Roman Catholic Church, Dominican Order, *Paroisse canadienne-française*, pp. 47–52, 68–69.
57 See Roman Catholic Church, Dominican Order, *Paroisse canadienne-française*, pp. 5, 25, 47–52, 68–69, 102–03. Plourde, "Les Dominicains," pp. 26–30. On conflicts between French Canadians and the Irish-American Catholic hierarchy, see Roby, *Les Franco-Américains*, pp. 155–83.
58 Roby, *Les Franco-Américains*, p. 33. Auburn's French Canadians got their own parish in 1902 and those of Lewiston's Little Canada in 1907.
59 See Rumilly, *Histoire des Franco-Américains*, pp. 113, 118, 120, 127. Mallet.
60 Roman Catholic Church, Dominican Order, *Paroisse canadienne-française,* pp. 96–100. Rumilly, *Histoire des Franco-Américains,* p. 166.
61 Franco-American Collection, University of Southern Maine Lewiston-Auburn College: File for Bibliography—Louis J. Martel.
62 Paul Paré, "Les vingt premières années," pp. 82–83, 93. Montmarquet. Tardivel.
63 The best attempt is Petrin.
64 On Franco-Americans as Democrats, see Beale and Bissonnette, *Political Parties as Products of Their Environments*.
65 Mallet.
66 Information on this important character can be found in Rumilly, *Histoire des Franco-Américains*, especially p. 36.
67 The Lewiston mayors' addresses and the city marshals' reports in the city's Annual Reports indicate the centrality of the liquor issue.
68 Macdonald, pp. 245–79. For an example of racism, see Wood to Lee.
69 On the low rate of naturalization among French Canadians, see Sepunik, "A Profile of Franco-American Political Attitudes in New England," 1968. The percentage of voters was tabulated from Lewiston, City Clerk's Office, *List of Voters, 1900.*
70 Lewiston, Records of the City Council; Annual Reports. Cox, pp. 104–05, 113. Paul Paré, "Les vingt premières années," p. 90.

IMMIGRANT DREAM—I

Susann Pelletier
Lewiston, Maine

Back then, the city where I was born
Gave little comfort.
It shook me with the clatter of looms
And night machines,
Blinded me with that immigrant dream
Burning—
Angry flames in men's eyes,
Soot and smoke in the bars
And on the altars
The stuff baked into daily bread.

When I read that the quality of mercy
Is not strained
Or how music is the food of love,
Fair Portia, beneath the wide, white porticos
Did not appear,
Nor Orsino on that Illyrian bank.
The dews of heaven did not rise
Sweet strains did not fall
And I saw only the tired stream
Of men and women
Treading through snowy streets
To the factories.

French people who built cathedrals—
LaMontagne, DeBlois, Thibault—
Their backs stooped now
With the weight of the dream,
Each carrying a black lunchbox.

Not trowels, mortar and stone
Or loads of shimmering glass
Not skeins of silk, wool, linen
For the woof and weft of a thousand flowers,
Virgins and homed horses.

Not even my father, once
A boy with no boots in the Maine winter,
Understood why the people were tramping
Over the old bridges
And gathering at mill doors.

But, then, my father is a maker of whole things
(Houses, fences and gates,
Tables and chairs
Cupboards and counters)
And when his saw sang through the board
And his hammer drove the nail,
The din of those mill machines was stilled,
I heard the sweetest strains of labor
And I saw how a world is crafted
By two steadfast hands.

GROWING UP IN BRUNSWICK IN THE 1930s AND 1940s

Raymond Duval
Brunswick, Maine

The town that I was born in—Brunswick, Maine—consisted of a substantial population of Franco-Americans. I was part of this ethnic group and proud of it. Not much has been written about our generation, born in the days of the Great Depression and probably among the last educated in both English and French in the state. The Catholic schools in the heavily French-Canadian towns taught French for half a day up until the 1950s. Economics and changes in Maine's scholastic requirements were probably the main reasons for dropping this half-day curriculum. Also, with the lack of vocational recruitment from the various societies of French nuns, the Catholic schools were forced to employ lay teachers, which greatly increased costs and led to the demise of French education.

I started at St. John's Parochial School in September 1938. St. John's had two classes for each level, from sub-primary through the eighth grade. We had a school population of approximately 600 students, and—before the fire of 1943—the school was three stories high.[1] It amazes me today to think that most of these kids spoke French back then. The Franco-American community of Brunswick chiefly lay within a rectangle made up of Mill Street, Maine Street, the railway, and Stanwood Street. This is the downtown area of Brunswick, northwest of Maine Street, between the Maine Central Railroad tracks and the Androscoggin River. In 1940 you could walk anywhere in this large neighborhood and hear French spoken.

We lived on Dunning Street, and my neighborhood was about 99 percent French-Canadian. French was the language in use, and I barely spoke English when I started school. I remember one day walking to school with Henry Bérubé, a neighborhood kid from Cushing Street, and discussing—in French—the definition of the English word "shower." My interpretation of the word was to take a bath and Henry argued that it meant it was raining. Obviously, we were both right, but at the time we were not that versed in the English language to know the double meaning. Coming from a bilingual group, the process of learning a second language was confusing!

Unlike today, most of us walked to school in the 1940s. Rural students were

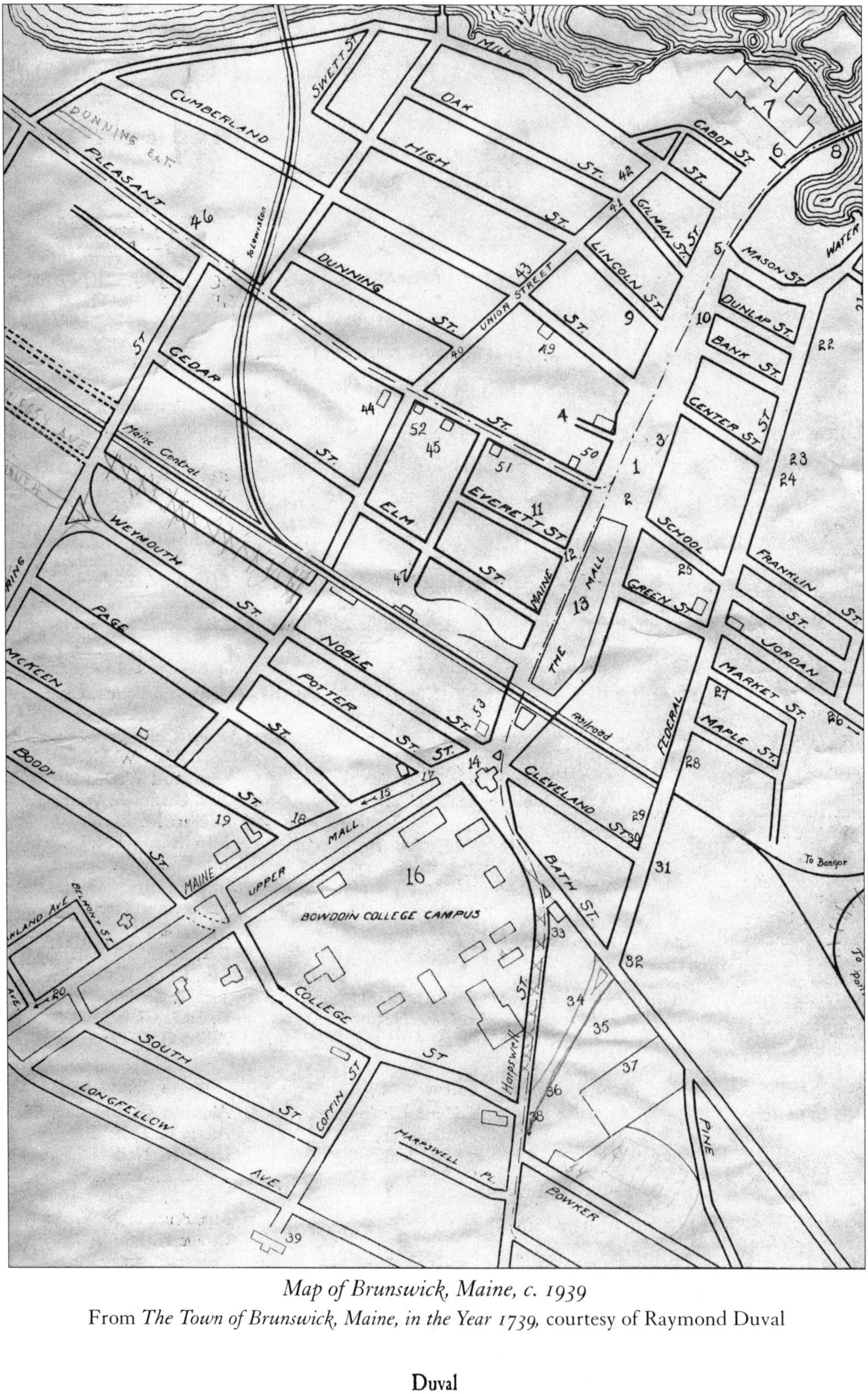

Map of Brunswick, Maine, c. 1939
From *The Town of Brunswick, Maine, in the Year 1739,* courtesy of Raymond Duval

bused, but us town kids hoofed it in a procession from all the neighborhoods to St. John's School on Pleasant Street. From Dunning Street, we would see other kids coming from Topsham Heights (another French-Canadian neighborhood) on the black railroad bridge over the Androscoggin River and along the railroad tracks to St. John's. Their parents used the same route to go to church on Sundays. It didn't matter the season of the year and, even after a hefty snowstorm, the Topsham Heights families would blaze a trail through the drifts along this same route. Instead of the black railroad bridge, some families used the swinging bridge over the Androscoggin from Topsham to Brunswick. This bridge was originally built for the workers of the Cabot Mill (later the Verney Mill). It's still in use today, but the foot population has greatly diminished, since most households own at least one automobile. The school busing system also eliminated much of the student foot traffic of the 1940s and 1950s.

Walking to school meant passing the time by kicking a rock or other object, like a soccer player does. During the winter, we would negotiate the snowbanks between the sidewalks and the streets. No self-respecting kid would use the sidewalks to school when the challenging snowbanks were part of our trail! We would climb the first snowbank and follow this route to school. Kid after kid could be seen navigating the snow mounds along the route to St. John's. Kids miss that today when they take the bus to school. After a snowstorm, the schoolyard would be pristine with a coat of new snow. Being one of the early arrivals, we would make a great circle in the fresh snow for a tag game. The circle would be completed with an intersecting cross that would quarter it and set the boundaries for the tag game. The players would enter the outer rim of the circle and the "it" player was stationed in the center and the tag game began. We burned a lot of energy this way before entering class.

When the school bell rang, announcing the beginning of school or the end of recess, each class assembled at the outside entrance in a single line. Boys and girls were segregated. The watchful eyes of the dedicated nuns kept the groups in silence and in order. The lower classes would enter first and the other classes would follow. In class, the boys sat on one side and the girls generally had the window side of the room. The French curriculum consisted mostly of *le catéchisme* (Catholic instruction), *l'histoire sainte* (Bible history), *la grammaire* (grammar), and *la lecture* (reading). Most of our textbooks were imported from Canada and the majority of the nuns were also educated in Canada. At St. John's, the Ursuline Nuns were assigned to our school—a teaching order that originally came from France to colonial Canada in the 1600s.

Pupils at the St. John the Baptist Parochial School wait for the noon bell on the steps of their church, c. 1939
From *The Town of Brunswick, Maine, in the Year 1739*, courtesy of Raymond Duval

A St. John the Baptist school picture, believed to be the third grade, May 1942. First step: Paul Bolduc, Louis Leclerc, Roland Laferriere, Roger Talbot, —, Leonard Place, Louis Roy, Leon Poulin, Raymond Letarte, Pierre Paul Michaud, and —. Second row: Edgar Lachance, Paul Talbot, Leonel "Spike" Dionne, Roger Duquesnoy, — Levasseur, Bertrand Bourassard, Raymond Duval, Phillip Levernois, Yves Deschaine, —, and —. Third row: —, Henri Berube, —, —, —, Maurice Lacharite, Wilfred Duquette, —, Channel Allard, —, François Lavallee. Back row: Sister, —, Emile Racine, Ralph Johnson, Phillip Pinette, —, —, —, —, Louis St. Pierre, and —.
Photograph courtesy of Raymond Duval

The Ursulines and various other communities of teaching nuns followed the French-Canadian migration to New England.

The Ursulines were dedicated and adequately educated, some more than others. They gave us all that they had, without prejudice and without pay. The progress of my education can be measured by the effort that I put into it, which wasn't much. I was not a good student, *per se*, because I found life outside of the academic arena too distracting. Also, my folks didn't fully understand the potential education had for our future. My dad had three years of formal education and my mother had eight years. Fortunately, they did believe enough in "schooling" to encourage us to continue our education. It was unfortunate and tragic to see some families urge their children to go to work and turn in their pay at the end of the week *en lieu* of continuing their education. We were not affluent, but we were rich in family values. We met the day-today struggle without complaining and had good, hardworking ethics coupled with strong pride. Most families met their financial obligations without welfare, which was almost nonexistent back then.

The kids in my day (circa 1940) played baseball, football, and hockey, but we also played other games and did other things that this generation has abandoned or found uninteresting. For instance, I have not witnessed our game of *kick la canne* (kick the can) since I was a kid—besides, it was played in the street and today that would be too dangerous! It's a hide-and-seek game where you placed an empty tin can on the ground with some weights inside, usually rocks, and have someone kick it as far as he or she could. The "it" player retrieves the can and brings it back to the original spot, while all the players scatter to hide before the can is placed back "home." During the hunt for those in hiding, if a player has the opportunity to run back "home" and kick the can, the "it" player has to bring the can back to home base. You become "it," if you are discovered and fail to return home to kick the can before the "it" player.

Played in the schoolyard and all around the neighborhood was another game we called *'tit bois*, which translates as "little wood." It was popular here in Brunswick with Franco-Americans, but I'm not sure of its origin or how popular this game was elsewhere. I have inquired with folks from other communities with similar backgrounds and found most were not familiar with this game. It was played with a cut-off broom handle and another short piece of wood—the *'tit bois*—cut from the same stock. You had fielders to catch the *'tit bois*, which was batted with the longer stick—much like you would in baseball. The person who caught the *'tit bois* would then become the batter, but there also were other ways scores could be added up and the batter could be replaced.[2]

In those days, automobile tires had rubber inner tubes. Used inner tubes were so plentiful that we could easily fashion a *fusil à élastique* or "rubber gun." First, we cut these tubes into elastic bands. Then, we fashioned a piece of wood into the shape of a rifle. You would "load" it by placing the rubber band at the tip-end of the rifle and stretching it back to be secured in the jaws of a clothespin mounted on the back. By releasing the clothespin, which was your trigger, the rubber band would set off as a projectile towards its mark. We had these available in different styles. A shot in the buttock usually gave you a sharp sting. You didn't want to hit anyone in the face with one of these because some of those rubber guns were pretty stiff and packed a wallop. Most kids were careful with these guns, but I wouldn't want our kids playing with them today!

How about recycling tin cans? With empty condensed milk cans (useful for this purpose because both ends were intact), we would take two and sink our heels between the ends until the cans rapped around from side to side of our shoes. Walking on the cement sidewalk with such equipment made just enough noise to irritate the whole neighborhood. Then we made stilts out of large juice cans. The juice cans were pieced at the top edge to allow rope to go through to make a loop long enough to use as a handle. You'd mount the large juice cans and hold on with to the rope handle and walk like you were on stilts. You also could make your bike sound like a motorcycle by cutting two strips of stiff cardboard, and then fasten the strips with two spring-latched clothespins to the bike frame so that the cardboard ends rubbed against the spokes.

These are just a sample of the stuff we use to do to pass the time away. Yes, we were noisy in the neighborhood and just being kids, but we were not *malfaisants* (evil-doers). We didn't have TV, so our imaginations ran without distraction. We could use some of that today! My pre-teen era of the 1930s and 1940s were wonderful years for me, and I cherish the memories of back then as well as the friends and neighbors I grew up with. Important years for most of us, I'm sure, and I wish everyone had such good memories!

1 The fire at St. John's parochial school happened on 6 May 1943.

2 For a complete description of the rules for *'tit bois*, see Claude Bonang, pp. 37-40. Also, see the following game description.

PETIT BOIS[1]

Claude Bonang
Brunswick, Maine
with Katie Camiré
Lewiston, Maine
Illustrations by Claude Bonang

As baseball became one of America's favorite past-times, some Maine Franco-Americans, particularly in the Brunswick-Topsham area, also entertained themselves with a game called *petit bois* (little wood), generally shortened to *'tit bois*. This springtime game was played in the French neighborhoods and at St. John's School—before and after school and during recess. It was favorably looked upon by the nuns because it involved counting, measuring, estimating, and adding!

First, a 16-inch (40-centimeter) section was cut off a broomstick and tapered to a rounded point at one end. From the remainder of the broom stick, a 4-inch (10-centimeter) section—the *petit bois*— was cut away. Next, the players would find an open area, where a groove was scratched in the dirt, with one end made a little deeper than the other, then another groove was scratched in the ground across it to form a "cross." Both groves were about equal in length. Although the number of players could vary, one person was "up" and served as the flipper/batter, and there were three or four fielders.

The batter placed the *petit bois* across the deepened groove of the cross and—placing the tapered end of the bat underneath—either flipped the *petit bois* into the air or along the ground toward the fielders. If it was flipped into the air and caught by a fielder, the batter was "out" and exchanged places with the fielder who made the catch. If not caught or if it was flipped along the ground, the batter then placed the bat in the horizontal groove and the retrieving fielder tried to hit it by throwing the *petit bois*. If successful, the two players exchanged places.

If not, the batter picked up the *petit bois* and hit it with the bat. If it was a miss, the batter was out, and a fielder took his or her place at bat. If it was hit and caught, the batter was out and exchanged places with the fielder who made the catch. If not caught, the batter estimated the distance (in bat lengths) from the center of the cross to the *petit bois*. The fielders could accept the estimate (the estimate thus becoming the

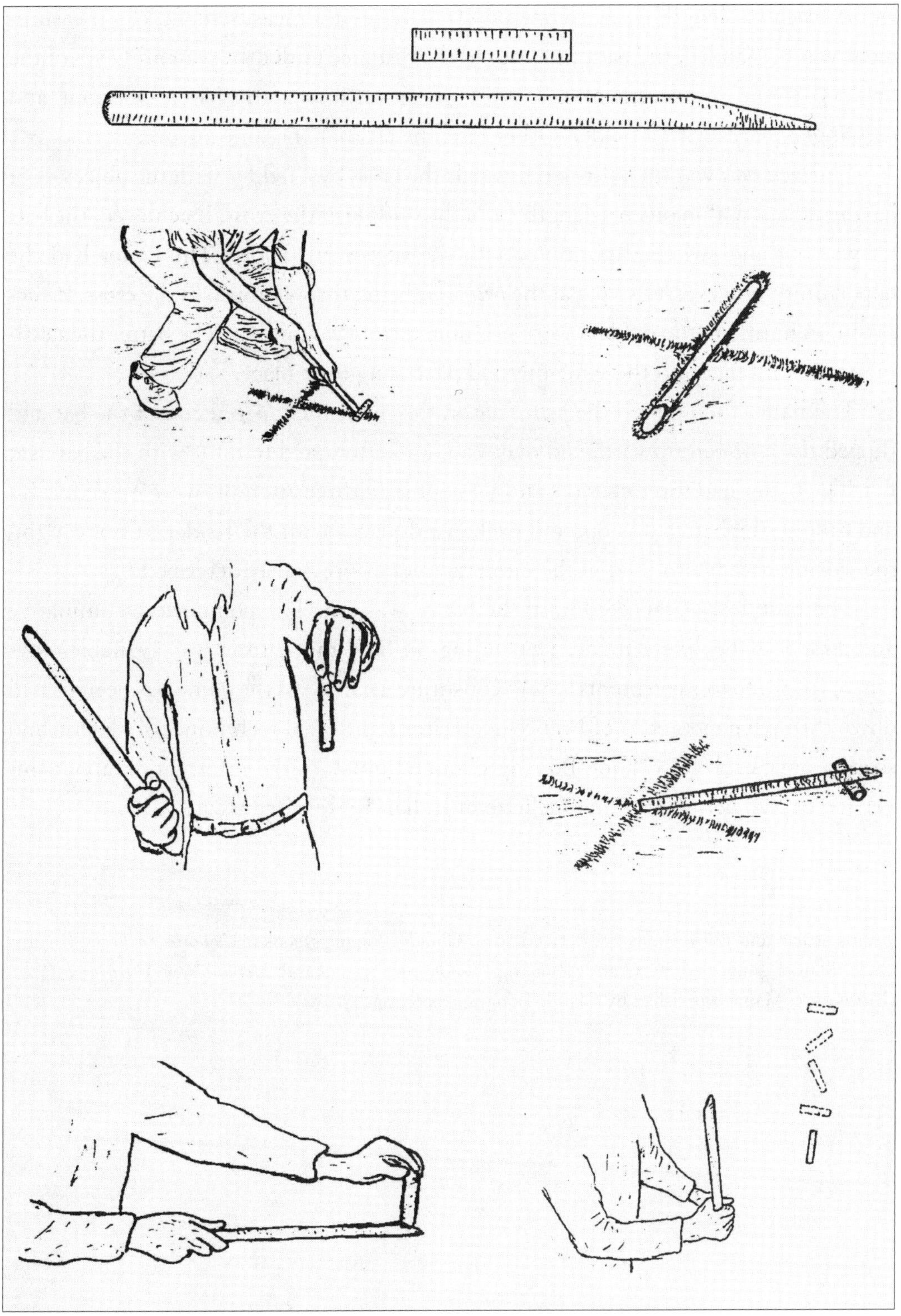

The game of petit bois
Illustration by Claude Bonang

score—each bat length equal to one point) or request a measurement. If a measurement was demanded, the batter measured the distance under the watchful eyes of the fielders. If the measurement fell short of the estimate, the batter was out and exchanged places with a fielder. Otherwise, the estimate became a score.

The *petit bois* was then thrown towards the cross by a fielder with the objective of having it land within one bat-length from the middle of the cross. If achieved, the batter was out and switched positions with the successful fielder. The batter had the opportunity, however, to swing at the *petit bois* being thrown towards the cross. If successful in hitting it, the fielders were prohibited from catching it. The batter then estimated the distance and the same method of scoring took place.

The batter then placed the *petit bois* on the tip of the tapered end of the bat and flipped the *petit bois* upward, end over end, and attempted to hit it with the bat as it fell. The batter had three chances and was out if all three attempts were missed. If hit and caught, the batter was out and exchanged places with the fielder. If not caught, the scoring was determined in the same manner as previously described.

The routine was repeated until the batter was out. The points were cumulative and added as they were made. Depending on how much time was available, anywhere from 100 to 1,000 points would constitute a game. As the game has been passed down through generations of Franco-Americans, different techniques of playing and scoring have evolved. Claude Bonang obtained much of the information about this version of *petit bois* from Phil Ouellette of Indian Rest in Brunswick, Maine.

1 This article and illustrations are derived from Claude Bonang's books, *Memories in Verse,* (Brunswick, Maine: Published by Claude Bonang, 1996), pp. 37–40, and *Memories in Verse and Prose,* (Brunswick, Maine: Published by Claude Bonang, 2006), pp. 27–29.

INTO THE HEART OF MAINE: A LOOK AT DEXTER'S FRANCO-AMERICAN COMMUNITY[1]

Dorothy Blanchard
Newcastle, Maine

Between 1840 and 1930 tens of thousands of French-speaking people made their way from Québec to Maine's industrial towns and cities. An examination of this migration reveals distinct settlement, occupational, and cultural patterns that seem to be similar throughout the state. But are they? To date most of the inquiry has focused on the *petits canadas* of Maine's larger cities, such as Lewiston, Biddeford, and Waterville, while the less visible, smaller centers are all but ignored.

One such community is Dexter, a small Penobscot County town whose ethnic composition is not widely known outside the local area. Yet, in the first decade of this century, nearly one-fourth of Dexter's population was Franco-American.[2] Generations of Franco families have lived and worked in Dexter, shaping and being shaped by this rural mill town. In some respects, their experiences mirror those of their compatriots in the urban-industrial areas of the state. But the small-town atmosphere has influenced certain aspects of their lives in ways that the city could not.

Geographically situated in a hilly area of central Maine, Dexter became a center of economic activity almost from its beginning. One of the reasons for its success was an abundant water supply. The town is bisected by the East Branch of the Sebasticook River, which flows out of Lake Wassookeag on its way to the Kennebec River. This stream, which drops 142 feet (43 meters) in three-quarters of a mile (1.2 kilometers), was immediately recognized by the first settlers as an important source of power.[3] It was this potential power source that influenced two Massachusetts men, Amos and Jeremiah Abbott, to choose the site for a mill. The woolen manufacturing business they started in 1820 was not only one of the state's earliest, but also one that was owned and operated by the same family for over 150 years.[4]

The stability and success of the Amos Abbott Company no doubt influenced other textile manufacturers to locate in Dexter, and four such businesses were operating by 1865. In addition there were two gristmills, a tannery, a foundry, and several saw mills.[5] It was this setting that greeted the first few French Canadians making their way into the central part of the state.

Amos Abbott Mill, Dexter, Maine, established 1820
Dexter Historical Society

Dexter's French Canadians came primarily from the Township of Tring in the Beauce area of Québec, just over the border from Maine.[6] Using the Canada Road (Route 201), they veered east into the central part of Maine, while others kept going south to the larger communities of Skowhegan, Waterville, and Augusta.[7] The railroad was extended from Newport to Dexter, in 1868, providing an important link to these Franco-American towns to the southwest and becoming the primary route of access.[8]

The timing of the Québec influx coincides with the expansion of industry in Dexter, but it is unclear whether the textile mills were the attraction. Geographer James Allen believes they were, but the assumption seems based on patterns of opportunity in New England's larger textile mill towns.[9] Most of Dexter's earliest immigrants were farmers or woodsmen and, when they first arrived, they continued to work in these occupations.[10] For example, the nine Cloutier brothers, who were among the first to arrive in the 1860s, "used axes to help clear this town, and (they) kept the Abbott mill supplied with wood."[11]

Table 1: Age and Occupation of French-Canadian Males in Dexter, Maine, 1870

	Age					
Occupation	**15–19**	**20–29**	**30–39**	**40–49**	**50–59**	**60+**
Millworkers	4	4	6	1	-	1
Farmers	-	-	1	-	1	-
Laborers	1	10	6	3	2	1

Source: U.S. Manuscript Census, 1870

Often unable to speak English and working at whatever jobs were available, most of the new immigrants became day laborers and remained at the bottom of the economic ladder (Table 1). Some younger men with families, as well as the few single males, found employment in the woolen mills in those early years. If women worked outside the home (and few did in the first two decades), it was in the mills. Several children as young as age ten worked there also.[12] The statistics reveal younger workers were employed more often in the woolen manufacturing industry.

In the decade from 1860 to 1870, Dexter's population grew by about 500 individuals. French Canadians accounted for one-third of the increase, or 5.7 percent of the total population.[13] In the 1870s Dexter actually lost population, but French Canadians, arriving in increasing numbers, made up approximately 10 percent of the total count.[14]

The town attracted other immigrants as well. People from England, Scotland, and Ireland had arrived before the Civil War, although their numbers did not equal those of the French Canadians. In addition, Anglophone Canadians from the Maritimes began to settle in central Maine about the same time. Most of these English-speaking immigrants generally found employment in the mills.[15]

Nearly all the French Canadians came to Dexter as family units.[16] Families with several children frequently joined relatives already living there in a classic example of chain migration: "An aunt and uncle came here first. Times were hard with so many children. Then the news was out: There were four mills here. They were hiring. There were jobs."[17]

The transience in those early years is indicated by the different French-Canadian surnames appearing in the manuscript census reports from 1860 to 1880.[18] Some of the new arrivals simply left after a few months, sometimes moving to the larger industrial cities to the southwest.[19] Perhaps they did not find the job opportunities they expected in Dexter, for many were employed as day laborers (Table 1). Most had no personal property, and only six families were listed as having any real estate. It is also possible that the woolen manufacturers were not willing to hire older individuals (only two men over forty worked in the industry during that first decade).[20]

These complex migration patterns, as well as Dexter's rural environment, not only affected individuals and families, but also influenced the French Canadians' social and institutional organization. The ethnic community was never large enough to support the diversity of businesses and institutions found in the *petits canadas* of Lewiston and Biddeford. But, as in those communities, the Roman Catholic Church played an important role in the lives of the immigrants in this period.

As early as 1845 a priest from Bangor visited Dexter to attend a dying person, and—while there—celebrated mass in the home of one of the few Catholic families. No regular services were held until 1871, by which time a large number of French-Canadian families had arrived, necessitating a more suitable place to worship. That year a church was constructed in High Street, and—as a mission—was attached first to the Waterville parish and later to the Skowhegan parish. French priests visited Dexter while it remained a mission, but when it was elevated to the status of a parish in 1893, the congregation was served by Irish priests.[21]

In many of New England's larger textile cities, conflicts arose between Irish Catholics and French Catholics. In Dexter, if such conflict existed, it is not very apparent.[22] A possible exception occurred in the 1920s, when an energetic Irish priest became very involved in the lives of his parishioners. A local Yankee described him as: "a busy and enthusiastic worker in the Parish for the material as well as the spiritual welfare of his people."[23] The same priest was thought by Franco-Americans to be "nosy" and "a dictator." Because the French "were not well educated, the priest felt he had to advise them in English. That caused a little trouble."[24]

It may have been the lack of a French priest that denied the essentially Franco-American parish another important institution—a Catholic school. The establishment of a church-sponsored school was often a priority in a growing Franco-American community; many of Maine's largest urban centers supported them. That Dexter lacked such an institution may be a reflection of the town's Catholic church being initially maintained as only a mission, as well as the Catholic community's size and rural isolation. Dexter and Millinocket, another Penobscot County town, were the largest Franco-American centers without any Catholic schools.[25]

Sometime prior to 1890 a school was constructed on Free Street that "was intended for a French [public] school, the idea being that by putting all French-speaking children in one school with a teacher who could speak the language, better progress would be made." This school lasted only a short time, however, with no reason given for its dissolution except for the notation that "it did not work and the idea was abandoned."[26] The 1890 town report states that the Free Street school "is now unoccupied." It seems to have been an attempt by the local education committee to smooth the way for mainstreaming young French-speaking students into the public school system. In 1890, of 537 pupils enrolled in public school, 149 (27 percent) were French Canadian.[27]

Young, French-speaking children, aged five or six, starting school for the first time, understandably had difficulty with lessons conducted in English, but most overcame the language barrier after about two years; in fact, they often skipped ahead to higher grade levels later.[28] Younger children encountered fewer problems if they had older brothers and sisters attending school. Experiencing the most difficulty were those older children attending English-speaking schools for the first time. Frustrated, they lost interest quickly, gave up, and went to work.[29]

It was a common practice to continue schooling until eighth grade. At that time, many children left to work in the mills, as any extra income the family could generate was welcome. But, by the 1920s, more and more Franco-Americans finished high school and a few managed a post-secondary degree. The latter came at great expense to the individual, and there were instances of students borrowing money from the priests to finish their education.[30]

Traditionally promoted by the Québec clergy, the French language was seen as important for maintaining a cultural identity in the new land. In general, the French Canadians who migrated to Maine have remained closer to their language and traditions than those in other New England states. But in Dexter, language retention proved more difficult because of the lack of French-language schools. Dexter, in fact, showed a higher degree of language assimilation than any other town surveyed in a 1974 study done by geographer James Allen.[31]

Most first-generation immigrants spoke French all their lives; some never learned English fluently, but they understood enough to get by. Conversations with friends were conducted in French, and their children learned to speak French at home. Second- or third-generation Franco-Americans generally spoke French until they went to school. Since lessons at school were taught in English, they were forced to adopt the new language rather quickly. Commonly, parents addressed their children in French, and the children answered in English.[32] Bilingualism tended to disappear by the third or fourth generations. Of particular interest were the family gatherings in which relatives from Lewiston participated. Recognizing that the city children attended parochial schools, one Dexter Franco-American recalled that "the cousins from Lewiston could barely speak English, but they spoke beautiful French."[33]

A common characteristic of French-Canadian communities is the high incidence of the Anglicizing of French names. There are many reasons for this, but in Dexter the motive most often cited was to facilitate communication. English-speaking people, especially employers, had difficulty spelling and pronouncing names that fell into certain letter combinations unfamiliar to them. Consequently, when they heard French-Canadian names, they spelled them as they sounded. Most of these changes were phonetic; for example, Rancourt became Ronco. Sometimes French Canadians changed their names voluntarily to help speed up the acculturation process, which they thought would guarantee a better job or improve their social status.[34]

Not all immigrants changed their names, however, and Dexter's Mount Pleasant Cemetery reveals both French and Anglicized versions of names. The cemetery itself is an interesting social comment on the status of French Canadians in the community.

A Sample of Franco Variations in Mount Pleasant Cemetery

Cloutier—Clukey	D'Amboise—Ambrose
Rancourt—Ronco	Daillon—Dyer
Giguere—Higgins	Poulliott—Pullyard

In the original section of the cemetery, all the French-Canadian graves are located in a corner next to the woods, while Yankee tombstones occupy the rest of the cemetery, which is on higher ground.

The social life of Dexter's Franco-Americans revolved around the church and the extended family. "We used to go down to Grove Street on Saturday night and one other night during the week to visit relatives. And we went *no matter what*. The [adults] sat in the kitchen and talked or played cards, while the children played outside with their cousins."[35] Singing and dancing provided entertainment for large family gatherings or special occasions. There always seemed to be someone who could play the piano or clog dance.[36]

Although work dominated the lives of most Franco-Americans, they always managed to find time for fun and socializing, and families remained close.[37] New Year's Eve was the holiday that brought the entire family together. Relatives, even those from distant towns, arrived to take part in a celebration that included visiting and sharing a meal. The traditional *tourtière* meat pies, still a holiday favorite, were served in nearly every Franco-American home.[38]

When the immigrants became less transient after 1880, the French-Canadian settlement in Dexter began to evolve into distinct patterns. They lived primarily in the neighborhoods around the mills: Grove Street and upper Church Street near the railway depot, and especially in the southern part of town—in the low area variously described as "The Hollow" or the "Lower End." This was an area of mixed tenements, boardinghouses, and individual residences.[39] Limited financial resources forced some immigrants to live with relatives until they could afford accommodations of their own. This meant that in Lower End the population density was much greater than in the rest of the town.

Before 1900 there was little mixing of the Yankee and French societies. The barriers of language, economics, and culture kept each ethnic group in separate sections of town.[40] But this dual society could not be maintained. Dexter's small size and rural nature encouraged cross-cultural contacts. All residents used the same post office and shopped in the same stores. In the workplace, members of both societies labored side by side. Most importantly, all school-age children were educated in the same schools. This assured a high rate of assimilation in the French-Canadian population.[41]

It was not a smooth process, however. Some Yankees viewed the growing numbers of Franco-Americans with suspicion. There was no outward display of hatred until the Ku Klux Klan, a growing national presence in the early 1920s, organized in Dexter. The KKK's membership consisted of residents of Dexter and surrounding towns, numbering at most about sixty. The local "klavern" received its charter from the national organization in 1924, although the group was active prior to that date.[42] The Klansmen conducted regular meetings in rented rooms in the Gerry building on Main Street and frequently marched through town dressed in their robes and hoods.[43] Occasionally the group held public meetings to which speakers were invited, and some Catholics attended, although they had little to say. The priest, on the other hand, was quite vocal, and he spent some time defending Roman Catholicism. About that time, an unfounded rumor circulated that a cache of weapons existed in the basement of the Catholic church.[44]

The fear and tension generated by these events culminated in the burning of a cross in Mount Pleasant Cemetery on Bryant's Hill. This act confused and terrified the children and angered the Catholic adults. Some of the young men went up to the

The Ku Klux Klan march down Maine Street in Dexter, Maine, 1924
Dexter Historical Society

cemetery and were involved in a scuffle.[45] But nothing more came of the incident, even though more cross-burnings followed. The Ku Klux Klan was active for only a few years in Dexter; after that, the anti-Catholic sentiment gradually diminished.[46]

Stabilization of the French-Canadian community brought a noticeable shift in occupational preferences. By 1900 more males were seeking employment in the woolen mills—steady work for heads of households with large families—their jobs often secured through relatives already working there.[47] In 1870 a majority of working males had been employed as day laborers and only 38 percent—mostly younger men—worked in the mills.[48] Thirty years later, the figures were reversed: 64 percent worked in the woolen manufacturing industry, and only 19 percent remained day laborers. In addition, by 1900 a few Franco-Americans had opened small shops and some held skilled or semi-skilled jobs (Table 2).

Dexter's woolen mills continued to prosper in the early years of the twentieth century. The Abbott mill, the Morrison Woolen Company, the Wassookeag Woolen Company, and Dumbarton Woolen Mills expanded after the turn of the century. By 1917 these businesses marketed their goods nationally, proclaiming the most modern machinery, fine workcraft, and superior products. In fifteen years of operation, the Morrison Woolen Company had doubled its capacity to fifty-nine broadlooms and eight sets of cards. At that time, the mill manufactured "high-class woolens" and employed about a hundred people. The Amos Abbott Company, by now a respected

Table 2: Age and Occupation, First- and Second-Generation Franco-American Males, 1900

	AGE					
OCCUPATION	15–19	20–29	30–39	40–49	50–59	60+
Merchants & Clerks	-	2	1	2	1	-
Farmers & Farm Laborers	-	-	3	1	2	3
Skilled Trade (Nonmill)	-	-	-	1	2	2
Millworkers	12	34	15	6	3	2
Day Laborers	-	2	5	3	7	5

Source: U.S. Manuscript Census, 1900; Dexter Town Directory, 1989–1999.

leader in the industry, operated eighty broadlooms and eight sets of large cards. The company had a monthly payroll of $12,000 and manufactured over a half-million yards of high-quality Mackinaw cloth before the outbreak of the First World War.[49]

Jobs in the textile industry became more specialized in the twentieth century. Entry-level positions occurred in the picker house or dye house, while certain skills were required for spinning and weaving. It was possible to advance (in terms of skill and wages) from entry-level spooler to weaver, spinner, loom-fixer, and eventually to "boss" or overseer of a section.[50] Dexter's Franco-American population found employment at all levels in the industry. There appeared to be no wage discrimination, and loyalty to a particular company was common. Many Franco-Americans worked their entire lives for a single woolen manufacturer.[51] More and more women also found themselves at the machines, as families struggled to make ends meet. Family size decreased during the second and third generations, but it was not uncommon for families to have from five to eight children in 1910.[52]

Children were still employed in the mills, as school attendance figures show.[53] For some this was part-time work, but for others it was the beginning of a career. During the 1920s, young people worried about getting "tied down to the mill" at an early age.[54] As this suggests, they were exploring alternatives to factory work, which was physically taxing; even children worked long hours. Frank Jock, who went to work as a teenager in the Dumbarton Mill, describes his duties:

> In 1913, in the fall, I went to work for Joe Higgins at the Dumbarton Mill as a filling carrier. I was getting $9.00 a week. I had to oil up the shafts, lug water to

the office, get the ice, get filling from the spinning room, take it down and steam it, pick up the waste, bag it up, weigh it and carry it out to the picker house, pick up the flyings, bag 'em up, and drag 'em up to the storehouse, sweep the floor and take empty bobbins upstairs.[55]

After 1880 Franco-Americans' willingness to put down roots also affected the social patterns of the ethnic community. Francos began to form organizations and to participate in community affairs, although to a limited extent. The fire company, especially, attracted several Dexter residents of French-Canadian descent.

Sports teams at the turn of the century also had a number of Franco-American participants. Records of organized baseball kept by Frank Jock show the popularity of the sport in central Maine between 1900 and 1920. Town teams, such as the "North Enders," the "South Enders," and various company teams from the mills, all played each other in games held on any available open land or pasture. In his book *Dexter Sports and Recreation*, James Wintle discusses the contributions of Dexter's citizens to leisure-time activities. Franco-American names appear throughout the book—especially after 1910—as outstanding athletes or members of musical and theater groups.[56] Sports and recreation appear to have played a significant role in their adaptation to life in the United States.

When the United States entered World War I in 1917, men from Dexter and surrounding towns enlisted in the army as part of Company A, 103rd Maine Infantry. There were seventy men in the company when it left town on 30 April 1917, many of them Franco-Americans. This was in contrast to widespread opposition to the war in Québec. In this context, the readiness of Dexter's Franco-Americans to enlist is a further example of their having put down roots in the United States. In a diary kept by one of the men, the activities of Company A are detailed throughout the course of the war, including major battles at Chateau Thierry and Belleau Wood.[57]

By 1930 the ethnic community in Dexter was vastly different from the small band of immigrants who arrived in the 1860s. Poor, lacking school-based education, and unorganized as a group at first, the French Canadians eventually put down roots in this central Maine town and found steady employment in the woolen mills. The community that evolved was characterized by a loose cohesiveness based on religious, linguistic, and cultural ties to French Canada. But it lacked the strong sense of *la survivance*—ardent *Québécois* cultural identity—found in the *petits canadas* of Lewiston and Biddeford. Dexter's small size, its rural nature, and its isolation from other Franco-American centers also influenced the ethnic community. That the Catholic district in that part of Maine remained a mission for nearly thirty years after the first immigrants arrived is certainly significant. Of even greater importance is the fact that St. Anne's parish did not have a resident French priest until 1931, even though the congregation was predominately Franco-American.

Thrust into an alien rural society that offered them steady employment, Dexter's French Canadians reacted by adjusting to their new surroundings as best they could. Finding little help from traditional institutions, they relied on each other for important social and cultural contact. Survival in rural Maine required that they adapt to the Yankee way of life. Hardworking and practical, Dexter's Franco-Americans did adapt, and they made generous contributions to the community while doing so. Their roots are deep, and underlying the assimilation process is a profound awareness of who they are and a strong commitment to the proud traditions of their French-Canadian heritage.

1 The original essay was researched and written as part of a senior seminar on Franco-American life and culture, which was taught by Professor C. Stewart Doty at the University of Maine in 1991. A version of this article was first published in the *Maine Historical Society Quarterly* in 1993, along with other essays developed in this seminar. Dorothy Blanchard, "Into the Heart of Maine: A Look at Dexter's Franco-American Community," *Maine Historical Society Quarterly* 33 (1), Summer 1993, pp. 20–39.
2 United States, Department of the Treasury, Bureau of the Census, *Thirteenth Census of the United States, 1910. Abstract in Supplement for Maine.* James Allen, "Franco-Americans in Maine," p. 47. I use the term "French Canadian" for events prior to 1900 and "Franco-American" for those afterwards.
3 Plummer, p. 12.
4 "Maine's Amos Abbott Company Is Still Family Owned After 140 Years," unidentified author, p. 9.
5 Plummer, p. 15.
6 Clatus Clukey, Jeannette Clukey, James Clukey, Anita Savage.
7 Allen, "Franco-Americans in Maine," p. 42.
8 Plummer, p. 23. Allen, "Franco-Americans in Maine," p. 39.
9 Allen, "Franco-Americans in Maine," p. 40.
10 United States, Department of the Treasury, Bureau of the Census, Manuscript Census, Dexter, Maine, 1870.
11 James Clukey.
12 United States, Department of the Treasury, Bureau of the Census, Manuscript Census, 1870.
13 United States, Department of the Treasury, Bureau of the Census, Manuscript Census, 1870.
14 United States, Department of the Treasury, Bureau of the Census, Manuscript Census, 1880.
15 United States, Department of the Treasury, Bureau of the Census, Manuscript Census, 1870.
16 United States, Department of the Treasury, Bureau of the Census, Manuscript Census, 1860, 1870, 1880.

17 Clatus Clukey.
18 United States, Department of the Treasury, Bureau of the Census, Manuscript Census, 1860, 1870, 1880.
19 Clatus Clukey, Jeannette Clukey, James Clukey, and Anita Savage.
20 United States, Department of the Treasury, Bureau of the Census, Manuscript Census, 1870.
21 Murphy, "A Brief History of St. Anne's Parish in Dexter."
22 Wade, "French and French Canadians in the U.S.," p. 147.
23 Plummer, p. 23.
24 Clatus Clukey and James Clukey.
25 Allen, "Franco-Americans in Maine," p. 50.
26 E. Alice Bradford, *Interesting Bits of Local History*, p. 18.
27 According to school committee figures, less than two-thirds of Dexter's school-age children attended school regularly. The rest, the committee reasoned, were working in the mills or hanging out on the streets. Town of Dexter, *Seventy-Fifth Annual Report*.
28 Jeannette Clukey.
29 Jeannette Clukey and Anita Savage.
30 Anita Savage.
31 Allen, "Franco-Americans in Maine," pp. 50, 60.
32 Clatus Clukey and Anita Savage.
33 Anita Savage.
34 Kempers and Maltais, pp. 4, 5.
35 Anita Savage.
36 James Clukey.
37 Clatus Clukey, Jeannette Clukey, James Clukey, and Anita Savage.
38 Anita Savage.
39 Anita Savage.
40 Clatus Clukey.
41 Allen, "Franco-Americans in Maine," p. 60.
42 Dexter Historical Society Archives.
43 Clatus Clukey, Jeannette Clukey, James Clukey, Anita Savage, and Richard Whitney.
44 Anita Savage.
45 Clatus Clukey and James Clukey.
46 Clatus Clukey, Jeannette Clukey, James Clukey, Anita Savage, and Richard Whitney.
47 Clatus Clukey.
48 United States, Department of the Treasury, Bureau of the Census, Manuscript Census, 1870.
49 Chamber of Commerce, Maine, "Progressive and Enterprising Dexter, Maine," pp. 61, 261, 263.
50 Clatus Clukey.
51 Clatus Clukey and James Clukey.
52 United States, Department of the Treasury, Bureau of the Census, Manuscript Census, 1910.
53 Town of Dexter, Report, 1888.
54 Haseltine, p. 32.
55 Frank Jock's description of his duties as a filling carrier appeared in James Wintle's *A History: Dexter Sports and Recreation*.
56 Frank Jock, description, pp. 12, 15.
57 Printed in installments twenty years later in *The Eastern Gazette*, the diary reveals the contributions Dexter's Franco-Americans made to the war effort. Frank Jock, diary.

SAWDUST IN MY EAR

Roland Lapointe
Augusta, Maine

My grandfather, Wilfrid Lapointe, was born in Lambton, Québec, in 1889. He worked in logging camps in the Lac Mégantic region, where he met and married Alexina (Elsie) Alcée Campeau (age sixteen), who had been employed as a cook in the *chantiers*. In 1913 they emigrated from Canada to settle in Waterville, Maine, where they purchased a farm. In 1938, they sold their property to Colby College and purchased another farm in Augusta, where they raised their thirteen children (seven sons and six daughters). This farm was located on Route 3, on either side of the Church Hill Road. In 1947 Wilfrid added a saw mill to the property, along the west bank of Riggs Brook, in order to supplement his income from farming. In addition to milk cows, Wilfrid employed a team of draft horses (Pete and Clyde) to work the farm in the summer and gather logs for the mill during the winter. He employed all his children in some form or fashion—either on the farm, in the mill, or both—as long as they lived at home. Most of the girls married and raised families of their own, while most of the boys took jobs at the Bates-Edwards cotton mill or the Statler paper mill in Augusta. The youngest went to college and went on to become a teacher. My father, Roland, and my uncle, Normand, continued to be employed in the operation of the mill and retail lumber business. In 1955 they purchased the saw mill from Wilfrid and went into business for themselves as Lapointe Brothers, Incorporated.

At the heart of the operation was a Lane mill with a 52-inch (132-centimeter) Disston circular blade saw, run by a 50-horsepower (37-kilowatt) electric motor. It was typical of the portable mills that had sprung up throughout Maine at the turn of the twentieth century. The mill building sat on posts with a wood floor and walls consisting of vertical boards on the north and west sides. You could see daylight between those boards and the roof leaked as well! The other two sides were open to the weather. The east side faced the brook and you could see piles of neatly stacked pine boards along both banks of the waterway.

Extending to the north of the mill building was the debarking shed. Logs would be loaded by forklift onto a series of three parallel timbers known as a "brow," then moved onto a carriage, run through the debarking machine, and dumped onto a second brow inside of the sawmill proper. The bark was carried out of the shed by means of a motor-driven steel chain laid in a wooden trough beneath the debarking machine. This chain was fitted with perpendicular wooden cleats, spaced every couple of feet (0.6 meter), to collect the pieces of bark that had been removed from the logs and move them to the northeast corner of the mill, where the bark was spread by tractor. This bark ended up covering much of the terrain behind the mill building. Further north, behind the mill, there were piles of logs and a small building that housed a blacksmith's forge for fabricating metal parts for the mill.

To the west of the mill building there was a wooden structure where lumber was stored for sale to customers. There were bins for pine boards that had been sorted by width and grade, as well as dimensional lumber—mainly spruce, but some pine, hemlock, and hardwood. Adjacent to that was a very small office and storage building. Inside was a very short counter from which my uncle Normand could wait on customers. It doubled as a lunch room for the mill crew. The storage building contained some odd doors, windows, and millwork special-ordered for various customers. At the south end of the mill, facing Route 3, was the pit. At that end were usually parked two flatbed trucks. One was a blue Ford F600 and the other a black International Harvester. Rough lumber was piled onto the Ford, while the other was used to receive slabs that would be bundled, stacked into piles, and shipped to the local paper mill.

It was during my high school years (1964–69) that I first worked with my father at the mill—on Saturdays during the school year and throughout the week during summer. I remember it being hot in summer and cold in winter. Mostly, I remember the winters. I would ride to work with my father and Wilfrid, and it would be barely light when we arrived. I would dress as warmly as I could with a pair of long-johns beneath my trousers, a warm coat, hat, gloves, and a pair of pack boots. On a typical day there would be a five-man crew.

My job would be to work in the "pit," where the rough lumber and slabs would emerge on a set of steel rollers or from the edger. Working with me was a man named Leo Jarvis. He was a tall, lean man. Leo did not own a car but walked five miles (eight kilometers) to work each day with a lunch basket under his arm. For his age, he was incredibly fit and never seemed to tire.

Between the pit area and the big saw was an edger and a radial arm-saw. With the arm-saw, a piece of wood could be trimmed to an even length—normally from 8 to 16 feet (2.5 to 5 meters). The edger was used to trim the live edges from the initial cuts of the log, after it was trimmed for length. This job fell to a man named Leavitt

Parlin. Mr. Parlin was a soft-spoken man of modest build and amiable demeanor. Some days he would deliver orders by pick-up truck.

At the far end of the mill my father operated the big saw and carriage. Assisting him at the other end of the carriage was my grandfather. By now in his mid-sixties, Wilfrid was armed with a short, 24-inch (61-centimeter) peavey. It had a wooden handle that he had carved himself from a piece of ash. The shaft was slender but strong, permitting a good grip even though three of his fingers had been shortened by a mishap with a surface planer some years before. Wilfrid's job was to roll logs onto the carriage when needed and to turn them at the proper times in preparation for the next cut of the saw.

Once the crew was assembled, putting the mill into operation during the winter was a sight to behold. The electric motor had once been equipped with an oil switch to control the inrush of electric current during start up. But after this device had outlived its useful life, my father replaced it with a regular disconnect switch *en lieu* of purchasing a more expensive replacement. Thereafter, on cold mornings, the mill would not start normally and, if attempted, the motor would merely sit there and hum loudly! On such occasions, my father would glance in the direction of Wilfrid, who would proceed to the area of the motor and reaching down, grasp the outside edges of the exposed v-belts firmly with his hands, and with sufficient force cause the steel shaft to begin to turn. For his part, my father would observe the big saw and, as soon as it began to turn, he would throw the switch—causing it to quickly accelerate to normal operating speed. At that point, it would be up to Wilfrid to withdraw his hands before they could be caught between the belts and sheaves, and then quickly return to his position on the far side of the brow. (I remember trying to duplicate this feat once when the mill was stopped, but without success.)

Once the mill was in operation, my father operated it with relentless determination until lunch. With the carriage in proper position, Wilfrid would plant his peavey into the next log in line and spin it sharply into place. Almost simultaneously, I would hear the sound of two metal "dogs" descend along steel uprights and jamb onto the top of the log with a "thump" and hold the log in place. My father secured one dog, Wilfrid the other. Manipulating a metal arm at his end of the carriage with his right hand, my father would manually advance the log into final position as he tugged on a wooden lever to advance the carriage with his left.

At his feet, my father kept a chainsaw. Often, the logs were too large in diameter for the 52-inch (132-centimeter) blade to cut completely through on the initial cut. In such a case, my father would place his left hand on the top of the log while reaching down for that chainsaw. In an instant, I would see him standing on the top of the log after he had brought the carriage back from the first cut, in order to finish it off with his chainsaw. I tried not to watch while he did this for fear he might fall, possibly landing into the unforgiving grasp of the big saw which was never far from the place he was working.

While the mill was in full operation, the sound inside was deafening. The floor vibrated with considerable force from the pulsing action of the powerful motor and saw. Depending on the types of lumber being sawn on a given day, the mill could easily sustain a production rate of from 2,000 to 2,500 board feet (7 to 9 cubic meters) in one hour. Mr. Jarvis and I would pile that output as neatly as we could onto one of the two trucks at the end of the pit—lumber to the right, slabs to the left. One day, I recall that we were making sills consisting of 8- by 8-inch (20- by 20-centimeter) pieces of hemlock or spruce 8- to 16-feet (2.5- to 5-meters) long. As I was carrying one by the middle onto the truck, I failed to notice that the truck had been parked so that there was a 12-inch (30-centimeter) gap between the end of the truck bed and the mill floor. The next thing I knew, I had fallen through that gap and was wedged tightly at the ribcage between the two—taking my breath away in an instant! Thankfully, it was nearly lunch time and that gave me an opportunity to recover—if only briefly.

At the appointed time we would gather in the office to consume whatever lunch we had as quickly as possible. Apart from food and a brief rest, the major blessing of lunch in the office was a chance to warm up, as this was the only building that was heated. (Typically, the big saw never stopped during the day, unless it was necessary to sharpen the teeth.) Mr. Jarvis would open up his lunch basket, which normally contained a quart jar of peaches and what seemed like an entire loaf of bread turned into sandwiches. This he normally consumed in less than fifteen minutes which was about all the time that was allotted!

Following this brief reprieve, the mill was quickly back into action until the end of the day or until my father had no additional logs left on the brow to be sawed, whichever was later! After the rest of the crew had departed, he would debark a brow full of logs for the following morning and make sure that the blower beneath the big saw was fully cleaned out. During the day, the sawdust would accumulate in a pit beneath the carriage and had to be forced out back by means of a large blower. However, if the sawdust pit was not cleaned out at the end of the day, it would freeze—causing problems the next day.

Nothing compared with getting back home after a day at the mill. After about thirty minutes, I regained the feeling of blood circulating through my feet. It took a bit longer for my body to stop vibrating in sympathy with the mill floor. There was almost always a ringing in my ears and usually a bit of sawdust as well. Supper tasted great, no matter what was on the menu, and I always slept a very sound sleep. Though my brief career at the mill ended after high school, I always regarded it as one of my most cherished life experiences and one which taught me the most.

Epilogue

Wilfrid continued to work at the saw mill most days, until it was eventually phased out of operation in the 1970s. He passed away in 1980 at age ninety. Elsie survived him by nearly twenty years, passing away in 1999 at age 101. By then, the business had gradually shifted from saw-milling to retail lumber and building supplies. In 1993 Lapointe Lumber built a second store in Gardiner, which included a big hardware store and several large storage buildings. In 1997 my father retired and sold his portion of the business to his brother Normand. Eventually, Normand sold his interest in the business to other family members. Presently, there are members of the fourth generation working at Lapointe Lumber.

FRANCO-AMERICAN AND LEBANESE TEXTILE WORKERS IN WATERVILLE, MAINE: LA SURVIVANCE ÉCONOMIQUE

Matthew Laflamme
Fairfield, Maine

Like many small, industrial cities in New England, Waterville was something of a boomtown in the first decades of the twentieth century. The Maine Central Railroad, Hathaway Shirt Manufacturing, Hollingsworth & Whitney Paper Company, Wyandotte Worsted Company, and Lockwood Manufacturing Company all grew considerably both in output and payroll in the years between 1900 and 1920.[1] Waterville's well-established Franco-American community reaped the benefits of this expansion, as did the newly arriving Lebanese immigrant community. For reasons demographic and geographic, these ethnic communities became especially associated with the cotton and worsted mills, respectively.[2] The size and relative prosperity of the Franco-American community almost enclosed the cotton mill within the enclave. Employment contacts were made within the community, French was the primary language on the shop floors, and those who gained the ranks of steward or foreman gained subsequent respect within the Franco-American community. For these workers, *la survivance* meant more than a sentimental preservation of their culture. In Waterville's industrial setting, the Franco-American community had an economic function as much as it had a social function. The Lebanese community, on the other hand, was never large enough to be a self-sufficient city-within-a-city. Its members' economic survival was dependent upon their ability to learn English and to function and interact in Yankee society. These demographic differences greatly affected the ways in which the two groups of workers related to their workplaces, but both were ultimately motivated by economic interests.

As long as mills were operating profitably and jobs were plentiful, Franco-American and Lebanese workers felt no need to recognize the potential value of economic cooperation and to close their social distance. Both of Waterville's textile operations were operating at maximum capacity during and after World War I, and the workers were generally content to live within their respective ethnic communities. After 1920, however, factors in the production of textiles began to change, and

Lockwood Cotton Mills, Waterville, Maine, 1911
Maine Historic Preservation Commission

as the industry began its descent across New England, the workers developed an interest in overcoming ethnic and geographical divisions to respond collectively to unfavorable conditions imposed by mill management.

The conditions in the New England textile industry of the 1920s were discouraging for those who attempted to organize workers. The high numbers of unemployed represented to employers a willing and able source of replacements for potential union organizers, and few workers were willing to join a union at the expense of losing their jobs. Thus, while the genesis of the widespread unionization can be seen in the desperate situation of the 1920s, the actual creation of formidable unions had to wait until employment conditions improved. After Franklin D. Roosevelt was elected in 1932 and his administration began addressing the concerns of U.S. labor, workers began recognizing the interests they shared with their co-workers of different ethnic backgrounds, and class-consciousness started to develop as a replacement to ethnic identity.

Described as "the dark decade," the years 1924–33 were difficult ones for textile workers in Waterville and across the country. Intense competition for machine-produced fabrics and technological advances forced layoffs, and millwork was no longer either abundant or steady.[3] The postwar slump affected industries nationwide, but New England textiles felt the effects with unusual severity. By the end of the decade some 120,000 of the region's textile workers were unemployed.[4] Thomas McMahon of the United Textile Workers (UTW) said in 1930 that: "There is, perhaps, more destitution and misery and degradation in the mill towns of New England today...than anywhere else in the United States."[5]

The UTW leaders felt the effects of the textile depression keenly, as its membership slumped. In Waterville and elsewhere, workers of different ethnic backgrounds were engaged in fierce competition for the remaining jobs. Although John Higham's study of nativism ended in 1925, the relations between textile workers of different ethnic backgrounds during this period would support his theory that nativism is driven primarily by economic factors. Rather than uniting with other workers to bargain collectively for wage stabilization and employment security, immigrant workers were forced to turn inward on the ethnic enclave as the source of economic security. At a time when labor organizations could have been most effective in improving the condition of the working class, the economic crisis helped to reinforce ethnic divisions.

Since its founding in 1901, the UTW had existed precariously close to insolvency and disbandment for decades. In New England, where its membership was divided along ethnic as well as craft lines, its history is particularly uninspiring. A series of failed strike attempts, resulting from the inability of the union to enlist the support of more than a small percentage of the workers in any single mill, cost the union popular support in the first decade of the century. In the years before World War I, competition from the National Amalgamation of Textile Operatives and the Industrial Workers of the World also limited the UTW's organizational success.[6]

Only during the wartime production boom was the union able to achieve any significant success. The employment stability offered by government textile contracts encouraged record numbers of workers to become union members. Total membership of cotton workers peaked in 1920 at over 110,000, representing more than one-fourth of all eligible employees. Of these, more than 80,000 were members of the UTW. In the cities where the UTW was the dominant union, such as Manchester and Lowell, systematic attempts were made to break through ethnic barriers by using union representatives of different immigrant groups as organizers.[7] The notion of a multicultural union was beginning to appeal to workers who had been previously unwilling to compromise their own culture for another worker's economic security.

The brief period of UTW advancement was short-lived, however. In 1922 the

National Cotton Manufacturers Association, which represented most of New England's cotton mills, issued a united challenge to the growing unions. When the association announced in January that it would support its members who decided to cut wages, the union was forced to respond. By mid-February locals from all over New England were picketing, and both the union and the mill owners had settled in for a long strike. Neither side, however, realized that the stalemate would continue into November in some areas. The strike ended with wage levels being restored to their previous levels, but the union's victory was not without great cost. The length of the strike taxed the commitment of many union members to the organization, and the UTW became increasingly impotent in its negotiations with employers in the years that followed.[8] By 1930, when Thomas McMahon, the union's president, issued his statement on the desperate condition of New England's textile workers, the organization was virtually powerless. Workers who were living hand-to-mouth were difficult to convince of the long-term benefits of unionization.

In Waterville, UTW attempts to involve Lockwood workers in the 1922 strike proved fruitless, and the organization's failures over the course of the summer hardened the resistance of these workers to the union.[9] An additional problem for the union was the perception of immigrant workers that the organization was unconcerned about their special circumstances. At the same time as the UTW was actively courting immigrant workers, the American Federation of Labor (AFL) was taking a strong stand in favor of immigration restriction. It was clear to the union leadership that continuing immigration was keeping wages low and undermining the bargaining power of the organization, but this stand also risked alienating the immigrant already at work in the United States. Particularly when the discussion turned to racist comparisons of "superior American workers" and "inferior stock," the immigrant worker was unable to support the union wholeheartedly.[10]

The UTW's crisis continued into the early years of the Great Depression, and the situation in Waterville was similar to that of other textile cities. Attempts at organizing Waterville's workers met with no success in the 1920s, and without any history of organization, the prospects of unionizing the Lockwood and Wyandotte mills were even bleaker than in most other parts of New England. As the depression began to be felt in the city, employment was too scarce for workers to jeopardize their opportunities by involving themselves in unions. Reports to the *American Federationist* during 1931 and 1932 on the state of Waterville's employment situation almost invariably discussed new layoffs in the textile mills.[11]

When U.S. workers helped to elect President Roosevelt in 1932, it was due more to frustration with the previous administration than to any labor policy which Roosevelt himself had proposed. In fact, he remained uncertain, into the first year of his presidency, of what role labor should play in any recovery legislation. It was due primarily to the influence of Raymond Moley and Senator Robert Wagner that the president agreed to include collective bargaining legislation in the National Industrial Recovery Act (NIRA).[12] For union leaders, weary after years of struggling to gain recognition of workers' interests, the passage of the NIRA was indeed a ray of hope. Of particular interest was section 7(a) of the Act, which reads, in part:

> Employees shall have the right to self-organization, to form, join, or assist labor organizations, to bargain collectively through representatives of their own choosing, and to engage in concerted activities, for the purpose of collective bargaining or other mutual aid or protection.[13]

Hailed by AFL President William Green as the "Magna Carta of American Labor," this single sentence had a profound impact on U.S. workers.[14] Not only did it expressly encourage organization, but it raised workers' expectations for improved conditions to a point where they would refuse to be disappointed. In July, the optimism of the textile unionists was further bolstered by the passage of the first National Recovery Administration's Code of Fair Competition which applied specifically to the cotton textile industry. The code established minimum wages and maximum hours for workers in textile mills and prohibited child labor for those less than sixteen years of age. A new, multi-level structure was also adopted for handling employee grievances. Each mill was instructed to create an Industrial Relations Committee to address internal controversies. Each of these committees would be overseen by a State Industrial Relations Board, and the entire structure would be directed and controlled by the new Cotton Textile National Industrial Relations Board (CTNIRB). Referred to as the Bruere Board, after its chairman, economist Robert Bruere, the CTNIRB was quickly recognized by the UTW as a tool of the manufacturing interests. In fact, the three members of the board had been selected on the recommendation of the Cotton Textile Institute, representing the industry. President McMahon was criticized by union members for failing to demand UTW representation on the board.[15]

Still, the response to the passage of the NIRA and the Codes of Fair Competition was immediate and vigorous among unionists. The reduction of the workweek allowed more individuals to share the available work, and the job security promised by section 7(a) led more of these workers to join the union. Robert Daggett reported to the *American Federationist* in October 1933 that "Organization campaign is under way with all unions cooperating. Some few workers have been taken on in the textile mills."[16] For many Waterville workers this marked the beginning of long associations with the labor movement. George Jabar, a Lebanese-American who was to become an organizer and statewide labor leader, recalled his introduction to organized labor "as an active participant in 1933 with the Roosevelt-Truman era under the NRA."[17]

But disenchantment with the promises of the National Recovery Administration (NRA) and the labor relations boards was quick to follow when returns failed to live up to expectations. Under the codes, the workweek had been reduced to a maximum of forty hours, but the failure to adjust wages meant that individual workers were taking home smaller checks each week when previous levels had been barely enough. More significantly, mill owners were circumventing the effectiveness of the provisions with layoffs and stretchouts—assigning more machines to a single worker—to reduce their labor costs. The main disappointment, however, was the realization that, for all the good intentions of code 7(a), labor had little more influence than before. The code gave them the authority to bargain collectively, but management was not obligated to listen, nor was there any encouragement for them to do so. Complaints regarding stretchouts and speedups, when brought to the attention of mill management, fell on deaf ears, and local union leaders were forced to bring their concerns to a higher authority.

The United Textile Workers remained dissatisfied with the Bruere Board's response to union grievances, and on 30 May 1934 the union announced that a general strike in the cotton industry would be called if further action to redress complaints was not taken. The union explained that "for more than a year the workers in the textile mills had been denied the rights supposedly given them under Section 7(a) because of the weak and unsatisfactory nature of the industrial relations board set up to handle complaints of the workers under the code and labor disputes."[18] They demanded an end to the stretchouts and the appointment of a UTW representative to the Bruere Board.

This tension continued throughout the summer, and when the Cotton Textile Institute requested permission of the NRA to authorize a general reduction in machine hours, any gains made by the union were threatened. UTW Vice President Francis Gorman seized this issue to step into the forefront of the union leadership. McMahon had long been criticized for his willingness to concede demands which were fundamental to the UTW's success, and Gorman represented a younger, more confrontational branch of the union.[19]

The union succeeded in appointing a member to the Bruere Board in August, but by this time Gorman and the UTW leadership had an even more valuable bargaining chip. In mid-July the Alabama State Council of Textile Workers, which had affiliated with the UTW only recently, launched a statewide walkout. When the impasse extended into autumn, both the national union and manufacturers across the country were surprised and impressed by the commitment of the Alabama workers.[20]

Inspired by this show of solidarity, Gorman continued to hold out the threat of a general strike in his negotiations with industry representatives. The problem of the stretchout and wage differentials continued to be sticking points, however, and Gorman called for UTW members to begin the walkout on Tuesday, September 4, following Labor Day weekend. Nationally, more than 175,000 participated on the first day of the strike, but in Maine the response was less emphatic. In Waterville there was 100 percent participation among the Lebanese-led union in the Wyandotte Mill, and the plant remained closed for the duration of the strike. The Lockwood Mill, on the other hand, saw only about 300 of the 1,100 cotton mill workers leave their jobs.[21]

In light of the marked difference between strike participation at these two mills, it is important not to make the familiar mistake of interpreting these numbers in terms of innate cultural inclinations. Cotton mill workers, whether Franco-American or not, were more difficult to organize than woolen and worsted mill employees for reasons inherent in cotton production. The presence of large numbers of women at the Lockwood Mill, many of whom were temporary and spare hands rather than career employees, made this workforce much less interested in long-term goals than the male-dominated workforce at the Wyandotte. Because the hiring of spare hands often depended on winning the favor of an overseer, these workers were unwilling to jeopardize personal relationships with their bosses by striking. Single women who expected eventually to become housewives and mothers were primarily interested in short-term employment opportunities, and were less concerned than full-time workers about the future of work conditions in the cotton mill. Working women who were already married could expect to require leaves when children were born, and, once again, rehiring depended on a positive relationship with management.[22] During the mid-1920s the AFL began to realize the importance of involving women in the activities of the union. Especially in cotton textiles, women were recognized as the weak link in forming a strong union.[23] Although they had the most to gain in the creation of a powerful voice for the workers, they also had the most to lose should such efforts fail.

For Franco-Americans who had previously turned to the community for support during times of crisis, redirecting their interests toward national unions and the federal government was a new experience. When it is applied to labor organizations, however, the notion of *survivance* de-emphasizes the economic interests of Franco-American workers. Cultural preservation was not practiced for its own sake, at the expense of economic advancement. Rather, the Franco-American neighborhood was itself a defense against economic crisis. Franco-American grocers would extend credit which could not be obtained elsewhere, *L'Association d'Epargne* (the Savings Association) could offer loans to those in need, and Franco-American physicians and lawyers extended medical and legal help to those who could not afford the rates charged outside of the community.[24]

Separating the social and economic functions of the Franco-American community is not simple, and it certainly was not so for workers in the 1930s. They were forced to choose between their traditional support system and a new one which, despite its logic, represented a foreign territory. The decision of Franco-American workers to unionize was further complicated by the position of the clergy. Father Marchand of Lewiston, the leader and mentor of one of the state's largest Franco-American parishes, urged his parishioners to reject the claims of union organizers.[25] He and other Franco-American priests were perhaps concerned that the separation of social and economic interests by Franco-American workers would diminish their own influence in the community.

At the worsted mill, the decision for Lebanese workers to join the union was less difficult. The vast majority of these workers were men who had invested years of labor into reaching the best jobs in the mill, and the union offered a measure of potential stability for jobs which were intended to be careers. The Lebanese community, despite its intimacy, was not large enough to support its working class in a time of general crisis, and the union offered a larger community which could serve this function. Because the Lebanese-Americans had learned the English language and were perhaps more familiar with the other cultures around them than were the Franco-Americans, they were also better equipped to participate in and even lead union activities. George Jabar recalled that he was chosen from among his co-workers to lead the organization drive at the Wyandotte mill, in part, because he was literate in both English and Arabic.[26]

Careful coordination of the strike at the national level provided for the organization of strikers into "flying squadrons" that had been organized in advance of the strike call. These groups were formed to picket mills which had been less successful in their organizational efforts. Under this structure, the responsibility fell to the woolen mill workers to organize pickets in conjunction with those few Lockwood cotton workers who were striking.[27]

The two primary labor leaders in this local conflict, then, were both weavers at the woolen mill: George Jabar, a Lebanese-American, and Joseph Poirier, a Franco-American. On September 11 they led some 200 picketers in a "peaceful protest" on the sidewalk outside the Lockwood Mill.[28] The following day they gained momentum as new members and thousands of spectators joined in. Jabar marched with 300 picketers and gained 125 new members.[29] They were able to close the night shift completely, and many of the previously undecided were convinced to leave their jobs.

A tenacious group of workers resisted the efforts of the strikers, however, and the mill continued to operate at reduced capacity until September 17. On this date, the first acts of violence took place when several windows in the mill were broken by picketers, several men reported being assaulted upon leaving work, and one man was arrested and charged with inciting a riot.[30] The National Guard had already been called into Lewiston and Lawrence, among other places, and strikers had been killed in clashes in Georgia and Rhode Island. The mayor of Waterville did not consider the events in his city to merit such attention. The following day, however, the situation exploded. The *Waterville Morning Sentinel* reported:

> The worst riot ever staged in this usually quiet Kennebec Valley City took place shortly after dawn yesterday when a mob of over 300 men and women barraged the Lockwood Manufacturing Company with stones, chased employees from the plant, and engaged in hand-to-hand battles with police who managed to stave off the first sensational attack by unionized forces in the current textile strike uprising. Six men were arrested as a result of the demonstration which saw frenzied men and women resisting officers and in some instances hurling stones at them. Two official cars were stoned during the demonstration and only tear gas dispersed the mob.[31]

George Jabar's account of the incident is significantly milder than was reported in the conservative, anti-labor *Sentinel*, but both versions agreed that the episode was enough to convince the remaining workers to leave their jobs.[32] The National Guard was called into the city for the remaining week of the strike, and there were no more notable confrontations. With both mills completely shut down, the picketing was curtailed and Waterville's flying squadrons continued on to other cities in the region.

On September 5 Roosevelt had appointed a committee to study the textile industry and the issues of the strike. Headed by former New Hampshire Governor John Winant, this board of inquiry faced an impossible task and was given a minimal amount of time to complete it. When the board forwarded its recommendations to the president on September 20, the union was offered almost no substantive concessions. Among the provisions were the replacement of the Bruere Board with a more-neutral Textile Labor Relations Board (TLRB), further study of the stretchout problem, and a recommendation that employers take back all striking workers. Despite the hollowness of this settlement, the union was seriously overextended in the previous two weeks, and Gorman was forced to accept the terms.

Although the strike failed to gain any immediate improvements in working conditions, the mobilization of textile workers nationwide under the banner of the UTW was a significant development. Rather than retreating under the weight of the strike settlement, the union and its members continued to demand recognition. In the months that followed, the new TLRB was inundated with thousands of official complaints regarding hiring practices, stretchouts, speedups, and the dismissal of union members. This redirection of workers' concerns from the local to the national level is an important legacy of the 1934 general strike.

In the wake of the strike, many mills systematically and blatantly ignored the Winant Board's recommendation that strikers be offered the opportunity to return to work. In Waterville, however, the Lockwood management expressed its willingness to take back all employees who were working the week prior to the strike. At least for the week ending September 29, there were no complaints regarding discrimination in rehiring. In the weeks that followed, however, a government order for which the mill had been operating at near maximum capacity was completed, and the payroll was cut almost in half. When these new layoffs were announced, union members began to exhibit the fact that their class-consciousness had not been crushed by the strike settlement. Official complaints were filed with the TLRB by forty-five Lockwood employees; of these, forty-three were Franco-Americans.[33]

The issues addressed in these complaints primarily related to the decisions made by overseers regarding which employees would continue to work and which would be laid off at the completion of the government order. Related to this issue were several complaints of stretchout, which allowed management to lay off even more workers. When the company displayed its unwillingness to negotiate with representatives of the union, the UTW initiated a formal inquiry, and an independent examiner was appointed to hear the testimony of both the union members and the company.

Representing the union in the hearing was UTW Vice President Horace Riviere of Providence. Riviere was an old associate of Thomas McMahon and he was one of the first and most prominent Franco-American union leaders. Since his earliest days in the union he had provided an important link between the national union and groups of Franco-American workers. He perfected this role during the 1922 strike in Manchester, New Hampshire, when he helped to maintain the commitment of the city's textile workers for more than ten months.[34] Riviere was also familiar with the workers in Waterville, whom he had attempted to organize—albeit unsuccessfully—during the early 1920s. His assignment to the Lockwood hearing was clearly a similar attempt to bridge the gap between Franco-American loyalties to culture and class.

The hearing took place over five days in December 1934 at the City Court House. Richard C. Evarts of Boston was the examiner, and Riviere used the testimony of the workers to demonstrate that the Lockwood Mill was implementing a "scientific method of discrimination against the members of our union."[35] Unlike the mills that had patently refused to allow strikers to return to work, the Lockwood Mill had temporarily restored employment to its pre-strike levels. For this reason, Riviere regarded the systematic imposition of layoffs as a more-evasive or "scientific" method of discrimination. In fact, this description contains a great deal of truth. The collective work hours of the forty-five complainants listed in the record of the hearing decreased significantly and steadily after the middle of October. For the week ending October 13, these forty-five workers were employed for a total of 1,536 hours, an average of more than thirty-four hours each. Four weeks later, this group worked a total of only ninety-six hours.[36] The company's claim that layoffs were imposed without regard to union membership could not account for such a drastic reduction in employment. When the strike ended and work resumed, 65 percent of the Lockwood Mill's employees were members of the union; at the time of the hearing in December, layoffs had reduced this figure to 33 percent.[37]

In the context of the trial, however, it was more difficult to prove individual cases of discrimination. Overseers were able to testify that the employees who were retained during the layoffs were the best and most productive workers in the department, or that the economic hardships of some individuals led the company to decide to keep them in their jobs. The subjective hiring practices used at the Lockwood and most other mills made it difficult for the union to prove that its members were being discriminated against solely on the basis of their membership. Thus, the union was not vindicated when Evarts concluded: "There are cases of discrimination, not due to any system promulgated by management, but rather to the action of individual overseers."[38] Since the hearing was limited to examining the specific issue of discrimination against the union, it was necessary to prove a conscious and systematic effort on the part of the mill's management to remove union members from the workforce.

The most obvious case of discrimination that Evarts identified occurred in the cloth room, where four inspectors who had been hired during the strike were rehired when four strikers were laid off.[39] The examiner recommended—in accordance with the previous recommendation of the Winant Board—that the strikers be returned to their jobs. Other incidents were less overtly discriminatory. In the spinning department four doffers were forced to share two jobs, two working one week and the other two the next week. At the same time, two of their co-workers who had not joined the union were retained full time. Since no one had technically been laid off, the discrimination was less clear, although it still certainly existed. A third example took place in the weave room, where battery hands were being required to tend sixty-two looms each rather than the usual forty-eight to fifty-two. This stretchout allowed the overseer to lay off one of every five battery hands, and union members complained that they were the first to be dismissed.

The workers' testimony during this hearing displays a great deal of knowledge about the details of federal labor regulations and the specific issues of the strike. Far from the *Portland Press Herald* report of "peaceful, law abiding class of citizens" who "never become agitators," these Franco-Americans had developed a passionate interest in the rights of the working class. In his closing remarks, Horace Riviere described the operation of the UTW:

> The United Textile Workers of America is an up-to-date organization, and we have developed what we call the industrial form of organization, from the sweeper up to the loom-fixers, and every [one] of these employees is eligible to the membership in the organization.[40]

When Evarts interrupted at this point to ask—"Does that idea come from England?"—he provided a poignant reversal of roles. While these Franco-American workers had grasped and accepted the concept of industrial organization, the government-appointed examiner was unable to see it as anything but foreign. For those who believed Franco-Americans lacked the aptitude for labor organization, this was overwhelming evidence that they had developed a new sense of class consciousness. *la survivance* was an economic formula that had served them well, but for many at this time the union offered a new sense of security and indeed a new community centered, not on a shared past, but on common interests in the present and future.

1 On the industrial history of Waterville, see Campbell; Whittemore; and Margaret Bernier.

2 The Franco-American neighborhood, referred to as "The Plains" and located at Waterville's south end, was adjacent to the Lockwood cotton mill. Cotton manufacturing, furthermore, was especially labor-intensive, and French-Canadian women and children were a welcome supplement to the Lockwood mill's labor pool. The Lebanese immigrants who arrived around the turn of the century were primarily men, and most settled in the neighborhood surrounding the new woolen mill. Wool weavers were more likely to be men, and some of these men may have had experience weaving silk before emigrating to the U.S. For more on the settlement and development of Waterville's ethnic communities, see Fecteau; Matthew Laflamme; Margaret Bernier; Mavrinac; Ezhaya; Hooglund. Note that the term "Lebanese" was not used in Waterville at this time. The U.S. Immigration and Naturalization Service considered them "Turks," as they had come from the Ottoman Empire at that time, but they considered themselves geographically "Syrian" and religiously "Maronite." After Lebanon gained independence, following World War II, the term "Lebanese" gained popularity and is most widely used today.

3 American Federation of Labor.

4 Bernstein, *The Lean Years*, p. 255.

5 Adamic (1938), p. 263.

6 For a more detailed history of the early years of the UTW, see Lahne, pp. 189–215.

7 Kelly, p. 91.

8 On the history of the 1922 strike, see Lahne, pp. 205–09; Kelly, pp. 91–92; Doty, *The First Franco-Americans*, p. 24.

9 Horace Riviere's reports to the *American Federationist* in the fall of 1921 suggest that he was making a serious effort to organize Lockwood workers, but at the time of the 1922 strikes there was no evidence of participation in Waterville. *American Federationist*, Volume 28, August 1921, p. 684; September 1921, p. 800; October 1921, p. 883.

10 Hoyem; AFL President Samuel Gompers also complained that immigration was harmful to the American working-class. *American Federationist*, June 1923, pp. 489–93.

11 The *American Federationist*'s correspondent in Waterville, Robert Daggett, included optimistic news in his reports whenever there was any to recount, but his reports on the layoff situation during these years was dour and frank: "at Waterville, Maine, industries are not taking on people and there are no signs of business improvement," July 1932, p. 816; "Pulp and paper, woolen and cotton mills, railroad shops and stores have been laying off workers," March 1933, p. 305.

12 Bernstein, *The Turbulent Years*, pp. 31–35. Bernstein, *The New Deal Collective Bargaining Policy,* pp. 33–39. Leuchtenburg, 106–110.

13 National Industrial Recovery Act (49 Stat. 449), 1933.

14 Bernstein, *The Turbulent Years*, p. 300.

15 Bernstein, *The Turbulent Years*, pp. 300–01.

16 *American Federationist*, October 1933, pp. 1117–18.

17 Jabar, interview by O'Leary, p. 574001B.

18 Lahne, p. 225. *American Federationist*, November 1934, "The Plan of Action of the Textile Strike," p. 1369.

19 Bernstein, *The Turbulent Years*, p. 298.

20 Lahne, p. 226.

21 *Waterville Morning Sentinel*, 7 September 1934, p. 1.

22 Labor historians generally agree that, under subjective hiring practices, women workers were more vulnerable to the whims of the bosses. In addition to being responsible for homemaking and childbirth, both of which could affect a woman's ability to do her job, women were also sometimes subjected to sexual pressure from the overseer. As one industrial worker in Chicago remembered: "You could get along swell if you let the boss slap you on the behind and feel you up." Anna Novak, p. 63. It was this same need to please the boss that discouraged women from participating openly in union activities.

23 See Cook; Green.

24 Marcou.

25 *Portland Press Herald*, 6 September 1934, p. 8.

26 Jabar, interview with Lavin.

27 Jabar, interview with O'Leary, p. 574003. The union explained its strategy in the journal, *American Federationist*, November 1934, p. 1372: "Every worker had to be ready to fight not only in his own mill but in the mill next door or in the mill in the next town. Every worker was ready.... The members of each local union were organized into squads of ten. Over each ten men or women was a squad leader. The squad leader was at all times in command of his group; he knew where his men were and what they were doing. He was responsible for their safety and their conduct. The squad leaders reported to and received orders from the union strike committees. This meant a direct contact between the union ranks..."

28 *Waterville Morning Sentinel*, 12 September 1934, p. 1.

29 *Waterville Morning Sentinel*, 13 September 1934, p. 1.

30 *Waterville Morning Sentinel*, 18 September 1934, p. 1.

31 *Waterville Morning Sentinel*, 20 September 1934, p. 1.

32 Jabar explained the incident this way: "We were picketing the other side of the street [from the Lockwood]...a fellow by the name of Picard hollared, 'Let's go get those scabs!' There was a rush into the plant and they chased the workers all over...local cop fired tear gas into the wind, knocked himself out, that's all that happened. It lasted probably ten or fifteen minutes." Jabar, O'Leary interview. In an interview with Margaret Bernier ten years later, Jabar further dissociated the strikers and the violence: "The state troopers came out with large billyclubs, and they had some tear gas. There were more people on the sides watching the pickets than there were picketers. Somebody in that crowd threw a stone into the plant, because some of the people were going in. That started, what we'd call, a minor skirmish. So a lot of the pickets and people who weren't involved in the strike went in and ran through the mills; so all the people came out. The state troopers got all together, and they fired tear gas into the crowd. They fired it, and it went against them and knocked them out." Margaret Bernier, pp. 70–71.

33 United States, National Recovery Administration, Record of the Inquiry, pp. 910–12.

34 For a brief biography of Riviere, see Kelly, pp. 89–98.

35 United States, National Recovery Administration, Record of the Inquiry, p. 949.

36 United States, National Recovery Administration, Record of the Inquiry, pp. 910–12.

37 United States, National Recovery Administration, Record of the Inquiry, p. 944.

38 United States, National Recovery Administration, Report of Examiner.

39 United States, National Recovery Administration, Record of the Inquiry, pp. 739–46.

40 United States, National Recovery Administration, Record of the Inquiry, pp. 953–54.

"JE NE REGRETTE RIEN" FRANCO-AMERICAN WOMEN IN MAINE: SURVIVAL, RESILIENCY, AND COMMUNITY

Celeste DeRoche
Vero Beach, Florida

Mary Ann Lebel was born in 1907 in Van Buren, Maine. One of seven children, she did not learn to speak English until she started grammar school when she was nine years old. She attended Van Buren High School for only one year. After she left high school, her mother sent her to sewing school for three months. She became an accomplished seamstress and later made all of her family's clothes, including her husband's dress suits. She survived two husbands. The first died in 1961; he had been disabled in a horse and wagon accident, and she nursed him for fifteen years. During his illness she supported the family by doing the home and farm chores. She cared for their one son as well as foster children. She also had a milk route. She did the milking and haying, and drove the truck and wagon. From her large garden she canned all the family's food. Never once did she think that anyone would find her life special. When asked about the Great Depression, she puzzled for a moment before saying that "she really never had time to be depressed." If she were given a chance to live her life over again she would not do anything any differently. "Why regret?" she asked. "What is past is past and what is coming up is coming and we don't know it! I regret nothing."[1]

Historians, like anthropologists and sociologists, use theories to offer explanation. Theories can be useful tools for understanding change over time. Immigration historians often include in their descriptions "push" and "pull" factors to identify why people leave certain areas and how they choose their destinations. But always behind the theories are real people and real stories. Historians need both the theories and stories to come close to the past.

This essay seeks to take the theories of immigration history and the experiences of Franco women to expand our knowledge of Maine history. Franco women like Mary Ann Lebel have always played an active and imaginative part of the state's development and life. But their presence is rarely acknowledged and their efforts only occasionally recognized. Theirs is a history that needs to be rescued from the oblivion it is usually consigned to, while at the same time it needs to be saved from being just a litany of achievements and contributions. The history of Franco-American women in Maine is as complicated as their individual lives were. For every general statement about why they came, where they lived, how they worked, and what they thought, there are exceptions and contradictions. Rather than being discouraging, the complexity offers the opportunity to uncover the reality of these women's lives.

Recent scholarship on the lives of immigrant and ethnic women demonstrates a rich continuum of experience. We know more than we ever did about immigrant women. Thanks to the work of numerous historians, we now have detailed and layered accounts of the immigration of women from Ireland, Italy, Japan, Jewish Eastern Europe, Korea, Mexico, and Eastern Central Europe.[2] These works underscore how class, ethnicity, and time of migrations shaped important variations in women's experiences. Their focus on the experience of immigrant women also demonstrates the gendered nature of the immigrant experience. Many histories of immigrants in the United States begin with the experiences of migratory men disguised as genderless humans. Yet the experience of immigrant women reminds us of the centrality of gender. Immigrant women could not isolate gender from other dimensions of their life. As historian Donna Gabaccia described, "Immigrant women...carried with them not merely Italian or German or Japanese ways, but also the distinctive female traditions found within their native cultures." Immigrant women were constantly blending the old with the new in a creative invention of an "ethnic" female identity.[3]

Often relegated to "landscape roles" in Maine history, Franco women need to be moved to the center. Franco women not only survived the often difficult migration process but also adapted to life in a new country with an often graceful resiliency that shaped the community they helped to build. Their survival, resiliency, and community provide a compelling story. Nowadays we think that we have invented the conversation about diversity and its role in American culture and life. But Franco-American women in Maine wrestled with issues of multiculturalism long before it had a name. Perhaps knowing their history can help us find our answers or at the very least sharpen our questions.

Survival

Back then, the city where I was born
Gave little comfort.
It shook me with the clatter of looms
And night machines,
Blinded me with that immigrant dream
Burning—[4]

The first task was getting here safely. Like Mexican-American immigrants, Franco-Americans did not have to board a ship to get to the United States. They did not, as so many other immigrant groups did, enter the U.S. through Ellis Island. Like Mexican-American immigrant women, Franco women could make the border journeys overland. Lucy Blouin recounted the migration of her grandparents to Lewiston. They traveled in a wagon with wooden wheels. Frequent stops were essential so the wheels would stay cool and not catch fire.[5] For the second generation, the story of how their parents or grandparents came to Maine often played a vital role in their own identity. Emma Tourangeau, a Franco-American woman from Westbrook, Maine, found in the story of her grandparents' migration to Maine a source for tenacious survival.

> The Mailly family came to Maine to help the French-Canadian procure their usual "way of living." From the pulpit one Sunday Fr. DeCelles [the first pastor of St. Hyacinth's, the French Roman Catholic Church in Westbrook] brought up the problem of the customary French bread and asked for one of the parishioners to go to Quebec and locate a French bread baker, bring him back to Saccarrappa to teach the method of bread-making. A Mr. Nadeau offered to go to Quebec and after awhile persuaded my grandfather, Dominique Mailly who had a bakery in St. Sauveur to come to Saccarrappa and teach this trade to someone.[6]

As was so often the case, Emma's grandfather came alone, leaving his wife and five children in Québec. He told his wife that if he were successful he would send for her and the children. However, as Emma remembers the story, her grandmother had her own ideas about how the migration would take place. And in the decision of Elizabeth Lepine Mailly we can see the fine tracings that move out in a web as a stereotype is shattered, in much the same way as a crack in a windshield spreads from the point of impact. One of the most common stereotypes of late-nineteenth-century and early twentieth-century French-Canadian women is that they were passive, compliant, and docile women, easily ruled by fathers, husbands, and the parish priest. The history of Franco-American women has been so difficult to uncover because it is assumed that the actions and choices of the men in the French-Canadian migration also told us the truth about the women. This is only partially true. The French-Canadian women who immigrated were active participants in the unfolding drama of the developing Franco-American presence in Maine. Their choices and actions contributed to the growth of a vital cultural piece of Maine history.

Emma's grandmother didn't wait for her husband to tell her when to come to Maine. Instead, Elizabeth Mailly took her migration and that of her children's into her own hands. "After a couple of months she became impatient, sold all of their belongings, took the children out of school, and left for the States. This was all unbeknown to my grandfather."[7] Elizabeth arrived just as her husband was preparing to return to Québec for them. Their future in Westbrook was sealed by the fact that "Grandmother often told us that she had never saved enough to take the family back to Canada."[8]

Like the influx of Eastern European Jews to the United States in the 1880s, many of the French Canadians who came to Maine after 1880 arrived with the intention of staying permanently. This had not always been the case. For instance in Lewiston, Maine, from 1860 to 1880 the French-Canadian population moved frequently between Lewiston, other U.S. cities, and Québec.[9] Only between 1880 and 1900 did the members of the "Québec Diaspora" begin settling permanently in cities like Lewiston. During this period French-Canadian institutions such as French parishes and schools, fraternal organizations, and French language newspapers developed in the city.[10] In Jackman, Maine, permanent settlement by French Canadians was even later. Located on a historic immigration route, the Canada Road, Jackman did not attract permanent French-Canadian settlement until after the coming of the Canadian Pacific Railroad's Short Line in 1888 and the establishment of *la paroisse St. Antoine de Padoue* in 1892. French parishes helped provide the infrastructure the immigrants needed to make the transition from life in rural Québec to industrial cities in Maine.[11]

Much of Franco-American historiography has focused on efforts to promote cultural survival or *la survivance*. The leaders of the first generation of French-Canadian immigrants created a definite and specific code of ethnicity which they believed would ensure the survival of their culture. Their ideological rhetoric was *qui perd sa langue, perd sa foi—he who loses his language loses his faith. La survivance* became the organizing principle for life in Maine's *petits canadas*. Many French-Canadian immigrants who settled permanently in New England set out to adapt to their new surroundings. They integrated rapidly into American society. But many immigrants reacted warily to their new environment. Leaders who developed a theory, derived from nineteenth-century Québec *survivance* ideology, about the group's life and culture influenced a majority of those who resisted assimilation. This theory had its roots in the continuation of the struggle against the assimilation that began in Quebec in the aftermath of the British Conquest (1760).

> According to this view, Franco-Americans may have ignored the call of the land—that is, the agrarian life for which they were supposedly destined—and left their native country, but they would continue to exist and prosper as a people if they cherished and safeguarded the other elements of their French-Canadian heritage, namely their mother tongue, Catholic faith, and customs. To do this, it was important to remain attached to traditional ways, and it was absolutely essential to combat the godlessness, materialism, and promiscuity they believed existed all around them.[12]

Leaders assumed the promotion of *la survivance* in the developing Franco-American communities. With its emphasis on religion and language as integral to retaining French Catholic identity, *la survivance* provided critical structure and support for a generation adjusting to a new way of life.[13] In cities like Biddeford and Lewiston, French newspapers played a prominent role in reminding Franco-Americans of the need to resist assimilation. French parish priests were another essential element in the cause of retaining cultural norms for the French-speaking community.

The leaders of the immigrant generation valued cultural survival. They understood their primary role in the developing Franco-American communities to be guardians of their cultural heritage, specifically defined as their language and religion. Active promotion of their French-Canadian past and translating this past into a useable present in a new country and culture was their priority for ensuring their future.

Franco-American historiography's examination of *la survivance* neglects an analysis of whether the model functioned effectively for all Franco-Americans. Did people subscribe to the tenets of *survivance?* How did people incorporate the elements of the model into their lives? While Franco-American elites may have subscribed to the paradigm, did other groups within the community do the same? Scholarship to date on *la survivance* has focused primarily on the formal institutions within Franco communities. The role of the Catholic church and parochial school and by extension priests and religious women has been examined.[14] How people translated what they heard at church and school into the fabric of their daily lives remains unclear. What did *la survivance* mean to people? Did they have a conscious understanding of the concept? Did they organize their lives around its precepts? Was *la survivance* the only way or even a major way they understood their ethnicity?

For Franco-American women, *la survivance* did not provide a neat or tidy solution to life in a new country. Despite what the leaders of the immigrant generation may have thought, a hermetic Franco-American culture did not develop. Rather, permeable *cultures* rooted in generation, gender, and region, class and personal experience evolved. Historian Vicki Ruiz notes: "People navigate across cultural boundaries and consciously make decisions with regard to the production of culture." Franco-American women not only survived but they flourished because they made choices. They and their children picked, borrowed, retained, and abandoned as they created distinctive cultural forms.[15] The history of Franco-American women underscores historian Yves Frenette's insistence on "the need for a broader perspective on the shaping of Franco-American history."[16]

If we are to capture the experience of Franco women we need to look beyond the traditional foci of formal organizations like church and school. We need to expand our search for *survivance* to include informal organizations, like neighborhood networks, which often provided extensive mutual assistance. The usual feminist edifice of "separate spheres" does not apply in the lives of immigrant women. The "inextricable nature" of family life and wage work which lies at the heart of the histories of immigrant women explodes and exposes the false oppositions of the public/private dichotomy.[17] It is the texture of Franco women's lives that needs to be captured. How did they see themselves? How did they socialize their children? How did they participate in neighborhood life? How did they create their own sense of values within the home and in the neighborhood?[18]

Resiliency

The dews of heaven did not rise
Sweet strains did not fall
And I saw only the tired stream
Of men and women
Treading through snowy streets
To the factories.[19]

If you stand on Brown Street in Westbrook, Maine, and look west you will see a substantial brick building with numerous windows. The former Dana Warp textile mill sits quietly by the Presumpscot River. Turning from this same spot and looking east you will see looming the S. D. Warren paper mill. As is the case in so many Maine towns, the history of immigration and ethnicity is intimately connected with Maine's geography, specifically, its abundance of powerful rivers. The story of many immigrants is ultimately linked to the changes wrought by industrialization. For Franco-American women who journeyed to Maine, important aspects of their story began in Britain in the eighteenth century when the flying shuttle, the spinning jenny, the water frame, and the spinning mule made the production of cloth a mechanized process.

While women have always worked, in the eighteenth and into the early nineteenth century their labor was confined almost entirely to the domestic setting, where it was unpaid labor. Women's work in this larger family economy was crucial for family survival. With the rise of the cotton textile industry between 1820 and 1860 large numbers of young single women left their farm homes to work in the burgeoning mill towns.[20]

By the mid-1840s, as greater demands were made on mill operatives, U.S.-born employees began to abandon millwork. For a short period, Irish immigrants filled their places. Increasingly, throughout New England, mill owners looked north for a steady supply of unskilled workers. With the post-Civil War boom in textiles, factory managers began to draw on the abundant human resources of Québec. The relative proximity of New England and the availability of cheap, rapid transportation by rail contributed to a dramatic migration.[21] From 1865 to 1900 approximately 350,000 French-Canadians came to New England and settled permanently.[22]

In essence the French-Canadian migration was a regional exodus, largely of family units, by a traditionally transient populace. Of all the immigrant groups, only the French-Canadians and Mexicans crossed no ocean and completed their regional moves in a matter of one or two days. In the minds of the French-Canadian migrants, the border barely existed, and the proximity of the mother country had far-reaching effects on the evolution of the ethnic group.[23]

An agricultural crisis in Québec coupled with overpopulation in some regions left the rural population with few employment prospects. The completion of the Grand Trunk Railroad made the rapidly industrializing mill town of Maine and New England a logical destination.

With the mechanization of the production of cloth, an employee did not need to know English or to understand the entire series of processes and technical innovations figuring in the mechanical transformation of raw fibers. The only thing a new employee had to learn was a single movement, a single operation, and to repeat it without stopping. The *Québécois* emigrants found in Maine mills a simple occupation open to them. Relatives were often already at work and could help them find jobs, housing, and a ready social life for the few hours left after the long workday.[24] French-Canadian women were a significant portion of this labor force.

Work became a place where Franco women grappled with questions of identity and negotiated answers. In many ways they looked to their parents' experience—in particular their mothers'—for a measure of what they should do. Yet they also looked at the preceding generation's lives and made different choices. The picture that emerges of Franco women is more complex, shaded, and nuanced than what is often assumed. Work outside of the home did not necessarily bring with it economic independence or personal autonomy. For Franco-American working-class women, work life and family life were inextricably linked. As working daughters, these women contributed to a family economy that needed their wages but didn't often leave room for choice or freedom. Work was often an extension of family responsibility. And the physical demands of millwork, as well as its accompanying tedium and boredom, did not necessarily provide a personally fulfilling work experience.

Estelle Bouchard grew up in Lewiston and clearly remembered how the rhythms of millwork provided the cadence for life.

I was brought up in the Hill Block in Lewiston. You see, there were three major mills. There was the Bates Mill, the Hill Mill, and the Androscoggin Mill. And

Women millworkers, weave room, Bates Mill, Lewiston, Maine, c. 1900
Franco-American Collection, University of Southern Maine, Lewiston-Auburn College[25]

> then one street lower was the Continental Mill. And each of these mills built a block of apartment buildings directly in back of the mill so that the people they brought in could live in those apartment buildings. At 3:00 P.M. everybody would come out, and the whole of Canal Street was invaded with workers. We were playing in the yards there, and the people would come by with their lunch boxes. This was very much a part of what I grew up with, the millworkers going in at 2:30, the other shift coming out at 3:00. Then, later that night, we would hear them on summer evenings at 11:00 coming out. This was very much a part of my surroundings—my mother's stories about how it was to work in the mill...and how hard they would work.[26]

The working conditions inside the mill were far from pleasant. Besides the monotonous and tiring nature of the work, there was the ever-present cotton dust suspended in the air and the constant noise of the machines. Alice Blais described the wearing noise that accompanied the workers eight to ten hours a day.

> There was not a lot of socializing going on in the mill. We worked very hard, and you didn't leave [your work] a lot. There was a lot of noise in the mills. It was worse than the noise in the shoe shops. If someone wasn't used to it, he was nearly deaf when he left. When there were fifty to sixty machines in the same room, they all made the same noise. What a racket that made.[27]

Cecile Doyon, who worked in the mill from the time when she was a child, found the mill sounds particularly fatiguing. She recalled a strategy the operatives used to combat the relentless sound.

> If you wanted to talk to someone, you had to talk in his ear. It came to a point where there was a rhythm to it, and we'd start to sing to that rhythm when the work was going fine, but when the work was going badly, there was no singing.[28]

For a city dependent on one industry, there was no singing if the industry experienced problems. With the Great Depression came work slow-downs and layoffs. Franco-American families like Cecile Doyon's were faced with difficult choices. As often happened, it was the women who bore the brunt of the difficult compromises.

> We suffered some.... I can remember one time, right after the last boy in the family was born. I had just had him, and my husband wasn't working at all. I saw the second man (one of the bosses) in the mill go by. After the baby was born, I couldn't go back to work right away, so I said to my husband, "Go ask him [the boss] if he will give you a job." He hadn't worked for two weeks, and so he went. And I said, as he started to go, "If he doesn't have any work for you, ask him if he has any for me." The man didn't want to take my husband, and he said, "Tell your wife to come. Tell her to come Monday." He knew I had more experience than my husband. I'd been working in the mill since I was fourteen years old. My husband hadn't worked long in the mill, so the boss knew I could do the work better than he could. My husband didn't like it too much because he had to take care of the baby. The baby was eight weeks old. The man doing the hiring wanted

me to work the third shift. During the day, I took care of the kids and the baby, and at night I had to work. My husband helped me in the daytime because then he wasn't working. I tried to sleep in the day when he was in the house. I could sleep once in a while—two or three hours sometimes. Then I'd go to work, and when I came home, I had to make the bread.[29]

For French-Canadian families, both working wives and working children contributed to the income necessary for the family's survival. The image of the male breadwinner providing through his work for the economic sustenance of the family was far from the reality. Claudia Emond knew firsthand the rigors of a family income. She was the last of twelve children born to Bellesemere and Eugene Breton on a one-hundred-acre tract in Thetford Mines, Québec. The farm was a spacious one and Claudia remembered her childhood as "J'ai une belle enfance; jamais les troubles." She was a child without a care. She grew up on the farm with her parents, three sisters, and one brother. The seven other children were already married and gone. Some had children before Claudia was born.[30]

Claudia and her family moved between Biddeford, Maine, and Thetford Mines several times before returning to settle permanently in Biddeford in 1927. When she returned to Biddeford she was sixteen. She found a job at the York mills where she worked sixty-four hours a week as a weaver. Her weekly income was nine dollars. As a weaver, she was required to stand before the giant looms from six in the morning until 5:30 P.M. She received a thirty-minute break for lunch and two other ten-minute breaks. She quit her weaving job after one year and returned to Thetford Mines for a four-month respite. When she returned to Biddeford she married Amedée Emond. Claudia didn't return to millwork until after the births of her four children.

In 1935 she began working again, this time as a winder in the Bates Mill, which was formerly the York Mill. As a winder she took the thread and attached it to the machine, the first step in the textile-making process. Claudia learned her job during unpaid training sessions. She found the job "easy" but it still meant she worked forty hours each week on her feet, except for the half-hour supper break and two twenty-minute breaks.

For the most part, personal independence did not result from taking a job. Franco-American women worked primarily in an attempt to enhance the standard of living of their families. The jobs they were able to find were characterized by low pay, low skill, low security, and low mobility. Personal safety could not be guaranteed as

Grace Pedneault Curtis learned with her first job.

> I started to work when I was a senior in high school. Trying to work in the dime store which was a Woolworth's uptown to earn money for a graduation dress. But I didn't last there very long, and the manager was overly friendly to a very unsophisticated, young girl. And all I had to do was to go home and tell my mother, "I don't want to work there anymore." And she didn't say one other word. That's fine. So she must have heard of the man's reputation. So that was my first job. I was very uncomfortable. I was not too sophisticated, and we won't go into....[31]

Entering the world of paid labor meant encountering danger and learning compromise. It was not necessarily a satisfying experience. For many Franco-American women, work outside of the home was a necessity if the family was to be housed, clothed, and fed. And while, especially from the late-nineteenth to the middle of the twentieth century, most Franco women worked in mills and factories, a few women did create better possibilities for themselves.

Emma Tourangeau of Westbrook, Maine, did not expect that her life would be linked with that of the S. D. Warren Company. She had explicitly decided that she did not want to work at the mill. Given the stories her mother had told her of her years at the Dana Warp Mill, Emma knew that millwork was not what she wanted for herself. As the eldest in a family with seven younger siblings, there was never any question that she would go to work and contribute to the family economy. She was able to stay in school long enough to receive her high school diploma. After she graduated, her father took her to S.D. Warren where he worked. He wanted her to see the young women sorting paper. Emma remembered, "One glance convinced me that I just did not want to spend days doing that kind of work."[32]

Despite her father's insistent desire that Emma join him in working at the mill, Emma decided she wanted more education. She gave piano lessons, played in a band with her father and brother, and saved the one hundred dollars required for tuition at Miss Elinor Moody's Private Business School. She studied bookkeeping, shorthand, typewriting, and advanced English. Successfully completing this one-year program, Emma secured a job in the freight office of the Maine Central Railroad at Union Station in Portland. Her salary was $7.00 a week.

Yet Emma's resolute goal of avoiding employ at S. D. Warren, or any mill for that matter, was interrupted by the gendered exigencies of family life and responsibility.

In 1906 Emma's father was permanently disabled in an accident at the mill where he had worked since 1883. John E. Warren, agent of the Warren mill, approached Emma. He asked her to come to work at the mill. Mr. Warren's motives were not completely altruistic or beneficent. Shortly after Emma's father's accident, Mr. Warren visited the family and insisted that Mr. Tourangeau sign a paper stipulating that he would never sue the mill. Emma remembered this as a traumatic moment for her father. "My father cried. He said, 'Mr. Warren, you did enough for me and my family. Why did you ask me—why do you fear that I'm going to sue—I'd never sue the Company.'"[33]

Emma recalled that while the mill paid her father's doctor bills, he did not receive any salary or worker's compensation. Instead, he received a promise from Mr. Warren: "Well, he [John E. Warren] said, 'I'll tell you, Mr. Tourangeau, I'll promise you that as long as there is a Tourangeau, they'll get a job at S. D. Warren Mills.'"[34] Emma was the first Tourangeau to benefit from this promise—though at the time she remained unconvinced that it was a positive move. She recalled her move to S. D. Warren and all the ambivalence and apprehension that surrounded the decision.

> They sent for me, you know, to go down and see him [John Warren]. So I had to go on a Saturday when I wasn't working. I told Mr. Warren, "I don't want to go down—to come down here to work. I like where I am." "Yes, you're paying carfare, and you have to wear better clothes, and you have to bring your lunch. Why not come in here, and you can go home to lunch." And I said, "No. I don't want to come."[35]

Emma found other considerations besides the ability to go home for lunch more critical. Central to these was the pride she felt at having carved out for herself a professional identity that liked having to wear "better clothes." Emma respected her current boss and "I liked to go downtown at noon, walk to the stores. I used to love to go to the library to get some books."[36] Mr. Warren continued to insist. He wanted Emma to leave her job immediately and come to the mill. Perhaps he felt some guilt at the accident; perhaps he really thought a job at the mill was a better opportunity for Emma. Yet Emma remained cautious and concerned. She told Warren: "I'd have to give them two weeks notice. I can't leave them this way, because I might want to come back here."[37] But to her great-grandniece, seventy-six years after this difficult period in her life, Emma admitted the more complicated nature of her anxieties, a poignant and telling acknowledgement of the imbalance of power between a prominent businessman and a young ethnic woman with a primary commitment to the well-being of her family.

> I made all kinds of excuses. I didn't want to go down. I was scared of the Warren people. To me they were just like the King. You know? My father worked there, and my father had a good position. We had a good home. I was afraid the whole thing would crumble up if I went down to work. I said, "What if I can't do the job and they discharged me?" I had all kinds of bad dreams about the job.[38]

Emma tried to allay her uneasiness by getting Mr. Warren to "...make it all right with Mr. Fletcher that if I don't like the job [at S. D. Warren] that I could come back." Through a combination of her sheer doggedness and tenacious determination to maintain some control over her future while meeting her family obligations, Emma convinced Mr. Warren to agree to her terms. She worked a two-week notice at her job with the Maine Central Railroad and then went to work at S. D. Warren. Her tenure at the Warren mill almost ended before it even began. On her first day of work Emma reported to a Mr. Caldwell, the office manager. When Emma inquired about Mr. Warren on her first day on the job, Mr. Caldwell was quick to assert his authority. He answered her inquiry by saying: "Well, Missy, you won't have nothing more to do with Mr. Warren. He's the agent. I'm the one that runs the office. I'm going to put you to work."[39] Mr. Caldwell then assigned Emma to her new job on the switchboard.

> And, so believe me—you wouldn't believe this—he took me to this little room. There was a high chair. It was a switchboard. A switchboard. I said, "Well, I didn't come here to be a switch operator—to be a telephone operator. I never saw a switchboard before," I said. And there was a sign there that said telephone and the number and all that. "Yes, you see, but you're going to learn. We're going to have someone teach you." I said, "I don't want to have anybody teach me. I don't want to be a switchboard operator. I didn't come here to be a switch-telephone operator." So he said, "You are certainly one person that knows what you want." "I don't want to be a switch operator." I said, "I'll go right back to Portland where I belong. I'm a secretary," I said. "I want to do what I like to do...." Well, he said, "All right. Get out."

So what was I going to do when a man tells me the first day of work to get out? I went in and sat in Mr. Warren's office, and so I waited about—a long time. Finally, he came in. Well, he says, "Hello, Emma. Well, what can I do for you?" "I came in to tell you that I'm going back to Portland. Mr. Caldwell put me on the switchboard and I don't want to be a switch operator. Haven't you got any other job for me?" He said, "I didn't tell him to put you on the switchboard." I said, "What do you want me to do? I came here to be—you know what I came here to do." So then he called in Mr. Barrow. He was the Assistant Superintendent of the mill. So I met him, and he took me in his office—private office, and, "Well, let's have our first letter, Emma." And he gave me the first letter, and "Come with me," and there was a desk with the typewriter. I was there for forty-six years. I came home, when I retired, and I brought home with me that desk and my chair.[40]

Maybe Mr. Caldwell was just establishing his authority as the boss and meant Emma no harm. With the chasm of time gone by, it is difficult to attribute motives and intentions. Yet a true fact is that Emma was the first French person or Catholic to work in the front office at S. D. Warren. Her father had been the first French man hired at the mill. Emma's father encouraged her to be a paper sorter because he was sure she would never get hired to work in the front office.[41] Emma was willing to risk losing her job in standing up to Mr. Caldwell. It isn't clear from her interview with her great-grandniece or her memoir what compelled Emma to take this risk. Did she know Mr. Warren would back her up? Did Emma think Warren would fear her father would file a lawsuit if Emma were fired? Perhaps Emma's business school training had instilled a professional sense of her abilities allowing her to stand her ground. Whatever the reason or probably reasons, Emma was able to negotiate a successful outcome for herself.

For the women who worked unskilled jobs at the Westbrook mills, life was quite different. Most Franco-American women in Westbrook found work at the textile mill. While they didn't face the outright discrimination that marked Emma's encounter with Mr. Caldwell, in contrast, the owner of the textile mill made clear his position by saying that he hoped when he got to heaven there would be only Republicans and Congregationalists.[42]

Franco-American women in Maine were not reluctant to join the paid labor force if it meant their families would be fed and younger siblings could stay in school. Paid labor did not provide exciting careers. Work was tedious and at times physically dangerous. And if a job brought a measure of prestige, as it did for Emma Tourangeau, she worked long hours to sustain an intangible reward. Franco women coped with the unpleasantness of their work lives by focusing on their sense of pride and accomplishment in enabling their families to survive. Work was a means to an end rather than an end in itself. Franco-American women didn't ignore the reality of low wages or discrimination. They focused instead on the dignity they found in surviving and shaping their lives to the best of their ability.

Community

The din of those mill machines was stilled,
I heard the sweetest strains of labor
And I saw how a world is crafted
By two steadfast hands.[43]

Franco-American women in Maine were community builders. Whether at work in the mills, hanging laundry in their backyards or tenement porches, or attending church functions, they were keenly attuned to developing bonds that would sustain themselves and their families through the often uncertain flow of everyday life. It is usually to institution-building rather then community-building that historians give their greatest attention. Institutions are more visible. Community can be intangible, vague, and difficult to pinpoint. For the most part historians do not like vague. In their effort to establish themselves as responsible professionals with important contributions to make, historians eschew the nebulous. In his novel, *Invisible Man*, Ralph Ellison had his protagonist muse about the nature of history.

> All things, it is said, are duly recorded—all things of importance, that is. But not quite, for actually it is only the known, the seen, the heard and only those events that the recorder regards as important that are put down. What did they ever think of us transitory ones?...birds of passage who were too obscure for learned classification, too silent for the most sensitive recorders of sound; of natures too ambiguous for the most ambiguous words, and too distant from the centers of historical decision to sign or even to applaud the signers of historical documents? We who write no novels, histories or other books. What about us....[44]

Historians, particularly historians of women, are paying more attention to the ambiguous words of women far distant from "historical" decision. In an effort to capture the experiences of people who leave behind little documentation of their efforts, historians are examining issues and questions that previously have been deemed of little importance.

In an effort to understand the culture and community Franco-American women created and sustained, one place to start is to look at their neighborhood life. Especially for working-class Franco women who usually had little time to join organizations, neighborhood life provided a pivotal connection.

Historians of immigrant communities have recognized the importance of the ethnic neighborhood. John Bodnar in his important synthesis of immigrant history noted: "Just by going about his mundane duties in a neighborhood a New York City Jew could feel 'unthreatened.' Neighborhoods such as Flatbush, the East Bronx, and Brownsville, acquired a 'persona' all their own."[45] More recently historians of immigrant women have come to recognize another important aspect of neighborhood life. Ardis Cameron in her study of the working women who went on strike in Lawrence, Massachusetts, in 1882 and again in 1912 found that a common neighborhood life prepared these women to organize on their own behalf. Sharing recipes, childcare, shopping strategies, and recreation, the immigrant women of Lawrence created links with one another across ethnic lines. Cameron argued "such links, formed as women sought to provide for their families and hold life together, would provide the foundation for community solidarity during the strike of 1912."[46]

Cameron's analysis strikes at a central and important point. Most of the emphasis on ethnic neighborhoods in Franco-American historiography has been to determine how the "Little Canadas" protected and sustained ethnic identity.[47] Cameron pushes us to acknowledge that neighborhood connections had a gendered dimension in addition to an ethnic component. Uncovering the neighborhood networks that women created and the female traditions of reciprocity and association that women utilized in their day-to-day lives can break open the myriad and prolific ways that Franco women created community and adapted it to their own needs. Cameron found in Lawrence a "latticework of relationships" that enabled women to train and protect children, care for the sick, feed the hungry, "keep" house, and provide for families and neighbors.[48] Franco-American women in Westbrook, Lewiston, Biddeford, Dexter, Fort Kent, and all the Little Canadas in between used their ethnic enclaves to improve life for themselves, their families, their neighbors, and the larger community.

Looking out for one another, helping one another, and just enjoying each other's company—elements of ethnic neighborhood life long overlooked by historians—created a sense of power and autonomy lacking in other areas of their lives. Denied choice or freedom in their work lives, the public space of the neighborhood found women creating relationships that ultimately empowered them to take active roles in neighborhood life. Whether functioning as midwife for her neighbors, political consultant for aspiring candidates seeking the French vote, or simply as a member of a neighborhood club, Franco women remembered a history often overlooked because it didn't involve permanent institution building. The pulse of life in the Little Canadas was monitored closely by Franco women. Paying attention to its daily beat enriched and expanded their lives.

Emma Tourangeau remembered Sundays best: "My father and my mother entertained people every single Sunday. Every single Sunday we had people for dinner at our house."[49] Social gatherings provided the backbone of neighborhood life and family gatherings were its centerpiece. These gatherings were an occasion to have fun together but they also cemented relationships that were essential to the family's well-being. *Family* was understood broadly, so family gatherings included friends, neighbors, and co-workers as well as blood relations.

Emma remembered in careful detail the elements of these Sunday events, which always included a meal.

> I loved to think of Sundays. My mother with her white apron on, cold roast pork, a lovely dinner. And then we would wash the dishes. We were four girls, you know, and we got along so well. And, then, people used to come. My mother used to make molasses candies. She used to make white candy. Popcorn balls in the wintertime. My father would have men in to play cards, and the women used to get together and talk.[50]

Emma recalled that this social life included both family and friends. If you didn't have much family, friends became even more important and visiting became a vital tradition.

> We didn't have much family. My mother only had a sister. Her brothers had gone. My father didn't have...relatives. Had an old uncle. My old uncle used to come. But I used to bring my friends, and I would—it was a kind of tradition among

the French people. If you went calling on Sunday afternoon, they asked you to stay for supper. So I was very fussy where I used to go Sunday afternoons. I'd always go someplace that would be better than I was going to have at home. I'd pick out different houses, you know, to go to.[51]

Later in her life, Emma took all these memories of Sunday gatherings, with their special foods and meals and created a cookbook. With an emphasis on old French-Canadian recipes, *Aunt Emma's Island Cookbook* featured all the food Emma remembered best and associated with the web of relationships that sustained her and her family. Collecting and saving the recipes seemed to be Emma's way of maintaining a connection with this central experience in her own history. Emma's recipes were one of her most treasured inheritances. She considered them "some sort of heirloom, like the old 'spinning wheel,' and the mother's 'wedding ring.'"[52]

Emma found a permanent way to mark the significance of food and social gatherings in her life, but for many other Franco-American women visiting also provided the cornerstone of their recreation. Dottie Hawkes remembered that visiting and playing cards often went hand-in-hand.

Back then I remember when we were young, my mother used to play cards a lot. They would go to the Old Westbrook Tavern and play cards; and the Sliscos lived down below us, and she used to like to play. We've always played cards and we still play cards. I remember Mother used to have Aunt Clara—she wasn't our aunt, but, you know, people you know so well—she used to—they'd come upstairs, and my mother would go downstairs, and they'd play cards. My mother and father and Clara and Carl with the Guitards or, you know.[53]

Josephine DeRoche LaBrecque remembered the sustaining importance of getting together.

That's all there was in those days. You know? There was no radio, no TV, dirt roads, so they got together. And what got me is when they would get together, everyone would bring their kids, and they were small babies. They'd lay them on the bed, you know. They'd have a ball—they'd have a dance in the house. It was really fun. You couldn't see them do that today.[54]

Like Dottie Hawkes's memory of her parents, Josephine remembered how important friends were to her mother. Josephine's mother belonged to a group of women who gathered weekly to visit. As Josephine put it, "They had something like a club."[55] Josephine's mother didn't drive, so Josephine would drive her to the gathering. Playing cards, talking, and just enjoying each other's company—this weekly social event brought women together and into each other's lives. Josephine related that spirits ran high for these women when they got together. "They went to this one house, and there was a circular—it was an apartment house. There was a circular stairway. I'll never forget it. They laughed. Coming down they—somebody dared my mother to ride the rail. She did!"[56]

Josephine continued the tradition of her mother's social group. She joined a group in the late 1930s that met weekly to socialize and to knit together. The club, which doesn't have a name, started before she was married and is still in existence. For most of that time Josephine, like her mother, attended every week. "The only reason I don't belong to it now is because I don't drive at night."[57]

Enjoying each other's company could also help when more serious matters needed attention. A prominent memory for both Dottie Hawkes and Josephine LaBrecque, who have been friends since they were young girls, was looking for work together. When they were in their early twenties and trying to get hired at S. D. Warren Paper Mill, they would go to the mill together every morning. Since this was in the latter years of the Great Depression, work was scarce and the young women became accustomed to hearing, "I'm sorry, ladies, the situation is just the same,"[58] which meant there was no work. While not getting any work was a worry, the young women didn't waste an opportunity to enjoy each other's company. As Dottie told it: "We always had our tennis rackets, and we'd go over and play tennis."[59]

As Josephine LaBrecque and Dottie Hawkes's actions testify, working-class women often carved out of daily life a sphere of pleasure that belied the harsh reality of looking for work. Their friendship and playing tennis when work was unavailable helped sustain them through the lean years of the depression and the daily cycle of seeking employment. Historian Kathy Peiss was among the first to identity the critical nature of leisure. She articulated what Josephine and Dottie lived: "Leisure activities may affirm the cultural patterns embedded in other institutions, but they may also offer an arena for the articulation of different values and behaviors."[60] Life in Westbrook's Little Canada offered Franco women different possibilities for creating values and behaviors that would afford a sustaining way of life. Their leisure time offered them the opportunity to affirm the value of relationships and spending time together. As Peiss also noted, women's time differed from men's. Women's leisure was often intertwined with the rhythms of household labor and the relations of kinship.[61] For Franco women, Sunday dinners, visiting, playing cards, and even playing tennis cleared a space and created a culture that enabled them to survive and even find some delight in the shadow of the mills.

Franco-American women also found ways to express more publicly the culture and community they were creating. Camille Lessard-Bissonette captured the experience of millwork in her novel *Canuck,* published in 1935. Lessard-Bissonette was born in Sainte-Julie-de-Mégantic in the Province of Quebec. She graduated from high school at sixteen and taught in a country school for the next three years. In 1904 she migrated to Lewiston with her family and went to work in the textile mills. During the last two years of her four years of millwork she wrote for the local French language newspaper, *Le Messager*. In 1908 she became a member of the paper's editorial staff and established the women's page. In 1912, when she moved with her family to Alberta, Canada, she continued to send chronicles and travel notes to the newspaper for publication as a regular column. She would write articles for *Le Messager* for forty years.

Lessard-Bissonette's novel *Canuck* foreshadowed the second wave of "White feminism" that would emerge in the mid-twentieth century by situating its main character, Victoria Labranche, as a young Franco millworker who embodies a defiant attitude toward life. She refuses to be cowed by a patriarchal father, she refuses a return to Canada with her parents, and she would not be tied to the home as the ideology of the Roman Catholic church demanded as the proper location for women in the first half of this century. In many ways Lessard-Bissonette created a representation of a traditional Franco-American woman, yet with significant details she was also pointing to a conception of a female Franco identity that included room for rebelliousness and self-pride. With *Canuck* Lessard-Bissonette began to imagine a feminist era that would include Franco women.

In her own life Camille Lessard-Bissonette found inspiration for the rebelliousness she included in her fiction. During the worst of the Great Depression she was hired as a colonization agent for the Louisville and Nashville Railroad Company of Louisville, Kentucky. The company wanted to establish a French colony along its line in northwest Florida. Lessard-Bissonette's job was to study the conditions of land near Pensacola, Florida. She had to become conversant about the soil conditions, weather, and the kind of seedings that would flourish in that climate. The trains became her home for the next decade. She traveled anyplace in this country where there were French-speaking people, trying to interest them in relocating. She read all of the French language newspapers. With her railroad pass she was able to visit family in California and Alberta and return to Lewiston. After her retirement she returned to California and lived in Long Beach in order to be close to the ocean. She frequently commented that: "I was a very lucky French-Canadian woman!"[62]

As much as luck, hard work provided the opportunities that Lessard-Bissonette enjoyed. For Franco-American women of all class backgrounds, creating and sustaining their culture and community required persistent efforts. Few were more zealous or committed to furthering the acceptance and appreciation of Franco-American contributions to the State of Maine than journalist, poet, and dramatic arts supporter, Charlotte Michaud. Born in 1898 in Lewiston, she was the daughter of Joseph Michaud and Amanda Simard Michaud. She attended Sts. Peter and Paul Parochial School and graduated from Lewiston High School in 1916. From early childhood she was tutored in music and dance and taught these arts in the early 1920s when the family lived at Old Orchard Beach. She taught weekly dance classes at Old Orchard Beach and Sanford, Maine, and she also served as the church organist at St. Margaret's-by-the-Sea Catholic Church at Old Orchard Beach.

In the mid-1920s the family returned to Lewiston. Michaud was mentored by L. N. Gendreau, a journalist with the French language newspaper in Lewiston, *Le Messager.* After Mr. Gendreau's death Charlotte succeeded him at *Le Messager,* where she contributed to the newspaper for the next twenty-five years. Charlotte Michaud had the added distinction of being the first Franco-American woman to be employed by the *Lewiston Evening Journal.* She was a reporter for the *Journal* for seventeen years. She specialized in reporting the news of the Franco-American community, but she also wrote a column on "The Dance" for several years and was a frequent contributor to the weekly magazine published by the newspaper. In the early 1940s Michaud became the Lewiston-Auburn correspondent for the Gannett newspapers in Portland. She remained with the Gannett Company until her retirement in late 1963.

Through her journalism, commitment to cultural activities and organizations, and public service on the Lewiston Historical Commission, Michaud contributed to the continuation and evolution of a Franco-American sensibility. Long before the ethnic pride revivals of the 1960s, Michaud wrote article after article tracing the presence and contributions of French Canadians and Franco-Americans to life in

Lewiston. In 1939, for the *Lewiston Journal's Illustrated Magazine,* Michaud wrote a multi-part series on the Catholic order of religious women, the Sisters of Charity, or the Gray Nuns, as they were commonly called. A French-Canadian order, the Sisters of Charity were instrumental in bringing quality medical care to Lewiston in the late decades of the nineteenth century.[63] Michaud never lost an opportunity to define as "news" important changes in Lewiston's Franco-American community. She wrote with perception and insightful analysis about the changing dynamics between Lewiston's Franco and Anglo communities in an article noting the increasing number of Franco-Americans attending Bates College, a private liberal-arts college located in Lewiston.[64]

Charlotte Michaud's long career in journalism allowed her the opportunity to watch perceptions change. She remembered from her early days at the Lewiston newspaper that a Franco-American woman's picture was never used on the society page until she made a submission. After that it became more common. Charlotte, by the very nature of her efforts, often was the bridge between Lewiston's Franco community and the "Yankees." She summed up her efforts saying: "For me, my great satisfaction was that I made 'my people' better known to the community as a whole. I quote 'my people' because so often it got so my news editors would say: 'Would your people be interested in this?'"[65]

Sharing Charlotte Michaud's commitment to "her people" and their complex past, the current generation of Franco-Americans has Madeleine Giguère to thank for saving, creating, and cataloguing the elements of a useable past. Also a Lewiston native, Giguère attended local schools and then graduated from the College of New Rochelle, Fordham University, and Columbia University. A sociologist by training, Giguère taught at St. Joseph's College, St. John's University, Boston College, and the University of Southern Maine (USM), where she retired as Professor Emerita of Sociology. She was the first to offer courses in Franco-American studies at USM and among her numerous publications, most are related to the sociology of Franco-American identity and demographics.

Madeleine Giguère was committed to the idea that: "As part of knowing who we are, we need to know our heritage, we need to be able to explore it, and in order to do this, we need to have a source of information."[66] To that end, Giguère—after her retirement from teaching at USM in 1990—became the volunteer director of the Franco-American Heritage Center (now called the Franco-American Collection) at USM's Lewiston-Auburn College. She began by cataloguing books but her responsi-

Madeleine Giguère (center), cutting the ribbon at the dedication of the expanded Franco-American Collection and the Reading Room named in her honor. University of Southern Maine, Lewiston-Auburn College, 7 December 2001. Congressman John Baldacci (back left), USM President Richard Pattenaude (right), USM/L-A Dean Betty Robinson (left foreground).
Franco-American Collection, University of Southern Maine, Lewiston-Auburn College[68]

bilities quickly grew: "I didn't know it would be such a long job," she observed with a laugh, six years later."[67] Giguère oversaw a collection that included 1,600 books, 1,700 photos, and countless newspaper articles—all pertaining to Franco-American culture. Admired as the "godmother of Franco-American history," Madeleine Giguère recognized that a viable Franco-American future depended on preserving the past. Like Charlotte Michaud, Madeleine Giguère talked about the importance of ethnic identity and the culture-building efforts of Franco-American women, well before multiculturalism or diversity became a common watchword.

Survival, resiliency, community—all three elements were necessary for the French-Canadian women who made the trek to Maine. They arrived with simple goals: A better life for themselves and their families. From mother to daughter came the will to survive, the resilient desire to prevail, and the determined effort to form communities that would last. Maine is a richer, deeper, and better place for their efforts.

1 Milton.
2 Diner. Gabaccia, *From Sicily to Elizabeth Street.* Yans-McLaughlin. Evelyn Nakano Glenn. Susan Glenn. Weinberg, *The World of Our Mothers.* Yu and Phillips. Blea. Morawska.
3 Gabaccia, *From the Other* Side, xi–xii.
4 Susann Pelletier, "Immigrant Dream." See pp, 127–28 for the full poem.
5 Blouin, p. 9.
6 Tourangeau, unpublished manuscript, p. 2.
7 Tourangeau, unpublished manuscript, p. 2.
8 Tourangeau, unpublished manuscript, p. 2.
9 Richard, "Out of 'Little Canada,'" p. 17.
10 Richard, "Out of 'Little Canada,'" p. 18.
11 Forgue.
12 Brault, *The French-Canadian Heritage in New England*, pp. 65–66.
13 Felix Albert.
14 Quintal, *Les Franco-Americains et Leurs Institutions Scolaires*; *Religion Catholique et Appartenance Franco-Americaine, Franco-Americans and Religion.*
15 Ruiz, p. xvi.
16 Frenette, pp. 198–229.
17 Ruiz, p. xvi.
18 Weinberg, "The Treatment of Women in Immigration History, pp. 25–69.
19 Pelletier, "Immigrant Dream." See pp, 127–28 for the full poem.
20 Dublin, *Women at Work*, p. 1; *Farm to Factory*; *Transforming Women's Work.*
21 Brault, *The French-Canadian Heritage in New England*, p. 54.
22 Vicero, *Immigration of French Canadians to New England, 1840–1900*, p. 195. For a more detailed account of the migration of French Canadians see Roby, *Les Franco-Américains de la Nouvelle-Angleterre,* and Weil, *Les Franco-Américains, 1860–1980.*
23 Frenette, "Understanding the French Canadians of Lewiston, 1860–1900," p. 201.
24 Anctil, "The Franco-Americans of New England," pp. 46–47.
25 Franco-American Collection: 19-I, Lewiston Mills, Box 4, Photos, File of Mill Exhibit, 2003. Donated by the Lewiston Historical Commission.
26 Searles and others, p. 19.
27 Searles and others, p. 22.
28 Searles and others, p. 25.
29 Searles and others, p. 26.
30 Anne Lucey.
31 Curtis, Grace Pedneault.
32 Tourangeau, unpublished manuscript, p. 7.
33 Tourangeau, interview.
34 Tourangeau, interview.
35 Tourangeau, interview.
36 Tourangeau, interview.
37 Tourangeau, interview.
38 Tourangeau, interview.
39 Tourangeau, interview.
40 Tourangeau, interview.

41 Tourangeau, interview.
42 Dana.
43 Pelletier, "Immigrant Dream."
44 Ellison, *Invisible Man*, p. 332.
45 Bodnar, p. 179.
46 Cameron, *Radicals of the Worst Sort*, p. 111.
47 Quintal, *The Little Canadas of New England.*
48 Cameron, *Radicals of the Worst Sort*, p. 110.
49 Tourangeau, interview.
50 Tourangeau, interview.
51 Tourangeau, interview.
52 Tourangeau, *Aunt Emma's Island Cookbook*, p. 85.
53 Hawkes.
54 LaBrecque, Interview, 30 October 1993.
55 LaBrecque, Interview, 30 October 1993.
56 LaBrecque, Interview, 30 October 1993.
57 LaBrecque, Interview, 30 October 1993.
58 Josephine DeRoche LaBrecque, interview with author, August 16, 1993.
59 Hawkes.
60 Peiss, p. 4.
61 Peiss, p. 5.
62 Schideler, pp. 29–43. Lapointe.
63 Charlotte Michaud, "Mother d'Youville."
64 Charlotte Michaud, "Increasing Number of Franco-Americans Interested in Bates."
65 Charlotte Michaud, unpublished correspondence with JoAnne Lapointe.
66 Giguère, "Remarks on the Occasion of the Formal Opening of the Franco-American Reading Room."
67 Yetter.
68 Franco-American Collection: File for Biography, Madeleine Giguère.

A LA MÉMOIRE DE NOS ANCÊTRES

(In Memory of Our Ancestors)

Mercedes Gastonguay
Lewiston, Maine

This oil painting is a tribute to our Franco-American ancestors who labored to make the Lewiston-Auburn area what it is today. Depicted on this 46" x 54" (117 cm by 137 cm) canvas are scenes of their arrival from Canada and their life in Lewiston and Auburn. The scene is set on an old parchment map with the Androscoggin River surging throughout the painting.

In the upper-left corner of the antique map we see a *Québécois* village and farmland, indicating the origin of their journey to the United States. A sugar shack rests on a maple leaf to show one important aspect of their heritage. From their homeland, the Canadian National Railroad meanders to the Auburn Trestle, where it culminates in a scene of immigrants arriving at the Grand Trunk Railway Station.

Work was the main focus of life for these immigrants and their reason for coming here; therefore, it is highlighted in the largest antique photo. The Androscoggin River runs through the scenes of toiling shoe shop workers and textile employees, dividing the industries unique to each of the Twin Cities. To the left of the river, in Auburn, appear five shops, namely, Foss-Packard, Lunn & Sweet, Wise & Cooper, Fitz Brothers, and Cushman. In Lewiston, east of the Androscoggin, looms a colorful composite of five buildings that includes the Libby, Continental, Androscoggin, Bates, and Hill textile mills.

Sunlight focuses on a panoramic view of *Le Petit Canada*, where traditional family life is portrayed in a typical apartment. In this scene the mother prepares dinner on a woodstove while the children play on the bare wood floor. Typical for women of this culture, she remains at home to care for her children, prepare meals, and maintain the household. A crucifix and a holy picture are hanging on the kitchen wall. These religious symbols were present in most homes, where it was common practice to kneel around the table in family prayer.

The Dominican Block, founded in 1881, was the first school serving Canadian children. This building also offered a social center and a temporary place of worship for the Franco population. Saints Peter and Paul and St. Mary's Roman Catholic

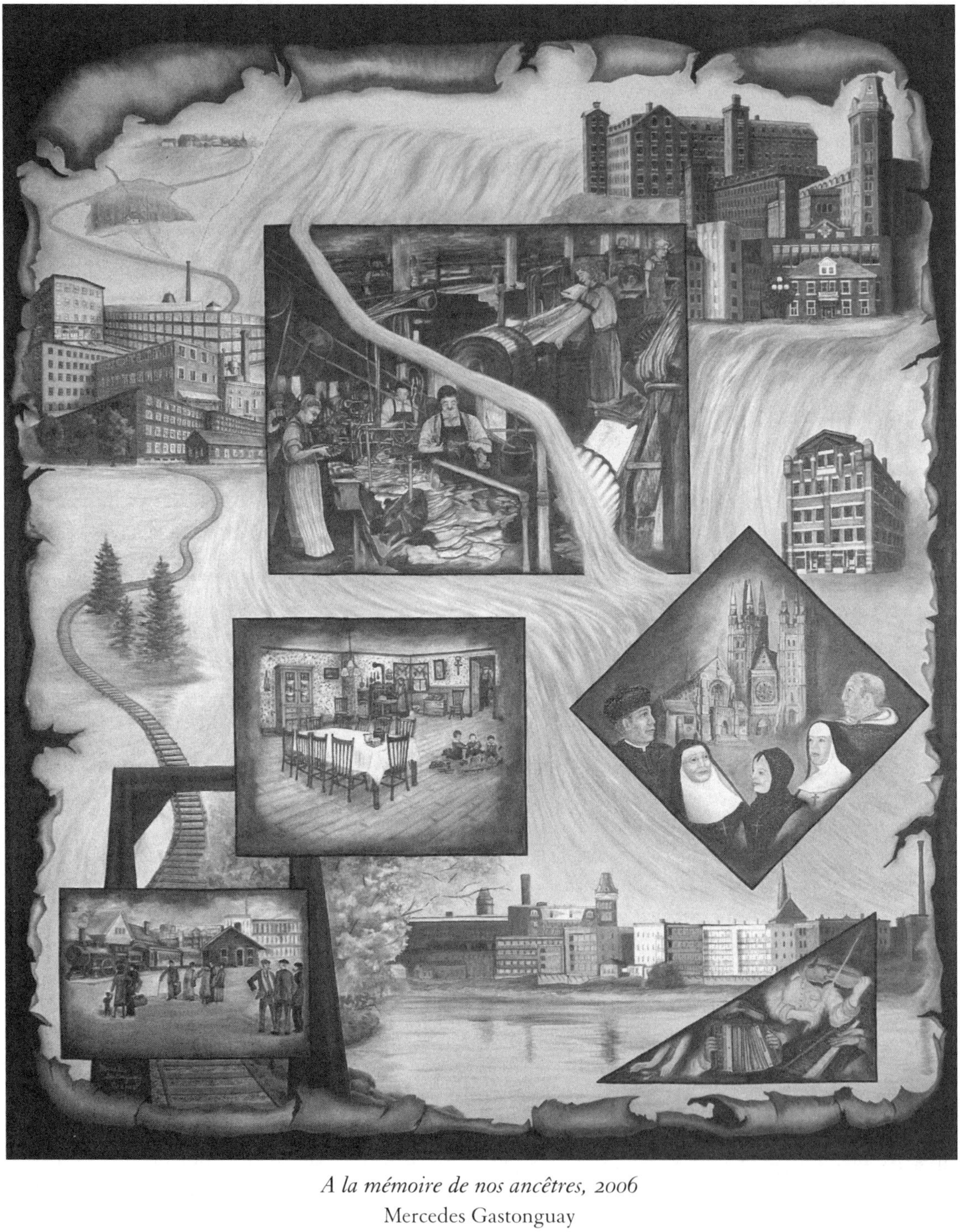

A la mémoire de nos ancêtres, 2006
Mercedes Gastonguay

churches eventually became the centers of worship for the Franco-Americans. Gazing at the churches are representatives of the religious men and women who came to serve the Franco-American faithful: a secular priest, an Ursuline sister, a Sister of Charity, a Dominican sister, and a Dominican priest.

There was little time for recreation because of the long and grueling hours spent at work. Although slight of time, it included the joyful family gatherings filled with song and music. Popular instruments at the time included the accordion, the harmonica, the violin, the piano, and the spoons. Many of the musicians were self-taught and shared their talent with future generations.

A la mémoire de nos ancêtres holds a special place in the heart of the artist, Mercedes Gastonguay. Creating this painting allowed her to travel back to Oxford Street, where her mother's family began their new life in the United States. Let us celebrate our ancestors today by remembering their courage, devotion, struggles, joys, and perseverance.[1]

1 Sources for *A la mémoire de nos ancêtres* include the University of Southern Maine's Franco-American Collection at Lewiston-Auburn College, Charlotte Michaud and Adelard Janelle's *Historic Lewiston: Franco-American Origins*, and Robert Rumily's *Histoire des Franco-Américains*.

THE FRENCH CATHOLICS IN MAINE

Father Clement Thibodeau
Caribou, Maine

I once got "into trouble" with Bishop Amedée Proulx, the late auxiliary bishop of Portland, for some remarks made about the differences between the French-speaking people of Aroostook County and those of the mill towns of central and southern Maine. The bishop and I were ordained to the priesthood in the same ceremony and were considered classmates, although we had not studied in the same seminary. The bishop was born and brought up in Sanford by French-Canadian immigrant parents. I was born and brought up in Caribou in a farm family where the land had been in the family for four generations. Interviewed by the writer of a small book on the French-Americans in Maine, *Quiet Presence* by Dyke Hendrickson of the Portland newspapers, I had said that the French in northern Maine did not consider themselves immigrants, having been there before Canada ever existed as a political entity. Acadians from the St. John Valley seemed to have more of a sense of *roots* and security. On the other hand, the French in the mill towns often talked about "going back home" to Canada, as if they did not have any ownership of the place here. The bishop thought I had a sense of superiority and looked down on the people from southern Maine, and he said so![1]

Franco-American Catholics have been more numerous in the mid- and southern sections of Maine than in the St. John River Valley in northern Maine.[2] The urban communities of Waterville, Augusta, Lewiston, Brunswick, Rumford, Westbrook, Biddeford, and Sanford received, albeit with some misgivings at times, substantial waves of immigrants from the Province of Quebec (and Prince Edward Island in the case of Rumford) as human-power for the industrial revolution in the textile, paper-manufacturing, and shoe-making industries of those cities and towns. After the turn of the century, a veritable flood-tide of Canadian immigrants came to augment the French-speaking working class of those cities. The numbers of new arrivals diminished during the Great Depression of the late 1920s and the decade of the 1930s. During and after World War II, relatively small numbers immigrated to Maine from the Province of Quebec.

Laymen and women, led by their priests, built mighty and influential church

St. Bruno's Roman Catholic Church in Van Buren:
The oldest French-Canadian and Acadian parish in the State of Maine, 1838.
St. Bruno's Church, Van Buren, Maine

institutions. Spacious and well-appointed parish churches were constructed, along with elegant rectories to house the clergy in the comfort to which the people thought these men had a right by reason of their rank in the community. Out of the meager wages of working men and women, money was collected, and funds were raised for the building and operation of parochial schools, the chief function of which was to assure that Franco-American children would not only be taught the rudiments of the Catholic faith, but that the French language would be preserved as the guarantor of that same faith.

The slogan "*Perdre sa langue c'est perdre sa foi*" (Loss of the language leads to the loss of the faith) echoed from the pulpits of those French churches time and time again. So closely identified were the Catholic faith and the French language that the same evangelical fervor served to promote both. The "Melting Pot" ideal of the broader U.S. culture was firmly and even fiercely rejected by church leaders because they understood any kind of meltdown to result in just one outcome: a Protestant America. Franco-American Catholics, like other ethnic minorities in the United States, resisted assimilation for fear of losing their religious identity.

Of the 139 Roman Catholic parishes and 55 missions existing in the Diocese of Portland in 1997, 61 parishes and 14 missions were established to serve predominantly French-speaking Catholics. That same year, there were 123 priests in Maine of French parentage, out of a total of 265 priests. Sisters and brothers with French family names in religious communities far outnumber those from other origins.

The oldest parish in the state of Maine established for a predominantly French-speaking population is St. Bruno in Van Buren (1838). The second oldest is Ste. Luce in Upper Frenchville (1843).[3] After the Civil War, French Canadians came to the textile towns of central and southern Maine in great numbers. One year alone (1870) saw three new parishes for French Catholics: Saints Peter and Paul in Lewiston, St. Joseph in Biddeford, and St. Louis in Fort Kent. Lay men and women have entered the professions and risen to positions of leadership in business and industry. Higher education and the state government have many French Catholics in positions of responsibility.

In 1904 the Marist Fathers in Van Buren obtained a charter from the State of Maine for a degree-granting college for men, which they established in Van Buren—across the street from the parish of St. Bruno. St. Mary's College continued to function until 1926, when the Marist Fathers reduced their mission to that of teaching only in the Boy's High School, a public school for boys in the town of Van Buren. St. Mary's College had some distinguished alumni, lay and clergy, some of whom were not natives of the Valley, notably Monsignor George Johnson, vicar general of the Diocese of Portland under five bishops, and Monsignor Philip Desjardins, late pastor of St. Hyacinth in Westbrook and trusted advisor to Bishop McCarthy and Bishop Feeney.

Not all French people in Maine are Catholics today. A small number of Huguenots settled in Maine and became influential in business and in the law. The late federal Judge Gignoux of Portland came from a French Protestant family. The DeMonts of Portland are descendants of one of the earliest founders of Acadia (Nova Scotia), a French territory that once claimed sovereignty over lands and people all the way to the mouth of the Kennebec River at Bath. The late Marguerite Yourcenar of Mount Desert Island, the first woman to be elected as one of the *40 Immortals,* members of the ancient and prestigious Académie Française, was not a Catholic.

There are a number of families with French names in Maine who have become members of Protestant churches. Some Thibodeau women of my grandfather's generation abandoned the practice of the Catholic faith when they married non-

Catholics in Fort Fairfield, Easton, and Houlton. In Caribou, some Thibodeaus of my generation were members of the United Pentecostal Church. A certain number of French Catholics became isolated from the Catholic communities when they settled in areas that did not have a Catholic parish nearby or when they did not feel welcome at long-established "Irish" parishes. When Catholics lived without a supportive community of their co-religionists for a long time, they often ceased to identify themselves as Catholic. Their descendants had no connection with the Catholic roots of their ancestors, so they simply dropped out. In some English-language Catholic parishes, French-speaking Catholics felt alienated when they could not go to confession in French. The devotional life of the church was not familiar to them, so they fell away from religious practice. It was a complex process.

During the long tenure of Cardinal Gibbons in Baltimore (1877 to 1921), the Catholic hierarchy in the United States pursued a deliberate policy of "Americanization" over the various ethnic groups of Catholics who came to America. The largest numbers of Catholic immigrants after the American Civil War were Germans from Bavaria and Austria. They settled mostly in the Midwest and the upper Midwest of the United States. The majority of them were farmers; they formed themselves into parish communities with German-speaking clergy. In some cases, such as Indianapolis and Milwaukee, they even had German-speaking bishops, as long as those bishops could be kept on a short leash by the dominant Irish-American hierarchs like Cardinal Gibbons.

Gibbons was a southerner, born in the United States, but his family had moved back to Ireland during his childhood. After the early death of her husband, his mother again moved the family to America, settling in New Orleans. Later in life Gibbons came back to Baltimore, where he had been born, and studied for the priesthood. He became vicar apostolic of North Carolina and bishop of Richmond, Virginia. He was the youngest bishop in the world at the First Vatican Council in 1870. Eventually he was appointed archbishop of Baltimore and was later a cardinal.

Gibbons had unusually sharp administrative and diplomatic skills, having learned to live peacefully with Protestants in the South. The Archdiocese of Baltimore at the time included Washington, D.C. He was an intimate of presidents, particularly William Henry Harrison, Theodore Roosevelt, and William Howard Taft. He firmly believed that the Catholic church would make better strides in the United States if the non-English-speaking immigrants were "Americanized" quickly and rid themselves of their "foreign cultures," which he believed kept them isolated from mainstream U.S. society. He had vast influence at the Vatican and within the U.S. hierarchy. He saw to it that most bishops appointed in the United States favored the policy of "Americanization."

As archbishop of Baltimore, Cardinal Gibbons enjoyed the prestige of that office. Baltimore was the base for the first Catholic bishop in the United States, the Most Reverend John Carroll (1790–1815). The archbishop of Baltimore was never officially granted the title of primate of the Catholic hierarchy in the United States, but unofficially the archbishop often functioned in that capacity, holding some sort of rank over all the other bishops and archbishops in the United States. An archbishop has no direct jurisdiction over other bishops, but an archbishop does exercise some influence both at home and in Rome.

The first Roman Catholic parish in Maine was established in 1798 at Damariscotta Mills in what is now the town of Newcastle—on the coast. Irish immigrants had come there as well-to-do landowners or as merchants involved in the lucrative transoceanic lumber market. It has the oldest Catholic church in New England and still serves as the parish church. St. Denis in North Whitefield was established in 1818 for Irish farmers settled at the headwaters of the Sheepscot River. In 1830 the Catholics in Portland, mostly of Irish descent, were given the parish of St. Dominic. St. Mary's parish in Augusta came into existence in 1834 to serve Catholics coming into the newly established state capital. That same year, Bishop Fenwick of Boston had created a parish in southern Aroostook County for an Irish farming community in Benedicta, Maine. In 1857 the first Catholic parish was set up in Lewiston: St. Joseph. This increasing activity led to the need for new administrative structures.

Bishop Jean Lefevre de Cheverus (1768–1836), a French Jesuit, after whom a high school in Portland is named, had been the first bishop of Boston from 1808 to 1823, with jurisdiction over all the Catholics in New England. In 1853 the Holy See decided to establish two suffragan dioceses for the Province of Boston: One in Portland for Maine and New Hampshire, and the other in Burlington for the State of Vermont. Louis de Goesbriand (1816–99), a French cleric, was appointed bishop for Vermont, since most of the Catholics in that state were French at the time. In 1855 David Bacon (1813–74) was consecrated at St. Dominic Church in Portland and began to develop the structures of his new diocese in Maine and New Hampshire. In 1884 the Diocese of Manchester, New Hampshire, was separated at the request of the second bishop of Portland, the Right Reverend James Healy (1830–1900), the first African-American priest to become a bishop in the United States.

Bishop Walsh (1906–24) in Portland was known to have promoted a policy of "Americanization" for the ethnic Catholics of Maine. Of course, the Irish were ethnics, too, but most of them spoke English, so they were already "Americanized." It has been said among the French that Bishop Walsh wanted to set up an Irish parish next door to every French church to promote the demise of the French!

In 1981, when I went from the French parish of Notre Dame in Waterville to the Irish parish of St. Mary's in Bangor, I was the first non-Irish priest to become pastor there. The elderly Irish members of the parish said to me: "But, you're not Irish, Father!" But for my thirty-fifth anniversary, they gave me a trip to Ireland!

In 1842, by virtue of the Webster-Ashburton Treaty, the boundary between British interests and U.S. enterprises in the Northeast was finally established. The St. John River in northern Maine, between Grand Falls, New Brunswick, and St. Francis, Maine, became the international boundary. The French-speaking communities of Acadian settlers who had been there since the 1770s found themselves divided by this political demarcation. The river had united these people of the valley since they had first come there after having been dispossessed of their farms for a second time in history. From 1842, the bishop of Boston, and—after 1855—the bishop of Portland, each had allowed the parishes in the valley to be headed by the bishop of St. John, New Brunswick, since the clergy of northern Maine were not eager to recognize the jurisdiction of the bishop of Boston even after the boundary settlement. The "Melting Pot" ideal did not appeal to these French-speaking priests in northern Aroostook County. In fact, it was not until 1870 that official jurisdiction was transferred to the bishop of Portland for those parishes in the St. John Valley.

French-speaking clergy came to the State of Maine from various places. At first, most of them came from Canada—with or without leave of their bishops. Some just "showed up" here and began to serve. Canonical niceties were often ignored. A few came from Québec to the lumber camps of northern Maine during the winter months and stayed to establish new parishes in Aroostook County, such as Father Joseph Marcoux (died 1918), founder of the Wallagrass and Eagle Lake parishes. A few were sent by Canadian bishops at the request of U.S. bishops, such as the Monsignor Arthur Décary (died 1957) to Fort Kent and his brother Zénon Décary (died 1940) to Presque Isle. Some came from France or Belgium or even Holland, mostly ex-members of religious orders that had been disbanded by anti-clerical laws in those countries. These included Fathers Alvery and Semery, the Reverend Monsignor Vital Nonorgues (died 1961), and his brother Father Louis Nonorgues (died 1921). They were truly twentieth-century political refugees to America.

Women's religious communities also enriched the Catholic church in Maine, as they, too, came after anti-clerical legislation took hold in France after 1903–04. During those years, the civil governments in France, Belgium, and Holland became very hostile to the Catholic religion. Laws were enacted to disband the communities of religious priests, brothers, and sisters. Some priests from religious orders came to the United States and became diocesan priests. The Daughters of Wisdom brought the gift of their aristocratic and elegant family backgrounds to the boarding and day schools of northern Aroostook in Ste. Agathe and Madawaska. The Sisters of St. Joseph-de-Lyon came to establish St. Joseph's Academy for girls in South Berwick, a boarding school for girls in Jackman, along with a hospital in that same town. They eventually served many parishes in Maine as teachers in parochial schools, as directors of religious education, and as pastoral associates.

The Servants of the Immaculate Heart of Mary, popularly known as the Good Shepherd Sisters, came to Van Buren and St. Joseph's parish in Biddeford from Québec. They established the first "Foundling Hospital" or Home for Unwed Mothers at St. Andre's Home on the Pool Road in Biddeford. The Gray Nuns still provide compassionate and quality health care services through several marvelous institutions in Lewiston, notably St. Mary's Medical Center. The Ladies of the Congregation of Notre Dame from Montréal for a time had a Catholic school in Lewiston.

The Sisters of the Presentation of Mary still provide leadership and staff for a number of parish schools, such as those at Lewiston, Saco, and Augusta. They even taught in the public schools in St. John and Fort Kent at one time. The Daughters of Wisdom and the Good Shepherd Sisters still do so in the St. John Valley. The Ursuline Sisters served four parish schools and ran a boarding school for high-school girls in Waterville, with parish schools in Caribou, Brunswick, Sanford, and Springvale.

Other French, Canadian, or Franco-American sisters who serve in Maine are the Little Franciscan Sisters of Mary, the Dominican Sisters of the Roman Congregation in Lewiston and Sabattus, and the Sisters of the Holy Rosary (formerly in Upper Frenchville) who still reside in Portland and Old Orchard Beach. The Sisters of Mercy, too, although not known as a French-speaking order, have had a great influence on Franco-American Catholics in Maine, primarily through their schools—St. Joseph's Academy in Portland and St. Joseph College in Windham—as well as through their hospitals—the former Madigan in Houlton and the prestigious Mercy Medical Center in Portland.

The Brothers of Christian Instruction based in Alfred provided elementary and high-school education for boys in Waterville, Biddeford, and Sanford. At one time, they operated a degree-granting college, LaMennais College in Alfred, where many teaching sisters were able to fulfill the State of Maine requirements for teacher certification. In 1960, the college was transferred to Canton, Ohio, and is now Walsh University, named after Bishop Emmet Walsh of Youngstown, Ohio.

Years ago an older, blue-blooded WASP lawyer in Sanford, Maine, Judge Willard, told the story, most likely apocryphal, of the Yankee farmer in the area who objected very strongly to the French-speaking immigrants in his town. He said: "If the English language was good enough for Jesus Christ, it ought to be good enough for those damned Canadians!"

Prejudice and discrimination are common and expected against newcomers to a settled region. Mix in the volatile issues of linguistic and religious differences and you are bound to have raging fires. Anglo mill managers in Sanford and Springvale sometimes employed the young children of their French-Canadian workers to also work in the mills. When federal inspectors were to come to enforce the child labor laws as they existed even in those early days, the managers, given advance notice by the inspectors, often gave a few hours off to those child laborers so they could go swimming in the millpond. The managers would proudly point out to the inspector how generous the company was in "allowing children from the neighborhood" to swim on company property! Later, these same managers looked down on these children, who grew up virtually illiterate since they had not been able to get an education.

Father John McGinnis, the Irish pastor at St. Ignatius in Sanford, who spoke French better than the French-Canadian immigrants to that town, was often called upon by the police in Sanford to help calm some conflict, either at the mill or outside one of the many taverns, when some French Canadians got involved in a "donnybrook" with Irish and/or Yankee co-workers of the mill. Many "Irish" priests in Maine were well schooled in the French language, having been educated in the multi-discipline schools of the Jesuits and at the Sulpician Seminaries in France or in Montréal. These compassionate parish priests took a special interest in these immigrants when they were still without their own priests to serve them in many towns. However, in a few unfortunate instances these immigrants were disdained by the "Irish" clergy and told to "learn English fast or go back where you came from!"

The French clergy, too, often practiced a self-imposed ghetto for themselves and their flocks. They isolated themselves even from their fellow Catholics who were not

French. Their perception was that the "Irish" clergy was in the business of "sheep stealing" from the French parishes. The pastor of Saint Mary's parish in Old Town allegedly would pretend to be weeping in his church when some French people from St. Joseph would stop in for a visit to the Blessed Sacrament. When asked why he was weeping, it's reported that he would groan over the small numbers who attended his church and he would invite those French parishioners from St. Joseph to register at St. Mary!

Parish schools in French parishes often taught the children only in French—in a deliberate effort to protect and to promote the French language, again as a vehicle for protecting and promoting the Catholic faith in an environment perceived to be hostile to Catholic interests. In Springvale, I once watched with amusement as the principal of the school gave a severe tongue-lashing to an English-speaking eighth-grade boy, in French! When the boy had gone back into the school, I opened the rectory door and said to the principal, "Serves you right! He did not understand a word you said!" She responded to me, "He understood my tone of voice!" The pastor there wanted me to speak only in French to the altar boys. He said it would promote vocations to the priesthood! I retorted that I would rather have them understand my instructions.

Some French-language parishes in Maine kept insisting on French only in their sermons and devotions even after the perceived "threats" to the faith had passed. In Lewiston, in Waterville, in Augusta, and in Biddeford, for example, if a French Catholic married a non-French person, the family usually ended up going to the "Irish" parish.

When I was ordained in 1958 there were two "tracks" for clergy assignments and promotions in the diocese. If a priest had grown up in a French parish, he was destined to serve as a pastor, at least, only in a French parish; and the Irish, vice versa. That year, French-speaking curates were still waiting to become pastors after twenty-five years of ordination. If one was "Irish," he could become a pastor after twelve to thirteen years, since there were more "Irish" parishes than French parishes to which one might have access to a pastorate.

Bishop Feeney (1946–69) began quietly to change this when he appointed some well-connected French priests to a hitherto Irish parish. Archbishop Gerety (1966–74) went ahead boldly with a freer policy. Bishop O'Leary (1970–88) and Bishop Joseph (1988–2003) picked freely across the lines of ethnic background for appointments and promotions. Father Maurice Lebel was the first French-speaking priest to be pastor at St. John's in Bangor since the days of Father John Bapst (1853–60), but he was a Jesuit, so ethnicity didn't count for them![4]

In Maine the lines of division between the Irish and the French clergy were never really as rigid as they were in other places. Shortly after my ordination I attended the funeral of a priest in Rochester, New Hampshire. At the grave for the committal prayers, a young priest yanked me to the other side of the grave from where I had been standing. He said, "That is the Irish side!"

Some French-speaking priests in Maine were "considered Irish" because they had grown up in an Irish parish. Father Arthur St. Pierre, who died in 1995, was always on the Irish track. He had grown up at St. Charles in Brunswick after the pastor at St. John's had expelled him from the parish school because his father had chosen to transfer the older daughter to the public schools when she went into the sixth grade so she would learn English in time to go to high school in the public system. The family had gone over to St. Charles and they were considered Irish after that! So, Father St. Pierre became a pastor at a younger age than the French priests, and he always served in Irish parishes.

As one of the French priests, I have tried always to be sensitive to the presence of non-French-speaking priests at the gatherings of the clergy. Some of the French priests would insist on carrying on in French even when an English-speaking priest would come to join the conversation. I attempted to steer the conversation into English, sometimes earning the scorn of the French.

Bishop Michael Côté (1995–2002), related by blood to both Father Josephat Sevigny and the late Bishop Proulx, had been one of my former altar boys, but became auxiliary bishop of Portland and my "Father" in the church! I have a profound honor and respect for him. I wonder if the Irish maidens of St. Patrick's in Lewiston referred to him as the "French bishop," as they did toward Bishop Proulx? I think not; those days have passed. In 2003 he went on to become bishop of Norwich, Connecticut.

What a treasure—first for Franco-American Catholics in Maine, then for other Catholics, and now even beyond the boundaries of the Catholic church! The French-speaking religious have left an indelible mark on all the people of Maine. The promised land of freedom and opportunity has been good for French Catholics in Maine, despite their minority status and their struggles to get a foothold in an area dominated by Protestants, who were often hostile to all Catholics and especially to French-speaking Catholics.

1 These reflections are offered as my thoughts about the experiences of French Catholics in Maine. My origins among the French people of northern Aroostook County place me primarily among the Acadians of that region, while my college education and professional life locate me among the descendants of French Canadians in central and southern Maine. Perhaps other Franco-American Catholics see themselves differently. With due respect for regional differences, I attempt to contribute one perspective on that experience.

2 The Acadians in northern Maine have called themselves *Français*. The French in southern Maine have called themselves *Canadiens,* even after several generations in the United States and even after having become U.S. citizens. It took me some time to realize that those terms often have little to do with political nationality or even with country of origin. In both cases the terms merely mean: *I speak French!*

3 Editor's note: Earlier parishes for Native American speakers of French had been established in Maine. In this case, Reverend Thibodeau refers to parishes established in Maine for French Canadians and Acadians.

4 The Jesuits belong to a religious order. When they serve in a diocese, they are not subject to the rules of precedence for promotion like diocesan clergy.

NEGOTIATING ETHNIC IDENTITY: ST. JEAN-BAPTISTE DAY CELEBRATIONS IN FRANCOPHONE LEWISTON, MAINE

Mark Paul Richard

Plattsburgh, New York

On 24 June 1897, the feast day of St. Jean-Baptiste, an estimated 2,000 French Canadians paraded through the streets of Lewiston, Maine. Ten bands accompanied them. Flags of France and the United States adorned the city; huge, decorated arches curved above its streets. On this day, while honoring the patron saint of French Canadians, Lewiston's French-speakers also celebrated the twenty-fifth anniversary of their mutual-benefit society, the Institut Jacques-Cartier. After attending mass at Saint-Pierre (St. Peter's) Church, 300 uniformed members of the society marched alongside a replica of the ship Jacques Cartier had sailed to the New World. The procession passed through the magnificent evergreen archway the Institut had constructed in front of its meeting hall. A banner on the structure stated emphatically: "Not foreigners but Americans, Let us be fair." It was on St. Jean-Baptiste Day that French Canadians in Lewiston typically argued that maintaining their language and their traditions did not preclude them from being loyal residents of the United States. Commonly heard and seen during St. Jean-Baptiste Day celebrations in the 1880s and 1890s, the slogan *"Loyaux mais Français"* (Loyal but French) made two important statements.[1] It announced that French Canadians were modifying their social identity in the United States; more significantly, it asserted that *francophones* were doing so on their own terms.

French Canadians had moved to Lewiston as part of the Québec migration, during which nearly a million persons took up residence in the United States by 1930. They concentrated in the textile mill towns of New England, such as Lewiston, where they succeeded the Irish as the predominant source of unskilled labor after the Civil War. French-Canadian descendants comprised nearly one-fourth of Lewiston's population by 1880, approximately one-half by 1900, and about three-fifths by 1930.[2]

French Canadians of Lewiston had formed the Institut Jacques-Cartier in May 1874 as a literary club and mutual-aid society. That same year, members of the Institut traveled to Montréal, along with over 10,000 French-Canadian migrants from other

St. Jean-Baptiste Day celebration, Lewiston, Maine, 24 June 1897: Members of the Institute Jacques Cartier and a team of horses in front of a float bearing a replica of La Grande Hermine, *the ship Jacques Cartier sailed to the New World.*
Photograph by Joseph Dignard, Franco-American Collection, University of Southern Maine, Lewiston-Auburn College[3]

parts of the United States, to celebrate St. Jean-Baptiste Day and to *fête* the fortieth anniversary of the Montréal Société Saint-Jean-Baptiste. Its ethnic pride aroused by the event, the Institut organized Lewiston's first public celebration of St. Jean-Baptiste Day the next year.[4]

Celebrations of St. Jean-Baptiste Day connected French-speakers in the United States and Canada. On these occasions, in honor of their patron saint, French Canadians on both sides of the international border celebrated their common heritage. Periodically, *francophones* from Lewiston and other New England cities traveled to Québec to join festivities organized in *le pays natal* (the native country). On one such occasion, which took place in Quebec City in 1889, Dr. Louis Martel of Lewiston underscored the shared roots of North America's *francophones* by calling the provincial capital *le berceau de notre nationalité* (the cradle of our nationality). Speaking at the same event, Québec Prime Minister Honoré Mercier urged French

Canadians in the United States to maintain their language and their faith: "Parlez français et soyez catholiques; les Anglais et les Américains respectent toujours les Français qui ont le courage de parler leur langue et de professer leur religion."[5] Sometimes, as in 1885, clergy from Québec came to preach in Lewiston on St. Jean-Baptiste Day. In 1896 Lewiston's celebration culminated with 800 people viewing the play, *Félix Poutré*, which focused on problems between *anglophones* and *francophones* during the 1837 rebellions in Canada; these problems must have resonated with Lewiston's French-speakers who faced anti-Catholic, anti-immigrant hostility from Protestant Yankees of the United States.[6] Whether in Québec or Lewiston, the issue of *survivance* (ethnic preservation) was always a central theme of St. Jean-Baptiste Day.

Scholars of the Québec migration to New England have focused on St. Jean-Baptiste Day celebrations as illustrations of *survivance*. While ethnic preservation was indeed a major theme of this feast day, so was entry into U.S. society. On St. Jean-Baptiste Day, Lewiston French Canadians promoted their ethnic heritage while asserting their loyalty to the United States. By doing so, French Canadians in the U.S. departed from those in *le pays natal*.

Neither the Province of Quebec nor the nation-state of Canada had an official flag until the mid-twentieth century. Since Canadians lacked national colors, the English, in 1854, "nous imposèrent le tricolore de la révolution française parce que Napoléon III s'alliait avec l'Angleterre contre la Russie,"[7] explained *Le Messager*, the French-language newspaper of Lewiston, on St. Jean-Baptiste Day in 1952. French Canadians, the newspaper further explained, continued to use the three colors of France in their celebrations, even after the English stopped doing so in 1870, following the Franco-Prussian War. To symbolize their French heritage on St. Jean-Baptiste Day, Lewiston's French-Canadian residents typically hung the Tricolor of France throughout the city. They also symbolized their loyalty to the United States by decorating their homes and businesses with the Stars and Stripes. Thus, the flags of France and the United States symbolically expressed the intertwined identities of Lewiston's *Canadiens* (French Canadians).[8] As the blue-white-red colors of France overlapped the U.S. red-white-blue, Lewiston *francophones* conveyed their noncompeting loyalties in their adopted country.

They emphasized this point with the slogan: *Loyaux mais Français*. The variation, *Loyaux mais Canadiens-Français*, which appeared on the banner that the Institut Jacques-Cartier unfurled during celebrations, made the same point.[9] Both slogans conveyed the loyalties of French-Canadian residents of the United States. Both also revealed that the *Canadiens* perceived their ethnic identity could be socially constructed and that, as a minority in an *anglophone* milieu, they were actively negotiating that identity in the host society.

Integral to the process of negotiation was identification with France during St. Jean-Baptiste Day celebrations. Emphasizing ties to France represented a departure, on the part of *francophones* in the United States, from their kin and kith in Québec. This was because French Canada had lost its ties to France after the British conquest of 1760. French-speakers in Lewiston found it expedient to resurrect those ties. While the practice may have reflected courtesy on the part of French Canadians wishing to be inclusive and respectful of their French religious leaders, the custom of paying homage to France predated the 1881 arrival of the French Dominicans in Lewiston. During the first local celebration of St. Jean-Baptiste Day in 1875, for example, the decorations on the speakers' platform included the flags of France and the United States, and the band played *la Marseillaise* during the afternoon picnic.[10]

Identification with France also served as a way for Lewiston's French-speaking residents to highlight the shared roots and patriotism of the United States and Canada. During St. Jean-Baptiste Day celebrations, parades included allegorical chariots featuring French-Canadian, French, and U.S. themes. For example, a young boy dressed in lambskin portraying St. Jean-Baptiste typically stood next to a lamb on one float, while on another, as in 1890, local French Canadians might pose as Revolutionary War figures Marquis de Lafayette and George Washington, even though Canada had stayed outside of both the U.S. and French revolutions. In addition to the symbols, the discourse of Lewiston's *francophone* population underscored the historic ties between the French and U.S. peoples. On St. Jean-Baptiste Day in 1897, Dr. Martel noted: "When this nation was yet in childhood and struggling for her rights, for her independence, Canada's mother, France, came to the aid of the thirteen colonies." Martel also pointed out that the French had played an important role in exploring New England's coast and other areas of what eventually became the United States. By harking back to their French roots, French-Canadian elites like Dr. Martel argued for acceptance in the United States. This strategy also gave evidence that their identity as French Canadians was evolving in the United States in ways that distinguished them from Francophones in Canada. By the turn of the century, in fact, increasing numbers of Lewiston's *Canadiens* began referring to themselves as Franco-Americans.[11]

Alfred Auger, St. Jean-Baptiste Day, Lewiston, Maine, 24 June 1890:
Alfred portrays St. Jean-Baptiste, dressed in a lambskin, next to a lamb.
Franco-American Collection, University of Southern Maine, Lewiston-Auburn College[12]

During the 1897 St. Jean-Baptiste Day celebration, attorney Émile Tardivel explained what he felt French Canadians most wanted in the United States: "Ce que nous voulons, pardessus toutes choses, c'est conserver notre langue et nos traditions dans la vie privée et parler la langue du pays et nous soumettre aux institutions américaines dans la vie publique."[13] He asserted that French Canadians had the right to preserve their ethnicity, just as Anglo-Americans had the right to preserve their heritage: "Nous entendons rester Canadiens tout comme les descendants des premiers colons anglais de la Nouvelle-Angleterre sont restés puritains, c'est-à-dire par tradition, par amour des ancêtres."[14] Contending that the strength of the United States lay in its diversity, Tardivel argued against those who tried to make the U.S. heterogeneous: "En effet, chaque nationalité, avec ses qualités, distinctives et son activité propre, contribue au développement matériel et moral de l'Union."[15] And, as an example: "Que serait, je vous le demande, l'industrie de la Nouvelle-Angleterre sans les bras irlandais et canadiens?"[16] The St. Jean-Baptiste Day celebrations provided the forum through which Lewiston *francophones* negotiated their place in the host society.

As French-speakers grew more numerous in the "Spindle City," non-French-Canadian businesses and politicians also became involved in St. Jean-Baptiste Day events. By the mid-1880s, if not earlier, U.S. businesses that employed French-Canadian clerks decorated their establishments for the occasion. Civic leaders, including Lewiston's mayor and members of the board of aldermen and common council, often joined the parade and lakeside picnic, as well as the evening ceremonies usually held at Lewiston City Hall. The participation of local politicians and businesses in St. Jean-Baptiste Day activities testified to the growing economic and political influence of Lewiston's French-Canadian population at the end of the nineteenth century. So did signs like *"Ici on parle français"* (French is spoken here), which appeared in the shop windows of U.S. businesses.[17] It is important to remember that change was not unidirectional: It did not take place only among the migrant population.

As French Canadians grew more numerous in Lewiston, and became naturalized citizens and voters, they increasingly gained access to positions in Lewiston city government in the early twentieth century. That access allowed them to exert influence in the conduct of local affairs, an influence which occasionally helped them to thwart actions prejudicial to their ethnic group. An incident from June 1901 illustrates this trend. During a meeting of Lewiston city officials, the Anglo-American mayor asked Franco-Americans to cancel their St. Jean-Baptiste Day celebration because he feared delegates from across the state might bring smallpox to Lewiston. A Franco-American on the board of health, Vital Ouellette, supported the idea. Then Ouellette asked about the planned Fourth of July celebration, which would follow two weeks later: "À cette question le silence se fait et tranquillement l'on aborde un autre sujet,"[18] reported *Le Messager*.[19]

During the first two decades of the twentieth century, the Catholic church became the predominant battleground within which ethnic differences were contested. One of the bitterest conflicts was the Corporation Sole controversy, during which Franco-Americans from Maine struggled with the Irish bishop, Louis Walsh, for administrative control of the state's Catholic parishes and institutions. Franco-Americans feared Walsh would use their funds to pursue his goal of assimilating them into U.S. society. They wanted to exercise control over their own institutions, just as the *fabriques*—or parish corporations—had in Québec. Subjected to bitter attacks in the French-language press during the controversy, Walsh interdicted six men, including the editor of *Le Messager*, and he forbade national societies like the Institut Jacques-Cartier from entering churches with their banners and insignias, something they typically did on French-Canadian feast days such as that of St. Jean-Baptiste.[20]

Following Walsh's interdiction of six *Canadiens* in 1911, "*la Cause Nationale*" (the National Cause) became the central topic of St. Jean-Baptiste Day speeches for at least a half decade. Whereas past speeches had focused on the place of Franco-Americans in the larger U.S. society, they now centered on their minority status in Maine. One of the interdicted, journalist Alfred Bonneau of Biddeford, Maine, promoted *la Cause Nationale* in 1911, asking Franco-Americans of the Lewiston-Auburn area to withhold funds from the Diocese of Portland and to support instead their parish schools. At Lewiston's St. Jean-Baptiste Day celebrations in 1915 and 1916, Bonneau continued to promote *la Cause Nationale*. In 1916 he argued that the situation of Maine's Franco-Americans was similar to that of French Canadians in Ontario.[21] Bonneau's remark referred to legislation against the use of the French language in the public schools of Canada's most populous province.

In short, the conflict with Bishop Walsh caused a shift in the principal theme of St. Jean-Baptiste Day speeches: Rather than focus on the participation of "loyal" *francophones* in U.S. society, as before, keynote speakers now addressed the conflict with the Irish hierarchy of Maine, particularly over the issue of preserving the French language. Thus, Walsh's efforts to push for "Americanization" precipitated ethnic tension and conflict, and, if anything, had the effect of increasing the determination of Lewiston's Franco-Americans to control the terms and pace of their entry into U.S. society.

Despite the efforts of Franco-Americans to learn English in communities like Lewiston, xenophobic tensions led Maine and other New England states to pass legislation pushing English-language instruction during and after World War I. Nativists in the Maine legislature passed a law in 1919, requiring English as "the basic language of instruction" in the state's public and private high schools. During a speech on St. Jean-Baptiste Day in the following year, Lewiston attorney Fernand Despins pointed out the irony of U.S. involvement in World War I, ostensibly to promote democracy, while zealots pushing Americanization worked to deny those of French-Canadian descent the ability to speak French in the United States. Like his predecessors on St. Jean-Baptiste Day in the late-nineteenth century, Despins argued in 1920 that preserving the French language and French-Canadian traditions was not incompatible with loyalty to the United States.[22]

The affirmation *Loyaux mais Français* still rang true. To Despins and to most other Franco-Americans in Lewiston, preserving ethnic traditions and becoming participants in the host society did not represent dichotomous goals. This belief and the resumption of heavy migration from Québec fortified Lewiston Franco-Americans in the 1920s against not only the Americanization program of Bishop Walsh, but also against the resurgence of the Ku Klux Klan.

During public celebrations of St. Jean-Baptiste Day in the 1920s and 1930s, Lewiston Franco-Americans continued to assert their identity in the face of the Americanization movement. Sometimes they needed a little prodding from *Le Messager*. In 1922, the year that the Institut Jacques-Cartier celebrated its fiftieth anniversary, *Le Messager* encouraged readers: "Ne craignons pas de montrer qui nous sommes, en portant à nos boutonnières, un petit ruban tricolore, demain, jour de la St-Jean-Baptiste et dimanche, fête du cinquantenaire de l'Institut."[23] Residents of the *petit canada* (Little Canada) near the industrial section of Lewiston decorated their homes, and the Franco-American societies paraded to Saint-Pierre Church for mass, during which Dominican prior Arsène Roy emphasized the importance of preserving the French language in order to retain the Catholic faith. The following year, when *Le Messager* reminded readers of the upcoming feast day of St. Jean-Baptiste, it asked them to decorate their homes with flags and banners "aux couleurs nationales et américaines, qui après tout sont les mêmes."[24] Thus, it made explicit what *francophones* had conveyed through their symbols since the late-nineteenth century, namely that their identities as French-Canadian descendants and U.S. citizens were closely intertwined. The French-language newspaper also asked Franco-Americans to sport buttons of the maple leaf or Tricolor. Despite the presence of the Ku Klux Klan in the Lewiston area, one thousand men, women, and children marched in the St. Jean-

Baptiste Day parade in 1923 to and from Saint-Pierre Church, which was decorated with the flags of France and the United States.[25]

An industrial crisis in Lewiston in 1924, as well as cross burnings and Klan parades in the Lewiston area, probably discouraged the organization of a St. Jean-Baptiste Day celebration in that year. Other evidence suggests that Franco-Americans did not fear public demonstrations in that tumultuous year, for 1,000 children paraded through Lewiston's streets in September to celebrate the opening of the new school of Saint-Pierre parish. From 1925 to 1927 about 2,000 to 3,000 Franco-American children paraded on St. Jean-Baptiste Day, carrying flags of the United States and either a flag or *boutonnière* of the Tricolor. After watching the children pass in 1926, *Le Messager* pointed out the symbolism they expressed when it stated that the U.S. flag "est également tricolore et comprend le bleu, le blanc et le rouge."[26] For a population negotiating its identity in the United States, this symbolism spoke volumes. So did the singing of both "O Canada" and the "The Star-Spangled Banner" following the St. Jean-Baptiste Day banquet of 1938, anthems that Franco-Americans probably sang at celebrations in other years as well.[27]

By the middle of the twentieth century, the advent of television, the closing of textile mills, changes in the Catholic church stemming from Vatican II, and continued discrimination against and the increased assimilation of *francophones* in the post-World War II era all contributed to declining ethnic identification among members of Lewiston's Franco-American community. Franco-Americans came to view ethnic preservation and participation in the host society as incompatible objectives. When these previously intertwined goals diverged, Franco-Americans loosened their connection with Québec, younger generations became unilingual English-speakers, their parochial schools declined, their parishes introduced English masses, and St. Jean-Baptiste Day programs attracted fewer youth and became smaller with each passing year.[28]

During the 1950s and 1960s St. Jean-Baptiste Day speakers lamented the growing Anglicization of the Franco-American community. On St. Jean-Baptiste Day in 1951, Pastor Félix Martin of Sainte-Croix (Holy Cross) parish argued the need to continue speaking and reading French in order to preserve the language. He contended that mixed marriages threatened cultural survival: "Dans ces unions, celui qui cède, ce n'est pas le conjoint de langue anglaise, mais celui de langue française."[29] In 1956 Sacré-Coeur (Sacred Heart) parish of Auburn offered the St. Jean-Baptiste Day mass, and its pastor, Théodore Bouthot, "exhorta les parents à parler et faire parler français à leurs enfants au sein de la famille."[30] At the evening banquet, Bouthot spoke, as had so many St. Jean-Baptiste Day orators before him, of preserving the French language, Catholic faith, and French-Canadian traditions. Like him, Pastor Wilfrid Ouellette of Auburn's Saint-Louis parish argued on St. Jean-Baptiste Day in 1959 that a significant problem for *survivance* was that too many Franco-American children no longer heard the French language spoken in their homes. Romeo Boisvert, state senator from Lewiston and president of *Le Messager*, asked those who attended the St. Jean-Baptiste Day banquet in 1961 to help youth to develop their French-language skills through reading and conversation.[31]

During the 1963 St. Jean-Baptiste Day celebration, funeral director Raoul Pinette acknowledged cultural realities when he stated that, in the aftermath of World War II, Franco-Americans were losing their language and their culture. During the postwar period in which the United States experienced great scientific progress, technological advances had brought radios, phonographs, and televisions into the homes of Franco-Americans, he noted. One social consequence of such technological progress, Pinette pointed out, was that children attending Franco-American schools in 1963 spoke English in the courtyards, quite unlike what they had done twenty and forty years previously.[32]

St. Jean-Baptiste Day parades ended in the 1960s. By 1969 a mass and banquet were the only means by which Lewiston Franco-Americans celebrated the feast day of French Canadians. Only two St. Jean-Baptiste Day celebrations appear to have taken place in the Lewiston area in the 1970s and 1980s. In 1975 *l'Unité Franco-Américaine* (Franco-American Unity), a federation of nearly thirty societies from Lewiston and Auburn founded in the previous year, organized a St. Jean-Baptiste Day celebration at Our Lady of the Rosary Church in Sabattus, which the Franco-American societies of Lewiston and Auburn attended. Assisted by Franco-American pastors from the local area, Canadian-born Dominican Pastor Raymond Laframboise offered an outdoor mass to 500 people; following the mass, 350 persons stayed to enjoy a bean supper and evening program of dance and music, marking the only public celebration of the feast day of French Canadians in the 1970s.[33]

In 1983 the Canadian-born Dominican pastor of Saint-Pierre Church, Roger Gabriel Blain, planned a special mass for St. Jean-Baptiste Day. Le Centre d'Héritage Franco-Américain (now the University of Southern Maine's Franco-American Collection), founded in the early 1970s, co-sponsored the celebration, which included a social hour, buffet, and evening program. Surely it was no coincidence that French-

Canadian pastors helped Lewiston-area Franco-Americans to organize public celebrations of St. Jean-Baptiste Day in 1975 and 1983. The Canadianization of the Dominican order in the early 1900s had led to a steady supply of French-Canadian pastors to Lewiston, and they had helped the city preserve its ethnic identity.[34] The 1975 and 1983 activities comprised, however, the last public celebrations of St. Jean-Baptiste Day in Lewiston.

But, reflecting a curve in the road from Franco-American to "American," the feast day reappeared as a private celebration in the 1990s. At the request of Franco-American residents, Maison Marcotte, an independent living center, commemorated St. Jean-Baptiste Day in the 1990s with ethnic food such as *tortière* (meat pie, usually made with pork), the singing of French songs, and waltzing. In 1997 the journalist reporting on Maison Marcotte's celebration, while somewhat trivializing it in her conclusion, hinted at how far Franco-Americans had diverged from French Canadians in Québec: "Although the holiday has evolved to focus on separatist aspirations in Quebec, at Maison Marcotte it seems to have become a time for eating birthday cake and reminiscing."[35] Most importantly, the public celebrations of St. Jean-Baptiste Day in 1975 and 1983, as well as the private celebrations at Maison Marcotte in the 1990s, suggest modest attempts at ethnic renewal. They also suggest that the road to assimilation is not linear.

To conclude, celebrations of St. Jean-Baptiste Day reflect the changing identity of Lewiston's French-Canadian descendants from 1875 to the present. What we learn from their experiences is that the process of acculturation and assimilation in the United States is a dynamic one. Lewiston's celebrations of St. Jean-Baptiste Day reveal that individuals of French-Canadian birth and background actively negotiated their identity in the host society and were indeed historical actors in their own right.

1 *Le Messager*, 2 July 1885, p. 1; 29 June 1897, p. 6. *Lewiston Evening Journal,* 24 June 1892, p. 5; 4 July 1895, p. 12; 24 June 1897, p. 7.

2 Lavoie, p. 53. *U.S. Census*, 1880. Vicero, p. 343. Bernard, p. 6. For general accounts of French-Canadian migrants and their descendants in the northeastern United States, see Rumilly, Brault, Weil, Roby (1990 and 2000), and Chartier (1991 and 2000).

3 Franco-American Collection: Celebrations, St. Jean Baptiste Celebrations, file for nineteenth century.

4 *Le Messager*, 29 June 1897, p. 5. Roby, "Émigrés canadiens-français," p. 136. *Paroisse Canadienne-Française de Lewiston,* unidentified author, p. 95.

5 Speak French and be Catholic; the English and the Americans always respect the French who have

the courage to speak their language and to profess their faith.

6 *Le Messager,* 24 June 1880; 2 July 1885, p. 1; 27 June 1889, p. 5; 7 April 1893; 4 February 1896; 23 June 1896; 26 June 1896, p. 2. *Lewiston Evening Journal*, 13 January 1896, p. 8; 20 January 1896, p. 7.

7 "...imposed upon us the Tricolor of the French Revolution because Napoleon III was allied with England against Russia." This was during the Crimean War (1853–56).

8 *Le Messager*, 2 July 1885, p. 1; 8 July 1886, p. 1; édition spéciale Saint-Jean-Baptiste, 24 June 1952. *Lewiston Evening Journal,* 22 June 1882; 27 June 1893, p. 8; 24 June 1897, pp. 5, 7. English-language newspaper clipping inserted into Roman Catholic Church, The Dominican Fathers, *La Chronique des Dominicains*, Volume 2, 28 June 1886, p. 44; Volume 4, 1892, p. 27. After a long search to determine why Catholic French Canadians adopted the Tricolor, the symbol of the "godless" French Republic, I came upon *Le Messager*'s 1952 account. Whether accurate or not, the newspaper's explanation reveals that the *Canadiens* had lacked a flag of their own and had had to choose one. Appropriating the Tricolor in the United States served the purposes of French Canadians, not only in asserting their French identity, but also in arguing for acceptance in their adopted country based upon the historical ties between the French and U.S. peoples.

9 *Le Messager*, 2 July 1885, p. 1; 8 July 1886, p. 1. *Lewiston Evening Journal*, 24 June 1875; 7 October 1889; 24 June 1892, p. 5; 4 July 1895, p. 12.

10 *La Marseillaise* is the French national anthem. *Lewiston Evening Journal*, 24 June 1875.

11 *Lewiston Evening Journal*, 24 June 1890; 24 June 1897, p. 5. French-language newspaper clipping inserted into Roman Catholic Church, The Dominican Fathers, *La Chronique des Dominicains*, Volume 3, 1890, p. 212. *Le Messager*, 23 August 1895; 13 November 1896, p. 2; 15 January 1897.

12 Franco-American Collection: Biography, Alfred Auger, donated by Juliette Boisvert Cloutier.

13 "What we want, above all things, is to conserve our language and our traditions in private life and to speak the language of the country and to submit to American institutions in public life."

14 "We intend to remain French Canadian just as the descendants of the first English colonists of New England have remained Puritan, that is to say by tradition, by love for ancestors."

15 "In effect, each nationality, with its distinctive qualities and its own activity, contributes to the material and moral development of the Union."

16 "What would New England industry be, I ask you, without Irish and French-Canadian workers?" *Le Messager,* 2 July 1897, p. 7.

17 *Le Messager,* 8 July 1886, p. 1. French-language newspaper clipping inserted into Roman Catholic Church, The Dominican Fathers, *La Chronique des Dominicains*, Volume 3, 1890, p. 212; Volume 4, 1892, p. 27. Alexandre-Louis Mothon, 1893, cited in Plourde, *Dominicains au Canada,* p. 112.

18 "On this question there is silence and quietly the subject changes."

19 *Le Messager*, 21 June 1901, p. 6.

20 Guignard, pp. 113–30. Roby, *Les Franco-Américains de la Nouvelle-Angleterre (1776–1930)*, p. 264. *Le Messager,* 15 May 1911, p. 4; 2 June 1911, p. 1.

21 *Le Messager*, 26 June 1911, p. 4; 25 June 1915, p. 1; 26 June 1916, p. 8.

22 Maine, *Acts and Resolves, 1919*, Chapter 146. *Le Messager,* 25 June 1920, p. 1. During the Americanization campaign of and following World War I, Connecticut in 1918 and Rhode Island in 1922 stipulated that English serve as the language of instruction in public and private schools. Roby, *Les Franco-Américains de la Nouvelle-Angleterre (1776–1930)*, pp. 291–92, 299–300. In the nineteenth and early twentieth centuries, Canadian provinces outside of Quebec—including Ontario, New Brunswick, Manitoba, Alberta, and Saskatchewan—also enacted legislation to curb or to eliminate bilingual instruction in their schools. Discrimination against the French language in Canada factored

into the decision of many French Canadians not to participate in the "war for democracy."
23 "Let us not be afraid to show who we are, by wearing a small tricolor ribbon on our lapels, tomorrow, Saint John the Baptist Day and Sunday, the fiftieth anniversary of the institute."
24 "...in the national and American colors, which after all are the same."
25 *Le Messager*, 23 June 1922, p. 8; 26 June 1922, pp. 1, 3; 28 June 1922, p. 4; 22 June 1923, p. 6; 25 June 1923, p. 1. *Lewiston Daily Sun*, 25 June 1923, p. 12. On the Ku Klux Klan in New England, see Doty, "How Many Frenchmen Does It Take to...?," pp. 92–94.
26 "...is equally tricolor and consists of blue, white and red."
27 *Le Messager*, 20 June 1924, p. 6; 8 September 1924, p. 1; 26 June 1925, p. 1; 25 June 1926, p. 1; 24 June 1927, p. 1. *Lewiston Daily Sun*, 27 June 1938, p. 12.
28 Boucher, p. 38.
29 "In these marriages, the one who gives in is not the English-speaking spouse but the French-speaking one."
30 "...exhorted parents to speak and to have their children speak French within the family."
31 Marcel Blouin, "Il faut retrouver le climat français dit le curé Martin," *Le Messager*, 25 June 1951, pp. 3, 10. *Le Messager*, 28 June 1956, p. B–2; 22 June 1959, p. 2; 19 June 1961, p. 12.
32 J. C. Larochelle, "Lewiston et Auburn fêtent La Saint-Jean-Baptiste," *Le Messager*, 20 June 1963, p. 5.
33 *Le Messager*, 23 June 1966, p. 1. *Lewiston Daily Sun*, 20 June 1969, p. 2. Paul Paré, "L'Unité Franco-Américaine: C'est pour tout le monde," *L'Unité,* Winter 1977–1978, pp. 1, 7. *L'Unité,* Spring 1978, p. 1. Roman Catholic Church, The Dominican Fathers, *La Chronique des Dominicains,* Volume 17, 23 June 1975, pp. 290–91. Plourde, *Qui sont-ils et d'o∫ viennent-ils?* p. 222.
34 Tom Robustelli, "French People Should Have a Holiday, Too, Says Sen. Charette," *Lewiston Journal*, 26 March 1982, p. 8. *Lewiston Daily Sun*, 2 June 1983, p. 12. Roman Catholic Church, Diocese of Maine, Chancery Archives, St. Peter's Parish File. On the Dominicans in Lewiston, see Mark Richard, *From Canadian to American*.
35 Carol Clapp, "St. Jean Still Remembered in Lewiston," *Sun Journal*, 25 June 1997, pp. 1A, 8A.

DONAT LABBÉ—WOODS COOK

Yvon Labbé
Old Town, Maine

Donat Labbé was born in Beauceville, Québec, and was orphaned at age two. He married Marie-Rose Labbé in 1936. They bought a proverbial thirty-acre farm, which could not support a family. Their first son was born in 1938, so Donat went to work during the fall and winter logging seasons in the woods of Abitibi as a cook's assistant, then in Gaspésie during World War II (1939–45) and, from 1947, in the Maine woods—as the best bread maker in the region! He inherited most of his old-time, hearty *bucheron* (woodsman) recipes as an apprentice to woods cook Siméon Poirier of Rang St-Pierre, where the Labbé farm was located.

Donat Labbé, Eustis, Maine, c. 1951
Photograph courtesy of Yvon Labbé

The recipes below are taken from a seriously yellowing booklet, added to as the years went by, from the late 1940s to the early 1950s, and seldom used thereafter since they were committed to memory and he was able to practice his discipline with a pinch of this and *une poignée* of that. His clientele sometimes numbered over two hundred, three meals a day!

Donat relocated the family to Maine in 1950, believing at the time that he would lose his U.S. work permit if he didn't make the move. His children—Huguette, Marcel, and Yvon—started school in Stratton, Maine. Six months later, Donat and Rose permanently moved their family to Madison, Maine, where their youngest daughter, Liliane, was born in 1953. Donat retired in 1976, at the age of sixty-three, due to ill health. He died soon afterwards from a brain tumor that had been caused by inhaling flour dust for more than forty years. His funeral was attended by hundreds of visitors from the generations that he had nourished.

Right: Bisquette et Muffins

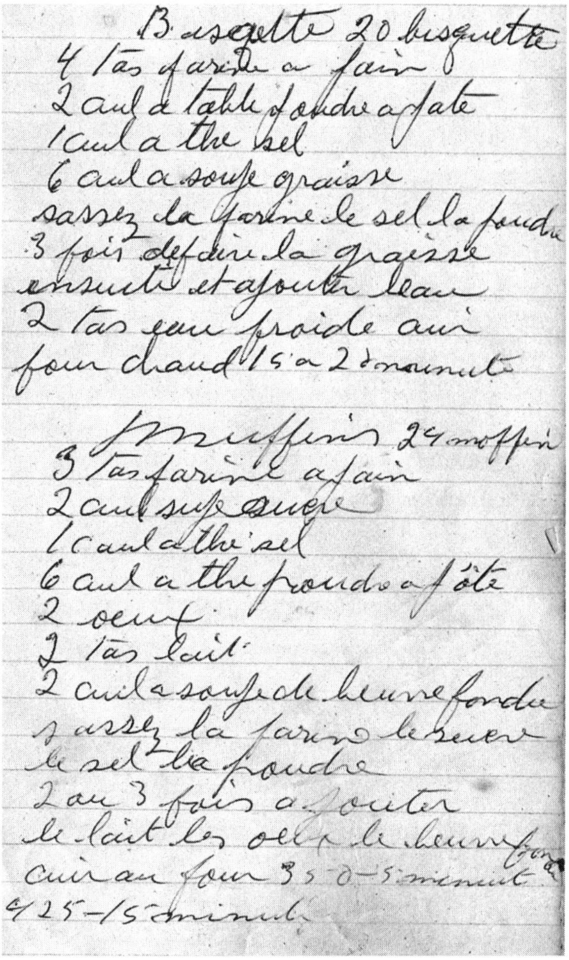
Bisquette 20 bisquette
4 tas farine a pain
2 cul a table poudre a pâte
1 cul a the sel
6 cul a soupe graisse
sassez la farine le sel la poudre
3 fois défaire la graisse
ensuite et ajouter leau
2 tas eau froide au
four chaud 15 a 20 minutes

Muffins 24 muffin
3 tas farine a pain
2 cul sup sucre
1 cul a the sel
6 cul a the poudre a pâte
2 oeuf
2 tas lait
2 cul a soupe de beurre fondu
sassez la farine le sucre
le sel la poudre
2 ou 3 fois ajouter
le lait les oeufs le beurre
cuir au four 350–5 minutes
425–15 minutes

Below: Tarte au sucre brun (brown sugar pie) and Pâte a tarte (pie dough)

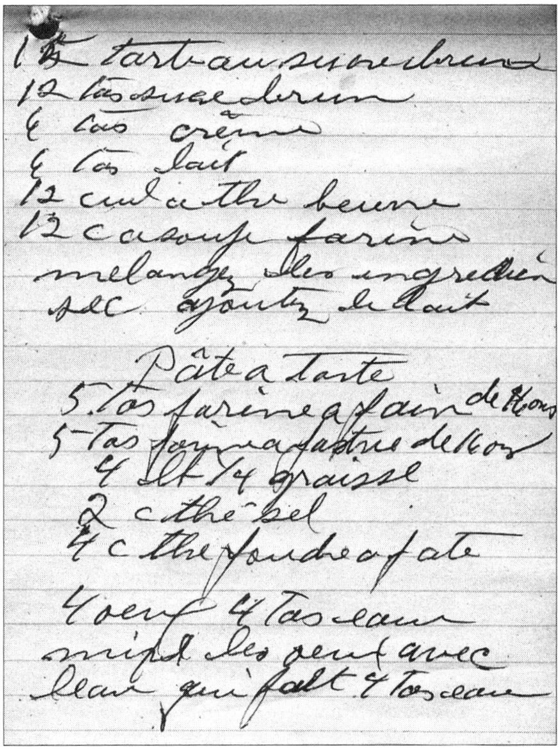
1 tarte au sucre brun
1/2 tas sucre brun
1/4 tas crème
1/4 tas lait
1/2 cul a the beurre
1/2 c a soupe farine
melangez les ingredients
sel ajoutez le lait

Pâte a tarte
5 tas farine a pain de Kon
5 tas farine a pâtisserie de Kon
4 lb 1/4 graisse
2 c the sel
4 c the poudre a pâte
4 oeuf 4 tas eau
mixez les oeufs avec
leau qui fait 4 tas eau

THE JACKMAN AND MOOSE RIVER MISSION: FROM FRANCE TO AMERICA WITH THE SISTERS OF ST. JOSEPH OF LYONS, 1904–1932

Gérard Forgue
Norridgewock, Maine

The twin communities of Jackman and Moose River had grown into an active railroad and lumber nexus with the construction of the "Short Line" of the Canadian Pacific Railroad (CP) through Maine in 1885. With the establishment of the CP depot in Jackman, the Yankee population had been significantly augmented by the French-Canadian workforce. In response to the arrival of these families, Jackman's parish of St. Antoine de Padoue had grown under the guidance of Father Joseph Forest, a missionary priest from Montréal who had moved into Maine's Diocese of Portland to fulfill this need.[1]

By the start of the twentieth century the final piece to be added to the parish of St. Antoine de Padoue was a school. Indeed, the need for a parish school became a dire necessity because of the dynamic growth of the French-Canadian and Franco-American population that had taken place to fulfill the needs of the booming timber industry. The dominant ideology that guided the formation of the school was embodied in the expression: *Qui perd sa langue perd sa foi* (whoever loses their language, loses their faith).[2] So, it was not surprising that Jackman's missionary priest would turn to his home province in search of an educational staff in April 1904. In two years Father Forest was able to present the Diocese of Portland with a *fait accompli*—a contract to be signed between the diocese and the Sisters of St. Joseph of Lyons (CSJ) in France. The sisters were to staff the Sacred Heart Convent, a boarding and parish school slated to open that autumn.[3]

Father Forest got the CSJ to Jackman via a most unusual route. Ordinarily, contact with them would have come through the diocesan offices in Portland. Instead, Father Forest contacted them through the Diocese of Quebec. It happened this way: Sister Benedicte and Marie Theophile of the CSJ were in Fall River, Massachusetts, searching for a diocese that would accept them as a religious teaching order.[4] Of the many contacts that they had, one was with Bishop Louis-Nazaire Bégin of Québec. In 1904 Bégin told the sisters that he had no opening for them in his diocese, but knew that Father Joseph Forest's parish in Maine was French-Canadian and in need of a religious teaching order to staff a new school opening in September 1906. Bégin vouched for Father Forest's character and that of his parishioners, who only recently crossed the frontier to settle themselves in Jackman. He implied that if they accepted this mission, he would welcome them to fill a Québec mission when one became available.[5]

To the CSJ, Bishop Bégin was the cream of Canadian bishops, so they wasted no time in contacting Father Forest.[6] An agreement was quickly reached. First, they would teach primarily in English, the diocese's official language. Secondly, even though they had never taught boys in France, they would run a boarding school, teaching and boarding boys up to the age of thirteen. They wrote:

> Do you know that I believe myself already in the Maine Forests? Sister Marie Théophile laughs with all her heart and sees herself already in the woods, at the head of a regiment of boys.[7]

Does it not seem odd that an order of nuns from France would choose to cross the Atlantic and come to the wilderness of the Maine woods? The sisters' Religious Institute of St. Joseph had been founded by a Jesuit missionary in the 1640s as the first community of women to be established "in any capacity other than a contemplative lifestyle, well protected by cloisted walls."[8] It was given canonical status in 1650, and in 1666 King Louis XIV delivered his letters of patents authorizing and affirming the establishment of the institute.[9] Except for a period of twelve years, during and immediately following the French Revolution, the CSJ spread throughout every diocese in France.[10]

However, in the late-nineteenth and early twentieth centuries, major reforms took place in France, following the now infamous Dreyfus Affair, in which Jewish army officer Alfred Dreyfus had been wrongly convicted of espionage. A major crackdown ensued against the Roman Catholic church because it not only had been vehemently anti-Semitic, but its sympathy had lain with the regular army that had persecuted Dreyfus.[11] France's most sweeping reforms came in the area of religious instruction and education. Just prior to the Dreyfus Affair, the majority of French schools had religious instructors. Following it, in an attempt to reform society, all religious orders—as teachers—were banned in France by a series of laws which have become known as the Combes Laws, named after French Premier Justin-Louis-Émile Combes (1902–05), who oversaw the separation of church and state.[12]

Indeed, the period after 1879 saw scores of religious orders, male and female, arriving from France to Québec and French-speaking North America. At that time the continent had an expanding French frontier, which was attractive to the religious and cultural needs of the dispossessed French religious orders.[13] St. Antoine de Padoue was part of this French-speaking frontier. The years from 1903 to 1904, which coincided with the arrival of the Sisters of St. Joseph in Fall River and the roots of the Jackman Mission, marked the height of the anti-clerical movement in France.[14] In this milieu it is not surprising that the sisters came looking to establish a mission and would listen to the advice of Bishop Bégin. Bégin had admitted a dozen or so new French refugee communities of religious professionals into his diocese between 1899 and 1905.[15] So, it is no accident that Father Forest initiated the process culminating with the CSJ establishment in St. Antoine de Padoue through Bishop Bégin in Québec, rather then Bishop O'Connell in Maine.

On 30 August 1906 eight sisters left France for the wilds of northwestern Maine.[16] Upon their arrival in New York they were greeted by the family of Sister Nicéphore and two sisters of Philadelphia.[17] All eight then went on to Philadelphia, where two of the nuns stayed to perfect their English before joining the others in Jackman. They then headed to Maine by way of New York and Boston.

When they arrived in Boston, they recalled that it was impossible to understand and to make themselves understood: "We were desperate to retrieve our baggage and have it transported to the Central Maine Depot, where we were to leave from."[18] They persevered and found their way from Boston to Portland: "They felt that if they didn't laugh they would certainly cry."[19] There, a man came up to them and said: "Are you the Sisters of St. Joseph?"[20]

With his help, they made the necessary train connections to reach Jackman on 17 September 1906 at 2:00 A.M. A word of advice to the next group who would be following them to Jackman and the Moose River Valley was included in the first communication back to Lyons: The next group should land in Halifax, Nova Scotia, not New York. From there, they could connect with the Canadian Pacific Railway and be in Jackman in only eight hours.[21]

One of the nuns recorded their initial reaction to Jackman:

What? Exile! We have the illusion of having one foot in France. Listen: Jackman is in the middle of the Maine forests and counts, approximately, in the main parish, with about eighty-five families, a majority of which are Canadians, the remainder comprised of Americans and Irish. The Canadians all speak French...they are excited to have Sisters from France, Sisters who can teach our children to make their first communion in French.... One cannot read anything so beautiful in the pages of the Propagation of the Faith as that which is going on here.[22]

She went on to say that Jackman was a true mission, indeed that the parish was bigger than Spain.[23] In each of the missions, she added, they had a telephone hookup with the *presbytère* (church office) in Jackman:

We would have been in admiration, except that tears welled up in our eyes as, last night, at the benediction of the Saint Sacrement, we saw first hand the poverty of the ornaments of the alter, the torn veil, etc.[24]

The nuns were particularly impressed by the beauty and isolation of Jackman:

The sky is full of stars. The pine trees smell good. But what cold! Our teeth chatter and our breath is taken away.[25]

She went on to say that Jackman was located close to the border and next to Moose River, which got its name from the river which flowed through both towns. There were many lakes in the area. In the middle of Jackman lay Wood Pond, where Father Forest went to fish. The mission comprised an area of 100 square miles (259 sq km). During the winter Father Forest traveled to the lumber camps to minister to the woodsmen.[26]

She finished by saying that only the day before the nuns had received their baggage. There had been a mix-up between New York and Portland and the baggage had been returned to New York before finding its way back to Jackman. They had French coffee that morning, and they wanted to make their provisions from France last until the end of days.[27]

On 24 September 1906, seven days after they had arrived in Jackman, school opened. They had sixty students in attendance, thirty-six boarders and twenty-four day students. They would have had more students except that many French Canadians had already sent their children back to Québec to school, plus there had been an epidemic of whooping cough in the area.[28]

The classes were very complicated, as there were some students who spoke only English, others only French, and still others—the majority—who spoke both. "In the beginning, it was incredibly hard."[29] "The children appeared willing and eager to learn, but they had been very, very spoiled by their parents."[30] The habits (dress) of the nuns intimidated some of the students, as most had never seen nuns before.

Sister Charles-Emile taught French as a foreign language. Her class consisted of nineteen boys and thirteen girls. The teachers were somewhat overwhelmed. They were only six; they needed at least six additional teachers.[31] Most of the boys, who ranged in age from twelve to fourteen, were bigger than she was.[32]

Another problem encountered by Sister Charles-Emile was the accent of the French-speakers.[33] Sisters Nicéphore and Saint-Léon watched the boys at night, Sisters Mercédès and Charles-Emile watched the girls. The title *Mère* (mother) that the students gave them was well deserved. They received word from Sisters Marie du Calvaire and Philoména, who were studying English at Chestnut Hill, near Boston: Both wished they could extend their stay as long as possible.[34]

There was one young girl, however, who brought much joy to Sister Charles-Emile. The girl knew no French, her English accent was different from the other students, and was difficult for the sister to understand. Although not her student in the classroom, Sister Charles-Emile developed a technique which enabled them to communicate while she supervised the girl at night. Writing one word on a slate, Sister Charles-Emile would ask the girl to say it out loud before copying it onto her slate as a pretext of helping the girl study. The technique enabled Sister Charles-Emile to not only learn this young girl's accent, but also to learn additional English words herself.[35]

The sisters were excited to get news from France that reinforcements were on their way. All hoped that they would remember to bring warm clothes. A request had been received in Jackman—from Philadelphia—for French language teachers. This request had been forwarded to Lyons. The sisters in Jackman told their mother superior that they wanted her to come and visit them, and were anxiously awaiting the additional help.[36]

The reinforcements left France in November 1906 and arrived in Halifax the next month. Heeding the advice of the first group, they connected with the Canadian Pacific Railroad, and arrived in Jackman at 2:30 A.M. to be greeted at the station by

Sisters of St. Joseph of Lyons, Sacred Heart Convent, Jackman, Maine, c. 1914–40
Archives, Sisters of St. Joseph of Lyons (CSJ)
Provincialate and Christian Life Center, Winslow, Maine

Father Joseph Forest with Sisters Nicéphore and Mercédès.[37]

Once this new group was settled in, the organization of the classes was finalized. The lay teacher, Miss Grafft, taught all grammar and lectured in all classes, assuring that English was the language of instruction. Sister Charles-Emile passed on the French classes to a new arrival and was assigned to assist Miss Grafft in English, math, history, and geography. Every day, there were religion classes.[38] There were a few additional boarders, but no specific number is mentioned.[39]

In 1912 the mother superior from Lyons visited the mission of Jackman and Moose River. It was on this occasion that the purchase of Sacred Heart Convent by the CSJ was finalized.[40] Once the outstanding debt had been paid, the remaining money (approximately $4,000) was forwarded to the parish accounts. When the student population outgrew available space at Sacred Heart Convent, this money was undoubtedly used for seed money when the new parish school was constructed.

In 1914 the parish school of St. Antoine de Padoue opened its doors, as the student population had outgrown the available space at the convent. From that time on, all classes were taught at the parish school. The CSJ and boarders lived in the convent. In 1914–15, a new wing was added to the convent to board male students.[41]

The school operated in the following manner. Classes were conducted in a coeducational environment, but all recreation was separate. This meant that the male and female students each had an indoor space, located in the basement of the parish school, and an outdoor space, as well as separate living quarters after 1914–15. Unfortunately, there are no complete enrollment figures for either the convent or the parish school.[42]

The Financial and Enrollment Ledgers of the CSJ, however, do allow a glimpse of the growth of enrollment. Starting with sixty students in the 1906–07 academic year, enrollment followed the same general trend of the community's population growth and development. By the 1913–14 academic years, total enrollment reached 240 students. This was the year that both the new parish school and the Jackman Lumber Company opened.

With both the Jackman Lumber Company's mills in Jackman and Moose River and the Kellogg Lumber Company at Long Pond in full operation, school enrollment reached 374 students in 1927. Following the closing of the Jackman Lumber Company mills in 1927 and the scaled-down operations at the Kellogg Lumber Company by 1932, school enrollment dipped to 296 in 1931–32.[43]

The Financial and Enrollment Ledgers of the CSJ for 1924–30 also tell us a lot about the students of Sacred Heart Convent and the parish school. For each of the years the Convent School had 180–220 boarding students. At least 25 percent of these boarders came from Lewiston/Auburn. At least 10 percent were boarders from Jackman itself. Almost every one of the missions supplied two or three boarding students. Almost all the rest came from towns throughout Maine. Every year five to ten students came from other states or from Canada.[44]

The numbers of these boarders clearly demonstrate that the CSJ greatly influenced not only the *survivance* of the Parish of St. Antoine de Padoue and the mission from 1906 to 1930, but also played an important role in many parishes along the Canada Road migration route into Maine. The celebrated adage, "whoever loses their language loses their faith," had an important impact in this small Franco-American parish in northwestern Maine—far beyond its usually applied significance in the large urban parishes of southern New England.

St. Antoine de Padoue Parish Church and Sacred Heart Convent, Jackman, Maine, c. 1940
Maine Historic Preservation Commission

1 Father Joseph Forest was born on 28 March 1861 in St. Roch de l'Achigan, Québec. He completed his studies at Collège de l'Achigan, with additional studies at the Grand Séminaire, and was ordained in 1887 by Édouard-Charles Fabre, Bishop of Montréal. Following his first duties as vicar in Beauharnois from 1887 to 1888, he decided to follow many of his countrymen, both religious and non-religious, as they immigrated to New England. From 1888 to 1892, Father Forest served in Fitchburg (Massachusetts) and Westbrook (Maine). In September 1892, at the age of thirty, Father Forest assumed the duties of administrator for the newly created parish of St. Antoine de Padoue in Jackman, Maine, where he was to remain until his death in 1940. Arthur Dubois. Forest.

2 Weil, pp. 9–13, and throughout; Guignard, p. 125.

3 The following is an excerpt of a letter located at the Diocese of Portland, in the Correspondence File, Edward Hurley, Vicar General, to Father Joseph Forest, 20 June 1906: "Your letter addressed to His Grace relative to the contract which you wish to enter into with les Soeurs de St. Joseph de Lyon has been referred to me. I saw His Grace about the matter and he said that since you had built your school and are ready for the beginning of the school work in your parish you are permitted to go ahead with the preparations.... His Grace said that you had begun this work of the convent and school without his knowledge and therefore without his permission, and if he gives you permission now to make definite arrangements with these sisters so that you may have them for September it is because he does not wish to make difficulties for you and because he recognizes [*sic*] in this undertaking a proof of the zeal with which you have been administering the mission of Jackman for so many years." See also, "The Sisters of St. Joseph in the Diocese of Portland," unidentified author, p. 10. On opening day, sixty students—twenty-four boarders and thirty-six day students—ranging from six to fourteen years old, were enrolled in the school, from Kindergarten to sixth grade. Roman Catholic Church, Sisters of Saint Joseph, "Mission D'Amérique, Fondation de Jackman," October–December 1907, p. 331. See also

Larkin, p. 69. Note: The total number of students is different in Sister Larkin's work and *Le Regne de Dieu*. I have used the enrollment figures from *Le Regne de Dieu*.

4 Roman Catholic Church, Sisters of Saint Joseph, "Mission D'Amérique, Fondation du Canada," June 1907, pp. 180–88.

5 Roman Catholic Church, Sisters of Saint Joseph, "Mission D'Amérique, Fondation du Canada," July 1907, pp. 202–03.

6 Roman Catholic Church, Sisters of Saint Joseph, "Mission D'Amérique, Fondation du Canada," July 1907, p. 205.

7 Roman Catholic Church, Sisters of Saint Joseph, "Mission D'Amérique, Fondation du Canada," July 1907, pp. 206–13.

8 Janet Gagnon, p. 14.

9 Bois, p. 164. This book also contains a copy of the original letters of patents. It was internally published and distributed, and a copy is stored at the archives of the CSJ at the Provincialate and Christian Life Center in Winslow, Maine. Janet Gagnon, p. 14; Roman Catholic Church, Sisters of Saint Joseph, Diocese of Portland, p. 10.

10 Janet Gagnon, p. 14–15; Roman Catholic Church, Sisters of Saint Joseph, Diocese of Portland, pp. 10–11. For a broader understanding of the various waves of anticlerical sentiment in France, see Hansen; Laperrière, pp. 389–411.

11 Schecter; Laperrière, pp. 393–97.

12 Laperrière, p. 391.

13 Laperrière, pp. 397–409. There is also a list, at the end of the article, in which he has identified a total of fifty-four male and female orders that came to Québec between 1837–1914. Of this total, 28 arrived between 1892 and 1914.

14 Laperrière, pp. 389–90; Roman Catholic Church, Sisters of Saint Joseph, "Mission D'Amérique, Fondation du Canada," January and March 1907, pp. 101–79.

15 Laperrière, p. 398.

16 Roman Catholic Church, Sisters of Saint Joseph, "Mission D'Amérique, Fondation de Jackman," October 1907, p. 298. They were: Sister Marie-Philippine (Superior), Charles-Emile, Marie du Calvaire et Philoména (from the diocese of Lyons, France), Sister Louis-Marie et Mércèdes (from the diocese of Autun, France), Sister Nicéphore (from the diocese of Aleppo, Syria), and Sister Saint-Léon (from the diocese of Cesaria, Little Armenia-Cilicia). An interesting side note should be added here. On one of my many trips to Jackman, I took the opportunity to visit Father Forest's mausoleum, where he and his brother, Father Arthur Forest, are buried. I am relatively cognizant of the cemetery layout, but I had never been conscious of the names on the tombstones. On this particular trip to the Jackman Cemetery, I noticed a set of tombstones that made a square around the mausoleum. When I looked at the names, they were the names of many of the original sisters that had come over to staff the Jackman and Moose River Mission, giving final testimonial of their faith in the church and its messenger, Father Joseph Forest.

17 Roman Catholic Church, Sisters of Saint Joseph, "Mission D'Amérique, Fondation de Jackman," October 1907, p. 300. In 1832, the CSJ had established a mission at Carondelet, St. Louis. This mission had expanded to Chestnut Hill, Philadelphia, in 1847. These missions were, by this time, independent of the Mother House in Lyons, France.

18 "Nous désespérions de pourvoir retirer nos bagages pour les faire transporter au dépôt central du Maine, d'ou nous devions repartir." Roman Catholic Church, Sisters of Saint Joseph, "Mission D'Amérique, Fondation de Jackman," October 1907, p. 303.

19 "C'était tellement drôle que nous en rions pour n'en pas pleurer." Roman Catholic Church, Sisters of Saint Joseph, "Mission D'Amérique, Fondation de Jackman," October 1907, p. 304.
20 "Ne seriez-vous pas des Soeurs de St. Joseph?" Roman Catholic Church, Sisters of Saint Joseph, "Mission D'Amérique, Fondation de Jackman," October 1907, p. 304
21 Roman Catholic Church, Sisters of Saint Joseph, "Mission D'Amérique, Fondation de Jackman," October 1907, p. 305.
22 "Mais que dis-je...; exil.... Nous aurons presque l'illusion d'avoir un pied en France. Ecoutez: Jackman est au milieu des forêts du Maine et ne comte environ, pour la paroisse proprement dite, que quatre-vingt familles, en majeure partie canadiennes, le reste comprend des Américains et des Irlandais. Les Canadiens parlent tous français.... Ils sont ravis d'avoir des Soeurs de France; des Soeurs 'qui pourront faire à nos enfants la première Communion en français'.... On ne lit rien d'aussi beau dans les livres de la Propagation de la Foi, que ce qui se passe ici." Roman Catholic Church, Sisters of Saint Joseph, "Mission D'Amérique, Fondation de Jackman," October 1907, p. 306.
23 Roman Catholic Church, Sisters of Saint Joseph, "Mission D'Amérique, Fondation de Jackman," October 1907, p. 306.
24 "Nous en avons été ravis, mais les larmes nous sont venues aux yeux quand, hier au soir, à la bénédiction du Saint-Sacrement, nous avons vu la pauvreté des ornements de l'autel: le voile tout déchiré." Roman Catholic Church, Sisters of Saint Joseph, "Mission D'Amérique, Fondation de Jackman," October 1907, p. 307.
25 "Le ciel était plein d'étoiles: les sapins sentaient bon; mais quel froid de loup!... On claquait des dents et la respiration manquait...." Roman Catholic Church, Sisters of Saint Joseph, "Mission D'Amérique, Fondation de Jackman," October 1907, p. 311.
26 Roman Catholic Church, Sisters of Saint Joseph, "Mission D'Amérique, Fondation de Jackman," October 1907, pp. 311–13.
27 Roman Catholic Church, Sisters of Saint Joseph, "Mission D'Amérique, Fondation de Jackman," November 1907, p. 332.
28 Roman Catholic Church, Sisters of Saint Joseph, "Mission D'Amérique, Fondation de Jackman," November 1907, pp. 330–31.
29 Roman Catholic Church, Sisters of Saint Joseph, "Mission D'Amérique, Fondation de Jackman," November 1907, p. 331.
30 Roman Catholic Church, Sisters of Saint Joseph, "Mission D'Amérique, Fondation de Jackman," November 1907, p. 332.
31 Roman Catholic Church, Sisters of Saint Joseph, "Mission D'Amérique, Fondation de Jackman," November 1907, pp. 332–33.
32 Roman Catholic Church, Sisters of Saint Joseph, "Mission D'Amérique, Fondation de Jackman," November 1907, p. 334.
33 Roman Catholic Church, Sisters of Saint Joseph, "Mission D'Amérique, Fondation de Jackman," November 1907, p. 335.
34 Roman Catholic Church, Sisters of Saint Joseph, "Mission D'Amérique, Fondation de Jackman," November 1907, pp. 337–38.
35 Roman Catholic Church, Sisters of Saint Joseph, "Mission D'Amérique, Fondation de Jackman," November 1907, pp. 338–39.
36 Roman Catholic Church, Sisters of Saint Joseph, "Mission D'Amérique, Fondation de Jackman," November 1907, pp. 340–41.
37 They were: Sister Marie-Joseph (from Sacré Coeur, Paris, France), Marguerite-Aglaé, et

Anthelmine (all from the diocese of Lyons, France). Roman Catholic Church, Sisters of Saint Joseph, "Mission D'Amérique, Fondation de Jackman," November 1907, pp. 365–69.

38 Roman Catholic Church, Sisters of Saint Joseph, "Mission D'Amérique, Fondation de Jackman," November 1907, pp. 368–69; October 1907, p. 306. Here it is mentioned that all aspects of religious education could be taught in French. It is of note that Guy Laperrière states that in Québec, these same types of teaching orders had to attend indoctrination into Québec religion and society before they were allowed to teach. Laperrière, p. 407. In the parish Antoine de Padoue, no indoctrination was required, as they were put to work immediately.

39 No mention was made of when Christmas vacation had taken place, except that the students had returned on 3 January 1907. Roman Catholic Church, Sisters of Saint Joseph, "Mission D'Amérique, Fondation de Jackman," December 1907, p. 373.

40 Monsignor Walsh, Portland, to Superiéure, Sister Marie-Philippine, Parish St. Antoine de Padoue, Jackman, Maine, 27 March 1912.This letter is in the hands of the CSJ Archives, Provincialate and Christian Life Center, Winslow, Maine. The letter is in both French and English. Also, see Sisters of St. Joseph of Lyons, Financial and Enrollment Ledgers: 1906–1967, p. 100. There are two of these ledgers which are a running account of all debit and credit transactions and other materials. Some of this other material is a description of events leading up to the purchase of the Convent of the Sacred Heart for $16,000.

41 Bernier, pp. 1–3

42 Bernier, pp. 1–3, and Gérard Forgue's conversations with Sisters Germaine and Aline while researching at the Provincialate Archives. Both sisters had attended, as boarders, the parish school, St. Antoine de Padoue, in the 1920s and 1930s. They later taught there in the 1940s, 1950s, and 1960s, with Sister Germaine also teaching at the Mexico (Maine) Mission.

43 Derived from Roman Catholic Church, Sisters of Saint Joseph, Financial and Enrollment Ledgers. They contain biographical enrollment information for six academic years, 1924–25 through 1929–30, listing such information as student and parent(s) home address, enrollment and boarding cost per student as well as miscellaneous expenses. For the academic years 1930–31 through 1966–67, complete enrollment figures are available. For additional school information see Jackman Bicentennial Committee, 95–115. Sprague, pp. 69–71.

44 Roman Catholic Church, Sisters of Saint Joseph, Financial and Enrollment Ledgers.

A NEW HOME

Paul Caron
Lewiston Maine

My musical theater play, *Lewiston: A New Home,* depicts the story of a Franco-American girl and her Irish-American beau living in Lewiston, Maine. Through their eyes, we see the development of the city from a prospering mill town to a city that strives to adapt to the changes at the end of the twentieth century. These are two songs from the musical.

Lewiston, A New Home,
Program, Lewiston Bicentennial Committee, 1995
From Paul Caron

The song, "A New Home," is set in the early twentieth century and focuses on a first-generation Irish-American boy telling his father's story of coming to America and helping to build the canals and the mills. The second part of the song has a Canadian immigrant girl moving to Lewiston due to economic hardships back home. Her story

is in French. The chorus states how the city has welcomed people of different nationalities throughout its history. The welcome may have been less than generous at first, but through time and patience, any person who is willing to work and help build the city is accepted in the community.

Vocals - Page 3
A New Home
Coda
119
me! ff We have found a new home where the fu - ture is bright For our
125
child - ren and their child - ren too. It's a world that is good, filled with hope and with
132
light. This ci - ty is our gift to you! We have trav - eled this far to
139
seek a new life, For the chance to be hap - py and free. To let go of the
146
past with its heart - aches and strife In a ci - ty that wel comes me
153
! In a ci - ty that wel comes me
160
!

"The Factory Waltz" depicts the life of a millworker during the heyday of Bates Manufacturing in Lewiston, Maine. The song is in three parts. The first part shows how workers rationalize their everyday work by making it seem better than it actually is. The second part describes the exact methods used to create the fabric. The

third part is the reality section where life in the mill can be overbearing, tiring, and based on an endless routine. This routine is played in three-quarter time, hence the title of the waltz. Orchestrally, the song has sounds based on mill noises I remember hearing when living and walking by the mills as a child.

Vocals
Factory Waltz
D.C. al Coda
123
And we bear it well 'til the fi - nal bell at the end of the day.
Coda
131
waltz ! The mill life, for me is like one two and three, for that is the
f
138
beat ff of the fac - tor - y waltz !
4
4

A CHILDHOOD MEMORY[1]

Helen Lévesque
Auburn, Maine

I grew up in a French-Canadian family in Lewiston, Maine, between the First and Second World Wars. We were a three-generation household that lived in an English-speaking neighborhood. My maternal grandparents lived with us during the winter. French was the language in our home, even though my grandparents understood and spoke English. However, I was expected to speak French in the house, even though I spoke more and more English as I played outdoors with the other children and went to public school.

I attended public school for three years before my parents decided it was time for me to be exposed to French in school, as well as at home! There were choices to be made: Either I had to be a day student at Sts. Peter's and Paul's parochial school in Lewiston or to be a boarder at the Ave Maria Convent in Sabattus. The parochial school offered a half-day of instruction in French and a half-day in English. The convent school followed the French system of dividing the week with classes on Monday–Tuesday–Wednesday mornings and on Thursday–Friday–Saturday mornings. You could go home for the weekend on Saturday if you had been a "good girl." I did not find the convent school schedule or the décor appealing, so I was allowed to attend parochial school.

Of course, nothing is ever problem-free. I had to catch up on three years of French language instruction; so I was tutored by a Dominican nun—Sister François d'Assise. The tutoring continued on a weekly basis for many years. I was expected to write a composition in French every week! The extra homework and the mandatory uniform did not make me a "happy camper," but I did survive through eighth grade. Little did I realize then that I would eventually earn my living teaching French!

Besides learning a little history about the French and Indian Wars and the defeat of Montcalm on the Plains of Abraham, I had not thought much about the widespread dispersion of the Francos throughout the North American continent. However, I knew how the need for factory workers in the U.S. in the mid-nineteenth century encouraged Canadians to emigrate, find jobs in the mills, and make their homes in factory towns such as Lewiston.

The wide interests and talents of the emigrants from the areas around Québec and the St. Lawrence River Valley manifested themselves in the societies that were established as the Canadians settled down in the United States. Two of these organizations for the ladies were Les Dames de Ste. Anne and Les Enfants de Marie. For the men, there were Les Défenseurs and the St. Vincent de Paul Society. Singing and acting groups such as L'Orphéon and Le Foyer Musical were very active. Members of the Franco community supported and participated in these societies.

I remember the celebration of the birthday of St. John the Baptist on June 24 each year. There was a parade, and a little boy—usually with blond curly hair—was chosen to ride in the parade as John the Baptist. There were also the snowshoe clubs whose members wore very distinctive attire—coats and pants of grey with broad colored stripes around the chest, and tasseled hats. Whenever there was a convention, the clubs had various athletic events such as snowshoe races, members walking from their homes to the convention sites, and a parade—usually on Sunday to attend mass.

In the 1930s, 1940s, and 1950s, Sunday services were well attended. At Sts. Peter's and Paul's, masses were held in the lower church. If you were a little late, you had difficulty finding a seat. One of my uncles was an usher and I can still see him, in my mind's eye, raising his left arm to indicate a vacant seat. There was a brief homily at every mass and there were five or six services beginning at 7:00 A.M. on Sunday—a far cry from today's attendance! I composed a poem of these memories when I was a teenager in the 1940s:

Midnight Mass at St. Peter's and St. Paul's

The stars glitter in the cold midnight sky,
The crunch of feet on the snow and the murmur of voices break the silence of the
night,
The heavy oaken doors open,
The crowd surges forward,
The annual drama is about to begin.
The faithful fill the church,
The voices of the choir blend with the organ music,
The golden vestments of the celebrants shimmer in the soft light,
The scent of pine and fur branches mingle with the incense,
The soloist sings "Minuit Chrétien,"

The joyous sound of "Adeste Fideles" echos against the vaulted ceilings, as the congregation leaves for home, to gather with family and friends for the traditional *réveillon*.

After World War II, things changed dramatically. The young people had experienced the great wide wonderful world in North America and in Europe. Congress had enacted the G.I. Bill of Rights, which gave them the opportunity to get a college education. English became the language of the home. The Francos became members of the local service clubs. They became politically active. This process is still alive and well.

Another milestone was Russia's launching of *Sputnik*, which shook up the political and educational establishments to the degree that Congress enacted the National Defense Education Act to improve the training of science, math, and foreign language teachers in the late 1950s and early 1960s. This piece of legislation sent me to the University of California–Berkeley for language education, followed by ten weeks in France the next summer. I remember one of the institute professors told me that I spoke French with a Norman accent. I was surprised that the accent would persist through several generations—from 1645 when the first Lévesque, who was from Normandy, came to the New World, to the present day.

Before coming to Auburn, I taught several years in Lewiston, spent a year in Japan teaching in the U.S. Army dependant school, and traveled extensively during vacations. I now enjoy my retirement. In my eighty years of living I have learned that life is a kaleidoscope of experiences!

[1] A version of this memoir was composed for a course on French North America at the University of Southern Maine's Lewiston Auburn College in Autumn 2006.

MAINE'S CORPORATION SOLE CONTROVERSY*

Michael Guignard
Biddeford, Maine

It is fashionable today to describe white "ethnics" in the United States as a monolithic group, even though conflict within that "group" has far from disappeared.[1] In fact, this interethnic conflict had usually been underemphasized, as historians have focused primarily on contention between third- and fourth-generation citizens and new immigrants. Yet, discord among the various ethnic communities—based on social, economic, or religious issues—was a common occurrence.

Conflict in the religious sphere was due primarily to the fact that the predominantly Irish-American Catholic church hierarchy was strongly assimilationist.[2] Faced with an "anti-papist" nativism because of the alleged foreignness of Catholicism, the Irish hierarchy attempted to "Americanize" the church. This policy was resisted by other Catholic immigrant groups who considered their native language and culture an integral part of their religious life. The French Canadians, in particular, fervently believed that a loss of one's language and culture would inevitably entail a loss of one's faith.[3] Consequently, religious conflict between this group and the Irish clergy was rife.[4]

The Franco-Americans won their first victory in a long struggle in the 1870s when the Catholic hierarchy in New England decided on the principle that the parish priest would use the language spoken by the majority of the congregation. But contention continued as some pastors refused to abide by the guideline. The Irish clergy's persistent Americanization efforts led the Franco-Americans and other groups to appeal their case to Rome. The pope ruled that ethnic parishes were to be retained for first-generation immigrants.[5]

Despite Rome's pronouncements, however, the Irish hierarchy continued its efforts to Americanize the church and even "labored for years under the threat of heresy," when it disregarded a papal bull that condemned their policies.[6] Constantly appealing to Rome and pointing to nonassimilationist clergy in other countries, Franco-Americans vigorously continued to resist the Irish-American clergy.

As one would expect, most major controversies between the two groups centered around the failure of the Irish hierarchy to establish Franco-American ethnic parishes and to appoint French priests to predominantly French-speaking parishes. The French wanted national parishes composed of one ethnic group only. Instead, Irish bishops established territorial parishes which administered to all Catholics within a certain district. The immediate issues of the "Corporation Sole" controversy focused on ownership of parish property. The underlying cause of this conflict, however, was Franco-American abhorrence of the assimilationist Irish clergy.

The term "Corporation Sole" referred to an 1887 state law that made the bishop of Portland "sole" owner of all parish property in his diocese. Church authorities had presented the bill in Augusta in an effort to better establish the church's financial credit. The old system of individual parish ownership had proven unsatisfactory as a number of parishes found themselves hopelessly bankrupt and unable to borrow additional funds.

Franco-American distaste for this "Corporation Sole" resulted from their experience in Québec. There, each parish was run by a *fabrique*, a church council composed of the pastor and members of the parish (representatives elected by the congregation). It was this *fabrique* that owned parish property in Québec and supervised its maintenance.[7] The Franco-Americans, who in Québec had had a voice in their parish school, were also disturbed when these schools were put under more centralized control by Maine diocesan authorities in 1897.

Nevertheless, the fact that there was no opposition to the "Corporation Sole" among the French until 1907 shows that they were not particularly concerned over who owned parish property. This peaceful period can be traced to James Healy, bishop of Portland from 1875 to 1901, who tempered the American hierarchy's assimilationist outlook. He held a "special affection" for the French, mastered their language, and lavished a great deal of attention and money on their parishes.[8]

After his death, Bishop Healy was succeeded by William O'Connell. No organized opposition developed against O'Connell, although there was some bitterness among the French that "one of their own" had not been appointed, and O'Connell left the diocese in 1906—before French dislike for him had crystallized. By 1904, however, several of his policies had drawn sharp criticism from Franco-Americans.[9]

The succession of Louis Walsh to the bishopric of Portland in 1906 signaled the beginning of the "Corporation Sole" controversy. Franco-Americans had vociferously advocated the appointment of a French bishop and even sent a delegation to Rome to plead their case, after one French priest had hired a canonist from Rome "to investigate the possibility of appointing a French Canadian Bishop to the diocese."[10] The

Bishop Louis Walsh of Portland, Maine, c. 1910
Maine Historic Preservation Commission

Lewiston (Maine) newspaper, *Le Messager,* embittered by Walsh's selection, counseled its readers that the French had simply lost a battle and that the struggle was just beginning.[11] To make matters worse, Walsh now had to deal with the Comité Permanent de la Cause Nationale du Maine (the Standing Committee of the Nationalist Cause in Maine). Established by a Franco-American convention in March 1906, several months before Walsh became bishop, the goals of the Comité were for the establishment of French ethnic parishes and schools.[12] Bishop Walsh also inherited the ill-will accumulated during O'Connell's rule.

Bishop Walsh, from all indications, was a strongly assimilationist cleric. He had incurred the enmity of French-Americans while serving as director of the Boston archdiocesan school system. Soon after becoming bishop of Portland, Walsh "began to implement his assimilationist aims." His Americanization efforts even brought him into conflict with the small Maine Catholic Slovak community.[13] Kenneth Woodbury has tried to minimize Bishop Walsh's assimilationist bias:

> The Reverend Louis S. Walsh...created fourteen French-Canadian parishes with the assignment of French-Canadian priests. There is no record of any pastor other than one of French-Canadian descent being assigned to a French-Canadian parish.[14]

When one considers that Bishop Walsh created thirty-six parishes and that almost 80 percent of his flock was Franco-American, Woodbury's assertion loses some of its significance.[15] The fact that no Irish pastors were ever appointed to a French church is misleading, because—in several instances—they were appointed to predominantly French parishes not classified as ethnic.[16] A number of Irish curates were also assigned to predominantly French parishes, such as Sacred Heart in Waterville and St. Ignatius in Sanford.[17] Moreover, Bishop Walsh made no effort to transfer Irish pastors who had previously been appointed to French parishes.[18]

Woodbury also makes a special effort to point out that the bishop took pains to voluntarily appoint French priests to 50 percent of his diocesan council seats. Woodbury does not tell us that Walsh appointed an Irish vicar-general and glosses over the fact that the council had no decision-making power. In fact, he admits that the role of council was a point of contention between the two groups.[19]

Bishop Walsh's diary and letters indicate his strong preference for English-language religious ceremonies. His diary is full of newspaper clippings describing his participation in St. Patrick's Day, Holy Name Society, and Knights of Columbus ceremonies. Never once does Walsh hint that he ever participated in festivities honoring St. Jean-Baptiste, the French-Canadian patron saint, or in ceremonies of French societies. When he was present at the dedication of a French church, however, he did speak in both languages.

The first crisis of Walsh's rule came late in 1906.[20] In 1905 Bishop O'Connell had decided to split St. Francis-de-Sales parish in Waterville to form the non-ethnic Sacred Heart parish. O'Connell had appointed an Irish pastor to the new parish although French parishioners outnumbered the Irish six to one. The French refused to worship in the new parish and were supported by the ethnic church's pastor. In the face of opposition, O'Connell reversed his decision and allowed the French to worship at St. Francis-de-Sales again.

Bishop Walsh decided to follow O'Connell's original plan. When the three Franco-American priests on the diocesan council accused him of changing O'Connell's policy, Walsh denied it emphatically. He was insulted by the opposition of Fathers Félix Trudel, Pierre Dupont, and Narcisse Charland, and was angered by their alleged mendacity. He asked the apostolic delegate if Charland was the bishop of Waterville, and characterized his course as "unreasonable" and "irreverent" and his statements "false" and "absurd." In a letter to Charland, Walsh told him to force his parishioners to go to the Irish church, expressed his dismay at Charland's attempt to communicate directly with the apostolic delegate, and blamed the whole controversy on him.[21] The French press saw the incident as another attempt by the Irish to "Saxonize" their children.[22]

In his first meeting with the Comité Permanent Walsh stated plainly that he would not tolerate any insubordination within his diocese. He refused to recognize the group and criticized the French for their impudence in appointing such a body. He warned them not to interfere in any parish affairs.[23]

On 24 June 1907, three weeks after their meeting with Walsh, the Franco-Americans held a second convention. Unable to have a Frenchman appointed bishop and faced with Walsh's adamant position, Franco-Americans at the Waterville convention voiced anticlerical sentiments.[24] The convention shocked French priests by its hostility toward diocese authorities and marked the end of clerical participation in Franco-American conventions. Even a small number of laity found the proceedings too extreme.[25] The convention reiterated the Franco-American belief that their language fortified their faith. The delegates severely criticized Walsh and asked for lay control of church property. When a Franco-American became bishop of the Manchester diocese in New Hampshire in 1907, French dissatisfaction in Maine rose sharply.

The Brunswick Convention of October 1909 brought the first systematic attack on the "Corporation Sole."[26] Franco-American opposition to the law was predicated on the fact that title to churches and schools they had built belonged, not to them, but to an Irish bishop. They believed that Walsh was draining French parishes of funds to further assimilationist goals. Led by Godfroy Dupré, the delegates decided to introduce a bill to the legislature to change the "Corporation Sole" law.[27]

Soon after this convention, Bishop Walsh traveled to Brunswick to hear French-Canadian grievances. His conciliatory gesture was not reciprocated; a French-Canadian crowd hurling insults at the bishop attempted to enter the presbytery where Walsh was staying, "causing the bishop to secure the doors." Shaken by such shocking behavior, Walsh became less inclined to compromise with the increasingly adamant French Canadians. The French press lauded the incident and advocated similar actions in the future.[28]

After 1906 the French press became increasingly critical of the bishop, accusing him of closing French schools and orphanages and of preventing French national societies from entering church in full regalia. In Walsh's defense, these charges, while true, must be qualified. Walsh was an excellent administrator who abhorred inefficiency. The schools and orphanages which he closed he considered too small and "miserably inadequate."[29] He simply wished to consolidate these institutions, but such action spelled doom for ethnic institutions. Walsh's sense of duty overrode his distaste for the hostile French reaction that he knew would ensue. His stand on national societies was consistent with the 1889 Congress of Baltimore, although it was impolitic to apply that restriction.[30]

Walsh's passion for confidentiality also hurt his reputation among the French. For instance, the superior of the Good Shepherd sisters in Biddeford told the bishop in 1907 that their convent would never be completed unless the parish bought it from the Québec order.[31] When Walsh suggested such a move two years later, he was accused of wishing to evict the French nuns.[32] Many other false charges were viciously hurled at Walsh by Franco-American extremists.

The French press constantly denounced the bishop for not appointing French priests to French parishes. It printed letters from irate Franco-Americans who could no longer tolerate English sermons.[33] *La Justice* of Biddeford often cited a church with a large French congregation and advocated the appointment of a French priest.[34] Both *La Justice* and *Le Messager* of Lewiston ran the letters of Godfroy Dupré vigorously attacking Walsh. The papers also printed each other's editorials and often ran the same news items. The more radical *Le Messager* began to mock the bishop as "His Excellency" and denounced him for refusing to meet with the *Comité*.[35] The Lewiston paper often asserted that one need not know English to enter heaven and advocated the creation of a separate ethnic diocese for Maine's French.[36]

Not all of Maine's French shared the press' sentiments, however. Westbrook parish priest Father Dugré supported Walsh and was denounced by *Le Messager*.[37] The Dominican Fathers of St. Peter-St. Paul's parish in Lewiston founded the *Courier du Maine* in 1906 to support the bishop. This order was considered assimilationist by Franco-American leaders, who then urged French parishioners to cease contributing to that church's building fund.

Bishop Walsh kept informed of the French press' attacks. As early as 1907, he ordered a priest to warn the editor of *Le Messager* about his scandalous articles.[38] He rejoiced upon hearing that the apostolic delegate had refused to give the pope's blessing to the "agitators" in Brunswick and their convention. Walsh continually criticized the two priests—Charland and Dupont—and warned them not to associate with Dr. Jean-Louis Fortier, whom he considered a "firebrand" for his "seditious and schismatical" statements.[39]

Legislative hearings on a bill submitted on the part of the Comité began on 7 March 1911. Defended by Dupré, the bill provided for the establishment of a lay council to administer parish property. Dupré presented petitions to the legislature signed by 7,500 Franco-Americans from twenty cities and asserted that the efforts of the Comité were supported by a large majority of French ethnics.

The arguments of Dupré were distinctly anticlerical. He accused diocesan officials of living in luxury while the French labored in poverty. He even intimated that some pastors were stealing parish funds. Dupré also addressed himself to the legislature's reluctance to interfere in church affairs by reminding them that they had meddled in 1887. Ending his oration, Dupré urged the legislature to end the bishop's "organized tyranny" and maintained that Maine had no room for a king.[40] Although the French were irked by Walsh, their objections were based on anti-Irish feeling, not anti-clericalism. The sentiments of Dupré were shared by few Franco-Americans.

The bishop's lawyers argued that they were not assembled to hear French grievances but to examine the merits of the "Corporation Sole" law. Several bankers testified against the bill, stressing that the church's good credit rating would be endangered by its passage. Bishop Walsh testified that only a few Franco-Americans opposed the "Corporation Sole." He defended his priests against the accusations of Dupré, and amid applause, asserted that never a cent had been misappropriated by the clergy. He described how the "Corporation Sole" allowed him to maintain small churches in rural areas that could not support themselves and maintained that French parishes were the chief beneficiary of the "Corporation Sole."[41]

Even though the French in Maine were indeed opposed to the "Corporation Sole," Walsh's statement that ethnic parishes benefited from the law was probably valid. Franco-American parishes were never notable for their good administration. Schools, orphanages, cemeteries, convents, and novitiates were often in debt. When the ethnic parish of St. Joseph's in Biddeford was being constructed, Bishop Healy had to supply funds to finish its construction.[42] Dupré and his cohorts never mentioned this.

While testifying, Walsh was a model of composure and equanimity. His diary reveals his true feelings, however. He was angered by his antagonists' attacks, and for good reason, as we have seen from the comments of Dupré. He considered his enemies "agitators" whose "vicious, malicious attacks" on the church and probity of the clergy deserved excommunication.[43] He felt that the Comité was appealing to "popular prejudices" and denounced the vicious attacks of Dupré on the clergy.[44] He mistakenly believed that most Franco-Americans supported the "Corporation Sole."[45] Throughout the agitation, Walsh was confident that the law would be retained.[46] It was, and by a great majority. His main regrets were that the hearings were made public and that the press had exaggerated the whole affair.[47]

An interesting aspect of Walsh's behavior is the amount of pressure he exerted on the French clergy to publicly renounce *la Cause Nationale* and his general attitude toward them. As late as 1911 he continued to blame Charland for the excesses of the conflict.[48] He constantly urged Dupont to castigate his good friend, the editor of *La Justice*.[49] In his meetings with Dupont and Charland, Walsh would criticize them for appealing the Franco-American cause directly to Rome.[50] He was suspicious of both priests throughout the controversy, although it was obvious by mid-1911 that they, too, were concerned about the excesses of the Comité. His constant pressure against several French priests worsened relations between the French community and the diocese.

In 1911 the French press became openly anticlerical. It called Walsh a barbarous assimilator and accused him of bribing legislators to vote against their bill.[51] *Le Messager* called the bishop a tyrant, a despot, and a Francophobe, and accused him of trying to trick the pope concerning the merits of their bill. The press urged the French faithful to close their pocketbooks to diocesan collections.[52] *Le Messager* maintained that their schools were being converted into Irish institutions and that Irish priests were constantly insulting French parishioners.[53] *Le Messager* and *La Justice* also provided forums for Dupré's unrelenting criticism of French clergy who attacked the Comité. Dupré and the papers held special contempt for the Oblates who, while preaching retreats in the diocese, severely criticized the Comité and the French people.[54]

Despite these attacks on the clergy, the French directly involved in the movement still maintained that they were loyal Catholics bearing allegiance to Rome. They stressed that their petition to the legislature had questioned only the bishop's civil authority, not his spiritual hegemony. They constantly pointed out that the "Corporation Sole" was not a universal manner of holding church property.[55]

Because of the French press's scandalous statements, Walsh asked the diocesan censor to check to see if the church should publicly condemn these newspapers. Certainly the bishop had cause for his action. But to anyone familiar with *La Justice* and *Le Messager* such a step seemed particularly paradoxical, for both papers had always been fervently Catholic. In fact, the two French editors cared so much for the faith of Franco-Americans that they felt compelled to hurl aspersions at a bishop whose policies they felt would lead to a general loss of faith among the French.[56]

By early April 1911 Walsh could no longer tolerate the excesses of the Comité. He wrote to two Biddeford priests telling them to warn the executive members of the Comité that they faced interdiction.[57] (Interdiction is the step before excommunication which deprives the interdicted of the right to receive the sacraments until retraction of the offensive statements.) When they did not desist in their action, he publicly interdicted them on 14 May 1911. Six men were interdicted: Albert Maynard, Alfred Bonneau (editor of *La Justice*), Jean-Baptiste Couture (editor of *Le Messager*), Alfred Béland, George Précourt, and Godfroy Dupré. This action sparked renewed controversy. The six said they were interdicted because they presented a bill to the legislature. They called the action an arbitrary imposition of tyranny.[58] Walsh's diary, however, indicates that the six were interdicted because of the scandal they had caused in the church. At first the French newspapers mocked the interdiction letter and vowed not to be intimidated. They denied that they had been informed of the impending interdiction.

The bishop's interdiction letter was also sharply attacked because it warned Franco-American societies not to attend the convention of the Comité. The Comité felt the bishop was trying to disrupt their Biddeford Convention scheduled to begin on 7 June 1911.[59] The bishop had the power to recall a society's chaplain if it disobeyed. This worried the Comité since it had formulated intricate plans by which society members could attend the convention without officially representing their associations. It urged all French societies to send delegates.

Walsh was very cooperative with the French clergy in explaining his action but refused to correspond directly with those interdicted. When Bonneau, Couture, and Maynard wrote to Walsh asking for a clarification of his position, Walsh answered their queries through parish priests.[60] The six men appealed their interdiction to Rome, as they had done in their fight against the "Corporation Sole." Walsh shrugged off this appeal, as he had the previous one, but his anger at the interdicted increased because they appealed over his head.[61]

Jean-Baptiste Couture, editor of Le Messager, *Lewiston, Maine, c. 1910*
Franco-American Collection, University of Southern Maine,
Lewiston-Auburn College[62]

The interdiction split the Franco-Americans of New England. By 1912 regional meetings of Franco-Americans were considering excluding the interdicted.[63] In Biddeford, where five of the six resided, the interdiction caused renewed interest in the "Corporation Sole." Except for Dupré, all those interdicted were widely respected in the community.[64] Although it is unlikely that the bulk of the French populace supported the extremism of the Comité, Walsh's actions, judging from the turnout at the June Convention, seems to have been interpreted as an attempt to discredit *la survivance*. Walsh knew that his action would spark renewed controversy, but felt it his duty to issue the interdiction, regardless.

The Biddeford Convention of June 1911 was a huge success. Over 350 delegates, representing 110 societies and 18 cities—the largest turnout ever—attended.[65] They criticized Walsh for appointing an allegedly anti-French superintendent of parish schools and vowed to carry on the fight against the "Corporation Sole." The delegates and townspeople signed petitions advocating a change in the law. Dupré, having little faith in their appeal to Rome, suggested that the Comité agitate for a state referendum on the question. Dupré added that once the French laymen had the opportunity to control church and school finances, they could improve their schools and buy books similar to those used in public schools. Thus, Dupré viewed the controversy primarily in anti-clerical terms; he did not oppose the Irish because they were assimilationist but because they were priests. It is very likely that he had little support among the delegates since Franco-Americans traditionally had great respect for the clergy. One delegate interviewed, Napoleon Nadeau, told me that Dupré was disliked by Biddeford's Franco-Americans. This antipathy was caused, in part, by Dupré's propensity for stirring up controversy. Nadeau's motivation in attending the convention was to register a protest against Bishop Walsh's policies. He had checked with Father Louis Bergeron before attending (a procedure followed by his friends)[66] and was given the go-ahead. The delegates renewed their pledge not to give any money to diocesan appeals. Observers from Québec promised the delegates the continued support of that province's French citizens.

Bishop Walsh followed the convention closely and dismissed it as an "insulting crowd" causing "public scandal." He stated that the convention was not representative and was made up primarily of "impromptu societies." He accused the members of the Comité of political ambitions and asserted that most of the delegates came from Biddeford. Of the delegates and the French people as a whole he wrote: "The people have no sympathy at all with these leaders but are easily deceived and at times misled."[67] This attitude toward the French, obviously, did much to fuel the controversy for Franco-Americans. Their attacks on the bishop often complained that he treated them condescendingly.[68] None of Walsh's observations about the conventions were completely accurate. If Walsh felt that "the Canadians," as he referred to Franco-Americans sometimes, were "un-American" and would bring nativist feeling against the church, the convention should have calmed his fears. The Stars and Stripes hung in the convention hall along with the French Tricolor. The "Star Spangled Banner" was sung, as well as French-Canadian hymns. Before adjourning, the delegates renewed their allegiance to church and country.

As the convention ended, word was received that Dr. Fortier had died and was being refused church burial by Walsh, despite Father Charland's pleas. The convention dedicated the first hours of the June 8 evening session to him, adjourning in his memory, and attended a mass at St. Joseph's in his honor. Many delegates went to

Waterville to attend Fortier's funeral. Fortier's wife was given a choice of having her husband buried in church (without banners, music, or ceremony) or at a private affair in their home where French societies could be present (it was customary for such societies to attend their member's funerals). His wife chose the latter, saying her husband had lived as a good Catholic without the Irish hierarchy and would go to heaven without them. Charland officiated and 2,000 people gathered to pay their last respects.[69]

Walsh's action infuriated the French, who accused him of punishing Fortier for having gone to Rome to seek a Franco-American bishop. The bishop explained in his diary that he followed this course because Fortier had never retracted his scandalous statements.[70] Even though he had "suspicions about an attempt at a great religious celebration at Fortier's funeral" before making his decision, Walsh made it, regardless of French reaction, because he felt it was his duty. His courageous stand won him the apostolic delegate's support.[71]

Bishop Walsh received his first setback in October 1911, when the pope issued a new decree indicating his preference for the parish corporation. Walsh was not perturbed at this decision against "Corporation Sole"; he had never been an ideological supporter of the system. His defense had always been predicated on his firm belief in the absolute authority of the church and its ministers. It was inconceivable to him that laymen could question and even defy the church. As he once wrote to Charland: "In the Catholic church the people are not to think and say and do as they like but they are to follow and obey the church."[72] The French press gloated over the "new decree...ad nauseam."[73] They felt that Rome had vindicated their position and Dupré promised to present another bill to the legislature.[74]

Meanwhile, the interdiction issue was left unresolved. The French press became increasingly impatient at papal delay and began printing articles questioning its allegiance to Rome.[75] It continually carried unsigned articles denouncing Walsh.[76] It is probable that, in the latter half of 1911, the radicals of *La Cause Nationale* lost a good deal of support. The "Corporation Sole" impasse was now, after papal intervention, in the process of being settled. In addition, Bishop Walsh seems to have become more circumspect in his dealing with the French by late 1911. No new incidents of Irish "tyranny" were reported in *La Justice* or *Le Messager* during this period. In any case, by December, *Le Messager* was hurling diatribes at French priests and laity, who—it said—were fawning before the bishop.[77]

The bitterness between the diocese and the leaders of *La Cause Nationale* continued throughout 1912. All the major French societies refused to parade on St. Jean-Baptiste Day as a protest against the French clergy who supported Walsh. The French press continued to hurl diatribes at Walsh while the latter denounced them privately in his diary. Relations with Dupont became particularly strained because Walsh, not without reason, believed that Dupont was secretly financing the Comité.[78]

In February 1912 Rome sustained Walsh's interdiction.[79] In April the now-conciliatory bishop wrote to those interdicted offering a compromise over "Corporation Sole." The Comité at first refused but eventually met with the bishop on 18 February 1913, in Biddeford. Walsh had called the meeting to prevent another battle before the legislature.[80] He felt that the continued controversy was hurting the image of the church; but the meeting proved fruitless. Still, the bishop's new conciliatory attitude provided hope for a settlement. In 1911 he had refused even to correspond with the interdicted laymen. Two years later he traveled twenty miles to meet with Béland, Bonneau, Maynard, and Précourt when they refused to come to Portland. (Dupré and Couture stayed away from their archenemy). The meeting was confidential, but Bonneau did report that the bishop was affable.

Because no agreement was achieved, the French again presented another bill to the legislature. The issue was slightly different this time. Although defending the "Corporation Sole" at the hearing, Walsh was ready to back a parish corporation consisting of himself, the vicar-general, the pastor, and two laymen appointed by these three. The French leaders advocated a corporation composed of the bishop, the pastor and three laymen elected by the parish. Dupré again attacked the clergy during the hearings and accused them of only wanting French money. After speaking with French leaders, one reporter covering the hearings wrote that these men were reasonable and not anticlerical.[81] The bishop again offered to compromise and invited the *Comité* to meet with three Franco-American priests. They refused. The legislature ruled in Walsh's favor and the Walsh-backed parish cooperation system was soon made law.

The next Franco-American convention was held in Augusta on 18 September 1913. The convention was subdued and its tone less virulent. The French seemed satisfied with the parish corporation law and the main issue in Augusta was about parish schools. Bonneau even admitted that it had been a mistake to go before the legislature with their grievances; the French could have had a fair hearing in church courts without any damaging publicity.[82] Although he characterized the convention as "the usual froth and blow," Walsh recognized the essential moderateness of the delegates.[83] One big change was the absence of Dupré at the convention. He had recently broken with the Comité because they refused to pay him for services rendered before the legislature. He tried to sue, but lost. One delegate at the convention referred to "ridiculous claims" of Dupré on the Comité.[84]

Financial burdens eventually spelled doom for the French movement. No longer supported by a majority of the French populace, the Comité ceased getting contributions. Funds from French Canada also dried up. In 1915 Walsh's great antagonist, Father Dupont, died. By 1916 Bonneau, Béland, Précourt, and Maynard had made a discreet submission to Walsh. *Le Messager* and *La Justice* ceased their combative tones.[85] The controversy, almost a decade old, had ended, but traces of the bitterness endangered by it can still be found today.[86]

* A version of this essay was first published by the Maine Hisorical Society. Michael Guignard, "Maine's Corporation Sole Controversy," in *Maine Historical Society Newsletter* 2, Winter 1973, pp. 113–30.

1 Greeley, Chapter 5.
2 Maynard, p. 285.
3 Ducharme, p. 66.
4 Rumilly, pp. 14–21.
5 Lower, p. 359.
6 Handlin, p. 31.
7 Theriault, pp. 344–47.
8 Foley, p. 136. Theriault, pp. 158–62.
9 *La Justice,* November and December 1905; January 1906. *Le Messager,* January and February 1906.
10 Woodbury, pp. 260–69. Johnson, p. 7.
11 *Le Messager*, 25 August 1906.
12 *La Justice,* 15 March 1906.
13 James Allen, pp. 165, 237, 242.
14 Tatarczuk, p. 261.
15 W. Lucey, p. 300. James Allen, pp. 110–30.
16 Case of Sacred Heart Parish (Document Folio #6, Diocese of Portland Library), Sanford, Maine, 1968.
17 Case of Sacred Heart Parish.
18 St. Michael Parish Directory, 1922.
19 Woodbury, p. 262.
20 Case of Sacred Heart Parish.
21 Case of Sacred Heart Parish.
22 *Le Messager, La Justice,* January 1907 issues.
23 Walsh, Diary, 1 June 1907.
24 *Le Messager*, 26–29 June 1907.
25 *Le Messager*, 26 June 1907. Walsh, Diary, 25 June 1911.

26 *La Justice,* 7 October 1909.
27 *La Justice*, 7 October 1909.
28 Johnson, p. 6. *La Justice,* 28 October 1909, 24 November 1909.
29 Walsh, Diary, 28 May 1907.
30 Mason Wade, p. 185.
31 Walsh, Diary, 11 March 1907.
32 *Le Messager,* 28 July 1909.
33 *Le Messager,* 24 January 1907.
34 *La Justice,* 6 May 1909.
35 *Le Messager*, 16 March 1907.
36 *Le Messager*, 6 August 1909, 28 September 1909.
37 *Le Messager*, 7 April 1906.
38 Walsh, Diary, 8 June 1907.
39 Walsh, Diary, 20 March 1907, 8 June 1907, 19 September 1909, 27 September 1909, 20 March 1907, 8 June 1907, 24 April 1910.
40 *Biddeford Daily Journal* and *Biddeford Record*, 7–9 March 1911.
41 *Biddeford Daily Journal* and *Biddeford Record*, 8–9 March 1911.
42 Foley, pp. 154–66.
43 Walsh, Diary, 31 January 1911, 11 February 1911, 7 March 1911.
44 Walsh, Diary, 19 February 1911, 10 March 1911.
45 Walsh, Diary, 14 February 1911, 21 February 1911.
46 Walsh, to Madigan, 12 February 1911.
47 Walsh, to Falconio, 10 March 1911; to Dwight, 20 June 1911.
48 Walsh, to Falconio, 19 February 1911.
49 Lee, to Dupont, 16 August 1911.
50 Walsh, Diary, 23 January 1911.
51 *Le Messager*, 20 February 1911. *La Justice,* March 1911.
52 *Le Messager*, 8 May 1911, 12 June 1911, 2 August 1911.
53 *Le Messager*, 7 July 1911, 11 August 1911.
54 *Le Messager*, 20 March 1911, 10 April 1911, 15 July 1911.
55 *Le Messager*, 17 May 1911, 22 June 1911, 29 June 1911.
56 Walsh, to Desjardins, 3 July 1911.
57 Walsh, to Bergeron, 10 April 1911; to Dupont, 1 April 1911.
58 *Le Messager,* 5 May 1911, 29 May 1911, 21 June 1911.
59 *Le Messager*, 2 June 1911.
60 Walsh, to Dupont, 8 April 1911; to Leguennec, 24 May 1911; to Jacques, 24 May 1911.
61 Walsh, Diary, 20 May 1911.
62 Franco-American Collection: Biography, Jean-Baptiste Couture.
63 Rumilly, pp. 257, 279.
64 *Biddeford Record*, 15 May 1911. *Biddeford Daily Journal*, 10 June 1911.
65 *Biddeford Daily Journal*, 6 June 1911, 8 June 1911.
66 Nadeau, 28 March 1972.
67 Walsh, Diary, 7 June 1911, 9 June 1911, 17 June 1911.
68 *Le Messager,* 16 March 1907, 20 March 1911.
69 *Biddeford Daily Journal*, 6–9 June 1911.

70 Walsh, Diary, 5 June 1911, 7 June 1911.
71 Walsh, Diary, 7 June 1911, 1 July 1911.
72 Walsh, to Charland, 4 March 1908.
73 Walsh, Diary, 21 October 1911, 30 October 1911.
74 *Le Messager,* 22 October 1911, 24–31 October 1911.
75 *Le Messager*, 28 June 1911.
76 *Le Messager*, 15 November 1911.
77 *Le Messager*, 6 December 1911.
78 Walsh, Diary, 30 January 1912, 3 February 1912, 5 February 1912, 16 February 1912, 20 February 1912, 13 May 1912, 28 December 1912; to Walker, 29 March 1918.
79 Newspaper clipping in Walsh's Diary, origin unknown, between February 15 and 16, 1912.
80 Walsh, Diary, 19 April 1912.
81 *Biddeford Daily Journal*, 15 February 1913.
82 *Biddeford Daily Journal*, 20 September 1913.
83 Walsh, Diary, 30 September 1913.
84 Newspaper clipping from Walsh's Diary, adjacent to his entry for 12 September 1913.
85 The account of the demise of the Comité comes from Rumilly, pp. 287–89, and Johnson, pp. 9–10.
86 Walsh's diary and letters are at the diocese's chancery in Portland, Maine. Not surprisingly, the Diocese of Providence has destroyed all the primary source material concerning the similar Sentinelle Affair.

THE SUMMER I WAS THIRTEEN

Denis Ledoux
Lisbon Falls, Maine

The summer I was thirteen, already becoming the gangly adolescent I was to be, I drove into Lewiston with my mother to Vincent & Leblanc's clothing store on Lisbon Street, and together we bought more new clothes than I had ever had at one time.[1] Shirts, pants, underwear, socks, even handkerchiefs. The Oblates had been very precise—I was to have three of these items and two of those and I wasn't to forget to bring a raincoat.

New clothing piled up on the counter. My parents had three other children at home, each needing his or her share of new clothes for the approaching school year. My brother, Bill, was already in high school at St. Dom's and my two sisters, Claire and Rachel, were behind me, still at Ste. Bernadette. I thought of my father working for an hourly wage that never seemed enough, and yet—and yet the clothes made real that I was going away and I was thrilled to see them pile up.

Somehow my parents would manage. Hadn't they always?

My mother must have tabulated the expense in her mind, rounding the figures to see what the purchases were adding up to (*trois et cinq font huit*) and surely reminding herself that I would need enough clothing to have a change during the time it would take to mail soiled laundry home to be washed and then get it back.

All the clothing would require an identifying tag, we had been told in the letter that had come to us with the list of things I would have to bring. With that tag, I would become number 134. Even today, number 134 is, among all the possible numbers, somehow mine.

My family lived in the country and I was, in spite of my brother and my sisters, a boy who spent his days alone. I did not understand then that it was our different ways of being in the world, of carrying ourselves through our days, that separated us, made it impossible for us to be close. Often, especially with my brother, I felt solitary, wondering why we were not friends, not knowing that there was nothing he or I could do differently.

That summer, before Bucksport, I must, as was my habit, have taken long rides on my 24-inch (61 cm) Columbia bicycle, riding farther into the country between mowed fields and the encroaching woods that even then were gaining on the pastures. When on the Ridge (not far from home, towards Sabattus), perhaps I stopped and, looking towards Mt. Washington, 150 miles (241 kilometers) away in New Hampshire, I must have struggled with the fear and the loneliness that was surely closing in on me as the day approached when, with all the new clothes now marked with the number 134 tags that my *Mémère* Verreault had stitched on, I would leave my family. In a real way, I would never be part of that family again.

My world was about to change, not so much from what it had been—which, at thirteen, I knew it would as I moved tremulously into adolescence—but from that of my contemporaries themselves. The seminary we called Bucksport found its inspiration from some time other than the one in which we lived and my being here would turn me into a person more at home in the past than in the present, so that I would always have a nostalgia for a time other than mine, a nostalgia for a time that had never been mine.

That summer (1960), I rode my bike to the library, my basket full of books, novels set in colonial Williamsburg or perhaps in a French river town along the Mississippi (novels in which the French were always a backdrop for the "American" hero, always proud to be part of this great democratic America and no longer under the autocratic French regime). I was aware, as I rode down Route 125 into Lisbon Falls with a nickel safely in one of my shorts' pockets, that my parents had not loved books when they had been my age living in tenements in Lewiston, that my own love of books was forging something new for myself, something that would somehow take me away. It made me feel guilty somehow, this love of books which they did not share. It made me feel better and worse.

The library was housed in half of a storefront at the corner of Union and Main streets. It did not have a regular librarian but was supervised by older ladies who made a social event of the three afternoons a week the library was open from two to five. After I returned the books, as I walked up and down the front of the shelves that lined the wall looking for novels that interested me, I would listen to the old ladies talk in English. It still startled me then to hear older people speaking English as later it would grab my attention to hear young persons speaking French.

The old Yankee ladies checked out my books, hardly paying any attention to me. Then outside, I filled the basket that was affixed to the handlebar with my books and straddled my bicycle but I did not return home. Instead I went to a gas station on Route 196 (just in back of the library) that had a soda machine. There I reached into my shorts and pulled out the nickel I had brought with me. I inserted it into the soda machine and then quickly guided my choice of a six-ounce bottle down its horizontal channel. The cold water the soda bottle rested in splashed until the bottle reached the spot where I could pull it out. Then, the bottle, cold and wet in my hands, I heard the mechanism spring back in place. Only another nickel inserted into the machine would make it release another treasure—and it would not be my nickel as I was not given to extravagance.

It was that summer that my other *mémère* who lived upstairs—she had turned seventy-seven in May—had said to someone we did not know, pointing proudly to me, "Him go to *collège* September" and I had, as millions of children of immigrants growing up in a country that was not yet theirs, cringed at her lack of English, embarrassed by this woman who had not mastered—in spite of the sixty years she had already lived here—something so basic as the language that was spoken all around her. She was a woman who could barely read and write her own language, let alone the language she could not speak.

My grandmother, if she sensed the embarrassment of this tall, lean grandson next to her, did not let on, did not falter. Instead, she was engulfed by pride: she was the grandmother of a soon-to-be minor seminarian. Her grandson was going to the *collège*—in this instance, the Franco-Maine equivalent of the French-Canadian classical high school that had been a hallmark of French Canada since the English had changed forever what it meant to be French in North America. Her own son, my Uncle Lucien, had gone away at thirteen to a *collège*, a seminary, and had become a priest. Now, she had lived long enough to see a grandson go to the *collège,* him, in September.

"College?" the woman my *mémère* had spoken to asked. She turned to me—surely she must have said to herself, she could not have a conversation with my grandmother. This woman who could only speak her one English language, who was ignorant of the way 30 percent of Maine's population spoke, brushed my *mémère* to the side of her consciousness and turned to me and said, "You're a bit young to go to college, aren't you?"

"The *collège*," I explained, "is how we say high school in French." I did not say it referred to the classical-studies high school, usually seminaries that had been created all over French Canada and French New England. I did not know then that the English had severely constricted educational opportunities in French Canada but that, having secured *Canadien* loyalty in 1774 against the increasingly rebellious

Americans, with the promulgation of religious liberty (via the Act of Quebec), they could not then interfere with the development of seminaries without abrogating the very laws they had set in place.

The *Canadiens* (French Canadians had not come into existence yet) funneled their ambitious sons into the seminary system. And well they might focus their attention on the seminary system. The majority of Franco-American doctors, lawyers, and sundry professionals in the Lewiston of my childhood had all—or nearly all—gone through the Canadian seminary system. And this my grandmother knew as well as she knew that, if I went to the *collège*, I would not work in the mills all my life as she and my *pépère* had.

I was very young and I had no idea what anything would mean except that I would be far away and that I would be striving for something I thought—or at least I had been told—I wanted. And so I rode along the ridge on my Columbia bicycle, both fearful of leaving my family and very hopeful of what life would bring me. I was about to do what the best of French-Canadian boys had been doing for almost 200 years.

It was just that I was doing it in the wrong country—and in the wrong century.

1 This excerpt is drawn from a memoir of Denis Ledoux's seminary high-school years, *Simply Bucksport/A Seminary Life*.

Denis Ledoux and Father Jules Guy,
St. Joseph's Oblate Seminary High School, Bucksport, Maine, 1962.
Courtesy of Denis Ledoux

AN INTRODUCTION TO "LIFE IN THE MILLS," FROM *CANUCK*, A NOVEL BY CAMILLE LESSARD-BISSONNETTE

Linda Pervier
Brunswick, Maine

A mere handful of French-language novels were written in New England during nearly eighty years of heavy Canadian emigration that began about 1860. All were originally published as *feuilletons* (serial fiction) in the vibrant Franco-American press. Hundreds of newspapers were founded in the U.S. during the late-nineteenth and early twentieth centuries to disseminate local and global news in French, host debate on questions of political, social, and religious import, and help sustain ethnic identity. These papers were also a source of entertainment. Along with other light reading, papers such as *Le Messager* in Lewiston, Maine, ran serialized romances as regular fare, imported, with very few exceptions, from Québec and Europe.

The two strongest *feuilletons* written by Franco-New Englanders, *Jeanne la fileuse* (Jeanne the Spinner) and *Canuck*, merit attention today. *Jeanne la fileuse* was written by Honoré Beaugrand, founding publisher of *La République* of Boston and Fall River, and appeared around 1875 in Massachusetts. *Canuck* was written by Camille Lessard-Bissonnette under her *nom de plume*, Liane, for *Le Messager* in 1936.

Style elements in the sub-genre as a whole, including these two novels, pose challenges for the modern reader. In some examples, pages and even whole chapters are filled with statistics, lists, or recycled news articles. In *Jeanne la fileuse*, in particular, these elements abound. They are important to Beaugrand's polemical purpose; however, narrative tension is sacrificed. All the novels reinforce, to one degree or another, traditional mores and morality. While this was expected—even demanded—by the Franco-American Catholic readership of the time, didactic elements come off today as melodramatic or preachy. *Canuck* is not totally exempt in this, even though Lessard-Bissonnette successfully expanded, reshaped, and contradicted traditional perspectives in the novel and throughout her writings.

In the preface to the first bound edition of *Jeanne la fileuse* Beaugrand asks to be let off the literary hook. He admits his book is "less a novel and more a pamphlet," a variant to his steady output of editorials against *Québécois* propagandists critical of

Office staff of Le Messager, *Lewiston, Maine, c 1908. Left to Right: Back row—Corinne Gauthier (Mrs. Eugène Dumais), Loretta Vachon, Blanche Verville (Mrs. Alfred Sutton), and Camille Lessard (Mrs. Bissonnette); Middle row—F. X. Guay, Albert Bédard, Odule Laplante, Joseph Bélanger, L. N. Gendreau, M. Runeau; Front row—J. B. Couture (director), P. S. Guilbault (foreman), Henri Carpentier, Omer Gauvin, Arthur Brunelle.*
Franco-American Collection, University of Southern Maine, Lewiston-Auburn College[1]

emigration and unflattering in their portrayals of Canadians in exile.[2] Beaugrand doesn't hesitate, either, to ask readers to tolerate structural flaws that may crop up in his novel, published under pressure of daily deadlines.[3] Lessard-Bissonnette asks no favors, but she does take a rather sudden turn of plot to bring her story to its denouement.

Still, both Beaugrand's and Liane's stories contain poetic flashes. Intellectual energy and curiosity about the world are palpable in the writing of both authors.

Lessard-Bissonnette provides rich descriptive detail. In Beaugrand we glimpse a real talent, later to grace his folktales, for storytelling. Beaugrand's heroine, Jeanne Girard, is pallid—underdrawn and overidealized; but Lessard-Bissonnette's Victoria Labranche bristles with character. Most important, these two authors are deeply thoughtful about the immigrant experience and provide rare views of its realities.

Lessard-Bissonnette was twenty in 1904, when she came with her family from the Mauricie-Bois-Francs region of Canada to Maine to enter the textile industry. Theirs was a story played out innumerable times in Québec: The Lessard farm—along with the rural economy of the time—was failing, and Camille's illiterate parents had few options for the support of their many children apart from emigration. In Canada, Camille had been an excellent student and, from age sixteen, the district schoolteacher. About two years into the job of "drawing-in girl" (described in the following excerpt) at the Continental Mills in Lewiston, she needed a creative outlet and began writing in the evening, submitting articles to *Le Messager*. Publisher J. B. Couture took encouraging notice and hired her full time in 1908.

This was a big break for a young journalist, as the paper's readership extended far beyond Lewiston's city limits. Blessed with capable management from the start, *Le Messager* was published continuously from 1880 to 1966. At its height the journal was one of the most widely read French newspapers in the country, second only to *L'Avenir* of Manchester, New Hampshire—a remarkable feat in view of fierce competition from well-funded publications produced in larger immigrant communities in larger states and from popular Franco-American editions of *La Presse* and *La Patrie* from Canada.

Camille left Maine with her family for Alberta, Canada, in 1912. She would never return. She continued, however, to file travelogues and essays to *Le Messager*, all while crisscrossing the U.S.-Canadian border to pursue other careers. Thirty years after the "drawing-in girl" began writing for J. B. Couture, Liane sent him *Canuck*, her only novel. Richard Santerre describes a degree of buzz preceding its publication. A great favorite with readers, Lessard-Bissonnette's submissions were routinely announced in the paper weeks in advance. On 23 January 1936, this banner ran across three columns: "*S'en vient par LIANE comme feuilleton dans les colonnes du Messager le roman* Canuck. *La vie d'une jeune canadienne exclusivement écrit pour Le Messager*" (Coming soon to these pages: A serial novel by Liane, *Canuck*, the story of a Canadian girl, written exclusively for *Le Messager*).[4]

Set in rural Québec and Lowell, Massachusetts, *Canuck* was serialized throughout the spring months and published in book form soon after. Chapter one, "Life in the Mills," opens with evocative details of an arrival in the States by train and plunges into unromanticized descriptions of millwork and tenement living. Lessard-Bissonnette's realistic accounts are nearly unique in Franco-American literature and, as historian André Senécal notes, she alone, among the immigrant *romanciers*, came from the working class and could tell the authentic story.[5] In this opening segment there is a whiff, too, of family conflict that will propel events later on.

Camille Lessard-Bissonnette would have been pleased to be re-read in the twenty-first century and to be identified with Maine. In 1970, at age eighty-seven, quite blind and very frail, she was living in a retirement home in California. On September 1 (just months before her death), she wrote to a Maine friend and colleague, devoting a long postscript to reminiscences of her career in journalism. Writing in French (translated here), Lessard-Bissonnette refers to herself as "a woman whose heart still belongs to Lewiston," affirming that "*Le Messager* was always in my blood, in all my pores...I have remained faithful to it at all times, no matter where I was, even if life has kept me at a distance."[6]

1 Franco-American Collection: 19-H-Lewiston Media, Box-A, F, G-I-Messager, File for articles and pictures. The names have been assembled from a notation on the back of the picture and an enclosed typed description.

2 Beaugrand, p. 75.

3 Beaugrand, p. 78.

4 Santerre, p. 181.

5 Senécal, pp. 147–48.

6 Lessard-Bissonnette, letter to Charlotte Michaud.

"LIFE IN THE MILLS," EXCERPT FROM *CANUCK*

Camille Lessard-Bissonnette
Lewiston, Maine
Translation by Linda Pervier
Brunswick, Maine

It was a morning in early March in the year 1900. A railroad locomotive on the Boston & Maine line pulled in to Lowell, Massachusetts, hauling baggage cars and three compartments full of French-Canadian immigrants. The locomotive's nose pointed toward Boston; its engine huffed and puffed, and its well-worn wheels were squealing. Gradually the train slowed its advance and eventually stopped just 100 feet from the station.

Passengers swarmed like bees from the front and rear of the cars. They kicked and elbowed one another roughly, trying to get out as quickly as possible from the filthy dust- and smoke-laden air of the cars where they had been jammed for hours like sardines in a can. The rush toward the doors was also due, perhaps, to excitement—they had arrived, at last, in the United States!

Old, young, men, women, children—all had drawn faces and eyes tired from an interminable night spent on the benches of the rail convoy.

The men's arms were filled with large sacks, they wore packs on their backs, and their hands grasped overstuffed suitcases. Young girls dragged little ones along by the hand. The women carried balking babies in their arms. All of these people, like flocks of sheep rushing toward the fold, disappeared into the comfortable station, where lamps lit the evening before were still burning.

On this frosty March morning in 1900, it was the poorest of French-Canadians who disembarked at Lowell from the train on the Boston & Maine. The next day, this same train might well board a more fortunate class of Canadians at the 45th parallel: merchants, industrialists and professionals. They, too, would be coming to get their hands on the gold in Uncle Sam's coffers.

While the passengers climbed out of the cars, the brakemen mercilessly knocked around enormous boxes whose sides had been gimleted with holes through which cord had been passed to serve as handles. Without this detail, such boxes would not have been permitted on a passenger train. Trunks—small or large, new or rusted, tied

Cover of Canuck *by "Liane,"* nom de plume *of Camille Lessard-Bissonnette, published by* Le Messager, *1936*
Franco-American Collection, University of Southern Maine, Lewiston-Auburn College

around with clothesline, some with camel hair covers—were handled as harshly as the boxes. Male travelers closely watched the unloading of the baggage. All at once one of them would be heard to say, "That one, that's mine!" or else, "There's one—I hope all the others are there!" When all were accounted for, the owner would breathe a sigh of relief and take off to join his family in the station while a neighbor called out, in his turn, the same exclamations.

Inside the station the dominant sounds were babies crying, toddlers whining, and children chattering. As quickly as they could, mothers brought out bottles of milk to quiet the youngest ones. Bigger children opened bags filled with sandwiches, which they greedily devoured, smearing themselves with lard, butter and jam. The older girls, moistened towels in their hands, barely managed to keep the little ones' noses, chins, and fingers clean.

In a corner, the five members of a family huddled close to one another, worried, nervous. The father, Vital Labranche, was a tall, brown-haired man with sharp eyes and lips like the blades of a knife, giving the impression that one would not do well to step on his toes. He could have been forty.

The mother was a small, frail blonde with large, soft, dreamy eyes and the fearful mien of an animal expecting to have her throat slit at any moment. She must have been about the same age as her husband, but she looked fifty.

Victoria (who was called Vic) was a girl of fifteen, as long and thin as a flute, with eyes as deep as the night, and long tresses as black as a crow's wing. She had slender, artistic fingers that seemed displaced, attached as they were to the hands of this unrefined peasant girl. She would have been pretty had she been differently dressed. Her clothes reflected the general misery of her family's poverty—tasteful options in attire were not available to them. Nevertheless, her young, well-formed body stood erect in a defiant posture. An astute observer could have perceived a bravado about her lips and a challenge in her eyes, signaling that this one would not be led to the slaughter without a struggle.

Maurice, ten years old, was a handsome lad with the blond hair and dreamy eyes of his mother. He had fine features and an alert expression. He stuck close to Vic, as if sensing that she was the one he could count on for understanding and protection.

Besson, Maurice's twin brother, had pleurisy. Inadequately treated, the disease had weakened the boy's bones and lungs, leaving him a pitifully twisted hunchback. He was huddled on a bench, his pale, scrawny head resting on his mother's knees. He wasn't sleeping—his angelic little wax-white face was alert, his eyes wide open to take in everything—but he had used up all his strength.

"This is as good a spot as any," said Mr. Labranche. "You'll wait for me here while I go look for a place for us to stay. When I've found a house, I'll go buy beds, a stove, a table and chairs, some wood and provisions. Don't worry if that takes me the better part of the forenoon. When everything's ready I'll come back here with a wagon to get you and our boxes."

He buttoned up his heavy cardigan, jammed his hat down over his ears, pulled on his woolen mittens, and took off into the cold, gray morning while the others, without thought of eating or talking, remained seated on the station benches.

Vic, whose eyes were exploring everywhere, arose and looked out the window. "If you don't mind, Mama," she said, "I'm going to take a walk outside and look around a little. I'll be careful of the wagons and I won't go far. Furthermore, Father isn't due back soon—he won't know."

"Me too, I'm going," said Maurice, rising to join Vic without waiting for permission.

"You can certainly go for a walk and stretch your limbs," said Mother. "But I'm going to stay here and tend to Besson. He seems pretty worn out from the night on the train. Don't be gone too long, though—I'd worry."

Vic, with Maurice at her side, walked about the platform and stopped on the sidewalk in front of the station. She looked at the dirty street just awakening to the day, the rickety-looking gray houses, and the murky windowpanes where shades were being raised. A frown appeared on her face. The terrain along the length of the station formed a high bank, and Vic and Maurice climbed it. Once at the summit, Vic contemplated for a few moments the tenement buildings that all looked alike, the dusty shops, the smoky factories. Her lips formed these words: "So, this is '*les Etats*'! And this is where I'm going to live!" Maurice, younger, was less observant and, furthermore, he was too excited about this change of circumstances to stop to analyze it thoughtfully.

On the evening of that same day in March 1900, the Labranches found themselves settling into an apartment of four rooms on the fourth floor of a tenement. The rent was $3 a month. In the front, the apartment looked out over the dusty street. Behind the building ran the muddy waters of the mill canal, a waterway built of masonry upon which would grow neither bush nor blade of grass. On the inside of the tenement block, as well as on the outside, any speck of paint had long ago disappeared. The wood of the doors and windows looked gnawed around the edges, probably due to having been opened and closed too often and too roughly. The panes rattled where the putty had worn away. In some cases, the glass was missing entirely. Plaster had fallen from numerous places in the ceiling and walls, leaving cavities like ratholes where the lathes of the substructure were visible. The floorboards of soft wood were full of knots and splinters; on a rugless landing, barefoot children and floor-washers were bound to catch numerous slivers from the slightest friction.

The knobs on the doors of the wardrobes rattled—they were barely attached. And the locks didn't work. The corners of the wardrobe shelves as well as the inside and underside of the iron sink swarmed with cockroaches of every size and color. The faucet was green with corrosion, and not a trace of enamel remained.

Over the sink were two hooks intended for hanging a cup and a mirror. The plaster around them had fallen away, all the way down to the lathing, and cockroaches had found refuge in the resulting dirty holes. Near a window in the kitchen there was a tiny shelf which served to hold a lamp during the day. In the evening, at dusk, the lamp was lit and placed on the table to better light the room.

To conserve lamp oil, the tenement stairwells remained unlit. One groped one's way up and down, feeling for the steps with the feet, guided by the handrail. Over time the steps had become worn down and thin in the middle. Fragments of wood were missing, making the useable part of each step narrower and thus more dangerous. On many of the steps, a sturdy, full-sized adult was truly hard-pressed to find safe footing for his larger feet and greater weight.

The handrails were worn and shaky from use by unruly children who rode them as if they were hobby horses instead of descending on foot. Children with knives practiced their carving skills on the balusters supporting the handrails, just as the plaster walls served as canvases for young artists working in pencil.

At the bottom of the stairwell, there was neither a porch nor a stoop. A single stair step out the door, and there you were, on trodden ground, as the street had no sidewalk.

Arriving at their lodging, Vic had been curious to look around from one room to another. This had taken her one minute at most and, for the second time that day, she murmured, "So, this is '*les Etats*.' And this is where I'm going to live!" Anyone watching the girl at that moment would have observed a fine wrinkle creasing her brow, and a ray of revolt in her eyes.

The afternoon and evening were taken up with unpacking, unwrapping, setting up cots, installing the stove, and adjusting the stovepipe (a process accompanied by curses on the part of Mr. Labranche). The most urgent cleaning was done—washing out the wardrobes, scrubbing the sink—so they could get moved in as quickly as possible and be at the mill gates the next morning at six. There was no time to lose in starting to make money.

Labranche had been to the States in his youth and, as he had already learned the job of weaver, he was sure to have no difficulty in finding work. His wife was going to learn the same job, as was Victoria, because it paid the most. Maurice, who was big and tall for his age, would be passed off as fifteen years old. Instead of going to school, he too would find work, either in the carding room or in the spinning department where there was always a need for boys. As for Besson, he was too weak to go to school or to work in a factory. He was going to keep house. He would peel potatoes, wash dishes, and do other light work. Evenings and Sundays, Vic and her mother would take care of the meals, laundry, ironing, etc. With their life organized in this way, they should be able, in four or five years, to amass enough money to pay the mortgages on the farm in Québec and go back there to live.

And so began this life—that is, life in the mills—for the Labranche family.

Vital Labranche and his wife were each assigned a set of looms in the same section. This permitted the man to keep after his wife, pushing her to improve her work with the goal of fattening the pay envelopes. She did not rebel. Obedience was the life of peasant women in her country. She went along like an animal in the yoke, certainly feeling the lashes of the master's whip, but making no effort to escape them.

They had planned to have Vic learn weaving, too. But on the second day the girl had fainted, collapsing onto a loom. A shuttle punctured her shoulder before they

Weaving machine, Bates Mill, Lewiston, Maine, c. 1900
Franco-American Collection, University of Southern Maine, Lewiston-Auburn College[1]

were able to shut down the heavy machine, which normally ran all day without interruption. The wound healed, and they succeeded in getting Vic into the department where the heddles were threaded. Drawing in, as this work was called, is always done by women, no doubt because it requires a patient nature and soft-skinned delicate fingers to handle thousands of fine strands of cotton every day without breaking them.

In this department, iron frames are set up opposite the windows. An enormous iron roller filled with thread—a sort of giant spindle—is carted in by male workers (because strong arms are required) and loaded on to each frame. This roller is the warp beam. Then the drawing-in girls use hooks to thread each strand on each roller (and there are hundreds and hundreds of them, sometimes thousands) through the eyes of a set of metal or fiber heddles. Those of metal come in sets of up to fifteen in a tightly packed arrangement. To correctly set the strands for special patterns, one must follow instructions written down by the overseer. Most often the pattern is simple and, for an old hand, no written instructions are necessary.

After the heddles are threaded, the same strands must be fed with another kind of hook into the "dents" (a row of narrow eyelets) along a "reed," minding the pattern all the while. Then, each completed roller is tested in the weaving room. If by chance there is a mistake with a single strand—whether an eyelet somewhere along the reed has been overlooked, or a strand has been threaded into the tenth heddle when the instructions specified the fifth—the roller is returned to the drawer-in who made the error, and she must re-do the time-consuming task from scratch with no remuneration whatsoever. It is, then, of the greatest importance to pay careful attention to one's work and, furthermore, to acquire speed if each Saturday's pay envelope is to be nice and thick.

The department where Vic went to work as a drawing-in girl was on the fourth floor. From this part of the factory you could see some of the city through the wide windows. Seated at her work, very peaceful, away from the infernal racket of the weaving looms, Vic finally felt that she had made a first step forward since her arrival in the States.

At six o'clock, her work finished, she would pocket her heddle hook and reed hook, for fear that some rascal would steal them from her (they were costly to replace), and she would make her unhurried way toward the dark and ugly family dwelling.

At home, it was the same story every day. Mornings, they left around 5:30, carrying a light lunch for noontime because they had not been able to find employment near their tenement. They had had to take work in a mill situated some distance away, which did not permit them to come home for the midday meal.

Upon arriving home around 6:20 in the evening, they took the stairs at a run, in spite of the darkness. Maurice and Vic, with the zeal of youth, often climbed them four steps at a time, sometimes missing a step and losing their footing, getting back up, and carrying on in the same way. On such occasions, their father never failed to say, "You're not capable of walking up the stairs like everybody else? Anyone would think animals were stampeding, the way you pound up the steps!" Neither one of them ever responded to this valid remark, thus avoiding a scene.

Reaching the top of three long and steep staircases, the working Labranches slipped into the kitchen which also served as dining room, parlor, and, in a word, everything aside from the bedrooms. Besson pulled the table out from the wall before the family arrived, and the two little brothers took their places for meals in the space between the table and the wall. Vic was seated across from them. Her father sat at one end of the table, his back to the door, and his wife at the other, facing toward her husband.

At six o'clock, Besson would set five straight chairs around the table. On the oilskin tablecloth he placed five large ceramic or enameled metal plates with as many bowls and saucers, a large spoon next to each plate when there was soup or, if not, a knife and fork. There was only one small spoon, and it was planted in the sugar bowl in the middle of the table. Everyone used it to add sugar to his or her tea (in the Labranche household they had not heard of coffee). The sugar was used in strict moderation, under the close surveillance of the head of the household. A pot of syrup was placed on a small plate to keep it from getting the oilskin table covering sticky, which would damage its scant coat of varnish. A bottle of vinegar accompanied the sugar bowl when baked beans were served.

When the table was set, Besson went to a window and stared out into the street. The day had been very long and very boring, so all alone was he at the house, and he was eager to see his loved ones return.

After a few minutes of meditation with his nose pressed against the windowpane, he climbed onto a chair in order to reach the lamp on its shelf. Then he got down off the chair, exercising all the caution in the world, as if the lamp he carried were a treasure (heaven help the child if it had gotten away from him and been broken). He set the lamp on the chair seat and removed the globe, looking to see if it were good and clean. If not, he cleaned it with a large plug of twisted paper that he pushed inside it.

He turned the paper plug in such a way as to slide it against the inner surfaces of the glass, removing the smudges of smoke. This operation completed, he checked to see if the lamp contained enough oil for the evening, and he refilled it if needed. He raised the wick and trimmed it with scissors with the greatest of care so not to leave any tips that would smoke. Next, he took a splinter of wood from the wood box and held it to the hot coals behind the little door of the stove. When it caught fire, he used it to light the lamp, which he then gently set right in the middle of the table.

Besson always cooked the potatoes to perfection, and they were always ready on time. When the tines of a fork pushed into a potato proved to the little invalid that no one would be able to criticize his work, he emptied the cooking water into the sink, paying close attention not to scald himself. He placed the kettle on the back of the stove so it wouldn't get cold, and he slid the cover a little to the side to give the steam a chance to escape, preventing the potatoes from taking on a watery taste.

This done, the boy looked to see if everything was in its place. If nothing were missing, he'd go and stretch out in the only rocking chair in the house. This chair was a big luxury for the family. But Mrs. Labranche, tears in her eyes, had so insisted on it, that her husband had decided to spend a few bucks for a chair that would provide a little comfort for the poor little one whose days on earth were numbered.

So Besson took to the rocking chair and waited for his loved ones. He placed his thin arms on the armrests, tipped his head against its back, and closed his eyes, his beautiful big eyes so soft and so deep that they seemed to contemplate all of earth and heaven.

He had not quite fallen asleep when banging doors and running in the stairways told him that the folks were arriving home from the factory. As soon as she came in, his mother would look at him intently, anxiously, as if she were always surprised to find him yet alive each time she returned from the mill. His father glanced at him in a protective, worried way. Vic never failed to touch her hand to the child's head in passing. Only Maurice teased him. "Hello, Besson, is your supper ready?" he'd ask, "Are your potatoes cooked?"

While Mr. Labranche and Maurice took turns at the kitchen sink to wash their faces over the basin that had been placed there, Vic and her mother brought out the pots of meat, stew, hash, or soup that had been cooked the night before. They would remove the round lids from the top of the stove and place the pots over the holes, directly over the fire, so the food would reheat more quickly and supper would not be delayed.

Nearly a whole loaf of bread was cut into thick slices, and the reheated contents of the pots were poured into enamelware platters that were set on trivets in the center of the table. These preparations done, each one was ready to plunge in the serving spoon to fill his plate and devour his supper after a hard day of work.

There were never any pies or cakes or pastries. Not only would they have taken too much time to prepare, but also would have been too expensive. On the other hand, there was always on the table a pot of light syrup made of brown sugar. They would pour a small quantity of this syrup in a saucer and dip their bread in it, on one side only, and very lightly, so not to waste it. When they grew bored with the dessert of syrup, they would eat a kind of jelly made from common grade fruits (which the frost may have touched, but too briefly, apparently, to cause real damage). This conserve came in a tin bucket with a hinged lid, and the supply would last them a year or more.

The meal over, Vic and her mother would carry away the platters. Labranche would take off his shoes to relax his feet, retaining the heavy wool farmer's socks that smelled of sweat. He would fill his pouch with tobacco and cross the hall to go to play his nightly card game at the neighbor's. As soon as he had gone out, mother and daughter, without looking at each other, would let out a sigh of relief: They were assured of a few hours of peace. Labranche was a grouch, violent and quick-tempered. When he was around, they never knew what might set him off. He would invent problems just for the satisfaction of blowing up about them.

After supper Maurice would stick his nose in his books—schoolbooks belonging to his mother, who had been a little country schoolmarm. He didn't put them away until it was time for bed. Sometimes his mother or Vic would have him recite lessons and solve problems. All the lad ever spoke of was becoming a priest, and no one argued with him, although they wondered how his father would ever be persuaded to untie the purse-strings so Maurice would be able to enter the seminary preparatory school.

As for Besson, games and studying tired him. He'd hang by the door and tag along after his father, spending his evenings curled up in a chair, watching the men playing cards and smoking. Sometimes the smoke was so thick that his atrophied lungs exploded. Doubled over in a fit of coughing that brought blood to his lips, he would come back home and put himself to bed without complaint.

1 Franco-American Collection: 19-I Lewiston Mills, Box 4, various photos.

AN INTRODUCTION TO *CANUCK*: WHY READ IT NOW?[1]

Sylvie Charron
Farmington, Maine

Rhea Côté Robbins
Waterville, Maine

According to the 1990 census, persons of French origin constitute the fifth largest ancestry group in the United States, numbering 13.15 million.[2] Most French-Canadian immigrants arrived in New England between 1850 and 1920 to work in factories. Yet, novels written in French by Franco-Americans representing this vast New England immigrant group are exceedingly rare. *Canuck* is one brilliant exception.[3] It plays an essential historical and literary role, especially considering the scarcity of immigrant writing in French within the genre of U.S. novels. It sheds light on the effects of immigration as well as on the specific fate of French-Canadian immigrants to the United States at the turn of the century. In addition, this text is almost all that exists for the recovery of Franco-American women's voices at the turn of the twentieth century. It relates the life of millions of working women in New England factories and tenements, and provides a bridge for new generations to understand the immigration process.

Camille Lessard-Bissonnette emerged from a society and time firmly rooted in traditionalism and nationalism, having left Quebec in 1904 for Lewiston, Maine. Two years later, the teacher-turned-millworker-turned-journalist would begin to boldly articulate her views on a variety of topics such as the suffrage movement, racism, and national allegiance. In 1936 Lessard-Bissonnette, the novelist, would do much to explode cherished myths about French-Canadian society.

Canuck was written in *feuilleton* form in 1936 for the French newspaper *Le Messager* located in Lewiston, Maine. Soon after, the novel was published as a single volume and was so successful that a newspaper in Lawrence, Massachusetts, also featured it as *feuilleton* a year later.[4] The novel has fundamental historical, sociological, and literary value.

Camille was born in 1883 in Sainte-Julie-de-Mégantic, Québec, near the Maine border. She was bright and ambitious, finished her schooling at age sixteen and became a school teacher—even though her parents were illiterate.[5] In 1904 her teaching career was interrupted when her entire family immigrated to Lewiston to improve their condition (a factory worker in the U.S. would receive ten times the wage of a school teacher in Canada). Camille began work in the *Filature Continentale*, a textile mill where she worked for four years. She also started working as a columnist for the local paper in 1906 and was hired as editor for its *pages féminines* (women's pages) two years later. These pages were similar to pages commonly found in *Québécois* newspapers but, because Lessard-Bissonnette was familiar with working women's woes, she used her columns to affirm the right to work for equal pay, speak against family violence, demand the right to vote, and addressed many other social issues affecting women, marriage, and family. This journalistic writing helped sharpen her social views, until she published her only work of fiction—*Canuck*—for *Le Messager* almost thirty years later.

Canuck is a minutely descriptive and evocative novel, largely based on autobiographical material from Camille's life and the life of the larger community around her. It is written in precise, elegant French, sprinkled with a few vernacular expressions. It presents the perspective of an immigrant family struggling to establish a life in a less-than-welcoming host environment. For the student of French, this novel demonstrates that Franco-American literature in French can be easily understood and highly literate. It helps deconstruct the stereotype that New England French, somehow, is an obscure *patois*—not meriting public attention.

The word "Canuck" is a derogatory term used to refer to French-Canadian immigrants and was used by Lessard-Bissonnette to reclaim a positive identity. The novel is divided into twelve chapters of similar length, as can be expected from a *feuilleton*. The first six chapters, constituting a vivid and tightly woven whole, describe the arrival of an immigrant family to Lowell, their struggle to adapt, and their life until the death of Besson, a sickly but angelic child who keeps the family blessed—in a manner predating Jack Kerouac's main character in *Visions of Gerard*.[6] The realism of *Canuck* echoes Balzac or Flaubert and recreates the environment of work and home so vividly that the modern reader can recover this past in its most minute and compelling details—cockroaches, food culture, noisy looms, crowded spaces, tenements, poverty, and prejudice, countered by dignity, pride, *joie de vivre,* and a desire to succeed. When the child dies, the family returns to the family homestead in Canada while Vic, the young and courageous heroine, stays behind to continue working in factories and sending money to her family. One of her first priorities, consistent with tradition, is to pay for her younger brother's education towards the priesthood. At her father's death, she returns to the ancestral farm with the intention of running it, reversing expected gender roles. Camille Lessard-Bissonnette sets the beginning of her novel in Lowell, Massachusetts, rather than Lewiston, Maine, to create some geographical distance, but retains the year of her own immigration to Maine in 1900.

Chapter 7 represents a major shift in tone and point of view, since it is a first-person narrative—an intimate journal written by Vic, which spans five years of her life. It addresses the issue of love relationships, but demonstrates her inner strength. Vic's journal is the turning point of the book, before she re-enters Québec after her sojourn in the U.S. The journal draws the female reader into the story by its intimacy. The preface of the first edition states: "*Le chapitre 'Je T'aime, Jean!' nous bouleverse, tellement cela sonne vrai*" (the chapter moves us deeply because it rings so true).[7] The author shows how relationships develop in the culture and insists on Vic's chastity and morality. She stands up against the commonly held view that French women are "loose." She purposely undoes the suspicion that surrounds ethnic women and their sexuality.

The remaining four chapters return to a third-person narrative and tell of a temporary repatriation into Québec: they represent a quilt of multiple themes, incorporating folklore, myth, recipes, folk medicine, pig slaughtering, while also paying tribute to traditional values in the culture. Life in the country is romanticized, as was customary in the French-Canadian novels of the period, contrasting with the bleak view of the town and factory at the beginning of the novel. These chapters are sociologically relevant as a detailed and accurate depiction of rural life and French customs.

Chapters 9 (*Père L'allumette*) and 10 (*La vie d'un errant*) introduce an old beggar from Louisiana, who depends on the charity of his hosts but also provides the family/reader with stories from the wider *francophone* world. He is a wandering soul and healer, providing a long list of herbal medicines for the women of Lewiston. This list is a tribute to the Franco-American faith in folk medicine. The saga of his family and travels resemble a Greek tragedy, giving the tale mythical overtones.

Finally, the last two chapters of the novel serve as an epilogue with Vic's marriage to her benefactor, a benevolent, educated man substantially older than she. Vic also discovers that her farm is sitting on precious minerals, which enables her to sell the property at substantial profit, travel the world, and live happily ever after. Life on the farm, then, is not shown as entirely desirable, as would be the case in most French-

Canadian novels of the period. Camille Lessard-Bissonnette does not propose a return to the rural past and certainly not to the traditional situation of women.

In short, the novel tells a story of immigration, resettlement, and the many cultural shocks the French-Canadians faced when newly arrived in the U.S. The literary establishment has largely ignored immigrant women's writings, especially in cases such as *Canuck*, because the text was not written in English and does not belong to either the U.S. or French tradition. Current criticism is re-evaluating the importance of immigrant writing, border-crossing, and writings by women like Lessard-Bissonnette.

Canuck is a particularly bold piece because it criticizes the traditional dependence of women on their fathers or husbands, their constant fear and silencing. Camille Lessard-Bissonnette proposes a new kind of Franco-American heroine: young, smart, independent, ambitious, and self-reliant, while respectful of contemporary morality and religion. The author challenges the patriarchy inherent in a French culture largely ruled by the priesthood and the supremacy of the adult male. She also examines the discrimination faced by newcomers. She describes their poverty and their desire for social promotion. She examines the stereotypes (typified by the title), the more prominent and recognizable elements of the culture, and goes beyond to add realistic dimension to the stereotypes by presenting a full-bodied view of the values and belief systems of the culture.

Canuck is also characteristic of immigrant writing and border-crossing in the way it weaves life and text. Camille Lessard-Bissonnette was herself a free spirit who moved often and traveled widely in the U.S. and Canada. Her mobility, geographical distance, and time separation from her subject played a part in her formation as a writer. She wrote *Canuck* while working as colonization agent for the Louisville and Nashville Railroad, the head office of which was located in Louisville, Kentucky.

The writing, in turn, serves as repatriation into the culture for the reader, generations removed from the original voices. Ethnic writing is an act of taboo (telling family secrets) and breaking taboo at the same time. A difficulty of writing the oral tradition is that the nature of writing does not easily resemble the oral tradition of storytelling. Oral tradition, myth, and storytelling may explain why Camille wrote in mixed genres. The absence of books in the home, the inter-textuality of the oral tradition—folklore, songs, medicines, recipes, poems, complaints—lends itself to the mixed genres.

Camille Lessard-Bissonnette's work is complex because she writes about the cultural "Other," in French, as a woman, and as an *émigré*. She "reversed the stereotype of submission...invalidates the external naming process that makes them outsiders" through her act of writing, and particularly by writing in mixed genres.[8] She opposes the traditional in literature and the patriarchy in the culture.

In the first half of *Canuck*, Vic challenges her father and the dominant ethos. She demonstrates her courage by leaving her family. She does it to keep her wages and help her mother and siblings, while still adhering to traditional values by supporting her brother's aspirations towards the priesthood. *Canuck* exemplifies border-crossings and re-entry into the culture. Camille, through her writing, stands up against the oppression of women long before the Quiet Revolution in Québec gave women "a newly rediscovered female mythology."[9] Camille Lessard-Bissonnette also points out that Vic's freedom is linked to the financial independence gained from her comparatively high wages in U.S. factories. These wages are the necessary basis for social promotion and respect: "*nous permettre de vivre comme du monde*!" (...permit us to make our way in the world.) Without financial independence, Vic could not rebel against her father's stinginess, the constant humiliation, or the physical harm that keeps the family in poverty and fear. Through her heroine, the author enunciates a new mythology of the French-speaking woman on the North American continent and denounces the oppression of the women within the culture.

Finally, *Canuck* deserves reading for its colorful representation of culture. Camille Lessard-Bissonnette includes oral tradition, family life, seasonal rites, folk medicines, folk tales, history, death and burial rites, religion, and more. She pays tribute to the culture renewed. It is very much her patchwork and her quilt. Her signature as a writer grew organically out of her cultural past, lived and redefined. *Canuck* serves the double purpose of breaking the bonds that keep women in their place by its form and its message.

A quilt is cut from squares of the past which a seamstress sews in the present, using a traditional pattern or devising one of her own, for future use by herself or for others, and still the quilt goes on much longer than she does; a writer like Camille, takes pieces of women's lives, the culture's oral traditions, the language and its nuances, the men and their redemptions, healing medicines, gossip, the dark side of life, the fortunate, and pieces together a story, quilted by her design—pieces of the past, in her present/presence for our future use.

1 For a complete translation of *Canuck*, as well as *Françaises d'Amérique* and *La Jeune Franco-Américaine*, see *Canuck and Other Stories*, Rheta Press, 2006. The above introduction is from this work, pp. 5–10. For the full French transcription of *Canuck*, *Françaises d'Amérique*, and *La Jeune Franco-Américaine*, visit the Franco-American Women's Institute website: http://www.fawi.net/Transcriptions/Transcriptions.html).

2 For the 1990 census, see Chartier, *The Franco-Americans of New England*, p. 417. Also Brault, pp. 1–2 (1980 census).

3 "Only a few Franco-American novels have been written in French, perhaps a dozen in all, and about half of them were published in the years from 1935 to 1960." Chartier, *The Franco-Americans of New England*, p. 318.

4 Shideler, p. 98.

5 Shideler, p. 114.

6 Jack Kerouac is considered one of the foremost Franco-American and U.S. writers of the beat generation. *Visions of Gerard* describes his growing up in Lowell's *petit canada* in the 1950s.

7 Lessard-Bissonnette, *Canuck*.

8 Lippard, p. 202.

9 Gilbert-Lewis, p. 8.

FRANCO-AMERICANS AND THE INTERNATIONAL PAPER COMPANY STRIKE OF 1910[1]

Anders Larson
South Portland, Maine

In the spring of 1910 several hundred millworkers at the International Paper Mill in Livermore Falls held a successful thirteen-week strike, conducted without a single dollar in the treasury of the union. In nearby Rumford Falls, the strike, under somewhat similar conditions, failed dramatically. Even more significant than the victory in Livermore Falls was the identity of the community's striking workers: The largest ethnic group represented in the work force was Franco-American. Long regarded as difficult to organize into labor unions, Franco-Americans supported this action as members of the International Brotherhood of Paper Makers and the International Brotherhood of Pulp, Sulfite, and Paper Mill Workers.

Among historians, turn-of-the-century Franco-Americans were reputed to be difficult to organize. The behavior of the paper workers of Rumford Falls and Livermore Falls challenges this perspective. A comparison of the two communities suggests that it was not the character of any single ethnic group that determined the outcome of the strike; rather it was the overall mix of gender and nationality—and the attitude of the community itself toward organized labor.

The pulp and paper industry was expanding in both size and number of employees at the turn of the century in Maine. Between 1899 and 1909 the number of mills grew from 35 to 45, and the number of wage earners from 4,851 to 8,647. In 1909 pulp and paper production led the rest of the state's industries in the value of its final product, and its mills employed 10.8 percent of the state's 79,955 wage earners.[2]

The paper industry's work force was more homogeneous in terms of sex and age than the average for both Maine and U.S. industries. In the state's pulp and paper industry, men made up 94.4 percent, women 5.4 percent, and children 0.2 percent of the work force.[3] By comparison, in the New England textile industry, women outnumbered men almost two to one.

Until 1893 there were no labor organizations in the paper industry. In that year the paper machine tenders were given a charter by the American Federation of Labor

(AFL) and were called the United Brotherhood of Papermakers. These tenders essentially dominated the workers in the mills, having the "power to hire and fire any member of the crew without appeal." Papermakers were soon added to the charter, which caused the tenders to break away and form the International Paper Machine Tenders Union in 1899. These two unions merged in 1902 to form the International Brotherhood of Paper Makers (IBPM).[4]

In 1906 the unskilled and semi-skilled pulp and paper mill workers formed the International Brotherhood of Pulp, Sulphite, and Paper Mill Workers union (IBPSPM), but they were denied a charter by the AFL. The rift between the IBPM and the IBPSPM came to a head in a strike against the International Paper Company in 1908. The IBPM walked out to protest a wage reduction, while the IBPSPM accepted the new wage and continued to work in the mills. The IBPM strike ended in failure, and—by 1909—this ongoing feud had nearly ruined both unions. Between 1908 and 1909 the number of organized papermakers dropped from 4,300 to 1,000 members, while unionized pulp and paper mill workers overall fell from 4,500 to 1,000 members.[5]

The failure of the 1908 strike and the subsequent decline of both unions led to a peace between the two unions in June 1909. The following month the AFL gave the IBPSPM a charter, accepting them into their ranks with the IBPM, and the two unions agreed to support each other in future labor disputes. By 1911 IBPM membership stood at 2,400 and IBPSPM membership had reached 2,800. Both unions were chartered in Livermore Falls and Rumford Falls.[6]

The towns of Rumford Falls and Livermore Falls had developed into industrial settlements at the end of the nineteenth century. The mills in Rumford Falls drew workers from not only its own borders, but also from the town of Mexico across the Androscoggin River. For their part, the cluster of mills in the area of Livermore Falls, Riley, and Otis Falls (Chisholm) drew workers from their own locales, as well as from nearby Livermore and Jay.

By 1906 Rumford Falls hosted five paper, pulp, and sulfite mills—all situated on the Androscoggin River. The largest of International Paper's three mills each day produced 190 tons (172 metric tons) of paper, 70 tons (64 metric tons) of newsprint, and 120 tons (109 metric tons) of bag and envelope paper. The latter products were sent to the adjacent Continental Paper Bag Company, an independent concern.[7] International Paper also operated a sulfite mill, which daily produced 130 tons (118 metric tons) of pulp, along with a groundwood mill producing 100 tons (91 metric

Bag-making machines, Continental Mill, Rumford, Maine, 1921
Maine Historic Preservation Commission

tons) of pulp. Finally, there was the Oxford Paper Company, another independent mill, which—in 1902—secured a contract from the U.S. Post Office and produced 3 million postcards per day for them.[8]

Rumford Falls's population grew from 898 in 1890 to 3,770 at the turn of the century, and by 1910—the year of the strike—6,777 people lived there. The area became a "melting pot for people of many nationalities." An agent in Providence, Rhode Island, was employed to "steer incoming Italians northward to Rumford." Along with Italians came Poles, Scots, Lithuanians, Irish, English Canadians, and French Canadians. Textile mills in other parts of New England were paying five to six cents

International Paper Company Mill, Rumford Falls, Maine, 1915
Maine Historic Preservation Commission

an hour, but labor brokers for the mills in Rumford Falls were paying 10 cents an hour, in order to attract workers to such an out-of-the-way place.[9]

This ethnic variety fractured the work force, as each group found solidarity among its own members. Thus, each area of town became known for the nationality of the people inhabiting it—Italians in Smithsville, Poles and Russians along River Street, and Irish on Waldo Street. Each group inherited a stereotypical label: "Canucks" or "Frogs" for Canadian French, "Dago or Wop" for Italians, "PIs" for those from the Maritime Provinces generally, "Skishmen" for those from New Brunswick, "Bluenose" for those from Nova Scotia, and "Herring Choker" for those from Prince Edward Island. Among Catholics, the French-speaking parishioners attended St. John's, while the Irish, Lithuanians, and Poles went to St. Athanasius Church, which was known as the "Irish" church.[10]

Rumford's elites were not exactly benevolent in their attitudes toward these new arrivals. The local paper, the *Rumford Times*, upon whose board sat Waldo Pettengill, one of the mills' financial backers, published an editorial characterizing the new immigrants as the "beaten from beaten races," representing "the worst failure in the struggle for existence." The editor felt that "next to the liquor problem, immigration is the most serious problem American people have to contend with." Yet the Yankee community was itself divided in its impressions of the changes the mills brought to Rumford Falls.[11]

In his history of Rumford, John Leane gives us a flavor for the changes the town was experiencing, along with insights into the dynamics of the town's elite. Some townspeople characterized Pettengill as one of the "ring of big city financiers who have taken over the town." Critics of the new paper-industry elite formed their own newspaper. The *Rumford Citizen*, voiced concerns about the "elements of feudalism" created primarily by Hugh Chisholm, founder of the Oxford Paper Company and co-founder of the International Paper Company. The paper argued that a few wealthy men in Rumford Falls "control all enterprise, fix wages and costs of both rented and owned houses."[12] They drove the point home with the following editorial:

> The Rumford Falls Power Co. owns the land, America Realty Co. owns the forests, the Light and Water Co. owns the lights and water, Rumford Falls Realty Co. owns the houses for rent, the Dunton Lumber Co. owns the timber for building houses, the Rail Road Co. owns the transportation, the Banks control finances, the Corporations own the mills and control the labor, and Hugh J. Chisholm owns and controls them all.[13]

Published from 1905 to 1907, the *Rumford Citizen* folded for lack of support: "After 1907, little criticism of H. J. Chisholm was heard in Rumford."[14] The town council itself took a conservative stand similar to that of Pettengill.

Livermore Falls also went through some dramatic changes around the turn of the century. In 1883 there were only three houses in the town, but by 1912 there were over 1,000 dwellings. The first paper mill appeared in Livermore Falls in 1888, soon followed by a pulp mill and a sulfite mill, with a second pulp mill located in the neighboring town of Riley. By 1910 the nearby town of Chisholm, named after the "man who did so much to develop the paper industry at Rumford Falls," also contained a large mill with nine newsprint machines and one wrapping-paper machine. All these mills were along the banks of the Androscoggin River and were owned and operated by the International Paper Company.[15]

The labor force in the paper mills of Rumford Falls was considerably more varied than that of Livermore Falls.[16] In Livermore Falls, there were only two major ethnic groups: Franco-Americans and Yankees, as well as 4 percent fewer non-

English-speaking workers and 10 percent fewer women than Rumford Falls. The Franco-American population in the Livermore Falls paper industry was substantially larger than that of Rumford, where Franco-Americans and Yankees combined made up only 53 percent of the labor force.[17]

A significant challenge for labor organizers at the Rumford mills was the ethnic diversity of the work force. There were 276 Russian, Lithuanian, Polish, and Lettish workers. Only 117 of these workers spoke English (44 percent), only one owned property, and the majority had immigrated within the previous ten years. This ethnic diversity did not exist in the labor force of the Livermore Falls mills, where Europeans numbered only 44 (8 percent) of the paper industry workers.[18]

Home ownership (Tables 1 and 2) was more frequent among paper industry workers in Livermore Falls than in Rumford. In Livermore Falls 20 percent of paper workers owned houses, with ownership among the three major ethnic groups about equal. These figures suggest a less transient population with a greater stake in the community. In Rumford Falls, home ownership was only 11 percent for all paper industry workers and was not equal among the different ethnic groups.[19]

In 1910 International Paper Company workers in the northeast part of the United States held a successful thirteen-week strike involving several thousand millworkers. The IBPM and the IBPSPM supported each other in the strike and effectively slowed paper production to such an extent that IP officials were forced to negotiate. The most important reason for the strike was over union recognition.[20]

Table 1: Ethnicity in Rumford

Ethnic Group	Total	Homeowner[a]	Women
French-Canada Born	327 (23 percent)	39	79
French-Canadian Parent(s)	125 (8 percent)	46	50
U.S. Born	361 (22 percent)	62	21
Other[b]	776 (47 percent)	43	32
Totals	1,589 (100 percent)	190	182[c]

[a]These figures include all workers who lived in houses that they or their immediate family owned. They do not include the Continental Company.
[b]Includes English, Scottish, Italian, Irish, German, Danish, Swedish, French, Turkish, Norwegian, Russian, Lithuanian, Polish, and Lettish.
[c]168 of these women were employed at the Continental Paper Bag Company, which did not participate in the IP strike.

Table 2: Ethnicity in Livermore Falls

Ethnic Group	*Total*	*Homeowner*[a]
French-Canada Born	209 (40 percent)	40
French-Canadian Parent(s)	29 (6 percent)	11
U.S. Born	201 (8 percent)	41
English-Canada Born	40 (8 percent)	10
Other	44 (8 percent)	3
Total	523 (100 percent)	105

[a]The figures include all workers who lived in houses that they or their immediate family owned.

Table 3: Ethnicity in Rumford Paper Mills (Pulp, Sulfur, Paper), Including Oxford Paper

Ethnic Group	*Total*	*Homeowner*	*Women*
French-Canada Born	251 (20 percent)	28	7
French-Canadian Parent(s)	46 (4 percent)	23	1
U.S. Born	284 (23 percent)	45	3
Other	669 (54 percent)	39	3
Totals	1,250 (100 percent)	135	14

Table 4: Ethnicity in Livermore Falls Paper Mill (International Paper)

Ethnic Group	*Total*	*Homeowner*[a]
French-Canada Born	128 (48 percent)	32
French-Canadian Parent(s)	18 (7 percent)	8
U.S. Born	90 (11 percent)	11
English-Canada Born	19 (7 percent)	1
Other	14 (5 percent)	1
Total	269 (100 percent)	53

Sources: U.S. Census Manuscript

There were many challenges facing union workers as strike preparations were made. Following the unsuccessful 1908 strike, the company had established an elaborate spy system to discourage union participation. Spies reported union men to the International Paper Company and the men would then find a "blue card" (pink slip) attached to their timecards.[21]

The IP strike began in Cornith, New York on 9 March 1910 and spread readily to other mills in the region. The *Paper Trade Journal* put the number of affected workers at 7,000 throughout the Northeast. Although IP was able to keep many of its mills producing, albeit under capacity and with scab labor, negotiations were underway with the two unions by the end of April. By May 21, the company and the unions reached an agreement. The union called off the strike, and workers began returning to work on May 23. The company agreed to end Sunday work and gave a 5 percent increase in pay beginning in August. It recognized the unions as the legal representatives of the workers and allowed workers who had participated in the strike to return to their jobs—"without discrimination, until all strikers are hired," before the company hired any others.[22] In the papermaking mills of Livermore Falls and Rumford Falls, however, workers had two different experiences in the course of this strike.

By March 21, 400 to 500 men were out of work in Livermore Falls, half of them striking and the other half idled by the shutdown.[23] The striking workers were active, sometimes even violent, in supporting the strike. On March 25, 250 strike sympathizers hurled rocks at arriving scabs and, the following day, a crowd of roughly 200 strikers met the trains carrying scabs at the Chisholm station. Although the union did not condone violence, workers were eager to express their determination to "keep out the scabs."[24]

The town of Livermore Falls also was more receptive than Rumford to union organizers. During the early stages of the strike, the Livermore Falls Board of Trade met with union representatives to exchange information and to discuss their respective concerns. Among the nine men on the board were three bearing Franco-American names: A. A. Merscreau, Napoleon L'Hereux, and the Reverend Father Desjardins, pastor at Saint Rose de Lima parish in Livermore Falls.[25]

Reacting cautiously to the strike and the ensuing violence, the town of Livermore Falls called in Androscoggin County Sheriff Hastings from the shiretown in Auburn. When asked by IP to deputize the company's loyal workers, Hastings refused, explaining that he did not want to take sides. Instead, he conferred with the strikers and millworkers in an attempt to get their cooperation in securing the peace. He was not entirely successful. At the end of March the town selectmen ordered in the militia, which had to be brought in from Farmington in Franklin County, because 75 percent of the militia of Androscoggin County was out on strike. During the rest of the strike, there were only a few relatively insignificant fights, most of them among young boys looking for fun. Two of the more serious encounters involved four men of Franco-American descent.[26]

During the course of the strike, union leaders stopped in Livermore Falls from time to time, enroute to Rumford, to reaffirm the union's goals and to generate enthusiasm for the strike. J. T. Carey, president of the IBPM, arrived in town on April 4, and succeeded in procuring the Dreamland Theater for a rally. Before a crowd of 800 strikers and sympathizers, he denounced IP for its vicious antiunion policies.[27]

On May 21 the strike ended, and two days later 75 percent of the striking workers were back on the job at the Livermore Falls mills. The *Paper Trade Journal* estimated, and the *Lewiston Journal* agreed, that a total of about 400 workers were idled. According to the figures of the Thirteenth Census, this would include most of the paper workers in the Livermore Falls area (Tables 4 and 5). It is important to note that the Livermore Falls workers participated primarily out of sympathy for the strikers in IP's New York mills. Although the grievances were probably the same throughout the region, the Livermore Falls walkout demonstrated a strong sense of solidarity with the union and what it stood for.

The situation in Rumford Falls was very different. An important consideration in comparing the experiences in Rumford Falls and Livermore Falls was the mood among the community leaders in the two towns. Judging from the coverage of the strike given in the *Rumford Falls Times*, the *Lewiston Evening Journal*, and the *Paper Trade Journal*, the town of Rumford Falls was more hostile to union organizers.

The *Times*, Rumford's weekly paper, published many articles and editorials with a definite anti-union flavor. The first was an editorial from the president of the International Brotherhood of Stationary Firemen, who claimed that J. T. Carey, president of the IBPM, wanted to create an "Industrial Organization of the millworkers." He charged that Carey was "untruthful and prone to seek self-interests." In late March J. H. Malin, president of the IBPSPM, and G. J. Schneider, vice president of the IBPM, were both driven out of Rumford Falls by a "citizen's delegation," members of which informed the organizers that "their disturbance of labor in the town would not be tolerated." A *Times* editorial, titled "The Rumford Way," praised the action as a proper method of dealing with "agitators," since neither the town nor the workers could afford the hardships a strike would bring. Malin and Schneider returned to Rumford two days later with a police escort.[28]

Not only did union organizers face outright physical hostility in Rumford, they had to contend with more subtle forms of exclusion by the community. In their search for a place to hold meetings, the organizers often found it necessary to meet in the streets or in empty lots. In March, Schneider obtained permission to use the Salvation Army building to hold an organizing meeting, but the lessee blocked it at the last moment. On April 9 the *Times* reported that Carey had to address a crowd in a vacant lot on Waldo Street. Carey moved across the river to Mexico to organize but encountered the same difficulty in obtaining a hall. Two Mexico town assessors asked him to leave, but he refused.[29]

Although in the end the effort failed, the ambitious organizing in Rumford Falls was not without its successes. On March 24 Schneider was able to sign up eight men for his union, in addition to the thirty-five who registered the previous night. The following day he mused that the "people of Rumford find I'm not so bad," and claimed to have "already forty names to start a local union of paper makers." Schneider noted that the "pulp workers [were] also being organized." On April 4 Carey ordered a strike, but only three or four participated. The following day at McMermamin Hall workers voted 150 to 51 not to strike. This event proved to be the last major effort by the union organizers in Rumford Falls. The *Times* reported, on May 7, that there would be no strike at Rumford; the "final attempt died when Carey, Malin, and a dozen lieutenants left town." Labeling the organizers "parasites of industry, trying to outlaw the right of the employees to make a living," the editor crowed that the "men of Rumford have displayed a higher sense of duty to their wives and children than the men of Livermore, Glens Falls, and other places."[30]

Although it is difficult to determine definitely, the predominance of Franco-Americans in the Livermore Falls labor force strongly suggests that their participation was crucial for the success of the strike. However, what emerged as the decisive factor in comparing Rumford Falls and Livermore Falls is not the behavior of any single ethnic group, but the overall gender and ethnic diversity of the labor force. The more diverse labor force in Rumford Falls proved more difficult to organize. Livermore Falls had only two ethnic groups of numerical significance: Franco-Americans and English-speaking natives.

In addition to the difference in the ethnic composition of Rumford Falls and Livermore Falls, differences in elite attitudes also were crucial to the outcome of the strike and the attempt to organize. The relatively small class of landowners and industrialists who controlled Rumford Falls knew it was in their interest to keep workers ethnically divided and unorganized, and they played a major role in hindering union efforts to organize workers. This elite group controlled the press and used it to persuade workers that unions were self-serving. The message from city leaders was that unions were infringing on workers' right to work. The company successfully alienated wage earners from the unions, while neighborhood segregation kept these same wage earners divided by ethnicity.

Table 5: Livermore Falls Pulp Mill (International Paper)

Ethnic Group	*Total*	*Homeowner*
French-Canada Born	80 (33 percent)	8
French-Canadian Parent(s)	10 (4 percent)	3
U.S. Born	102 (44 percent)	30
English-Canadian Born	19 (8 percent)	5
Other[a]	29 (11 percent)	2
Totals	240 (100 percent)	48

[a]Other here represents Irish, French, Italian, Danish, Russian, Hungarian, and Austrian

Table 6: Rumford Sulfur Mill (International Paper)

Ethnic Group	*Total*	*Homeowner*
French-Canada Born	5 (18 percent)	2
French-Canadian Parent(s)	1 (4 percent)	1
U.S. Born	12 (43 percent)	3
English-Canadian & Others	10 (35 percent)	1
Totals	28 (100 percent)	7

Table 7: Rumford Pulp Mill (International Paper)

Ethnic Group	*Total*	*Homeowner*
French-Canada Born	13 (18 percent)	2
French-Canadian Parent(s)	2 (4 percent)	-
U.S. Born	5 (7 percent)	-
English-Canadian & Others	54 (73 percent)	1
Totals	74 (100 percent)	3

Sources: U.S. Census Manuscript

The active participation of Franco-Americans in the IP strike helps to dispel the myth that they were anti-union, an assumption that evidently stems from studies of early immigrants working the textile industry.

Most studies of Franco-American union participation have focused on the textile industry, where Franco-Americans were quite visible. Yet the work force in this industry was diverse with respect to both ethnicity and gender; in particular, it employed a large number of women. For example, figures for the year 1900 in the

New England towns of Fall River, Lawrence, Lowell, Manchester, and New Bedford show that Franco-American women outnumbered Franco-American men almost two to one in the mills. Largely for these reasons, the textile industry as a whole was not successfully organized until after World War I.[31]

It is important to recognize the specific challenges women and, in particular, ethnic women, faced when it came to labor organizing and membership in unions. Historian Colette Hyman notes that "by its very structure, the organized labor movement at the turn of the century all but excluded working women."[32] Labor leaders often reiterated the prevailing belief that women belonged at home and that it was unnecessary for the wife to contribute to the support of the family by working.

Despite this view, women, again particularly ethnic women, were joining the labor force in large numbers. The response to their presence ranged from benign neglect to efforts aimed at driving them out of factory and mill work.[33] When labor leaders organized women, the major incentive was the need to protect the earning power of men.[34] So it would seem that the frequent lack of women's activism in unions was largely a product of poor organization on the part of the labor movement itself.

It is unclear from the available documents whether any attempt was made to organize the women millworkers of Livermore Falls and Rumford Falls. But given the propensity of historians to generalize about Franco-Americans based on the trade-union movement in the textile industry, where women constituted such a large part of the work force, the Rumford Falls and Livermore Falls examples take on additional importance. Studies of textile industry towns suggest that Franco-American women were difficult to organize. But was this also true of Franco-American men?

1 A version of this article was first published in the *Maine Historical Society Quarterly.* Anders Larson, "Franco-Americans and the International Paper Company Strike of 1910," *Maine Historical Society Quarterly* 33 (1), Summer 1993, pp. 40–60.

2 Employment in the industry in 1909 was quite steady, with a peak of 8,841 in December and a low of 8,334 in September, a decline of only 507 workers (5.7 percent). United States, Treasury Department, Bureau of the Census, *Thirteenth Census,* Maine, 1910, *Abstract with Maine Supplement*, pp. 457, 634, 635.

3 For all Maine industries, men averaged 75.8 percent, women 22.5 percent, and children (under 16) 1.7 percent of the total work force. Nationally, the work force was made up of 71.8 percent men, 19.5 percent women, and 2.4 percent children. United States, Treasury Department, Bureau of the Census, *Thirteenth Census,* Maine, 1910, *Abstract with Maine Supplement*, pp. 455, 457–59, 620.

4 Harry Graham, pp. 1–5. James Gross.

5 Harry Graham. Wolman, pp. 116–17.
6 James Gross. Charles O'Leary, pp. 137–41.
7 United States, Treasury Department, Bureau of the Census, *Thirteenth Census,* Maine, 1910.
8 Leane, pp. 40–41.
9 Leane, pp. 42–43, 571–75.
10 Leane, pp. 43–44.
11 *Rumford Times*, no date.
12 Leane, pp. 45–48.
13 Leane, pp. 45–48.
14 Leane, pp. 45–48.
15 Lawrence, pp. 18–19.
16 With respect to the mills in Rumford Falls, this census surveyed the towns of Rumford Falls, Rumford Village, and Mexico. For the mills near Livermore Falls, the towns of Livermore, East Livermore, Chesterville, and Jay were examined. In the Rumford census, no distinction was made between International Paper and Oxford Paper company employees; only the type of mill—pulp, paper, chemical/sulfite, or bag/envelope—was distinguished. In Livermore Falls, all mills were owned by IP. For statistical purposes, it will be assumed that the labor force in the paper mills of Rumford (Oxford and IP) was similar in composition. United States, Treasury Department, Bureau of the Census, *Thirteenth Census,* Maine, 1910.
17 Of the 1,634 paper industry workers in the Rumford mills, 182 (11 percent) were women and only 4 (0.02 percent) were under the age of sixteen; this number of women employees was higher than the state average of 5.4 percent. The Franco-American population in the Livermore Falls paper industry—55 percent in the paper mill and 37 percent in the pulp mills (46 percent overall)—was substantially larger than Rumford's 297 Franco-American paper mill employees (24 percent), excluding the Continental Company's 190 additional Franco-Americans. United States, Treasury Department, United States, Treasury Department, Bureau of the Census, *Thirteenth Census,* Maine, 1910.
18 United States, Treasury Department, Bureau of the Census, *Thirteenth Census,* Maine, 1910.
19 United States, Treasury Department, Bureau of the Census, *Thirteenth U.S. Census*, Maine, 1910.
20 Leane, p. 188. Harry Graham, p. 5.
21 Leane, p. 188. Harry Graham, p. 5.
22 *Paper Trade Journal*, 24 March 1910; 26 May 1910. *Lewiston Evening Journal*, 23 May 1910. IP's position on the 1908 strike, according to President A. N. Burbank, was that the two unions held an "antagonistic attitude" toward the company. An editor in the pro-business *Paper Trade Journal* felt that union leaders had no real reason to strike and were simply out to "wreak vengeance." It was the "absence of a good cause [that had] defeated the men in 1908," and the paper predicted that the same weakness "fore doomed" the 1910 attempt by "bad leaders to wreak personal spite on the company."
23 In Livermore Falls, the pulp mills were less affected than the paper mills: 60 men continued to work in the Livermore Falls pulp mill and 100 at the Riley pulp mill. Interestingly, these were the mills that contained the lowest percentage of Franco-Americans (37 percent, as compared to 55 percent in the paper mills). The two IP pulp mills at Livermore Falls and Riley continued to supply the ten-machine paper mill in Chisholm. *Lewiston Evening Journal,* 21 March 1910, 22 March 1910.
24 *Lewiston Evening Journal*, 25 March 1910, 26 March 1910.
25 *Lewiston Evening Journal*, 25 March 1910, 29 March 1910.
26 *Lewiston Evening Journal,* 26 March 1910, 29 March 1910.
27 *Lewiston Evening Journal*, 5 April 1910.

28 *Rumford Falls Times,* 19 March 1910, 26 March 1910.
29 *Lewiston Evening Journal*, 25 March 1910, 4 April 1910. *Rumford Falls Times*, 9 April 1910.
30 *Lewiston Evening Journal*, 24 March 1910, 25 March 1910, 4 April 1910, 5 April 1910. *Rumford Falls Times*, 9 April 1910; 7 May 1910.
31 Brault, *French-Canadian Heritage*, pp. 61, 63.
32 Hyman, p. 23.
33 Tax, pp. 36–37.
34 Kessler-Harris, p. 156.

AN EXCERPT FROM *PAPA MARTEL*[1]

Gérard Robichaud
Auburn, Maine

Gérard Robichaud is the author of *Papa Martel*, a novel that is a "story in ten parts." Originally published by Doubleday Publishers in 1961, the story tells of a French family in Lewiston, Maine, in the early 1900s. They cope with each other and with a culture in which they feel slightly unsure, facing a wide array of problems that we face even today. It is truly a story where reality meets fiction. In this excerpt, a new baby has been born into the household. Gerry is currently working on a sequel to *Papa Martel*. —Chase Hébert

The next morning, at dawn, one by one, the children came running out of their cold rooms to finish their dressing near the hot stove. First thing they saw, each in turn, was the nurse, in a plain white smock, tall, thin, and wordless. Laurent and Maurice looked at one another, then nodded in agreement, and Laurent cleared his throat, but Thérèse simply walked up to her.

"Good morning, nurse," she said.

As if awakened by this, she answered, "Good morning," and then she smiled. She pointed toward the table and the children saw that she was ready for them with flapjacks, French toast, maple syrup, tea, and milk. Now suddenly, Thérèse became shy—this nurse seemed so cold—and she sat at the table and the others did the same, and they ate and looked at one another, asking with their eyes the terrible question, and signaled to Laurent—was he not the oldest?—to ask the terrible question. He cleared his throat, but Louis himself came bouncing out of Maman's room. He was clean-shaven, there was a glimmer of a tear in his eyes, but his voice sang out.

"My children, straight from heaven she came, a precious little bundle of a girl!"

Everyone cheered, except the nurse.

"And Maman?" asked Thérèse.

"Didn't I promise you that she'd be all right? Well, she is!"

Everyone cheered, and the nurse smiled.

"Mon Dieu!" she murmured. "It's only another baby!"

"Ah," said Louis, "but this is a Martel baby!"

Gérard Robichaud and Dani Potvin, Auburn, Maine, September 2007
Photograph by Barry Rodrigue

He went up to the nurse, put his arms around her, squeezed her, and then, while the children roared in delight, he gave her a big wet kiss. She blushed.

"You are a crazy family!" she announced.

"Papa!" screamed Thérèse, "can we visit? Can we, please?"

"For sure!" said Louis.

For sure, my children, you can visit, but Maman is resting, and so is the new baby from the long voyage to this earth, and, my children, it is the time for the quiet moment and for the use of the tip of the toes, and time to go in, as if in church at High Mass, and to go in turn, one by one, Marie, the youngest to be first, and then Thérèse, and then the boys, and to say: "Bienvenue, p'tite soeur!" but to themselves, not to the whole world—yet. For these two are tired from their long night. Oh, yes, one might kiss Maman, but gently, and the baby too, very gently.... And while they did this, it was time for him to unwrap the silver cup for the new baby, as he had for all the others, and he did, and now he put it on the table for the children to admire....

1 This excerpt came from Gérard Robichaud's novel, *Papa Martel* (Orono: University of Maine Press, 2003), pp. 34–35. We appreciate author Gérard Robichaud's and publisher Michael Alpert's permission to reprint it.

J'AIMAIS

Jean-Paul Poulain
Augusta, Maine

Many folks popularly associate the French settlers of North America with intricate fiddle music, jigs, and reels. While true—especially for rural areas where people made all of their own music—there are other traditions of French music in the Americas. The Franco-American and Acadian migrants who came to central and southern Maine lived for the most part in cities. There, they came into greater contact with vaudeville, cabarets, phonographs, and radios. French city folks not only were influenced by these urban traditions, but also influenced the traditions themselves. These included famous singers and songwriters like "La Bolduc" from Québec. Until he passed away in 2007, Jean-Paul Poulain was among the best Franco-American songwriters and composers in this rich tradition of cabaret music. —Barry Rodrigue

J'Aimais

J'aimais t'écrire des lettres enflammées,
J'aimais te faire rire et te charmer,
J'aimais te montrer combien belle est la vie
Jusqu' à l'envie de ton premier baiser.
J'aimais te rencontrer dans ce café,
J'aimais regarder tes jambes se croiser,
J'aimais caresser ta peau de déesse
Pour que j'y laisse tous mes baisers.

Pourquoi se revoir sans sentiment?
Pourquoi se revoir plus tard ou maintenant?
Après ce départ pour l'émotion sans limite,
Il vaut bien mieux pour nous deux que je te quitte
Car la fin de ce beau voyage est arrivé
Même si je crois que je t'aimais.

J'aimais danser au rythme de nos deux corps,
J'aimais qu'on s'oublie dans notre lit,
J'aimais qu'on s'aime encore et toujours plus fort
Jusqu' à la mort de nos envies.
J'aimais voir tes larmes fuir tes yeux mouillés,
J'aimais voir combien pour toi je comptais,
J'aimais pouvoir te consoler d'un regard
Jusqu'au départ de tes regrets.

Pourquoi se revoir sans sentiment?
Pourquoi se revoir plus tard ou maintenant?
Après ce départ pour un amour hypocrite,
Il vaut bien mieux pour nous deux que je te quitte.
Car si l'envie est ta rage, je préfère t'oublier
Même se je crois que je t'aimais.

English Translation—I Used To Love

I used to love to write you impassioned letters,
I used to love to make you laugh and charm you,
I used to show you how beautiful life is
Up to the point of craving your first kiss.
I used to love meeting you in this café,
I used to love watching you cross your legs,
I used to love caressing your goddess-like skin
That I might leave all of my kisses there.

Why see each other again without feeling?
Why see each other now or later?
After this departure for limitless feeling,
It's much better for both of us that I leave you,
Because the end has come for this beautiful voyage,
Even if I believe that I used to love you.

I used to love to dance to the rhythm of our two bodies,
I used to love that we let go ourselves in bed,
I used to love that we still loved one another even harder
Up to the death of our cravings.
I used to love to see your tears fleeing from your moist eyes,
I used to love to see how much I meant to you,
I used to love being able to console you with a single glance
Up to the point when your regrets left you.

Why see each other without feelings?
Why see each other now or later?
After this departure for a hypocritical love,
It's much better for both of us that I leave you.
For if longing is your rage, I prefer to forget you,
Even if I believe I used to love you.

Jean-Paul Poulain, music CD album cover, Le Droit D'Aimer
(Augusta, Maine: Mërilda Recordings, 1996)

PASSING THE FLAME

Cindy Larock
Lewiston, Maine

When I am asked what inspires me as an artist, the answer is simple: the music. To me, dancing is what happens when the right tune—the right mix of melody and rhythm—enters in through my ears, percolates down through my heart, and comes out my feet. There's little or no brain involvement.

That, I'm convinced, is what spawned *la gigue*—or stepdancing, as it's known in English. The fiddling sometimes got so hot, back on those long, frosty winter nights in La Beauce, that it precipitated a kind of kinetic combustion. It might start as simple foot tapping, but at some point, the buoyancy took over and the "victims" were on their feet, jigging away with joyous abandon. It was not premeditated. It just happened, because it had to happen.

That's why I tend to squirm when someone asks me to perform before an audience. Stepdancing, in its natural state, is not about performing. It's about communing, about catching the spirit of the music and going along for the ride.

And this is what I try to impress on my dance students. Whether it is a young adult I'm coaching on the intricacies of the *valse-clog* or a roomful of schoolchildren learning to master a *grande chaine*, I tell them that first and foremost, they should be having fun. And, more often than not, they do.

I became interested in pursuing the study of French-Canadian traditional dance many years ago when, through my avid involvement in New England contradancing, I became aware that much of the best Maine contradance music, in my estimation, was made up of tunes from French Canada, the land of my own paternal ethnic roots. I then became determined to find out as much as I could about the dance styles that went along with this music, with the hope of reintroducing traditional *Québécois* dance to my own native community of Lewiston, where a formerly vibrant Franco music and dance heritage had approached extinction.

I eventually crossed paths with Benoit Bourque, who—as both a musician and a dancer—was a leading figure on the dynamic Québec folk scene. I soon realized that Benoit was not only a gifted artist but was also a wonderfully inspiring teacher who shared the same "Dance is nothing if not joy" philosophy that fueled my own passion

Cindy Larock practices a valse-clog *with* Québécois *dance master Benoit Bourque, on the planks of the Bates Mill, Lewiston, Maine, c. 1997.*
Photograph by Jere DeWaters

for the art. I applied for and was awarded an apprenticeship with him through the Maine Arts Commission's Traditional Arts Apprenticeship Program, and that opened the door for an extended mentoring relationship through which I not only expanded my own dance capabilities, but—more important—was able to spark a new interest in the French-Canadian heritage among Francos and non-Francos alike as I "shared" him liberally at community workshops, house parties, and concerts. Benoit, the prototypical Québec *bonhomme*, proved to be an ideal role model for the aspiring young jiggers that I had myself started to coach and the perfect "magnet" to lure others out onto the floor for a *quadrille* or *contre danse*.

I now am mentoring my own apprentices and getting particular satisfaction that my current *protégé,* Donna (Roy) Casavant—another Lewiston native— is passing the steps on down to her young daughter and son as soon as she learns them from me. Even her husband has caught the spirit, and—as a result—Mainers from Freeport to Waterville to Bangor were treated to inspired jigging performances by La Famille Casavant within six months of their having taken their first percussive Franco step. Furthermore, they were accompanied at these appearances by young Maine fiddlers whose command of the old-time jigs and reels far belied their tender years.

This all bodes well for the future of *la gigue* in Maine. I feel secure that when my knees go in a few years and my energy dissipates, the dancing will go on. And on.

I am deeply indebted to the Maine Arts Commission for giving me the opportunity to reclaim and pass on my cultural heritage, to Benoit for nurturing the flame, and, most important, to the musicians of Canada and Maine, past, present, and future, for providing the muse.

FRENCH-CANADIAN GENEALOGICAL RESEARCH

Bob Chenard
Waterville, Maine

For many French-Canadians, even most of them, learning their genealogy is not just a hobby—it's nearly an obsession, which explains the success of so many genealogical societies dedicated to French-Canadian and Acadian genealogy in Québec and New Brunswick. In the United States there are several genealogy societies for French-Canadian research—most of them located in the New England states of Rhode Island, Connecticut, New Hampshire, Vermont, and Maine. Oddly enough, Massachusetts (the New England state that received the largest number of French-Canadian immigrants) has no such society. Nonetheless, the New England Genealogical and Historical Society in Boston maintains a good reference library of French-Canadian books and records. Upstate New York, which also has a sizable number of French-Canadian connections, has a dedicated French-Canadian genealogy society. For the rest of the country, there are such societies in Louisiana, California, Minnesota, and Michigan.

Of the 15,000 or so French immigrants into New France, from the beginning of the first settlement in 1604 to the mid-1750s, many returned to France and a large number either never married or had no progeny. The remaining 8,500 became the ancestors of an estimated 10 million descendants living today in North America—about half in the United States. As a consequence of the British "closing the door" to any new French immigration from the old country after their conquest of Canada in 1760, Québec became an isolated French-Catholic region for several generations. Eventually, Irish families migrated into Québec at the turn of the nineteenth century and were well received by the French Catholics of Québec—since they shared a common faith, resulting in many French-Irish marriages. Although the earliest settlers in New France were mainly from France, a small number of them had roots in England, Belgium, Switzerland, Italy, Portugal, Spain, the Basque regions, Germany, and even Poland. Some of these immigrants and their descendants also married into the local Native American population almost from the beginning of the colony to this day. Thus, the roots of those who have French-Canadian ancestry are varied and colorful.

French-Canadian genealogical research is a challenge in some ways, particularly for those who cannot read French—since all the original records in Québec are written in that language. Despite the fact that the records kept by the church in Québec have no equals anywhere in the world, research into these original documents can be formidable for several reasons. First, the handwriting in the ancient records is difficult to read. Second, the variations in spelling of surnames and the common use of *dit* or "so-called" surnames often make tracing a lineage from one generation to the next a challenge. But the completeness of the genealogical record of the French-Canadians is without doubt the best in the Western world. It is common for a typical descendant of this population to identify in his or her research upwards of 4,000 direct ancestors back to the early seventeenth century and earlier. Except for some church records that were lost to fire, flood, rodents, and insects, or accidental destruction, the vast majority of all church records from the mid-1630s to the present are complete for baptisms, marriages, and funerals.

For the past twenty-five years, I have dedicated myself to researching the lineage of the French-Canadian immigrants into central Maine, particularly the greater Kennebec River Valley—from Jackman to Gardiner, including the communities of Skowhegan, Madison, Waterville, Winslow, and Augusta. From this research, I have concluded that about 85 percent of the French-Canadians who migrated, prior to 1900, into the Kennebec Valley originated from one Québec county—Beauce.

Thus, my current research is to prepare a complete record of all the birth/baptism and death/funeral records in all the towns in Beauce County from the earliest in 1738 up to 1876. This compilation will be an invaluable source of documentation for those researching their Beauce ancestry. It will contain over 75,000 records in a large database covering almost 140 years and will make research quick and easy, regardless of ability with the French language. The immigrants from Beauce County not only migrated into central Maine, but also to almost every part of New England, as evidenced by the church records of such towns as Worcester and Lowell (Massachusetts), Woonsocket and Central Falls (Rhode Island), Manchester and many other towns in New Hampshire, as well as other places in New England.

I have also researched other parts of Maine—such as in the large French-Canadian towns of Lewiston-Auburn, Biddeford, Sanford, Old Town, Orono, Brunswick, and Dexter. Finally, as to my current genealogical research, below is a listing of thirty-two things I have learned from my work into the original church records of Beauce County, Québec:

1. Some of the eighteenth-century records are either damaged (torn or water-stained) or missing entirely.

2. Information in the records is more standardized by the early nineteenth century.

3. There are some errors in the original records, but—for the most part—they are very reliable. Errors of major consequence are less than 0.5 percent of the total. Thus, we can assume that the church records in Québec are 99.5 percent reliable.

4. Without other compilations of records, such as Cyprien Tanguay's *Dictionnaire généalogique des familles canadiennes françaises*, which covers the period up to 1780, some records would not be readable because they have deteriorated since the time Tanguay did his compilation back in the 1850s and 1860s.

5. At the end of each year, a copy of the church records was sent to the court house (civil authorities) as designated for a parish or community. This duplication of records helped the survival of these church registers, where one or the other were lost or destroyed.

6. Sometimes multiple baptisms (from two to five) are grouped into one entry during the eighteenth century. After about 1790 each baptism or death record stands alone in the register, except for occasional multiple births.

7. Family (last) names are spelled multiple ways and thus not standardized, making it difficult to compile in a modern computer data base. The best way around this is to use the most common spelling in use today. In a few cases, it's better to use two common versions—the original name and the so-called *dit* name, for example: Vachon and Pomerleau, Dupuis and Gilbert, Lagueux and Charpentier.

8. Numerous Native Americans—mainly Algonquin, Abenaki, and some Iroquois—settled in the area of Beauce County, where many had their children baptized and some were married in the church. There were few recorded marriages between the French Canadians and the Native Americans who did not live in the towns in the old days, but there were some that occurred "in the woods," according to the records.

9. Most Native Americans had no family surnames, just individual names. Church officials often filled this gap (to the European mind) by writing in "sauvage" or "sauvagesse," which lacks some of the negative connotation that the word has in English. They also usually gave the tribal connection—Abenaki, Iroquois, Algonquin, etc.

10. The Native Americans who lived in Beauce County mostly came from

Acadia, including Abenaki from Maine. Some may have been Algonquins. The few Iroquois were mainly from New York.

11. Indexes to the registers are not always to be believed. There are occasional errors.

12. Handwriting and spelling improved over the years. Quality of the records also improved.

13. *Dit* names were used for many families all through the seventeenth, eighteenth, and nineteenth centuries.

14. Most multiple births (twins/triplets) ended in death shortly after birth prior to the twentieth century.

15. Wives who died young (eighteen to forty) typically died of childbirth in the years before 1900.

16. Many children also died in their youth—most typically prior to age ten.

17. In the eighteenth century, few adults lived past age seventy. By the nineteenth century, adults lived into their seventies, eighties, and nineties, along with a few instances of centenarians.

18. A married couple was more likely to lose children born to them later in life. In other words, the older the mother was when she gave birth, the more likely the child would die. Stillbirths and others are listed in the registers list as *anonyme.*

19. Most families had numerous children. Some couples lost most of their children; some as many as fifteen out of eighteen.

20. Most men were farmers—*cultivateurs.* In the eighteenth-century records, the trades of men were rarely listed unless they were notaries, judges, soldiers, or police *(capitaine de milice)*. By the nineteenth century, most records include the trade of the husband or father.

21. Fathers were rarely present at the baptisms of their children. Most baptism records ended as: *"Le père absent."* Jokingly, perhaps they didn't want that "troublemaker" around.

22. Few signatures on parish records are found in the eighteenth century—other than that of the officiating priest. By the nineteenth century signatures are quite common, especially for persons of importance to their community such as attorneys, judges, merchants, notaries, doctors, and some craftsmen.

23. An unbaptized infant was usually buried in an area dedicated for such in the parish cemetery—not with others who were baptized.

24. A married woman kept her maiden name in all church records. Even at

death, the records give her maiden name. She is listed only as the wife or widow of her husband or late husband. The names of her parents are not given.

25. The age of a person in a funeral (death) record is often not reliable as evidenced from baptismal records of those individuals.

26. Similar to our custom of filing intentions, a couple planning to marry went to a notary to make a marriage contract—typically a few days or even several months before their church or religious marriage. In cases where both the church and copy of the civil record was destroyed, researchers often find a copy of their marriage contract in the records of notaries. Those records give the names of the parents and where they came from.

27. In eighteenth-century records, the name of the mother was often included in the baptism of an illegitimate child. In the nineteenth century and later the parents are given as *inconnus* or unknown.

28. As is true today, some couples had children before or shortly after they were legally married.

29. Illegitimate births were rare in the eighteenth century but became more common in the nineteenth century.

30. Unfortunately, many illegitimate children somehow tended to die at an early age.

31. In the eighteenth century, children were typically baptized a couple days after birth to several days, weeks, or even months. By the nineteenth century, infants were usually baptized as soon as possible or within two days of their birth.

32. The Québec church records are superior to all others in the Western world for the "common" folks. In most countries, such records were kept only for royalty and the like.

"DOWN THE PLAINS," AN EXCERPT[1]

Rhea Côté Robbins
Waterville, Maine

BUANDERIE DE FALL RIVER! FALL RIVER LAUNDRY, No. 24, rue Hartwell, Collette et manchettes, 2 cents, pièce tapis battus et nettoyés à la vapeur, 4 cents la verge. Linge lavé, empesé, repassé ou non, au gré des clients. On va chercher sans frais tous les paquets à domicile....
—*L'Indépendant*, 4ième année, No. 3 Foi, loyauté, progrès, Fall River, Mass, 20 janvier, 1888.

Collette et manchettes, 2 cents

Perfect, present, future tense. In French. Everything in French. Even if it is in English, it is still in French. A layer of French living laid over by layers of popular culture or popular culture covered by living done in French. Intertwined. I wish I had a happier story to tell, but I've made my peace with its ugliness. It is a truthful, unpretty face. I have learned to love the story I hated. One of the deep reverberations that I must reacquaint myself with. Legends. Customs. Recipes. Folktales. Stories. Songs. Futuristic visions. I have visions of perfect, present, future tense. What am I in the future of my Franco-American womaning? Do I learn the language? Do I write my way to freedom? Will I be understood by even myself, I wonder, let alone someone without a cultural blueprint. I am scared. Afraid of the outcome. The judgments. The pronouncements. Some have more of the inner sanctum secret passwords than others. Some have the original recipes.

Some can sing. Some know the essence of the moment told in French words. I can hear the heartbeat of Québec. I can hear the St. Lawrence River, *le fleuve St. Laurent,* running in my bloodstream. I am giant and I have out-of-the-body experiences picking up tankers on the St. Lawrence looking down from the thirteenth floor of Le Concorde. I eat the soup, bread, *plat principal,* and dessert without a bit of explanation necessary. I climb on my knees the prayer stairs at Ste. Anne de Beaupré. I am close to Jean Côté's grave on l'Île d'Orléans. He arrived just yesterday—1600 something. I married the very distant cousin. I eat the soup. I bake the bread. I am a *couseuse*. I make bold the colors in my house. I get dizzy admiring the roofs in Québec. The colors on the houses leave me breathless. I have been shamed to white, but I vow to return to the palette of true colors. I dream the visions of young women in French. Equanimity in the cultural unearthing of their legacy of the near millennium. Do-it-to-yourself archeology. The cookbook of life rendered for what it is. That which sustains the generations to come. Pride, not shame in the female cook pot. Modern day tapestry of living unparalleled in its boasts. *On parle français, ici* the commercial advertisements read. Understood, at last.

I talk about losing a piece of one's body and it is like losing a piece of one's self in their culture. Changed forever, but you continue to live just the same. You take it all in stride. I chose to tattoo pressed flowers over my mastectomy scar. Just like in the poster made famous by the woman depicting the female crucifixion, salvation for all, in the skyline pose. Naked to the waist, outdoors and celebrating single-breastedness. Culture women, Franco-American women, in the folds of nature and the future, celebrating the newly designed and defined selves. That present, future, tense. Maybe, not perfect, but who would want it?

Am I willing to give more weight to the dark side of story rather than the good side of story—although the dark is as necessary as the light. My fears are what intrude. Because in each story is the light and the dark. The evil and the good.

I want to tell someone something and one day I need to tell it from over here with that day's rations of embellishments, and then the next day I have a different view of what I want to say about the same thing because I've changed and I've become better seasoned in my own passage through the personal truths. I can understand the event in a different light. I am impressed with what I choose to tell and what I choose to not tell and then when I tell the story, how it sometimes doesn't even come close to what it is I experienced or what happened. Words are slippery. Slimy. Gooey. Slick. Silky. A breath of air on the wind. Utterances echoing. I am struck with what a story is about. (The Franco-American and Acadian festivals in the summer whispering our fame.) Usually not what actually took place because people have a way of not corroborating their stories. (Everyone's recipe for *tourtière* is different.) They need to tell their version to protect their interests. (Stewed tomatoes as signature.) Or, they just cannot tell a good story or put the right words to the experience. (Immigration as person denied in a land of forget-who-you-were, you're-here-now story.) Whoever they are writing or telling the story to does not have the time or the patience to listen to them. They tell the long version when a shorter version could be said. (How do you spell your name mill boss says to M. Poulin, the nonreader and nonwriter. P-O-O-L-E-R, the mill boss tells him.) When you draw it is a matter of seeing more than a matter of moving the pencil or charcoal to do what you want. Some skill of the hand is needed to record the seeing, but it is in the seeing the thing drawn is recorded. The event of a tree standing there in all its glory of autumn. The river coming into focus for the duration of the winter months as the leaves shed their camouflage and the river's disappearing act in the spring of the year when the trees regain their composure of leaves once again. (Reclaiming one's right to one's culture and singing one's songs. The forces of tradition blowing against the shores of modernity. What flashes across your mind is the view of dancers dancing the *gigues* while you shop the aisles in the grocery store. The women all around you speak in French or Franglais. They say the French culture is dead. Are these people ghosts?) Regeneration. The sign of nature to us that we too are hopefuls in possibilities of becoming new people.

To write, is to see. To record. To believe in the belonging to the telling. To express. To explain. (Even if only to oneself.) Acquire. Words are paint. Words as picture. Dad always said, "One picture is worth a thousand words." It is only one picture and a thousand words are a thousand words with the possibility of multiplication, proliferation, exponential growth because of their suggestive lucidity.

So we tell and retell. Telling has nothing to do with competing. Or being beat down because the telling does not match a criteria of some other kind of telling. (*No Adam in Eden* by Grace Metalious or *Canuck* by Camille Lessard-Bissonnette telling.) Telling is its own story and its own reward. The story has its birth in our way of being and not to doubt our experience just because someone has a formula for themselves and their story. My story is of me as I represent the bloodline of the *grand-mères*. (Raining down through the centuries like crashing waves of consciousness coming to being. When I walked the streets of Angers, France, I did not know that the woman immigrant who began the line of women on my maman's side lived here centuries before.)

Like I can remember the curve in the road which I can see from my windows in my house with all the years I've looked out onto the road with my thoughts. Thinking of my maman's death, my father's death, the years of traffic going by, the seasons changing under my gaze, the steeples visible in the distance, my children, my brothers, and their lives. My brother's death. Me, as a young maman, as a cancer patient, with my husband coming home on that road. The train tracks which cross the road's path. The yellow lines newly painted and fading with the passing time and traffic. I stand in the house and the road has not moved or changed, but yet I see the road very differently now than when I first lived here with my hopes set on high. Sorry, but that is not the way the bend in the road goes. The road is resolute and real. (One million *Québécois* immigrated to the northeast United States between the years 1820 and 1920 all with descendants today living in the entire Northeast.) It is me standing at the window looking at its curve imposing my meaning on the view. My thoughts floating heavenward, becoming golden letters in the book of life.

Like the heartbeat, no matter what, passed on from generation to generation. I have the French language and the French way of being in Maine. A historical me. One who was born into a life. Lives. Moving toward the white light that sucks up the soul. We are full of smells in our souls of those things which we live with in our lifetimes. That is why our sense of smell is so acute. Like our eyes which are windows into our soul, our sense of smell is how we find our way home. (The frenzied supper hour. The salt-porked beans.) Our five senses are like the petals of a star in the heavens, or a star fish on the beach, or the inside of an apple cut to reveal its inner heart's core of truth star. Our own five-pointed starness of head and limbs echo the central being of unity to which we all belong in relation to the other five-pointed beings and their placement. Their constancy of change in the sky. Who we are when we move together. The five senses are our points of being inside of the other physically five appendages. We are all stars. All *vedettes*. In our own universes. We are entities and parts of constellations.

Living does a little twisty dance all over expectations and the story changes from the one you have in your head. (I will be French in Maine, Franco-American female, and proud of it.) So it all becomes more story. Or song. Lamentations. War wounds. Epitaph. What we choose to see when we look is what is really there—disappointment and celebration. We can remain aloof, outside, cold, indifferent; or we can belong, praise, recognize, sing alleluias. We can reject. Accept at will. Disagree with. Affirm. We belong to the story plane much like we belong to the picture plane. Depth of field and focus. Good lighting. Bad lighting. Shadow. Sun. Dark. The shifting sands of conversing. Telling. Storying. Each one comes to us and we are filters of the future. We decide what will be seen and heard only so much as we carefully choose the words which do the telling.

For someone to doubt the telling or to devalue the telling of a story makes telling difficult for the one doing story. And also for the one who refuses a story's life. Clear, careful, concise. Clean. With a mind to multiple views of the same view. And the passing years. That is how we tell a story. That is how we become future.

Fin

1 "Down the Plains" appears in Rhea Côté-Robbins' *Wednesday's Child,* pp. 80–85.

CALICE

Greg Chabot
Waterville, Maine

(The scene is set in rural Maine in the 1930s. It is summertime. The woman is standing in the long driveway that goes up from the main road to her farmhouse. The scene really only needs a large rock somewhere near center stage on which the woman can sit. The woman can be anywhere from forty to fifty years old. She is dressed appropriately for a poor farm woman of the times. She should seem nervous and uneasy.)

Femme: (Looking off in the distance). Isn't it pretty? A big beautiful lake with deep, dark blue water. (Pause.) They say that where rich people live, you have to pay lots of money to get a view like this. Lots and lots of money. (Pause.) And it's right here for us. Right in our front yard. Just about. You'd think that we'd spend all day just sitting out here gazing at it. I bet you that's what rich people do. (Pause.) Unless they decide to go swimming or out in a sailboat. Have you ever seen a sailboat? There was one right here on the lake a couple of summers ago. Big one, too. Didn't belong to anyone from around here, that's for sure. They said someone from New York had come up here for the summer and rented one of the camps on the other side of the lake.

Doesn't make any sense to me. Can you imagine coming all the way from New York just to find a lake. They had to be rich—or crazy. (Pause.) It's about the same thing if you ask me—rich and crazy. Only rich people can do crazy things without something happening to them. They can do the dumbest things and people think it's cute or clever or smart. If we did what they do, we'd get put in jail or in the nut house. Maybe they'd just lock us up in a room like they've done with Uncle Johnny.

Poor Uncle Johnny. I remember seeing him walk around in his potato fields. He owned the farm right next to my father's. Back then, we'd see him talking to himself and laugh at him behind his back. "He's got money in the bank, that one," my mother used to say. That's what talking to yourself was supposed to mean. I guess he was one of the richest people in town. That's not saying much because just about everyone else is dead broke. So a rich man here would probably be dirt poor just about any place else. But we always treated Uncle Johnny like he was important. The priest even chose his house to hold the first mass here—before we had a real church of our own. Uncle Johnny had the biggest house, so we'd go to mass in his living room.

Poor Uncle Johnny. Now, he's locked up in a room with only a straight chair in the middle and bars on the window and a bucket for a toilet. He spends all his time catching flies and eating them. (She shows how Uncle Johnny catches and eats flies with his hands. She shudders a bit.) It gives me the creeps when I watch him. Makes me sad, too, to think that somebody's life can end up like that. Doesn't make sense to me. (Pause.) I wonder if rich people go nuts. When I'd see them on their sailboat, it seemed that they couldn't have problems. They had this big beautiful boat that just moved by itself—that glided on the water and took them wherever they wanted to go. And they didn't have to lift a finger. That's what life is like for them, I bet. They can go wherever they want and do whatever they want without having to work or do anything at all. Not like us. (Pause.)

We started working on the farm almost as soon as we could walk. And we'll keep on working until the day we die. When I was just tiny, they used to send me out to the barn to get eggs or out in the fields to pick wild strawberries or blueberries. When I got older, I had to help Mama do the housework and take care of the younger kids. There's no way Mama could have done all of that by herself. Not with all the kids she had. I didn't mind working. It made the time go by a lot faster than just sitting around doing nothing. But with all the chores I had, I never got a chance to go to school like the youngest ones. They'd always get in the way and we never knew quite what to do with them. So we'd pack them off to school.

Back then, we used to think it was some kind of punishment for them. Being stuck inside that big stone building all day without being able to go out and do anything you wanted to. Getting yelled at by the nuns because you were stupid. (Pause.) Now, I know that I was the one being punished. The younger ones were all able to get away from here and do something with their lives. I don't even know how to read or write, so here I stay. Stuck forever.

My Pierre is a good man. That's not the problem. He only drinks a little and he's always been good to me. Always. He got his own farm in no time at all. But I was seventeen when I married him. So it feels like the only thing I did was change houses. One day, I was working like a slave for my mama and papa. The next day, I was working like a slave at my own house. There was a difference, though. For a while. Back then, there weren't as many kids at my house. But it didn't take long for the place to fill up. One after the other they came. Sixteen in all. There are thirteen left.

We lost three. We've been lucky in a way. Fortunat's wife had twenty-two kids. Lost six. Three when they were babies and three more because of some kind of accident on the farm. (Pause.) I'm surprised we don't end up having more die on us than that. People aren't meant to have that many kids—seems to me. (Pause.) Just can't take care of them.

Besides, all those pregnancies do something to you. One after the other like that, they take all the strength out of you. I'm not sure what it is exactly but we lose something—and we never get it back. Maybe if we had a chance to rest a bit—maybe it wouldn't be so bad. But you can't rest on a farm—not if you want to have enough to eat. So you get right back up and go back to work. But you're never the same. And still, you keep on doing it until there's nothing left inside.

That's how Mama died. At forty-six. She'd already had seventeen kids and she was pregnant again. There was trouble when she went into labor. The baby—my brother Zimie—was fine. But it was different for Mama. They couldn't stop the bleeding. The midwife even got the doctor to come over, but he couldn't do anything. She died the next day—bled white and dry, they said.

Those words have always scared me to death. "Bled white and dry." It was true, though. I saw Mama the night before she died and she was as white as snow. I didn't get to see her again because I had to take care of the little ones. (Pause.) But that's no way to die. Not after you've worked like a dog for your whole life and after sacrificing and praying and always trying to do your best. Mama deserved a lot better than that. For sure.

I had put that whole scene out of my mind for years. But now, that picture that I have of her—white as snow—keeps coming back to me. A lot. Maybe it's because I'm almost the same age as she was when she died—I don't know. (Pause.) My last one did give me no end of trouble. It all took hours—and when he decided to come out, it was feet first. (Pause.) I was sure he was going to die. And the midwife and the others, they were sure I was the one who wasn't going to make it. (Pause.) Good thing everybody was wrong. (Pause.) But it was a close call, I tell you that. (Slightly longer pause. Femme should appear even more nervous and on edge. She's not sure what to do or say. She could burst into tears.)

That's why I really don't know what I'm going to do this time around. (Pause.) And how it will all turn out. (She sighs.) I'm pregnant again. At least, I'm pretty sure I am. I'm on my way to see the midwife just to see what she'll say. (Pause.) But I really don't need her to tell me what's going on inside. (Pause.) Women always seem to know when they're pregnant. Right away, just about. I knew every other time and I was always right. (Pause.) Don't see why it would be any different now.

This will be the seventeenth. (Pause.) I told Pierre I didn't want to. That it wasn't a good time. But you know how men are—once they get it in their heads, there's not much that can stop them. That night, we went to a party at his brother Leo's. He had a couple of drinks. Not enough to get him drunk but more than enough to give him quite the urge. We got back here and he was on me in no time at all, calling me every sweet name he could think of. That's when I told him I was afraid I'd get pregnant. But when men get like that, they get real hard of hearing, that's for sure. (Pause.) It was over in no time. That's when he fell asleep and starting snoring loud enough to wake the neighbors. And that's when I started worrying. I haven't stopped worrying since. (Pause.)

But this time, for the first time, I started getting mad, too. Foot-stomping, wall-hitting, curse-screaming mad. And that hasn't stopped either. Goddammit, enough's enough. Is that all life is for us? Cleaning, cooking, and spreading your legs every once in a while to let another kid pop out? If that's all we're good for, then we're no better than Mickey Michaud's fat sow. Sitting in our sties. Watching the world go by through the slats in the fence. And always trying to recover from the last batch of kids before the next one comes along.

Never seemed to bother me before—being like Mickey's sow. It was our duty to be like that, do all those sow things, they'd tell us. And I believed them. My own mama told me that—and played the sow herself for years. How was I supposed to think any different?

But something happened after my youngest was born. It wasn't just here (she indicates her stomach). Things started going wrong up here (she indicates her head). And it changed me a lot. I didn't want to do anything any more. Not even take care of my baby. And every once in a while, I'd get these ideas, these urges. (Pause.) When I think back on it now, it scares the daylights out of me—the living daylights. I didn't get out of bed for a couple of weeks at least. Pierre had the doctor come but he said I wasn't really sick—that it was all in my head. So when Pierre saw that I wasn't getting any better, he called the priest.

Well, the priest comes over and talks to me for I don't know how long in that priest language they use. And his point was that it was a really good thing to be a sow. That's not what he actually said. Priests have a way with words, you know. But that's what he really meant.

He starts telling me that I'm like the Blessed Virgin Mary. She had to sacrifice and suffer and go through pain and misery—just like me. Just like all mothers do. As if that's all we were made for or good for. As if we didn't deserve to be happy. I was supposed to trust her and pray to her, he said. Well, I don't have anything against the Blessed Virgin Mary, but with just one kid, there's no way she can know what it's like to have a dozen or more. And her little boy was the son of God. Come on, he couldn't have given her that much trouble, now could he? I wonder if she'd still be "Blessed" after a couple of days trying to keep up with my Clifford and Johnny and Gilman. Those three together are enough to drive anybody over the edge.

And then the priest starts telling me how she suffered because her only son died. Well, we lost three kids, Pierre and me. Eva—she got the flu one winter and there was so much snow that we couldn't take her anywhere and the doctor couldn't make it to our house, so she died. Maxime broke through the ice on the lake one winter and drowned—and the other one (Pause. As if she'd rather not remember)—the other one got run over. Pierre was backing up on the big tractor. (Pause.) And he couldn't see Peewee—that's what we called him—because he was so small and the tractor was up so high. And that tractor made so much damned noise that he didn't hear anything either. Pierre ended up running over his own little boy. (Pause.) Our little boy. So I think that maybe we could teach the Virgin Mary a thing or two about suffering if she's looking for lessons.

When that priest was here, I was still all messed up. I couldn't think straight—couldn't make sense out of it like I can now. So I just kept quiet. Never said a word. For some reason, he didn't like that very much. I guess I was supposed to break down in tears or beg him for forgiveness or something like that. But I didn't because I just couldn't seem to get my head together. So he got mad. And he started threatening me with hell like all the priests do when they think you're not listening to them and they want you to be a sow again. That's where I was going to end up, he said. Especially if we tried to do things so I wouldn't have any more children. Because it was a mortal sin, he said, to use anything or do anything that would prevent me from getting pregnant. (Pause.) As if I had even given that any thought. As if I was going to jump on Pierre and drag him into the bedroom the minute he left. Besides, I didn't understand half of what he was talking about.

It was only later, when I started feeling more like myself again, that what he said practically drove me to drink. He's had a damned girlfriend ever since he came to town seven years ago. That Chamberland woman who's as big as our old milk cow.

And all those years he's been fooling around with her, she's never gotten pregnant—not even once. Now that's a miracle if I've ever seen one. But it doesn't bother him one bit to tell everybody else that they'll go to hell for doing exactly what he's been doing for years. Damned hypocrite. (Pause.) That's where the real mortal sin is. Not with us. We'd do it to keep from starving. He's doing it to keep from getting caught.

But like I said, it was long after the priest left that I started putting all of this together. My little sister Yvette came to visit not long after that. That's when I realized that I really hated being a sow. My little sister with her husband and their big store in Massachusetts and their big house and their big new car and their nice new store-bought clothes. They were here for four days and they spent more money than we do in four years. She's been married fifteen years, my little sister Yvette. And she has two kids—a boy and a girl. That's it. And it's not because she's been luckier than me. There's a lot more than luck involved, that's for sure. (Pause.) And you know, she looked pretty happy for someone who was committing one mortal sin after another and who was going right straight to hell for eternity at the end of her days. Didn't seem to bother her at all.

It was during her visit that I promised myself I wouldn't live a sow-life any more. I figured if she could do it, so could I. And I've done pretty good until now. I've promised myself to do even better after this one is born. (Pause.) The other night, I dreamed about Mama again. I saw her on her deathbed—white as a sheet—bled white and dry. After a while, I saw myself in her place—bled white and dry. It scared me so much that I still haven't gotten over it. So I know that this one's going to be my last one, that's for sure. (Pause.) One way or another, this one will be my last. (She gets up and looks at the lake.) The lake is even prettier than usual today, don't you think? Look how the sun shines on it. You'd swear that the top was covered with diamonds. Real, sparkling diamonds. The kind rich people wear. (Pause, she exits slowly.)

—Rideau—

THE LANE ROAD, 1958

Susann Pelletier
Lewiston, Maine

I remember the Brule's dairy farm,
Down the hill, beside the snowy pasture:
Big barn painted red,
A hundred cows within—Holsteins, Guernseys, Jerseys—
All those
Wet noses and steaming breaths,
Low moos and swooshing tails,
All that
Cud-munching and hoof-shuffling,
In time with the warmth, the cold,
A hundred cows keeping our secrets:

How my brother, Norman, swooped down,
Ragged, angel-like,
From the hayloft to the ground,
Not once,
But three times in a single December week.
(These, we later called
His "luckier streak of accidents.")

How I sneaked around the old grain bins,
Lifted lids and stole away home
With the tiny mice I had caught,
Wriggling in a shoe box.
(These, we later heard,
Rustling in cupboards, scuttling inside the walls,
As the cat yawned, curled up and slept.)

How my sister Nancy and Phil, the farmer's son, tussled
Away the winter dusks in the hay.
(Same Phil who greeted her thirty-five years later
With a startling full-mouth kiss
Outside his Hostess delivery truck.)

The cows watched and nodded,
Eyes wide and kind and unjudging
As old goddesses,
Only stirring and whispering
Briefly
These tales, these lessons,
As we opened the milkroom door,
And slipped into the barn.

WHAT WE GATHER IN NOVEMBER

Susann Pelletier
Lewiston, Maine

On the next roof,
Steam is rising this November morning.
The barn swallow, orange breast of summer, is gone
Its song a thousand miles south of this sunrise,
Its daub-and-wattle nest on the beam
Abandoned.

Frost holds now its bright jewels—
Emerald, sapphire, topaz—
On the grass,
Ice, its diamonds on the water pail,
Long after sun up.

My brother Norman has slept in the shed again—
In a room he made of old boards,
A discarded door, a padlock;
Furnished with an army cot, two chairs.
("Was he warm?" I wonder from my bed.)

Weeks ago, when he let me in,
I looked at the trinkets on his windowsill,
Took in their iridescences:
The white ceramic horse Mémère had given him,
The silver lighter,
The guitar pick of horn,
The gleaming crow feather....

Outside his door, last night,
I sat for a long time,
Listening to him play
The harmonica, the guitar,
Listening to him sing:
"How many seas must the white dove sail,
Before it sleeps in the sand?
The answer, my friend, is blowin' in the wind...."

Finding our way around my mother's sadness,
We gather jewels from November sun,
Build rooms,
Sing songs to rough walls
In the moonlight.

HOW MANY FRENCHMEN DOES IT TAKE TO...?*

C. Stewart Doty
Alburquerque, New Mexico

Since World War I, "dumb Frenchman" jokes have been pervasive in the northeast United States. "How many Frenchmen does it take to screw in a light bulb?" queries the most familiar of the genre. The expected answer: "Three, one to put the bulb in the socket, and two to turn the ladder."

In all regions other than the Northeast, "French jokes" invariably are erotic, as in "French kiss" or "French tickler." In a milder one, a Frenchman says, "I know one thousand positions for making love." "Boy, that's something," replies an impressed American. "I only know one position. The woman lies down on her back, and the man lies down on top of her." "Eh bien!" exclaims the Frenchman, "One thousand and one."

The "sexy Frenchmen" in these jokes may be too preoccupied, but they are intelligent, clever, and bearers of *savoir faire*. In the Northeast, people do not tell these "sexy Frenchman" jokes. They tell the ethnic slurs of "dumb Frenchman" jokes, which differ in nature from other regional ethnic humor such as "Yankee jokes." In "dumb Frenchman" jokes, the Franco-American is the target of the joke. In Yankee jokes, the "out-of-stater," or non-Yankee, is the target of the joke.

I had not thought of these jokes for years. But in 1992 I was asked to be an expert witness in a discrimination case filed by a Franco-American. In his workplace the plaintiff had experienced "dumb Frenchman" jokes, the term "frog" used as an ethnic slur, and hostility to spoken French.

The attorneys for the plaintiff believed that a history of discrimination against Franco-Americans would show those acts to be discriminatory. I prepared such a history and gave depositions on it. Such research and testimony was a new experience for me, but academic historians are becoming commonplace as expert witnesses. In a widely publicized case of the 1980s, *Equal Opportunity Commission v. Sears, Roebuck, & Co.*, some historians testified on behalf of the company's women workers, while others supported management.[1] A decade later, historians testified both for and against a proposed Disney Corporation's Civil War theme park in northern Virginia.

My study of the history of discrimination against Franco-America, as developed for the legal battle in Maine, taught me three lessons.

First, it demonstrated that humanities disciplines and research techniques can and should have practical uses. The humanities are not simply a cultural ornament, trivialized as less "real" than the natural and social sciences.

Second, the research for the case unexpectedly revealed that colleges and universities were intimately involved in the history of discrimination. Academics in the humanities and social sciences helped create discrimination. Later, academics have worked to overturn that discrimination.

Third, for the many faculty members who teach Franco-American students, particularly common in the public colleges and universities of the Northeast, the documentation prepared for the case reveals the "forgotten" or "unknown" history of discrimination against Franco-Americans.

I believe that many faculty members, especially in the humanities, have and can develop comparable "useable" knowledge. I hope that this demonstration of the use of the history of discrimination inspires others to use their knowledge.

I begin with some of the highlights of discrimination against Franco-Americans.[2] In that summary, I document the critical role of schools, colleges, and academics in both the development and the decline of discrimination.

Historical research on Franco-Americans indicates that discrimination against them began with the expansion of their population into the United States in the late-nineteenth century.[3] Until the Civil War, the only significant populations of native French residents in the United States were the Acadians of northern Maine and western Louisiana, as well as the descendants of French-Canadian fur traders and loggers in the Midwest and West.

Between the Civil War and 1900, however, these Franco-Americans were joined by 500,000 more French Canadians who settled almost exclusively in the textile and papermaking cities of the Northeast. They constituted the first major non-English-speaking immigrant group in that region. These immigrants composed up to 60 percent of the population .in such small textile and paper-manufacturing cities as Cohoes in New York; Chicopee, Lowell, Worcester, and Holyoke in Massachusetts; Woonsocket and Central Falls in Rhode Island; Manchester and Nashua in New Hampshire; the mill towns of Connecticut's Quinebaug River Valley; and Biddeford and Lewiston in Maine.

Native Yankees responded to those large numbers with prejudice and discrimination. As early as 1881 the widely circulated *Twelfth Annual Report of the Massachusetts Bureau of Statistics of Labor* characterized Franco-Americans as "the Chinese of the Eastern States." Franco-Americans throughout the Northeast protested that characterization, but it became standard among members of the Yankee establishment. The report legitimized discrimination against Franco-Americans—and marked the beginning of Franco-American ethnic consciousness. Mass meetings of Franco-Americans protesting the report led to the establishment of the first permanent advocacy organizations.[4]

In its discrimination against Franco-Americans, the Yankee establishment was almost immediately joined by Irish-Americans—the immigrant wave that immediately preceded the Franco-Americans of the mill migration era.

Irish-Americans discriminated against newly arriving Franco-Americans in two ways. In industries dominated by Irish-Americans, Franco-Americans were limited in opportunities for advancement to better jobs. Irish-Americans frequently viewed Franco-Americans as the "Chinese of the Eastern States," in competition with Irish-Americans for jobs. Fights between the two groups were common in textile and papermaking towns.[5]

A second area of Irish-American discrimination against Franco-Americans was within the Roman Catholic church. In the 1890 to 1930 era, Franco-American Catholics—determined to preserve the French-speaking, lay-controlled parishes of their native Québec—frequently battled Irish-American bishops opposed to both the French language and lay control. In particularly bitter struggles in Connecticut, Maine, and Rhode Island, Franco-Americans used civil disobedience, legislative action, and appeal to the courts to get their way. Sometimes they won, but usually the Irish-American bishops triumphed.

One of the leaders in this Franco-American struggle was Dr. J. L. Fortier of Waterville, Maine. When he died at the height of the fight in 1911, his Irish-American bishop refused to allow a mass for him or let his body to be buried in a Catholic cemetery unless his widow repudiated the cause. To that demand she replied: "*Mon mari a fait sa vie sans l'évêque; il ira bien au ciel sans lui*."[6]

After World War I, these struggles were exacerbated by the building of "English" Catholic churches in competition with the existing "French" Catholic churches throughout the Northeast. Eight kilometers (five miles) from my campus at the University of Maine, for instance, "English" St. Mary's broke off from "French" St. Joseph's to form a new parish one block away in Old Town, Maine. The contemporary shortage of priests has now caused the two parishes to recombine into a single new parish, appropriately named "Holy Family."

Many Franco-Americans perceive continuing discrimination by Irish-Americans. Currently, in those New England states where Franco-Americans constitute over 30 percent of the population, only the dioceses of Manchester and Providence have Franco-American bishops. Maine Catholics have been overwhelmingly Franco-American, but their diocese has yet to have a Franco-American appointed bishop (only two auxiliary bishops).

The most intense discrimination against Franco-Americans occurred after World War I. At the war's end, right-wing politicians found political success through a nation-wide drive against recent immigrants—often termed "hyphenated Americans"—and political radicals. The Yankee intellectual elite that participated in this nativism opposed immigration from southern and eastern Europe. It was especially hostile to Franco-Americans, out of fear that New England was being taken over by them. As early as 1900, *Boston Transcript* journalist Rollin Lynde Hartt worried that "Puritan" New England is becoming a "Romish New France."[7] This movement was dubbed "Americanism."

Where did intellectuals in academic institutions stand in this era? The "Americanism" movement frequently relied on research by academics to justify discrimination. Academics produced scholarly and academic racism, full of footnotes and social science data—the "political correctness" of that era.

In 1918–19 H. B. Woolston, University of Washington professor of sociology, claimed that in "physical vigor, intellectual ability, self-control, moral integrity, sympathy, cooperation, leadership, perseverance, efficiency, aspiration" Franco-Americans ranked seventh among ethnic groups, well behind first-ranked "Native White Americans" and fourth-ranked "Polish and Russian Hebrews," but ahead of tenth-ranked "Negroes." In 1926 a longtime professor of sociology at the University of Minnesota and Indiana University, Clifford Kirkpatrick, alarmed his readers with the information that 48.1 percent of French Canadians were "retarded"—almost twice the percentage of native-born English-speaking Americans.[8]

Especially hostile to Franco-Americans was Madison Grant, who advocated causes as varied as South African apartheid and the preservation of California redwood trees. His book, *The Passing of the Great Race*, warned that the Nordic race was being replaced by lesser races, such as "Alpine" French Canadians. Not surprisingly, the book was translated into German during the Nazi era. In his book, Grant told his many readers that French Canadians were but "a poor and ignorant community of little more importance to the world at large than are the Negroes of the South."[9]

In another work of Grant's, *The Alien in Our Midst* (1930), sociologist and Unitarian-Universalist peace activist Robert Dexter predicted that Franco-Americans "will culturally and religiously control the New England state," thanks to the fecundity of their families and their "philosophy of separatism." Even worse, University of Buffalo professor of sociology—and consultant for the United States Census Bureau—Niles Carpenter warned in 1927 that, if the number of French Canadians in the Northeast continue to increase at its current rate for another ten years, the United States might be faced with "plebiscites of the sort which have been held in Upper Silesia and Transylvania" resulting "in the transfer of a considerable portion of the territory of the United States to...Canada."[10]

This elite, intellectual, and academic prejudice and discrimination against Franco-Americans framed the social context for students during their college years—and was echoed by writers of juvenile fiction. Generations of well-brought-up boys read adventure fiction set in the Maine woods, written by members of the Yankee Protestant establishment, and informed by the denigration of Franco-Americans. In that fiction for boys, one historian tells us, "French Canadians...are treated almost as contemptuously as they are frequently depicted as evil, dirty, and simply as the villain."[11]

Far more lasting in impact than the writings of upper-class intellectuals was the "Americanism" movement's English-only campaign. Beginning in the 1920s, New England employers and state legislators adopted policies and laws to forbid French as a language of instruction in school and as a language of the workplace. Most of the English-only legislation of the 1920s was ultimately repealed or declared unconstitutional, but it left a permanent legacy of hostility to spoken French—another form of discrimination.

Most contemporary Franco-Americans have memories of being punished for speaking French in school or the workplace. Even worse for many of them was their experience in the French language classes of secondary schools, colleges, and universities. Their teachers—for whom "Parisian" French was a second language—"corrected" the pronunciation of these native French-speakers. Imagine the impact—comparable to North American English-speakers being corrected for their failure to speak British English or teachers of Spanish in the southwestern U.S. demanding that their Spanish-speaking students adopt Castilian pronunciation! Even today it is commonplace for French teachers in the Northeast to insist that their Franco-American students speak "Parisian" French.

The discriminatory banning and belittling of spoken North American French in schools and colleges fostered low Franco-American self-esteem. Almost every business and office in the Northeast continues to have "closet" French-speakers, apprehensive of speaking the "wrong" language. Richard Beach, past president of the Association for Canadian Studies in the United States, tells of a poignant encounter shortly after his arrival in Plattsburg, New York:

> While conversing with an elderly teller at a local bank, I detected what was a very slight French accent. Trying to be polite and wanting to please, I began speaking French. Her reaction startled me; she seemed horrified. She looked around suspiciously and in a low voice asked me not to tell anyone that she was in fact originally French Canadian. Sadly, she considered her heritage to be an embarrassment and degrading. She was not alone in that time in trying to camouflage, or even deny, her origins—an attitude fostered to some extent by a population locally that for a variety of reasons frowned or looked down upon immigrants in general and French Canadians in particular.[12]

Beach's experience is hardly an isolated case. Sadly, stories like that are commonplace and persistent. Franco-Americans, such as novelist Jack Kerouac, hid the fact that they were Franco-American. "Believe me," Kerouac recalled in 1950, "I'll never hide it again, as I once did, say in high school, when I first began 'Englishing myself' to coin a term" (*Me faire un Anglais*).[13] Only in 1991 did Bates College, in the heart of French-speaking Lewiston, Maine, restore the right of its Franco-American clerical and maintenance staff to speak French in the workplace.[14]

A more sinister effect of the "Americanism" movement was its trickle-down effect in legitimating, broadening, popularizing, and intensifying discrimination against Franco-Americans in the Northeast. One sign was the appearance of the "dumb Frenchman" joke. Another sign was the introduction of the term "frog." Scholars opposed to discrimination found that the term was brought back from France by American soldiers and applied as an ethnic slur to Franco-Americans. These scholars found that such usage is limited to the Northeast. Indeed, the word is not associated with Franco-Americans elsewhere in North America. Neither Cajuns in Louisiana nor *Québécois* and Acadians in Canada are called "frogs." In the West and upper Midwest, the term "frog" is used only to describe people from France. For most people in Maine and the Northeast since World War I, however, "frog" can only be understood as an ethnic slur against Franco-Americans.[15]

Perhaps the most sinister aspect of this nativist campaign against Franco-Americans was the rise of the Ku Klux Klan throughout New England in the 1920s. At its peak of membership in 1925, the Klan had as many as 37,000 members in Rhode Island; 65,590 in Connecticut; 75,000 in New Hampshire; 80,301 in Vermont; 130,780 in Massachusetts; and 150,141 in Maine. Probably no other political movement in New England's history had the Ku Klux Klan's success and membership. Yet it has been virtually ignored by scholars.

In New England, the Klan appealed to Protestant clergy, businessmen, members of the Masons and Odd Fellows, and farmers. Unlike in the American South, the Klan's target in New England was French Catholics and Jews. "It's all so simple," a Klan-affiliated Maine clergyman told a writer for *Collier's* magazine in 1923, "It's the rising of a Protestant people to take back what is their own." A brochure announcing a Massachusetts Klan meeting in Worcester's venerable Mechanics Hall told potential attendees that the Klan merely stood for "Americanism" and "public schools," surely items of appeal to "a native, white, gentile, Protestant American."[16] The Klan sought to end state funding of parochial schools and extend English-only legislation.

Throughout New England, rallies with thousands of hooded participants and cross-burnings were common in cities and towns, big and small. In Maine, Franco-American loggers of the Industrial Workers of the World (IWW) turned back forty hooded Klansmen from Greenville in the zero temperatures of February 1924. In Fairfield, Maine, on 1 July 1924, Ku Klux Klan forces and Franco-Americans battled each other with rocks and clubs before a fiery cross was torn down. In September 1924 Franco-Americans defended Biddeford from the Ku Klux Klan storming the bridge from Saco. It is also generally conceded that Owen Brewster was elected governor of Maine only through the Klan's efforts. In September 1924 nearly one hundred people were injured by stones and buckshot in Klan versus anti-Klan clashes in Lancaster, Spencer, and Haverill, Massachusetts, just kilometers from the Concord of Emerson and Thoreau. In October 1924 stoning and destruction of cars ended a Klan rally in nearby Worcester. The year 1925 saw similar outbreaks at Northbridge and Dedham. In Rhode Island, Lucien Sansouci, a reporter for *La Tribune* of Woonsocket, claimed to be branded by Klansmen after he was caught observing one of their rallies in 1924. Large Rhode Island Klan rallies in such towns as Rhodes-on-Pawtuxet, Greenville, and East Greenwich caused the *Providence News* to warn—in French: "*Le Ku Klux Klan declare la guerre aux candidats catholiques. Il se ligue avec le parti républicain. Ce qu'il importe de faire.*"[17] Southeastern New Hampshire had a similarly large Klan movement, strong enough to make believable a hoax that the Klan had captured and branded a Rochester man.[18]

Yankee New England may have forgotten the Ku Klux Klan or relegated it to benighted regions somewhere else. Older Franco-Americans, however, can quickly recall the trauma they and their parents experienced at the hands of the Klan in those dark years. They remember, as children, being hidden under beds and in closets and behind locked doors in the darkened houses of the *petits canadas* of the Northeast.

Thanks to the nativism begun in the 1920s and other forms of discrimination, Franco-Americans have been remarkably unsuccessful in New England politics until the twenty-first century. Even though 30 percent of Maine voters are of Franco-American heritage, there has never been an openly Franco-American governor, U.S. senator, or member of Congress (Senator Margaret Chase Smith's electoral success was won by her concealment of her Franco-American heritage, and a Franco-American was elected in the 2nd District after this article was first published). Nor have New Hampshire and Massachusetts elected Franco-Americans as governors or senators. Only in Rhode Island have Franco-Americans had much political success. Even there, however, no Franco-American has been elected governor or U.S. senator since the 1930s.[19]

How did Franco-Americans respond to scholarly discrimination by the Yankee intellectual elite, the rise of "the dumb Frenchman joke" and the ethnic slur "frog," the English-only campaigns in school and workplace, and the impact of the Ku Klux Klan on politics? Their most frequent response to this pattern of discrimination and exclusion was to "assimilate," that is to abandon French language, customs, and even religion in favor of English ones. Some even Anglicized their names—Boisvert became Greenwood, Lévesque became Bishop, Pinette became Spruce, St. Pierre became St. Peter or even Stone, and Grenier became Green.[20] Some denied knowledge of French and told "dumb Frenchman" jokes.

Too often Franco-Americans have paid a price either for assimilating or concealing the "French Fact" of their lives. Assimilating, middle-aged Franco-Americans frequently regret their rootlessness. A sign of the agony are the frequently heard "bridge stories." Over the years I have collected Maine accounts of irrational fright and fear of falling as one crosses a bridge between the "French" neighborhood and the "English" one—as in crossing over from French Island to Old Town, from Lewiston to Auburn, and from the French to English side of the Presumpscot River in Westbrook. Similar stories are told in other New England states.

One more factor contributed to creating the post-World War I discrimination against Franco-Americans. That was the decline of the textile industry, the major employer of Franco-Americans, in the Northeast. This permanent downturn not only made others resent Franco-Americans as competitors for a shrinking number of jobs, but it trapped Franco-Americans in the Northeast in a continued low standard of living, low level of education, and limited opportunity.

With the Great Depression of the 1930s, the same became true for Acadians in the potato-growing regions of Northern Maine. Moreover, when Franco-American workers tried to protect their interests in a declining economy by joining trade unions, they were discriminated against for that. *Roughing the Uppers*, the 1992 video of the Auburn, Maine, shoe strike of 1937, demonstrates that the strike not only pitted labor against management, it pitted Franco-Americans against the Yankee establishment and non-Franco-American strike-breakers. Indeed, we only know what any of the strike organizers said because one of their major speeches was translated into French and published in the Franco-American newspaper *Le Messager*. None of the speech appears in the English-language Lewiston newspapers.[21]

Life was better for Franco-Americans employed and living in papermaking cities and, especially, in other parts of the nation. West Coast Franco-Americans experience little or no discrimination. Indeed, being Franco-American and speaking French is considered an asset in the West—where Spanish-speakers are discriminated against.

Whatever general process of "embourgeoisization" had occurred for Franco-Americans in the Northeast, it dates only from the 1950s. Much of that was created by opportunities opened for them by the new and expanded state colleges and universities created in those years.

Historic patterns of discrimination may now be changing, thanks to Franco-American self-awareness and to greater sensitivity by members of other groups, and, once again, colleges and universities have been the centers for change. Much of the academic research on Franco-Americans in the first part of this century was racist. Yet it is more recent research by academics that has documented the origins of the ethnic slur, "frog," and the beginnings of the "dumb Frenchman" joke.

By the 1970s and 1980s academics increasingly valued North American French language, literature, and history. The 1950s leader in this appreciation was surely Smith College Professor Marine Leland. Her pioneering work has been followed by the works of members of the Northeast Council for Quebec Studies and its successor organization, the American Council for Quebec Studies.

The 1970s saw the establishment of French/English bilingual education programs in Maine, New Hampshire, and Vermont; the publication of scholarly and literary material on Franco-Americans by the National Materials Development Center for French and Portuguese; and consciousness-raising scholarly colloquia organized by the French Institute of Assumption College—founded at the turn of the century as a Franco-American school. Between 1979 and 1981 the University of Maine, funded by the National Endowment for the Humanities, conducted the Canadian-Franco-American Studies Project for secondary and post-secondary teachers.[22]

More than one commentator has noted that the civil rights and anti-war movements of the 1960s created *une nouvelle identité* (a new identity) for Franco-Americans, a new cultural identity of pride in being Franco-American and in speaking French. Since 1970 leaders in that new identity have included those associated with the University of Maine's Franco-American Resource and Opportunity Group, or FAROG. In a not-quite-monthly newspaper called *Le FAROG Forum*, this group of Franco-Americans turned "frog" back on the detractors as a term of Franco-American pride and new identity, in defiance of its use as an ethnic slur. So widespread is Franco-American resentment of the "frog" designation, however, that in recent years Franco-American legislators in Maine forced the *Forum* to change its telephone number from 581-FROG.[23] To be more inclusive in its appeal, the newspaper recently changed its name to *Le Forum*.

Still more recently the controversy in 1992–93 surrounding radio-commentator "Frenchie" (Ernie Gagne) illustrates the rival strategies Franco-Americans use in responding to discrimination.[24] For seven years "Frenchie" had told "dumb Frenchman" jokes on radio station WBLM, a radio station widely heard in southern Maine and New Hampshire. A typical joke, told in French-accented English, is that he had been hired by the station to count the number of compact disks in the station's library. Unfortunately, he lost count after getting to three. The station had long ignored objections to such "humor." That changed in January 1993 when an Augusta attorney and a director of the Holocaust Human Rights Center of Maine objected to "Frenchie" and his ethnic jokes, then filed complaints with the Maine Human Rights Commission and the Federal Communications Commission against radio station WBLM.

A few Franco-Americans and some members of the broadcast and print media saw "Frenchie's" work as harmless humor and viewed objections to it as violations of the freedom of speech. Indeed, a particularly intemperate editorial in the Manchester, New Hampshire, *Union-Leader*—perhaps the most right-wing daily newspaper in New England—claimed that Franco-Americans "thoroughly enjoy" such ethnic jokes with themselves as the target, because they "have an expansive sense of humor and an ability to laugh at themselves that derives from quiet self-confidence."[25] This editorial, more than "Frenchie's" jokes, mobilized Franco-Americans. Manchester's *Association Canada-Américain* (ACA), a leading advocacy group for Franco-Americans, organized protest rallies in Manchester, New Hampshire, and Lewiston, Maine. The ACA and other Franco-American advocacy groups heightened awareness that "Frenchie's" work constituted objectionable ethnic stereotyping. So widespread were the objections that "Frenchie" withdrew his services from WBLM.

This struggle heightened Franco-American ethnic-consciousness and pride. Although some Franco-Americans sympathized with "Frenchie," most resented the "dumb Frenchman" jokes, just as they resented the term "frog," as signs of historical discrimination. The mixed reaction to "Frenchie" struck a particularly sensitive nerve in political reporter Paul Carrier. Writing in the Portland *Press Herald*, Carrier recalled his happiness and pride of growing up in the French and *francophone* heritage in Massachusetts. Then he wrote:

> Now I live in Maine, and this is a far different place. Here, people with French accents are routinely ridiculed on a Portland radio station that wouldn't dream of reviving *Amos and Andy.* Here, an assistant attorney general recalls an Augusta landlady who initially declined to rent him an apartment because she thought his wife was French Canadian. Here, "dumb Frenchman" jokes are so commonplace that even the most "politically correct" among us feel free to tell them. Here, I periodically get anonymous hate mail at work from a newspaper reader who, seeing my French surname in by-lines, regales me with unsigned diatribes that use "French" and "Catholic" as slurs. Here, Franco-American cashiers who make an honest mistake have been conditioned to apologize for being French, as if their errors are genetic. Here, students without a trace of French ancestry sometimes explain away their failings by telling teachers, "Oh, I'm French sometimes." And here, misguided Franco-Americans laugh louder than anyone else at mean-spirited insults that are thinly disguised as humor.[26]

"Sadly," Carrier continued, "these insults do not take place in Massachusetts simply because the African American, Hispanic, Portuguese-American, and Southeast Asian populations there provide larger, more convenient targets."[27]

An even more recent reaction to the historic discrimination against Franco-Americans was the first discrimination suit filed by a Franco-American against an employer. In 1988, Steffan Duplessis, a bilingual Franco-American of Acadian ancestry, became a residential advisor at the Penobscot Job Corps Center, a division of the Training and Development Corporation in Bangor, Maine. According to his complaint, things went well for him through the end of 1989. He won raises and promotions. He received the center's Outstanding Staff Award.

Following one of his promotions, a resentful co-worker placed on his desk a ceramic frog with a crown. Then it got worse. After he objected to smoking by others in his workplace, co-workers responded by harassing him as a Franco-American. A copy of the memorandum banning smoking was placed on his desk with the inscription, "To your health, Frog." From then on, he received written and oral "frog" slurs, ethnic insults, "dumb Frenchman" jokes, and objections to his speaking in French with French-speaking clients. After several months, he threatened to take this ethnic harassment to the Maine Human Rights Commission (MHRC). Simultaneously, the company was "reorganized," and Duplessis was terminated. He filed complaints with the MHRC and the Equal Employment Opportunity Commission alleging that he had been discriminated against on the basis of ancestry. By May 1992 the MHRC was unable to bring about reconciliation and the EEOC issued a "Right to Sue" letter.[28]

When the case was tried in July 1993 the attorneys representing Duplessis' employer gave a different version of these events. According to them, Duplessis was a "creative and energetic" but "unpopular and controversial" employee. He was "insufferably arrogant," "incourteous" in speaking French in the presence of non-French-speakers, "strident about the non-smoking issue," and had a job history of professional failure. In short, Duplessis was a "mediocre employee" whose arrogance prevented him from getting along with his co-workers and made him "ineffective with students." His employer, described as "hypersensitive" to "diversity issues," fired him on grounds of poor performance, not bias.[29]

On 24 July 1993 the court decided against Duplessis. It agreed that the Job Corps Center "was not a model of cultural acceptance" and that "ethnic jokes and slurs occurred," but insisted that Duplessis "failed to prove that the treatment [accorded him], if unfair, was motivated by plaintiff's ancestry." Although several

Franco-American and other witnesses corroborated Duplessis's complaint, other Franco-American witnesses assured the court that they were not offended by "dumb Frenchman" jokes or "frog" as an ethnic slur. That contradiction, like Duplessis's own use of "frog" as a self-identifier when he was a member of F.A.R.O.G. as a student at the University of Maine, clearly puzzled the judge.[30] The case was not appealed.

The court's puzzled verdict provides little guidance for the rest of us. The verdict, as described in the press, suggests that sometimes the term "frog" and "dumb Frenchman" jokes are harmless. If Franco-Americans tell "dumb Frenchman" jokes and use "frog" as a self-identifier, it may be all right for others to use "frog" in any way they choose. The verdict coincided with a national debate on the use of "nigger," "bitch," and "whore" by so-called "gangster" rap musicians.[31] If Black people use "nigger" and if women use "bitch" and "whore," can anyone else use those terms, even as slurs, in the face of what we have learned from the civil rights and women's movements?

One unexpected discovery in this history of discrimination against Franco-Americans is the central role of Franco-American faculty. Academics helped to create the discrimination and helped to combat it. In the first half of the twentieth century, academics provided countless "scientific" studies showing that Franco-Americans were inferior in intellect and character to Americans of northern European descent. More recent academic research has challenged that view. In the past, many academic teachers of French denigrated the speaking of North American French. More recent teachers of French value the language of North American "native speakers."

In the past, colleges and universities fostered prejudice and discrimination. Now colleges and universities foster Franco-American pride. In these ethnic struggles, academics have chosen sides. The debate over whether "political correctness" means courtesy and civility or the invasion of freedom of speech is but one illustration of a continuing debate on these issues. Another is the debate over the value and accuracy of such academic works as *The Bell Curve*.

Academics cannot avoid playing a role in this continuing debate. One would think that events of the past thirty years in America would have made historic discrimination and ethnic slurs things of the past. Those things should have ended or have been dampened by the civil rights movement of the 1960s, the influence of Martin Luther King, Jr., and Malcolm X, civil rights legislation, and the rise of the women's movement. Yet the "Frenchie" controversy and the Duplessis case show that in the Northeast discrimination against Franco-Americans continues—the "dumb Frenchman" joke, the ethnic slur of "frog," the hesitancy to speak French in public, and the willingness to equate "Frenchness" with ineptness.

As an academic, those cases gave me an opportunity to draw on my own work and that of other scholars to fight against ethnic discrimination. Most faculty have similar opportunities—in our classroom conduct, in the books we assign students to read, and in our own research—to help end the years of discrimination against Franco-Americans and other ethnic groups.

Even "Frenchie" finally got the message. He briefly came back on the air in 1994, but the butt of his "French" jokes now had become the Yankee boss or arrogant "out-of-stater." If he can get the message, maybe academics and the students and communities they influence can, too.

* A version of this essay first appeared in 1995. C. Stewart Doty, "How Many Frenchmen Does It Take to....?" in *Thought and Action* 11 (2), Fall 1995, pp. 85–104.

1 Novick.

2 There is no major historical work on discrimination against Franco-Americans, nor does their story appear in the standard histories on discrimination and nativism. This is even true of Higham's exemplary work, *Strangers in the Land*. See also Perlmutter, *Divided We Fall*.

3 For general accounts of the history of Franco-Americans, see: Brault; Poteet; Chartier, *Histoire des Franco-Américains de la Nouvelle-Angleterre*; Doty, *The First Franco-Americans*; Roby, *Les Franco-Américains de la Nouvelle-Angleterre*; Weil. For the most thorough and up-to-date bibliography of recent work on Franco-Americans, see Frenette and Roby, pp. 129–64.

4 For the impact of the Wright report, see Weil, pp. 119–27; Roby, *Les Franco-Américains de la Nouvelle-Angleterre*, pp. 185–89; Brault, pp. 67–68; Wright, *Uniform Hours of Labor*, pp. 150–51.

5 This rivalry is a recurrent theme in Doty, *The First Franco Americans*; Weil; and Roby, *Les Franco-Américains de la Nouvelle-Angleterre*. For an alternative view, see Hartford.

6 "My husband lived his life without the Bishop's influence. He will get to Heaven well enough without it, too." For the struggle with the church in this paragraph and the following paragraphs, see Weil, pp. 150–61, 194–96; Brault, pp. 68–73, 87–88. The Fortier quote comes from Rumilly, *Histoire des Franco-Américains*, p. 262: translation by Doty.

7 Hartt, p. 628.

8 Kirkpatrick, p. 40. Woolston as quoted by Drachsler, p. 42.

9 Grant, pp. 72–73.

10 R. Dexter, pp. 70–79. Carpenter, pp. 128–29.

11 D. Smith, p. 197.

12 Beach.

13 Letter dated 8 September 1950 from Jack Kerouac to Yvonne Le Maître, originally published in *Le F.A.R.O.G. Forum* 11 (8), May–June 1984, p. 15, as reprinted in Poteet, p. 447.

14 "Bates Ends Rule against Workers Speaking French," *Le F.A.R.O.G. Forum* 19 (1), October–December, 1991, p. 8.
15 On the use of "frog," see Casssidy and Hall, II: p. 581. *The Oxford English Dictionary*, VI: pp. 208–09. Mencken, pp. 595–96.
16 F. Collins, pp. 12–13. "Ku Klux Stirs Worcester," *New York Times*, 24 September 1923, pp. 3–4.
17 "The Ku Klux Klan has declared war on Catholic candidates. It is in league with the Republican Party. It knows what it has to do."
18 For an overview of the Ku Klux Klan, see Wyn Wade. For New England membership figures and Klan activity in Maine, see Breton, pp. 170–210; Blanchard, pp. 20–39; and Spugnardi. For Massachusetts, see the following articles in the *New York Times*: "Fifty Hurt in Two Bay State Klan Battles; In One 500 Foes Clash with 200 Knights," 30 July 1924, p. 1:7; "Three Shot in Attack on Klansmen by Crowd After Initiation Ceremonies Near Haverhill," 31 July 1924, p. 1:3; "Klan Clash Prisoners Are Jailed and Fined," 1 August 1924, p. 1:5; "More Arrests Made in Klan Rioting," 2 August 1924, p. 10:5; "Finds 13 Guilty in Klan Riot," 19 August 1924, p. 35:2; "Mob of 800 in Worcester Beats Klansmen and Wrecks Cars After Order's Big Meeting," 19 October 1924, p. 1:2; "To Investigate Klan Riot," 20 October 1924, p. 18:1; "Beseige 150 Klansmen," 29 April 1925, p. 23:2; "300 Klansmen Stoned in Massachusetts," May 1925, p. 14:2; "Two Klan Foes Beaten," 29 April 1925, p. 10:2; "Held for Klan Riots," 21 June 1925, p. 15:2; "Scores Are Hurt in Bay State Klan Riot; Three Arrested After Siege in Farmhouse," 3 August 1925, p. 1:4; "Five Shot Near Klan Field," 11 August 1925, p. 12:3; "16 Klansmen Held for Bay State Riot," 12 August 1925, p. 23:3; "1,000 in Bay State Engage in Klan Row," 13 August 1925, p. 23:5. See also Wolkovich-Valkavicius, pp. 61–80. For New Hampshire, see Goetz, pp. 245–63. For Rhode Island, see "Threat to Bomb Movies," *New York Times*, 18 January 1923, p. 9:4; "Says Klan Branded Him," *New York Times*, 6 August 1924, p. 17:3; Sullivan, pp. 74–82; N. Smith, pp. 35–45.
19 For a brief discussion of Franco-American politics, see Doty, *The First Franco Americans*, pp. 155–58.
20 For a discussion of name-changing, see Forget, as reprinted in Poteet, pp. 322–37.
21 Branham, Francoeur, and Surkis.
22 Chartier, pp. 330–53.
23 E. Peterson, "Dial 581–FROG," pp. 185–93; "Diversity in Franco-American Identity Politics," pp. 58–67.
24 The paragraphs on the "Frenchie" controversy are drawn from various articles in *Le F.A.R.O.G. Forum*, (20) 2, January-February 1993.
25 Drawn from various articles in *Le FAROG Forum* 20 (2), January-February 1993.
26 Carrier, p. 10.
27 Carrier, p. 10.
28 United States, District Court, District of Maine, Complaint of *Steffan T. Duplessis*.
29 Opening arguments of Attorneys Bernard Kubetz and George Schelling on 12 July 1993, in United States, District Court, District of Maine, Complaint of *Steffan T. Duplessis*.
30 See, for example, "Brutality as a Teen Fashion Statement," *Newsweek*, 23 August 1993, p. 61; Matsuda and others; MacKinnon.
31 "Franco-American Loses Lawsuit," *Bangor Daily News*, 26 August 1993, p. 5.

THE LESSONS OF LIVING IN A FRANCOPHOBIC WORLD

Pat LaMarche
Yarmouth, Maine

Not all that long ago, I spent about a week staring at my parent's wedding picture. The 3rd of July in the year of our Lord nineteen hundred and fifty-two, Paul Henri LaMarche married an Irish girl just outside Boston, Massachusetts. Shortly after the event and before the subsequent Sunday would allow for another such intercultural marriage, the church burned to the ground.

No one believed it was suspicious, no one but my mother, that is. If you believe in divine intervention—or retribution in this case—then you might agree with her. She often mused that God had burnt it down so that no other such mistakes could be made in his name.

My dad's family was made up of North American longtimers. The earliest LaMarche on this continent was a soldier who had come to the New World at the "royal request" in the seventeenth century. My great-grandfather had only made the journey to the United States about fifty years before my parents' wedding. And my grandfather, Hormisdas LaMarche, was a Boston cop. Not just any cop mind you—a mounted policeman. To this day, walking through Boston and seeing those officers high atop their beautiful horses evokes a certain awe and admiration. So, even though my dad's family had no money and little education, they had attitude.

When my dad joined the navy, against his dad's will because he was too young, he got out of the little world he lived in and saw a new one. Returning to Boston from the South Pacific, he decided to attend a dance, where he'd meet new girls—different girls from those he had known all his life. His sisters had very French names: Bernadette and Lorraine. So, when my parents met and my mom's name was Genevieve, it might have thrown my dad off; she didn't really have an Irish girl's name. Still, it didn't slow my French grandparents down at all when it came to asking her background. And, when they learned that she was Irish, they tried to put an end to the relationship.

My Irish-American mom lived in a house so small that "you had to go outside to change your mind!" They had chickens in the back yard that my grandmother killed when they would splurge and eat meat. My grandfather died of old age when my mom was only seventeen. Both her parents had come off the boat from Ireland, and my grandmother, decades younger than her husband, ran the household as my grandfather aged.

My mom grew up with every accommodation poverty could provide. Down by the marshes that bordered Boston, they were the first folks on her street to even try living there year-round. During the Great Depression she sold bleach-water my grandmother mixed up in their kitchen's soapstone sink, while my grandmother worked cleaning other people's houses so that her own children could eat. My Uuncle Buddy died of tuberculosis when my mom was a little girl, and all her other older brothers fought in World War II.

By comparison, my dad's family, which lived in their established Boston neighborhood, with a mom that stayed home and cared for the kids while her husband worked as a policeman, stood much higher on the social ladder. When the LaMarche's learned that my dad intended to marry this Irish girl they threw a *sabot*!—This famine family would only sully their far more regal and established bloodline.

I heard these stories all the time during my youth. My dad would tease my mom that his parents never wanted him to marry her. My mother fought the stigmatization that these remarks caused. Honoring my dad's traditions, we had meat pie every Christmas Eve, but my mom would call it "Irish-French meat pie" and, if my dad wanted some, he called it that too.

Still, the sentiment remained. The French were better than everybody else. Lafayette and the revolution, Louis the XIV, Joan of Arc, even Ireland's patron saint—Patrick—were all from France. French food, French wine, French language classes in schools. The French just had a legacy that the exploited and famished Irish didn't share. And that was the attitude my mother endured and which influenced my world.

We had settled in Rhode Island, but then one day, my dad moved our entire family to Maine, and the attitude we encountered because of our ethnicity stunned me. I had grown up hearing ethnic jokes. Most of the jokes ridiculed Eastern Europeans or Hispanics—the newest waves of immigrants historically have taken the brunt of such cultural abuse. My mother, herself a victim of such scorn, wouldn't abide such things and wouldn't tolerate her kids' participation in such a ritual. Consequently, no such joke was ever told in my house.

It was halfway through my freshman year in high school that we moved to Bangor, and I became the brunt of a host of insulting jokes. I didn't understand. Why me? The answer: What did I expect with a French name like LaMarche? None of it made sense. No surprise here: the reputation of the French in Maine was that of mental defectives, and I clearly was too stupid to get the joke.

My classmates made disparaging comments about my intellectual abilities. I had transferred into the school with nothing but *As* on my report card; my dad had just taken the position of chief of pediatrics at Eastern Maine Medical Center, my brother had just been accepted at Yale University's graduate program in Physics, did I really seem stupid? I didn't necessarily feel the need to share these facts with my new harassers, but how on earth could it be so instantly assumed that my intellect was impaired?

I met other "French" kids: Cormier, Bourgoin, and Côté—all of them accepted the ribbing as though it was deserved. This prejudice confounded me. Then I noticed a few more things about Bangor: No bagel shops, no Portuguese bakeries, no kosher delis, no Chinese markets, no Mexican food. No ethnics. I went up to one of the other "French" kids and asked, where are the immigrants? (Really asking: "Where's the replacement fodder for ridicule.") What immigrants? We were it.

I was confounded. There hadn't been any immigrants since the seventeenth century? Appalled, I decided my dad hadn't just found the end of the earth, he actually expected us to live there. Don't misunderstand me. I'm with my mom on this. I abhor the practice of ridiculing and maligning folks based on cultural differences, but that doesn't change the fact that "pickin' on the new guys" has long stirred the melting pot in which we live, and I had come to a place that hadn't added a new flavor to the pot in hundreds of years.

My classmates informed me that when it came to the time-honored tradition of insulting somebody because they were different, there were only two groups available: the French and the Indians. Ah-ha, the Indians!

My confusion had kept me from realizing that some immigrants had made it to Bangor. Back in Rhode Island, where I came from, lots of Indians worked at my dad's lab. And while I felt bad that they were maligned, I reveled in the great news for the community—at least there'd be Indian food. I met some of these kids at my school. I met Pardillas and Sockebesons to name two. But wait, these Indians weren't immigrants, these Indians were Natives!

Native Americans and the French comprised Bangor's euphemistic lower class?

But they'd been here so long; in the case of the Natives, here forever. And even though we shared the distinction of being the "ethnics," we didn't even get the perks of ethnic minority status. We had no restaurants, no private languages muttered in secret behind the mocking majority, and no hangouts.

All we had were jokes. Did you hear about the French astronaut who wanted to go to the sun? How about the French guy who's car broke down in the desert? Yeah, well there's that one with the three Frenchmen on the deserted island....

It took me years to remember Renoir, Jules Verne, Madame Curie, Louis Pasteur, and so many other brilliant French people who changed the world for the better. I probably forgot all about them until I left Maine and went to college, because mentioning them wouldn't have done any good. An argument based on their brilliance wouldn't have dispelled theories of intellectual inferiority in my high school: Prejudice is itself the lack of reasoned decision-making.

But moving to Bangor, Maine, was like stepping back in time. We moved back through old resentments, centuries of immigration and intermarriage, to a time when the country's newer arrivals still inhabited their homelands.

The only time since my school days that I again experienced disdain for being French happened when the United States waged war with Iraq. And the French government stood up to us. But this time I wouldn't tolerate it in my presence. This time I stopped people who bullied and ridiculed the country of my ancestry. This time I fought the ethnic taunts and degrading comments with logic and truth. I don't know that standing up for my ancestry and ethnicity had any effect, but I had learned a valuable lesson from having my dad's name and being a Franco growing up in Maine. I learned what it was like to be my mom decades before, and to be Irish in Boston.

FRENCH JOKES

Question: Why does a Frenchman have only one egg for breakfast?
Answer: One is "un oeuf!"

Question: What are the three kinds of bears in northern Maine?
Answer: Brown bears, black bears, and jalberts.

—Overheard on the streets, over the years

A common motif running through many accounts in this collection is the contrast between good humor and hurtful humor. To some younger readers, this might seem like a quaint issue of the past or even something with which they are not familiar. One of the jokes that we grew up with in the 1960s, at the height of the civil rights movement, ran as follows:

Question: Why are the French in Maine and the Blacks in Alabama?
Answer: Alabama had first choice....

These kinds of attacks say a lot about the dominant society's view of both Franco-Americans and African Americans in Maine at a time when the Anglo-American elite's power base was coming under seige in a large movement of national reform.

—Barry Rodrigue, editor

WHEN FUNNY MIGHT NOT BE....

Ernie Gagné
Lewiston, Maine

I'm confused. As hard as I try, I just cannot comprehend what is deemed politically correct anymore when it comes to humor. Just when I think that I've figured it out, something occurs that forces me to rethink what I thought. After careful consideration and reflection, I nearly convinced myself that perhaps I was wrong when I made fun of my own heritage on Portland's WBLM radio a few years back. Maybe my opponents were right when they claimed that I, as WBLM's "Frenchie" was not considering the oppression and difficult times that my ancestors and other immigrants from Canada faced when they arrived in the United States in the early 1900s. After all, as a younger man, I was not subjected to the ridicule and discrimination they endured and I should have known better than to portray a stereotypical "dumb Frenchman" in public. Yet history, hypocrisy, and that little voice in my head tell me that it's only a joke and that everyone ought to lighten up. Somebody help me!

As far back as I can remember, I have told jokes. Typically, I just repeat funny stories or riddles that have been told to me and admittedly, I have repeated some bad jokes about sensitive topics, some that I no longer find funny, such as jokes about child abuse or the Holocaust. As a more mature and responsible adult, I have gained a better understanding as to what may or may not be considered humorous; or at least I think I have. I feel this way because of what I've learned from society. I found it funny when Jews such as Joey Bishop or David Brenner made fun of other Jews. I found it funny when Blacks such as Richard Pryor or Eddie Murphy ridiculed other Blacks. And so, as a full-fledged member of the Franco-American community, I thought it would be safe to pick on my own French heritage in order to get a few yucks.

For over seven years, it was safe. However, I unknowingly offended a small group of "frogs" who accidentally tripped over a prerecorded bit we had done at WBLM which eventually led to my all but forced resignation from relating humorous anecdotes on the radio. I hope you're not offended because I referred to other Franco-Americans as "frogs" because it's politically correct now. In a guest column in the *Lewiston Sun-Journal* (13 November 2005), Jan Plourde Barrett (an admitted Franco) writes that "Being a Frog is actually something to celebrate." She'll get no argument from me, and her statement will certainly be welcomed by the members of the directors that run the La Kermese Festival in Biddeford, Maine and the writers of the *FAROG Forum,* a French-rooted newspaper based at the Franco-American Centre in Orono, Maine. Ironically, however, many members and representatives from the Biddeford festival and Orono newspaper were very vocal in protesting the existence of the fictional radio character I played, though they were also guilty of poking fun at their own heritage, and nearly all of them had admittedly never heard a single word I ever said on the air.

Both of these organizations implemented humor to promote their products. A few members of the festival donned frog costumes and proudly marched in parades, while others wore hats and t-shirts with frog emblems decorating them. If you wish to contact the FAROG newspaper, just dial the number 207-581-FROG on your phone, or pick up a copy and see if they still use frogs to make up the Canadian fleur-de-lis. Both outfits have created humorous promotional pieces, I applaud them for their work, and I am not offended at all by the way they have used humor to depict the French. I am offended by the hypocrisy they reveal and the double standard they live by.

Humor is a tool that has played a major role in society. It has been used in the workplace as a roundabout way of stating opinions. In the film *Modern Times*, Charlie Chaplin used humor in order to point out many of the faults and issues that white-collar workers faced during the depression era. This was his way of combating problems facing society. (As "Frenchie," I had no agenda other than trying to make people laugh.) Other forms of workplace humor included editorial cartoons by artists such as Art Young and Fred Wright. These editorial cartoonists allowed employees to make fun of the bosses and "take their revenge consciously and unconsciously." By telling and retelling jokes in and about the workplace, the "deep resentment came out into the open"[1]

Humor was a major part of U.S. culture during the burlesque years and that influence is still felt today. Burlesque humor is considered to be satirical and ridicules a type of speech or writing. In the 1840s, burlesque works such as plays and non-musicals poked fun at operas and social patterns of the upper classes.[2] Burlesque humor was also very influential in establishing the role of women: "Without question...burlesque's principal legacy as a cultural form was its establishment that forever changed the role of woman on the American stage and later influenced her role on the screen" and "called attention to the entire question of the 'place' of woman in American society."[3] The idea of women undressing in these shows was a marketing stroke that was created to keep the audiences interested.

Writer Thomas Haliburton made a living by implementing humor towards people in the Canadian Maritimes. *The Clockmaker* is a collection of newspaper columns that Haliburton wrote back in the mid-1800s that involved his alter-ego in the form of Sam Slick. Slick was a Yankee traveling salesman who sold clocks, and his favorite sales circuit was in Nova Scotia, where he referred to the local people as "Bluenoses." There are a few meanings of a Nova Scotia bluenose. A couple have to do with the potatoes in Nova Scotia, but one also involves over-indulgence of rum. Along with these hints of their character, Haliburton suggested that Nova Scotians were lazy and lacked a proper work ethic. Haliburton did not truly believe that they were lazy, but used the power of his pen to try to persuade them to keep up with the times. Nova Scotia had many resources available to them commercially and Haliburton wanted the bluenoses to think big, like the Yankees to the south were doing. This was his way of using humor to make a point rather than to publicly ridicule someone for not seeing an issue the way he did. Today, Nova Scotians are still referred to as Bluenoses.

Humor truly is everywhere, and in some areas, it's easy to get away with making fun of certain groups because they are the majority. Catholics and Christians are generally easy targets because there are so many and they're all over the world. Recently, I attended a performance by entertainer and activist Utah Phillips, at the University of Southern Maine's Lewiston-Auburn College, where I go to school. Phillips made a back-handed remark towards Christians when he stated that most Christians were hypocrites. After Phillips made the comment, many, if not most, in the audience laughed or at least chuckled.

As a good-humored thick-skinned Catholic and a Christian, I normally allow comments like that to roll off my shoulders, but his general comment bothered me enough that I brought it up to a professor at the college. I asked him if the reaction from the crowd would have been the same if the comment would have been made about Muslims or Jews. I could care less that someone is making fun of my religion, as long as all religions are fair game. The professor replied that Christians can be made fun of because of their roots in this country and that Christians in the United States have never been oppressed. My thought process is that if making fun of someone is wrong, then it's wrong! Period! One cannot be selective and decide for everyone else who can and cannot be made fun of. I have personally selected a few areas that I feel are not funny anymore, particularly where many people have been killed or damaged by the actions of others, but that's my decision. I am not going to demand that everyone follows my lead. I simply ask that those who protest making fun of one particular group understand that they are not the humor police and should not decide what groups are targets over others.

Politicians, on the other hand, are fair game. First of all, they have entered a world that is open to ridicule. They chose to be in the public eye under public scrutiny. The same cannot be said about other topics that make good or bad humor. We are all born with a certain skin color, with particular traits and characteristics that we have no control over and cannot change. However, even political humor can hurt because we must remember that the politicians are human, too (most of them, anyway).

In the 17 November 2004 edition of the *Washington Post*, editorial cartoonist Pat Oliphant attempted to depict Condaleeza Rice, then newly appointed secretary of state, as a parrot of President Bush. However, in his caricature of Dr. Rice, who is an African American, Oliphant draws her with very large lips, a characteristic that is used as a stereotype of Blacks. Had Dr. Rice been a member of the Democratic party, I assure you that liberal supporters such as Jesse Jackson would have protested the editorial, and that in itself is comical. Therefore, it's safer to joke about politicians than Blacks—unless, of course, you're Black.

Here's where I'm confused again. If the "n" word is so demeaning and deplorable, why is it still used in movies that are written by, directed by, and produced by the members of the race that abhor the word? If it's an offensive word, don't use or promote it. I can understand the use of the "n" word where it is necessary in a film that documents history, but I do not see the humor when Black comedians use the word they supposedly hate so much to refer to other Blacks. However, the use of this word among Blacks does not seem to be considered offensive among the culture. I was not as fortunate as I faced a small group of Francos that were offended.

This forces me to ask the following question: Why were the Franco-Americans so upset about the humor I used on the radio while other cultures seem to accept ridicule from their own? I do not know the answer. I do not believe that the French are without a sense of humor at all, since I have told jokes using characters' names such as Pierre and Émile for as long as I can remember, and I have told them to French descendants of all walks of life, including my grandparents, their elderly friends, the local priests, and educators.

Never was I told that they were offended by the stories, because almost all of the people I know, regardless of their ethnicity, have a sense of self-deprecation. They understand that I am not attempting to discredit the Franco-Americans; in fact, most of them have told me that some of the stories I tell remind them of their past. They recall certain times or instances in their life, either back home in Canada or after they immigrated to the United States. Many of the jokes I told my grandfather lead to conversations with him about history. He came to Maine from Canada when he was only twelve years old. He lived through the oppression that haunted the French in the 1900s, but never lost his sense of humor and never took himself so seriously that he could not laugh at himself.

I had no resentments, at least before the whole "Frenchie" episode began, but I think I did immediately after I left the airways. I resented how a few people could form such a negative opinion of something without ever hearing *what* was said and *how* it was said. It was reported to them that I was literally bashing the entire Franco community in Maine, but actually I had been simply regurgitating jokes that had been told to me into scenarios that fit the irreverent morning radio show format. This is a routine that I had been doing for over seven years before anyone objected. If I was that offensive, do you think that it would have taken over seven years before someone complained? The whole "Frenchie" episode taught me a few lessons. I have a better understanding of what the Franco-Americans went through when they arrived in the U.S. I have read stories of how unfairly they were treated in places like the mills and schools. However, they were not alone in their oppression. Jews, Blacks, women, Irish, Polish, and others have all faced hard times in this country, yet it seems as though they have all been able to maintain their sense of humor. Generally speaking, so have the French, save a few.

I'm still confused as to what constitutes humor today. Is it okay to tell jokes about gays if you're gay? Is it only permissible to tell Black jokes if you're Black? Is it safe for a White man to poke fun at any group other than White men? I suppose it depends on your audience. Meanwhile, did you hear the one about the....

1 Buhle, p. 3.
2 Kenrick, p.1
3 R. Allen, pp. 258–59.

ONE OF FRENCHIE'S STORIES: IN HEAT

Ernie Gagné
Lewiston, Maine

One hot summer day, Réjean Sainson Skidoo went to one of Lewiston's more famous bars along with his dog. Of course, the bar did not allow animals, so Skidoo tied her to a tree out front. After a short while, a policeman entered the bar and wanted to know who the dog belonged to. Skidoo told the officer that the dog was his and asked what the problem was.

"Your dog is in heat," said the policeman.

Skidoo replied, "No, sir, my dog is in the shade, I tied her there myself."

Sensing that Skidoo did not quite understand, the police officer said, "I mean your dog needs to get bred."

With a confused look on his face, Skidoo said, "I'm sorry, sir, but my dog ate right before we came here, and most dogs don't eat bread."

The policeman gave up trying to say what he meant in a polite way and stated, "Your dog needs to have sex!"

"Go ahead," said Skidoo, "I always wanted a police dog!"

Courtesy of Ernie Gagné, Reindeer Records
and the University of Southern Maine's Franco-American Collection

LA GRAINE POUSSE

Normand Dubé
Caribou, Maine

Il faut mouiller la terre
Pour que la graine pousse.
Alors,
Laissez-moi pleurer
Dans le fleuve
De mon passé
Où j'ai pris le chemin des émigrés
Avec mes souvenirs
Comme compagnons.

Laissez-moi pleurer
De villes en villages
Dans la verdure
Remplie de promesses, de cœur,
Et d'une foi
Plantée dans la croix.
Laissez-moi pleurer
L'héritage
De la solitude
Tamponnée de vaillance d'honnêteté
Dans un langage de métiers:
Weaver
Stitcher
Digger
O.K.
Lumberjack
Boss
Chum
Too Bad!

Normand Dubé at the Soirée Grand Ménage, *organized by the Franco-American Centre, University of Maine, Orono, c. 1982–83*
Photograph by Yvon Labbé

J'ai pris une femme.
C'est mon désennui
C'est mon devoir.
J'ai pris une femme
Venue du grand pays
De mon histoire.

Créature d'habitant
Compagne de lit,
Mère de mes enfants
Et semeuse de vie!
Tu es mon partage et mon soutien.
Tu es mon ménage. Je suis ton bien.

Je sens l'exil et le Grand Tronc.
Je chante les provinces et les états.
Je respire les chantiers, les rangs de patates et le Petit Canada.
Je récite le pater, l'Angelus et l'Ave Maria.
Je fête Champlain, Évangéline, Sainte Anne et Ferdinand Gagnon.
Je respecte la loi et les commandements.
Je satisfais ma routine et ma nostalgie.

Et puis,
Je me meurs de ces émotions
Traqué dans l'idéal des ambitions.
Je me meurs des inspirations
Traqué dans l'entrave des aspirations.
Je me meurs d'une fondation
Traqué dans le devoir et l'immersion.
Il faut mouiller la terre
Pour que la graine pousse, Alors,
Laissez-moi pleurer
Par les ruelles
De chez-nous
Où la sécheresse du mensonge
Y semait
Lex faux espoirs.
Laissez-moi pleurer
Entre les bloques
Aux bardeaux dépeinturés
Où, la fertilité de mon enfance
Était gênée
Par des voyages déroutés
Laissez-moi pleurer
Dans perrons et des passages
Où, dans ma langue singulière
J'apprenais les mots d'usage :

Puanteur
Crasse
Punaise
Crève faim
Pourriture
Colon
Petit pain
Misère.

La femme est mon comfort
D'amant et de mari
L'amour de toute une vie
La femme est le ressort
Qui contourne mes conflits :
Passions et délies.
Elle est la grande messe
De chaque matin
Elle est la sagesse
Des jours bénis
Tu es ma raison nuptiale
Et ma rubrique familiale.
Je sens l'église et l'école paroissiale.
Je chante le grégorien et La Bonne Chanson.
Je respire les filatures et les hôpitaux.
Je récite mes blasphèmes et les litanies.
Je fête la Saint-Jean et les vendredi.
Je respecte la grand'tante et Monsieur le Curé.
Je satisfais mon intempérance et la belle Félicité.

Et puis,
Je me meurs l'esprit brisé,
Blessé par l'ignorance du préjugé.
Je me meurs le cœur brisé,
Blessé aux mains des bien-aimés.

Je me meurs l'âme brisée
Blessé par la conscience de ma timidité.

Il faut mouiller la terre
Pour que la graine pousse.
Alors, Laissez-moi pleurer
Sur le béton
Des nos nouveaux soucis

Ou la folie de nos désirs
Sera la mesure
De mes plaisirs et mon entrain.

Laissez-moi pleurer
Au cœur
De nos cœurs
Où, dans une langue bien précise,
Retentiront
Des mots plus choisis:
Fierté
Amour
Force
Bonheur
Fraternité
Connaissance
Fertilité
Honneur

Je sens la rencontre et les grandes écoles.
Je chante nos clochers et nos violons.
Je respire la besogne et la santé.
Je récite mes vers et mon crédo.
Je fête chaque jour et mes petits-enfants.
Je satisfais mes folies et les tiennes.
Je respecte tous ceux qui veulent s'aimer.

Il y a des enfants
Qui veulent sourire
Se réjouir
Et se souvenir
Se faire réjouir
Et se faire souvenir
Se nourrir, courir et grandir.

Il y a des adolescents
Qui veulent se déprendre
Se comprendre
Et s'entendre
Se faire comprendre
Et se faire entendre
Se détendre.

Il y a des jeunes gens
Qui veulent se concrétiser
Se parler
Et se toucher
Se faire parler
Et se faire toucher
S'idéaliser et s'aimer.

Il y a des femmes
Qui veulent se libérer
Se mériter
Et s'admirer
Se faire mériter
Et se faire admirer
Se destiner.
Il y a des hommes
Qui veulent s'enhardir
Se valoir
Et se matérialiser

Produire et reproduire.
Je n'ai pas d'illusions.
Hier n'était pas toute tempête
Et aujourd'hui n'est pas tout beau temps.
Tant qu'à demain,
La graine aura poussé
Dans une terre bien mouillée.
Mais, ça sera à d'autres de pleurer.

The Seed Sprouts by Normand Dubé—English translation by Normand Beaupré

One has to wet the soil
To make the seed sprout.
So,
Let me cry
In the river
Of my past
Where I took the road of the emigrants
With my memories
As companions.

Let me cry
From cities to villages
In the greenery
Filled with promises, with heartfelt feelings,
And with faith
Planted in the cross.
Let me cry
The heritage
Of solitude
Mopped with the bravery of honesty
In a language of trades:
Weaver
Stitcher
Digger

O.K.
Lumberjack
Boss
Chum
Too Bad!

I took a bride.
It's my relief from boredom
It's my duty.
I took a bride
Who came from the grand old country
Of my history.

Creature-woman of a habitant
Bed companion,
Mother of my children
And sower of life!
You are my portion and my help.
You are my household. I'm your possessions.
I experience the exile and the Grand Trunk.
I sing of the provinces and the States.
I breathe the lumber camps, the rows of potatoes and Little Canada.
I recite the Pater, the Angelus and the Ave Maria.
Celebrate Champlain, Évangéline, Saint Anne, and Ferdinand Gagnon.
I respect the law and the commandments.
I satisfy my routine and my nostalgia.

And then,
I'm dying for these emotions
Hunted down in the ideal of my ambitions.
I'm dying for inspiration
Hunted down in the constraint of long breaths.
I'm dying for a foundation
Hunted down in the duty of immersion.
One must wet the soil

To make the seed sprout. So,
Let me cry
In the lanes
Of home
Where the dryness of the lie
Sowed there
False hopes.
Let me cry
Between the blocks
With faded shingles
Where, the fertility of my childhood
Was hampered
By diverted trips
Let me cry
On the doorsteps and the hallways
Where, in my singular language
I used to learn everyday words:

Stench
Filth
Bed bug
Down-and-out
Rottenness
Settler
Small dough
Misery.

The woman is my comfort
Of lover and husband
The love of an entire life
The woman is the force
That skirts my conflicts:
Passions and offenses
She is the high mass
Of every morning

She is the wisdom
Of blessed days
You are my nuptial reason for being
And my familial rubric.
I feel inside me the church and the parochial school.
I sing Gregorian chant and La Bonne Chanson.
I breathe the cotton mills and the hospitals.
I recite my swear words and the litany.
I celebrate Saint John the Baptist day and the Fridays.
I respect great aunt and the pastor, Monsieur le Curé.
I satisfy my intemperance and the beautiful Felicity.

And then,
I die with a broken spirit,
Injured by the ignorance of prejudice.
I die with a broken heart,
Injured by the hands of well-loved ones.
I die with a broken soul
Injured by the conscience of my timidity.

One must water the soil
For the seed to sprout.
Then, Let me cry
On the concrete
Of our new worries

Where the madness of our desires
Will be the measure
Of my pleasures and my drive.

Let me cry
At the very heart
Of our hearts
Where, in a very precise language
Will resonate

Words better chosen:
Pride
Love
Strength
Happiness
Fraternity
Knowledge
Fertility
Honor

I feel inside me the getting together and the upper-grade schools.
I sing our bells and our violins.
I breathe the drudgery and health.
I recite my verses and my credo.
I celebrate each day and my grandchildren.
I satisfy my follies and yours.
I respect all those who want to love one another.
There are children
Who want to smile
Have fun
And remember
To be made to have fun
And to be made to remember
Nourish oneself, run and grow up.

There are adolescents
Who want to manage on their own
Know themselves
And get along
Make themselves understood
And make themselves heard
Relax.

There are young people
Who want to materialize

Talk to one another
And touch one another
To make themselves talk
And make themselves touched by others
To idealize themselves and to love themselves.

There are women
Who want to liberate themselves
To be of merit to themselves
And admire themselves
To make themselves be worthy
And to make themselves admired
To destine themselves.
There are men
Who want to harden themselves
To be worthy
And to materialize
To show themselves off to their best advantage
And to make themselves be materialized
Produce and reproduce.
I have no illusions.
Yesterday was not all tempest and storm
And today is not all fair weather.
As for tomorrow,
The seed will have sprouted
In a well-drenched soil.
But, it will be up to others to cry.

EVERYTHING'S JUST FINOPHOBIA

Greg Chabot
Waterville, Maine

There's only one thing that terrifies Francos more than abject misery—and that's boundless joy. It scares us so much that we try to avoid being happy as much as possible. If Happiness decides to pay us a visit, we hide and turn off the lights to make it look like no one's home. If he's inconsiderate enough to waltz right in without being invited, we politely tell him that the neighbor's house is much nicer and more comfortable. Besides, everybody there speaks English, so THAT's where he really belongs. We even volunteer to go with him right up to the back steps (wouldn't be proper for us to use the front door) so he won't get lost.

Thanks to a whole bunch of influences, we are convinced that we don't have the right to be happy. For example, we've always been told that life is a vale of tears and sorrow. And we've heard over and over that our suffering on earth today helps us do penance for the sins we commit, meaning that we'll spend less time in Purgatory tomorrow. I guess the people who kept repeating this nonsense thought it would make life more bearable. Unfortunately, what it really did was create a no-win situation that gives us a choice, not between joy and suffering, but between different levels and intensities of suffering. The more miserable we are in life, the less we'll have to suffer in the afterlife. The easier we have it today, the more we'll be weeping and gnashing our teeth later on. Some choice. Happiness isn't even an option.

We also know that a surfeit of happiness can easily make the gods jealous. If and when that happens, all the gods get together to find horrible ways to punish us. It never takes very long. A couple of glasses of elixir and they've got so many ideas that they're all trying to talk at once. We go to bed a picture of health. We wake up with a dozen or so diseases—and with no teeth or hair. We go to work at our "big bucks" job only to discover that the company went bankrupt overnight. So we trudge back home and set the place on fire because we forget to put out one of the cigarettes that we've started chain-smoking ever since we lost our job and our health. If you don't believe me, check out what happened to Job. And God actually liked him.

To avoid the disasters that happiness typically unleashes, we can choose one of the following tactics. First, we can try to be miserable throughout our entire lives. This is the ideal option, even though it's tough to fully implement. But I've known a good number of Francos who succeeded in being absolutely miserable 97 percent of the time. They also drastically reduced the number of potential catastrophes by sharing their misery with all of their relatives and a bunch of total strangers.

Those of us who are not as brave or as terminally grouchy can try to stay happy for as short a time as possible, if we are unfortunate enough to be visited by good fortune. (Imagine what a shrink could do with that sentence.) This can be accomplished easily enough by treating minor annoyances as if they were major disasters.

A pen runs out of ink right in the middle of a sentence. "Just my luck."

Our favorite T.V. show is pre-empted for an in-depth discussion of the economic policies of the new Estonian government. "I told you it wasn't going to be my day. And besides, the coffee I made this morning tasted like dishwater. Boy, when things go wrong.... And everything was going along just fine for awhile."

The advantage of this approach is that after implementing it enough times, we start believing that we are indeed doomed to misfortune. This makes us more and more unhappy until we can adopt the first strategy outlined above, i.e., to be miserable throughout our entire lives.

The third approach should be reserved for dire emergencies. In spite of our best efforts, the heavens, at their cruelest, may punish us by forcing us to endure long periods of unabated prosperity and happiness. We immediately try both approaches previously discussed without success. In that case, there's nothing else to do. We must simply pretend to be as miserable as everybody else, even if it's not true. We can use statements like: "You probably think owning a Rolls Royce is fun. Well let me tell you, the damned thing is nowhere near as reliable as my old Chevy. I'd get rid of it in a minute, but I'd probably lose my shirt in the deal." Or else: "Sure, it's an impressive house, but it takes almost everything I make just to heat the damn thing." We can also allude to the only thing that scares Francos even more than happiness: THE FUTURE. All we have to do is say: "I'm afraid I'll end up paying quite a price for all this good fortune some day" to bring us right back down to the level of every other Franco-American until the moment that the gods take pity on us by giving us back our blessed and comforting misery.

This terror of being happy creates major obstacles for us when we try to build a future. Futures must be planned before they are built. They must have clear objectives and well-defined goals. In other words, we must state exactly what we want and where we are going if we expect to get there. And that's precisely our problem. As Francos, we can't state what we want because we're scared to death that we may actually get it.

RESEARCH NOTE: MAINE "JIM CROW"? THE FORGOTTEN MAINE CONSTITUTIONAL AMENDMENT OF 1891

Rebecca Dirnfeld
Vancouver, British Columbia

No person shall have the right to vote or be eligible to office under the constitution of this state, who shall not be able to read the constitution in the English language, and write his name.... —Amendment XXIX, Chapter 109, Maine State Constitution

On 3 April 1891 the Maine State Legislature voted that this proposed constitutional amendment for the State of Maine be submitted to referendum. Essentially, it mandated an educational qualification for voters, similar to the "Jim Crow" laws being adopted in the South to prevent African-American political life. At the time, an immigrant to Maine did not need to speak English to be naturalized, have the right to vote, or to hold office.

This had important implications because numerous French-speaking and Catholic communities had been incorporated into Maine as a result of the border adjustments of the 1842 Treaty of Washington. The largest "immigrant" communities in Maine were the French-Canadians and Acadians, who were the primary target of this amendment. Interestingly, there was no landslide victory for the referendum, it being adopted by only 60 percent of the voters.

As part of the state's consolidated statutes, this amendment presented the United States as a melting pot in which different cultures dissolved to form a new Anglo-Protestant one. The French-Canadian and Acadian community viewed identity in another way, seeing themselves as French and Catholic, as well as "American." The debate surrounding this amendment needs to be further explored, as it reflected a clash of cultures that forced the Franco-American community to reflect upon its own identity. The amendment vanishes fom the Maine Constitution in 1982–83, presumably as a result of the civil rights movement and resulting federal voting reforms.

(Rebecca is researching this topic for her thesis and for publication; any information would be greatly appreciated. She can be contacted in care of her academic advisor: Dr. Béatrice Craig, Office 306, 157 Séraphin Marion, Ottawa, Ontario, Canada K1N 6N5; or by e-mail at: bcraig@uottawa.ca).

A SHORT AUTOBIOGRAPHY FOR MY DAUGHTER[1]

Raymond Luc Levasseur
Sanford, Maine

(Author's Note: My first daughter, Carmen, was born in January 1976 while I was underground. This autobiography was written that same year—in haste, during a long night, at a time when it appeared my survival chances were slim. I wanted to leave her a sense of who she came from. It's crudely written and the temptation to rewrite it is great. But I won't. It is what it is—one man's glimpse in the mirror and his infant daughter's eyes—and then taking unskilled pen to paper. While underground, my partner gave birth to two

Card with watercolor of Carmen Levasseur reading the autobiography
Illustration by Pat Levasseur

more daughters, Simone and Rosa. I remained underground with my family until captured in 1984. Then I spent twenty years in prison. I returned home to Maine in 2004—in time to attend Carmen's wedding and my mother's funeral mass. Carmen is a student at the New York University graduate school of Social Work. My mother was the last *mémère* of this family to make real *tourtière et creton*. Each was proud of the other, and—in their own ways—of their French-Canadian blood.)

I was born 10 October 1946 in Sanford, Maine, a mill town, at the end of World War II. All of the family is French, which is to say our people came either directly or indirectly from Québec. Our family is deeply rooted in the working class, having to have worked for survival primarily in the mills and shoe factories.

My father, Paul, was born in Québec, the French nation in Canada. He migrated to the United States with his family when he was five years old. What brought them to this country was the prospect of work in the mills. Everyone around Sanford in those days worked in the textile mills of the Goodall family or in shoe shops. As the oldest child, my father had to quit school to work and help support the family. There was a certain anger he carried within himself from that point on, because he felt he had not gotten enough education. He joined the Army Air Force during World War II, went back to work in the mills as a mechanic after the war, but then reenlisted for what he felt was more opportunity than was offered in Sanford to someone with limited education and background.

My mother was born in a house in Springvale, Maine, one of three children. She dropped out of school at a young age to work in mills and shoe shops. My *pépère* and *mémère* Lizotte were also millworkers, both having had to quit school when they were just kids to work in the mills. Mémère was also a fortuneteller and was known for miles around by people who had come to her to have their fortunes read and look into the future. Folks appreciated her advice.

My brother Jim was born less than a year after me, in 1947. We worked briefly as laborers together, but he usually drove heavy equipment for construction companies when the work was there. His wife Sandy worked in one of the old Goodall mills that has long been converted into another type of manufacturing process. Your cousin Tracey is their only child and a beautiful little girl.

I grew up in Springvale, close to the mills and factories, which were near the Mousam River. My earliest school years were in Notre Dame, a neighborhood

Catholic school, which most of the French-Canadian kids attended. The classes were taught by nuns who were very strict and taught a lot of religious doctrine along with everything else. I hated it, and after getting slapped around by the nuns too many times, my brother and I switched over to public school. This was in the sixth grade. During this change, I lost the ability to speak the French language fluently—something I've since come to regret.

I did most things other neighborhood boys did growing up in a small town—played ball, played war, rode my bike, explored the surrounding woods and nearby river, sold newspapers, went junk-picking in the local dumps, and collected returnable bottles for the 2 or 3 cents return. My brother was usually my constant companion. I fired my first weapon when I was about ten years old. It was a .22 rifle. That was an important event for a kid—a big advance over a BB gun. In school, I was not a very good student, most of my reading being limited to comic books.

I did all sorts of odd jobs as a kid, but my first real taste of wage labor came when I was thirteen years old. I got a social security card and worked in the Kennebunk blueberry fields for three weeks one extremely hot August. Whole families worked there. A big truck would pick us up in Sanford and carry us to the fields. "Raking" the berries was backbreaking work. The following summers, when school was out, I worked in the area apple orchards: haying, pruning, thinning, and picking. My first hourly wage was 87 1/2 cents an hour. But anything was better than working in the mills.

In high school I was placed in a course of study without being consulted in any meaningful way. The studies were uninteresting to me and I got poor grades, though I eventually graduated in 1964. I had no direction in high school, and not knowing what I wanted out of school just led me to drift along. The closest I came to generating any real motivation was when I played football. I loved the excitement and contact of the game. High school was largely a waste of time in preparing me for life in the real world. In the end, it became just a place to socialize with friends. In the end, it was useless.

After graduation and with no prospects for more schooling, I had to start supporting myself as best I could. As with my family before me, that meant taking a job in a mill. I had to lie about my age on the application form because I was under eighteen—the legal minimum age to work in a mill. My first job was on third shift at $1.54 an hour. I worked a machine that made shoeheels. It was a hard, sweaty job in which the machine was speeded-up to push workers to the limits of their strengths.

At the end of a shift on this machine, the only feeling left was exhaustion. Being in the mill was to be continually subjected to the by-products of production—noise so deafening that you had to scream to get the attention of a fellow worker or foreman. There were chemical by-products that poisoned the air and got on your skin, and always a grueling pace on the machinery. In looking back, I know that things were the way they were because the interest of the bosses was in making profits and not the health and welfare of us workers. I didn't know it at the time, but this is capitalist production where workers are used like a piece of machinery then discarded—just like they did with my *pépère*.

During the time I worked this mill, I took to drinking, gambling, and fighting with a crowd that was pretty much in the same situation I was. You feel trapped after awhile. The mill being as bad as it was and seeing no other opportunity, I packed a bag of clothes and hitched to Boston, Massachusetts, to see if I could find work. This was the fall of 1964. I was seventeen years old. I had little money when I got to Boston, but I did get a place to stay with other guys in a small apartment, where I slept on the couch. I had adventure in mind, but also had to get out and find a job right away. This I did at the Boston Fish Pier, working on the loading dock. I worked for the same company for over a year, loading and unloading trucks and working in the warehouse. It was better than the mill and it was steady.

In other ways I lived pretty irresponsibly and was jailed briefly a couple of times for minor hassles. For awhile I got the nickname "Animal" because I was in so many fights. These were nights of drinking wine and cough medicine, dancing, partying, and thinking only of the moment and the excitement the next day would bring.

While I was not aware of the political situation that existed at the time, I did get to meet lots of different people and began to see some of the racism that existed in that particular city and to hear talk of the civil rights movement. Bob Dylan's music was the poetry I heard. There was city survival, music, drugs—and a war going on that I had little interest in. With the cops looking for me and facing the draft, I enlisted in the army. I was nineteen years old.

I went through basic training in the cold New Jersey winter of 1966 at Fort Dix. I qualified as expert with the M-14 rifle and like every other solider there, I was trained to kill. After my initial training, I was sent to Fort Bragg, North Carolina, to await shipment to Vietnam. We left on a troop ship and I was to remain in Vietnam for a year, which was most of 1967. I was stationed with the 91st FDS in the Long Binh/Bien Hoa area and with the 11th Armored Calvary in Black Horse near

Xuan Loc. This experience in Vietnam radically altered my life and left an impression on my heart and mind that is with me to this day.

Until 1967, I had never stopped to examine the role of the U.S. government in Vietnam or any other country. The impact on me was not so much from seeing countless deaths, but from seeing and being part of a foreign occupation army using its powerful weapons to destroy everything that was Vietnamese. To take what didn't belong to it. From choppers I saw the bomb-destroyed countryside, while in villages I saw slums, people living in poverty with not enough food and having to eat garbage from the GI mess. Women and young girls were forced into prostitution, heavy drug use, and always, the children who begged from the U.S. soldiers who got extra combat pay for being there. Everywhere were people crippled by the war—with no arms or legs—the walking wounded for others to see and be fearful that it might happen to them. It seemed as if every man, woman, and child had lost someone in the war. There was a lot of disease. I couldn't tell what the diseases were, but you can tell that people are sick when their skin has open sores and they are underweight or don't breathe right.

The occupation by U.S. soldiers was death and destruction for Vietnam, not freedom, as the politicians would have had us believe. It was Ho Chi Minh and the National Liberation Front (NLF) that offered the Vietnamese people their independence and freedom from foreign occupation. The GIs directed their arrogance and racism towards the Vietnamese people, their culture, and daily lives. Every day, we'd see the big bombers leave Bien Hoa air base for strikes in North Vietnam. By the week's end, we could only read about the death and destruction they had caused in the army newspaper, *Stars and Stripes*. I've often wondered what a pilot felt like to kill people he couldn't see.

On a convoy coming out of Black Horse one day, lead vehicles were hit by a land mine. We ground to an uneasy halt as a med-evac chopper took out those that had been killed or injured. We couldn't see the enemy, so we opened fire on the rubber trees. About this time, I found out my friend Brins was missing in action. It was awhile before they found his body by a downed chopper on the side of a mountain. I got back stateside in time to go to his funeral. There was death on both sides, but the Vietnamese people suffered much more. They were also the strongest with the will to win.

In that kind of situation, when you see much suffering, and you know that there is much more that is worse beyond imagination, then you have to ask why, and you have to come up with some answers that go beyond government propaganda. I saw the U.S. government and the big corporations that profited from the war as being guilty—beyond doubt—of murder and a campaign of genocide against the Vietnamese people. When the children die, when they are born deformed because of poverty and war, when the innocent suffer, then the war-makers must be held responsible.

Someone who helped me put things in a political perspective was a British anarchist in my unit named Chris Henson. We spent countless hours together as close friends, rapping and analyzing. He got me to thinking on my own and to read (though there wasn't too much to read while I was there). He told me about imperialism and that this was an imperialist war. I gained more insight. For the first time in my life I was asking important questions of myself. I felt like I was growing with a deeper consciousness.

I got back in the States on Christmas Eve 1967. After leave, I was stationed at Fort Campbell, Kentucky, where I was honorably discharged on 12 September 1968. I had been taking night classes at Austin Peay State University prior to my discharge and decided to attend the university full time. While going to school, I lived in Clarksville, Tennessee.

I wanted to do what I could to help end the war, so I became politically active with the Southern Student Organizing Committee (SSOC), and some of us started an "underground" paper called *The Wall*. I gained experience as a political organizer. It was an exciting time to be involved with people in struggles for workers' rights, student rights, the Black liberation movement, organizing women, and trying to stop the war. I read, wrote, spoke, and discussed—all the while gaining organizational skills. Most important, I developed a friendship with some of the first truly revolutionary people I had ever met.

On 9 February 1969, local and state police kicked in the door to my apartment and arrested me for the sale of marijuana. I was eventually sentenced to five years in prison for selling $7 of marijuana to an undercover agent. I had been set up. I was thrown in jail, but was able to post bail and was released before the start of my trial.

After my arrest, the landlord said too many Black people were coming to my apartment and I was evicted. I was expelled from the university and prohibited from entering any part of the campus. I tried to find work around town, but couldn't because I had been blacklisted (part of our work with the SSOC had been to support local workers in an important strike for union recognition). We put out one more issue of *The Wall*, got a visit from the Secret Service, who wanted to know of my relationship with Chris, and when the local police put us under constant surveillance and appeared to be gearing up for another bust, most of us who had been working together split up and left the area.

I returned to Boston and got an apartment in Dorchester. I arrived with $9 in my pocket and worked the labor pool for a week, until I got hired back on again at the Fish Pier. This time I mostly drove a truck. I knew now that I was facing serious jail time. I had no money or influence to get me a break. Instead of trying to deal straightforwardly with the situation, I started doing drugs, "ups" and "psychedelics," many times going to work without sleep. I would walk the street a lot, especially in Cambridge, feeling like a trapped animal. This was "Woodstock Summer" with hippies and giant rock festivals. I went to several of them, including Woodstock. The music was great.

I hitched back to Tennessee for my trial on 30 September 1969. That was a mistake. The two-day trial was conducted in an atmosphere of controlled hysteria. My court-appointed lawyer was totally unprepared. I was found guilty by a jury of old people who were scared half to death by the prosecutor's tactics. I got five years in the Tennessee State Penitentiary—the maximum sentence at that time. I was told that I would be tried again on another minor marijuana charge and then taken to Montgomery County Jail. Later, I was to write a story about this trial called "Theatre of the Absurd," but everything I wrote in prison (except for some poems and a couple of short stories) is now in the hands of the FBI.

The government called Vietnam a "military conflict," when it was really mass murder. They also like to call the legal/court/prison system their "criminal justice" system, when it's an organized system of class and race oppression. It is a machine, like the war machine, that grinds down the poor and protects the rich. When people die in Third World countries such as Vietnam or South Africa or Argentina, it is the corporate rich—ITT, Gulf, GM, IBM, etc.—that profit. While it is the Black child who goes hungry and the poor who are chained and imprisoned—it is the ruling class that benefits. It is they that go to the good schools and live in fine homes.

Jail brought this class conflict into sharper focus for me. My own situation became worse for the next six months. It was a hard life in very bad living conditions. The cells were overridden with mice and other vermin. The food was horrible—a poor diet usually served cold in bread pans that we ate with the same plastic spoon. Many prisoners got sick, but there was no proper health care. There was no exercise or recreation or work. We were always locked up in the tanks where our cells were located. Visits were a half hour, once a week; if you got a visitor, you saw them (but couldn't touch) through a thick, grimy, plate-glass window set in a steel partition. It was often cold in the cells; but when the heat was turned up, it became unbearable because of poor ventilation. The mental anguish was hard to deal with: despair, paranoia, and incredible loneliness. Sometimes I would lie on my bunk for hours, looking at the wall, just maintaining enough control to keep from slamming my fist into it. Time never passed so slowly.

In jail I always gave a part of each day to reading—study, really. Most often it was philosophy, as well as revolutionary and other political writings. We had many discussions of a political nature and, though nothing developed too much in a group sense, I think that among the prisoners that came through the jail at this time, they gained more of an awareness of their place in this exploitive system—why things were the way they were for us and so many others, and what might be done to change the situation.

In March 1970 I was brought, without notice, to the same courthouse for another trial. In the many months since my first trial, my lawyer had never come to see me nor did he answer any of my letters asking to see him, if there was to be a second trial. I tried to have him dismissed from the case on these grounds, but the judge wouldn't hear of it. The second trial was much like the first and my lawyer never appealed the second conviction.

Back in the county jail, things got worse. I had already lost between 10 to 15 kilos (20 to 30 pounds) from the inadequate diet and intestinal sickness (an illness many of us got from the food). One evening meal, the guards tried to give us bologna sandwiches that were spoiled—or rotten, I should say. Three tanks of prisoners rebelled by throwing food out onto the walkway and declaring a hunger strike until the food was improved. Black and White prisoners united—overcoming the racism that prevailed in jail—and, after some discussion with the sheriff, we were promised a better diet.

I'll never know if the food improved in the long run, because in two days an illegal order was issued by the court, transferring me for "safekeeping" to the Tennessee State Prison in Nashville. Just that initial show of strength and solidarity among the prisoners was enough for the powers that be to move against me. This was near Easter 1970.

After being transferred to the prison in Nashville, I was placed in a segregation unit for the first few days. Segregation is the worst place to be in a prison. I was put on the old death row, just a few cells away from the electric chair. It was a frightening place to be. I didn't know anyone or what was to happen to me. The feeling of total isolation is hard for prisoners. There were all sorts of noises—screaming, raving, hysterical laughter. Some prisoners just stare at and talk to the walls.

In a few days, I was sent to classification, where they decide what to do with you. I was given a haircut, and then made to shave and dress in prison gray shirt and pants. My living quarters were an overcrowded bay area stuffed with prisoners. I met Bill Allen here, a light in a very dark and bleak situation. He and his partners were strong, intelligent, militant, Pan-Africanist and creative. They would later escape. Bill is Black. Because I was spending time with him, rapping, meeting other brothers, playing basketball (the only White there to do so), and eating in the mess hall together, I was sent straight from the classification unit to a special long-term segregation unit on Death Row. This was racism. This was in the days of "Jim Crow," where racial segregation was illegal on the books, but in fact was practiced widely. In prison, racism is intense.

The prison administration had a stake in seeing that Black and White prisoners were kept divided. They played on the racist fears of prisoners, making their control of the prisoners that much easier. When you are too busy fighting each other, you forget about fighting the real enemy and injustice remains unchallenged.

I was put in segregation, not knowing how long I'd be there. We were locked in our cells most of the time. We call it "Lock Down." When we did get out, it was for an hour, one prisoner at a time. All you could do was walk the length of the catwalk in front of the cells. The walk was encased with mesh wire. Later, we were able to go outside to a small enclosed yard in small groups. This was the exercise area for the prisoners sentenced to die in the electric chair. We shared it with them. This is where I really got to know Jesse X and Ernest, two really fine brothers from Memphis who were on death row.

I spent a great deal of my cell time reading and studying. Friends were sending me books from the outside. Some would get passed around inside. Once in a while I would pick some up from Bill or others. I read mostly revolutionary writings: Marx, Lenin, Mao, Ho Chi Minh, Comrade Che, Franz Fanon, Bakunin, Nkrumah, etc. I read much history and about present-day liberation movements. I read philosophy, poetry, and literature, also radical papers, when I could get them. The reading stimulated my thinking and made me excited about the possibilities of what people can do with their lives.

It was during this time of imprisonment that my political consciousness and commitment evolved into a revolutionary life. It was the most radical and extensive change I'd ever experienced, and it happened within those segregation cells of the Tennessee State Prison—amid the suffering of the "wretched of the earth." In the beginning, it gave real political definition to my situation and what I saw around me, to the far ends of the earth—I became a vehicle of revolutionary principle and action, a part of the liberation process—along with millions of others, a worker and a fighter.

I believe that some of the most important developments in my thinking at the time were: 1) Acquiring a Marxist-Leninist method of analysis—a class analysis to interpret events and history as well as our own background, the background of our family, and the family of workers and other oppressed people; central to this was seeing how capitalism and imperialism function, as well as developing a view of a socialist society rather than the one we're stuck with now; 2) Identifying racism as the most vicious kind of oppression—one that threatens every movement that struggles for freedom; 3) Ironically, within the all-male world of prison, I gained a better understanding of how sexism is used against women and the need for us to fight it if we really want to change things for the better; 4) Gaining a better understanding of the principles and practice of armed struggle and revolution, in which some use of violence is made necessary because of prevailing conditions. We cannot win without armed struggle. I studied guerrilla warfare as one part of revolution and military conflict; 5) Recognizing the need for mass organizing and party-building to some degree, organizing people in the workplace, the neighborhoods, schools, even in prisons; 6) That the most oppressed people lead the struggle. Whether here among Black and Latino people and as much of the working class as can be organized, or, internationally with Third World nation struggles from South Africa to Central America to China to Puerto Rico.

I got a real education in prison. The suffering that was everyone's within those walls strengthened my will to resist. I learned well.

Conditions went from bad to worse in June 1970. One morning, I woke to the sound of rattling chains. The prisoners on Death Row were being taken from their cells, handcuffed, chained, and then removed from the block. I was able to get a glimpse of Ernest as he was chained. I found out later they were transferred to Brushy Mountain super-maximum security prison. The prison no one wants to end up in.

The rest of us in the block not sentenced to death were later removed and placed in Unit VI, another segregation unit located by itself in a small building in the center of the prison. On one side of this building was the "Hole," used for prisoners doing disciplinary sentences. On the other side, which is where they put me, was the long-term segregation cells. Once again, I had no idea how long I'd be there.

This unit was a nightmare that left a deep impression on me. At first we spent twenty-four hours of every day locked in tiny cells in this prison within a prison. I talked to people I couldn't see. I couldn't see outside, not even to any other part of prison, only the walls. Time and space got very blurred. Twice a week, you would be taken down the end of the tier for a quick shower, where you could catch a glimpse of another human being as you walked by the other cells. By July they allowed us into a small exercise yard attached to the end of the building, which had very high walls and was covered with a thick wire/chain mesh. It became so hot, and with nothing to do there, most prisoners stopped using it.

Here again, the noise was unbearable, prisoners screaming, crying, threatening to one degree or another. It presented an assault to your sanity. Every day was difficult and the longer you stayed in segregation the harder it got. This was supposed to be solitary confinement, and it was for awhile, but there were times when the unit became so crowded they doubled us up. During these times, I shared a cell with several different people. One was a man in his late forties, doing time for shooting a bill collector who tried to repossess his family's furniture. He could not read or write, so I would write the letters home to his wife for him. He was a very lonely man who loved and missed his wife very much. He had never been away from her before. As he explained his feelings to me, I would try to write them in the letters he sent home. It was very sad.

Another person who briefly shared a cell with me was a much younger man, around eighteen years old. He was facing a disciplinary hearing, as well as criminal charges, for assault. He was a likeable young man who had been totally gripped by terror—the fear of rape being forced on him at the hands of other prisoners. As he explained it to me, he had arrived at the prison very young and with no friends. In classification, he was approached by some older prisoners who wanted him as a sexual partner. He refused, but began to fear for his life as threats were made against him. He was threatened with being forced to submit to sexual acts. Finally, when one of the prisoners who threatened him made advances in the yard, the prisoner turned on him and fractured his skull with a baseball bat. The bully was taken to the hospital in serious condition and the young prisoner was taken to segregation. You could still see on his face and hear in his voice the fear he felt of being sexually assaulted. It's not good that we have to live with violence, but this prisoner did the right thing when he defended himself.

Another prisoner I shared a cell with during this period was also a victim of the brutal environment of prison. He was a very depressed and angry person, doing a sixty-year sentence for armed robbery. He was about twenty to twenty-one years old and felt cheated by the system—his arms were covered with scar tissue where he'd cut himself up in the past. Now, facing a lengthy time in segregation, he decided to hurt himself badly enough to end up in the medical ward, where rumors had it conditions were better. He explained his plan and asked me to watch for the guard and, when he was hurt badly enough, I was to yell for the guards to get him to medical.

I watched as he broke a large wedge-shaped piece of glass from a jar. He sat on the bunk and pushed the glass into his stomach, slowly at first, then all the way in. Blood spurted out on to his hands and the floor. He then took a pocket comb and pushed the glass wedge in further. At this point, he fell back against the bunk and it seemed as he were going to loose consciousness. When I yelled to the guards that a man was hurt, a guard came down the tier, looked at the blood and who was injured then said, "Oh, it's him again," then walked off. It took awhile, but finally a group of guards showed up with a stretcher. No one asked me what happened. No one really cared. I later heard this prisoner had hurt himself more seriously than he planned to. Eventually, he ended up in a padded cell in the medical ward.

Bill Allen passed through the segregation unit about this time. I couldn't see him, but was able to talk to him through the air vents. He was being transferred to Brushy Mountain and sent me some books before shipping out. Books were worth their weight in gold.

I filed a writ of *habeas corpus* in court, declaring that I had been illegally confined in segregation without due process (that is—without a proper hearing or court order) and that the conditions there were very bad, constituting cruel and unusual punishment. Shortly after, I was ordered released to the regular prison population, which—for me—meant going back to classification, a process that had never been completed. I returned to the overcrowded bay area where tensions were running high because of the bad conditions. It was a violent place of fights, knifings, rapes, and robberies. There was plenty of gambling and drugs, and a whole lot of scared, depressed people. The toilets and sinks were constantly overflowing, even backing-up into our sleeping area. Bugs were everywhere.

My charge partner from Clarksville was in classification when I got there. Frank is Black. We bunked near each other and ate our meals together, once again violating the "Jim Crow" unwritten rules. From the racist administration's point of view, we were making a serious mistake. They hate it when Blacks and Whites hang together—"Salt and Pepper." Without notice, I was put in one of the segregation cells in classification. One of the guards, "Hacks" we used to call them, said the reason was "because I didn't stay with my own kind." Next day, I was brought to the "Bull Pen" area, where the administration offices were. Through a window, the deputy warden (a racist dog known for his repressive tactics with prisoners) waved a piece of paper saying that it was a death-threat against me signed by an anonymous prisoner. The gist of it, he said, was that if I didn't stay away from Black prisoners I would be killed. The deputy warden said I should hang around with my "own kind."

I was then placed back in the segregation area, near some notoriously racist prisoners. Next day, I got my first "shank" (a homemade prison knife) and prepared to defend myself against any attacks. Tension-filled days passed. It becomes really hard to tell when you're just being careful and when there is too much paranoia involved. You start to feel more like some kind of animal in a concrete jungle. Without further incident, about a month later, I went before the classification board. They said I was a troublemaker and wanted to send me straight to Brushy (me, with no prior record). One young counselor finally convinced the others that I should be given a chance to remain in Nashville. Of course, my opinion counted for nothing. So I was sent into population with no job and a lot of cell time.

A few days before my twenty-fourth birthday, I was taken by a goon squad to a reclassification hearing. They said I was too much trouble and would have to be sent to Brushy Mountain (in the mountains of East Tennessee). They insisted that the order to transfer me came from outside the prison administration in Nashville. I spent the next two weeks in Unit VI Seg, then I was chained and shipped to Brushy. Bad times were on the horizon.

My biggest "crime" in Nashville had been to associate with Bill, my brother Rico, Tim Barkley, and others, who were considered to be militant and who would not kiss the boots of those who oppressed them. My being White and standing up to their racist policies was considered a serious threat—a threat to shake up things and create the potential for change, to be able to free ourselves, even in small ways.

Brushy was the end of the line. The "House of the Dead," it couldn't get much worse. Most times we were locked in our cells, except for meals. There was hardly any work and the tensions were running high because of lockups, overcrowding, racism, and deprivation. Arguments and fights were continuous. I read and studied as much as I could, but outside books and literature were prohibited. When we were able to get out of our cells, I got into pretty good shape running, lifting weights, and boxing. I tried not to waste a minute of time. I prepared myself for each new day, because I thought things might blow up at any moment. And I prepared for my eventual release.

In early 1971 I went before the parole board, which granted me parole on the condition that I leave the State of Tennessee. The parole board was made up of three older, White businessmen-types who knew nothing of the workings and conditions of the prisons—and didn't care anyway. They didn't represent the kind of people us prisoners came from. I applied first to Massachusetts, but even though I lined up a job, I was denied, which caused a three-month delay in my release. Finally, after twenty months, I was granted parole to Maine, where your *mémère* had helped to set up a parole plan that the state accepted. Initially, it was to pump gas for minimum wage and crash on the couch in her apartment.

So I moved in with your *mémère* and my *mémère*, who was also living there at the time. My first job was with Genest Concrete, making concrete blocks and cement pipes. It was hard work, dirty and requiring long hours (fifteen hours my first day). I worked there until September 1971, when I took a job as a carpenter in Kennebunkport, along the coast. I made enough money to eat, pay the rent, and keep my newly purchased panel truck on the road. The truck was red, a relic from the past, but I loved it. Before the truck, I had used a borrowed bicycle. Before that, I hitched.

But time started to weigh heavily on me. I never really stopped doing time. George Jackson (Black Panther and revolutionary) was murdered on 21 August 1971 and, just days after starting my new carpenter job, the Attica Prison uprising and massacre happened on September 9–13. The impact of these and other historic events in our struggle seemed to be with me every waking moment. The rage shook me from within.

I was laid off from the carpenter job a few days before Christmas. I had to eat, so I got a job, luckily, as a construction laborer, working with light steel and putting up a building. I worked with my brother on this job. Cold, I worked until January 1972, when I made a move that would enable me to become politically active and still be able to eat. I enrolled as a student at the University of Maine in Augusta.

After the first or second day at the university, I met Roger—another Vietnam veteran and a former chopper pilot—and we moved into an apartment together on Sand Hill. Within weeks we were organizing against the war in Vietnam and revitalized the Maine Chapter of the Vietnam Veterans against the War (VVAW), a national organization. We felt very strongly against the war and, based on our experiences in Vietnam, we had credibility among the people who helped to organize resistance to the war. At that time, the air war—dropping millions of tons of bombs on the Vietnamese people—was in full swing.

Our political work consisted mostly of regrouping veterans from various communities, organizing demonstrations, and doing political education through films, literature, and speaking gigs. Our focus was on the air war and how U.S. imperialism was destroying the nation of Vietnam. We called for total withdrawal of all U.S. forces. A high point of this activity in Augusta was the rally, march, and demonstration that we organized when Vice President Agnew appeared at the Maine Republican Convention. About 1,000 protestors participated. Many of us surrounded the building where the convention was held and demonstrated in a very militant spirit. We let Agnew know that he and the war policies he helped carry out were very much opposed by lots of people. I was glad to see that over many months of organizing that a sizable number of people supported a free and independent Vietnam. The culmination of this struggle was South Vietnam's liberation by revolutionary forces, when they marched into Saigon (now Ho Chi Minh City) in April 1975.

Because war hurts so many people, some of us in VVAW decided to go out to the veteran's hospital in Togus to see if we could help some of the Vietnam vets. I remembered how bad it could be in a veteran's hospital because my *pépère* had been there when I was around seventeen. I remember going out to visit him and he begged that we take him home, because the people who ran the hospital didn't care about him. He didn't want to die forgotten in some corner. In a few weeks, we went back to get him, to bring him home.

Now we went back to this hospital and found young vets who were having serious problems with their lives, a lot of it with drug and alcohol abuse, just sitting in a ward, forgotten men, not being helped at all. We couldn't do too much for them; we had no money or power. But we did become friends with these young brothers. I took some of them over to the Rap and Rescue Center in town, where I worked as a drug counselor and coordinator. A couple of times, we took them to a camp on a nearby lake; sometimes we'd just have a beer together and rap.

Around May 1972 I decided to leave VVAW. The organization had been a significant anti-war organization, but weakened from internal hassles. It hadn't broadened its political and community activities enough. In Maine, besides opposing the war, there was not much of a base to do more. I wanted to do more than work against the war, because I saw different problems and solutions being connected. Through that spring and summer, I continued working as a drug counselor with young people in the community. I picked up food and rent money by working first for the state forestry department planting seedling pine trees and then as a construction laborer.

I received a full scholarship at the university for most of 1972 and all of the 1973 academic year. It was a work-study grant, so I did janitorial work on campus during the day. Although the particular studies did not interest me much, I did study initially and received good grades. One reason I put some real effort into my studies, at first, was to prove to myself that I could do college work. My father, who was very demanding, would at times ridicule my brother and me for doing so poorly in school when we were young. He would call us stupid and say that this has always been the lot of most French-Canadian people. He would point out the men sweeping the town streets and say we'd end up doing the same (as far as I'm concerned there is nothing wrong with keeping a town clean). The university was, at first, a simple test for me—to see if I could make it in the "acceptable" world of higher learning. It was just an intellectual exercise. I had no other well-defined goal, as I studied and took my exams.

In September 1972 a small group of us from the university distributed thousands of leaflets commemorating the first anniversary of the Attica rebellion and massacre (a year earlier, prisoners had taken over Attica Prison in New York to protest terrible living conditions and inhumane treatment from guards; they said they would no longer allow themselves to be treated like beasts). Governor and ruling-class member Rockefeller ordered the police to attack. They murdered dozens, including brothers Sam Melville and L. D. Barkley. This leaflet action was the beginning of a prison support group we called "The Committee to Secure Justice for Prisoners." Early efforts consisted of working with prisoners at the Maine State Prison in Thomaston, helping them to form a prisoners' "union." We did outreach in the Kennebec County Jail, helping to set up drug and literacy programs. We did public education in communities and tried to interest people in working with us. Eventually, we joined efforts with another, similar organization called SCAR. From then on, we were all SCAR. The whole effort was done primarily by ex-prisoners and prisoners with a few supporters. We like to say that our work was done "in the spirit of George Jackson."

Through the winter/spring of 1973 our work continued and expanded in some areas. Unfortunately, by spring, I was getting into a bad drug thing, mostly speed, trying to keep the animal inside me from shaking his cage so much. It's very, very destructive. I knew this, but played with it anyway. I remember sitting in my unheated apartment all night long, feeling guilty and sick, playing games with sanity, waiting for the morning sun. Dawn meant more speed and another day to cut university classes.

I got away from the drug thing at the end of the school year and away from Maine. I traveled with Wally up into Québec and then across the Trans-Canada highway to British Columbia and the Canadian Rocky Mountains. This is one of the most beautiful areas I'd ever seen. On my own, from there, I hitched into Vancouver City to the jazz clubs in Gastown, then out to Vancouver Island and Long Beach to watch the 10:00 P.M. sunsets and whales from a driftwood beach shelter. I re-entered the U.S. at Port Angeles in Washington State, hitched down the coast into the rain forest and the Oregon dunes, then into northern California and on to Big Sur and L.A. In the Bay Area, I stayed with a friend in Berkeley. I left Berkeley for the Sierra Nevada Mountains, Lake Tahoe, and Reno. Then Utah, Colorado, and the Rockies, where I hiked the trails to small lakes and old gold mines. I hitched to Nashville to see friends and pay respects to honky-tonk Broadway, then it was back to Portland, Maine—near broke, but feeling a whole lot better.

I ended up living on Munjoy Hill in Portland with your mama and friends Joel and Casey. I was happy to be with them. I also hustled onto the university payroll for the rest of the summer and part of the following year. Several of us did this, and it helped pay our expenses while working with SCAR. And work we did.

We set up a base of operations in Portland, getting to know people in the community and expanding our programs. We opened a storefront; put out a paper called *Scar'd Times*; did a lot of work with prisoners, including the prisoners' "union" at the Maine State Prison; began a community bail fund; did paralegal work with prisoners; and got jobs, housing, and food when we could put it together. We raised funds through outdoor rock festivals and concerts; supported the Attica brothers; did much political education work throughout the area; taught karate to kids and adults; supported welfare rights and other struggles that tried to develop in people something to be proud of and fight for.

It was the early '70s when I got started in Shotokan Karate. I worked my ass off, initially going to classes at the university and later in the same day at the dojo in town.

It wasn't work after awhile. It was enjoyment that involved work. What I related to in this traditional style of karate was the ability you could develop to use your mind and body in a disciplined way. There was an inner strength to be brought out, the ability and power to concentrate and focus your energy and power. And the physical skills you develop served the needs of good health and self-defense, again, in a disciplined way. The spirit of karate is something you carry with you in many aspects of life. Every self-respecting political organization should have some sort of martial arts training.

After reaching Brown Belt, I began to teach karate classes to a group of people, most of whom were connected to SCAR. I also taught a class to young kids in the Kennedy Park/Bayside projects. I loved doing this, because I saw some of these people begin to pick up basic skills they needed to get into the spirit of karate and defend themselves. For the kids, that meant accomplishing something in a positive way and seeing themselves as brothers and sisters. The way things are in the projects, this was a good beginning.

In August 1974 your mama and I went to Tennessee in an old clunker that died on us somewhere outside of Nashville. On the way down, we went by the now-abandoned Brushy Mountain Prison with a mountain ledge for a rear wall. We climbed the walls and could see my old cell. The prison still showed the effects of the riot that had closed it down. The deaths of guards and prisoners could be felt in the air, an evil place.

We stayed at a friend's farm for a week, drinking homemade beer, picking cantaloupe for breakfast, and relaxing—something I find hard to do. We hitched back through the Smoky Mountains and stopped at a flat piece of ground called Maryland to visit your grandma and grandpa. It was like a honeymoon before the marriage.

This was a time that became a turning point for me. I began to work less for SCAR. I had done much with SCAR, but now felt it was time to work on some other projects. I still worked with the bail fund, taught karate, but stayed away from SCAR's storefront and meetings. I intensified my own karate training. I still practice it.

A lot of my energy went into the bookstore "Redstar North," a political bookstore that a few of us had opened in the west end of Portland. We fixed up an old shoe repair shop, and what little money I had was tied up in books and rent. The storefront was painted bright red. Dickie had made a red star with the word "North" carved under it, which was proudly displayed in the front of the store. The books we had covered subjects such as Marxism and revolution, Third World and labor struggles, Black liberation, feminism, people's history, prison, etc. All kinds of good stuff, children's books too! An important part of our work was the "Free Books to Prisoners Program." We sent them free to prisoners all around the country and wrote letters as well. The response of prisoners was tremendous. We continued to try for a strong political dialogue and relationship and sent out many books. It was a good effort, but short-lived.

There was a lot of repression in the late-1960s on through the mid-1970s. The government and police killed a lot of revolutionaries and imprisoned many more. If you worked among the people, you could become a target. In Portland there was supposed to be a "death squad" of policemen that got together to kill certain ex-prisoners. This came out in public hearings. Rumors abounded as to who was on "the list." Rumor had it that SCAR people were on it. Some members were attacked and beat-up. There were threats and arrests. The police made no secret that they were watching us. I began carrying a gun, and—as an ex-prisoner—this meant I was breaking the law.

In the fall of 1974 I met with others who wanted to form a guerrilla unit that would operate "underground" and engage in armed attacks against the state. We planned and participated in one such action that worked well. We then increased our membership. But then made serious errors. I have felt for a long time that my initial mistake was in leaving Portland (and the political work I was doing there) for what was an obscure plan to develop ourselves underground. After the first successful action, very little positive development took place and one result was a loose group of people that was wide open to mistakes in strategy and actions. It was doomed to failure.

In March 1975 I was arrested in Rhode Island with Cameron Bishop, a political fugitive. The charges were illegal possession of weapons and conspiracy to commit robbery. We were imprisoned at the Adult Correctional Institution (ACI) in Cranston, Rhode Island. Cameron was soon extradited to Colorado to face federal charges of sabotage. He was accused of blowing up transmission towers leading to a weapons plant that made armaments for the military during the Vietnam War. Since this action came during the war years, it was a particularly righteous action.

I was in ACI for about a month, a miserable prison destined for another riot. Eventually, friends put up my bail and I got out in April. Mama met me outside. We stayed the night together, and this is when you were conceived, Little One! Cameron was still imprisoned in Colorado, so I went to Denver to help his defense committee.

I was there for a few weeks, during a very intense time when the Chicano community was being attacked. The federal court house was bombed and we were under surveillance by the police. After his family finally got Cam out on bail, we had a talk, and then I left. I haven't seen him since.

Upon returning to the East Coast, I met again with people who were interested in doing armed actions, who wanted to try to build a serious resistance unit. It was during this time that I wrote *Seize the Time*, a view on armed struggle and revolution. Experience is a great teacher and, since that piece of writing, I've had many experiences which have been instructive. We've learned by doing. I have since been re-analyzing our situation and the revolutionary struggle of which we are a part.

Since the fall of 1974 I have participated in armed attacks against the enemy state and U.S imperialism. I worked and struggled with others to contribute something to the advancement of socialist revolution. I fight with the vision of a world in which there are no poor and no bosses, in which the workers are in control. I have become one of the workers in the Internationale, with a gun in hand. Since 1975 I have been pursed by the police, the FBI, and others. I know that they would imprison or shoot me if they got the chance. That is why I now write these words. In January 1976 you were born. This was one of the happiest days of my life, it always will be.

Little One, when you are healthy and happy, that pleases me. We struggle now so that all peoples will have good health and happiness. Our struggle means we must fight oppression and suffering. I hope that you grow to be strong and proud and to have a heart for the people. I hope that the world will be a better place to live for everyone and that you will be conscious of the need to struggle to create such a world.

I love you. Papa (1976)

1 A version of this article was first published in 1992. Raymond Luc Levasseur, "A Short Autobiography for My Daughter," in *Le FAROG Forum*, April-May 1992.

Ray Levasseur, his daughter Carmen, and grand-daughter Farran, Portland, Maine, 2004
Photograph by Simone Levasseur

UNDER WINTERY CONSTELLATIONS

Susann Pelletier
Lewiston, Maine

I.

Eleven-year-old boy –
thin shadow
    that you are,
your day's work at the brickyard is done....

Under wintery constellations of lit windows
    at twilight, walking past the "blocks" where
    Eddie and Theresa and Gerry and Willy live,
    and lean now over their books and lessons...

Under twenty or so dim street lights,
    at dusk, walking past Église St. Pierre, where
    the widows, Mmes. Gilbert and Thibault, light candles
    and genuflect and pray, where
    the organist M. Parent practices for Sunday mass....

Under moon-lit spires of cold stone,
    at dark, walking past the drift of ghostly notes,
    past shop windows mirroring a sturdy boy,
    with bare hands and head,
    with ragged coat....

Now, you run up the walkway,
            the wooden steps,
                        the hallway stairs

Home.

Under the halo of kitchen light,
    opening the package you carry, extending your hands,
    giving this gift to your almost-blind mother,
    her tears of gladness fall, as you exclaim:
    "V'la le fromage! V'la le pain!"....
    Here is the cheese! Here is the bread....

II.

Eleven-year-old boy, working outdoors
Blue eyes tearing with the wind's whip, the dust of bricks,
    counting and loading,
            pulling wagons,
    unloading....

Count you could, and multiply, and divide
Best in your fifth-grade class in arithmetic
Solving problems
Your teacher faltered over at the board
During this—your final year of school....

That story often told as a moral lesson, about what? What?!
I wondered,
Hearing you, father, at eighty, your blue eyes welling up, again
    Dragging me in....

Was the lesson:

    "We give what we can?"
  or " We lose what we hope for?"
    or was it: "Love will bless us with tears?"

A CEUX QUI M'ONT OFFENSÉ

Jean-Paul Poulain

Augusta, Maine

Growing up Roman Catholic, Jean-Paul Poulain was drawn into a web of events to which children should never be exposed. Between the ages of ten and fourteen, he was sexually abused by a priest. Thinking he was alone in the tragedy, Jean-Paul was later horrified to discover that about thirty other boys had also been abused by this man of the cloth. Seeking some form of justice and closure for this abuse often placed Jean-Paul in opposition to the Franco-American mainstream. Not just a matter of a "cover up," conservative Franco-Americans possess a very proud state of mind and prefer not to publicly condemn their traditional leaders. So, it was no surprise that Jean-Paul, after these secrets had been revealed, was told that while it was admirable that he had come forward, it would have been better if he had remained silent about these dark matters. To deal with such a fragile, emotionally sensitive situation, Jean-Paul wrote this song, "A ceux qui m'ont offensé," or, "To Those Who Have Offended Me." This song has stirred up a range of sentiments. Some establishments have asked Jean-Paul not to perform the song, and his CDs have been removed from the shelves of various retailers. Universities, however, have welcomed his song of tragedy and truth.[1] —Chase Hébert

A ceux qui m'ont offensé

Je lègue mon mépris à ceux qui m'ont offensé
Qui ont fait de ma vie une culpabilité.
Le temps de l'innocence s'est trop tôt arrêté
Au gré de vos démences, semence de vanité.
Je n'ai au rendez-vous de mes souvenirs d'enfance
Qu'un trop-plein de dégoût et l'envie de vengeance.
Mes nuits pauvres en sommeil sont de vos images agitées
Car elles laissent en éveil ce que je ne peux effacer.

Comment puis-je pardonner
A ceux qui m'ont offensé
A ceux en qui j'avais confiance
A ceux qui m'ont condamné
A cet amour sans substance
A cette enfance dérobée.
Comment puis-je vous pardonner?

Votre autorité respectable vous a permis
De jouer contre mon gré vos jeux sans interdits.
Et quand je priais Dieu de protéger mon innocence,
Il récompensait mon voeu de sa divine absence.
Vous m'avez tant sali que ma mémoire est pleine
De toutes vos fantaisies innomables et malsaines.

Comment puis-je pardonner
A ceux qui m'ont offensé
A ceux en qui j'avais confiance
A ceux qui m'ont condamné.
Puis-je appeler ça de la chance
De pouvoir encore en parler?
Comment puis-je vous pardonner?

Quand vous abusiez de ce petit garçon,
Vous êtiez sans pitié; je serai sans pardon.

English Translation—For Those Who Have Offended Me

I bequeath my contempt to those who have offended me,
Who have filled my life with guilt.
The time of innocence stopped too soon,
Drifting with your madness, the seeds of vanity.
At the rendez-vous of my childhood memories,
I have but an overflow of disgust and a feeling of vengeance.

My nights deprived of sleep are filled with your agitated images,
Since all that I cannot erase remains wide awake.

How can I forgive
Those who have offended me,
Those whom I trusted,
Those who have condemned me,
To this love without substance,
To this stolen childhood.
How can I forgive you?

Your respectable authority allowed you
To play your games—against my wishes—without prohibitions.
And when I prayed God to protect my innocence,
He recompensed my vow with his divine absence.
You soiled me so much that my memory is filled
With all your unspeakable and unwholesome fantasies.

How can I forgive
Those who have offended me,
Those whom I trusted,
Those who condemned me.
Can I call this luck
To be able to still speak of it?
How can I forgive you?

When you abused this little boy,
You were without pity; I will be without forgiveness.

1 This song introduction was derived from Chase Hébert's interview with Jean-Paul Poulain in Augusta, Maine, on 19 December 2006. The cassette tape-recording and transcription of the interview are held in the University of Southern Maine's Franco-American Collection at Lewiston-Auburn College.

FRANCO-AMERICAN IDENTITY AT THE UNIVERSITY OF MAINE[1]

Michael Serizawa Brown
Seattle, Washington

The establishment of the Franco-American program at the University of Maine and the resurgence of French ethnic pride were the results of a confluence of events originating in both Québec and in the United States. Among them were a history of denigration of French heritage in New England, the social and political upheavals in the United States during the 1960s, and the experiences of individual Franco-Americans.

During the nineteenth century, approximately 500,000 French Canadians emigrated from Québec to New England. In Québec they had enjoyed a rich and varied tradition forged with the land. When emigrants arrived in New England, however, they faced an unfamiliar and often hostile world, and they reacted by staunchly resisting assimilation. They clung to their ethnic and cultural heritage, adopting a strategy of *survivance*—the preservation of the French-Canadian language, culture, and religion—in the new land. *Survivance* propagated itself through institutional structures that affected every aspect of Franco-American life. In New England, these included ethnic-centered neighborhoods, the extended family, numerous social organizations, the Franco-American press, and the Catholic church, each of which played a pivotal role in encouraging a strong sense of ethnic identity.[2]

Despite its enormous role in maintaining Franco-American culture, *survivance* began to wane after World War I and the "Americanization" campaigns of the 1920s. The weakening of traditional institutions came with more rapid assimilation as French-Canadian immigrants, hoping for material gain, adopted mainstream U.S. traditions.[3] The resulting loss of cultural identity, however, deprived them of an important bulwark that had sheltered the earlier Franco immigrants from the harsh experiences they had endured in the mills and neighborhoods of Yankee New England. While *survivance* eroded, the hardships of life, most apparent in educational and workplace disadvantages, persisted.[4] By the 1960s, there were only scattered remnants of the once ubiquitous efforts to preserve French ethnic identity.

The post-Second World War period, however, brought many events that affected

U.S. popular consciousness and contributed to a revival of *survivance*. In 1958, as the Cold War began to intensify, the Soviet Union launched *Sputnik*, the earth's first orbiting satellite. The Russians' success made many U.S. citizens realize the need for improvements in education in order to maintain parity with Soviet science and technology. Between 1958 and 1971 the federal government inaugurated a series of programs that encouraged bilingual education and indirectly aided Francos who sought government help to preserve their cultural heritage. The PACE Fabric Project in northern Maine, for example, became one of the first bilingual education programs that received a federal grant to help French-speaking children.

Additional federal efforts provided further impetus behind this change. In 1964 Congress passed the Civil Rights Act and, in the following year, it enacted the Elementary and Secondary Education Act (ESEA), which provided funding for bilingual education programs. In 1971 President Richard Nixon promulgated Executive Orders 11246 and 111375, requiring agencies receiving federal funds to apportion them according to local population characteristics, including ethnicity and native language. In 1972 Congress approved an "Ethnic Heritage Studies Program" and mandated bilingual education programs under Title VII of the ESEA and the Emergency School Aid Act.[5]

Meanwhile, social and political activism intensified around the country as the civil rights movement, the peace movement, the women's movement, the environmental movement, and other efforts advocating for reform arose. Networks and personal connections among those who participated in the various movements, moreover, reinforced the broader momentum for social and political change in both the public and the private sectors.[6]

In Maine, the state university system began to encourage ethnic and cultural diversity. In November 1971 the University of Maine's Board of Trustees created an Affirmative Action Office, actively recruited Black students from large urban areas outside of the state, assigned a foreign student advisor for international students and, for the first time in its history, began a formal program for hosting students from other countries.[7] Students themselves, moreover, worked for cultural diversity. Examples were the Chinese Students Association at the University of Maine in Orono, which offered Mandarin language lessons during the winter of 1971, and Native American students, who established their own organization.[8]

The events encouraged Franco-Americans at the University of Maine who were trying to redefine their own ethnic identity. Between 1969 and 1971 they held a series

FAROG students, University of Maine, Orono, 1978. Left to right:
Front row—Ludger Duplessis, Mary Ann Cyr, Andrew Sabol, Yvon Labbé;
Back row—Daniel Parent, Marc Morin, Kevin Duplessis.
Franco-American Centre, University of Maine, Orono

of meetings at a snack bar in Orono, where they shared experiences and tried to define a new Franco-American consciousness. They found inspiration not only in the political events of the time both in the United States and in Canada—where there was a struggle to create an autonomous Québec—as well as in the beginnings of a new phase of *survivance* in different parts of New England. New bilingual education programs had begun in northern Maine; a "Franco-American Week" took place in Lowell, Massachusetts; and the outspoken French/English bilingual newspaper, *Observations*, was established in Lewiston. Additional inspiration came from the activities of the Centre d'Heritage Franco-Américain (today's Franco-American Collection at the University of Southern Maine), the Club Richelieu, the Légion de Marie, and the Société St. Jean-Baptiste. In 1972 the Orono students created an organization that eventually became the Franco-American Resources Opportunity Group (FAROG).[9]

The path was not entirely trouble-free, however. Tension arose from the participation of Anglo-Americans in the meetings. Another, more fundamental tension arose from relations between males and females. Franco women were beginning to assert themselves not only as members of a minority group, but also as females.[10] Inspired not only by the civil rights movement, but also by the women's movement, the female Francos sought new ways of defining both ethnic and gender identity. Claire Bolduc, for one, believed that her own experience with the "sisterhood" contributed to her participation in Franco-American activities.[11] "We looked at our mothers' lives and decided that was not what we wanted," Bolduc recalled. Women students realized that "it wasn't right to give men all the power" because "that would be as bad as letting the French be put down."[12] At the same time, they also tried to come to terms not only with sexism in the United States, but also with sexism in their own French culture. Consequently, their goal was to define an identity that would preserve their French ethnic heritage while also claiming gender equality with male Francos. In Bolduc's words: "It was really confusing.... Are you a woman first, or a French person first?" The women—four of the group's five core members—regularly participated in campus women's meetings and made it clear to males that they would not accept subordinate status: "Let's talk different ways, let's invent ways to use our own culture," was Bolduc's response to the times.[13]

FAROG also drew sustenance from the conscious choices individual members made about defining themselves. Yvon Labbé was born in 1938 in Quebec, where his father worked as a cook for logging crews. At age eleven, when he and his family moved to Stratton, Maine, he spoke only French. After attending seventh and eighth grades at St. Georges-de-Beauce (Québec) he studied for five years at a U.S. high school in Madison, Maine, where everyone spoke only English in the classroom. Although the teachers in Québec had told him that he was very bright, those in Madison informed Labbé that "there was something wrong" with him: They made him feel as though he could not speak correctly and that his thinking was skewed. Labbé faced other obstacles as well. Anglo classmates teased him because, to them, his name sounded like "Yvonne," an Anglo name for girls and women, To stop the teasing, he adopted the name "Ivan," withdrew from his classmates, and hid his French heritage.[14]

The undergraduate education Labbé experienced also encouraged him to deny his *Québécois* background. In 1963 he finished his baccalaureate and, two years later, matriculated into the University of Maine's graduate program in the College of Education. He received a U.S. Department of Defense scholarship to study in France and, while there, diligently erased his *Québécois* accent. After he completed his graduate studies in 1968, he taught French in Wellesley, Massachusetts, and gradually began to rebel against the thought of teaching French, his mother tongue, as if it were a "foreign language."[15] He had begun to reject the idea that his French-Canadian heritage was culturally inferior.

Claire Bolduc, like Labbé, gradually came to affirm her French ethnicity. Born in Eagle Lake, Maine, in 1946, Bolduc went to school in Québec until the third grade and then in northern Maine between fourth and twelfth grades. In 1963, after graduating as salutatorian of her high school class and winning a scholarship, she enrolled at St. Joseph's College in North Windham, Maine, where she became politically conscious, participating in various activities including student government, the French Club, and the Judicial Board.[16] In 1970, by the time Bolduc joined other Francos in FAROG, she was a veteran of the women's movement, had performed in street theater, and knew how to use language as a consciousness-raising tool. She was also well aware of the stigma attached to French-Canadian ethnicity. In elementary school, for example, she had learned about Anglo-American prejudice when a teacher punished her for speaking French outside of the classroom; the teacher made her write, one hundred times: "I will not speak French." As a college student, Bolduc noticed that nowhere was there evidence of French contributions to the State of Maine; people who held the most prestigious jobs were Anglo-Americans, and that those who held the most menial, French.[17] In 1970 she met members of FAROG in Orono, where they all began to realize that they shared similar experiences in wrestling with their French heritage. Among them was Liliane Labbé, sister of Yvon Labbé and a core member of the group, who had embraced her French background even in elementary school; she had been known in her neighborhood as "the French kid" because of her insistence on speaking French. As people like Bolduc and Labbé became aware of a shared history of ethnic denigration, they became determined to articulate a new French identity.[18]

As the Orono group joined in a common purpose, they drew inspiration not only from the various movements occurring around the nation, but also from their contact with other Franco-Americans. In late 1972, when the *Bangor Daily News*, a newspaper originating in a town a few miles from Orono, printed an article about the rise of Franco-American ethnic consciousness at the University of Maine, FAROG gained fame among other Francos. The article, "'Frog Power': Ethnic Identity Forms," mentioned green "Frog Power" bumper stickers that FAROG was distributing and described the Orono students as being among the most vocal in the state. The article resulted in a flurry of letters from Franco-Americans across New England. François

Beaudet, a French language teacher in Rhode Island, for example, wrote to FAROG, asking for some bumper stickers and information on how he could help the group. Ethelyn LaGassey Montgomery of East Millinocket, Maine, made a similar request and sent words of encouragement, as did Robert Massé, chef at the Hyde School in Bath.[19]

Having resolved to organize, the group still had to find a practical means for transforming ideals into reality. In 1970 Yvon Labbé and other members of FAROG met with University of Maine President Winthrop Libby. Over several meetings that spanned a period of months, the students and the president carried on informal discussions about the condition of Franco-Americans at the university. During the initial meetings, the young Franco-Americans asked for nothing of the University. The president, however, became personally involved, as the meetings made him increasingly aware of the discrepancies between the lives of Anglos and Francos.[20]

In April 1972 the group distributed a campus-wide survey to ascertain administrators' attitudes toward the establishment of a Franco-American program. In his response to the survey, the president was highly supportive. He acknowledged that the University of Maine had provided only "lip service" to the Franco-American community and that it must, in the future, make a "major, concentrated effort... to understand and appreciate the contributions of the Franco-Americans to the culture of the Northeast." The French population, he further asserted, "could become a source of great strength to the University...[and to] the State." Libby recommended, among other things, support of research projects about Franco-Americans, a "massive program" to teach conversational French to both undergraduates and adults, a Franco-American studies program, counseling for children from French backgrounds, recruitment of Franco-Americans for professional positions, and television programs to explain Franco-American culture to all Maine citizens.[21]

President Libby's support was based on his understanding that the cultural oppression was due in large part to ignorance. Libby acknowledged in a public address that he himself had unintentionally helped perpetuate "second-class citizenship" for Francos and that his Anglo background prejudiced him "against recognizing the tremendous contributions of the Franco-American to our culture." In late 1971, when the University of Maine received a federal grant for supplementing its personnel, President Libby allocated a portion to establish what would become the university's formal Franco-American program.[22]

Other university administrators were also committed to helping Franco-

Americans. Gerald Herlihy, director of the university's Onward program, whose purpose was to assist students from low-income and other non-traditional backgrounds, provided some of the initial support. Herlihy met with Labbé, Vice President Jim Clark, Foreign Languages Professor Robert Rioux, and several Franco-American students to discuss the needs of Francos. In 1971 Herlihy hired Labbé and three other Francos to visit students of French heritage in northern Maine high schools. Kristine Dahlberg, assistant dean of student affairs, also helped. She believed that the status of Franco-Americans had to be redefined and in late 1971 became involved in hiring Labbé as the first coordinator of the newly founded Franco-American program. Ruth Benson, the affirmative action officer for the University of Maine System, encouraged the Franco-American group to supply statistics demonstrating concrete examples of social and economic discrimination.[23]

Soon, the new Franco-American program enjoyed significant successes. Among them were the establishment of a program office, the compilation of a library and archive of Franco-American materials, the organization of a clearinghouse for statewide exchanges of information about Francos, and a cluster of university courses on Franco-American culture.[24] The program's journal, *Le FAROG Forum*, articulated Franco-American issues to a broad audience using material ranging from poetry to letters, opinions, and scholarly articles from different parts of the French-speaking world. By the late 1980s the paper had subscribers not only in Maine but also in other New England states, Québec, and France.

Perhaps the greatest success story of the Franco-American students, however, was the broad lesson they taught to posterity. Responding to the confluence of events in the 1960s and early 1970s, they reinvented and rearticulated their ethnicity; dissatisfied with the denigrated identity that had been forced upon them, they showed that it was possible to redefine themselves on their own terms.

The experience of emigration; the rise, decline, and rise again of *la survivance* in New England; the social and political upheavals of the 1960s; and the life experiences of individual Franco leaders led to the beginnings of the Franco-American program at the University of Maine. FAROG's genesis was the culmination of a complex process that originated in both Franco-American traditions and in the contemporary historical context.

1 A version of this essay initially came out in 1997. Michael Serizawa Brown, "Franco-American Identity at the University of Maine," *Maine History* 36 (3-4), Winter-Spring 1997, pp. 106–19.

2 Giguère, Vol. 3, pp. 1–7; Vol. 4, pp. 255–61.
3 Weil, pp. 96, 148, 151–52, 154. LeMaire, pp. 30, 35.
4 Armstrong, pp. 2–4, 9. Armstrong and others, p. 3. Giguère, Vol. 3, p. 7. St. Pierre, 29 December 1990. Herlihy, 23 January 1991. Bolduc to WCBB-TV, Lewiston, 15 May 1972.
5 Brault, pp. 172–76. Weil, p. 215.
6 Yvon Labbé, 30 December 1990. Bolduc, 29 March 1991. Donovan, pp. 9, 141–45. Evans, pp. 156–211. Gitlin, pp. 362–76.
7 Giguère to Donald McNeil, c. 1970–71. Herlihy, 23 January 1991. *Maine Campus*, 21 September 1967, p. 3; 26 October 1967, p. 3; 9 August 1972, p. 2.
8 *Maine Campus*, 3 December 1971, p. 5. Herlihy.
9 Yvon Labbé, 12 October and 30 December. Bolduc, 29 March 1991. Brault, pp. 172, 183. *Observations*, 15 July 1972, p. 14.
10 Yvon Labbé, 27 November 1990. Claire Bolduc, 8 November 1990, 4 January 1991.
11 Bolduc, 8 November 1990. Yvon Labbé, 12 October and 10 November 1990.
12 Bolduc, 8 November 1990, 27 March 1991.
13 Bolduc, 8 November 1990, 27 March 1991.
14 Yvon Labbé, Interview, 12 October 1990.
15 Yvon Labbé to Dahlberg; Labbé, 12 October and 10 November 1990.
16 Bolduc, Undated resume, c. 1970–72.
17 Bolduc, 8 November 1990.
18 Bolduc, 8 November 1990. Liliane Labbé, 19 June 1991.
19 Beaudet, 22 October 1972. Montgomery, 21 October 1972.
20 Yvon Labbé, 27 November 1990.
21 Armstrong and others, Appendix M.
22 Yvon Labbé, 12 October 1990, 20 December 1972. Shriver, p. 1. Montgomery, 13 November 1972. Libby, 16 November 1972.
23 Armstrong and others, p. 2, Appendix M. Herlihy, 23 January 1991.
24 Yvon Labbé and Dahlberg, p. 2. Yvon Labbé, 12 October 1990.

BEAU FROG

Peter Archambault
Orono, Maine

Artists often get inspiration for their drawings from social events or from their own personal experiences. Peter Archambault was no different. Employed by the University of Maine's Graphics Department in the mid-1970s, he was approached by Yvon Labbé, editor of the *FAROG Forum*—a new Franco-American journal. Yvon wanted a cartoon series to uplift the pride of Franco-Americans. They chose to use the frog image, as a way to transform this negative image into a positive one. After a few dry sketches, *Beau Frog* was born. Whenever in need of inspiration, Archambault would attend university or other local events to obtain fresh material to lampoon. *Beau Frog* not only represented events but socially important issues as well. The series ran for many years.[1] —Corinna Miller

Beau Frog # 1, FAROG Forum, *Orono, Maine, May 1976*
By Peter Archambault, from the Franco-American Centre, University of Maine at Orono

Beau Frog: "Calling Forth the Sprits," FAROG Forum, *Orono, Maine, January 1977*
By Peter Archambault, from the Franco-American Centre, University of Maine at Orono

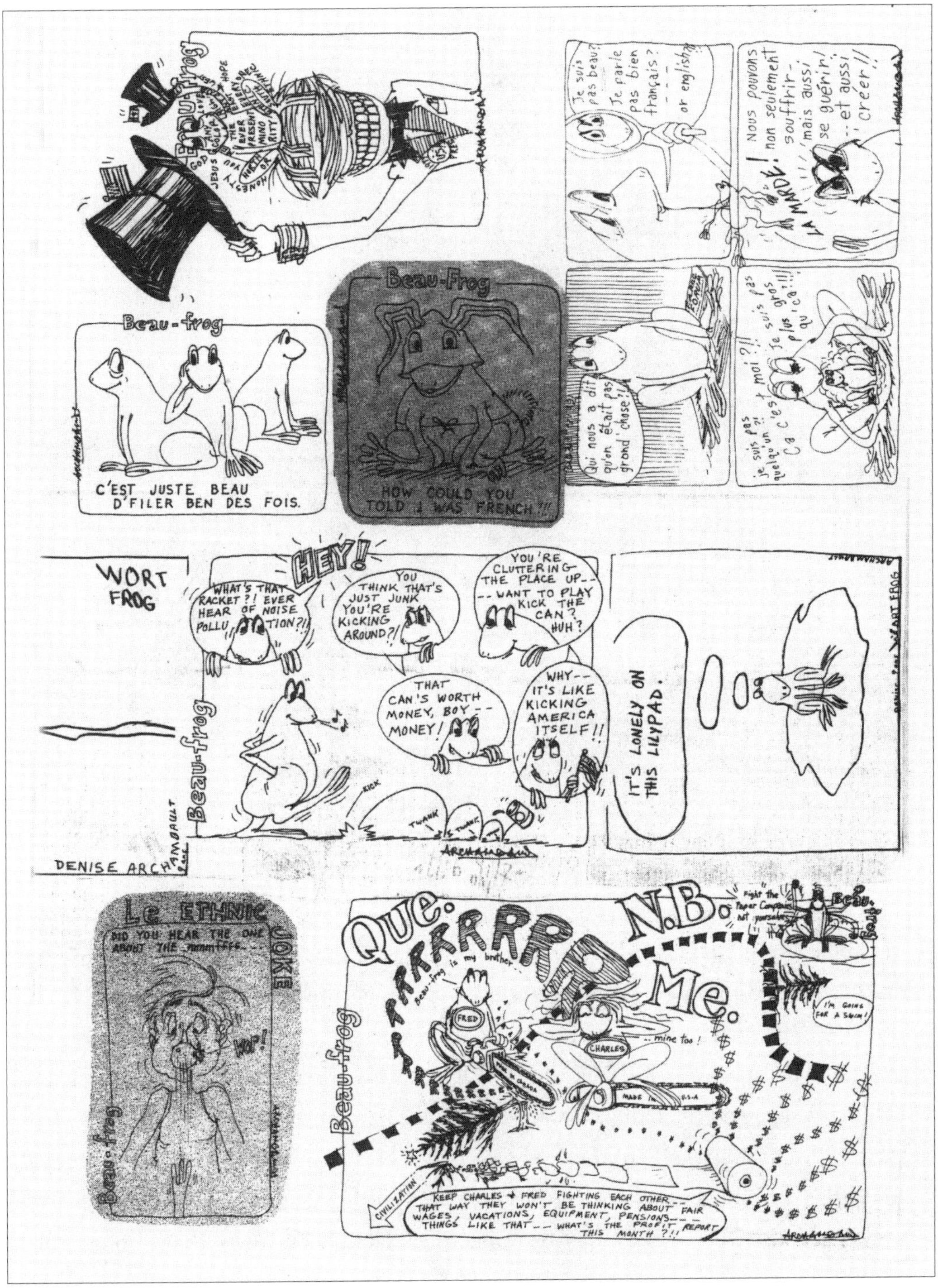
Beau-Frog
Beau-frog
C'EST JUSTE BEAU
D'FILER BEN DES FOIS.
Beau-Frog
HOW COULD YOU
TOLD I WAS FRENCH ?!!
Je suis pas beau?
Je parle pas bien français? --- or english?!
LA MARDE!
Nous pouvons non seulement souffrir- mais aussi se guérir! .. et aussi créer!!
Qui nous a dit qu'on était pas grand' chose?!!
je suis pas quelqu'un?! moi?!! Je suis pas plus gros qu'ça!!!
Ça c'est
WORT FROG
Beau-frog
HEY!
WHAT'S THAT RACKET?! EVER HEAR OF NOISE POLLUTION?!
YOU THINK THAT'S JUST JUNK YOU'RE KICKING AROUND?!
YOU'RE CLUTTERING THE PLACE UP-- --WANT TO PLAY KICK THE CAN? HUH?
THAT CAN'S WORTH MONEY, BOY-- MONEY!
WHY-- IT'S LIKE KICKING AMERICA ITSELF!!
KICK
TWANK
TWANK
IT'S LONELY ON THIS LILYPAD.
DENISE ARCHAMBAULT
Le ETHNIC JOKE
DID YOU HEAR THE ONE ABOUT THE mmmfff---
Beau-frog
QUE.
N.B.
Me.
RRRRRR
Beau-frog is my brother..
..mine too!
FRED
CHARLES
MADE IN CANADA
MADE IN U.S.A
Fight the Paper Companies not yourselves
Beau-frog
I'M GOING FOR A SWIM!
CIVILIZATION
KEEP CHARLES + FRED FIGHTING EACH OTHER-- THAT WAY THEY WON'T BE THINKING ABOUT FAIR WAGES, VACATIONS, EQUIPMENT, PENSIONS--- THINGS LIKE THAT-- WHAT'S THE PROFIT REPORT THIS MONTH ?!!
Beau-frog

Beau Frog and Maine's KKK, FAROG Forum, *Orono, Maine, c 1980.*
By Peter Archambault, from the Franco-American Centre, University of Maine at Orono

In the early 1970s when FAROG was being given birth, a group of FAROG students were visiting households in the Old Town area in search of live Francos. In one house, a FAROGer was going by a desk in an ante room on which there was a big and heavy metal stamper. Curious, as all FAROGers were, he wondered about the stamp which might be produced, placed a piece of paper in it, and pressed down on the handle. He brought the results to the FAROG office at the university where we were all impressed with the embossed finding—"the Milford Women's Auxiliary of the KKK"—goes to show that it may have been the lack of curiosity that almost killed the FROG. —Yvon Labbé.

1 This introduction was assembled from the flyer "Calling Forth the Spirits," the Franco-American Centre, University of Maine at Orono, 17 January 1983.

Stamp impression, KKK Women's Auxiliary, Milford, Maine
From Yvon Labbé and the Franco-American Centre,
University of Maine at Orono

OUT OF THE SHADOWS[1]

Yvon Labbé
Orono, Maine

We all vaguely know that the French have been in this region since colonial times, when the European superpowers warred and struggled over real estate on this continent—property not their own. In fact, for more than a century, the newly arrived French immigrants to Turtle Island referred to this region of the continent, including what is now Maine, as *la Nouvelle France* (New France). It should not be forgotten that French missionaries had already established themselves in what is now called New England. The door having been opened by Jacques Cartier and Samuel de Champlain, the latter having founded the first European settlement on Turtle Island in 1604—on an island he named Sainte Croix. Oblivious to the fate reserved for them and succeeding generations of their French flock, missionaries proceeded with the colonizing of aboriginals, eroding or replacing, to various degrees, traditional ways that had evolved over thousands of years. The French of that day, and Francos of today, were not immunized against arrogance, prejudice, and even racism. Or even against the denial of our own cultural and language inheritance.

Nonetheless, as the English succeeded in dominating the continent region by region, the French retreated and—eventually—surrendered. During the *Grand Dérangement* (the Great Dispersal) of the 1750s, the Acadians were gathered and herded on ships, many of which barely floated. They were then dispersed, families separated, dispossessed and exiled far from their homes. They ended up all over the hemisphere, including at the tip of South America. But we may know them best for their settlement of the bayou region of what is today Louisiana, as well as Le Madawaska in the border region of northern Maine/Nouveau Brunswick. The latter area was settled by Acadians who had escaped from the British in Nova Scotia by going north for a generation to what is now Fredericton, but were displaced again—in 1785—by Loyalists fleeing the successful Revolutionary War to the south.

Their cousins, the French in Québec, having given up the territory to the English following their defeat on the Plaines d'Abraham in 1759, were dealt with differently. Their numbers being greater than the Acadians (and greater than the English for that matter), and having developed both an urban and agricultural society with a panoply of institutions controlled by the Catholic church, these *fidèles* (faithful) were ripe for absentee management by English authorities, who made good use of the church's institutions as an instrument for crowd control. The church made a deal with the English—if the church kept its flock under control, it would be allowed its religious institutions and the French language. That crowd control was implemented very successfully and was in full operation for more than two centuries, until the *Révolution Tranquille* (the Quiet Revolution) of the 1960s and 1970s in Québec.

I find it ironical and paradoxical that the seventeenth-century superpower, France, which was well on its way to colonizing the whole continent and its aboriginals, found its French settlers recolonized by the English by the second half of the eighteenth century. France then forgot its conquered and exiled settlers in its *Nouveau Monde* (New World) until it emerged from this amnesia some 200 years later—specifically and very publicly in 1967 with the very loud "Vive le Québec Libre" (Long Live Free Québec) uttered by Président de la France, le Général De Gaulle.

During this interval between the British Conquest and De Gaulle's exhortation, a great migration of French-Canadian cheap labor pressed a tidal wave of Québec workers from the farms to the mills of the U.S. Northeast—at the invitation of the textile industrialists to the south. During the latter part of the nineteenth century, more than half the population of Québec sought greener pastures in the U.S. More than one million uprooted themselves for the trek south—many with the thought of returning to *la patrie* (the homeland) someday. This represented a massive exodus for French Canada, and a threatening influx for Maine local and regional authorities.

Francos currently make up about 30 to 40 percent of the state's population. About 100,000 remain French-speakers. We are of Québec and Acadian heritage, identities forged on this continent—initially as invaders and colonizers. We are the product of generations of those who fueled the Maine economic engine as invited cheap labor during the latter part of the nineteenth century. Our forebears—Lafayette, Rochambeau, Paul Revere (a.k.a. Paul Rivoire, son of Gascon Rivoire)—participated in and made possible the birth of this democracy. Our forebears also fought for the North during the Civil War as other French Canadians worked on production lines for this defining event. Even more have volunteered since and paid the ultimate price.

Yet despite our rich contribution to the building of this state, ours have yet to reach the top managerial levels of government. Never, despite comprising 30 to 40 percent of Maine's population, has a Maine governor of Franco heritage been elected.

Only once has a congressional seat been filled by a Franco Mainer. And never has one of us occupied the post of full bishop of the Portland diocese. Never! Auxiliary, yes. Full, no!—even though more than 70 percent of the Catholics in Maine are of French heritage. While Francos have been absent from the top Catholic post in Portland, the diocese has for generations taken the cream of our young people, and—for generations—has sent them elsewhere in the world to colonize other people.

This injustice has continued as our communities sank into invisibility. There has been a cost to this "official" invisibility and its attendant political powerlessness. The current State of Maine Franco identity is the result of accommodation, cultural devaluation, and derision. Until recently, "dumb frog" jokes were heard in classrooms and in public—in higher and lower education. Check the school textbooks in Maine "higher and lower" education, and try to find our history, our literature, our language. Ask teachers in your community about Franco contributions to the building of the state and its institutions. Higher education has yet to produce them in any significant way. In the 1980s, a much celebrated video about lumbering in Maine, *From Stump to Ship,* was aired and perceived as representing Maine lumbering history.[2] My father and most of the men in my family worked in the Maine woods and on the river drives most of their lives, for decades, going back into the nineteenth century. He and other Franco workers were not represented in that video.

We have been told that we don't have a real culture or a real language. We have generally grown to believe it as we continue to live and work within our depressed and shame-based identity, with our borrowed names, with faces not our own—the makings of political eunuchs clearly manifested in our lack of political success—and, more politely, the makings of a minority psychology with accompanying codependency. We wanted to be accepted, to improve our economic and social condition. We wanted something better for our children. We wanted to belong. But there was a price. We were asked to give up crucial pieces of ourselves. These surrendered pieces have thus far limited our access to full self-realization and full expression in all human activity: social, governmental, economic, and educational. A consequence may very well be, as many have told me over the years, that Maine Francos have a higher toll of mental health issues and problems with self-destructive behaviors—alcohol, tobacco, and other substance abuses. There is already plentiful literature that has examined and studied the consequences and impact of colonization, prejudice, and repression on conquered, colonized, and devalued cultural communities in the region.

Over the last ten years, our public institutions have been piously organizing diversity initiatives, mostly based and focused on skin pigmentation—not on understanding and appreciation of the selves under that skin. And in Maine, where the population is already popularly perceived as "diversityless" and homogeneous, homogenized and "McDonaldized," leaders have not the eyes to see us, nor the knowledge to value us. And from there, it seems easy to deny our existence as a cultural/language community worthy of attention and study.

As I write, a disappearing generation is leaving with our history, our folklore, our music, and our language. Until recently most University of Maine academicians were oblivious to our presence and our numbers—a continuation of what we have known since the foundation of the institution in 1865. It is a university and an educational system that Francos have been supporting and depending on to fulfill a public mandate—the generation and dissemination of knowledge about Maine people—all of them. The token initiatives to date do not produce higher education graduates able to convey to the current generation of young Francos and others what our generations have contributed and produced. Barring few exceptions, the work of higher education in Maine currently ignores nearly one-half of the state's population.

Among the exceptions that I have found thus far are the self-serving higher education consultants who are hired by politicians to unravel the socio-political behavior of Francos in order to win elections. They know more about our behavior and predispositions at the voting booth than we do. Franco aspirants to top political offices are loath to use such measures, since they are a product of longstanding self-effacing Franco processes.

The obvious remedy is an education with Franco "essence" built into it. But Maine higher education has yet to produce a history that integrates the rich diversity of Maine peoples. Our labor history (and we were mostly working class) generally still rots in the mill cellars of major Franco communities or lies fallow in local budding and unfunded historical initiatives. Such is the fallout of historical prejudice: low ceilings, stunted and ailing expression, closeted creativity, shame, fear of discovery and exposure, and hesitation. All this, as we try to claim and use our cultural and language inheritance and our bilingual skills, while also trying to avoid public denigration and rejection. The price of our Franco story remaining uncollected and untold is that our collective voice remains mute. This is a condition which, on one hand, nullifies our control over our political voice. On the other hand, it makes our community predictable and manageable by politicians and higher-education assimilators who devise all sorts of solutions to abstract issues of diversity, but are blind to the diverse Maine communities that surround them.

It is of no help to Francos that our North American cultural heritage dates to the pre-French revolutionary period, giving us a more than healthy respect for what we perceive as duly constituted authority: the company foreman, the teacher, the priest, or the pope. All had and have domain over us. They all have rights over our identity. In Québec and Acadia, social hierarchies had expressions for it: "C'est pas du monde de not' classe ça!" (Those are not our kind of people!) or "C'est pas not' place!" (It's not our place!). These notions migrated with us and were nurtured in Maine as rationales for immobility. While the socio-political space allotted the Franco identity in Maine was restricted and small, relegated essentially to the Franco parish and the Little Canada, Francos gave themselves the illusion of power, however little, by accepting and accommodating their lot as outsiders and temporaries—temporally and spiritually. The reward would come later—much, much later. We would have to learn to laugh at ourselves in the meantime.

Well! What happened to reduce a culture and a language honed and transmitted over more than a thousand years to such low standing? What happened to the cultural tools of self- and community management, the moral compass fired by a belief system attached to land, faith, and fierce pride? What happened to the genius of our culture, its capacity to invent, innovate, and renew itself? What happened to the language?—Ours—that expressed *notre vécu*, our living reality and experience? What happened to the power of our identity in fulfilling our duties as citizens in this democracy? As the French in Québec embraced their fate following *la Conquête* (the Conquest)—with the able assistance of church authorities and their teachings—a sense of fatality and futility began to ingrain itself in the culture, and eventually was manifested in the language.

Fond of proverbs and adages that explain and express socio-economic and cultural ceilings, one saying in particular has dogged the French in North America to this day: "On est né pour être petit pain, on ne peut pas s'attendre à la boulangerie" (We are born to be little breads; we cannot expect the bakery). These kinds of expressions reveal an incapacitating mindset that dates to the British conquest. Such a colonized worldview made it easier for external bigotry to gain a foothold in Franco society, as Francos established themselves in Maine among a new group of Anglos who seemed to have a divine right to power in this budding democracy.

Our families' overland migration to the States was joined by hordes of other immigrants from across the oceans. This "invasion" provided a challenge in the last half of the nineteenth century to the Anglo-Yankee establishment. The welcome mat in Maine was not out. This is evidenced by the land grant university founded in the midst of that migration with a mission that was primarily to meet the agricultural needs of Maine. This should have been of interest to Francos, who believed in education and who had irreducible bonds to *la terre* (the land). But the new university established a community network using the Grange system, which did not welcome Francos or Catholics. Indeed, the University of Maine's ignorance of Francos persevered until it was breached only in recent years.

We came from Acadia, from eastern and western Québec. In Maine, we settled on farms, worked in the woods, and settled along Maine rivers by the tens of thousands to work in the textile mills. Having experienced English Protestant-style conquest and exile in Québec and Acadia for generations, our people came—whole villages and families recruited by Maine and New England mill agents. Uprooted, and nearly overnight, they left *la terre* and crowded into mill housing. From there, they soon set up schools, built churches, and hospitals, and founded newspapers (more than 200 in New England in little more than fifty years). In fact, Francos built a whole socio-cultural support system in order to ensure survival within their identity. Their schools became bilingual and provided the possibility of an education through college for their children—and many children there were. Enough to please mill authorities, as they were put to work, and enough to scare the same authorities as these children grew and continued to add to the Franco ranks and swell the community with a nonpreferred identity.

The ignorance propagated by the Maine public education system was not accidental. The goal was to assimilate us and melt us. But into what? Would we be better citizens as retreaded Anglos? Not by a long shot. The dominant Anglo society preferred us to be nonentities, rather than competitors. If we were lacking in worth—having no history, no real culture, and no real language—it became easier to dispossess and disenfranchise us. As this erosion gained ground, it caused us to be complicit in our own devaluation, as our shame-based public education—built on a twice-conquered history—supported negative images—individual and collective.

A series of actions and events at the turn of the twentieth century started the process of cultural sterilization. At first, the Francos "circled their wagons" and sought refuge in French-language societies and associations for mutual support. This resistance intensified Anglo–Yankee reaction. I remember reading demeaning descriptions of these Franco movements in many municipal reports. Descriptions of Franco workers represented them as just barely above the level of beasts of burden. Attacks also came from their own Catholic church.

Late in the nineteenth century, the high Catholic clergy in the United States became politically threatened by the socio-cultural makeup of their newly arrived flock from Europe and Canada. In particular, these migrants spoke a diversity of languages. In our case, the bishop of the Diocese of Portland proceeded to assign *anglophone* priests to Franco-national parishes. Francos and their leaders eventually gathered their courage and refused. Further, they embarked on a ten-year struggle to keep control of their parish properties and funds. The bishop claimed that he alone had the legal right to all parish properties and monies. Francos sought legislative redress, then took their issue up the church hierarchy, eventually to the pope. They were excommunicated. Francos lost a major political battle that struck at the center of their cultural identity—*la perte de leur salut* (the loss of their eternal salvation). These excommunications inaugurated decades of shame that lowered the ceilings on Franco identity in Maine, which were repeated in Rhode Island in the 1920s with similar results, more guilt, and more shame.

In fact, with the entry into the twentieth century, Franco identity was assaulted by a series of attacks and events that pushed them back into their neighborhoods, their Little Canadas, and the safety of their kitchens and *sociétés* (clubs). Beginning with the 1920s, and for the next fifty years, the Ku Klux Klan found Franco-Catholics to be an easy target for their bigotry. In the 1920s an anti-language bill found fertile ground in the Maine Legislature and with a governor who was a KKK sympathizer. The law prohibited the teaching of subject matter in any language other than English in our public schools. It stayed on the books until 1976, when Franco legislators, led by Elmer Violette and Émilien Lévesque, were able to persuade their colleagues to recognize the injustice and strike down the offensive law.

Public-school authorities then invented ways to discourage French from being spoken on school grounds or in school corridors: Being moved to the end of lunch lines, writing hundreds of times on the blackboard that no French will be spoken, as well as other shame-based inventions fashioned from ignorance. French could be spoken in the classroom, where it was taught as a "foreign" language by teachers who had received teaching certificates from institutions that had chosen to ignore our presence. The results were predictable. Research over the last twenty years has clearly demonstrated that learning and using two languages simultaneously is beneficial to

Ku Klux Klan hood from Saco, Maine, c. 1925[3]
Franco-American Centre, Univesity of Maine (Orono)
Courtesy of Yvon Labbé & Lisa Desjardins Michaud

both languages and, moreover, beneficial to the learner. The anti-language law, given the size of the Franco population in Maine, was essentially an anti-French law. It further demeaned and diminished the public voice of Francos. It added another ceiling of prejudice, which created further invisibility for our community, as its members sought to keep succeeding generations out of harm's way, out of reach of psychological assaults on Franco identity.

We accommodated. We changed our names. Boileau for some became an unrecognizable translation. So did Vaillancourt, Boisvert, Pinette, Savoy, as did so many others. The attributes of our identity—our culture and language—were further undermined by wars and the Great Depression—*la Crise*. It was a period of time when Francos could have produced leaders who could have been successful in the

Maine political arena and—with that—overcome the negative socio-political forces that were keeping us as *petits pains* (little breads). During the first fifty years of the twentieth century, Francos should have taken their places as managers of the "bakery"—*la boulangerie*. It did not happen.

Names such as Bérubé, Béliveau, Dutremble, and Violette were candidates for the posts of governor and congressperson. No success! A Proulx came close to occupying the post of full bishop. No success there, either. Then, with the onset of the Great Depression and World War II, Francos were finding that they were no longer able to support two systems of education out of working-class wages. By the 1960s their bilingual schools had, for the most part, disappeared. Their societies became increasingly moribund and, worse, drinking clubs. I believe many of those societies, formally serving as protective ramparts, became stifling cages without exits. By the 1960s Francos were experiencing another conquest, another exile. Another identity, another face other than their own was being imposed. Ignorant of our contributions, our literature and folklore, our history, our cultural and language assets, the public education system had nearly succeeded in erasing us from the public place.

As the 1960s marched in, we had become mostly silent, colorless, and hidden. A shame-based education and socialization process fed the silent invisibility. And complicit in all this was an indifferent public university system entrenched in its 100-plus years of ignorance regarding this community, which makes up 30 to 40 percent of Maine's population. It is then understandable that books—published following Franco stirrings of the early 1970s—wore names that reflected this situation—titles such as *Quiet Presence,* the *Chinese of the East,* and *Les Nègres Blancs d'Amériques* (America's White Niggers)—unflattering as they were. Maine history and Maine literature texts also were published by university professors that did not recognize or include the 30 to 40 percent of the state that is Franco. Some Franco community groups were discussing class-action suits for institutional discrimination. In the early 1970s a publication entitled *Le FAROG Forum* emerged from a student and community group at the University of Maine. The group challenged the traditional engrained attitudes and products put forward by faculty and the Franco community. This kind of activism began to achieve some results. In the late 1980s a re-edition of a previously Franco-less anthology of Maine writers was published with "newly found" Franco authors.[4] There have been other changes for the better since, with the installation of more enlightened administrations and new initiatives dealing with Maine Franco-Americans. But the proof of ownership of our heritage, its history, culture, and language, will be in the eating of the pudding. Will it be authentic, will it taste like us, or will we be served another cultural uniform with further "McDonaldization"?

Renowned Acadian writer Antonine Maillet tells us that it takes a thousand years to kill a culture, a hundred years to kill a word: "On est pas fort, mais on est pas mort!" (We're not strong, but we ain't dead yet!) In spite of my words, there is yet hope. *Un réveil* (a wakeup) has to take place, responsibility for ourselves has to be assumed, and we must insist on participation within our identity. It's the only one we have. If we continue to wear another's identity, we can never hope to be as magnificent in it as the real owners. We must reclaim our history, our culture, and its language, as well as our voice, and rid ourselves of the shame-based masks. Then will we be able to take our place, with our identity, with full appurtenance and participation in this democracy and its institutions. The latest assault on our identity by "English only" advocates was successfully repulsed by Francos in 1998.

We are openly finding and reconnecting with our cultural backbone where we really live and create: "Only preferred models need apply or speak up" will no longer be our manacles. Moreover, regarding language, Madame Maillet says that we have but one authentic choice, and that is: "de parler avec la langue qu'on a dans la bouche" (to express ourselves with our own voice). Prior to meeting Antonine Maillet, *Le FAROG Forum*, in 1974, had already chosen its motto: "Afin d'être en pleine possession de ses moyens" (Be in full command of one's own tools of self-expression). An inspired choice. That motto was the beginning of our seeing ourselves as shapers of ourselves and our environment, and not as *petits pains*. That motto is the beginning of our being perceived and perceiving ourselves as an important resource possessing an important cultural and language capital.

We may yet have a part in shaping Maine and its future in a proactive manner. It is vastly superior to the cultural uniforms and the "McDonaldization"—millions served looking and tasting all the same—that had been tailored for us. I believe that within our Franco identity, we will make the highest quality contribution to our community and our society. There are currently a number of Franco-related initiatives underway at Maine colleges and universities. As these purportedly deal with our language and culture, it is important that community Francos maintain a constant dialogue with these same initiatives. As the owners, the least we can expect is that these Franco-American initiatives reflect authentically who we are, and not who they are.

Rhea Côté Robbins, Yvon Labbé, and Jim Bishop at Le Centre Franco-Américain, Orono, Maine, 1992. Photograph from the Franco-American Centre, University of Maine at Orono

In conclusion, as Franco-Americans shed the *petits pains* mindset, rebuild a shame-based identity into one that is assertive, creative, productive, and useful, break through the historically prescribed ceilings and their impoverishing limits, decolonize ourselves and push for access to the highest levels of institutions, and put to work cultural tools and a belief system honed over more than a 1,000 years, then will our historical invisibility cease to loom as a shadow over Maine. It is also then that future generations will have access to the accumulated wisdom of this community and reclaim ancestry and our full participation in this democracy within our identity. We deserve it, and Maine deserves us. We, Franco-American citizens, also love and want our full measure of life, liberty, and the pursuit of happiness—within our identity, of course. *Excusez-là*.

1 A version of this essay was originally published in 1999. Yvon Labbé, "It's time for Franco-Americans to Rise," *Lewiston Sun Journal,* 5 December 1999.
2 Ames.
3 Leroy "Bud" Waco, a retired builder from Saco, found several KKK hoods in the attic of a home that he was remodeling. He sent one of them to the Franco-American Centre at the University of Maine, where it is on display. He also sent a report about Saco and the KKK.
4 The first edition was Robert Lecker and Kathleen Brown's *An Anthology of Maine Literature*, which was published in 1982; the revised edition was Jeff Fischer's *Maine Speaks: An Anthology of Maine Literature* in 1989.

PHOTO-DOCUMENTARY: FRANCO-AMERICAN WORK TRADITIONS

Jere DeWaters
Portland, Maine

These two photographs are from the exhibit and booklet, *The Franco-American Work Experience, Lewiston-Auburn, Maine, 1994*. Funded by a grant from the Maine Arts Commission, this documentary project focused on twenty different large and small enterprises that have traditionally employed Franco-Americans, as well as those that are owned by Franco-Americans. The exhibition focused on many facets—work environments, daily tasks, making things, family connections, social environments, and in many cases, skill and stamina. The study resulted in a portfolio of thirty black-and-white photographs for the Franco-American Collection at the University of Southern Maine's Lewiston-Auburn College.

Émile Lacasse, Jr., brushing egg wash on the tourtières at Lacasse's Bakery, Lewiston, Maine, 1994
Photograph by Jere DeWaters

Tourtière (pork pie) was traditionally served in French-Canadian homes on Christmas Eve after midnight mass. In the days before refrigeration, families would wait until cold weather to slaughter their livestock, making meat pies a seasonal specialty. Today, *tourtière* is prepared year-round but still serves as a traditional Christmas feature.

Bob Pelletier preparing to make boudin,
E. W. Mailhot Sausage Company, Lewiston, Maine, 1994
Photograph by Jere DeWaters

Boudin or blood sausage is a traditional Franco-American specialty made from pig's blood, milk, lard, onions, and spices. As part of the thrifty farm economy, nothing in the butchering process was wasted.

A QUÉBEC SOLDIER IN MAINE[1]

Barry Rodrigue
Bath, Maine

In the autumn of 1991 I got a frantic call from Forest Friends Nursery School in Montville. Their administrator told me that my gravestone had arrived. Half the kids were asking the teacher who had died, half were asking who was going to die, one little boy had peed on the packing crate, and another had locked herself in the broom closet until the gravestone would go away. The school administrator told me that I could pick it up anytime, the sooner the better. I quickly drove from Belfast to collect the stone. Over that winter I kept the two hundred pounds of granite in the trunk of my car, and the extra 91 kilograms of weight helped me through some really icy spots on Route 143. I waited for spring thaw to place it in the Orono cemetery. It wasn't my stone. It belonged to my great-great-great uncle, Georges DesRochers, who had been a soldier in the Civil War.

I'd never been particularly interested in the Civil War in high school history classes. All our ancestors had been in Canada, so what was the point? Then one Memorial Day I noticed a corroded plaque from the Grand Army of the Republic on my great-great grandfather's grave. So I went to the Maine State Archives and looked through their Civil War index. Surprisingly enough, I found over a dozen relatives who had come down from Canada to join the Union army. It turned out that one of them had been accused of desertion. That began my quest to get the true story and a memorial for *mon onc'* Georges.

The DesRochers had come to Canada in the 1600s and settled around Trois Rivières. Some of them moved to the Beauce in the 1820s, then to Maine in the 1830s. Michel DesRochers and Mathilde Saucier first settled with their children in Waterville, where Father Moïse Fortin found them among the small colony of *canadiens* when he visited in 1840. The family moved to the Forks in the 1840s, then settled in Orono by 1855. Michel was a professional hunter and trapper, but had become infirm. The sons supported the family by woods work in the thriving timber industry on the Penobscot River. When Fort Sumter fell in 1861, four of them enlisted in the Union army.

Such an enlistment of foreign nationals in Yankee regiments wasn't unusual, and the Union army overall included up to 30,000 French Canadians.[2] Maine recruited

Photograph from the attic of the Grenier–Rodrigue family home in Augusta, Maine, and believed to be one of the DesRochers brothers during the Civil War.
Photograph courtesy of Peter Grenier, Gardiner, Maine

more soldiers on a per capita basis than any other state. The bounties paid to enlistees by the local and state governments nearly bankrupted the state treasury, it taking decades to pay back the bonds issued to cover the bounties. Women and children had to take on men's work to supply the Union and themselves. It is tempting to believe that Michel and Mathilde's republican sentiments also motivated their children to enlist during their adopted country's hour of need.

Georges DesRochers enlisted in Bangor in Company I of the 18th Maine Volunteer Infantry in 1862, as did his brothers, Ovide and Charles. James, another brother, enlisted in the 11th Maine Infantry, which contained the biggest men of any Civil War regiment–woods and mill workers from the upper Penobscot River Valley. Even the DesRochers cousins in Waterville enlisted: Henry and Charles W. DesRochers joined the 3rd Maine Infantry, which met with disaster in the advanced position of the Peach Orchard at Gettysburg. The kid brothers, Louis and Henry, took on men's work to help the family. And ironically, many of the DesRochers' "Cajun" cousins who had migrated down the Mississippi in the previous century fought for the Confederacy in the regiments of the "Louisiana Tigers" during this terrible war.

Upon reaching Washington, D.C., the army commanders realized that the federal capital was vulnerable to Confederate attack. The 18th Maine was one of the infantry regiments retained to fire heavy artillery pieces and was renamed the 1st Maine Heavy Artillery. For two years they guarded Washington from behind their large-bore Rodman guns. Lee's thrust into the Union at Gettysburg proved the wisdom of this garrison force. However, after Lee's failure to carry the war into the Union, General Grant began his move into the Confederacy and called the defenders of the capital into action.

During the assault on Richmond in 1864, the heavy artillery regiments in Washington, D.C., were brought into battle as infantry units. By this time some of the war-torn regiments had been whittled down to as few as a hundred men. These veteran combat units were amazed to see 1,800-man regiments march into action dressed in their red-trimmed artillery uniforms and under the crossed cannon of their battle flags. Not a small amount of resentment was directed at these regiments, as if they themselves had made the decision to "loaf" in the capital during the first half of the war. The artillery regiments resolved to prove themselves.

The first engagement took place at the Battle of Laurel Hill on 19 May 1864 near Spottsylvania Court House. Georges and his brothers Ovide received gunshot wounds and each had a leg amputated on the battlefield. Georges survived the first amputation to his knee and then a second operation to his thigh in July 1864. However, Ovide died of wounds at Emery Hospital in Washington, D.C., a month later and was buried at the newly designated Arlington National Cemetery. Ovide left his wife Susan Gagné and their four-year-old daughter Emma in Bangor.

Amazingly, Charles DesRochers was not wounded. He had entered Company I as a corporal and rose through the ranks to become their quartermaster sergeant. Charles even survived the infantry charge of 18 June 1864 at the Siege of Petersburg, where the 1st Maine Heavy Artillery "...made for itself a record it did not seek." Their regimental historian described how "...the earth was literally torn with iron and lead...the field became a burning, seething, crashing, hissing hell...the men involuntarily pulled their cap visors down over their eyes and advanced against the storm."[3] The 1st Maine Heavy Artillery suffered the worst casualties of any regiment in any single battle of the Civil War. Indeed, their losses surpassed the renowned "Charge of the Light Brigade" of a decade earlier in the Crimea. Charles died in 1876, working as a lumberman in Pennsylvania. He is buried with his wife, Jennie, under a hemlock tree in Mt. Hope Cemetery in Bangor.

Georges, however, was not as fortunate. After the second amputation, he went on furlough to visit his family for Christmas in Orono. Georges' seven-year-old nephew, Lonnie Rodrigue, sold candy (made by his mother) on the Maine Central Railroad, and it must have been difficult for Lonnie to recognize his Uncle Georges when they met in a railroad car one cold winter morning in 1864. Georges had been 5 feet 7 inches (171 centimeters) tall with gray eyes and black hair, but the war had changed him dramatically. His leg became infected again, and he had to undergo a third amputation. Not being able to report back to his regiment in time, the U.S. marshal was dispatched from Bangor to arrest him as a deserter. Georges wrote his commander that he was sick and could not report for duty in person; instead he "reported by mail" until his death at his mother's home on 20 February 1865.

Their elderly mother, Mathilde, was not able to support herself, so she received Georges' pension until she passed away in 1898. Her surviving children moved away to the West. As the family trickled away from Maine, Uncle Georges' grave was forgotten on the banks of the Stillwater River.

A cloud hung over his grave. I discovered that it has remained unmarked—whether due to the family's poverty and migration or because of the "taint" of implied desertion. So I began correspondence with the U.S. Veterans Administration, cleared up the oversight, and finally received Uncle Georges' gravestone. The 12th of April 1991 was the 131st anniversary of the start of the Civil War, and Uncle Georges finally got more than just a red carnation on that day.[4]

(On 11–12 April 1992, Barry Rodrigue organized the conference, Beyond the French and Indian Wars: The Impact of Wartime on the Franco-American and Native American Communities, which was sponsored by the Franco-American Centre at the University of Maine, Orono, and the Penobscot Nation. The dedication of Georges DesRochers' gravestone was one of the conference activities).

1 A version of this article appeared in 1992. Barry Rodrigue, "Overdue Commemoration for a Civil War Soldier," in the *Kennebec Journal* (Augusta, Maine), 28 March 1992, p. A-9. Another version of the article plus reports on the conference, Beyond the French and Indian Wars, appeared in the *FAROG Forum* (Orono, Maine) in 1992–93.

2 This estimate of the number of Canadians in the Union army was made in a fit of postwar patriotism, so probably half this number would be more accurate.

3 Shaw.

4 A file on the conference Beyond the French and Indian Wars is held at the Univesity of Southern Maine's Franco-American Collection at Lewiston-Auburn College.

THE SILENT PLAYGROUND

Ross and Judy Paradis
Frenchville, Maine

The "Silent Playground" depicts the discrimination against native-born and majority-population descendants of French Canadians and Acadians in the St. John Valley by the English-speaking authorities, especially in the schools in the extreme northern part of Aroostook. The effort to eradicate a language and a culture was well intentioned, but misinformed at best, and cruel, psychologically damaging, and long-lasting at worst. The attempts at linguistic and cultural cleansing were sanctioned by the government of Maine and its Department of Education. The anti-French movement ranks as one of the darkest chapters in the history of the state.

On April Fools' Day, 1919, the Maine State Legislature, greatly influenced by the Ku Klux Klan, passed a bill that prohibited the use of French in public schools outside of high-school French classes. This bill was one more manifestation of the paranoia that gripped the WASP establishment in the state, which was bent on suppressing the perceived threat posed by any group of immigrants that did not fit the narrow confines of the White-Anglo-Saxon Protestant model.

Naturally, the *émigrés* coming down from Québec seeking work in the textile mills of central and southern Maine were not well received, not only because they were seen as taking jobs away from U.S. citizens but also because they spoke only French and worshipped in the Roman Catholic faith. Furthermore, they were perceived as being staunchly resistant to any kind of assimilation into the "Great Melting Pot" by setting up *petits canadas* in the major textile centers of Lewiston, Waterville, and Augusta. Never mind that the massive infusion of cheap new laborers was needed to quench the thirst of the thriving mills in those urban centers and that the French-Canadian population brought a dogged work ethic that was ideal for the demands of those mills, the increasing French Canadians were *personae non gratae*.

The discrimination of the 1919 law, which today's more enlightened and sensitive society could very well label linguistic and cultural "cleansing," was not limited to the prospering textile centers. Its roots also extended to the vast rural areas of the state—all the way up to the St. John Valley in northern Maine, where French Acadians were not a minority but an overwhelming majority.

Starting in 1785 a steady stream of Acadians with family names such as Cyr, Daigle, and Hébert set up farms on the southern side of the St. John River. These were refugees of the Grand Dérangement thirty years before. There is no denying that the order from British Governor Lawrence to destroy the Acadian settlement at Grand Pré, Nova Scotia, in 1755, was ethnic cleansing. The strategy is one that unfortunately has been used throughout history to eliminate various peoples. In the sad story of the Acadians, homes were burned to the ground to eliminate the possibility of the rightful owners of the property ever reclaiming their birthright. In more recent times, Nazi attempts to annihilate the Jews and other "undesirable" populations of Europe in the 1930s and 1940s, as well as the Serbian attempt to purge Albanians from Kosovo in the 1990's, are analogous to the systematic elimination of the Acadians from their prosperous enclave 200 years earlier.

Men, women, and children were separated and shipped out from Grand Pré on different vessels, a move that made future reunification very difficult, if not impossible. Thousands of the expelled died from starvation or disease brought about by the abominable conditions aboard ship. Those who survived the ordeal were dispersed down the Eastern Seaboard—all the way to the bayous of Louisiana. Some Acadians managed to escape the English troops and flee west to New Brunswick and Québec. A few even were relocated to France, the land of their ancestors.

The Acadian tragedy is a cruel reminder of the fact that even the most pacific and neutral peoples are too often the victims of old hostilities between nations. The Acadians had gone from being French citizens to English subjects. They were a non-violent people who did not want to swear allegiance to any country. They wanted to love one another, raise their children, practice their religion, and be left alone.

The original Acadian residents on the south shore of the St. John River were still very much tied to Canada. Statehood for Maine would occur only in 1820, but—even then—the northern boundary of the state was not officially determined. It was only in 1842, when the Webster-Ashburton Treaty was signed in Washington, D.C., that the inhabitants of the growing villages that later became Madawaska, Van Buren, Frenchville, and Fort Kent realized that their allegiance was now to be to the United States and not to English-controlled Canada.

Once the border dispute was settled, the residents on the Maine side of St. John Valley did their best to embrace United States citizenship and get involved in the new way of life. In what must have been a frenzied rush to manifest their now unquestioned allegiance, the village of Van Buren, itself named after President Martin Van

Buren, chose other famous names for many of its streets: Washington, Jefferson, Harrison, and McKinley.

Other towns honored Maine political figures that had played a major, positive role in the St. John Valley. After being known as Dionne Plantation and Chataqua in its early days, the large area between Madawaska and Fort Kent was renamed after Major William Dickey, a distinguished and influential figure from downstate who had moved to the valley and had represented that northern district very well in Augusta. The town's new name, Dickeyville, was indeed a fitting tribute to the good major who had stood up for the rights of the fledgling Maine communities in his days as state representative. Then, one evening, the selectmen of Dickeyville voted to change the name of their town again, not as an affront to the beloved and popular Dickey but rather as recognition of the town's overwhelmingly French population. Thus, Dickeyville became forevermore Frenchville.

Even as it was making a sincere effort to become civically and politically correct, the St. John Valley desired to maintain its distinctive character. Religion, family, language, and love of the land were still the pillars of their Acadian culture. Devoutly Catholic, the residents of the valley looked to French Canada and even to France and other French-speaking European countries to send priests and nuns to serve in the missions and parishes that were being founded along the international border. For example, the legendary Father Charles Sweron, a native of Belgium, became the first pastor of Ste. Luce Parish in Frenchville in 1843 and shepherded his flock for decades. Likewise, the Daughters of Wisdom, a missionary order from France, answered the call for service in the valley, sending four pioneering sisters to Ste. Agathe, where they proceeded to build a convent school and a medical clinic that were so much needed in the area. The older churches that dominate the landscape today owe their design and beauty to architects from Québec. The church, parish hall, and convent school were as indispensable to townspeople as its civic institutions. In fact, these institutions often merged, but later developed conflict with state institutions, especially the Department of Education.

In the last half of the nineteenth century and the early years of the twentieth century, the state worked out a unique agreement with the convent schools, which were authorized to deliver state-approved curricula within their walls—in the absence of public schools. As a result, these state-approved schools were allowed to use the early part of the school day to teach religion or ethics. The administrative staff was exclusively religious personnel, and the teaching positions were filled mainly by nuns, priests, or brothers, with a few lay people, usually women who wished to supplement their family income. Even after the state built public schools, religious personnel filled many of the administrative and teaching positions, and religion was still taught. The state turned a blind eye to this clear violation of the separation of church and state, preferring to tolerate the *status quo*, which seemed to be working quite well. However, in the early 1970s Jehovah's Witness parents complained to state officials that the Catholic religion was being taught in their children's schools (Maine School Administrative District 33—Frenchville and Ste. Agathe). So, the Department of Education finally forbade this long-lasting practice of religious teaching in the valley's public schools.

The Department of Education had also been tolerant of the use of French in the public schools, as long as the students were making reasonable progress in the acquisition of English. It was slow going in the first decades after the Webster-Ashburton Treaty, when local teachers' command of English was mediocre. But as the English proficiency of the teaching staff improved, the students accelerated their progress in English. Veteran teachers with strong bilingual skills and knowledge of language acquisition wisely used the French-language skills that the students had acquired at home to facilitate the transference of those skills to their learning of English. Children were allowed to speak their native French in school until they could perform in English. Those who were comfortable in French and had been praised for their use of their native language were the most receptive to English and invariably went on to excel in their second language, without losing their first language or feeling inferior while using it.

Then, there came the misguided law of 1919, which was more about eradicating French than promoting excellence in English. In developing rules to implement the law, the Department of Education and its agents became virtual language police, often insensitive or even brutal in their anti-French crusade. The horror stories repeated themselves throughout the valley and spawned resistance to authority, feelings of inferiority, and lack of motivation in learning any language, especially the one that had been forcibly imposed—English. Instead of bringing about excellence in English, the new order bred resentment and mediocrity. It often alienated the homes, where children had been nurtured in French with all the positive feelings of self-worth, from the schools, where these same children were made to reject their language and the comfort that had come with it.

Although they knew deep down that what the Department of Education was imposing on their schools was misguided, psychologically detrimental, and educationally counterproductive, many teachers reluctantly accepted the new order and became the enforcers of the edicts from Augusta. A minority resisted, as best they could, without bringing the wrath of authorities down on themselves.

Former educator Bernadette Sirois Charette, still mentally sharp at age ninety-two, remembers it all so well: "He came down on her like a ton of bricks," she said, recounting an incident involving a colleague, Rita Violette. Ms. Violette had discovered, during English spelling, that if a child got stuck on a word, the student's knowledge of French could be most helpful. "Think French," she would say, and out would pop the correct spelling of the word. What a find! What a coup! She was ecstatic that this discovery was facilitating her students' ability to learn, using what they already knew—the age-old building on the child's knowledge base.

However, Superintendent of Schools Charles O'Connell, an *anglophone*, was not so thrilled. He gave poor Rita a severe tongue-lashing and forbade her to do that again. She was not to let her students think that there was any value to the beautiful French language spoken in the home, at church, and in the business community. O'Connell was adamant in his belief that hanging onto French made students stupid and that it had to be eradicated at all costs. He joined the others in adopting the position that French hinders the proper acquisition of English.

Students developed some remarkable coping skills when faced with the dictatorial imposition of the Department of Education and its agents. Secret groups sprang up to systematically keep their use of English in school at a minimum, never volunteering answers in class and answering only when questioned directly. "You deny me my native language: I'll be damned if I will readily adopt yours"—such was their secret code.

Modern science, especially research in language acquisition has totally dispelled the fallacy promoted by O'Connell and so many others like him in the education establishment of the state. Two-way immersion programs in the schools of Madawaska and Van Buren, based on successful models in Ontario and New Brunswick, have proven that the stronger the knowledge and use of French among the students, then the better will be the acquisition of English. After all, the English language is indebted to French for 54 percent of its vocabulary words, a fact that once inspired a French humorist to say: "English is just badly pronounced French."

Unfortunately, the reign of terror that prevailed for half a century in Maine wreaked havoc on the learning of many French students. In order to survive in school, they had to discard their native language or risk flunking, being mislabeled as retarded, or—at worst—being expelled, no matter the age. All this at a time of life when frustration and resentment also could manifest themselves in so many disruptive ways.

Administrators like O'Connell had zero tolerance or patience for the monolingual five year olds entering school. Teachers were told that they could be fired on the spot if they did not insist that their students discard their French tongue. Sadly, old fallacies regarding the acquisition of languages continue to this day in some schools. It's a daily battle to manage French immersion programs when unenlightened administrators and school board members reject the findings of science and the successes of well-run language programs. Heaven forbid that a child is diagnosed as having a learning disability! The question often asked of the parents is: "Do you speak French in front of your children?" The corresponding advice is to cease and desist the practice immediately. Are there no learning-disabled in strictly monolingual schools? What about the fifty-two or so French-speaking countries? Are all their students learning-disabled? Hardly!

In our parents' generation, adults spoke English at a third-grade level, but they conversed in French throughout the day and conducted business very well in that language. To ask them to model English to their children as they progressed beyond that level was not only ridiculous, but also a complete misuse of the parents' talents. They often spoke a beautiful and sophisticated French that enabled them to converse with the French-speaking world and benefit from the rich literature written in French. A wise and practical use of existing talents would have been to encourage the parents to continue expanding their children's knowledge of French by using the language at home and delegating the learning of English to the schools—and let there be no misunderstanding and friction between the two!

Lucky for many of us now fluently bilingual in English and French that our parents ignored the racist and linguistically deficient advice thrown at them by misguided educators and insisted that we learn both languages. Many young parents today also insist on the same language goals, often teaching French first to their young children, knowing full well that they will learn English soon enough and that the process will be made easier by their prior knowledge of French.

The half century of suppression of the French language continued unabated in educational institutions all over the valley. In Ste. Agathe a brand-new kindergarten teacher, Sister Jean Marc (Thérèse Ayotte), a native of the area, found herself in the strange predicament of having to post children at the windows and doors to warn her if administrators were coming. They would surely misunderstand her having to use French to bring many children to learn English. A high percentage of her students started school knowing only French, since many U.S. men would marry Canadian women from the French-speaking areas of New Brunswick (right across the river) and Province of Quebec (only a half hour away). These intermarriages provided a steady stream of French-speakers. In addition, until the late 1950s, there were few English-language radio and television stations. Those who had radios and TV sets invariably chose the closer and clearer French-Canadian stations.

The majority of men and women teachers of the day were bilingual. How unfortunate that, instead of being allowed to teach to the needs of their students, they were threatened with loss of position if they failed to greet their students in English only! The 1919 law wreaked havoc with the shy, inhibited, scared monolingual children, and what a guilt-trip was laid on their parents. A huge problem was created where none existed before.

Only three years out of high school when she started teaching, Sister Jean Marc still had vivid memories of her own survival under a repressive regime that she was expected to support. She remembered the many children who had quit before eighth grade because school was so frustrating and frightening. Attending a one-room schoolhouse next to her home, she sometimes would count up to forty students playing in her yard during lunch, since they could easily hear the school bell and make it back to class on time. Adult supervision was not required.

She also remembered the infamous ticket system used to punish those who insisted on speaking French. All the students were given fifteen tickets each at the beginning of the week. Whenever they were caught speaking French, they had to give up a ticket to the students catching them in the act. Many children would not join group play for fear of uttering a word or phrase in French and being punished by the forfeiture of a ticket.

Whitey, an underachieving little bully, would win a prize week after week for accumulating the most tickets. One day when the teacher arrived in class after lunch, she found most of the girls in tears. She insisted on being told what was wrong. Finally a little girl stood up and blurted in French: "Whitey hurt us in our crotch!" Indeed, the young ruffian would come up to the girls with a stick, put the piece of wood between their legs, and pull up until they cried out in pain—in French, of course. *Et voilà*, that's how he would accumulate the most tickets! That particular day he had gotten greedy and was caught. The hated ticket system quickly disappeared from the school after that incident.

Grand Isle and Lille schools had their own unique version of the ticket scenario, according to publisher Don Lévesque of the *St. John Valley Times*. In the 1950s, fifth and sixth graders were allotted a certain amount of "chips" that consisted of rolls of perforated tickets:

> You added to your stack of "chips" by catching a classmate speaking French, sticking out your hand, and saying "Bewyse!" She or he then had to give you a "chip." Students with a certain number of "chips" on Friday afternoon had no homework on the weekend. Others, like me, who lacked the required number of "chips" always had homework on the weekend.

This "chips" system also led to many quarrels after each recess or lunch period. Small groups of students gathered around the nun's desk with one screaming: "I bewysed him and he didn't give me a chip!"

> "I didn't speak French!" shouted another.
> "Yes, you did!"
> "What did I say?"
> "You said, 'Viens icitte!'"
> "BEWYSE!"
> "No, sir, that's not fair! I only said what you said!"
> "You spoke French—I heard you."

Lévesque says: "The nun was the final judge. Some students, and it seems to me they were mostly girls, would be dangerously enthusiastic about 'bewysing' everybody for very minor transgressions. The combined reward of no homework and kissing up to the teacher was irresistible for some students.

> It was not until I became an adult and was thinking back on this experience that I realized that "Bewyse" was in fact "Be wise"—as in "Be wise! Speak English."

Lévesque also remembers having to write "I will not speak French" many, many times on the chalkboard in elementary school. He has had the last word as a newspaperman, however, writing a weekly column entitled, "Mon cinq cents" (My Five Cents) blending the local *patois* with English as he expounds on his favorite topics.

Many boys turned around the drudgery of copying lines by applying their native ingenuity, simultaneously using three or four chalks or pencils at a time when the teacher was not looking. Some perfected the art to the point where all the lines looked very much alike.

The students would adapt very well, too, when the Department of Education inspectors showed up during recess to make sure that the "rule" was enforced. When a black car pulled into the schoolyard and the two black-suited men emerged, the students would stop speaking French, but rather than switch to English they would continue playing in silence. The whole yard would become a silent playground. One wonders if those inspectors ever wondered why no sound emanated from the children at play.

It was in 1969 that the fifty-year "English Only" law was erased from the books. Representatives Émilien Lévesque of Madawaska and Léon Lebel of Van Buren joined Senator Elmer Violette, also of Van Buren, in presenting a bill that would finally put an end to the racist law that had spawned frustration, anger, and psychological scars among several generations of students.

Violette even gave part of his speech on this topic to the senate in French. After his remarks *en français*, he told his colleagues: "Imagine you are a five-year-old child and you had to listen to a language you had never heard before. How much of what I said did you understand?" After his speech, the senate voted unanimously to repeal the "English Only" law. Lévesque and Lebel were equally persuasive in the house, which also voted overwhelmingly to end the reign of terror on Maine's Franco-American students.

The resounding vote in the legislature ushered in a period of reconciliation, innovative language programs, and sound methodology for preserving the regional French language while acquiring English. The results of this more sensitive and reasonable approach have led to pride in heritage and dramatic results in producing very competent bilingual students, who take no back seat in English proficiency to those schooled strictly in a monolingual setting. In fact, the former often become the best students in both English and French.

Since 1969 there have been very few challenges to the new law, which treated the regional French language as an asset that was worthy of expansion beyond just traditional high-school French programs. Furthermore, it treated French as being instrumental in fostering positive attitudes towards the English language and any other language offered. Only Representative Tom Shields of Auburn dared present, in the late 1990s, a newer form of "English Only" legislation. His bill met with stiff resistance among the Franco-Americans in the legislature and even among the majority of *anglophone* lawmakers. After a passionate hearing, Shield's proposed legislation was resoundingly defeated in committee.

Meanwhile, also in the late 1960s, something else was happening in the St. John Valley schools. Dr. Patrick Babin (curriculum director for the Madawaska, Frenchville, and Ste. Agathe schools—MSAD 33) had come to the realization that, despite the strictest enforcement of "English Only," scores in English had been plummeting for years, children were unhappy, and the dropout rate was alarming. Obviously, something was very wrong.

The recipient of a Ford Fellowship, Babin decided to explore similar bilingual populations all over the country. The fellowship included a generous traveling budget that took him to bilingual states like Massachusetts, California, Texas, Hawaii, and Louisiana, even allowing him a very beneficial stay at Harvard University. During his year away studying bilingualism and multilingualism, Babin sent back weekly columns to the *Valley Times*, giving positive feedback to the people of the St. John Valley about the treasure that was still in their grasp but had been under attack for years.

Armed with sound pedagogical data and the very latest research, Babin approached the MSAD 33 Board of Directors, Superintendent J. Raymond Brennick, as well as school administrators and teachers to write an application for a federal grant under Title VII, on behalf of the district and the Madawaska School Department. Dr. Babin said he was shocked that the grant application was approved, since precedence and political clout favored the Spanish-English applications in the larger states of the Southwest and West. The grant to the St. John Valley school districts was the first major French-English bilingual program in the country. The rest is history!

The grant enabled the two school departments to conduct intensive workshops in the summer of 1969 for their faculty and administrators, as the first step in implementing the far-reaching language goals of the grant. These goals included attitude and self-image change, openness to new approaches in language teaching, the identification of leadership and creative skills, and a strong infusion of the teamwork necessary to deliver a truly bilingual program. It was foreseen that this program would enhance both the regional French of students and accelerate their learning of English, the second language. Sensitive training, conducted by nationally recognized experts, proved somewhat painful and confusing to many of the instructors and administrators, who were literally being asked to abandon the *modus operandi* of several years, under the old "English Only" law, and embark on a new radical, but very promising, endeavor aimed at producing more competent students in two languages.

At the end of the training session in late July 1969, a remarkable transformation had taken place. There was a palpable *esprit de corps* as well as a growing can-do attitude among the attendees, who had started the session with long-entrenched attitudes about the French language and culture. After some intense soul-searching, the faculties of the different schools were united in their willingness to give the new program their best efforts. A veteran language teacher, who assessed the situation very well, uttered the most poignant comment that summarized the weeks of training: "I thank God that I am now given the chance to undo all the damage I did for so many years trying to teach language skills under a faulty system," she remarked.

The rather generous federal grant was for a transitional program, whereby the participating schools were allowed to use French in their respective classes to facilitate comprehension of the subject matter and a gradual improvement of English. Instead of suppressing their native French language, students were now encouraged to use it to hone their English language skills. Although the ultimate goal was English proficiency, the PACE-FABRIC Program had as a pleasant side product a dramatic turnaround in the students' attitudes about being French and speaking French.

An increasingly positive self-image and validation of their primary language made them thankful for this new respect and consequently more apt to maintain and improve their French language, while consciously and willingly improving their command of English. The old defiant code: "You deny me my native language, I'll be damned if I will readily adopt yours" was replaced by "You respect me and my language, and I will respect yours and try to learn it well."

A sharp, dramatic rise in the students' English scores soon manifested itself in the Madawaska, Frenchville, and Ste. Agathe schools, a transformation that surprised and thrilled students, parents, teachers, and administrators alike, and drew laudatory assessments from the federal agencies. The Title VII program had succeeded way beyond the original expectations. The success of PACE-FABRIC encouraged the St. John Valley school districts to pursue other federal grants to promote bilingualism among their students. MSAD 24 (Van Buren and Grand Isle) teamed up with MSAD 33 in another successful application and resulting grant.

Then, these two MSADs joined the Madawaska School Department, in the late 1990s, to apply for a two-way immersion federal grant to implement a program similar to the very successful Ontario models, used not only in that province but also extensively in New Brunswick. Although MSAD 27 in Fort Kent was invited to join in the application, the district's superintendent and school board declined, just as they had in the 1970s and 1980s. To this day that district lags behind the other valley entities in the effectiveness of their limited French programs, much to the chagrin of many of their students who aspire to more challenging French curricula.

Receiving the approval of the federal agency for what became known as *L'Acadien du Haut St-Jean* (The Acadian of the Upper St. John) proved to be easier than approval in the three educational signatories to the grant. The Madawaska and Van Buren school committees overwhelmingly and enthusiastically approved the $5 million grant. However, MSAD 33 was influenced by "English Only" activists who mounted a negative, concerted effort to derail the program before it even started. The district's school board turned down the program by a one-vote majority.

Ironically, the Dr. Lévesque Elementary School in MSAD 33 had several teachers with French degrees and was best equipped to deliver the immersion program. Also, MSAD 33 was supposed to be the funding agency, as it had been for the earlier federally financed language programs. Moreover, Gil Albert, the writer of the grant and the eminently qualified director of the bilingual grant that had served both MSADs 33 and 24 so well, but which was in its last year, still maintained an office at the . Lévesque School and was slated to head the new program out of the same location.

After the MSAD 33 school board vote, the fate of *l'Acadien du Haut St-Jean* hung in the balance. Would the federal funds be cut back drastically? Or, even worse, would the Feds abort the process entirely? Fortunately, the program survived with full funding; the money that would have served three districts would now be expended in two districts—$5 million over five years. MSAD 24 became the funding agency, and the Madawaska School Department provided Albert a spacious office at its brand-new elementary school.

Frenchville and Ste. Agathe have not yet recovered from the divisive struggle between immersion proponents and the opponents of a program they badly misunderstood. Friendships were destroyed and family relationships seriously threatened. MSAD 33 could only watch from the sidelines as the immersion program flourished in neighboring districts, first at the elementary level, then at the middle- and high-school levels.

Most of the parents in MSAD 33 really wanted the program and felt let down by their elected officials and some administrators and teachers. Many wanted their district to allow their children to participate in immersion courses in nearby Madawaska. When the superintendent refused, some bought property in Madawaska, established a primary residence there, and then transferred their children to the Madawaska schools.

Recent articles in prominent news magazines have included research that backs up earlier studies of language acquisition and demonstrates why well-run immersion programs have been so successful. For example, in the 19 February 1996 issue of *Newsweek*, Patricia Kuhl of the University of Washington presented her extensive research on the subject. Her studies show that babies can be multilingual, if taught different languages simultaneously from birth: "A child taught a second language after the age of ten or so is unlikely ever to speak it as a native," she maintains.

In the first decade of the twenty-first century, after years of struggle to maintain the French culture and language in Maine, there is an ever-increasing pride in being of French ancestry, as well as a renaissance and strengthening of our ancestral language. Historical societies and clubs have rededicated themselves to the preservation of the French way of life. *Etre français et parler la langue, ça c'est quelque chose*![1] The Maine State Legislature now celebrates Franco-American Day at the State House every year, an all-day celebration that showcases the proud heritage of over 40 percent of the population of the state and is a great hit for both Francos and non-Francos. The event has done much to dispel the inferiority complex that has existed for too long among Franco-Americans and replaced it with a positive self-image. Finally, they can join the rest of the population of Maine as equals—the state is that much better for it.

1 Being French and speaking the language, now that's something!

MÉMÈRE (GRANDMOTHER)[1]

Raymond Luc Levasseur
Sanford, Maine

the blues say if you born under a bad sign you got trouble
you born in the shadow of the mills
you born near a river
and you got more trouble still

mémère walked thru that shadow
to work at 13
to work you understand
as a child
to breathe that dust
work that machine
& to find her husband
who'd been there since 13

an unlucky # you say?
no
French-Canadian French-speaking catholic
proud sensitive loving hardworking &
exploited

1 of 11 children
who had children
who took in other children &
bro & I
when the next generation of woman
went into mills & shoe factories

that alone should tell you something bout strength

she read the cards &
told the fortunes
for those with broken hearts
dismal jobs & uncertain futures

when urban renewal flattened their apt
they built a small house in the country
that was pleasant for a spell till
the mill caught up with pépère &
he'd breathe hard & shake & sometimes fall
in the chicken coop
then I'd come to lift him in my arms &
put him in the kitchen
where mémère cleaned him up &
rolled a bull durham
which she had to hold
cause his hands shook so much

she took him to the v.a.
but neither could stand the shock
of neglect
so he came home to die

the govt gave her the coffin flag &
$22 a month pension
not enuff for eye drops she'd say
then the little house was gone &
to avoid the poor house on the hill
she moved in with her daughter, my ma
who worked 2 jobs to keep the wolf
from the door

mémère burned the holy candle
when I was in 'nam &
put it out with relief

when I returned only
to light it again
the day I got out of prison

she loved all her children
holding each of us
to her bosom
over decades of time
thru each sickness
celebration &
bout with the blues

her dream was that
we'd finish school
("no quitting" she'd say)
& make the great escape
from the mills
which some did & some didn't
back home where women still
hold up half the sky
but without unions
on assembly lines
that boss says is for
"soft brains and nimble fingers"
makin circuit boards 'stead a shoes
with husbands more quick to split &
where stamps help feed the kids

she die while I was underground
the fbi hangin from trees
at catholic cementery
cause they knew I was close
to her
but I wasn't there
didn't even know she'd died

till some pig laid it on me
trying to pry out information

before death she'd been sick
with the feds at the docs
probing how much could she take
how many questions to ask
an old mill woman
of the docs
who'd received their flyer
with our kids on it
saying snitch if these kids
come to you sick

but all she said was
"I hope I see him before I die"
see—with her eyes filled with
glaucoma & cataracts & cornea trouble
damn near blind
pigs gone she'd retrieve
her magnifying glass &
look at the pictures
of underground children
I'd sent her
incl her namesake
simone eva

that she'd never met
but loved
cause we felt it
cross the shadows &
troubles
mémère's love
helped hold us strong.

1 "Mémère" was first published in *Hauling up the Morning*, Tim Blunk and Ray Levasseur, editors, (Trenton, New Jersey: Red Sea Press, 1990), pp. 117–21.

TOURTIÈRE (MEAT PIE)

Philomène Létourneau Simard
Lewiston, Maine

Diane Simard McKenney
Lewiston, Maine

Each family in Franco-America has a carefully guarded secret for making their *tourtières*. Luckily, one family from the Beauce is willing to share!

- 2 lbs. ground meat (pork/beef combo)
- 1/4 teaspoon nutmeg
- 1/4 teaspoon black pepper
- 1/2 cup chopped onion
- 1 cup water
- 1/4 teaspoon allspice
- 1 tablespoon salt
- 2 cups mashed potato

Cook all but the mashed potato together on top of stove for two hours. Add the cooked potato to the mix and let cool (allows flavors to blend). Make into pie.

Philomène Létourneau Simard was from the Beauce in Québec and moved to Lewiston, Maine, in the 1920s. Her grandchildren and great-grandchildren delighted in her *tourtières* and in the fudge that she could be counted on to bring to family get-togethers. She was also well loved for her exquisite sewing and quilting, a talent that was inherited by several of her grandchildren.

VOICING MÉMÈRE

Kristin Langellier
Orono, Maine

> We may feel superior to [grandmothers] because they are less well-educated or were old-fashioned (we like that as well); often we are taught not to take them seriously. So now when they are safely out of our lives, we use the memory of them to evoke nostalgia-less assimilated ethnicity, less complicated times, the security of ascribed relationships.[1]

For feminists concerned with women's lives and the subject of aging, the figure of the grandmother requires sustained analysis.[2] My project is to take grandmothers seriously, Franco-American grandmothers in particular, through a study of how daughters and granddaughters write *mémère* stories in *Le Forum,* a bilingual newspaper published at the University of Maine. I have argued that these stories arouse nostalgia for a more traditional ethnic past, the ideal of the patriarchal family, and the heroic mother as a cultural icon.[3] As the "traditional ethnic woman," the Franco-American *mémère* serves to guarantee "who we are" through the reproductive labor of producing children and the cultural labor of producing foods, religious rituals, holiday traditions, and family storytelling. *Mémères* and *mémère* stories reproduce the Franco-American family in the fusion of the father's story and mother's body: "You write what your father speaks, just as you eat what your mother cooks."[4] *Mémère* stories serve *la survivance,* a struggle for French ethnic survival in North America, by casting the grandmother as hero/ine in the fight for the preservation of a people and a past. But they also do much more: As storytelling across generations, they negotiate gender roles for Maine Franco-American women in the present and future.

If *mémère* stories speak the narrative of the fathers and sons, they are nonetheless written by mothers and daughters. How do we tell our grandmothers' stories without constructing them as either mythic mothers or martyrs? How are *mémère* stories a complex performance in which mothers are remembered by daughters whose lives at the end of the twentieth century differ significantly from the family women who have come before them? For Franco-American women, this storytelling presents both a narrative and a gendered challenge: to navigate the constraints of the master narrative of the heroic mother of French Canadian/Franco-American/Maine mythology; and to negotiate the impasse of feminist confrontation with the "traditional ethnic woman." Storytelling constitutes the *one who tells* as surely as the *one whose story is told*. How are mothers and daughters positioned within the ongoing struggle to co-create selves? "Telling the story of one's life who is intertwined in one's own, in terms different from her own, is often a morally delicate project, requiring accommodation and tact and ability to leave room for her account even as one claims room for one's own."[5]

I examine sixteen *mémère* stories written by family women and published in *Le Forum* between 1977 and 1994.[6] Although not all writers identify where their *mémères* lived, when writers specify their locations, Maine is well represented in stories from Biddeford, Waterville, Fort Kent, Caribou, Wallagrass, Rumford, and Old Town.[7] I read these stories from the motherline, first in the sense of how a daughter thinks back through her mother within established traditions of women's storytelling.[8] Second, the motherline addresses the "emotional attunement and mutual recognition that stretches across a continuity established by three generations."[9] This three-generational continuity rejects the mother-daughter struggle between two generations, a model in which older women such as *mémères* are expressly missing. The motherline embraces the possibility for women to psychically inhabit different generations simultaneously. Questions of "Who is speaking?" and "Who is listening?" blur in the motherline—for who is the mother and who is the daughter in *mémère* stories which are told by women who are themselves mothers and grandmothers? By examining how mothers and daughters negotiate their invisibility and idealization within their own storytelling, we can better understand *mémère* stories as strategic responses to the French father's stories.

Embodied Memoir: Strategies of Telling Mémère Stories

In 1917 Pheobe Ouellette married Thomas Marin. By 1937 she had carried and delivered eighteen children. After her first child was born the doctor told her she would never be able to have any more children because she nearly bled to death. Two of her eighteen children died shortly after they were born. One son died before he was old enough to marry and have children. Being a devout Catholic she could not practice birth control. One of my aunts asked her one time why she had so many children. Her reply was, "Because I didn't want anyone to take my place." Pheobe, my maternal grandmother, was buried on the day before Mother's Day in 1986 and 89 years old. At the time of her death, she had 11 surviving children, 104 grandchildren, 150 great-grandchildren, and several great-great-grandchildren. (Kimberly Cook)

Pheobe's is a story of heroic fecundity, but all the more so when the reader finds in the next paragraph that her husband died in 1937, leaving her a widow to raise sixteen children. We are overwhelmed with an excess of numbers, large numbers, numbers without names, styled with a dearth of emotion and elaboration in the narrative. And Pheobe's story is like other *mémère* stories in the collection, which likewise report large numbers of births (12, 14, 8, 12, 17, 10, 12, 12) but also deaths—of infants, children, grown children, husbands, and parents, embedded within long lives that many *mémères* live (89, 91, 97, 81, 91 years). Survivor stories indeed. But with Dorothy Allison: "I thought about their one-note references to those they lost, never mentioning the loss of their own hopes, their own futures."[10] Pheobe's brief narrative reveals some textual strategies of *mémère* stories, specifically, who is numbered and who is named, how sparse is evaluation, and how spare emotion, and how muted the *mémères'* voices in the (grand)daughters' stories.

Naming Mémère(s)

Who is named in *mémère* stories, and under what circumstances? Clarified as the writer's maternal grandmother, this woman is called Pheobe rather than *Mémère* by her granddaughter. Claudia, Victoria, Jeannine, and Antoinette are other *mémères* who are named in *Le Forum* stories. These names individuate each woman and partially extrude their family role. Like the author of "Missing Alice," they address the mother by her first name: "I write to you in order to remember what I have never known."[11] Cook describes Pheobe as a woman about whom she knows little but would like to know more fully. First names distinguish women from their relations with men and intimate an identity which precedes, surpasses, and follows their mothering roles. Two other *mémère* stories suggest the dynamic relationship of name and role in their titles, "*Mémère*: The Life of a Franco American *Woman*" from Biddeford, and "The Story of a *Woman*: A Biography of Antoinette Milotte Messier," written by her granddaughter. In this naming of names the humility of *mémères* is partially mitigated by their (grand)daughters' pride and tribute.

Intriguingly, the most highly developed characterization of a *mémère*, including hints of sexuality and desire, is titled "A Canadian Matriarch"—and it employs only the pronoun "she." This story emphasizes tales of a mischievous child and then "belle of the town," a "stunning beauty" with "*savoir faire*" who one time dated a "rich" young man and another time stayed out until 5:00 A.M. Notably, her mothering role is subordinated and narrated only near the end of the story in that one-note way

Allison captured: "Three girls were born here but died shortly after birth. Then the booming town of Cohoes, New York, beckoned them to join the French colony there. Here eight more children were born and raised." Within the corpus, five other stories use *mémère*, with or without a last name. On one woman is bestowed the honorary title of *Mémère* Jane, a third wife who had no children of her own but raised her husband's six children. *Mémère* Jane recalls the many women who did not survive to become *mémères* because of their early deaths.

Undoubtedly *mémère* stories serve *la survivance*, but the narrative strategies of naming confer visibility and significance on Franco-American women and on each woman within a patriarchal culture and in a newspaper which overwhelmingly features men. Moreover, these daughters narrate individual lives from within a collectivistic culture which discourages personal storytelling, particularly for women. And by contrast to *mémères*, children are not named, a strategy that strikingly distinguishes these stories from African-American women's narratives, where names of children and kinship relations are painstakingly laid out and elaborated, a strategy of survival within African-American slave history, when marriage was proscribed, names changed by owners, rape a common practice, and family members deliberately divided.[12] Within the *mémère* corpus, just two narratives name children, one designating family resistance to the practice of Americanizing their French names: "At home [Biddeford], too, [Claudia] spoke only French with her husband, three daughters, and one son. Their names reflected the Franco influence" (Lucey). Considered strategically, not naming children may serve several functions: To retain the narrative focus on *mémères*; to deflect attention from the narrating (grand)daughter; to downplay Americanization; or to enact a childrearing belief to treat all the children with equal value. Perhaps most significantly, naming *mémère*s but not their children distinguishes the motherline of cross-generational continuity among women from patrimony's fatherline. In *mémère* stories, men and children play supporting roles in women's dramas.

Speaking for My Mother/Myself

Mémères reproduce the Franco-American family literally—one can only be a *mémère* if one has children, by birth or marriage. Beyond the numbers of children, *mémère* stories are characterized by actions and events in which *mémères* "do and make do"—all the work family women do to make a home and make a living. Annie Ernaux sardonically comments on how the lifetime of rural Catholics in France is split into successive stages when people become "old enough to..." first, take Holy Communion, and last, "die." She concludes: "In our lives nothing is thought, everything is done."[13] Similarly, *mémère* stories are dramas wherein *mémères* speak through their actions, as mothers' labor is enumerated and documented by the narrating (grand)daughters. These stories often display a pattern of gendered telling identified by Michaela Di Leonardo among Italian Americans: Women talked about mothers' labor whereas men highlighted their nurturant activities.[14] *Mémère* stories make visible not just family work but also the daily cultural and economic work that Franco women have done. Daughters do not downplay, but indeed underline their mothers' work with little romance or nostalgia.

But what did the *mémères* think and feel about all they do? We rarely hear their voices, and more rarely still their thoughts. In narrative terms, we have event-centered narratives with little personal evaluation of what happened and little emotion, whether the events were births, deaths, or hard work. Consider again Pheobe's story where her *mémère* is given a single sentence to speak. When an aunt asked Pheobe why she had so many children, she replied: "Because I didn't want anyone to take my place." What do we hear and not hear in this reply? Its meaning suggests a multitude of silences in *mémère* stories about women's place. Her place may be taken by another woman—through an annulment of their marriage? Through her husband's extramarital affair? Through her own death? Less directly, this could be a statement of her "doing her (wifely) duty" at the risk of her own health, even life. As the youngest child of the youngest child of this woman, Cook further fleshes out the motherline: "As I grew up, especially after I became a mother, I realized how terribly difficult life must have been for Pheobe. Life is hard enough now in the 1980s as a single parent with one or two children." In becoming a mother herself, the younger mother identifies with the older mother. The granddaughter speaks for her mother and herself, in recognition, in emotional attunement, in shared identity.

But this speaking for my mother/myself is not a simple biological, developmental identification because it is culturally and historically situated. Cook continues:

> ...as my feminist consciousness grew, so did my realization that if these strong women had not suffered the oppression of the Catholic patriarchy I would not exist today. If my grandmother had had contraceptives at her disposal, as we do today, how many people would not exist now? How many of those eighteen pregnancies would have been voluntarily terminated had that been a viable alter-

native? These are questions whose answers I will never know, perhaps for the better!

In the motherline, the same continuity differentiates itself as the granddaughter imagines another voice for her mother, a questioning voice: Then and now, before feminism and after. Notably, abortion is referenced but not written. Cook neither requires an answer nor expects her grandmother to answer these questions in the same way as she herself might from a different point in historical time and cultural space. Her narrative strategy embodies the desire to give tribute to her *mémère's* life but also to negotiate the identity issues of her own adulthood, for example, between economic opportunities and threats to (single) motherhood, and within the personal and social options opened by feminisms.

Other *mémère* stories engage in emotional identification of (grand)daughters with their mothers. The tribute to Victoria Gagnon St. Germain Daigle is characterized by its sustained empathy for a mother of nine who suffered the loss of her husband and a life of relentless poverty. "Many a night I heard my mother cry," writes Blanche St. Germain Michaud, whose family moved between Wallagrass (Maine), Fall River (Massuchusetts), Eagle Lake (Maine), and Waterville (Maine). She expresses gratitude for her mother's insistence, against her stepfather's wishes, that her four youngest daughters receive an education. Her mother worked winters as a lumber-camp cook "to keep us in school." In this storytelling strategy, access to a mother's thoughts and feelings are indirect and embodied in the daughter's voice in absence of her mother's voice. Another writer constructs her mother's final assessment of her own life in Biddeford (Maine): "For Claudia, her life was complete. It was beautiful and it sometimes was ugly. Yet, for all her woes, she knows in her heart she did all that was possible to survive a difficult and trying life" (Lucey). Notably, *mémère* stories witness narrators working within constraints of their point of view as daughters to imagine their mothers' and *mémères'* lives. They adhere to documentary-like reconstruction at the same time they engage in imaginative creation.

Speaking to Mémeres

Mémeres are occasionally quoted in the stories, for example:

> "*Non, non, vous êtes en vacances*" [No, no, you're on vacation," in response to offers of help from grandchildren] (Morin-Scribner).

> "*Ah, bien, les patates sont déjà épluchées et il y a un rôti que je veux faire cuisiner*" ["Ah, well, the potatoes are already peeled and there's a roast I want to cook," declining an invitation to go out for dinner] (Morin-Scribner).

> "You call that pea soup, Lucie? This is not fit for the *cochons* [pigs]!" (Hatch, "*Soupe Aux Pois*").

> "*Regarde la bonne femme*. Her *mari* has been dead for six months and she is walking in public wearing a pink dress with no sleeves." [About a widow she sees outside her window] (Hatch, "*Mémère* Thibodeau").

Admittedly, these quotations position *mémères* as self-sacrificing, as scolding, as complaining. However, until I collected these quotations together, I did not realize that they are either in French or a mixture of French and English. Cook elaborates that "I never had a conversation with my grandmother Pheobe; she spoke very little English and I spoke very little French." It is worth emphasizing that the daughters and granddaughters who write their *mémères*' stories may not speak or understand French, nor might their audience of family members or *Le Forum* readers. This loss of language in the motherline may significantly contribute to the muting of the *mémères'* voices.

In *mémère* stories (grand)daughters sometimes speak to their *mémères*, addressing them from beyond the grave. With this strategy, (grand)daughters may say what was not said in life, while their *mémère* was alive. Marie Martel Hatch imagines a little *visite* with her *mémère* in which she says the following:

> You know, *Mémère*, ethnicity is popular today and people everywhere have grown proud of their immigrant roots. Your own granddaughters are trying to recreate the dishes that were served to us as children in your home and your great-grandchildren have studied French in high school and at college. Some speak it fluently and are equally familiar with Paris, Montreal, and [con]tribute to the support of their families as you did, and women with your good business sense enjoy great prestige.

This third-generation granddaughter functions as the "redeemer" of the first-generation immigrant grandmother. Hatch speaks *about* her *mémère* to reconstruct a cultural past, and she speaks *to mémère* to value her and herself as Franco-American. She continues: "Then, as I repeat this litany, I will sense her approbation and know that if I could but see her, her left eye would be closed in a saucy French wink: 'You bet, Marie. You bet.'" Earlier, Hatch has written of the Anglicisms creeping into her *mémère*'s French: "sometimes I would blanch at 'you bet' or 'gee whiz,' common slang expressions of the day that even I recognized to be inappropriate for a gray-haired French lady." With this storytelling strategy, the granddaughter creates a scene of mutual recognition and acceptance in addition to a hyphenated Franco-American identity in verbal language (English) and nonverbal gesture (French). She also broaches the limits of personal narrative by constructing a fictive dialogue with her deceased *mémère*.

Mémères Speak for Themselves

Let me close with one example in the corpus in which a *mémère* speaks for herself. In a piece entitled, "A Second Chance," Lanette Landry Petrie of Old Town (Maine) reflects on being one of ten children, the mother of two daughters, and now grandmother to one granddaughter. From her *mémère* and mother she inherited child-rearing practices based in the need for order, authority, and control, a pattern she not only witnesses as changing when her daughter becomes a mother but also in her own embodiment of the *mémère* role. It is a change that Petrie welcomes. She concludes:

> I feel like being a grandmother is a special gift from God to reward you for doing the best you could. It is wonderful to share friendship with adult daughters and even more wonderful to share their children. I feel I've been given a second chance.

Petrie returns us to the ambiguity of the motherline as we ask: "In age, who is mother? Who is daughter?"[15] In simultaneously inhabiting different generations of cultural women, Petrie revisits her experience as a daughter, forgives herself for errors she may have made as a mother, and experiences being a grandmother as a new opportunity for personal growth. Here the *mémère*'s voice is written in a prospective rather than retrospective direction. Her story introduces the possibility of *mémère* stories as ways to imagine a future as well as to document a past. This strategy joins other ways of voicing *mémères*—naming *mémères*, speaking for my mother/myself, and speaking to *mémères*—to suggest that grandmother stories cannot be understood only as nostalgia for a more ethnic past nor simply as mourning or honoring of departed mothers. Rather *mémère* stories are an ongoing creation of the motherline over and across generations of Franco-American women. What other stories might we tell about *mémères* and might *mémères* tell about themselves? Telling *mémère* stories embodies multiple meanings for being a Franco-American woman in Maine today, stories of both continuities and change.

1 Cooper, p. 10.
2 Woodward, p. 151.
3 Langellier, "Performing Family Stories, Forming Cultural Identity," pp. 56–73.
4 Miller, p. 34.
5 Narayan, p. 9.
6 The narratives examined for this essay are from Rhea Côté Robbins and others, an anthology of women's writings from *Le Forum*. The sixteen *mémère* stories include: "Mémère: The Life of a Franco American Woman" by Anne Lucey (1987); "A Tribute to Pheobe" by Kimberly Cook (1987); "Une Immense Joie" by Stephanie Vire (1993); "Notre Heritage Vivant or My Grandmother (1977); "A Canadian Matriarch" by Monica Comeau (1981); "Ma Belle Petite Mémère" by Nicole Morin-Schribner (1977); "Soupe Aux Pois" by Marie Martel Hatch (1991); "A Tribute to My Incredible Mother—Victoria Gagnon St. Germaine Daigle" by Blanche "Queen" St. Germaine Michaud (1988); "Mémère Thibodeau" by Marie Martel Hatch (1989); "A Second Chance" by Lanette Landry Petrie (1993); "The Tea Party" by Lanette Landry Petrie (1993); "The Story of a Woman: A Biography of Antoinette Milotte Messier" by Armanda Barney Messier (1994); "Melasse, D'la M'lasse" by Venney Bolduc (1986); "Focus on Christine: Une Faute du Passe" by Christine Rouleau-Nedik (1977); "Alphonse and Jeannine" by Arlene Pelletier Keaton (1989); and "Une Journée avec Mémère" by Arlene Pelletier Keaton (1994).
7 For work on Franco-American family storytelling in Maine, see Chapters One through Four in Langellier and Peterson, *Storytelling in Daily Life*.
8 Smith and Watson.
9 Woodward, p. 149.
10 Allison, p. 33.
11 Cole, in Woodward, p. 338.
12 Rollins, p. 1995. I thank Susan Bell for this observation and reference.
13 Erneaux, p. 50.
14 Di Leonardo.
15 Woodward, p. 324.

ON BECOMING A FRANCO-AMERICAN

Richard Pattenaude
Gorham, Maine

In 1991, I was just learning the ropes as the new president of the University of Southern Maine. As a native of Seattle, Washington, I had little detailed knowledge of Maine, other than to know it was a beautiful place and that the university had an important role to play in its future. I'd spent the previous six years in Connecticut, and had heard many good things about Maine and was excited to be here. Early that fall, I pulled into the parking lot at the University of Maine at Augusta for a trustees' meeting. The fellow guarding the parking area waved me to a stop. I rolled down the window, and he said: "It's really great to have a Franco-American president in the system!" He chuckled, and I moved on, thinking: "I wonder who he's talking about...." Then it registered—he means me!

Thinking of myself as a Franco-American had never been in the front of my mind, had never been part of how I'd defined myself in my first forty-five years. Growing up in the Northwest, our understanding of Canada is dominated by the British influence one encounters in neighboring Vancouver and Victoria. Visiting Victoria, B.C., is like going to a small city on the coast of England near London. We even pronounced our name in an Anglicized way, "Pat and nod." My father and his brother were the only Pattenaudes in the entire Seattle phone book!

Now, living in Maine, I had to confront and engage a heritage and a history that was only dimly part of my consciousness. Yes, I knew that my grandfather, Lejeur Pattenaude, had migrated from Quebec City in the 1870s to Robber's Roost, Washington (later to become Ellensburg). We were never sure why he came west—and to the United States; we just didn't get around to asking him. I was proud of being French, Canadian, and Irish (that's my grandmother's doing), but had little feeling for that heritage.

Maine has been an awakening and insightful discovery of who I am. Not all has been pleasant; I still find it enormously hard to comprehend why anyone would discriminate against Franco-Americans. It just doesn't make sense to someone from away. But that is clearly a powerful and troubling part of our history. Exploring towns like Lewiston and Biddeford, being contacted by historians and genealogists, and regularly being identified as a Franco-American has shifted and restructured my view of myself. I even no longer correct people when they "mispronounce" my name, using correct French. Through conversations, books, articles, and observation, I've begun to understand my history and to find a personal place in it. I understand that this will always be a partial and limited place; there is no way one can totally incorporate the experiences of those who grew up and were socialized in Maine. It also gives me pleasure to see Franco-American pride rise over the past years, and to help build an important research site such as the Franco-American Collection at the Lewiston-Auburn campus of USM.

This has been a positive experience for me. "Becoming Franco-American" has given me a past and a pride for my heritage. This is a great gift, particularly coming to me at a later age. Interestingly, I have also become sensitive to jibes and jokes about Franco-Americans. It has provided me insight to the feelings of others who are sometimes placed on the outside. Finally, in the great melting pot we live in, I now better understand the power and meaning of identity. This is a wonderful country and I am proud to be an American. And it is a testament to the spirit of America that at the same time I can also be proud to be a Franco-American.

SHE APPEARS[1]

Jim Bishop
Bangor, Maine

she appears

she takes the form
of my mother

she is setting the room
my room I suppose

aright

she pays no attention
to what's happened

that I heard a song
I tell her

start & stop & it was

no song but two things
rubbing together somewhere

& that a silence came over
me that was like drowning

or like rising to a foreign
surface & that I didn't care

if I came back that my children
were no longer mine & that
I had no hands

& she just goes on bringing
order my order

to the room she just goes on
in that country way knowing

words won't do her hands
will just touch the right

places in the room & I'll
be rescued she is earth

& whatever thereof & has been
able every time to bring me home

that way every time so far

1 "She Appears" is from *Mother Tongue*, a book of Jim Bishop's poetry.

LIVRES (BOOKS)

Maureen Perry
Lewiston, Maine

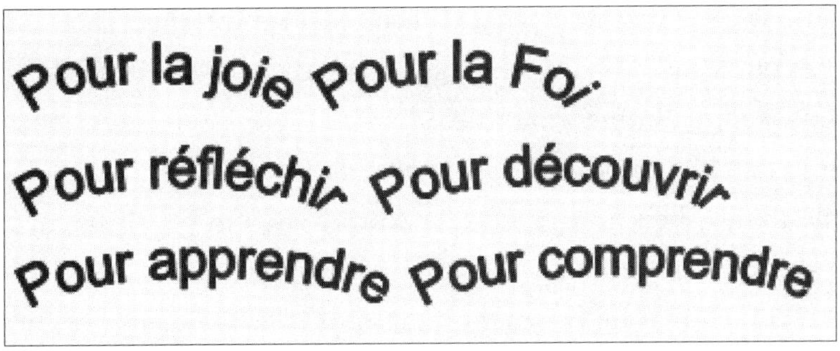

For pleasure / For Faith
To reflect / To discover
To learn / To understand

MY WRITING OF *LA SOUILLONNE*

Normand Beaupré
Biddeford, Maine

La Souillonne, monologue sur scène is the dramatic monologue of an elderly woman who lives with a male friend, "just for companionship," she says, and who pours out her heart while telling us about her life experiences. A former millworker, she knows what hard work is and what transpired in those mills. She talks about the traumatic loss of the only man she ever loved and the sad results of a love affair of one of her friends. All in all, this woman has had a very hard life. Scorned by her pastor and the entire neighborhood, she has managed to put together a whole litany of her views on the things she knows best. Her story is as funny as it is sad at times. The author claims that this woman is the amalgamation of all the marginalized, abused, and scorned women that he has met or heard of over the course of the years. She is the Franco-American version of *La Sagouine* by Acadian author Antonine Maillet (the long monologue of a washerwoman in her Acadian dialect). And like Maillet's play, *La Souillonne* is written in the dialect of her own region. The Souillonne (the slut/dirty woman) is direct in her speech and minces no words when she talks about some of the people that have crossed her path. The play is one long monologue on fourteen themes such as *les amouracheries du moulin, la boisson, les histouères du Christ, qui chus, and la canne de boutons* (infatuations in the mills, drinking, Christ's stories, who I am, and the button can).

I wrote this monologue in the short period of a month back in 2003. I believe I got started in late October and finished it November 25, according to my notes. I had been wanting to do this for quite some time, since I admired Antonine Maillet's *La Sagouine* and wished to emulate her work. She told me at one time that she had taken a chance in writing this play since she didn't know how and if it would be accepted in Québec. Writing in one's dialect is an invitation not only for derision but also for rejection by one's peers as well as academicians. But I so loved the character of la Souillonne in my first novel, *Le Petit Mangeur de Fleurs*, that I became convinced that it would make a perfect Franco-American *Sagouine*. However, would I be able to handle the Franco-American dialect, since it's basically an oral expression, not a written one? Putting long-standing sounds in my head into words was going to be a definite challenge.

However, the dialect was part and parcel of my own heritage. I had full possession of it in the sense that I knew what I was doing and felt comfortable with it, since I had learned through the years that dialects are not inferior to standard language modes. It's not a question of good or bad but rather of being the authentic expression of a people in a given region. It took me a long time to cast aside the disdain of some people for our dialect, especially academicians, since they totally rejected the spoken language of my people, who were proud of their heritage and their language. And I have to admit that I once shared this scorn. However, Antonine Maillet showed me the way with her fierce pride of the Acadian heritage. And I so wanted to prove to myself and to others that I could do it that I began writing the monologue and it flowed and flowed like a running stream and all my memories about being a Franco-American and all the stories I had heard about the Franco neighborhoods and the millworkers just came pouring out.

I have to say that I once worked in the mills myself and vowed not to spend the rest of my life doing what I considered slave labor. I know from first experience the toil that *la Souillonne* and the other millworkers endured. Sometimes I had to pause to find ideas or themes but they came after a few moments of going deep down within myself and remembering. Remembering about the way people talked, about words that stuck in my mind since they were colorful words such as *ratoureux, bilou, califourchon, cobberte, effats, fantasse, flaille,* and *tapon* (crafty, dust ball, the behind, cupboard, purchases, impolite, a man's fly, and wad). Besides, like *la Sagouine*, *la Souillonne* doesn't fully realize that she is the guardian of a glossary and a race. They're both pioneers and protectors of the heritage. I did it and I was proud of what I had accomplished. Then it took some time to find a publisher but I convinced them that it was worthwhile. Finally, I knew I had truly succeeded when the books started selling better than the others and one woman, a former millworker, actually thanked me for having written this book. She had indeed identified with *la Souillonne* and her stories.

(The première of *La Souillonne* was held on 14 April 2007 at the Franco-American Heritage Center in Lewiston, Maine. Marie Cormier of Oakland, Maine, played the title role.)

"QUI CHUS," EXCERPT FROM *LA SOUILLONNE*[1]

Normand Beaupré
Biddeford, Maine

Ben, c'est l'temps que j'vous dise qui chus. J'ai parlé de tout l'monde, mais j'ai pas parlé d'moé. J'veux vous dire qui chus vraiment. Pas que j'aime parler d'moé trop trop, mais chus une parsonne moé aussi. J'ai des sentiments et chus pas gnochonne. J'ai une tête sur mes épaules, vous l'saurez. Mais, chus faite comme chus faite, j'vas vous l'dire ben clairement. J'aime pas dire des histouères et pis abrier les choses. J'vas vous dire la franche vérité. Chus Maybelle Sansoucis. Ma mére m'a faite appelée Maybelle après sa chum, Maybelle Sarasin. J'ai grandi avec ça. Pas que j'aimais pas mon nom, mais y'en avait, surtout les gars, qui aimaient à m'dire, "*Maybelle pretty, maybe belle, grassy Maybelle*." Pas belle comme les fleurs ni même les pissenlittes. I' voulaient m'dire que j'étais belle comme l'harbe qui pousse. Des fois belle, des fois laite. C'est pour ça qu'on marche dessus l'harbe. J'en faisais pas d'cas d'eux-autres. Des vrais niaiseux. Dans c'temps-là, j'leur disais, "Mangez d'la béloné, bande de p'tits morveux." Aujourd'hui, j'leur dirais "Mangez d'la marde."

Quant au nom d'la Souillonne, ça m'vient du voisinage où j'reste. Ça fait cinquante-neuf ans que j'reste dans l'même voisinage. Dans la même paroisse. Sur la même rue. J'ai v'nue au monde au Canada. On a mouvé j'avais dix ans. Chus la plus jeune dans famille. On s'est env'nus aux États parce que ça marchait pus sa terre. Y'en avait qui crevaient dans nos cantons. Non, ça marchait pus pantoute les terres. Mon grand-pére, as-tu pleuré quand on s'est en allé. Y'é't'allé vivre avec un de ses garçons, mon oncle, Eugène. Lui, j'ai pas connu trop trop. Après ça, on a trouvé ce loyer au deuxième étage. Ça s'trouvait pas ben ben loin du moulin. Avec les années mon pére a pu ach'ter la maison du vieux grec, un monsieur Throumolos. Ça été la maison de mon pére et de ma mére. I' l'ont gagnée c'ta maison-là. Mon pére et ma mére s'ont arraché l'coeur à travailler pour gagner leur maison. Jamais j'la vendrai. Jamais. Après que mon pére est mort, i' faut l'dire, yé mort soûlon, mon pére, chus restée avec ma mére pendant vingt-trois ans. J'ai pardu mes fréres et ma soeur jeunes. J'ai travaillé au moulin pour supporter ma mére. Avait pas d'argent, ma mére, pas une cenne

Madame Maybelle
Une personne qui se débourre le cœur—a person who unloads, pours out her heart.
Drawn by Valérie Lachance, Alfred, Maine,
for *La Souillonne, monologue sur scène* by Normand Beaupré

après qu'avait enterré mon pére. Une bonne chance que la maison était payée. Ça lui avait coûté cher, ma mére. Pas d'assurance, mon pére créyait pas là d'dans. A' voulait i' donner un enterrement qui avait du bon sens parce qu'a' l'aimait mon pére malgré sa soûlerie. Pis, a' voulait pas que les autres disent qu'avait négligé son mari. "On dira pas que j'l'ai envoyé à pied," a' m'a dit. Pis, a' m'l'a répété des fois pis des fois, "On dira pas que j'l'ai envoyé à pied." Man' était faite comme ça. Que voulez-vous? Pauvre papa, yé pas parti à pied, yé parti en belle carrosse nouére.

Chus pas une pour me vanter. J'accepte les choses dans vie comme ça vient. Des fois, ça vient de dru, pas trop comme j'l'voudrais, mais on peut pas virer les choses de bord. Les choses sont toutes arrangées pour nous autres les créatures du bon Djieu. Qu'on l'veule ou qu'on l'veule pas, c'est comme ça, ça marche les choses. On peut chiâler, on peut s'fâcher, on peut s'révolter, mais ça changera pas les choses. Ben, moé, j'vas vous l'dire, j'prends ça comme ça vient. Faut pas s'en faire avec ça. Si on est né pour un p'tit pain, on va rester comme ça. *No matter what,* comme dit la Atkinson. Une ben bonne femme la Atkinson. A' s'mêle de ses affaires. A' toujours un bon mot pour moé. Y'en a qui l'aiment pas parce que c'est une Américaine, mais moé je l'aime. On s'défriche ensemble, moqué français moqué anglais. Y'en a qui disent qu'à la longue on va parde notre français si on continue à parler anglais. Que voulez-vous? On reste dans un pays en dehors du Canada et pis on parle anglais partout icitte. C'est vrai que presque tout l'monde qu'on connaît parle français, mais de plusse en plusse, les jeunes apprennnent l'anglais. Moé, j'trouve ça ben bon d'savoir les deux langues. Faut savoir s'débrouiller dans vie. On va parde son français seulement si on veut l'parde. Parsonne va nous l'arracher. C'est comme ça que j'pense. Chus faite comme ça.

J'vas vous raconter une p'tite histouère. J'ai eu une minoune pendant ben longtemps. Pis c'est comme ça que j'l'appelais. Minoune. Faut crère que nous autres les Canadiens, on trouve pas de noms pour nos chats et nos chattes: minou et minoune. Pourtant on en trouve pour nos chiens, nos perroquets, nos jouaux et même nos cochons. Ma tante avait un chien pis a l'appelait *Blackie*. On sait ben c'est parce qu'i' était nouére. A' l'aurait pu l'appeler Ti Nouére, mais c'était d'son affaire. Son frére à elle, mon oncle Ludger, qui restait au Rhode Island appelait son joual, la *Chestnut*. Ça aurait été étrange de l'appeler la Châtaigne. C'est un mot trop frança' d'France pour nous autres, il faut crère. Quant à son meilleur cochon, c'était vraiment une truie, i' l'appelait sa Verrâsse. Un tarme d'affection d'sa part. Pour en r'venir à mon histouére, ma minoune aimait pas les matous. A' les r'gârdait d'travers chaque fois qu'a' en rencontrait un. Les matous ratouraient pis ratouraient et voulaient ben l'avoir, la minoune. Mais, a' n'en voulait pas d'eux autres. Un jour, un gros matou jaune crotté et plein de gales s'met à courir après elle. A' l'a griffé dans face et a l'a mordu sur une oreille. Le matou a laissé sortir un cri si fort et si long que même les voisins l'ont entendu. I' pouvaient pas s'en empêcher. Un cri d'mort. La chatte s'était défendue comme une chatte sait l'faire. C'est parce qu'a' n'en voulait pas des matous, surtout des crottés galeux. C'est comme ça que j'voyais les hommes des fois. Crottés pis galeux. Ratoureurs aussi. Moé aussi j'aurais pas aimé me faire sauter su'l'dos par un vieux matou juste pour satisfaire sa démangeaison de coune. Chus peut-être mal faite, mais chus faite comme ça.

Allez pas crère que les hommes me font peur tout l'temps. Y'en a qui m'dégoûtent et pis y'en a qui m'laissent indifférente. Par contre, y'en a aussi que j'pourrais aimer à la longue si j'me laissais faire. Mais, y'en a pas trop de ceusses-là. C'est parce que j'en ai trop vu dans ma vie, trop de claques à pleine face, trop de coups d'poing, trop de faire pleurer une femme, trop de mauvais sang, trop de buveries, trop de sacres à pleine tête et trop de cochonneries. Pire, trop souvent des silences d'abandonnement. D'a-b-a-n-d-o-n-n-e-m-e-n-t! Mon Djieu! Ça reste collé dans l'gosier pis dans l'coeur trop longtemps. Chus faite comme ça.

Chus faite de guénilles parce que j'ai des années de guénilles dans l'sang. Guénilles à frotter, vieilles guénilles à porter, guénilles à tresser pour des tapis, guénilles dans l'coeur parce qu'on m'l'a déchiré si souvent. Chus faite de torchons parce que j'ai torché les planchers et les marches d'escaliers dans ma vie; torchons d'bécosses parce j'en ai-tu lavé des bécossses et des toilettes, torchons d'avoir tant torché les autres dans ma vie. On peut ben m'appeler la vieille torche. Chus faite de savon parce que chus pas la souillonne que l'monde pense; j'aime être propre. Avec du savon on peut laver et frotter; avec du savon dans l'âme on peut s'nettoyer l'coeur. Chus faite de bon pain chaud parce que j'en ai-tu fait du pain dans ma vie. Trois grosses cuites par semaine, comme ma mére me l'a montré. On était seulement trois dans not'e famille après que mes fréres et ma soeur sont morts, mais maman aimait donner du pain à ceusses qui en avaient pas ou très peu. Surtout les grosses familles qui s'passaient d'manger trop souvent. Bon pain chaud parce que la senteur reste collée après nous autres pour longtemps. Ça sent d'chez nous toute comme le piccalilli faite à maison. Bon pain chaud parce que j'en ai le souvenir dans l'fond de moé-même qui m'réchauffe et qui m'soulage. Chus faite de bonne soupe chaude: d'la soupe au chou, d'la soupe aux pois, d'la soupe au riz avec du jus d'tamates, d'la soupe au bouillon d'poule. C'est don' bon d'la soupe, surtout en hiver. L'hiver est longue par icitte pis i' fait frette itou surtout après les fêtes. Des frettes nouéres. Je r'gârde les gros bancs d'neige dehors. En vieillissant, on a besoin d'quoi d'chaud pour nous dégourdir et nous empêcher de penser qu'on devient de plusse en plusse seule dans l'monde. J'm'ennuie en hiver. D'la bonne soupe chaude, ça réchauffe le canayen. Chus faite de coton, pas de soie ni de dentelle. Ma parsonne est tissée de gros brins forts assez forts pour tiendre ben. J'déchire pas, j'endure comme du gros coton jaune du moulin et du beau coton d'indienne des poches à grains avec des p'tites fleurs dessus. Oui, chus faite aussi de fleurs surtout les fleurs savages qui nous coûtent rien. L'bon Djieu les met là juste pour nous autres pour les apprécier. I' faut seulement s'arrêter pis les r'gârder, vraiment les r'gârder, parce qu'on peut manquer des r'gârder. Les belles couleurs, les pétales doux comme d'la soie, les senteurs de fleurs qui viennent nous caresser les narines et le coeur. Oh! oui, chus faite de fleurs dans toutes mes cinq sens parce que j'veux vraiment sentir les fleurs avec toute mon corps: les toucher, les vouère, les sentir, les goûter et même les manger. J'veux m'faire caresser et m'laisser emporter par elles, les fleurs, au-d'là d'ma vie de chaque jour qui, des fois, est pas mal platte. Chus faite de bleu d'ciel parce que ma couleur favorite est bleu. Le bleu du ciel, le bleu de la Vierge, le bleu de la mer, le bleu d'un oiseau, le bleu des beluets et le bleu qui vient barcer ma tête quand j'ai des envies de m'ennuyer de ma mére, mon pére, mes fréres, ma soeur et surtout de mon Willé. Chus faite de prières parce que j'les dis souvent. Pas que j'aime à répéter des mots pis des mots pis des mots dans des livres de prières, mais j'aime surtout inventer mes prières à moé parce que ça vient du coeur et pas d'la bouche, et pis l'bon Djieu comprend c'que j'veux dire. Y'a pas besoin d'images saintes, de neuvaines pis des élas, l'bon Djieu. Chus faite de paroles parce que les mots sont faites pour nous autres les humains. Vous entendez pas les animaux parler avec des mots. Oh! oui, y'en a qui pensent que leurs pitous leur parlent, mais c'est seulement des accrères ça. Chus faite de paroles qui viennent du coeur parce que c'est les meilleures. Les mots du coeur en disent plusse que toutes les autres. Pas d'menteries, pas de s'en faire accrère, pas parler pour parler, mais paroles pures comme de l'or et franches comme le dire de mémère Tousignant. Mémère Tousignant, quelle bonne parsonne! A' f'rait pas mal à parsonne, pas même à une mouche. Un coeur d'or, la mémère. Jamais une mauvaise parole contre un autre; a' l'a toujours un bon mot pour tout l'monde. Moé, chus faite de la parole de mémère Tousignant. En plusse, chus faite de rêves. Pas des jongleries pis des choses qui font virer la tête. Non. Des rêves qui font rêver aux doux souvenirs du rire des amis et d'ceusses-là qu'on a aimés. Des

Little boy bringing Madame Maybelle wildflowers
Drawn by Valérie LaChance, Alfred, Maine, for *La Souillonne, monologue sur scène* by Normand Beaupré

rêves qu'un jour on aura un peu moins d'peine et un peu plusse d'amour. Des rêves d'être belle à la pensée des parsonnes qui m'trouvent laite parce qu'i' savent pas que chus belle en d'dans. Moé, j'l'sais. Willé le savait itou. Des rêves d'appartenir parce que quand on est méprisée par les autres, ça darde dans l'coeur. Des rêves que tout l'monde s'accorde. Pas d'chicanes à nulle part. Des rêves que messieurs les curés apprennent à pas faire mal au coeur de parsonne. Des rêves que Médée va jamais m'laisser. Et pis, chus faite d'enfants, des rires, des becs, des beaux yeux clairs des enfants. Les enfants que moé j'ai jamais eus. Les enfants que j'aurai jamais. J'l'sais que, de temps en temps, les enfants me donnent du fil à r'torde, pas toutes, mais y'en a. I' font pas ça par méchanc'té, je l'sais, mais ça m'fait mal quand même. C'est parce que j'les aime, les enfants. I' sont pas jeunes trop longtemps; i'grandissent, les enfants. Faut les prend'e et les aimer quand i' sont encore jeunes. J'm'rappelle un jour, un p'tit bonhomme est v'nu m'apporter des fleurs des champs jusqu'à ma porte. C'est Médée qui a ouvert la porte et pis i'm'a crié de v'nir vouère. J'l'avais entendu parler le p'tit. Y'avait pas plusse que dix ans. Y'a pas demandé de vouère la Souillonne. Madame Maybelle, y'a dit. Ça, ça m'a fait du bien au coeur. Y'avait d'l'air gêné le p'tit; y r'gârdait à terre. Mais, pour un moment, y'a l'ver la tête et j'ai vu ses beux yeux bruns, pareils à ceux de mon Willé. J'l'ai aimé toute d'suite le p'tit bonhomme aux fleurs des champs. Chus faite comme ça, que voulez-vous?

English Translation of "Qui Chus"—"Who I Am"

Well it's time that I tell you who I am. I've talked about everyone else, but I haven't talked about me.[2] I want to tell you who I really am. Not that I like to talk about myself too much, but I'm a person, too. I have feelings and I'm not dumb. I have a head on my shoulders, I'll have you know. I'm made the way I'm made and I say that with an open heart. I don't like to tell tales and cover things up. I'm going to tell you the plain truth about myself. I'm Maybelle Sansoucis. My mother named me after her chum Maybelle Sarasin. I grew up with that name. Not that I didn't like my name, but there were some, especially the guys, who just loved to tell me, "Maybe pretty, maybe *belle*, grassy Maybelle." Not pretty like the flowers not even the dandelions, you know, the piss-in-the-bed. They wanted to tell me that I was pretty like the grass that grows. Sometimes nice sometimes ugly. That's why we walk on grass. I didn't pay any attention to them. Real crackpots. Then I used to tell them "Go fly a kite, you snotty kids." Today I'd tell them straight out, "You bastards!"

As to the name Souillonne that some people call me, well, it comes from the neighborhood where I live. I've lived there fifty-nine years in the same parish and on the same street. I was born in Canada. We moved here when I was six years old. I was the youngest in the family. We came to the States because things weren't going so well on the farm. There were many in our village who were starving. No, it definitely wasn't working out for the people on those farms over there. Did my grandfather cry when we left for the States? He went to live with one of his boys, my uncle Eugène. I never got to know him too much. After that, we found this rent on the second floor. It wasn't too far from the mills. With time my father was able to buy the house from the old Greek, a man called Mr. Throumolos. It will always be my mother's and father's house. They earned it, I'll have you know. My father and my mother worked like dogs to finally earn the right to buy a house. I'll never sell it, no siree. After my father died, and I have to tell you he died a drunk, I stayed in the house with my mother for twenty-three years. I lost my brothers and my sister when they were still young. I worked in the mill to help support my mother. She didn't have any money, my poor mother, not a penny after she had buried my father. Good thing that the house was paid for. She shelled out a lot of money to bury him the way she wanted. No insurance, since my father didn't believe in that. She wanted so much to give him a proper burial because she loved my father in spite of his drunken binges. And she didn't want to hear the others say that she had neglected her husband. "People won't say that I sent him off poorly," she told me. She used to tell me that over and over again. Maman was made that way. What can I say. Poor Papa, he didn't go as a poor man, he went off in a beautiful black carriage with all the trappings.

I'm not one to show off. I take things in life as they come. Sometimes things come hard and fast, not like I would want them to, but we can't turn things around. Things are all prearranged for us, creatures of God that we are. Like it or not, that's how things are. We can crab about things, we can get angry and we can just rebel, but it won't change a darn thing. But as for me, I'm going to tell you, I take things as they come. We mustn't let things get the best of us. If you're born for little things in life you're going to stay like that no matter what. That's what Mrs. Atkinson used to say. She's such a lovely lady, Mrs. Atkinson. She always minds her own business. She always has a good word for me. There are those who don't like her because she's a Yankee, but not me. I really like her. We somehow learned how to understand one another half French half English. Some say that with time we're going to lose our French language if we continue to speak English. So, what do you want? We live in a country away from Canada and people speak English everywhere. It's true that almost everyone we know speaks French but more and more do we find that young people learn English. I have no problem with that. It's nice to be able to use two tongues. You have to know how to sort things out in life. We're going to lose our French only if we want to lose it. No one is going to grab it away from us. That's what I think about it and that's the way I am.

I'm going to tell you a little story. I had a cat once and I had her for a very long time. Her name was Minoune. I guess we French Canadians can't find names for our tom cats and our female cats so we call them minou and minoune. Yet, we find names for our dogs, our parrots, our horses, and even our pigs. My aunt had a dog that she named Blackie. Of course the dog was black. She could have called him *Ti Nouère* but that was her business. Her brother, my uncle Ludger, who lived in Rhode Island, named his horse "la Chestnut." It would have been odd for us Francos to call him by the real French name of *Châtaigne*. It's a word that's too Frenchy French for us. As for his favorite pig, really a sow, he called her *la Verrâsse*. A way of showing his affection for her.

Coming back to my story, my cat did not like tom cats. She looked at them with her mean eyes every time she met one. The tom cats prowled and prowled around her and really wanted to get her. But, she didn't want any part of them. One day, a big yellow tom cat real dirty and full of scabs started to run after her. She scratched him in the face and bit him on one ear. The tom cat let out such a loud and long scream that the entire neighborhood heard it. He couldn't help himself. A real deadly yell. She had defended herself like a cat knows how. It's because she didn't want any part of tom cats, especially the mangy dirty ones. Sometimes I see men exactly like that. Dirty and mangy. Prowlers, too. Me too, I wouldn't have liked to have an old tom cat jump on my back just to satisfy his coon cat's itching. I'm probably not the best person on earth, but that's the way I am.

Don't go thinking that I'm afraid of men all the time. There are some who disgust me while others leave me indifferent. On the other hand, there are some I could love with time if I would let myself go. But, there aren't too many of them. It's because I've seen too many things in my life, too many slaps in the face, too many blows with the fist, too many times making a woman cry, too much bad blood, too much drunkenness, too much swearing and hollering, and too many disgusting things. Worse, too often came the hurt of the hollow silence of abandonment. A-b-a-n-d-o-n-m-e-n-t! My Gawd! All of that stays stuck in the throat and in the heart too long. That's me, I'm made that way.

I'm made up of rags because I have years of rags in the blood. Rags for polishing, old rags to wear, rags to braid carpets, rags in the heart because it's been broken too many times. I'm made up of old rags to mop up things because I've washed many floors and stairs in my life; rags for cleaning toilets because did I ever wash toilet bowls and mop up after people in my life. I suppose that you could very well call me the old fat rag lady. I'm made up of soap because I'm not the dirty messy lady, the *souillonne*, that people think I am; I like to be clean. With soap and water we can wash and scrub; with soap in the soul we can clean the heart out. I'm made up of good warm bread. Did I ever bake bread in my life! Three big batches every week like my mother showed me. We were only three in the house after my brothers and my sister died but *maman* loved to give bread away to those who didn't have any at all or very little. Especially to large families who so often went hungry. Good warm bread because the smell stays with you and your clothing for quite a long time. It really smells of home just like the homemade piccalilli. Good warm bread because I still have the memory of it deep down inside of me that warms me up and comforts me. I'm made up of good hot soup: cabbage soup, pea soup, rice and tomato juice soup, and soup made with chicken broth. Soup is oh! so good especially in winter. Winter is so very long over here and it's cold, especially after the holidays. Bone chilling cold. I look outside and see the big snow banks. When you get old you need something warm to thaw you out and prevent you from thinking about being more and more alone in the world. I'm lonely in winter. Some good hot soup warms up the old *canayen* (that's a word that means the old Canadian noggin). I'm made up of cotton, not silk, not lace. The person that I am is woven of very strong threads, strong enough to last and to hold. I don't tear easily since I last and last like the heavy yellow cotton from the mills and the beautiful printed calico with nice little flowers that was used for grain bags. Oh! yes, I'm also made up of flowers especially the wildflowers that don't cost us a dime. God, *l'bon Dieu*, put them there just for us so that we can appreciate them. All you have to do is look at them, really look at them, because one can so easily miss seeing them. The beautiful colors with petals soft as silk, and the smell of the flowers that caress your nostrils and your heart. Oh! yes, I'm made up of flowers in all of my five senses because I really want to smell the flowers with all my body: touch them, see them, smell them, taste them, and even eat them. I want to be caressed by them and let myself be carried away by them beyond my everyday life that sometimes seems so dull. I'm made up of the blue of the sky because my favorite color is blue. Sky blue, the blue of the Virgin, the blue of the sea, the blue of a bird, the blue of blueberries and the blue that comes to lull my head when I feel blue since I miss my mother, my father, my brothers, my sister, and especially my Willie. I'm made up of prayers because I say them often. Not that I like to repeat word after word in prayer books, but I like to make up my own prayers since they come from the heart and not from the mouth. Anyways, God understands what I mean. He doesn't need holy pictures, novenas, and loud sighs. I'm made up of words because they're made for us humans. You won't hear animals speaking words. Oh! yes, there are some who claim that their sweet pets speak to them, but that's only bragging on their part. I'm made up of words that come from the heart because they're the best. Words straight from the heart say and mean more than all the others. No lies, no puffed up words, no talking for the sake of talking, just pure words golden and frank like the words of Mémère Tousignant. Mémère Tousignant, what a good person she is! She wouldn't hurt anyone, not even a fly. She has a real heart of gold that one. Never a bad word against anyone; always a good word for you. I'm made up of Mémère Tousignant's words. And I'm made up of dreams. Not daydreaming and things that make the head spin. No. Dreams that bring back the nice souvenirs of the laughter of friends and those that we have loved. Dreams that someday we'll have less sorrow and a bit more love. Dreams of being pretty in the mind of others who find me ugly because they don't know that inside

I'm beautiful. I know. Willie knew it. Dreams of belonging, because when you're put down by others, that's like a stab to the heart. Dreams that everyone will live in harmony. No fighting nowhere. Dreams that *Messieurs les curés,* all pastors, learn how not to hurt anyone. Dreams that Médée will never leave me. And on top of it all, I'm made up of children, of laughter, kisses, and the beautiful clear eyes of children. Children that I never had. Children that I will never have. I know that from time to time children give me a hard time, not all, but there's some. They don't do that because they're mean, but it hurts just the same. It's because I love them. They don't stay young too long; they grow up. You must take them as they are and love them while they're still young. I remember one day a little boy came to my door to bring me wildflowers. It was Médée who opened the door and then shouted to me to come and see the boy. I had heard the boy talking. He wasn't much older than ten. He didn't ask to see the *Souillonne.* Madame Maybelle, he said. That really did my heart good. He seemed shy; he was looking down. But for just a moment he raised his head and I saw his lovely brown eyes just like those of my Willie. I fell in love with him right on the spot, the little fellow with the wildflowers. I'm made that way, what else can I say? "Chus qui chus."

1 Extract from *La Souillonne, monologue sur scène* by Normand Beaupré, Llumina Press, Coral Springs, Florida, pp. 53-66.
2 "Qui chus" (Who I Am) is taken from *La Souillonne, monologue sur scène* by Normand Beaupré, pp. 53–66, and was translated by the author.

FRANCO-AMERICANS AND A CENTURY OF POLITICAL ELECTIONS, 1892–1992[1]

Madeleine Giguère
Lewiston, Maine

The French immigrants to New England in the nineteenth and twentieth centuries were familiar with the two-party system in Canada. In addition, as members of Catholic parishes, they had participated in the election of parish elders, the *marguilliers* who presided over the temporal affairs of the parish. Some of the immigrants became part of the electoral system early in their U.S. experience. Thus, Joseph Cyr was elected as a representative to the Maine State Legislature in 1845, three years after the Madawaska–Aroostook region was confirmed as a part of the State of Maine by the Webster–Ashburton Treaty. A generation later, in 1874, Charles Fontaine was elected to the Vermont State Legislature.

> In the late 1890s, Franco-Americans were elected to legislatures in each of the New England states. They gradually began to challenge Yankee and Irish control of local politics in virtually every mill town in the area. By 1907, in New Hampshire, there were eighteen Franco-Americans in the state legislature—by far the best political performance in New England.[2]

Others would consider Rhode Island to be the premier state of Franco-American political success—with its three Franco-American governors, several congressmen, and the first U.S. senator from New England (Félix Hébert, elected in 1928).[3] Yet, as David Walker said:

> The transition from Canadian to American politics was not easy. Political interest and activity was kept to a minimum by the language barrier, intense concern with economic betterment, and massive efforts to erect the basic institutions of ethnic identity: the French parish, church, school, press, and ethnic societies. Many considered their stay in the States temporary which strengthened their apolitical tendency.[4]

Indeed, between one-quarter to a half of the French-Canadian migrants returned to Canada. This led to great instability in the early Franco-American communities of New England and made authorities in both countries consider what could be done to better situate the migrants.

The volume of in-migration to the States was great. Some counties in Québec saw one-third of their farms lying fallow because of abandonment. The Québec and Canadian governments became concerned with this loss of people and established repatriation programs to persuade emigrants to return—onto new lands provided by the program. Québec and Canada even hired French Canadians living in the United States to recruit their compatriots to this resettlement plan. The best known of these agents were Ferdinand Gagnon and his brother-in-law Charles Lalime—one working for the Canadian government, the other for the Québec government. They crisscrossed New England with promises of land and support back in Canada. However, the conditions of the grants were somewhat onerous, including the need for the "repatriots" to have $150 in funds on hand. French Canadians returned to Canada, but usually of their own accord and under their own direction.

Although the repatriation program failed to greatly increase the numbers of French Canadians returning to their homeland, it did give impetus to a naturalization movement among the French in New England. Naturalization clubs were established to support those who wanted to become citizens of the United States—another state-sponsored vision seeking "stabilization" of the French-Canadian migrants. The former agent of repatriation, Ferdinand Gagnon, became an advocate of this approach. Yet, strongly committed to the French-Canadian culture, he preached naturalization without assimilation. In fact, the majority of French immigrants in the nineteenth century did not participate in the naturalization process because of language differences, economic striving, the building of ethnic institutions, and instability of residence.

The 1910 U.S. Census indicates that only 45 percent of the French born in Canada had been naturalized in the United States. By 1940, this number had grown to 56 percent and, by 1950, to 72 percent. The intervening experience of World War II (1939–45) had obviously forged new bonds between these French-Canadian migrants and their new country. By 1950 the majority of resident Francos in New England actually had been born in the United States, so the percentage of those who were citizens was substantially higher than just the 72 percent of naturalized French Canadians. Indeed, in 1970, only 13 percent of those who spoke French as their

Ferdinand Gagnon,
from his Biographie, éloge funèbre, pages choisies, *1940*

mother tongue were foreign-born. Today (1992), I estimate that at least 95 percent of Franco-Americans are U.S. citizens.

So, given this background, we arrive at the central question of my paper: Did Franco-Americans support one party or another? On the state level, an early pattern of politics among the French can be clearly seen. The ethnic antagonists of the French were the Irish and the Yankees. The voting behavior of the Francos seems to have been a product of how much these rivals were hated and/or feared.

> For example, a stronger political position for the Irish Democrats usually nurtured a sizeable French GOP (Republican) vote, as in Rhode Island. A weaker Irish Democratic party and a potent, more nativist Yankee Republican organization helped to produce more Franco-American Democrats, as was the case in Maine and Vermont.[5]

In 1992, in New England state legislatures, representatives with French surnames are overwhelmingly Democratic in Maine, Massachusetts, Connecticut, and Rhode Island; moderately Democratic in New Hampshire; and marginally Democratic in Vermont (Table 1).

David Walker, in his study of presidential voting patterns in thirty Franco-American communities from 1892 to 1924, found no consistent pattern of voting as a unit for either the Republican or Democratic presidential candidates (Table 2). Having supported the Democrats during the Cleveland years, there was a realignment of the French toward the Republicans in 1896, reflecting the conservatism of the Francos. In that year, Democratic presidential candidate William Jennings Bryan provoked unease among Francos with his support of a new monetary program based on the silver standard.[6] Shortly afterwards, Republican Theodore Roosevelt demonstrated friendliness toward the French, as evidenced by consular appointments that helped to further draw the French to the Republican party. Finally, disputes with the Irish Catholic hierarchy over churches and schools in the early twentieth century spilled over into presidential politics, with the Democrats being seen as the voice of the Irish. So, the period from 1896 to 1924 is described by many as the Franco-American's time of "leaning Republican."[7]

In 1928 a new era of political commitment for the Franco-Americans began with the candidacy of Al Smith for president. The French chose to ignore Smith's Irish origins and to concentrate on his Catholic, urban, and immigrant background. Smith lost the election, but he had brought many French people into the Democratic party. The economic troubles of the next decade, along with the working-class complexion of *la Franco-Americanie*, extended French support for the Democrats. Roosevelt's attractive personality and the solidarity experience of World War II intensified the attachment of Francos to the Democratic party. In Walker's thirty Democratic cities, only the Eisenhower personality and conservative policies were able to cut into the French commitment to the Democrats in the period from 1928 to 1960.

Again, in 1960, the French put away their antipathy to the Irish in order to support an Irish Democratic candidate—Jack Kennedy, especially after his Catholicism became an issue. This late development in the campaign was recognized by Kennedy's staff and he ended his campaign in the early morning hours of Election Day with a rally in the city park of Lewiston, Maine (later renamed Kennedy Park). On Election Day in 1960, JFK carried Walker's thirty Franco-American communities with 71 percent of the vote and carried Lewiston with 83 percent, the highest ever for Democrats—in both the thirty cities and in Lewiston.

If the Franco-Americans, in the period from 1896 to 1924, could be said to be "leaning Republican," then they can be said to be "leaning Democratic" in the period from 1928 to 1960. But Francos were never a block of "safe" votes that any party could count on in an electoral campaign. However, given this independent thinking, Franco-Americans have not been as successful in politics as one might think. Only in Rhode Island can Franco-Americans be said to have been very successful. From 1892 to 1992 they have not elected "one of their own" to statewide office in Vermont, nor often in Connecticut, Massachusetts, Maine, or even in New Hampshire, where a number of Franco politicians at the statewide level have tended to have short political lives.[8]

Josephat Benoit, a long-term mayor of Manchester, New Hampshire, cites eight reasons why Franco-Americans have not been as successful as they might have been in politics:

> Their timidity, lack of perseverance in defeat, prejudice against persons and groups who are aggressive and tenacious, jealousy among themselves and against other political groups, an inclination to hold political grudges, a disposition to verbal violence, a tendency to let their emotional feelings overcome reason, and a parsimony in investing work and money in the success of the party and its approved candidates.[9]

Andrew Greeley, a priest and sociologist interested in ethnicity, characterized the French-American political style as being very strong on contacting political representatives and consistent in high levels of voting (whatever the educational backgrounds), but weak in participating in political campaigns.[10] This makes Francos a difficult group to represent and probably contributes to their relative lack of political power.

What has been the pattern of Franco-American presidential votes since 1960? The data from Lewiston, Maine, will be used to give some insight into the tendencies of Francos in presidential elections since 1960. Lewiston is not a typical Franco-American city, but it is one with a culturally distinct Franco population. Among the larger French-ancestry cities, it is the one with the largest number and the largest proportion of French-speakers not only of the French-ancestry population, but also of the city as a whole (only Manchester, Worcester, and Woonsocket have a larger number

John F. Kennedy at the city park in Lewiston, Maine, 1960
Maine Historic Preservation Commission

of French-ancestry persons; yet, none of these cities have as many French-speakers in the home as does Lewiston.)[11]

Lewiston is a Democratic stronghold, having supported Democratic nominees since 1924. And even before that, it had voted for Wilson in 1912 and 1916, according to Ronald Bissonnette (Table 4). If we compare the Lewiston Democratic vote for president with that of Walker's thirty Franco-American cities (Tables 2 and 4), we find that the Lewiston Democratic percentage is consistently higher than that for the other Franco-American cities—by ten to sixteen percentage points higher in the period from 1924 to 1960.

The Democratic percentage in the Lewiston 1964 presidential election was the highest ever, perhaps an effect of the afterglow of the Kennedy promise and personality, but also a response to the programs which were put in place in the Johnson administration: the Economic Opportunity Act (with its emphasis on work and training), the National Defense Education Act, as well as a tax cut. The "Great Society" programs were attractive to a working class that comprises much of Lewiston's Franco-American constituency.

In evaluating Franco-American voters, Michael Guignard distinguishes between Franco-Americans with high ethnic involvement who vote for Franco-Americans in local elections and vote Democratic in state and national elections, on one hand, and the less ethnically identified who vote independently of ethnic affiliation at all levels. Guignard links the level of ethnic identification with class. Upward mobility leads to a lower level of ethnic identification and consequently more of a tendency to vote independent of party label. Voting one's middle-class or upper-class interest tends to induce voting for Republican candidates. On the other hand, a working-class orientation leads to higher levels of Democratic voting, not only out of tradition but because the Democratic party better expresses the interests of the working class.

The most Democratic precinct in the city of Lewiston is Ward VI, Precinct 1. It has consistently had higher percentages voting for the Democratic presidential candidate than the rest of the city (Tables 5 and 6). It is the area of the mills and the extended *petit canada*—what my father called "The Island," because it is bounded by Lewiston's canal system. It is a working-class precinct that voted over 70 percent Democratic in the Reagan elections, when the city as a whole was giving the Democrats only a small majority and a bare majority at that in 1984.

What was striking in Lewiston in 1992 was the substantial vote given to Independent presidential candidate Ross Perot in the city as a whole—31 percent. Perhaps even more surprising is the 30 percent of the vote that went to Perot in Ward VI, Precinct 1, which the Democrats only carried by a small majority (Table 6). In this election, the Lewiston Democrats failed to get a majority for their presidential candidate for the first time since 1920. By advocating a conservative economic program and projecting an engaging personality, Perot made a substantial impact on the culturally distinct Franco-American community of Lewiston, even on its most working-class precinct.

In summary, insofar as our data permits, we can say the following about Franco-American voting patterns over the century between 1892 and 1992. When they began arriving in New England in great numbers in 1892, Franco-Americans tended to support the Democratic party. They then tended to support Republicans in presidential elections from 1896 to 1924. Later, from 1928 to 1960, the French tended to support the Democrats again. Yet they were not and are not block voters for one party or the other. Since 1960 the data from one Franco-American city (Lewiston, Maine) suggests that they have tended to remain Democratic, especially those with a working-class orientation. But in 1992 Ross Perot attracted nearly a third of the citywide vote in the presidential election in this culturally distinct Franco-American city and nearly a third of the votes in its most highly democratic and working-class precinct.

Again we see that Franco-Americans are not "safe" party voters. An "intense individualism" hovers constantly over the electoral politics of Franco-Americans.[12] Whether in 1892 or in 1992, their individual votes must be won at each and every election!

Table 1: French Surnames in Legislatures of New England, 1990

State	Number of French Names	Percent of Legislature	Percent of Population of French Ancestry	Ratio, French Home-Speakers to State Population
Maine	27-28 24D/4R	15%	22.6%	6.6
New Hampshire	52-57 27D/19R 11 other	13%	23.4%	4.6
Vermont	12-13 7D/6R	7%	23.7%	3.1
Massachusetts	10-9 7D/1R 1D-R	6%	10.9%	2.1
Connecticut	3-5 4D/1R	2-3%	8%	1.6
Rhode Island	18 16D/2R	12%	16%	3.2

Sources: Madeleine Giguère's evaluation of surnames is listed first; the second number was generated by using the French origin surname list from Cyprien Tanguay's *Dictionnaire genealogigue des familles canadienne* and Reginald Olivier's *Your Ancient Canadian Family Ties*. The transcript of these (1978) is held at the Franco-American Collection, University of Southern Maine, Lewiston-Auburn College. Persons reporting their ancestry as first being French or French-Canadian and Persons age five and over who report speaking French at home are derived from the 1990 U.S. Census of Population and Housing, Summary Tape File 3A. *Maine Register, 1993–1994*, pp. 6–45. "Roster of the General Court, 1993–1994." "The 1993 Vermont Legislature," The *Sunday Rutland Herald* and the *Sunday Times Argus*, pp. 8–10. The *Boston Globe*, 5 November 1992, p. 38. The *Hartford Courant*, 5 November 1992, pp. 18–20. State of Rhode Island and Providence Plantations, "Elected Officials, 1993–1994."

Table 2: Selected Median Democratic Party Percentages of the Presidential Vote for Thirty Franco-American Communities, 1892–1960

1892	50%	1932	63%
1896	32%	1936	67%
1900	38%	1940	65%
1904	39%	1944	67%
1908	40%	1948	66%
1916	52%	1952	56%
1920	41%	1956	49%
1924	39%	1960	71%
1928	57%		

Source: David Walker, "The Presidential Politics of the Franco-Americans."

Table 3: Democratic Party Percentages of the Presidential Vote in Two Democratic Cities of Maine, Lewiston and Biddeford

Year	Lewiston	Biddeford
1952	66%	73%
1956	59%	66%
1960	83%	86%
1964	90%	91%
1968	86%	

Source: Michael Guignard, *The Franco-Americans*.

Table 4: Democratic Party Percentages of the Lewiston Republican-Democratic Vote for President, 1900—1968

1900	46%	1936	79%
1904	43%	1940	81%
1908	53%	1944	80%
1912	61%	1948	77%
1916	62%	1952	66%
1920	48%	1956	59%
1924	53%	1960	83%
1928	73%	1964	90%
1932	78%	1968	86%

Source: Ronald Bissonnette.

Table 5: Democratic Party Percentages of Presidential Vote in Lewiston and Its Ward VI, Precinct 1

Year	Lewiston	VI-1
1972	62%	76%
1976	71%	85%
1980	58%	74%

Source: William Vassar, pp. 10, 12, 14.

Table 6: Democratic Party Percentage of Presidential vote in Lewiston, Maine, 1984–92

Year	Lewiston	VI-1
1984	50%	72%
1988	56%	65%
1992	47%	54%
Perot	31%	30%

Source: *Lewiston Journal*, 7 November 1984, 9 November 1988. *Sun-Journal*, Lewiston, Maine, 5 November 1992.

1 This paper was a presentation at the meeting of the French Colonial History Society on 22 May 1993; the original paper is held at the Franco-American Collection of the University of Southern Maine's Lewiston-Auburn College.
2 Sepenuk, p. 215.
3 Rhode Island's Franco-American governors were Aram Pothier (Republican) in 1908, 1910, 1912, and 1924; Emery San Souci (Republican) in 1922; and Philip Noel (Democrat) in 1972 and 1974.
4 Walker, p. 210
5 Walker, p. 203.
6 In 1896 William Jennings Bryan and the Democratic Party supported the U.S. currency being changed from the gold standard to the silver standard.
7 President Woodrow Wilson, in 1916, got a small winning margin in the thirty Franco-American communities surveyed by David Walker, which led Walker to emphasize a "non-consistent pattern" rather than the Republican-leaning of the period.
8 In Maine, Republican Margaret Chase Smith down-played her French-Canadian origins to stay in office as U.S. Representative (1940–49) and Senator (1949–73). In Massachusetts, "Reagan Democrat" Edward King served as governor from 1979–83 and was said to have been a descendant of the French Roy (King) family. In Connecticut, William St. Onge was a Democrat who served in Congress from 1963–70. In New Hampshire, U.S. Representatives included Alphonse Roy (1938–39), Oliva Huot (1965–67), and Norman D'Amours (1975–85); all were Democrats.
9 Benoit, pp. 15–16.
10 Greeley, pp. 122–55.
11 In Social Science terms I am using Lewiston as an "ideal type."
12 Ducharme. Sepenuk, p. 219.

AD ASTRA PER ASPERA—
TO THE HEAVENS THROUGH HARDSHIP: THE FRANCO-AMERICAN RISE TO POLITICAL POWER IN MAINE

Christian Potholm
Brunswick, Maine

Although Maine is often written of as "the whitest state" in the Union, its ethnic mix is both varied and historically interesting—with wave after wave of European settlers following on the heels of centuries-old movement of Native American people through the state.[1] One thinks, for example, of the Swedes settling in New Sweden in Aroostook County, the Russians finding a home in Richmond, or the Greeks in Bangor. But in terms of the law of large numbers, there are three primary ethnic groups which have had ongoing and consistent political impact. These are the immigrants of English and Scots descent, the Irish-Americans, and the Franco-Americans. In Maine today, over 30 percent claim the first heritage, and approximately 20 percent claim the second and third.

The English arrived both by sea and by land, many coming up from the existing colony in Massachusetts and were generally, although not exclusively, Protestant. In the early period, they were joined by some Irish, many of whom were also Protestant. In the nineteenth century, however, the largest numbers of Irish immigrants were Catholic and arrived following the massive famine in Ireland.[2] While there were some attempts to settle these Irish in the countryside, most ended up in the major cities such as Portland and Bangor. And Lewiston! It is hard to imagine that one of the most Franco of Maine cities was considered an "Irish" town in mid-nineteenth-century Maine. Indeed, it is most ironic that the Irish, who built the great mill complex on the Androscoggin, also labored long and hard to link Maine to Québec by railroad. It was this railroad that brought so many French Canadians from Québec, a process duplicated in many other corners of New England.[3]

So many French Canadians came to Lewiston and the other great mill towns of Maine that, by the early twentieth century, French-speakers and their descendants became a majority or at least a plurality in Sanford, Saco, Biddeford, Brunswick, Westbrook, Lewiston, Auburn, Waterville, Skowhegan, and many other towns.

Although many students of Maine history concentrate on this later large in-migration, Mainers of French descent were among the first European visitors and inhabitants of the Pine Tree State as missionaries, trappers, hunters, traders, and explorers moved south and west from existing French settlements. And the forced movements of the Acadians from Atlantic Canada are well celebrated in both poetry and prose.[4]

From the perspective of Maine's political history, however, it was the influx of French Canadians in the latter decades of the nineteenth century that was politically more important because as time went on, they tended to bolster the minority Democratic party. While this is both an accepted fact and part of the storied mythology of Maine's political process, I have always thought that Franco overrepresentation in the Democratic party in Maine was due in part to the fact that the mill owners tended to be Republicans, rather than any common cause the French immigrants had in terms of political worldview with their Irish counterparts. The French and Irish had the common bond of the Catholic faith—although the French labored long and hard under the Irish domination of that institution in Maine—and their common situation, as exploited workers, accounted for their solidarity. As the French grew in importance in specific locales and were thus a vital part of the Maine State Legislature, Franco-Americans were seldom targeted by Republicans as possible allies and hence seemed to "belong" to the Democrats, by default, as much as by design.

But all of that changed in the early 1970s. Ironically, it was because of two very different men, one a venerated Democratic Titan, the other an often disappointed Republican seeker of major office, George Mitchell and Robert "Bob" Monks respectively.[5] This important tipping point in Maine's political history has been understudied and underappreciated. It all began with the 1970 gubernatorial race between the incumbent Ken Curtis and his Republican opponent, James "Jim" Erwin. This race was one of the closest in Maine history, with Curtis defeating Erwin by only 890 votes out of 325,000. Because of the close scrutiny of the ballots during the 1970 recount, there was a wealth of historical data, and George Mitchell, a former aide to Senator Ed Muskie and a Portland lawyer who had been involved in the recount process, presented his findings in a *Maine Sunday Telegram* article.[6] In his essay, "In Politics There Are Two Maines," Mitchell proved what many had already suspected, namely that the Democrats did well in urban areas and Republicans in rural ones. But the real surprise was that Democrats were much more likely to vote a straight party ticket than Republicans. This straight-ticket voting was made simple and easy by the presence of a "big box" at the top of the ballot. In that era, a voter, by checking this big box, automatically voted for all the members of that party.

The conventional wisdom was that more rural Republicans used this device than urban Democrats, but Mitchell demolished this assumption when he proved that 61 percent of Curtis voters had used the big box compared with only 48 percent of Republican voters who had used it in supporting Erwin. Moreover, Curtis had gotten only 55 percent of his big box vote from rural areas compared to 65 percent in urban areas. Mitchell talked, in good government terms, about the need for both parties to expand their appeal to the other's strongholds and affirmed the democratic process by calling for the end of the big box.

The Republicans were quick to see that the Democrats had a stark and discernible advantage and wanted to get rid of the big box for partisan as well as good government reasons. However, the Democrats were supremely uninterested in getting rid of that same advantage and there the matter languished until a millionaire industrialist and investor, Robert "Bob" Monks, came to Maine looking to become a U.S. senator.

Monks saw himself running for the seat then currently held by Margaret Chase Smith, believing she would retire at the end of her term in 1972. He saw that he would need every advantage he could get in order to defeat the probable Democratic nominee, the very popular second district congressman, William "Bill" Hathaway. Monks tried to recruit younger, vigorous, and "fresh" Republican faces to join him on the ticket—Bangor Mayor Bill Cohen in the 2nd Congressional District and Robert "Bob" Porteous in the 1st. He also mounted a vigorous court challenge to the big box.

On the Democratic side, there was by now a sharp division of opinion. Office-seekers at the top of the ticket, such as Hathaway, assumed that if Ed Muskie, who was running for president in 1972, was to get the nomination, having him at the head of the ticket would be a big boon. But many Democrats in the Maine State Legislature saw the removal of the big box as a way to break the Republican hold on the rural districts of Maine. In this, they would be proved stunningly correct. After the removal of the big box, Democrats would capture the Maine house in 1974 and never lose control of it (as of 2006)!

The big box would be removed by court order and, by the fall of 1972, the urban Democrats, especially the Franco-Americans, became "in play" for the first time in Maine political history. They would then become the most important bloc of swing voters, as their role and importance in deciding not just candidate elections but ballot measures would be greatly enhanced.

How and why did this happen?

Beginning with my practical political research in 1972—when I served as Bill Cohen's campaign manager—I noticed that the Franco-Americans in Maine often shared a common worldview with their Republican counterparts when it came to the role of government: The fear of growing governmental interference and greater taxation. This pattern was visible in polling, focus groups, political action, and examinations of the voters' inner landscapes. I think the explanation is two-fold: First, the French had long-standing and ongoing suspicions about government (both in France and Canada), and second, many of the Franco-American opinion leaders were often small-business owners and professional people.

While the first waves of Franco immigrants were working-class people drawn to the shoe and textile factories, successive waves of subsequent in-migrants were more likely to be small-business people and professionals. These were much more likely to look at the world differently than their earlier counterparts and were instinctively drawn to the Republican small-business perspective, even as they registered as Democrats.

The Franco-American small-business owners, however, seldom had Republican office seekers come directly to them with their small-government, lower-tax messages. Thus, they were somewhat prisoners within the Democratic party, taken for granted by many Democratic candidates for the major offices—governor, U.S. Senate, and U.S. Congress—and yet ignored by many Republican candidates for those same offices. The Democratic candidates often felt they did not need to campaign hard in the Franco areas, and the Republicans often did not even bother to try, assuming the Franco voters were a lost cause.

There was also another underlying aspect, and that was that some Franco-Americans from a particular area did not necessarily want a Franco-American from another area to succeed to an important position—be it governor, senator, or congressman. Thus, Elmer Violette did not receive the necessary support from Lewiston Franco-Americans when he ran for Congress in 1972, and Duke Dutremble did not receive the necessary support from Franco-Americans outside of Biddeford when he ran for Congress in 1994.[7] It was not until the seminal election of 2002 when Michael "Mike" Michaud defeated Kevin Raye for the 2nd Congressional District seat that an avowed Franco-American was elected to any of the major offices in the state.[8]

Congressman Michaud's victory ushered in what was to be a new era in the Pine

Tree State. From being taken for granted or ignored for major statewide office, the Franco-Americans have become the key ethnic group both in terms of electing others as well as one of their own. They have truly "Gone to the stars, through difficulties."

1 Even though African Americans make up less than 1 percent of the population of Maine, their heritage in the Pine Tree State is of note. See Elgersman-Lee, *Black Bangor*. In this "whitest" of states, there was an unexpectedly strong, cohesive African-American community (comprising nearly 1 percent of its population) in Irish-dominated Bangor, especially during the early decades of the twentieth century. Surprisingly, in the early years of the century, 95 percent of non-native-born African Americans were from Canada, most from New Brunswick, not the U.S. South or the Caribbean! See Elgersman-Lee, "What They Lack in Numbers," and Price and Talbot's *Maine's Visible Black History*. For a recent overview of the Native American experience in Maine, see Rolde, *Unsettled Past, Unsettled Future*, and Bourque, *Twelve Thousand Years*, and "Prehistoric Indians of Maine."

2 There is great irony in that great Irish tragedy: While millions of Irish peasant farmers and their families starved and millions more emigrated, Ireland as a whole continued to be a net exporter of grain and farm products! For the Maine experience of the early Irish immigrants, see Mundy, *Hard Times, Hard Men*, and Michael Connolly, *They Change Their Sky*.

3 See especially Faulker and Fearon-Faulkner, "Acadian Settlement." The date of the first French settlement on St. Croix Island was 1604 (it lasted only one year), sixteen years before the Pilgrims landed at Plymouth. In 1635 the French in Acadia (present-day Atlantic Canada) established Fort Pentagoet at the mouth of the Penobscot River, site of present-day Castine. A broader portrait of the later Franco migration to New England can be found in Quintal, *Steeples and Smokestacks*.

4 Beyond the human suffering and misery depicted in Longfellow's *Evangeline*, there are striking portraits of the historical forces that propelled the Acadian French to distant lands: Mahaffie, *A Land of Discord Always*. A less sympathetic note is sounded in Parkman, "1755–1763: Removal of the Acadians."

5 The following section is taken from, and the interested reader is urged to consult further, my previous writing on this subject: Potholm, *This Splendid Game*, pp. 61–136.

6 George Mitchell, "In Politics There Are Two Maines."

7 Potholm, *This Splendid Game*, pp. 95–136.

8 Potholm, "Up Ye Mighty Francos"; and for the importance of Michaud's victory see Potholm, "A Grand Moment." It should be noted that Congresswoman and Senator Margaret Chase Smith was at least one-half Franco-American (on her mother's side), but she never acknowledged that heritage until she was out of office.

FIRST CAMPAIGNS[1]

Georgette Bérubé
Lewiston, Maine

Saturday, 8:20 A.M., February 1970. I picked up the old ringing rotary phone and after the customary "Hello," a man's gruff voice said:

"This is Louis."

"Louis?" I asked.

"Louis Jalbert," came the imperious reply. He continued:

"I hear that you're thinking of running for the House [of Representatives]. I can tell you right now that you're not going to win. Now, if you're interested in politics, you should start by joining the County Democratic Women's Club. They're getting ready for a card party as a fund-raiser. You can help them set up the tables. That's where you start."

Little did he know that this was not what I had in mind. I subscribed to the saying: "Make policy, not coffee." After recovering from the initial shock I responded:

"How can you say this—you don't even know me nor what I am capable of serving in the legislature...."

But before I could continue, he interrupted: "My dear, I know everything about you, including the size of your underwear."

I was stunned!—Stunned at the insolence, particularly coming from the mouth of the so-called leader of the Democratic party. He then went on to explain, spelling out in graphic language, how "they" would defeat me in the primary election. Thus I was introduced to "Mr. Democrat" and to the world of politics.

Mr. Jalbert, or "Mr. D" as he liked to be called, had shown absolutely no interest in my views on issues so vital to the people of our city and state. Yet his attitude told me that his only concern was to ensure that the power to control not be eroded from his hands by someone with a mind of her own, if by a fluke she were elected. I say "she" because there had never been a woman elected to the house from Lewiston. My city's Democratic party leaders were a male-dominated "good old boy" club who followed orders. And I was subsequently told by a local member of "that" club, "what would a woman know about politics?" The ideals and goals that I cherished were suddenly shattered: nonetheless, they would guide me in my decision to seek office.

In doing so, I would discover that while there are those who, to seek control, misuse power, many more exist who are genuinely educated to easing the burdens of daily life for their fellow citizens—Louis Jalbert was not one of the latter.

After hanging up on me, my antagonist then called my husband at work and advised him to "keep the little woman at home to take care of the kiddies." Gerry was principled and had a strength of character gained from his family and his experience in the war. He did not back down when doing what was right was at issue. The caller was told in no uncertain terms that my family was supportive of the endeavor. Threats which initially were dismissed were to be proven prophetic in a few short years when "Mr. D" had the administrator of the hospital fire Gerry, a decision which was shortly thereafter rescinded because of the support the hospital staff gave to my husband.

Perhaps my mother was correct when she said to me after I had called to tell her of my interest in seeking elective office, "but why would you want to do that—they're not honest people." Heeding her advice might have saved me the aggravation stemming from the "take no prisoners" attitude of party loyalists. I was considered an intruder. But had I caved in, decided not to run, I would have been deprived of participation in a great adventure, working in the greatest democratic system in the world, and I would have missed the chance of making a positive impact on people's lives. It was bad enough that I had not sought permission to run, but worse, I was a woman perceived as wanting to usurp what up to that time had been a safe, secure male domain.

Textbooks do not teach what to expect in political campaigns. I found it offensive that instead of discussing issues that might separate us, tactics used by party "hacks" centered on removal of lawn signs, character assassination, and threats to supporters.

With regard to lawn signs, I was fortunate that my husband, brother, and friends would immediately replace them as fast as they were broken or taken away outright. One of my supporters called to tell me that the sign they had put up on their lawn had been taken. This was only one of many calls I received. They told me that shortly after dusk a car would pull up in front of the house, remove my campaign sign, and place it in their trunk. My husband and brother took my brother's car and waited and waited across the street from one of the homes. Surely enough, after dark a car pulled up, two men removed the sign and put it in their trunk. There was little my husband and brother could do—painted on the car was the word "Sheriff."

More frustrating was the pressure brought to businesses that had placed my posters in their shop windows or within their establishments. In one instance, the coercion occurred when a bar-restaurant owner placed a VOTE FOR GEORGETTE sign over the bar. The next day I received his frantic call—he had been told to remove "that broad's sign" or he might lose his liquor license. I suggested that he take it down, but I also reminded him that he would be voting in the secrecy of a voting booth. The secret ballot—what a godsend. Throughout that campaign and subsequent ones I would constantly stress that point.

Many overzealous campaign workers disregarded the protocol and in some cases the voters would be asked to sign several application forms which were then held until the next election, at which time a ballot would be picked up and brought to the voter, even though by that time he or she might be unable to physically vote. Easy to see how there could be a fraud.

During that first campaign I received a call from a man who said that his father had just voted by absentee ballot at Lewiston's largest nursing home. He questioned this since his father had been a "vegetable" for over one year. It was no exaggeration when, in a party caucus, "Mr. D" pridefully stated that "when the polls open on election day, I have 250 votes in my pocket," which roughly corresponded to the number of nursing home residents. I promised myself that if elected, I would introduce legislation to curb this abuse.

In the year 1970 selection of nominees in the primary elections was by an at-large voting district, meaning that the entire city of voters selected their party's nominee, as opposed to the current single-member district where the city is divided in districts and the voters select a candidate for their district only. Based on population, Lewiston was entitled to six house seats, with the six top vote-getters of each political party in the primary to face each other in the November general election. That saw fourteen Democrat candidates vying for the six seats, most having been selected by the party machine. Surprisingly, I placed third, assuring myself a place on the fall ballot.

On the evening of that November election, friends and supporters dropped by our home to wish me well. Election results had not as yet been tabulated, fueling some nervousness on my part, at least. My thoughts went back to the campaign. "Good luck, Mrs. Bérubé," "We need you up there in Augusta." Those words were also a reminder that, with winning, comes responsibility, for people place their trust in their elected officials and that belief should not be betrayed. All citizens ask is that you be honest with them, and make them proud that you serve them. Once having gained their approval, it is incumbent upon all those who serve the public to place personal agendas aside and partisan politics second to the people's wishes. It was that philosophy that led me not to oppose—as other Maine legislators did—the results of a term limit referendum supported by Maine residents which led me to depart the state senate in 1996.

I was also remembering that first outing at campaigning. It was eleven o'clock in the evening and the shifts were changing at Bates Mill, when there were still three shifts, or indeed any. Hundreds of people streamed in and out of these vast forbidding brick buildings. As I opened the car door to begin my walk toward the mill gate (it felt more as though I was walking the plank), I suddenly developed stage fright and did not move. Would I be rebuffed? After a gentle shove by my husband, who was also my chauffeur, I approached a man who was slowly walking toward his workplace, smoking a corncob pipe, swinging a black lunch pail. How many hundreds—no, thousands—had trudged these same worn sidewalks for little pay, few benefits, yet giving their all.

I handed him a campaign matchbook and said I would need his vote. Stopping to read the message on the cardboard ad, he took a puff from his pipe, looked up at me and said in French: "Une femme? Pourquoi pas." (A woman? Why not.) He then continued his slow pace to his all-night job. I thought that if I made it, my decisions would affect him and so many like him—what an awesome responsibility. I promised myself that I would not be a disappointment to him nor so many like him. "A woman? Why not!" became my campaign slogan.

My husband was now at my side, having parked the car, and his presence gave me encouragement. One man stopped and said, as I met him and others walking with him, "Never forget the working man, the one who works all the time. Don't take all of his earned money. But when a catastrophe hits him, such as losing his job, be there to help him through a difficult time."

I remember vividly that first foray into campaigning. None of us—family, friends—had ever campaigned. Needless to say, we were apprehensive.

My spirits buoyed by the encouraging comments that met me during this first campaign, I and my family charged into an uncharted political process with vigor and determination. It wasn't so bad after all; in fact, it was downright fun. However, had it not been for the gracious words of support from voters, I might not have continued.

Having made it through the primary, my election in November was nearly assured as no Republicans generally gained a seat—not since the mid-twentieth century. But having been victorious, I also attracted the wrath of those who had predicted my demise. "We'll defeat you with all the ammunition we have." This now rang hollow on the evening of the November election, particularly as the returns came in. The greatest pleasure on that November night came when I led the winners, having bested five other names on the ballot under the Democrat column, for I had received 12,133 votes, and Mr. Jalbert garnered 12,132 votes.

"Should we ask for a recount?" asked my husband with tongue in cheek.

As all of us unwound after the final results were announced, again I thought of the many people whom I had met at the factory gates, at their places of business, the elderly—all had entrusted me with their future. I prayed that I would never let them down and that I would represent them with the dignity they all deserved. I vowed never to benefit financially from my service and I did not—I still buy solid, used cars and I still live in the same house my husband and I bought forty-eight years ago. Nor would I forget my husband's only advice: "Remember that you'll get old someday, and never, never forget the military veteran."

A family friend and advisor said to me as he was leaving our home that exciting evening: "Remember this victory—there will never be another one like it." He was right.

And so, that evening of Tuesday, 3 November 1970, saw the culmination of a hectic campaign. The "Thank You" newspaper ad which I ran the next morning simply said:

PEOPLE OF LEWISTON, I LOVE YOU.
—GEORGETTE

The morning after our sweet victory, Lewiston was greeted by lawn signs which, as if by magic, had sprouted cardboard banners with the words: Thank you (signed Georgette). My husband had stapled those thank-you signs till the early morning hours—the election triumph was due in great part to him.

In 1972 a young mayor from Bangor, an unknown Republican to most in central Maine, came campaigning in Lewiston as the Republican nominee for Congress; he would later become a secretary of defense. He worked extremely hard while running against a man whom I thoroughly respected, having served with him in the state legislature. Democratic state Senator Elmer Violette from Van Buren was a Franco-American of Acadian descent, with deep convictions and integrity, who was expected to win hands down, counting heavily on the French-speaking Democrats of Lewiston who voted in large numbers, thus ensuring him a win. Candidate Cohen had picked up on the "take them for granted Francos" and he paid special attention to the citizens of this ethnic group. At that first election of his many to come, he had not carried the city that was so predominantly Democrat, but he had succeeded in making inroads, eroding the Democrat support and establishing his credibility.

That fall, I was privileged to campaign, as a volunteer, with Senator Violette, climbing flights of stairs in tenement buildings with him to visit workers on night shifts, hosting receptions in my home. Unknown to me at that time was the lukewarm support for his candidacy by the local political machine. On the night of the election I received a phone call from John Martin, who wanted to know how the vote count was going in Lewiston saying: "I can trust you to level with me."

After giving him the latest tally, which clearly indicated that Violette had a comfortable lead, John said: "It isn't enough, Georgette, he should have done better there. We were done in by some members of our own party." Indeed, candidate Cohen had eaten into the Democrat stronghold and he became the new congressman for Maine.

For a time I had felt that my party, the party of Roosevelt, Truman, and Kennedy, was bent on a more liberal course than the majority of enrolled Democrats wanted. Party caucuses and conventions became dominated by a vocal liberal minority whose philosophy was alien to the more moderate and fiscally conservative views of the people of my district. The overwhelming Democrat vote was taken for granted with little attention given to the city. To rectify this, I firmly believed that change must come from within.

And so, after much thought and knowing full well the political ramifications that my action would engender, on 8 September 1977, I announced at a press conference held in my home that I had sent a letter to Congressman Cohen urging him to seriously consider seeking the U.S. Senate seat the following year, a seat held by Senator William Hathaway. I did not want to cast aspersions on the senator, but I felt that his ultra-liberal voting record was not reflective of the views held by the Franco-American community and that Congressman Cohen had a more traditional approach more in tune with the citizens of my community. My letter read:

> Dear Congressman Cohen:
>
> From all accounts in the press it would appear that you have not arrived at a final decision on whether to seek the Governorship of our State or the U.S. Senate seat. As our Congressman, you have remembered the voters of my City of Lewiston as no other U.S. Representative has. During your first campaign I recall you said that when you were elected you would open an office locally in order to better

serve us and in turn have input from the citizens of this community—this you did after holding your victorious press conference here the day following the election thereby acknowledging the importance you have attached to our people. Your willingness to listen to our views on many issues, irrespective of Party affiliation, explains your victories.

Your views parallel my own philosophy and are reflective, I feel, of that of many of my fellow citizens of Lewiston—the very same people who value integrity and honesty in government, and individualism above partisan politics.

During the next crucial six years, major decisions will be made by our Senator: decisions involving national defense and security, energy, safeguarding private enterprise in productive employment while remembering the duties and privileges associated with all of our rights—these decisions will demand that we be given a choice of selecting a person who reflects the moderate thinking of so many people of my community and my State. From your years of proven service and experience for us in Washington, I feel that you are the person to do this—and so, although perhaps forward on my part, I nevertheless ask that you actively seek the Office of U.S. Senator. I stand ready to support you.

Sincerely,
Georgette B Bérubé

This announcement generated some vitriolic comments from the local party activists, which was expected. But the many positive comments wiped out the less-than-supportive ones. During the next few days I was comforted by the support and encouragement expressed by the people of my city. Of all the letters and notes I received, only three (two unsigned) chastised me for "daring to come out for a Republican." One of the unsigned letters bordered on the humorous. It came from the Androscoggin Democrat Women's Club (the "card-party group" that Louis Jalbert once suggested that I join instead of running for office), typed on onion paper, advising me that I and another Cohen supporter, who was a heavy contributor to the Democrat party, were being expelled from their group. No signature. Queried by the press for my reaction I said: "I feel as though I've been sent to the Gulag Archipelago."

My dues check of $2 was returned. So much indignation by some of the very people who had concealed their lack of support for their own congressional candidate!

A Democrat legislator called on Speaker Martin to remove me as chair of the

Audit and Program Review Committee. The crime? Endorsing a Republican! So much for freedom of thought. An editorial in the *Lewiston Daily Sun* read:

> Representative Bérubé is not the first nor will she be the last to endorse a candidate of the opposing party. The old politics called for such endorsements to be made in the backroom away from the public view. Mrs. Bérubé took no such route. She announced her support for Representative Cohen publicly. Actually, her "political sin" is not so much that she supports an opposition candidate, it is because she "went public." Still it is refreshing to have someone in politics take an action considered right, even though it could have embarrassing consequences. It will be interesting to see if our Lewiston lawmaker retains her chairmanship when the legislature reconvenes in January.

In 1979 a Democrat activist from Livermore Falls, Joseph Langlais, wrote to longtime party insider Harold Pachios, a fair man, saying:

> During the last year I've heard you say a number of times that the Party system is in trouble, the voters are shying away from Party politics and voting as Independents. I'd like to know why and what to do about it. Now here is a good reason: Georgette Bérubé was the first politician to come through for Bill Cohen, before he even announced. At the time, when we asked why this woman was tolerated as a Democrat, your answer was: "Everyone is entitled to a difference of opinion, and we don't bounce anyone out of the party because of it, or just because they don't agree with us." Now, my friend, we find that this woman is complimented with a co-chair on what some people consider an important committee. The question at this time, though we do not take action against a difference of opinion is it necessary to reward them for it? I think that there are many other Democrats more deserving: if not, then I would rather see a Republican in that position than Mrs. Bérubé. This is the kind of action that makes people say: "Politicians are all alike, put them in a bag and shake it and they all come out the same color regardless of their label." It was these so-called Democrats who supported Bill Cohen that sparked the anti-Hathaway vote in November and the Party is that much poorer because of it.

A response came from John Martin:

Dear Mr. Langlais,

I have received the copy of your letter to Hal Pachios regarding the appointment of Rep. Georgette Bérubé as house chairman of the Joint Standing Committee on Audit and Program Review. I realize that such an action may be difficult to understand to those who may not have all the facts. Although Rep. Bérubé had been the top vote-getter in Lewiston for some time, Bill Hathaway never once contacted her until she announced for Cohen. Only after her endorsement of Cohen did he finally bother to call her. Perhaps this was because of the various factions in Lewiston. Cohen also voiced strong support for the interest of Franco-Americans which Bill had never done. Rep. Bérubé is a conservative Democrat who was never at ease with Bill's more liberal philosophy. Also, she was offered a staff position with Cohen but refused. While I do not approve of her endorsement of Cohen, at least she had the honesty to do it openly before the Primary instead of after she was home free.

Further alienating her from the party would serve little purpose, since she is popular with her constituents and may be of assistance to the Democratic candidates in the future. As treasurer of Elmer Violette's congressional campaign I can attest to her strong support while many others sat on their hands.

I am sure this response will not satisfy you completely, but I hope it will help you to better understand my decision.

Pressure had been applied with John to remove me as chair, and to a legislator he responded: "While I do not approve of her decision, she is able and competent and she stays." John Martin, as the speaker of the house and one of the leading Democrats in the state had every right and opportunity to remove me from the chairmanship. That he did not seek retribution bespeaks volumes of the side of him that I got to know but that the public, especially the media, rarely saw. In the twenty-six years we served together at the capitol, John and I agreed on some issues and disagreed on others, but we were always straight with each other. I never forgot the fairness he showed during this especially trying time.

My announcement was made some seven months before the next primary election, and it was obvious that candidates would be found to run against me. Since the next election would be from the new single-member districts, the feeling was that I could be easily defeated. On the issue of single-member districts, while the machine did not support it, I had voted for this change since I believed that the elected officials

Georgette Bérubé, Lewiston, Maine, 2000
Staff photo, *Sun Journal,* Lewiston, Maine, in the
Franco-American Collection, University of Southern Maine, Lewiston-Auburn College[2]

from the new districts would be more responsive and accountable to their constituents; they would be the sole representative from a particular area, thereby accountable on their part instead of riding the coattails of others.

In announcing for Bill Cohen months ahead of the primary, I risked much, but I chose to do so before the next primary election thus allowing voters to be the judge. A candidate, Gerald Bouffard, was indeed found to oppose me and he was billed as "the Real Democrat." My faith in the fairness of the electorate was again rewarded when I was renominated in June 1978. The vote tally:

Bérubé	1,218
Bouffard	384

He had even lost his own precinct.

After reconvening in January 1979, during one of our Democrat caucuses, a then-flaming young liberal (who later changed to the Republican party—to the far right of the Republican party, I might add) suggested to the members that I leave the Democrat party.

I sent a note to Assistant Majority Leader Rodney Quinn, a veteran World War II bomber pilot who would later become Maine's secretary of state. My note said that I would be glad to oblige if he wanted me to do so. His response: "NO. By no means—and you and I both know that baboons applaud bananas. People so fast with the clap, deserve the 'clap' and that's the reason they need people like you and me to give some balance and directions."

1 This article is an excerpt from the autobiography of Georgette Bérubé, *Thank You Georgette* (Bloomington: Autohouse, 2005).
2 Franco-American Collection: Georgette Bérubé File.

MAINE FRANCO-AMERICANS IN POLITICS

John Martin
Eagle Lake, Maine

The first French landing, in 1604, took place on Ste. Croix Island, and—with it—a new era was ushered into Maine history. Today, about 25 percent of Maine's population is of Franco descent. The greatest number of Francos came from Québec to work in the mills in Old Town, Lewiston, Augusta, and Biddeford. The Acadians are an exception, having come to the St. John Valley because of their expulsion from Nova Scotia and New Brunswick by the British, as well as through various states and colonies in which they had been scattered, most notably through Québec.

The involvement of citizens of French descent in 400 years of Maine politics has been primarily at the local level—on town councils and school boards, as well as in various municipal positions. As you explore individual towns throughout Maine, you will find many French surnames in their history books—names like Boucher, Lausier, Binette, and Jalbert can be found prominently listed. Few have ventured into the realm of state-level politics, and even fewer have done it successfully. These French legislators who have walked the halls of the State House can be traced in the House and Senate Registers. However, those names, with few exceptions, are in the more recent history of Maine.

After Maine became a state in 1820, only one French individual was elected to state-wide office in the nineteenth and twentieth centuries—Dr. Alonzo Garcelon of Lewiston. Born to French Huguenot parents, he attended Bowdoin College and the Medical College of Ohio. Upon graduation, he returned to Lewiston to open a medical practice. Garcelon then served in the Maine House of Representatives from 1853 to 1854 and from 1857 to 1858, and then in the Maine Senate from 1855 to 1856. (This was when terms of office were shorter than today.) During the Civil War he served as a general in the Union Army. It was during the impeachment of President Andrew Johnson after the Civil War that Garcelon became disgusted with the Republican party and became a Democrat. As such, he served three years as governor of Maine, from 1879 to 1880. Garcelon also is credited as one of the founders of Bates College in Lewiston and is recognized as one of that city's most renowned residents. In over a century since Garcelon's time as governor, no resident of French decent went on to serve in statewide office, although at least eight French Mainers became candidates for governor, some even winning the Democratic party nomination. Only one, to my knowledge, sought the Republican nomination—Alexander LaFleaur, in 1956.

Congressman Michael Michaud has the unique distinction of being the first Frenchman elected to a congressional office here in Maine. He was first elected to serve in the U.S. House of Representatives in 2002 and has continued in that office. Michaud, from Medway, began his political career in 1980, when he was elected to serve in the Maine House of Representatives, a post he held until his election to the Maine Senate in 1994. During his second term in the senate, he was appointed to serve as chair of the legislature's Appropriations Committee and, in 2000, he was unanimously selected to serve as president of the senate. He left the senate in 2002 to serve in Congress. Michaud hails from a traditional French background. Like his father and grandfather before him, he began working at the Great Northern paper mill upon graduation from high school and continues to reside in the community in which he was born and raised.

My focus, however, is on in-state politics and service. Two prominent Franco-Americans have not only served our political system with distinction, but have gone on to further success on Maine's Supreme Court—Albert Béliveau of Rumford and Elmer Violette of Van Buren.

Albert Béliveau was born in the Little Canada of Lewiston. He entered the United States Army in 1917 and served as a lieutenant in the Judge Advocate General's Corp during the remainder of World War I. Upon returning home, he founded the Rumford American Legion post. Béliveau was very active in Democratic party politics and ran for the U.S. House of Representatives in 1928 and 1930. In 1935 he was appointed to the Maine Superior Court, the first lawyer of French-Canadian descent to serve on it. He remained on that bench for almost twenty years before he was appointed to the Maine Supreme Court in 1958, once again setting a record as the first French member of that court.

Elmer Violette came from the St. John Valley. He entered the political arena when he was elected to the Maine House of Representatives in 1942, then served in the U.S. Army Air Force during World War II, and returned to the house in 1946. Violette served in the Maine State Senate in 1964 and, in 1968, was a candidate for U.S. Senate. He proceeded to run for the U.S. House of Representatives in 1968. He was appointed to the Superior Court of Maine in 1973. His final role as a public servant came when he was appointed as a Maine Supreme Court justice in 1973. He served on the bench until his retirement in 1981.

Only three members of the French community have been elected to serve as leaders in the Maine legislative bodies—the house of representatives and the senate. I was elected as the first French speaker of the house in 1974, Dennis Dutremble was elected as president of the Maine senate in 1993, and Michael Michaud served as president of the senate in 2001. Over the years French legislators have served their communities proud in the halls of the State House, obtaining committee chair positions and articulating a much needed, well-respected voice on many key issues. Unfortunately, the level of French membership within the legislature has never truly been reflective of the French population of the state.

Some have suggested that Franco-Americans themselves are a cause of the problem since they are not like other ethnic groups in terms of "sticking together." Some have even suggested that they are politically jealous of one another's accomplishments. Sévérin Béliveau, son of Albert Béliveau, went on to his own illustrious career in Maine politics and once stated that: "We don't support and encourage our own people to the extent we should." However, I tend to disagree with that conclusion, and it certainly cannot be said by those of us who hail from the St. John Valley. Maine's French residents are known for their outstanding work ethic—excelling in whatever job they face. To hard-working millworkers, farmers, and lumber industry folks—the taking of valuable time to play politics in Augusta is simply a luxury they could not afford and, in some cases, couldn't really understand. How could others in similar situations pursue such frivolity?!

When I was first elected to the Maine House of Representatives in 1965, derogatory French jokes were common. The members who were of French descent very rarely spoke their native language amongst themselves and in the halls of the State House. The majority of the committee chairs were held by non-French members. There was no pride in having a French background—it was not newsworthy and very little was made of it, certainly nothing positive.

The tide began to change in the 1970s. I was elected minority leader in 1970, winning the position over another Franco-American, Louis Jalbert from Lewiston. This was clearly a race between a "Young Turk" against a "Party Stalwart," rather than ancestry, and our French heritage played no role in the race. Very little was made of the fact that I was French. My surname did not immediately point to being of French heritage, and I spoke with little to no French accent. Also, the fact that I was simply the leader of the minority party managed to shield me somewhat from the limelight.

I was elected speaker of the house in 1974—the first presiding officer of either chamber of Franco descent. The election came with a power shift in the house—from Republican-controlled to Democratic-controlled, the first of its kind in ten years. My election as the youngest speaker in a century was great fodder for the newspapers of Maine, as was the fact that the house was controlled by Democrats, the senate by Republicans, and the governor was an Independent—the first time in Maine's history. The papers focused on new leadership and budget squabbles.

When I was first elected as speaker, members would often wander into my office and ask if I had heard the latest French joke. My response was always the same—"Are you French?" If the answer was no, I would tell them: "I'll listen to your joke, as long as you use your own ethnic background as the brunt of it!" After a few months of this, the members quickly became aware of that rule, and after one term in office, it was never again an issue.

I remember vividly the first time members of the house heard me speak French to fellow French members. It was a side of me that few people in the State House had seen. For us, it was second nature—far more natural than speaking English. For non-French members, it was a novelty, one met with curiosity and criticism.

After a divisive debate in the house that subsequently played out dramatically in Maine newspapers across the state, I received a letter from an individual in Ellsworth, suggesting that I go back to my "lily pad" in northern Maine, clearly referencing my ethnic background, and using the word "frog" in the letter. It actually resulted in my being more stubborn on the issue that had prompted the newspaper articles in the first place.

The first real reference in any newspaper about my Franco-American background did not come until 1980, fifteen years after my election to the Maine house and six years after my appointment as speaker. The *Maine Sunday Telegram*, Maine's only statewide Sunday paper, profiled my life as speaker and a resident of northern Maine. It was only then that it was mentioned that I was the first French speaker, and a great deal was focused on the French community that I call home, Eagle Lake.

Fast-forward thirteen years to the election of Senator Duke Dutremble as senate president in 1993. The tide had already begun to change. The first newspaper articles regarding Dutremble prominently mentioned that he was the first senator of French descent to assume the head of the Maine senate. Stories were crafted about his French heritage and his bilingualism. It was something truly to be celebrated. Similarly, when Mike Michaud was elected to Congress in 2002, much coverage was devoted to his French heritage and Franco-American background. The early stories covering his congressional win all contained the fact that he was a time-clock-punching mill-worker and a Frenchman, the first ever to hold such a seat.

During the past forty years that I have walked the halls of the State House, I have seen the atmosphere around here change dramatically in regards to cultural heritage. Not only do people wear their ethnic backgrounds as a badge of honor, but respect is given to those who possess a unique ancestry. The French heritage is something to celebrate these days, as are Irish and Native American backgrounds, among others. These days, those of us who can speak a second language are no longer looked upon with curiosity, but rather, respect. Oftentimes we are sought out when a non-French-speaking member has to converse with a constituent in their district who only speaks French. Very few of the one hundred and eighty-six members of the legislature (house and senate combined) can claim that they have no French ancestry, whether they originally hail from Maine or not. Generally, one need only look as far as their grandparents for some French connection. As the French population of Maine has grown over the years, so has its representation and reputation within the State House.

For the last several years, Franco-American Day has been celebrated here at the State House, and all members, whether of French lineage or not, look forward to the events and celebrations of the day. It is a stark contrast from the days when derogatory French jokes were openly shared among the non-French members. The festivities include a bilingual session of the house and senate as well as traditional French music performed throughout the day. It is a celebration of our heritage and of our importance in the history of Maine politics: An importance not soon to be forgotten.

SINGING THE VERNACULAR, EXCERPTS

Paul Paré
Ogunquit, Maine, and
Fort Lauderdale, Florida

What is *Singing the Vernacular* about?

This memoir-novel takes the reader on two road trips undertaken by the same character about thirty years apart, both occurring in January, and both leading to self-discoveries and life-changing decisions. This is a coming-of-age story, as well as a coming-out story. The main character, Marc, just happens to experience them twice: The first time as a sixteen-year-old Catholic seminary student and the second time as a fifty-year-old closeted man whose wife of twenty-five years has just died.

The first road trip takes Marc on a train excursion during a fierce Québec snowstorm. It's a short holiday weekend during the early 1960s. Marc has been given permission to leave the seminary to visit his aunt, a nun and the family matriarch, stationed at a nearby hospital. During the snowbound weekend, he confronts doubts about his vocation to the priesthood, begins to question authority, and has his first sexual encounter with another man. He returns to the seminary full of guilt and uncertainty. During the second trip, Marc has just turned fifty and his wife of twenty-five years has just died. It is 1995. His three-week, last-minute escape from work and depression covers the vast desert landscape of the American Southwest. Marc winds up at a gay resort, hoping to connect with gay men and the lifestyle he denied himself all these years. He meets a wide array of men, makes friends, falls in love, has a few dissatisfying sexual experiences, and in the end, has to decide if he can go back to his old life.

The book is written in the first person and the chapters alternate between Marc's seminary life and his Southwest escapade as a fifty-year-old widower. Although many of the circumstances are real, a good number of the characters and situations are fictitious, which is why I prefer to call the work a memoir-novel.

In the first excerpt presented here, Marc has just checked himself into The Villa, a gay resort in Palm Springs, California. He's been driving through the Southwest for several days, not sure of what he really wants to do during this trip. He's very lonely and he's ready for company, desperate, in fact, to make that first contact with other gay men.

Getting Along Real Well

"Hello, my name is Jimmy Hoover. That's Hoover, just like the vacuum cleaner." With his hand outstretched, he jumped from his pool-side chair to greet me.

I instinctively shook his hand. "My name is Marc," came forward my automatic reply. I was really pleased by his friendliness.

"I always explain. I repeat, 'Hoover, just like the vacuum cleaner,' because so many people hear Jimmy Hoffa instead. I've tried James Hoover, but people still think of Hoffa. And, that leads to all kinds of jokes, and I'm so tired of them all. Sometimes I think I should just change my name. That would be so much easier. But, it *is* my name. Marc? Is that what you said?" He was still holding my hand, and he finally gave it a weak up and down movement, before letting go. "You have no idea how many people make a comment about Jimmy Hoffa. I say HooVER, with the emphasis on the 'ver,' and they still think of Jimmy Hoffa."

"That's amazing," I replied. My new friend gestured to an empty chair next to his, and I accepted his invitation.

"Or, they hear Hoover all right and then they start in on J. Edgar Hoover. Frankly, I don't know which one I hate the most, J. Edgar Hoover or Jimmy Hoffa."

"Yes, I see what you mean," I said meekly.

"It seems to me that, these days, people would have other points of reference. Jimmy Hoffa vanished twenty years ago. And Hoover? He's been out of the picture for decades. After all, this *is* 1995! You know what I mean."

It wasn't a question, but I nodded my head. "Yes, I know what you mean—Jimmy."

"That's it, just call me Jimmy. Good of you to remember, Marc. See? I remember your name, too. Even if I've been talking a fast streak. You know, so many people meet someone and they instantly forget their names. I think names are very important. That's Marc with a 'c' or a 'k'?"

"With a 'c,'" I replied.

"So, what you doing here, Marc?" He changed the conversation just like that.

"Ah—I guess—I don't know. Well, really, I know. I'm on vacation, and...."

Jimmy started laughing loudly. "I love to throw people off like that," he said.

At that moment I couldn't decide if this guy amused me or irritated the hell out of me. "What are *you* here for?" I said with a forced grin.

"Ah! That's good. Just turn it around. Good, very good. We're going to get along real well." He reached over and squeezed my upper arm.

"And, what's your last name, Marc with a 'c'?"

"Ah, it's Ladouceur," I replied. I hesitated as I always did when I had to give my name to an English-speaker. I pronounced it La-DEW-cer, with the accent on the middle syllable. In French, it would have been La-dew-SIR, with the accent on the last syllable and with a gentle roll of the final "r."

Jimmy didn't seem to notice the hesitation and there was no comment on my name. He kept on talking rapidly, telling me that he always took a vacation in January.

I hadn't given much thought to my last name for quite a while, it suddenly dawned on me. I spent so many years hating my last name. My mother, on the other hand, was so pleased with it. "Gentleness, softness, that's what your name means, you know," she kept telling me as a child. My father's family name was one of the things she found the most attractive about him, she often confided to me. To my father, she would say she was very disappointed that he hadn't lived up to it.

By the time I was ten years old, I had decided the name was too feminine, too sissy. Why couldn't my name be Ledoux, for example? I loved that name. Although it translated into 'the soft one,' it had nothing to so with softness, in my mind. I translated it as 'the nice guy' and that was the name I really wanted.

"January can be pretty chilly here, especially at night, but the days are truly gorgeous. You'll see," Jimmy said.

I realized he really had no interest in my last name and that was fine with me.

I dropped deeper into the patio chair and before I knew it we were chatting like old friends. We talked about the upcoming weekend, how it should be fun with a full house, how the long weekend would bring out the party spirit in all.

Our chairs were facing west, and I allowed the heat of the late afternoon sun to penetrate deep into my tired body. The wind died at that moment and the place fell quiet.

I found myself not paying much attention to the conversation. Jimmy continued to do most of the talking. I focused on the lush surroundings. The Villa was blessed with tall palm trees, the tallest I had seen so far in Southern California, and everywhere there were vivid tropical flowers. The pool was mated with a hot tub that seemed big enough to hold a dozen men. In the distance, a fountain faced the Spanish-style grillwork at the entrance of the compound. A soft brown paint covered the high stucco walls that surrounded the property.

Jimmy kept on talking. When he realized I wasn't paying attention, he turned the conversation around to match my inspection of the place.

"This was Elizabeth Arden's fat farm," he said. I wasn't sure who Elizabeth Arden was. The name was vaguely familiar; I assumed a Hollywood connection. I had learned quickly that so many things in Palm Springs were linked to a Hollywood personality in some way.

There were only two other men on the wide patio surrounding the pool and the hot tub. They occupied lounge chairs not very far from ours and they seemed to be napping. One had a straw hat down over his eyes while the other sported large sun glasses. Their arms were stretched out towards each other and their hands were touching, one resting lightly inside his companion's.

"Here, let me introduce you to these guys. They're from New York City." Jimmy broke the silence. "They're really very nice guys. A little too snooty for me, but still very nice." He sat up and whispered the last sentence to me, and I was surprised at how annoying I found it.

"No, don't disturb them. I think they're sleeping," I said to him.

"Well, you can meet them later." He sat back in his chair. "That's it, there are only three of us here, four with you, of course," Jimmy said. "But, it's only Thursday. This weekend, the place will be full."

"How long has it been a gay resort?" I asked.

"About fifteen years," he replied. "At least, I think that's what the brochures say," he added. "This is my third time here."

"This is my first time," I said. "It really is beautiful, the grounds, the rooms, everything's first class. I was really impressed with the cottages. I wonder if they are all alike," I said, beginning to warm up to Jimmy. I had come to Palm Springs to meet gay men, after all.

"Oh, yes the cottages are all alike. Not that I've seen them all, you know," he said with a wink. "They're all split into two units, with an atrium in between. Mine is right there." He pointed to the cottage closest to the hot tub, explaining he wanted to be close to "where the action is."

I found myself assessing my new friend. I guessed he was about thirty-five, just a bit overweight. He said he was out—"all the way out," as he put it. His manner was slightly effeminate, but his voice was not. He was wearing baggy shorts and a yellow tank top. His sandals were intricate and seemed heavy

He said he was from Atlanta, although from Pittsburgh originally. He worked as a court illustrator, making sketches of court proceedings for a chain of television stations. I told him I had been a newspaper reporter for almost ten years.

"I hate my job, I truly hate it," he volunteered. "It's all too serious. I've got to be accurate and faithful; I'm there instead of the camera," he said, confessing that he does caricatures on the side when nobody's watching. "It keeps me sane, you know. I focus on this or that trait of one of the jurors, or the judge, or a lawyer and then I play with it. Of course, I never turn those in."

"I know what you mean, Jimmy. Working in court is what made me into a true voyeur," I added.

"I keep the cartoons to myself. I have tons of them back home. I turn in the real drawings to my boss and most of the time I have no idea what happens to them, unless, of course I happen to be watching the late news that night and there they are, one or two drawings. And, I turned in dozens. It's just not very gratifying," Jimmy said.

"You're not listening to me," he said loudly. "I don't blame you, Marc. My life *is* boring.

I had closed my eyes briefly. "I'm sorry," I said. "The sun is getting strong and I left my sunglasses...."

He didn't let me finish my sentence. Jimmy had picked up where he left off and was describing one of his most recent assignments. My mind wandered back in time.

I should have been more sensitive to the fact that she was pregnant and that she felt insecure and vulnerable. I should also have been more circumspect. But the couple on the beach blanket in front of us was truly stunning, and neither Louise nor I could stop staring. We were both such voyeurs.

It was one of those perfect beach days in Maine and we were both proud that we had reserved it for just the two of us, having turned down my in-laws' weekly invitation to have Sunday dinner with them. We were congratulating each other once again when the gorgeous couple set themselves up between us and the incoming tide. My jaw dropped when I first saw the guy: early twenties, dark hair and deep eyes, a perfect tan, and the broadest shoulders I had ever seen. His girlfriend, equally striking, had a skimpy bikini, and her blond hair flowed all the way to her lower back. They had been there for about a half hour when they started making out. Louise and I gave each other a quick look and tried to make it less obvious that we were watching their every move. Within minutes, the couple was getting quite serious; they were practically having sex just a few feet from us.

Suddenly a strong wave washed up on their blanket and interrupted them. They both jumped up and I immediately noticed the guy's erection stretching his bathing trunks. "Wow!" I said much louder than I should have. At that moment, Louise slapped me directly in the face. I was stunned. She started crying. "Just because I'm big and all stretched out, you don't have to gawk at her just because one of her perfect little boobies jumped out of her bikini," she said to me.

The perfect couple picked up their blanket and beach gear, walking past us to a spot a few yards behind us. I watched the couple go by, my gaze attached to the guy's perfect round ass.

"I used to be pretty. At least that's what you used to tell me." I looked at Louise and realized how hurt she was. I felt terrible, yet I felt relieved that she hadn't noticed what had really caught my attention.

"Excuse me, I have to finish unpacking," I said to Jimmy as I got up from my chair. The sun had just hit the rim of the San Jacinto Mountains, and I could already feel the chill in the air.

"How long you here for?" he asked me.

"Probably through Monday or Tuesday, maybe even Wednesday." I knew my flight back home was Thursday night, but I didn't want to commit to any length of stay, not yet.

"Good, he replied. You'll meet lots of guys."

I waved to him. I was already yards from the pool area and he was still talking. I waved again. I decided he talked much too much.

In the second excerpt, Marc is returning to the seminary after visiting his Aunt the Nun. What was supposed to be a day-trip becomes an overnighter when his train is canceled due to a snowstorm. He has to spend the night with Richard, a deacon. The next day, his aunt tells Marc that the real reason she had invited him was to tell him in person that his mother is dying from cancer.

Hulking Gray Hills

Boarding went smoothly and I hastily took possession of the first vacant seat I could find. The noises of the train station were replaced by the muffled brushing of heavy clothing on upholstery and of leather valises one against the other. Hardly any of the passengers spoke as they hurried to settle themselves in, each one bearing, along with his or her baggage, a piece of the January chill collected while waiting on the platform.

While we were boarding, the doors remained open and the compartment swallowed up the frigid air. My seat happened to be a window seat, and I noticed, after I had laid claim to it, that the pane of glass was frosted on the outside. I tried to keep my shoulder away from the window, but the cold penetrated my coat. As it invaded my body, I started shivering.

I knew I was about to cry, and this time I didn't resist. I quickly reviewed my recent conversation with my aunt and found in it no consolation. I repeated to myself her final words, as she led me to the front door and the waiting taxicab.

"Why? Why? Why do I have to be strong?" I said out loud, not caring if anyone heard me. I knew that's what I should have said to my aunt as we uttered our final good-byes outside the *Hôtel-Dieu*. But I said nothing. I knew she'd have come up with some kind of answer that I didn't want to hear. At the time, I just wanted to get into the taxi and leave. But now, I wanted to yell out the question. I wanted to ask it again, and again, fully knowing that I wouldn't accept any answer. It was the question that mattered, only the question.

"Why? Why?" I repeated. But not so loud this time, becoming aware that someone might hear me.

I shut my eyes tightly. I removed my glasses and let the tears break through and flow freely down my face. The scarf around my neck captured the tears and held them there. I folded my arms. I held them close to my torso, yet I made no effort to control my breathing. I didn't care if anyone saw me. I didn't care if everyone on the train, or if anyone, anywhere, knew that I was weeping.

I deserved to cry. I had never felt so helpless, so abandoned. I deserved to cry.

"Why does she have to die?" I asked myself quietly again and again. "Why do I have to be strong?"

The train started moving and, as it gained momentum, the murmur of the engine and the swaying motion of the cars had a calming effect on me. After a long time, I stopped sobbing. I wiped my face with my scarf. I opened my eyes and, slowly looking around, discovered that no one was paying attention to me.

An older gentleman sitting across from me was already asleep. His legs stretched across the small space between our benches, well into the area that would have been occupied if another passenger had taken the seat next to me. I could smell the snow-soaked leather of his boots and wondered if my day-old clothes discharged an offensive odor.

Each bench could comfortably accommodate three persons and completing the trio on the seat facing mine were two young women who were caught up in a fast-paced conversation. The only person sharing my bench was a middle-aged man in a suit. A businessman, I thought. Very well groomed, very distinguished looking, he occupied the far end of the seat. He was reading a neatly folded newspaper.

I sighed deeply. At least I didn't create too much of a spectacle, I told myself.

Now that the train was moving, it felt warmer in the compartment. I unbuttoned my coat.

I continued to canvass my fellow passengers. There was a great variety, in age, size, dress, and comportment. No one seemed to pay much attention to his or her neighbor. Many occupied themselves with reading or conversation. Some simply stared vacantly ahead of them, while others catnapped.

Where are they all going? Who is waiting for them? How did they weather their weekend? How many little tragedies are they carrying inside them? I asked myself. I realized that my usual curiosity was as intense as ever and I made a clear decision that I was not about to strike up a conversation in an effort to feed it.

I was grateful for the anonymity. The turmoil of my weekend was not something I wanted to share with any of them, nor did I want to camouflage my anxiety with idle badinage with strangers.

It was at that moment that I realized there was no one to share any of it with. I had no really close friends at the seminary. I enjoyed the company of some of my classmates, and a few of the older seminarians were kind and helpful, but there was no one I considered a close friend.

Of course, I would discuss my mother's illness with my spiritual advisor, Father Blanchette. I already knew, though, what he would say: "We must pray, and you must remain strong." Father Blanchette and my Aunt the Nun were working out of the same guidebook.

Who else could I confide in? I pondered. The fact that I didn't have a single close friend at the seminary didn't upset me. I had taken that for granted from the start. In my entire life, I had never made friends easily. Why should that change at the seminary, a place as cold and impersonal as any I had ever seen?

And what about my father? I had no idea how he would deal with his wife's illness and death. My father and I had always maintained a good distance from each other. We had shared very little over the years and I doubted if this crisis would bring us closer.

As the train rolled on through the open countryside on its way to the remnants of the Appalachians that cradled the city of Sherbrooke, I kept pondering my fate: I was an only child who would soon become part orphan, a loner, working his way towards a vocation he doubted was truly his.

I stared out the window. Through the frost, I watched the endless plains of new snow pass by. The glow of the winter sun was already angled, even though it was only mid-afternoon. Often, a distant silo or a church steeple would sparkle, and I speculated how the people of those small, nameless places had dealt with the snowstorm of the past weekend.

I watched gusts of wind sweep up the dry snow here and there, adding some relief to the flat landscape. Occasionally, the snow clouds would swallow up the train, and we would blindly continue on our route for a while as my view vanished into a solid whiteness.

I felt a chill. The thought occurred to me that I was probably coming down with a cold. I pulled away from the window and leaned into the vacant space next to me.

Wisps of conversation caught my attention. The young women facing me were caught in a frantic exchange, each apparently trying to outdo the other with fresh information. I could only catch an infrequent word, but I could easily see how entrenched in the conversation each of them was. They were well dressed, nothing rich or fancy, but certainly not plain. I guessed they were in their mid-twenties. Where are they going? How had they spent their weekend? Are they friends, schoolmates, sisters? Part of me wanted to know.

One of them had my mother's profile. I pulled away and sat back in my seat, my eyes glued on the ladies. I could no longer hear any of their words, and my mind was free to imagine what the excitement was all about.

I thought of my mother and my aunt at that age. Some forty years before, they would have traveled this very route as they emigrated to the United States. My mother's retelling of her first trip to *les Etats*—her expression for the United States—was a colorful and entertaining ritual of my growing-up years. She and my aunt had escorted their mother and their younger siblings on this first trip to Maine.

My mother never talked of the uprooting of the family from their ancestral farm or of the uncertainty facing them in a strange land. She only remembered the excitement of the train trip, and, as the event aged with her, it became more and more of an escapade. With wide-open eyes and exaggerated motions, she would tell me how she and her sister sang songs and told stories to calm the young ones in their care, how they gossiped about those left behind, and how they envisioned their new home. It had been a long, tedious trip from the infertile farmlands of Québec through the thick forests of the New Hampshire mountains and finally into Lewiston, the city of tenements and smokestacks. For my mother and my aunt, however, it had been the adventure of their lives, an adventure embellished by time and the retelling.

I understood that I really didn't know my mother. The woman I knew was in her mid- forties and fifties, a wife and a mother. The child on the farm and at school, the teenager caring for her brothers and sisters, the young woman learning to live in a new land, negotiating the travails of a strange city, adapting to the workplace, falling in love and eventually marrying—that woman was a stranger to me, as would be the woman growing old gracefully and enjoying the calm of her later years.

The segment of her life that had been shared with me would wind up being but a small part of a life cut short by cancer. I resented the cancer deeply at that moment. I hated it.

The old man facing me woke up with a sudden cough. He coughed again and seemed to be having trouble catching his breath. He pulled his legs away from my seat and sat up, his torso arched forward.

"Are you all right?" I asked him in French. He nodded yes and patted his breast. He coughed a few more times, and he seemed to relax.

"Did you have a good weekend?" he asked me a moment later. "I am assuming you are going back to school after the holiday break," he added.

"Yes, thank you." I looked away from him and stared at the passing countryside. I really didn't feel like having a conversation. Frankly, I had a terrible weekend, I said to myself, as I absentmindedly examined the frosty figures that had formed on the edges of the window. I had a terrible weekend, I repeated.

The train cabin, by this time, was cozily warm. I listened to the soothing, muffled rhythm of the wheels as the train moved incessantly forward. I closed my eyes. There were no more tears, at least not for the moment. There was only fatigue and I gave in to it.

My sleep was not deep or total enough to allow me to dream. I remained on the brink of awareness, and my mind kept projecting short images, fragments of my weekend. Then, the train slowed down just a bit, but enough to alter the rhythm of its movement, and I became fully awake.

"*Pardon?*" The voice spoke in French and it came from the passenger next to me. "You are speaking to me?" he added.

"Excuse me? Oh. No, No. I'm sorry. I was simply thinking out loud," I replied. I must have been day-dreaming, I thought, wondering what I had said in my half-sleep.

He smiled and returned to his newspaper.

"Here," he said suddenly. "You can have this section. I've finished reading it."

I reached out to accept the newspaper, fearing that a refusal would be bad manners.

"*Merci. Merci beaucoup,*" I offered.

He smiled at me and kept his gaze on me. I thought he was waiting for me to say something else. I didn't know what to say, so I opened the newspaper and started reading—to my surprise—the sports pages.

In bold type, the lead story reported on the previous night's hockey game between the Canadiens and the Bruins. I was immediately transported to my introduction to Richard in my aunt's office. In one swift movement, the entire evening invaded my consciousness. It played before my eyes like a film in fast motion—up until the moment when, in bed, he pulled me to him. I saw myself cuddling with him, his arm draped over me, his body pressed against my back. The film stopped there and that image flicked over and over before my eyes. The film wouldn't go forward. It replayed the scene again and again. To my surprise, I didn't recoil. I felt warm and protected.

Gradually, the flashback faded away. My eyes focused on the newspaper and I read the entire article. I chuckled, thinking that it was probably the first time in my life that I paid any attention to the sports pages. The article was written from the

Montréal point of view and it glowingly described the victorious performance of the home team. The Bruins had to return to Boston in shame, the writer concluded. I imagined Richard reading the same article. I could see him reliving the game with all the bravado that was naturally his.

And, what will happen to him? I wondered. Where will he be assigned after his ordination? Will I ever see him again? I stared at the newspaper page and I saw Richard's engaging smile and his deeply set eyes staring back at me. He should be a very popular priest, I said to myself. A good priest too. Even though he likes to have someone to cuddle up with in bed on cold winter nights, added a nasty voice from the rear of my brain. At that moment, the image staring at me through the newsprint changed and I saw him shirtless at the foot of his bed, handing me a pair of old pajamas.

Suddenly, I had a new problem to deal with, as I felt an imminent erection. I became agitated, almost terrified. This is ridiculous, I said to myself. I found it difficult to breathe. I was beginning to perspire. This is ridiculous, I repeated. I leaned forward in my seat in order to breathe more easily.

I became angry. For the moment, I forgot the sadness I knew I should be feeling because of my mother. There was only anger. I couldn't decide if I was angry at my aunt, at Richard or at myself. In my mind, all three became one and I harbored, relished, even, a strong distaste for everything about the weekend.

Distracted, I stood up. My fellow passengers moved their legs out of the way in an automatic gesture. But I didn't move. I stood there, not knowing why, not knowing what to do. To my relief, I noticed that my hard-on hadn't materialized. My breathing gradually returned to normal.

The compartment darkened. I looked outside. The plains had been replaced by hulking gray hills. We had entered the foothills. Soon we would be in Sherbrooke. I realized that my trip was nearly over. I returned to a sitting position. I decided to put out of my mind all questions about my mother and my future. I would sit quietly until the train pulled into the station. I would walk up the hill to the seminary and I would wait.

BRUNSWICK: A BRIDGE AND ITS HISTORY
UN PONT ET SON HISTOIRE

Juliana L'Heureux
Brunswick, Maine

There's a rustic bridge stretched across the Androscoggin River in Maine—between Topsham and Brunswick—that is known by locals as the "Swinging Bridge." Rustic is a nice word for it, since it has frequently been in disrepair. Town records call it the "Androscoggin Pedestrian Bridge" and show it to have been built between 1891 and 1892 for textile and shoe millworkers who lived in Topsham but worked on the Brunswick side of the river. A narrow and beautiful bridge hidden amidst clusters of scrub trees, it spans a lovely section of the Androscoggin River, where the currents rush parallel with twisting Route 1 through Brunswick.

French-Canadian millworkers might have called it *le petit pont*. After all, it was built primarily to accommodate them. Thousands of French Canadians came to the Brunswick area during the height of Maine's industrial age, after the U.S. Civil War, when the Cabot Mill produced cotton textiles using the Androscoggin River's hydro energy. *Le petit pont* linked millworkers in their apartments on Topsham Island to their daily routines—going to jobs in Brunswick, to mass at St. John the Baptist Church on Pleasant Street, and to shops on Maine Street.

Apparently, there was no need to maintain the bridge after the mills closed or moved someplace else. Today *le petit pont* is a terrific backdrop for picture-taking or a place to find a cute stray cat. Otherwise, most living creatures hardly remember the bridge or the reason it was built in the first place. Imagine New England's economy today if the French Canadians had not helped build the amazing wealth of the mill moguls with their readily available labor. It's a rhetorical question, of course, but worth asking nonetheless.

Let's pretend *le petit pont* is a graphic timeline pictured in a history book. The date, 24 June 1604, should be printed on the far left side of the picture. On that evidently beautiful day, explorer Samuel de Champlain and the Huguenot entrepreneur Sieur de Monts established a settlement on Maine's Ste. Croix Island, located in the Ste. Croix River—between Calais in Washington County and St. Stephen's in New Brunswick. So began the "French Fact" in Maine, preceeding the Pilgrim settlement in Plymouth, Massachusetts, by sixteen years.

"Here seemed to be a paradise," wrote Champlain, describing Ste. Croix Island in his journals. That optimism changed over the winter of 1604 to 1605, when the men came down with scurvy and half died. Survivors of Ste. Croix Island relocated, with the help of the local Passamaquoddy people, to Port Royal in today's Nova Scotia. Of course, from there the French Acadians met with yet another horror in 1755, during the British expulsion—*Le Grand Dérangement*.

Brunswick's Franco-Americans mark the year 1867, about midway in the timeline bridge—between the St. Croix Island settlement and today. That's when the Cabot Mill began a major capital expansion to meet a growing market for cotton textiles. To quickly meet the labor needs, agents were sent to recruit workers from the Province de Québec. A core group of these French Canadians came to Brunswick from the L'Islet region, on the south (east) bank of the St. Lawrence River. Many others, however, came from every corner of Québec.

Le petit pont is an obvious metaphor for social change. Roads and railroads allowed peaceful migration and immigration for thousands of French Canadians, who came to Maine in search of a cash economy life. Barry Rodrigue, a University of Southern Maine researcher and professor, writes about the Old Canada Road, running through the jagged terrain of Jackman. *Habitants* who were too poor to travel by train made the arduous journey into Maine on horseback, in wagons, or on foot.

Le petit pont is a story about a structure and about the people who used it. People like Topsham native Jean Caron says her parents and family members relied on the bridge: "It was our lifeline to Brunswick." The bridge was constructed by John A. Roebling's Sons Company, the company that designed and built the world-famous Brooklyn Bridge and several other pioneering suspension bridges. It is recognized as a historic structure. But Brunswick's Franco-Americans today are nearly as invisible as the swinging bridge. Also, they need almost as much cultural restoration.

Like other Franco-Americans, they quickly assimilated. They are steadfast leaders in Midcoast Maine communities, content to remember their long history but not boast about it. Although French is hardly heard in Brunswick today, there are occasional "sightings," like hearing the song of an exceptional bird seldom seen in the vicinity. Overwhelmingly, French Canadians worked hard to became prosperous Franco-Americans, but they have amazingly disappeared into the economic progress of the region. French names are common in Maine cities and towns, like Brunswick, but the language and culture are buried somewhere beneath the surface. There's a

Le Petit Pont—*The Little Bridge, Topsham-Brunswick, Maine, 2004*
Photograph by Rosanne Crider

cultural awakening happening within a small group of writers, actors, and performers trying to raise awareness through original artistic work. Without substantial patrons, however, these creative efforts may be too late to have lasting impact. Most Franco-American audiences have crossed the metaphoric bridge and find it difficult, if not impossible, to go back.

With restoration, Brunswick's swinging bridge will complement the beautiful Androscoggin River. *Le petit pont* will, no doubt, be another highlight of Brunswick's rich historic past, just like the people it faithfully served.

LES NON NON BLUES

Josée Vachon
Brownville Junction, Maine

My son was able to speak French, English, and Spanish until the age of seven; at fourteen he's still comfortable with French, probably due to spending time in Quebec every summer for three to six weeks. Around the age of six he had asked me one evening if he could stay up a bit later, even though it was a school night. I said: "Non, non, non, y'a d'l'ecole demain!" And he said back: "Tu dis toujours non, non, non, maman!" The way he said it was so cute, and once I put him to bed, I sat down and penned the words to this song in no time flat. It's one of the most fun songs for me to perform in schools today.[1]

Les Non Non Blues

J'peux pas passer la journée d'vant la télévision
Ça vaut même pas la peine de d'mander la permission
Je sors dehors, mais j'rends maman encore mal à l'aise
"Regarde la belle grenouille, Maman."
—"Dehors, pis ça presse!"

Refrain: Papa aide moi—Maman ne me comprend pas—
Ah! Qu'c'est dur d'être un enfant,
C'est toujours, Non, non, non
Oui, j'ai les blues—les non non blues.

Y fait même pas noir mais c'est le temps de s'coucher
J'ai beaucoup d'énergie, je ne suis pas fatigué
J'essaie de la gagner avec mes yeux plein d'affection
"Maman, j'peux-tu rester debout?"
—"Y'en est pas question!"

Refrain: Papa aide moi—Maman ne me comprend pas....

Touche pas ci, touche pas ça,
J'ai pourtant rien cassé encore
C'est quoi qui n'va pas?

Mais ce matin, "Maman, pourrais-tu me lire un livre?"—OUI!
Ensuite j'demande un jus, et les réponses se poursuivent.—OUI!
J'ose demander si mon ami peut v'nir jouer ici.—OUI!
Voyons, qu'est-ce que j'ai fait, elle dit toujours "OUI, OUI, OUI!"

Papa, j'suis content—Maman me comprend—
Ah, parfois si j'pose la bonne question
C'est oui, oui, oui, j'n'ai plus les blues
Ah, parfois si j'pose la bonne question
C'est oui, ou—fini les non non blues—

English Translation—The No No Blues

I can't spend the day in front of the TV
Don't even try asking for permission
I go outside, but again annoy my mother—
"Check out this cool frog, Mom."
"Out—now!"

Refrain: Daddy help me—Mom doesn't understand
It's so hard to be a kid,
It's always, No, no, no
Yes, I've got the blues—the no no blues.

It's not even dark out, but already time for bed
I have so much energy, I'm not even tired
I try to win her over with my loving eyes
"Mom, can I stay up later?"
"That's out of the question!"

Refrain: Daddy help me....

Don't touch this, don't touch that,
I have yet to break something
What's the problem?

But this morning, "Mom, would you read to me?"—YES!
Then I ask for juice, and the answers continue—YES!
I dare ask if my friend can come over and play—YES!
I wonder what I'm doing, she just keeps saying: "YES, YES, YES!"

Daddy, I'm so happy—Mom understands me
Sometimes if I ask the right question
I get YES, YES, YES, no more blues
Sometimes if I ask the right question
I get YES, YES, YES—the no no blues are over—

1 Josée Vachon,. "Les non non blues,"*Ça fait rire les enfants*, CéVon Musique, CV–CD401, 1996.

ACADIAN PLOYES

Emily Clavet Ouellette Martin
St. Agatha, Maine

Sandra Dionne Croft
Lewiston, Maine

Ployes are an inexpensive way to feed large families—they replace bread at meals. This is how you make them.

Take 1 cup white flour and 1 cup buckwheat flour, add a dash of salt, and blend with a wooden spoon;
Add enough cold water to make a thick pancake mixture;
Add 1/2 teaspoon baking soda and 1/2 teaspoon baking power, and then let these two dissolve into the mixture—BE PATIENT!
Add enough VERY HOT water to make a thin pancake mixture.
Then scoop about 2 tablespoons on a HOT cast iron skillet and spread the batter evenly;
When it bubbles evenly, flip and cook on second side very briefly.
Spread with butter, roll, and enjoy!

Emily Clavet was from St. Agatha, Maine. This is her Acadian *ployes* recipe that she handed down to her granddaughter, Sandi Dionne. Sandi reports that her own daughter missed *ployes* when she went away to college and has now carried on the family tradition as well!

THE NEIGHBORHOOD

Michelle Morgan
Auburn, Maine

Lying in bed I listen on the alarm
radio to classical songs
I will never learn the names to
& sense the train coming before
I can hear it, twitching vibrations
in my muscles, pulsing tremors,
a washing machine chugging
off-kilter in the basement
making the light bulbs tremble.
The train comes bouldering over
the trestle above the falls, sound
amplifying off the gorged river.

I know the graffiti by heart,
its jagged red and black symbols,
its whitewashed blocks,
the Portland-Boston line.
During the day it is picturesque—
15¢ postcards, French immigrants
& the names of old mill
towns tattooed on my back.
My great-uncle Henry worked
on the canal before it became
a sewer of garbage & told
of the gangs that fought
with fists and rocks after church,
Poles against Irish,
bloody skirmishes.

When the classical hour is over
your old girlfriend's voice
wires out through the metallic
speaker, stamping at my head.
You are long asleep next
to me & hear nothing.
I used to half-hang myself
out of my bedroom window
the next street over & watch
the old tower light blink
at me through the trees,
my cigarette winking back
a delinquent S.O.S.

Those were the days of rope
swinging in the gully
& throwing pennies at Donnie's
window to wake him up
& climbing the eaves at the church
& dodging headlights in the bushes.

Now I watch the children trudging
along in the early morning to wait
at the bus stop on the corner
where I waited every morning
twenty years ago.
Nostalgia fits me like an old cliché,
but my days are numbered.
Like the freight cars rolling by
this land of the unceasing past,
I've jumped the bridge & disappeared.

WHY BOTHER?

Michael Parent

Portland, Maine

For nearly thirty years, I've made my living as a storyteller, singer, writer, and sometimes actor. For the past twenty years, I've increasingly focused on material related to my Franco-American heritage.

After living in Virginia for nearly two decades (and re-appreciating my birth culture's uniqueness from a distance), I returned to Maine in 1998 and now live less than an hour from Lewiston, my hometown. Since 1977 I've done hundreds of performances, more and more of them done bilingually since the mid-1980s. I've co-authored a book of translated and retold tales from the Franco-American tradition and had a number of stories included in various anthologies, some of which are also based in that tradition. I've made a storytelling audiotape and a musical CD, as well as written and performed three plays that are all grounded in my Franco-American heritage. So, I ask myself, how did I, a guy who stopped speaking French for many years, who was guilty of ridiculing my own culture at times, how did I come around to giving performances and producing materials grounded in that culture? In seeking the answer, I turn to my parents and grandparents, all now deceased.

My father, unsurprisingly, was a key figure and unwittingly (or perhaps more wittingly than I've often thought) played a major role in determining my path. Gérard Alexandre Parent represented the voice that said: "Deux langues c'est deux fois mieux" (Two languages are twice as good). The other voice, represented by people within and outside the Franco-American culture, proclaimed: "Le Bosse ne parle pas français" (The boss doesn't speak French).

My father believed that we should retain our language and cultural heritage. And I think he understood that language and culture are inextricably entwined. My parents, Gérard and Alice, did not insist that we speak French at home, but there was an unwritten rule in the family that we must speak French to our grandparents. My paternal grandparents, Ferdinand and Adéline Parent, were able to get by in English, but to speak to them *en Anglais* would have been considered disrespectful. We never spoke English to *Mémère* and *Pépère*, and we never called them Grandma and Grandpa. There was never any discussion about the matter because it wasn't an issue. Since we had regular contact with them, and always spoke French, that language was

Michael Parent at the Timpanogos Storytelling Festival in Utah, 2004
Tom Thurston, Festival Photographer

well grooved into our neural pathways. Even as a teenager, during the self-conscious "let's-be-American-and-assimilate-and-not-let-anybody-know-we're-Canucks" years, I was able to easily converse with my grandfather (my grandmother had died by then).

If my father represented the voice of preservation of language and culture, there were many others, in and out of the family, who represented the voice that believed that our Franco-American heritage held us back, economically and otherwise. Some of these people told their children to get busy learning English, that there was no point in speaking their own (the parents') language. Others used French as a "secret language" when they did not want their children to know what they were saying. It's not surprising, then, that many children in that next generation (mine) didn't learn more than a smattering of French, often the colorful curse words or oft-repeated phrases. All this, combined with the notion that their particular dialect, or accent, was not "real French" led to a conviction among many that the French language was a social and economic liability. It was a private community language that worked well within the community, but did no good when the speakers ventured into the wider, mostly English-speaking world of "the Bosses."

For many in that generation, it was thought impossible to swim in both the mainstream and their own inherited "birth-stream." A kind of "transitional confusion" resulted. After feeling quite at home in Canada for generations, they came to a place where the message was that "you can work here, but you don't really *belong* here. You can't speak English, and your French is of an inferior variety. You're misfits." So, in many families, spoken French stopped quite abruptly between one generation and the next. And the Franco-American culture gradually became more invisible. One generation resigned itself to never completely belonging, turned in on itself, but encouraged their children to do whatever it took to someday belong. If it meant putting aside language and culture, then so be it.

In the face of significant evidence that this second "voice" was right, that in an English-dominated society there wasn't much point in holding on to a language which only identified a person as lower working class and therefore doomed to a life in the textile mills or shoe shops, one could reasonably ask, why bother?

Why bother making the effort to retain our cultural identity if that very identity was a drawback, a sure-fire means of not getting ahead in the big world of the United States? Why bother re-connecting to one's heritage and culture if the wider world, as well as many members of that very culture and heritage, are almost completely indifferent to it? For those of us involved in the arts, why expend our creative energy on a culture and heritage that seems to be dying out? Since I can speak accurately only for myself in trying to answer these questions, I have to ask, more specifically, why have *I* decided to "bother"?

In the introduction to his novel, *Ireland*, Frank Delaney says:

> We merge our myths with our facts according to our feelings, we tell ourselves our own story. And no matter what we are told, we choose what we believe. All "truths" are only our truths, because we bring to the "facts" our feelings, our experiences, our wishes. Thus storytelling—from wherever it comes—forms a layer in the foundation of the world; and glinting in it we see the trace elements of every tribe on earth.[1]

So, let's have a look at my "tribe," tell at least part of its story, and see what "trace elements" emerge. My mother's family, the Fourniers, journeyed from Québec to Suncook, New Hampshire, and finally to Lewiston, Maine. My maternal grandfather, Honoré Fournier, eventually became an overseer in the rayon weaving room at the Bates Manufacturing Company textile mills. My father's family followed a similar route, leaving Québec for Salmon Falls, New Hampshire, and then on to Lewiston, where my paternal grandfather, Ferdinand Parent, eventually worked as a tailor, though all of his seven children but one (who became a priest) worked in the mills at one time or another.

My early childhood revolved around the tailor shop, which my Pépère and Papa operated in downtown Lewiston after my father's severe asthma forced him out of dusty millwork, and visits to Mémère and Pépère's house "out in the country" on Bailey Avenue. About three miles (five kilometers) from the center of town, it was the family gathering place on Sundays and special occasions—where the latest news, jokes, and stories were told—mostly in French.

The tailor shop occupied the front room of our first-floor apartment on Middle Street, aptly named since we were within shouting distance of the most important places in town. The Bates Street playground was a half block away. So was the Central Fire Station, where we were thrilled to watch the fire trucks go screaming out to fires and privileged to be their official "backer-uppers" when they returned—our words and gestures guiding these sparkling red behemoths into their parking spaces. The cathedral-like Saints Peter and Paul's Church stood a block and a half up

Ash Street from the firehouse and could be seen for miles around. Masses were said in Latin and French. Saints Peter and Paul's School, imposing but not as majestic, sat three blocks up Bates Street. Half the school day was conducted in French and half in English.

Most of the inhabitants of this little world were French-speaking, and I don't remember giving that any thought as a child. Only later, when I stepped into the wider world, did I realize this was perceived as an unusual situation by most English-speaking residents of the United States. Through the years, in my travels as a performer, I've met countless people who know of my French-Canadian heritage. But unless I tell them otherwise, they often assume that since I've spoken French since childhood and continue to do so, I must have grown up in Québec and later moved to the United States.

Very few U.S. residents are aware that, according to the 1990 census, the northeastern U.S. is home to over three million people of French heritage and that most of their ancestors came to the U.S. by way of French Canada. Many of the original immigrants from Québec, New Brunswick, and Nova Scotia intended to come to "the States" only briefly, make some money, stay out of trouble, and go back home. So they did not make a lot of noise—in public anyway. They banded together in their neighborhoods, spoke French, occasionally kicked up quite a ruckus singing and dancing, but mostly stayed to themselves. Self-expression through song and story was okay in private, for family and friends, but it was most often not okay in public. So it's not surprising that—even today—the mainstream of the U.S. of A. knows little of the Franco-Americans and their culture. Like cautious visitors unwilling to offend a powerful host, our people were reluctant to be the center of attention in a stranger's house. Their songs and stories were sung and told around their own fires but not when "strangers" or "the boss" or the boss's kind of people were around.

As a younger man, I wondered why my grandparents' and parents' generations did not manage to preserve their native French-speaking culture *and* smoothly assimilate into the larger English-speaking culture? Why, for instance, were they not able to mix with "the strangers" or shed their "Canuck" accents—speaking French and English equally well? Why did they seldom put their thoughts into writing? Perhaps a closer look at the "tribe" and a particular member of that "tribe," my father, will help shed some light on these matters.

During the course of a long-ago conversation, a few questions arose about a possible connection or interplay between oral traditions and "literacy" or "literateness" in a culture, specifically the Franco-American culture in the northeastern United States. When we refer to someone as a "literate person," we are usually talking about someone who possesses basic reading and writing skills, an illiterate person being one who does not. The term can also refer to people who are formally educated—people of letters—who can express themselves clearly in both verbal and written communication.

Is there—in fact—a direct connection or a kind of inverse proportion between a strong oral tradition and a more advanced kind of "literateness"? Is it possible for individuals within a primarily oral culture to acquire a facility for written expression and gain the support of that culture for their literary efforts? Why is it, for instance, that so many Franco-Americans of my parents' generation seem to be such able talkers and singers, but seldom seem to be proficient and enthusiastic writers? Within my own family, the Parents on my father's side, the Fourniers on my mother's, it's often said that certain members of the family are, or were, fine tellers of tales and jokes, and good singers. But very seldom did I hear, or do I hear, anyone referred to as a good writer—not only of letters to relatives but of poems, short stories, or even novels—a writer defined as a person whose main avenue for expressing thoughts and feelings is through the written word.

Put another way, is a culture full of good talkers and singers, who have had minimal formal education, less likely to produce people who write and thus perceive themselves as "writers"? Examining this question for a number of different cultures (the Irish spring to mind) could occupy us at great length. I prefer to examine my own tribe and, as I specified earlier, one member of that tribe.

I learned some years ago that my father, Gérard Parent (born in 1912 and died in 1983) had—as a young man—written a number of stories. I never heard him refer to these literary endeavors, though he was usually willing to sing a song at family gatherings or tell us stories at bedtime. I can barely imagine my Papa finishing up a story he'd written and showing it to people to get their reaction. Why? There may have been a number of factors, but I'd guess there was one "bottom line" and that is that Gerry Parent's own perception of himself was that he was not a "literate person." Therefore his attempts at self-expression were invested with only a private value. And why might that be?

My father's early childhood was spent in the tiny village of St. André-de-Restigouche on the Gaspé Peninsula in eastern Québec. When he was about ten years old, the family moved to New Hampshire and, later, to Maine, living in an immigrant culture where hard work and survival were primary values. Most members of the family, Gerry included, worked in the textile industry in Lewiston, Maine, where they eventually settled. The gifts of gab and song were also valued among a people who often had large families and thus many occasions for gathering in groups. There was a long tradition of song, story, and dance, and Gerry's strong voice, tenacious memory, and nimble feet allowed him a secure place within that tradition. There seemed little precedent in the family or culture, however, for people going off by themselves to write. So, Gerry wrote his stories, but only shared them with a small circle within his immediate family.

It's probably worth noting that his formal education ended after fifth grade and, though he continued to be a steady reader on a wide range of subjects throughout his life, he never seemed totally at home with the English language and grew more ill-at-ease with his native French. He often said: "*Le bon français, y'est parlé au Canada*" (The good French, it's spoken in Canada). Thus, his perception of himself, and the Franco-Americans of themselves, was as people who don't use either French or English very well. Not surprising, then, that putting one's thoughts and feelings into the written word was not encouraged. That would invite the kind of exposure and judgment that could only confirm their view of themselves as linguistically and "literately" unaccomplished. My Aunt Antoinette, my father's sister with whom he shared his stories, once said of his literary efforts: "His grammar wasn't good, but he had a lot of imagination. His stories were romantic, they were short stories, like literature. They were like—classics. He would've been real good with an education."

Other factors were certainly at play. Franco-Americans are not the only ethnic group where the struggle to make ends meet precludes the leisure time necessary for written artistic expression. A doctor from Thailand once told me that in his homeland, where the level of poverty is staggering, there is an abundance of oral tradition and almost no literary tradition. A friend of mine quoted her Dutch immigrant father as saying that: "Some people make their living with their heads, others with their hands."

Many immigrants who came to the U.S. to find work and new lives were more familiar and practiced in the "work of the hands" than in the "work of the head." Literary expression was not so much discouraged as it was just not an active part of my father's generation's blue-collar consciousness. That might explain why, a generation later, I feel more like I've done real work if I'm splitting wood, pounding nails, or any kind of "work of the hands" than I do learning a song, writing a story or play, or any "work of the head."

Not only did the Franco-Americans of my father's generation think of themselves primarily as workers, the northeastern mill town culture into which they slowly assimilated reinforced that notion. The mill owners wanted factory hands, not singers, poets, or writers. And oral expression, in the form of songs sung and stories told, was seen as something to be done among family and friends, not for strangers or a judgmental public.

The French Canadians who eventually became Franco-Americans and supplied the backbone of many textile mills in the northeastern United States possessed many personality traits that fostered an oral tradition, but those same traits may have inhibited the development of a literary tradition. For one thing, this was a people fond of group gatherings. Because of the size of their families, many people spent much of their lives living in a large group on a daily basis. And it wasn't unusual for families to gather at the home of a family member, usually the grandparents who were close by and whose house could accommodate the whole clan. They also tended to gather together in an ethnically homogeneous neighborhood called a *petit canada* (Little Canada)—another larger group experience that reinforced the sense of community or village. Add to this a rich body of folklore in both story and song, an attachment to the past, and a basic need to affiliate and communicate verbally, and what you have, unsurprisingly enough, is a group of people where talkers and singers are in abundance and writers are scarce.

If my *Papa,* Gerry Parent, was at all typical of the Franco-Americans of his generation, his experience suggests that very plausible connection between oral and literary traditions. He had the soul of a writer and was surrounded by people who had little incentive to write. I'm not suggesting that the preponderance of oral over literary expression in the Franco-American culture is good or bad, deplorable or admirable. I can only wish that I had been able to read my father's stories and been able to keep copies. I've long forgotten the ones he told me when I was a child, and I dearly wish he had been proud enough of, and supported enough in, his literary efforts to hang onto those stories and pass them on.

So, what does this mean for me and my generation? If he were able to articulate it, what would my Papa have me do with this impulse or inner urging that he felt, and that I also feel, to create stories, sing songs, and have those stories and songs say something about our tribe? In retrospect, I realize that I've had some clues about his feelings on that issue. A particularly memorable one came during my junior year in high school.

I was the goalie on our high-school hockey team. I came home after a particularly bad day on the rink and at school. He was sitting in his chair by the radio. I was frustrated and angry about the lousy day I'd had and began fulminating to no one in particular about how I was sick of school, sick of hockey, that I was about ready to quit school altogether and go to work in the mills like many other guys in town. When I paused for breath, I heard the distinctive squeak my Pa's chair made when he leaned forward. Though he had a powerful voice, he spoke softly and clearly on this occasion: "You're not gonna to quit school now, and you're not gonna work in the mills, ever." His tone made it clear there would be no discussion. He didn't have to say the words, but he got his message across—"You won't do what I did. You'll do better." He might even have added—"I did what I did so you could do better." He never prescribed or suggested what it was I should do. He trusted, I suppose, that I'd find that out for myself.

When I came home from college and told him and my Mama that I'd gotten some free language credits by passing a French exam, he did not say "I told you, two languages are better than one," but his slight nod and grin conveyed his pleasure at the news. When I told him, years later, that I had performed a story in French at a storytelling event in New York City, it was clear he was pleased. When I started writing and publishing stories, as well as performing them, he didn't say it, but perhaps it crossed his mind that his son was not working in the mills, that his son was in fact doing something that he, the son, loved doing, and that he was doing so in public, in the big wide world, doing something that he, Gerry Parent, had only felt free to do in private. I wish I could have told him that he was and continues to be a fine example. In a culture that only knew how to encourage some of his gifts, he at least tried to go beyond. He wrote the stories and showed them to somebody.

So, why do I bother writing and performing stories that reflect my culture, language, and heritage? Perhaps, because my father and others did what they could. And, in doing what they could, they opened the door to my being able to do what I can. It also became clear that I was the one who should be doing the very thing I wanted them to do. I should do well in both French and English, expressing myself verbally and in writing, because I could. And I can, precisely because they did their job. My grandparents and parents made the journey and did the work of building a new life in a strange place. As a result, I have the opportunity to tell the stories and sing the songs in public that they felt they could only sing in private, within the tribe. I can also choose to sing them and tell them around any fire. And when I do, whether for my own tribe or for other tribes, it feels like I'm somehow more myself, that my journey back to my birth culture brings me all the way back to who I really am. And it's been good to find that many people are willing to join me for part of the ride.

So, a large part of why I "bother" is to thank those hardy, loving people of my tribe for doing their "job" and to celebrate them not only for surviving but for telling me their stories and singing me their songs—and thus clearing the path for me to make the journey to my own "job." Their primary job was to survive in a place where they never truly belonged. Because they did that job so well, I've had the capacity and the opportunity to swim in the U.S. mainstream and in my Franco-American birth-stream. And I honor my tribe with every stroke.

1 Delaney, author's note, no page number.

CONTRIBUTORS

Peter Archambault is an accomplished artist who was born in Madawaska, Maine. He has exhibited his designs all over New England—in such places as Old Town and Bangor—as well as in the Maritime Provinces, Québec, and Louisiana. Peter attended the Boston School of Practical Arts and the Rhode Island School of Design. In the early 1960s he was employed at the University of Maine (Orono) in the Graphics Department, where the *FAROG Forum* approached him to design a cartoon series. The result was the cartoon character, "Beau Frog" (Beautiful Frog), which attempted to put reverse spin on the racist stereotypes of a frog and to turn them into positive reflections about Franco-Americans. Peter used the feelings and experiences that he observed in Maine at the time and expressed them in his drawings. He now lives in Moncton, New Brunswick.

Eva Ashland Roderick (Marie-Eve Asselin) was born in Gardiner, Maine, in 1892. Her family name had been changed by a Maine postmaster. She married Henry Roderick, Sr., in 1915 (her husband's family name had also been anglicized from Rodrigue). They had one son, Henry Roderick, Jr. Her grandson, Barry Rodrigue, co-edited this volume, *Voyages*, in part inspired by her stories. Eva worked in shoe shops all her life, retiring from the E. E. Taylor Shoe Corporation in Augusta in the 1960s. She passed away in 1965.

Luella Ashland Roderick (Luella Asselin) was born in Livermore Falls, Maine, in 1894. Her family name had been changed by a Maine postmaster. She married Lawrence Roderick in 1918 (her husband's family name had also been anglicized from Rodrigue). They had one son, Richard Roderick. Her grand-nephew, Barry Rodrigue, co-edited this volume, *Voyages*, in part inspired by her stories. Lou worked in shoe shops all her life, retiring from the E. E. Taylor Shoe Corporation in Augusta in the 1970s. She passed away in 1980.

Normand Beaupré was born in Maine of Franco-American parents and *Québécois* grandparents. After receiving his B.A. he entered Brown University where he earned both a masters and a doctorate in French literature. He is presently professor emeritus at the University of New England in Biddeford, Maine. Normand writes in French and in English, having published a bilingual book on folk art (French/ English), four works in French and two in English. He is presently doing research for a novel based on Vincent Van Gogh's time in Arles.

Georgette Beauparlant Bérubé (1927–2005) was a lifelong resident of Lewiston, Maine. For many years she worked in the family business, Beauparlant Furniture. She furthered her studies at the University of Maine at Augusta and the Maine School of Commerce, where she met her future husband, Gérard Bérubé. Georgette served in the Maine State Legislature for over a quarter century, longer than any woman in Maine history. She is remembered as a tireless advocate for the elderly, youth, and the working poor. As a legislator, she was a delegate on a number of missions to Québec to foster closer economic and cultural ties. Georgette also hosted a long-running local French radio program, *Le rendez-vous de la chanson,* which featured music from France, Québec, Acadia and Louisiana. Along with Madeleine Giguère, she was a founding member of the original Centre d'Héritage Franco-Américain, which became the Franco-American Collection at the University of Southern Maine's Lewiston-Auburn College. She was chair of the Collection's Board of Directors at the time of her death.

Jim Bishop grew up on French Island in Old Town. His father, Frederick, had legally changed his name from Lévesque to Bishop before Jim was born, so Jim became the first in his line with the Anglo surname. Curiously, he has two birth certificates, with different given names, and was known as Peter for the first eighteen years of his life. He is currently known as Pepé (not Pépère) Levesque to his five grandaughters. Formally retired, Jim continues to teach courses in the English Department at the University of Maine at Orono and serves as editor of a multicultural book series through the University of Maine Press. He and his wife Joanna live in Bangor, Maine.

Dorothy Blanchard was born in Dover-Foxcroft, with family ties to the town of Dexter. After raising a family, she re-enrolled at the University of Maine at Orono, graduating in 1993 with a B.A. in History (Canadian Studies). Dot has also written two local histories, *Along the Damariscotta* and *Old Sebec Lake*. She lives in Newcastle, Maine.

Donat Boisvert, a bilingual, Lewiston-born resident, is the coordinator of the Franco-American Collection, at the University of Southern Maine's Lewiston-Auburn College. He has served as director of Canadian Relations for the Maine State Legislature and administrative secretary for Maine's section of the International Association of French-Speaking Parliamentarians. Donat also was editor of Maine's French language, bimonthly newspaper, *L'Unité*. He has written numerous articles and prepared exhibits on the French in Maine.

Claude Bonang was born in Brunswick, Maine in 1930. He is a graduate of St. John's School (1944), Brunswick High School (1948), and Bowdoin College (1952). For thirty-two years, he taught Science at Brunswick High School, except for 1957–58, when he obtained a Master's Degree from Stanford University, and 1960–61, when he taught at the Paris American High School in France. After retiring in 1987, he taught five years as a part-time biology lab instructor at the University of Southern Maine. In 1992 he started a book of stories in verse about his family and about growing up in Brunswick, which he illustrated with pen-and-ink. The book, *Memories in Verse,* was published in 1996, followed by a second edition ten years later. Claude enjoys music (he plays the guitar, musical saw, bones, spoons, and harmonica), reading, writing, working on the computer, swimming, art, and photography. He lives with his wife Ann in Brunswick. They have two sons—Tim, a graduate of Colby, and Chris, who obtained his undergraduate degree at Stanford and his doctorate in applied physics at the University of California at Davis—and two grand-daughters.

Michael Serizawa Brown is an adjunct faculty member at Eastern Washington University, and at Washington State University. He teaches on Law as well as Asian and Legal History. He has published articles on Legal History and Asian-American History in a variety of academic journals, including the *University of West Los Angeles Law Review* and the *Pacific Northwest Quarterly*. His book, *Victorio Acosta Velasco: An American Life*, is one of perhaps a half dozen biographical (in contrast to autobiographical) works detailing the life of an Asian man in the United States. His Ph.D. (History) is from Washington State University, his J.D. (Law) from Temple University, his M.A. (History) from the University of Maine at Orono, and his B.A. (Art) from Whitman College in Washington State. Since the 1980s, Mike has been a fervent advocate of civil rights as a community activist and, following his membership in the bar, as an attorney. In his free time, he participates in regional and national figure skating competitions with his pairs-partner, Shelly Lane.

Katie Camiré is a student at the University of Southern Maine's Lewiston-Auburn College. She is an Arts and Humanities major with a minor in Global Studies. Currently, she works as a part-time staff-writer for the *Lewiston Sun Journal*. Much of her study focuses on her French and Lithuanian background.

Paul Caron is an associate professor of Education at the University of Southern Maine's Lewiston-Auburn College, where he teaches Mathematics and Physics. His research focuses on creative and authentic assessments in response to state and national standards. Paul combines his vocation of writing and music with teaching Mathematics and Science at the K–8 levels by designing projects in which students compose and record songs that feature content knowledge. He is also a composer and lyricist himself, having written music for an original production, *Lewiston: A New Home*, as well as liturgical songs. He is a theatrical director and musical director, as well as a performer, having played in such venues as Las Vegas, New York City, Quebec City, and Moscow, Russia. Paul has received awards for excellence in teaching and for writing music.

Greg Chabot was born in Waterville, Maine. After he received his formal education at Colby College, the University of Maine at Orono, and the University of Massachusetts/Amherst, he worked in theater and broadcasting. He first wrote a series of plays in the late 1970s, including *Un Jacques Cartier Errant, Chère Maman,* and *Sans Atout*. These plays, along with Greg's English translations, are available in *Un Jacques Cartier Errant / Jacques Cartier Discovers America*. He has also written a series of twenty-six essays about some of the most poignant francofoibles, called *Entre la Manie et la Phobie*, as well as a three-act play about a Sentinelle-type event entitled, *Qui perd sa langue*. Most recently, Greg completed seven of a projected twelve pieces in *Les Sacrés monologues*. He is also the director of the Franco-American theater group, Du monde d'à côté (Neighbors), which performs his works. He currently lives in South Hampton, New Hampshire, where he works as a freelance copywriter and communications consultant, specializing primarily in high-tech work.

Sylvie Charron received her Ph.D. from the University of Wisconsin and is professor of French at the University of Maine at Farmington. She has published extensively on nineteenth-century French literature and is interested in dissonant voices in literature, particularly voices calling for social change and expressing the condition of men and women at the margins of society. In recent years Sylvie has focused on regional and immigrant *francophone* literature. With Sue Huseman, she translated *The Marquise and Pauline* by George Sand, and analyzed and translated *Grapes of Despair* by Tahar Ben Jelloun (a Moroccan prize-winning author currently living in France) and *Canuck* by Camille Lessard-Bissonnette.

Robert Chenard was born in 1938 in Waterville, Maine. He is a graduate of the University of Maine at Orono. A retired federal employee, Bob now dedicates much of his spare time (outside of enjoying his grandchildren) doing French-Canadian genealogical research and giving presentations of his work. Since 1997 he has maintained a popular genealogical website, which can be accessed at (http://users.adelphia.net/~frenchcx). For this work, Bob has received awards and has been highlighted in several popular genealogical publications. He has also published reference works on St. Joseph's parish in Old Town and St. Francis-de-Sales parish in Waterville. Since 1989 he has written genealogy articles in *Le Forum* (Orono) and the *Morning Sentinel* (Waterville), as well as a booklet compiling the records of

Waterville's Halde Cemetery, the earliest Catholic cemetery in the area. Bob is the father of three daughters and seven grandsons/step-grandsons.

Emily Clavet Ouellette Martin was born in St. Agatha, Maine, in 1905. She married Archille Ouellette and they had two daughters. Emily was widowed at the age of twenty-eight when Archille passed away from tuberculosis. She later married Alfée Martin and together they added three more children to their family. In 1943 they moved to Lewiston. Emily worked at Clark Shoe in Auburn for many year. She passed away in 1996 at the age of ninety-one.

Rhea Côté Robbins, author of *Wednesday's Child*, a memoir which addresses the question of what does it mean to be Franco-American and female, grew up bilingually in Waterville, Maine, in the Franco-American neighborhood known as "down the Plains." She is an adjunct professor of Women's Studies and Franco-American Studies at the University of Maine in Orono. She has published many poems, articles, essays, and book reviews, and edited or co-edited other books as well. Rhea edits an online 'ezine, since 1997, titled, *moé pi toé* (me and you), which promotes the current writings of Franco-American women. She worked as editor of *Le Forum* from 1986 to 1996. She is founder and executive director of the Franco-American Women's Institute (http://www.fawi.net/), which promotes awareness about the contributions of Franco-American women to the culture, their families, and the communities. Her most recent project involved editing a volume of translations of earlier Franco-American women writers titled, *Canuck and Other Stories*.

Béatrice Craig was born in France. She attended the University of Lille, receiving a *licence* (B.A.) in English Language and Literature, then a *maitrise* (M.A.) in American Studies. She came to the University of Maine at Presque Isle as a French teaching assistant in 1973, where—as she is wont to say—there was nothing else to do, so she married the language lab assistant (who was also a local boy). Their first date was to go to see the potato harvest. Béatrice also found the topic of her thesis while there: The Madawaska French population. After three years in France with her husband, teaching high school, she, her husband, and their baby boy came back to Maine, where she enrolled in the Ph.D. program in Canadian and American History at the University of Maine. After completing her dissertation (*Family, Kinship, and Community Formation on the Canadian-American Border: Madawaska, 1785–1842*) and receiving her doctorate, Béatrice taught part time at the University of Maine at Orono, Bangor Community College, and the University of New Hampshire. Since 1985 she has been a member of the History Department at the University of Ottawa, where she is now a full professor and teaches Canadian History and the History of Women in the Western World (in French and English). She has never stopped working and publishing on the history of the Upper St. John Valley. In 1995, Béatrice was awarded a D.Litt. by the University of Maine at Fort Kent for her work. Her book—*Backwood Consumers and Homespun Capitalists: The Emergence of a Market Culture in Eastern Canada*—deals with the relationship of rural people and markets in the nineteenth century, using the Upper St. John Valley as a case study. She is currently working on a survey history of the Upper St. John Valley from 12,000 B.P. to the present. Her other research interests are women in business in Europe. Béatrice was the French-language secretary of the Canadian Historical Association from 1992 to 2002. In her spare time, she reads mystery novels, knits, and does woodwork. She enjoys traveling and loves to cook.

Don Cyr was born in Edmundston, New Brunswick. He is a dual citizen of Canada and the United States. He was the founder and president of the *Association Culturelle et Historique de Mont-Carmel* in Lille, Maine. He was also responsible for the restoration of a very large former Catholic church that is now a cultural museum, *Musee Culturelle du Mont-Carmel*, and responsible for restoration of the parish rectory, which is now his home. Don worked for three years for the U.S. National Park Service as administrator of the Maine Acadian Culture Project. He has been involved with the following boards: Maine Humanities Council, Maine Arts Commission, Maine/New Brunswick Legislature Committee, and the State House and Capitol Park Commission. Don has received the Phoenix Award from the Association of North American Travel Writers, the Maine Historic Preservation Award for the restoration of the former church in Lille, and the Acadian Achievement Award.

Mary Rice-DeFosse is professor of French at Bates College and teaches in the programs of Women and Gender Studies and American Cultural Studies. She did her doctoral work at Yale University and the École Normale Supérieure in Paris. Mary specializes in French literature of the nineteenth century, revolution, and social change. She has published on Sand, Tristan, Agoult, Nodier, and Flaubert. Currently she serves as chair of Women in French, an international professional organization for research on women writers of French expression. She also serves on the board of directors of the Franco-American Collection at the University of Southern Maine's Lewiston-Auburn College.

Céleste DeRoche is originally from Portland, Maine, but presently resides in Vero Beach, Florida. She holds a master's degree in Feminist Ethics and Theology from the Episcopal Divinity School in Cambridge, Massachusetts, as well as master's and doctoral degrees in United States History from the University of Maine in Orono. Currently, she serves on the board of the Florida State Historical Society and as the humanities consultant for Cracker Tales: An Oral History Project of Indian River County. Céleste is an adjunct faculty member for Barry University and Indian River Community College. Some of her teaching subjects include U.S. History, World History, Florida History, and Women in the Church. Her "Walking toward the Red Sky: Franco-American Women in Maine" appeared in Marli Weiner's *Of Place and Gender: Women in Maine History*.

Jere DeWaters was introduced to photography in the 1960s, while living in Portland (Maine). As a teenager, he discovered the companionship of a camera during long walks in the woods. While still pursuing landscape imagery with a large-format camera, he also has worked on several documentary projects with groups as diverse as the Shaker family at Sabbathday Lake and the Franco-American community of Lewiston and Auburn. Jere's produced photographic surveys for the towns of Camden-Rockport, Litchfield, and Monmouth. In 1997 his collaboration with writer Kathleen Mundell resulted in the Maine Arts Commission book, *Generations: The Traditional Arts Apprenticeship Program of Maine*, a collection of photographs and interviews with some of Maine's most renowned craftspeople. He holds degrees from Goddard College (Vermont) and Clark University (Massachusetts). Currently, he is an associate professor and coordinator of Photography at the University of Maine at Augusta.

Sandra Dionne Croft was born in Lewiston, Maine, in 1956. She married Bill Croft in 1976, and they raised two children. Sandi works at the University of Southern Maine's Lewiston-Auburn College. She enjoys hiking, kayaking, and gardening. She and Bill also enjoy riding their Harley!

Rebecca Dirnfeld is a native of Vancouver, British Columbia. She attended the University of British Columbia, where she completed her B.A. in History. Having been inspired by her parents to pursue a career in academia, she became interested in immigration and cultural history. An avid fan of the outdoors, Rebecca enjoys backpacking and day-hiking through the British Columbia wilderness, and would one day like to experience different mountainous regions of the world. She is currently enrolled in a Master's program in History at the University of Ottawa.

C. Stewart Doty is professor emeritus of History at the University of Maine at Orono, where he taught from 1964 until 1996. There, he received the juried 1994 Presidential Distinguished Research and Creative Achievement Award for his work on Franco-American history. He is the author of seven books, two of which are concerned with Franco-Americans. His most recent works are *Photographing Navajos: John Collier Jr. on the Reservation, 1948–1952* and *Orono, 1806–2006*. Stew was founding president of the Associated Faculties of the University of Maine and past president of the American Council for Québec Studies. Retired in Albuquerque, New Mexico, he lectures in two "life-long learning" programs for seniors and paints watercolors. For seven years he was hiking coordinator at his senior center.

Normand Dubé (1932–1988) was born in Van Buren, Maine, and attended high school in Lewiston. In 1956 he graduated from St. Michael's College in Winooski, Vermont, with a major in English, and two years later received a master's degree in English from the State University of New York in Albany. Normand completed a doctorate in foreign language instruction from Ohio State University in 1971 with his dissertation, *Guidelines for the Teaching of French to Franco-Americans*. Between 1971 and 1977 he was based in Fort Kent and served as director of the St. John Valley Bilingual Education Programs. Normand was then appointed director of the National Materials Development Center in Bedford, New Hampshire, where he served for six years, until 1981. Considered one of the leading Franco-American writers, he wrote thirty-two books in French and English. Some of Normand's many works include *Un Mot de Chez-Nous* (A Message from Home), which was written as an offshoot of his bilingual educational work. *Les nuages de ma pensée* (The Clouds in My Thoughts) is a book of poetry about the world around him.[1]

Raymond Duval was born in 1933 in Brunswick, Maine. The son of Wilfred and Eva Déhêtre Duval, Ray graduated from Brunswick High School in 1952 and from Portland University (now the University of Southern Maine) in 1956. He was a partner in the family business (Duval's Bakery) until he accepted the position of cashier with Maine Fidelity Life Insurance Company in Portland. In 1957 he married Georgette Caron of Lewiston. They have three children and ten grandchildren. In 1965 Ray joined the *Brunswick Record*, which later merged with the *Bath Daily Times* to become the *Times Record*. When he retired after thirty years of service, he was the newspaper's CFO and vice president. Ray maintains an accounting and tax service business. An avid chess player, he ran the Brunswick Chess Club for a number of years and was team captain. Woodworking and ship-modeling are also his hobbies. He is a communicant of St. John's Church and a member of the Knights of Columbus.

Alaric Faulkner is a historical archeologist and professor of Anthropology at the University of Maine (Orono), where he has taught since 1978. He received his B.A. in Anthropology at Harvard University in 1967 and his Ph.D. at Washington State University in 1972. Since coming to Maine, Ric has specilized in the Acadian settlement of this state, and has conducted major excavations on early French sites in Castine and Cushing. He has also assisted Barry Rodrigue in defining the early nineteenth-century route of the Old Canada Road, linking the northern end of the Boston Post Road to Québec. While he continues to do research on Acadian Maine, Ric is currently working on the later British fortifications of the Revolutionary War and the War of 1812 in Castine.

Gérard Forgue was born in Jackman, Maine, to a family that had been in the border region for generations. One of twelve children, he was educated in St. Antoine de Padoue's parish school and Forest Hills High School. Following a four-year enlistment in the U.S. Air Force, Gérard graduated from the University of Maine at Farmington in 1986. Two years later, he and his wife (Tammy Jo Martin) had twins—Nathan and Shantelle. With this major life change, Gérard became a "stay-at-home dad," but also managed to graduate with an M.A. in History from the University of Maine at Orono in 1994. Now living in Norridgewock with his family, Gérard has held positions ranging from registrar of voters to deputy town clerk. In 1995 he joined the Norridgewock Historical Society, became its president, and was a founding editor of the *Norridgewock Historical Society News*. His interest in local and regional affairs led to his being appointed by Governor Angus King to the Chaudière-Kennebec International Corridor Commission. A founding member of the Jackman and Moose River Historical Society and the Central Kennebec Heritage Council, he has also served as vice chair of the Skowhegan Heritage Council. He currently works as an assistant clerk at the Skowhegan District Court.

Yves Frenette is currently the director of the Centre for Research on French Canadian Culture at the University of Ottawa. Prior to that, he was a professor of History at York University's Glendon College in Toronto, Ontario, for eighteen years. He also has taught History at the University of Maine at Orono and at Bates College in Lewiston, Maine. Yves has written two books, edited eight others, and has published more than fifty articles and book chapters on various aspects of French-American history.

Michael "Ernie" Gagné is a native of Auburn, Maine, but now resides in Lewiston. He was fortunate to have been raised next-door to his grandparents, who immigrated to Maine from Québec. After twenty-five years in sales, he entered the University of Southern Maine's Lewiston-Auburn College, graduated in 2006 with an Arts and Humanities degree, and is entering the field of education as an elementary school teacher. From 1985 to 1993 Ernie played a fictitious character known as "Frenchie" on WBLM radio's morning show. Much of his material was based on family characters and the Franco-American culture that he grew up in. On the air, Frenchie was a popular, dimwitted character who made short, weekly appearances on the Portland-based station for over seven years. Unfortunately, his humor was interpreted by some as offensive and his radio act ended. After his departure from WBLM, Ernie made several appearances as Frenchie at private functions and businesses, providing some after-dinner entertainment based on the same characters that had frequented the airwaves. A collection of his radio appearances was made into a cassette, *Frenchie's Greatest Bits*, and he has compiled a dossier of his show and the controversy for USM's Franco-American Collection. Today, he is very busy working as a father, husband, and educator. He moonlights as a wedding/party disc-jockey on weekends and is the public address announcer for the Lewiston MAINEiacs hockey club of the Québec Major Junior Hockey League.

Mercedes Gastonguay was born and raised in Lewiston, Maine. Her Catholic heritage and religious upbringing has had a great impact on her work today. She attended Holy Cross parochial school. Her French language remained close to her, as she studied in both the French and English languages. Both of Mercedes' parents were originally from Canada and came to Lewiston in search of work. Mercedes does original artwork on commission in all subjects and media. She is noted for her pen-and-ink renderings and paintings of homes and businesses. Her talent and versatility have led her to many challenging projects including Maine seascapes and landscapes, rustic still lifes, portraits, florals, religious subjects, and scenes depicting her Franco-American heritage. Her works have been displayed throughout Maine, including the Nettie Ricker Art Gallery in the Maine State Building at Poland Spring. Mercedes and her students have also been invited annually to exhibit a variety of subjects and media in USM's Atrium Gallery at the University of Southern Maine's Lewiston-Auburn College. In addition, her Bates College campus prints are available at the Bates College bookstore. Mercedes has been teaching art to children and adults in her Apple Sass Hill Studio for over twenty-five years. A self-taught artist, she also credits outstanding workshop instructors for much of her education. Mercedes owns and operates JMG Art & Framing Inc.

David Ghere is an associate professor of History in the College of Education and Human Development at the University of Minnesota. He received a B.S. in Secondary Education and a M.Ed. in Social Studies from the University of Illinois before serving as a military simulation instructor and designer for the U.S. Army. He received an M.A. and a Ph.D. in History from the University of Maine at Orono, and was awarded a pre-doctoral fellowship to the Newberry Library. Dave has taught American and World History for sixteen years at the University of Minnesota, as well as six previous years at Jefferson Community College in Watertown, New York. He has a variety of publications on Native American history, developmental education, and active learning teaching methods. He is the creator of fifteen classroom simulations and conducts teacher workshops on the use of active learning teaching methods and the creation of classroom simulations.

Madeleine Giguère (1925–2004) was a prominent, life-long resident of Lewiston. An internationally recognized sociologist, she was known as *la marraine* (the godmother) of Maine's Franco-Americans. After her early education in Lewiston she went on to obtain higher degrees at the Ursulines' College of New Rochelle, Fordham University, and Columbia University. Madeleine had a long and distinguished academic career, specializing in ethnic and women's issues. She taught at St. Joseph's College and Boston College before accepting a position at the University of Southern Maine in 1967. At USM she established Franco-American Studies as an important part of her curriculum. The author and editor of numerous groundbreaking publications about Franco-Americans, Madeleine was an authority on the analysis of ethnic components of the U.S. census. Upon her retirement in 1990, she was instrumental in establishing the Franco-American Heritage Center (now known as the Franco-American Collection) at USM's Lewiston-Auburn College. From Governor Curtis to Governor King, Madeleine served on statewide committees defending women's rights and promoting Franco-American contributions to Maine's development. Her many awards and affiliations included her appointment to the Advisory Council on the Status of Women (1973), the U.S. Advisory Commission on Civil Rights (1979), and the Commission to Study the Development of Maine's Franco-American Resource, as well as receiving the Maryann Hartman Award for Women's Achievement (1997). In 1992 the Library of Congress recognized her for contributions to Acadian culture and, in 1986, Mayor Alfred Plourde of Lewiston acknowledged her for lifetime achievements on behalf of Maine's Franco-Americans. (By Donat Boisvert, Lewiston, Maine.)

Michael Guignard grew up in Biddeford, Maine, and attended local parochial schools and St. Louis High School, where he graduated in 1965 as a National Merit Scholar. He then attended Bowdoin College and received a B.A. degree in 1969. After he graduated Phi Beta Kappa, Michael did graduate work at Syracuse University and received his M.A. and Ph.D. in Social Science in 1972 and 1976 respectively, writing his dissertation on the Franco-Americans of Biddeford, Maine. In 1972–73 he taught History and Government at Cazenovia College in Cazenovia, New York, near Syracuse, and then spent three months during the summer of 1973 doing research in Biddeford on an NDEA summer stipend. Michael entered the United States Department of State as a Foreign Service officer in August 1973. He served in Tokyo (Japan), Montréal (Canada), San Jose (Costa Rica), and Naples (Italy) before retiring to work with an immigration law firm in Washington, D.C. While in Montréal and Naples he taught U.S. History and Government to university students. He is now fully retired and currently doing research on the history of St. Andre's Home, which served as a home for unwed mothers run by the Good Shepherd Sisters in Biddeford, Maine, from 1940 to 1976.

Chase Hébert was born in Lafayette, Louisiana, in 1984, but has spent most of his life in Maine in the Lewiston-Auburn area. He has recorded a professional music CD with his former band, Alteria, under the independent record label Reindeer Records from Portland, Maine. In 2004 his son—Aiden—was born. He currently is completing a B.A. at the University of Southern Maine's Lewiston-Auburn College as an Arts and Humanities major, with a concentration in French North American Studies.

Joseph Yvon Albert Labbé was born in humble circumstances outside Saint-Georges-de-Beauce, Québec. His mother, Marie Rose, managed a household with four children and a thirty-acre farm. His father, Donat, worked as a cook in Maine lumber camps. Yvon attended a French-Catholic, one-room school until age eleven. In 1950 his father moved the family to Maine, where Yvon experienced a multitude of cultural and emotional precipices, which in turn energized, fed, and gave shape to a process of emergence from the "ethnic closet." Following two years of eighth grade, five years of high school, stints in shoe shops, lumbering, and work in a paper mill, he entered college to study French as a "foreign" language. Yvon then taught in public schools for seven years. He left teaching, disillusioned, in 1969, and re-entered the university to earn a graduate degree in French Literature—North American and Continental French. During this time he began the long road back to his cultural identity and self-respect. He undertook a reclamation process of his name, his language, and his culture, and decided to use his duality both assertively and creatively. With three other students, the participation of community people, and after extensive lobbying of the University of Maine administration in Orono, they founded the Franco-American Office. It became better known by its soul name, FAROG (Franco-American Resource Opportunity Group). The mission of FAROG has been to make the French Fact of Maine visible and respected at the University of Maine, where it had been ignored and unknown—in a state that is 40 percent French. A bilingual, socio-cultural journal was introduced in order to build a public forum for the articulation and discussion of Franco-American issues and to integrate the new knowledge into the fabric of the university. Course models were developed, seminars were offered, and projects dealing with gerontology, mental health, substance abuse, and the media were implemented. Joseph Yvon Albert Labbé is still reclaiming his inheritance so that he can have access to more of his tools and talents for his personal and professional betterment.

Matthew Laflamme is a native of central Maine. He studied History at Holy Cross College, the University of Maine at Orono, and the Catholic University of America. Matt has consulted on projects for The History Factory and the National Archives. His research in Franco-American history sparked an interest in the history of ethnicity and race in America, which he continues to pursue.

Pat LaMarche is an author, educator, journalist, and broadcaster who has successfully managed business and charitable organizations and is well known for her innovative approach to public service. Pat has leveraged her popularity as radio personality "Genny Judge" to help provide food, heating oil, and medical treatment for many of her fellow Mainers, as well as support for the Maine National Guard and September 11 relief crews. In 1998 Pat ran for governor of Maine and, in 2004, she served as the Green Party's vice-presidential candidate. A graduate of Bangor's John Bapst High School and Boston College, she also pursued post-graduate studies at the University of Amsterdam. She is the proud mother of two college students, Rebecca and John. Pat's recent book, *Left Out in America*, is available online and at bookstores around the country.

Kristin Langellier is a Midwest Franco from Illinois who didn't understand she was French until she moved to Maine in 1980 and connected the dots to her French-Canadian roots. She is the granddaughter of Nelda Bouchard Provost, who bore six children; granddaughter of Agatha Cyrier Langellier, who bore seven children; daughter of Lenore who had ten children; and mother of one. At the University of Maine (Orono), Kristen is Mark and Marcia Bailey Professor where she teaches communication studies and women's studies. sheis a member of the Franco-American Studies faculty and the Somali Narrative Project. Her research focuses on narrative, including family storytelling, breast cancer narrative, quiltmaking culture, and women's storytelling. For her co-authored book (with Eric Peterson), *Storytelling in Daily Life: Performing Narrative*, she collected family stories from Franco-Americans in Maine. She has authored numerous other publications and served as editor of the *Text and Performance Quarterly*. She dedicates her essay, "Voicing Mémère," to her grandmothers and mother.

After completing a B.S. in Civil Engineering from Northeastern University in 1974, **Roland Lapointe** accepted a commission as a second lieutenant in the U.S. Army and served an initial tour of active duty with the 10th Combat Engineer Battalion in Germany. Upon his return to the United States, he was released from active duty and joined the Maine Army National Guard, completing a wide variety of assignments, including company, battalion, and brigade command. In 1990 Roland deployed to the Persian Gulf, during Operations Desert Shield/Desert Storm, where he served as battalion executive officer, 286th Combat Support Battalion. In 1996 he received his Master's Degree in Public Administration from the University of Maine at Orono. In 1997 he was promoted to the rank of colonel, and the following year accepted a short tour of active duty to attend the U.S. Army War College in Carlisle, Pennsylvania, from which he graduated in 1999. In 2004 Roland was transferred to the Retired Reserve after thirty years of commissioned service. In between active duty tours, he served in a wide variety of civilian assignments: base civil engineer, Naval Air Station Brunswick; director of public works and city engineer, City of Waterville; deputy director, Facilities Management, Department of Defense, Veterans and Emergency Management; director, Bureau of Veterans' Services, and resident engineer at Togus Veterans Administration Medical Center. He is now district engineer of the Waterville Sewerage District. Roland married Susanne Bourassa of Augusta in 1974 and they have two children.

Cindy Larock is a "Franco-Yankee" from Lewiston, Maine. She began studying the traditional dances of French Canada over two decades ago with such respected *Québécois* artists as Pierre Chartrand, Normand Legault, and Yvan Gagné. After apprenticing with *Québécois* master stepdancer and caller Benoit Bourque through the Maine Arts Commission, she was designated as a Master Artist by the commission in 2004. A theater graduate of Bates College, with a master's degree in Speech Arts and Theater Education from Adelphi University, Cindy served on the adjunct faculty of the Bates College Physical Education Department from the mid-1980s until 2001 as an instructor of ballroom and folk dance. She also taught a course entitled "New England Folk Dance: The French Connection" at the University of Southern Maine's Lewiston-Auburn College, where she served for many years on the board of directors of the Franco-American Collection. She was a founding member and director of the Maine-based troupe *La Plume de Ma Tante* Franco-New England Folk Dancers, who performed in the 1980s, and she regularly leads dance workshops at Maine's annual DownEast Country Dance Festival, as well as in classrooms statewide for students from kindergarten through high school. Five years ago she founded the youth folk dance ensemble *Les Pieds Rigolants* (The Giggling Feet), which she continues to coach and direct in performances throughout Maine.

Anders Larson received his B.A. in History from the University of Maine at Orono in 1992. He has been teaching Social Studies at Sanford Junior High School in Sanford, Maine, for ten years and became head of its Social Studies Department in 2004. When not teaching, he enjoys playing guitar, spending time with his family, and racing mountain bikes.

Because his paternal grandparents lived upstairs, **Denis Ledoux** grew up hearing tales of his extended family and of their history recounted by the family storyteller, his *mémère*. In 1989, he won the Maine Fiction Chapbook Award for *Mountain Dance and Other Stories*. His other titles include *What Became of Them and Other Stories from Franco-America*, *Lives in Translation: An Anthology of Contemporary Franco-American Writings*, which he edited, and *Turning Memories into Memoirs / A Handbook for Writing Lifestories*. He has won two Maine Writing Fellowship Awards (1991, 1996). Denis directs the Soleil Lifestory Network, an international group of lifestory writing professionals. He also coaches memoir writers and edits and co-authors memoirs. In 1996 Denis was named Lifewriting Professional of the Year by the Association of Personal Historians. He has taught Franco-American Studies at the university level and has been a guest lecturer at numerous colleges and universities on the subjects of cultural diversity and Franco North American culture and history. He has written a memoir of his seminary high school years, *Simply Bucksport / A Seminary Life*, and has also completed an unpublished book, *Here to Stay / The Story of my 17th-Century Ancestors*.

Camille Lessard-Bissonnette (1883–1970) was a young country school teacher when she moved from Québec to Lewiston, Maine, with her family in 1904. She went to work in the mills, but she also wrote for the local French language newspaper, *Le Messager*, and joined their staff in 1908. Four years later she moved with her family to Alberta, Canada, but continued her writing. In 1936 she published her celebrated novel, *Canuck*. She worked for the Louisville and Nashville Railroad Company, traveling widely and writing, and retired to California.

Philomène Létourneau Simard was born in 1902 in St. Hilaire-de-Dorset, Beauce, Québec. She and three of her sisters followed other family members to Lewiston, Maine, in the early 1920s to work in the Bates Mill. She married Joseph Simard in 1924 and raised four children in Lewiston. In the year of her fiftieth wedding anniversary, she separated from her husband and lived independently for twenty more years. She was small in stature but had a huge heart! She died in 1994 at the age of ninety-two.

Raymond Luc Levasseur was born on 10 October 1946 in Sanford, Maine, to a father born in Disraeli, Québec, and a mother (*née* Lizotte) born in Springvale, Maine. He grew up in the shadow of textile mills and shoe factories, and then served in the U.S. Army from 1965 to 1968, including a tour of duty in Vietnam in 1967. He has been a political activist since 1968, currently with the Portland Victory Gardens Project. Ray was imprisoned for twenty years for political offenses—actions taken to protest racist apartheid rule in South Africa and U.S. crimes against the people of Central America in the 1980s. He was released in 2004. Ray is father to three daughters and grandfather of two; he currently works in the plumbing trade.

Helen Lévesque is currently a retired educator who was born and raised in Lewiston, Maine. She attended parochial and public schools there, graduated from Regis College in Massachusetts (with a B.A. in Foreign Languages), and then received her master's degree from Catholic University in Spanish and Education. Under the National Defense Education Act in the late 1950s and 1960s, Helen attended the University of California at Berkley, where she studied French, and then the University of Besançon in Franche-Comté (France). She then taught at the U.S. Army Dependent School on the island of Hokkaido (Japan). Helen has traveled extensively and taught French and English for many years in the public schools of Auburn, Maine.

Writing about Franco-Americans is an avocation for **Juliana L'Heureux**, but from an "exterior" point of view. Born into an Italian and Ukrainian family in Baltimore City, Maryland, she grew up with heroic stories about the American Revolution and how the colonists' victory came about, in large part, because of their alliance with France—in particular, the French naval victory during the Battle of Yorktown in Maryland that brought the Revolutionary War to an end. So it was no surprise when Julie fell in love with a Franco-American sailor from Sanford, Maine, who was stationed with the U.S. Navy in Maryland. Julie and Richard moved back to Maine, but she was surprised at how Yankee views of French traditions didn't match up with her valiant images: "I've always believed the French brought culture and enlightenment to North America," she comments. So, Julie embarked on a two-decade career of writing about Franco-American heritage for the *Portland Press Herald* and other journals. Julie also is a registered nurse and executive director of the Community Health and Nursing Services' Home Health Care and Hospice in Brunswick, Maine. Additionally, she's an essayist and blogger. Her webpage and domain are (www.mainewriter.com).

Dean Louder is from the United States, by birth, but *Québécois* by adoption and preference. He was professor of Geography for thirty-two years (1971–2003) at Laval University in Québec.

He is currently retired but, as evidenced by his blog, "À travers l'Amérique," located on the website of the Conseil de la vie française en Amérique (www.cvfa.ca), Dean continues to pursue his quest of French America. In addition to numerous articles on the French experience in North America published in scholarly and popular reviews, he has, with colleagues, produced numerous other major works. Among them are *Le Québec et les francophones de la Nouvelle-Angleterre* and *French America: Mobility, Identity and Minority Experience across the Continent*. He was received as a member of *L'Ordre des francophones d'Amérique* by the Conseil de la langue française for his exceptional contribution to the spread and comprehension of French culture in North America. From the Mormon History Association, he received the T. Edgar Lyon award for his article "Canadian Mormon Identity and the French Fact" in 1991.

Nelson Madore was born at Eagle Lake, Maine. He attended Fort Kent Community High School. He has four brothers and three sisters, with all but one brother residing in Maine. He received several degrees from the University of Maine at Orono, including his B.A. in History and Government, his M.S. in History, and his C.A.S. in Social Studies. He then attended Vanderbilt University in Nashville, Tennessee, where he obtained his Ph.D. in Education Management. Since 1969 Nelson has been a professor of History, Government, and Management at Thomas College in Waterville. He served fifteen years on Waterville's Board of Education (twelve years as the chair), five years as mayor of Waterville, and two years on Maine's Ethics Commission. Nelson was a member of the Chaudière-Kennebec International Corridor Commission when it was established. He and his wife Paula share two daughters, Maren and Virginia. He is captivated by all aspects of nature, and enjoys the mountains, the coastline, and small town communities. He also enjoys freshwater fishing.

John Martin was born at Eagle Lake in 1941. He attended local schools and received his B.A. in History and Government from the University of Maine at Orono in 1963, then did advanced study in Political Science. The Aroostook Democrat was first elected to the Maine State House of Representatives in 1964 and served on the Joint Standing Committees on Taxation, State Government, and Appropriations and Financial Affairs. He was elected minority floor leader in 1971 and served in that position until becoming speaker in 1975. In addition, he has been president of the board of the Foundation for the State Legislatures, chair of the Regional Executive Committee of the Democrat State Legislative Leaders Association, chairman of the New England Caucus of State Legislatures, chair of The Land Use Regulation Commission, chair of the Intergovernmental Relations Commission, and president of the National Conference of State Legislatures, as well as other positions in that body. In 1992 John was chosen to serve an unprecedented tenth term as speaker of the house of the 116th Maine Legislature. He is an assistant professor of Political Science and Government at the University of Maine at Fort Kent and a member of the New England Political Science Association and the American Academy of Political Science. He is presently director of Enrollment Management for the University of Maine at Fort Kent. John's other activities include serving as treasurer of Northern Maine General Hospital, president of Ambulance Services, Inc., treasurer of the Eagle Lake Water and Sewer District, and president of Fish River Rural Health Systems. He presently serves as a Maine state senator.

Michael Michaud is the second of six children. He was raised in Medway and attended Schenck High School in East Millinocket. After graduation he followed in the footsteps of his father and grandfather, gaining employment at the Great Northern Paper Company. He is a thirty-year employee of GNP and is a member of United Steel Workers Local #4–00037 (formerly PACE Local #1–40037). Citing a desire to help clean up the badly polluted Penobscot River near his home, Mike was elected to the Maine House of Representatives in 1980, then went on to serve seven consecutive terms. He attended the John F. Kennedy School of Government Program for Senior Executives in State and Local Government at Harvard University, and—in 1989—Unity College awarded him a Doctor of Public Service. In December 2000 the Maine State Senate unanimously elected him its president. Two years later, he was elected to represent the Second Congressional District of Maine in Congress, the first recognized Franco-American from Maine elected to federal office. In the U.S. House of Representatives, Mike serves on the Veterans' Affairs Committee and others. He currently resides in East Millinocket, where he is remodeling his late grandmother's home.

Corinna Miller was born and raised in Durham, Maine. After attending high school in Brunswick, she worked in the food industry—where she held leadership positions in all aspects of her work. Knowing that her great-grandfather came from Beauce County in Québec in the late-1800s to work in the mills of Skowhegan, she started investigating her genealogy. The mother of two boys, she felt it was important that they know about their heritage. Cory is currently completing a B.A. in Arts and Humanities (with a minor in French North American Studies) at the University of Southern Maine's Lewiston-Auburn College. She was one of the co-ordinators for the Maine Social Forum in Lewiston and brought together the Franco-American community to celebrate at this event in July 2006. She plans to continue her research on Franco-America after graduation.

Michelle Morgan lives in Auburn and attends the University of Southern Maine in the M.A. program for American and New England Studies. Her Franco heritage passes through her mother's side from the Beaulieu and Richard families, who migrated from Rimouski (Québec) to Caribou and then Westbrook in Maine. Michelle's poems and artwork appears in over a dozen literary journals, including *The Aurorean, Off the Coast, Wolf Moon Journal, Plain Spoke, Pemmican* & *New Verse News,* as well as in the anthologies, *Belonging in Word & Picture* and *Outside Voices' 2008 Anthology of Younger American Poets*. She is also editor of the online literature /arts journal *Panamowa: A New Lit Order* (http://web.mac.com/newlitorder/).

Judy Ayotte Paradis, a native of Ste-Agathe, served in the Maine House of Representatives from 1986 to 1992 and in the senate from 1992 to 2000. She served on most of the major committees of the legislature. In the St. John Valley she co-founded—with her husband Ross—the "Save Our French" movement, which evolved into *Le Club Français*. Judy also founded the statewide Franco-American Hall of Fame. Always an advocate of the French language and culture, she relentlessly advocated for *le fait français au Maine* (the French Way of Maine) with willing legislators and staff at the capital, encouraging other people of French descent to acknowledge their heritage with pride. During her fourteen-year stay in Augusta, Judy became known as a champion of women and children's rights and a staunch advocate of universal health care. Before her legislative career, she taught French at Wisdom High School and Madawaska High School. She was elected to the Maine Women's Hall of Fame in 2004.

Rosaire "Ross" Paradis of Frenchville served as a Maine state representative for the 2nd District from 2000 to 2006. One of his priorities in the legislature was to fight for justice and equal rights for all of Maine's people, including the large Franco-American population that has contributed so much to the state. Ross created and chaired the annual Franco-American Day and Francophone Caucus at the capitol. He has been recognized for his support of minority rights and cultural diversity in Maine. Before becoming a legislator, he taught English, French, and Latin for thirty-six years at Wisdom High School in Ste-Agathe and Madawaska High School. Ross also served as Language Department chair at both schools. He has written many articles and columns in weekly and daily newspapers to promote the French language and culture. He is presently writing a play in French, *Papineau*, about a bogey-man in the St. John Valley in the early 1900s.

The parents of **Paul Paré** were French-Canadian immigrants to Maine. His father was a lumberjack and his mother worked in a shoe-shop. They were in their early forties when he was born in the concluding days of World War II. A sensitive only child, Paul was raised in Lewiston-Auburn and attended bilingual parochial schools. At age fourteen he was sent off to a seminary in Sherbrooke (Québec) because everyone (himself included) thought he should be a priest. Leaving the seminary at age twenty-one (their idea, not his), Paul went to work as a reporter for the *Evening Journal*, a daily newspaper in Lewiston, and was one of the founders of the Franco-American Festival in Lewiston. He started working at the Channel Ten television station and eventually produced a children's series for New Hampshire Public Television that won an Emmy in 1980. In New Hampshire he worked for non-profit organizations, including the Association Canado-Américaine, where he edited a bilingual quarterly magazine and produced a weekly French-language program for cable television. Married for twenty-five years, Paul raised four children and became a widower at age fifty. He came out of his depression and came out of the closet at about the same time. He and his partner own an antique shop in Ogunquit (Maine) that specializes in religious art. Paul says: "I can't get away from that seminary training!" In addition, they own a tax-preparation business in Ft. Lauderdale (Florida) and Lawrence (Massachusetts). Paul also works as the host at an Italian restaurant in Ogunquit and writes as often as he can.

Michael Parent, a Franco-American Mainer, has performed as a storyteller, singer, and actor, in both English and French, since 1977. He has been featured at many schools and libraries, festivals, and theaters throughout the U.S., as well as in Canada, France, Austria, New Zealand, Ireland, England, and Poland. Michael is a 1999 recipient of the National Storytelling Network's Circle of Excellence Award. After living in Virginia for many years, he returned to his home state of Maine in 1998, and now lives in Portland. He created an award-winning audio-tape, *Sundays at Grandma's*, based on stories collected from family and other members of the Franco-American community. He co-authored *Of Kings and Fools*, a book of translated and retold stories from the Franco-American tradition. Michael's original stories, many of which are rooted in that tradition, also have been included in various anthologies, such as *Heroes and Villains in American Literature*. His 2000 bilingual CD, *Chantons, Let's Sing*, includes songs from Franco-American culture, sung in an alternating French-English pattern, and have been distributed to schools throughout Maine. In 2001, Michael, along with Susan Poulin and Gordon Carlisle, premiered their original play, *A Frog Stuck in the Ice—A Franco-American Story*. Since the spring of 2004, he has been presenting his one-person show, *One More Thing*, a dramatic portrait of Jean-Paul Boisvert, a retired Franco-American millworker; this monologue has even been performed in old textile mills! He presents bilingual assemblies and workshops for students of French, part of an effort to keep the French language and music alive in Maine and beyond, and of spreading an appreciation of Franco-American culture. His website is at (www.michaelparent.com).

A native of Seattle (Washington), **Richard Pattenaude** earned his bachelor's degree in Economics from California's San Jose State University, followed by a Ph.D. in Political Science at the University of Colorado—with a specialty in U.S. Government and Public Administration. Initially, Rich served as a member of the Political Science faculty at Drake University (Iowa), then went on to become an associate vice-president at the State University of New York at Binghamton, a vice president at Central Connecticut State University, and—in 1991—president of the University of Southern Maine). Rich and his wife Michele have a daughter, Lauren, who is a 2004 graduate of New York University and presently lives in New York City. Believing that "a modern university should be of its community, not just in its community," Rich has put his words into action by also serving on the boards of the Portland Museum of Art, the World Affairs Council, Blue Cross/Blue Shield, the Maine Science & Technology Foundation, the Chamber of Commerce, the Portland Symphony Orchestra, and others. In 2007 he was appointed chancellor of the University of Maine System.

Susann Pelletier, a native of Lewiston, Maine, has been writing poems since she was eleven. Her work gives voice to her deep connections to family and place in Franco America, as well as her vision of social justice and dignity at home and beyond our borders. Her articles and poems have been published here and abroad in anthologies, literary journals, chapbooks, and political and environmental magazines. Susann works as a learning associate at The Writing Workshop at Bates College in Lewiston. She was one of eight Bates College faculty and staff members awarded Johnson Foundation grants in order to take part in its 2003–04 faculty seminars on *Islam & the Modern World*. Susann was awarded a second Johnson Foundation grant in 2004–05 in order to participate in faculty seminars on *Movements for Change*. A pacifist, Susann is committed to non-violent social change and is intensely distressed by U.S. domestic and international policies in the initial years of the third millenium (C.E.).

Born and raised in Lewiston, Maine, **Maureen Perry** enjoys playing with words—be they in French or in English. Words are but one means of expressing her heritage: Maureen works as a reference librarian for the University of Southern Maine's Lewiston-Auburn College and also serves on the board of directors of USM's Franco-American Collection.

Linda Pervier is a Maine native currently living in Vermont. She writes: "My mother's parents and older siblings were immigrants, but she was born in Connecticut, fully assimilated, and married to a Yankee boy. I grew up with only vague notions of my own Franco-American heritage." Since picking up the study of French in mid-life, however, every exposure to Canadian and U.S. *francophonie*, including pursuit of *la chanson française* for fun, has inspired self-discovery and—best of all—has prompted "renewed memories and stories from Mom." In 2006 Linda earned an M.A. degree in French from the University of Vermont, where she was a Graduate Teaching Fellow.

Christian Potholm is the DeAlva Stanwood Alexander Professor of Government at Bowdoin College (Brunswick, Maine). He previously taught at Vassar and Dartmouth. His books about Maine politics include: *An Insider's Guide to Maine Politics*, *The Delights of Democracy*, *"This Splendid Game": Maine Politics from 1940 to 2002*, and most recently, *Maine: The Dynamics of Political Development*. Long active on Maine's political scene, Chris has served as a chief strategist for Congressman and Senator Bill Cohen, Governor Angus King, and—most recently—Governor John Baldacci. His national polling firm, Command Research, has been involved in more than ninety successful ballot-measure and image-enhancement campaigns all across the U.S. The role of Franco-Americans in Maine politics is one of his primary research interests, inspired in large part by his mother-in-law, Claire Roby Quinlan.

Jean-Paul Poulain (1945–2007) was born in Augusta, Maine to Lucien "Bobby" Poulain and Mërilda Paré Poulain. His early days were filled with strong French sentiment, as both his mother and father were musicians and singers. His mother was a singer of traditional French and French-Canadian folk songs, while his father was an opera singer. Jean-Paul produced a television show, called *La Boite à Chansons* (The Song Box), which aired in Augusta, South Portland, and Biddeford. Selected for the Maine and New England Artist Touring Programs, Jean-Paul also was past president of L'Alliance Française de Portland. He received the Mariane Award from the French government in 1979, taught French through the University of Maine at Augusta's Adult Education Program, lectured and performed at the University of Southern Maine's Lewiston-Auburn College, and served as liaison agent on the Community Council of the Franco-American Centre at the University of Maine at Orono. More recently, Jean-Paul was appointed as the New England artistic director for the *WebMusic-MusiqueWeb* network. Although his very active life ended in 2007, when he was grievously murdered in Augusta, the rich legacy he left to Franco-Americans continues.

Mark Paul Richard is a native of Lewiston, Maine. He earned his A.B. degree in Government and Legal Studies from Bowdoin College, his M.A. in History from the University of Maine, and his Ph.D. in History from Duke University. He has taught at Landmark College, Northwestern State University of Louisiana, and the University of Maine at Fort Kent—prior to his current appointment at Plattsburgh State in New York. At SUNY Plattsburgh, Mark is associate professor of History and Canadian Studies and also serves as associate director of the Center for the Study of Canada/Institute on Québec Studies. His essay in this volume is part of a larger work that examines the acculturation of French-Canadian migrants and their Franco-American descendants in U.S. society.

Gérard Robichaud was born in St. Evariste, Québec, in 1908. After attending various New England grade schools, he went to seminary in Québec at the age of fourteen. At nineteen, he left seminary to move to New York, where he immersed himself in an education that included art, writing, and photography. In 1942 Gerry enlisted in the U.S. Army and was deployed to the South Pacific, where he served in Oahu (Hawaii) and Iwo Jima. Soon afterwards, he met his beloved wife, who passed away in 1988. After his discharge from the army, Gerry attended Columbia University, enrolling in their English program. From that point on, he began working on his two greatest literary achievements to date—*Papa Martel* in 1961, followed by *The Apple of His Eye* in 1965. He now lives in Auburn, Maine, and is writing a sequel to *Papa Martel.*

The Eurasian ancestors of **Barry Rodrigue** first came to what is now called Maine with the Champlain–DeMonts Expedition of 1604. In the New World, they intermarried with the Algonquin and Abenaki nations, Afro-Iberians, and even the Irish and English, but never with English Canadians or Yankees! Born in Lewiston, Barry was raised in Augusta and—after high school—left for Alaska, where he spent twenty years as a commercial fisheries worker, ethnographer, and journalist. The focus of his work is in the field of multicultural and global studies. Receiving a Fulbright Scholarship to study at Laval University in 1994,

Barry and his son—Kenaï—moved to Quebec City, where he completed a doctorate and worked as a geographer in the Laboratoire de géographie historique. In 2000 he was awarded a second Ph.D. from the University of Maine in History and Historical Archeology. An active socialist, Barry and his son travel widely, working on scholarly and community projects from Québec to the Caucasus. Presently an associate professor of Arts and Humanities at the University of Southern Maine (Lewiston-Auburn College), he serves as the scholar attached to its Franco-American Collection and director of French North American Studies. Barry and his wife, Pénélope Markle, live in Bath; they both enjoy reading science and science fiction, as well as hiking and exploring for minerals.

Diane Simard McKenney was born in Lewiston, Maine, married Neal McKenney in 1973, and they raised a son and daughter in Poland, Maine. She is completing a B.A. at the University of Southern Maine at Lewiston-Auburn.

Clement Thibodeau graduated from St. Francis College (University of New England) in Biddeford, Maine, in 1954 with a Bachelor of Arts. Studying theology at the University of Montréal (Grand Séminaire), he was awarded a bachelor degree in Theology in 1958. Rev. Thibodeau returned to Maine, where he became a part-time teacher at St. Ignatius High School in Sanford and St. Louis High School in Biddeford. Until 1975 he taught Religious Studies at Nasson College in Springvale and served as Chaplain with the Brothers of Christian Instruction in Alfred. Nasson College awarded him an honorary degree as Doctor of Humane Letters in 1975. Clementß preached annual retreats for priests in Burlington, Vermont, as well as in Springfield and Boston, Massachusetts; and also gave annual retreats for sisters and brothers in New York, Maine, and Colorado. He served as pastor at St. Mary's in Eagle Lake (1975–81), Notre Dame in Waterville (1981–87), St. Mary's in Bangor (1981–87), and St. Joseph's in Gardiner (1987–01). He retired in 2001 and lives in Caribou, where he serves a weekend ministry in parishes in Northern Maine.

Josée Vachon was born in Lac Mégantic (Québec) and raised in Brownville Junction, Maine. She has been singing about her Franco-American upbringing for nearly twenty-five years. She debuted her career in 1980, while a student at the University of Maine and its Franco-American Centre, quickly winning over audiences across New England, Canada, and France. Josée shares traditional and popular French folk songs, as well as originals she composed to represent her Franco-American culture. She has eleven solo recordings, plus two more with the female trio, *Chanterelle*. For eleven years, she also hosted *Bonjour!*—the most widely seen French-language television program produced in the U.S. She was invited to perform for various cultural television programs in France (*Le grand échiquier*), Québec, and New Brunswick. She has often performed at various language conferences and immersion weekends for teachers, such as the American Association of Teachers of French and the Conseil International des Études Francophones. Her awards include the National Culture through the Arts Award (1999) from New York State for her work in schools and a proclamation and key to the City of Woonsocket, Rhode Island. Josée and her Spanish-speaking husband spent the early years raising their children trilingually, and due to her fluency in Spanish, she often performs school assemblies in both French and Spanish.

1 The biographica sketch about Normand Dubé is derived from several sources, including Dugas; the obituary, "Normand C. Dubé, at fifty-six; teacher, writer, Franco-American activist," in the *Boston Globe*, 23 August 1988; and Quintal, *La Littérature Franco-Américaine*, pp. 176–77.

BIBLIOGRAPHY

Acadian Culture in Maine. Internet site: acim.umfk.maine.edu/preservation.html.

Adamic, Louis. *My America, 1922–1938*. New York: Harper & Row, 1938.

Albert, Félix. *Immigrant Odyssey: A French-Canadian Habitant in New England*. Orono: The University of Maine Press, 1991.

Albert, Renaud, comp. *A Franco-American Overview*, Vol. 1. Cambridge (Massachusetts): National Assessment and Dissemination Center for Bilingual/Bicultural Education, 1979.

Albert, Thomas. *Histoire du Madawaska*. Québec: Imprimerie franciscaine missionnaire, 1920.

Album Souvenir du cinquantenaire de l'Institut Jacques-Cartier. Lewiston: unidentified publisher, 1925.

Allain, Mathé and Carl Brasseaux, comps. *A Franco-American Overview: Lousiana*. Part 1, no. 5. Cambridge (Massachusetts): National Assessment and Dissemination Center for Bilingual/Bicultural Education, 1981.

_____. *A Franco-American Overview: Louisiana*. Part 2, vol. 6. Cambridge (Massachusetts): National Assessment and Dissemination Center for Bilingual/Bicultural Education, 1981.

_____. *A Franco-American Overview: Louisiana*. Part 3, vol. 7. Washington, D.C.: U.S. Department of Education, 1982.

Allen, James. "Catholics in Maine: A Social Geography." Ph.D Dissertation. Syracuse University, 1970.

_____. "Franco-Americans in Maine: A Geographical Perspective." *Acadiensis* 4 (autumn 1974), pp. 32–66.

Allen, R. *Horrible Pettiness: Burlesque and American Culture*. University of North Carolina Press, Chapel Hill, 1991.

Allen, William. "Account of Arnold's Expedition." *Collections of the Maine Historical Society*. Vol. 1. Portland: Maine Historical Society, 1831, 1865, pp. 499–532.

Allison, Dorothy. *Skin: Talking about Sex, Class, and Literature.* Ithaca (New York): Firebrand Books, 1994.

American Federation of Labor–Congress of Industrial Organizations, Maine State Federated Labor Council. "Six Decades of History, 1904–1963." Portland: Maine State Federated Labor Council, 1963.

Ames, Alfred. *From Stump to Ship*. Orono: University of Maine, 1985. Videocassette.

Anctil, Pierre. "The Franco-Americans of New England." *French America: Mobility, Identity, and Minority Experience Across the Continent*, Dean Louder and Eric Waddell, eds. Baton Rouge: Lousiana State University Press, 1993, pp. 33–52.

_____. comp. *A Franco-American Bibliography: New England*. Bedford (New Hampshire): National Materials Development Center, 1979.

Angers, Philippe. "La Beauce en 1775: La Veille De L'Invasion." In *Le Terroir* 5, no. 2 (June 1924), pp. 37–38.

Angers, Philippe and Robert Vézina. *Histoire de Saint-Georges de Beauce*. St-Georges-de-Beauce (Québec): published by the authors, 1935.

Archdeacon, Thomas, *Becoming American: An Ethnic History*. New York: The Free Press, 1983.

Armstrong, Steve. "A Presentation of Some Statistics Concerning Franco-Americans at

U.M.O." *Le FAROG Forum* (1972), pp. 2–4, 9.
Armstrong, Steve and others. "A Compelling Case for the Recognition of Franco-Americans in Maine Public Schools." *Le FAROG Forum* (1971), p. 3.
Arnold, Benedict. "Arnold's Account Sheets of the Quebec Expedition." *March to Quebec: Journals of the Members of Arnold's Expedition,* Kenneth Roberts, ed. Garden City (New York): Doubleday & Company, Inc., 1953, pp. 717–24.
_____. Journal, Part B. *March to Quebec: Journals of the Members of Arnold's Expedition,* Kenneth Roberts, ed. Garden City (New York): Doubleday & Co., Inc., 1953, pp. 45–61.
Arnold, Benedict and Eleazer Oswald, secretary. Journal, Part A. *American Archives*, vol. 3, Peter Force, ed., Washington, D.C.: M. St. Clair Clarke and Peter Force, 1840, pp. 1058–60.
Arsenault, Bona. *Histoire et Généalogie des Acadiens*. 7 vols. Ottawa: Lemeac, 1978.
Ashland-Roderick, Luella. Letter to Barry Roderick (Rodrigue), 2 April 1977. University of Southern Maine's Franco-American Collection in Lewiston.
_____. Oral History, with Gladys Roderick, in Augusta, Maine, c. 1977. University of Southern Maine's Franco-American Collection in Lewiston.
_____. Cookbook, Augusta, Maine, c. 1940. University of Southern Maine's Franco-American Collection in Lewiston.
Ashland-Roderick, Eva. Cookbook, Augusta, Maine, c. 1930. University of Southern Maine's Franco-American Collection in Lewiston.
Audubon, John. *Delineations of American Scenery and Character*. New York: G. A. Baker & Company, 1926.
Auger, A. "Wotton." Lewiston Public Library, Lewiston, Maine, 1947. Typescript.
Baby, François, Gabriel-Elzéar Taschereau, and Jenkin Williams. *Journal. Rapport de L'Archiviste de la Province de Québec pour 1927–28*, Ægidius Fauteux, ed. Québec: Province de Québec, 1928, pp. 431–75.
Barkan, Elliot. "French Canadians." *Harvard Encyclopedia of Ethnic Groups,* Stephen Thernstrom, ed. Cambridge: Belknap Press, 1981.
Barrett, J. "L-A's French Heritage Is Revitalized." *Lewiston Sun Journal*, 13 November 2005, p. D–3.
Barron, Hal. *Those Who Stayed Behind, Rural Society in Nineteenth-Century New England.* Cambridge (England): Cambridge University Press, 1984.
Barry, William. "Fires of Bigotry." *Down East* (October 1989), pp. 44 ff.
Baxter, James, ed. *Documentary History of the State of Maine*. 24 vols. Portland: Fred L. Tower Company, 1916.
Beach, Richard. "Ideas and Suggestions for Further Research on Québec and la Franco-américanité." *Le Québec et les francophones de la Nouvelle-Angleterre*, Dean Louder, ed. Québec: Laval University Press, 1991.
Beale, Steve. "Minority Group Politics in Maine." B.A. Honors Thesis, Bowdoin College,1964.
Beaudet, François. Letter to FAROG, 22 October 1972. Franco-American Centre, University of Maine at Orono.
Beaugrand, Honoré. *Jeanne la fileuse*. Bedford (New Hampshire): National Materials Development Center for French, 1980.
_____. Preface to the first bound edition, *Jeanne la fileuse; épisode de l'émigration franco-canadienne aux États-Unis*. Reprinted, Roger LeMoine, ed., Montréal: Fides, 1980.
Beaupré, Normand. *Before All Dignity Is Lost*. Coral Springs (Florida): Llumina Press, 2006.
_____. *Deux Femmes, Deux Rêves*. Coral Springs (Florida): Llumina Press, 2005.

_____. *L'Enclume et le couteau: The Life and Work of Adelard Coté, Folk Artist*. Photographs by Stephen Muskie. Manchester (New Hampshire): National Materials Development Center for French and Creole, 1982.
_____. *Lumineau*. Chicoutimi (Québec): Éditions JCL, 2002.
_____. *Marginal Enemies*. Coral Springs (Florida): Llumina Press, 2004.
_____. *Le Petit Mangeur de Fleurs*. Chicoutimi (Québec): Éditions JCL, 1999.
_____. *La Souillonne, monologue sur scène*. Coral Springs (Florida): Llumina Press, 2006.
Beauregard, Yves, Alain Laberge, and others. "Famille, parenté et colonisation en Nouvelle France." *Revue d'histoire de l'Amérique française* 39 (winter 1986), pp. 396–400.
Bélanger, France and others, eds. *La Beauce et les Beaucerons: Portraits d'une région, 1737–1987*. St-Joseph: La Société du patrimoine des Beaucerons, 1988.
Belluck, Pam. "Long Scorned in Maine, French Has Renaissance." *New York Times*, 4 June 2006, p. 20.
Benoit, Josaphat. *L'Ame Franco-Américaine*. Montréal: Édition Albert Lévesque, 1935.
_____. "Attitudes des Franco-Américains en politique." *Les Conférences de l'Institute Franco-Américain de Bowdoin College*, Gérard Brault, dir. Brunswick, Maine, 1961, pp. 7–19.
Bérnard, Lauréat Odilon. "A Political History of Lewiston, Maine (1930–39)." M.A. Thesis, University of Maine at Orono, 1949.
Bernier, Germaine, Sr. "Chronology of Events: Sisters of St. Joseph of Lyons, France, TD, 1906–1967." N.p., n.d. Copy held in the Archives, Sisters of St. Joseph of Lyon (CSJ), Provincialate and Christian Life Center, Winslow, Maine.
Bernier, Margaret. "A Labor Study of the Franco-American Community of Waterville, Maine, from 1890 to 1940." Senior Scholar Paper, Colby College, 1981.
Bernstein, Irving. *The Lean Years*. Boston: Houghton Mifflin, 1960.
_____. *The New Deal Collective Bargaining Policy*. New York: Da Capo Press, 1975.
_____. *Turbulent Years: A History of the American Worker, 1933–1941*. Boston: Houghton Mifflin, 1970.
Bérubé, Georgette. *Thank You Georgette*. Bloomington: Autohouse, 2005.
Bethel Historical Society (Bethel, Maine). "Yankee Mill Girls' Letters from Lewiston, 1868–1879." N.p., n.d.
Biaya, Pierre. *Les marges de l'aekoumène dans l'Est du Canada*. Québec: Laval University Press, 1967.
Biddeford Daily Journal. (Biddeford, Maine).
Biddeford Record. (Biddeford, Maine).
Bishop, Jim. *Mother Tongue.* Portland (Maine): Contraband Press, 1975.
Bissonnette, Ronald. "Political Parties As Products of Their Environments: A Case Study of Lewiston, Maine." Honors Thesis, University of Maine at Orono, 1977. Quoted in "Voting Patterns of Franco-Americans in Lewiston, Maine," by William Vassar, Senior Seminar in History, University of Maine at Orono, p. 9.
Blanchard, Dorothy. "Into the Heart of Maine: A Look at Dexter's Franco-American Community." *Maine Historical Society Quarterly* 33, no. 1 (summer 1993), pp. 20–39.
Blea, Irene. *La Chicana and the Intersection of Race, Class, and Gender*. New York: Praeger, 1992.
Blouin, Lucy. In *Immigrants from the North: Franco-Americans Recall the Settlement of Their Canadian Families in the Mill Towns of New England*, James Searles, ed. Bath, Maine: Hyde School, 1982.

Blazon, Gerald. "A Social History of the French-Canadian Community of Suncook, New Hampshire, 1870–1920." M.A. Thesis, University of New Hampshire, 1974.
Bodnar, John. *The Transplanted: A History of Immigrants in Urban America*. Bloomington: Indiana University Press, 1985.
Bois, Chanoine. *Les Soeurs de Saint Joseph: Filles du Petit Dessein de 1648 à 1949*. Lyons, (France): du SUD-EST, 46 rue de la chariet, 1950. Archives, Sisters of St. Joseph of Lyons (CSJ), France, Provincialate and Christian Life Center, Winslow, Maine.
Boisvert, Donat. "1879: Rapatriement ou naturalisation." *L'Unité* 7 (July–August 1974), pp. 10–11.
_____. Letter to WCBB–TV, Lewiston, Maine, 15 May 1972, Franco-American Centre, University of Maine, Orono.
_____. "L'impact des relations interparlementaires régionales sur la francophonie continentale." In *Bulletin Amérique*, 1990.
_____. "Le Maine francophone," *Assemblé Internationale des Parlementaires de Langue Française* (Paris), Fall 1990.
_____. "Place Ste-Marie: Une carrière en utilité." *L'Unité* 12 (October 1979), pp. 6–8.
Bolduc, Claire. Interview by Michael Brown, 8 November 1990, 27 March 1991, 4 January 1991, and 29 March 1991, Franco-American Centre, University of Maine at Orono.
_____. Résumé, c. 1970–72.
Bonang, Claude. *Memories in Verse*. Brunswick, Maine: Claude Bonang, 1996.
_____. *Memories in Verse and Prose*. Brunswick, Maine: Claude Bonang, 2006.
Bouchard, Gérard. "Family Structures and Geographic Mobility at Laterrière, 1851–1935." *Journal of Family History* 2 (December 1977), pp. 350–69.
_____. *Genèse des nations et cultures du nouveau monde*. Montréal: Boréal Express, 2000.
_____. *Quelques arpents d'Amérique, Population, économie, famille au Saguenay, 1838–1971*. Québec: Boréal Express, 1996.
Boucher, Jacqueline. "The Franco-American in Lewiston." Senior Thesis, Bates College, 1956.
Bouchette, Joseph. *Topographical Dictionary of the Province of Lower Canada*. London: Longman, Rees, Orme, Brown, Green, and Longman, 1832.
Bourque, Bruce. "Prehistoric Indians of Maine." *Maine the Pine Tree State from Prehistory to the Present*, Richard Judd, Edwin Churchill, and Joel Eastman, eds. Orono: University of Maine Press, 1995, pp. 12–30.
_____. *Twelve Thousand Years: American Indians in Maine*. Lincoln: University of Nebraska Press, 2004.
Bowen, William. *The Willamette Valley Migration and Settlement on the Oregon Frontier*. Seattle: University of Washington Press, 1978.
Bradford, E. Alice. *Interesting Bits of Local History*. N.p., 1929. Abbott Memorial Library, Dexter, Maine. Pamphlet.
Bradford, William. *Of Plymouth Plantation, 1620–1647*. New York: Alfred A. Knopf, 1952.
Branham, R., L. Francoeur, and W. Surkis. *Roughing the Uppers: the Great Shoe Strike of 1937*. Lewiston (Maine): Bates College, 1992. Videocassette.
Brault, Gérard. *The French-Canadian Heritage in New England*. Hanover (New Hampshire): University Press of New England, 1986.
Brebner, John. *The Neutral Yankees of Nova Scotia; A Marginal Colony During the Revolutionary Years*. New York: Columbia University Press, 1937.
Breton, R. "Red Scare: A Study in Maine Nativism, 1919–1925." M.A. Thesis, University of Maine at Orono, 1972.

Brousseau, Yves. "*Le FAROG Forum:* autopsie d'un journal d'éveil et de combat." M.A. Dissertation, Laval University, 1985.
Brown, Michael. "Franco-American Identity at the University of Maine." *Maine History* 36, nos. 3–4 (winter–spring 1997), pp. 106–19.
_____. "Revolution: The Coming of FAROG, 1970–1972." M.A. Thesis, University of Maine at Orono, 1992.
Bruegel, Martin. *Farm, Shop, Landing: The Rise of a Market Society in the Hudson Valley, 1780–1860*. Durham (North Carolina): Duke University Press, 2002.
Brunet, Henri. "Lettre de Henri Brunet à sa sœur, Boston, le 4e février, 1675." In Collection Clairambault, Public Archives of Canada, Ottawa MG7 I A5. Vol. 106, no. 864, pp. 68–69.
Brunswick, Town of. *The Town of Brunswick, Maine, in the Year 1739*. File material. Copy donated by Raymond Duval to the University of Southern Maine's Franco-American Collection at Lewiston-Auburn College.
Buerger, Geoffrey. "Williams, Thomas." *Dictionaire Biographique du Canada*, vol. 7, Francess Halpenny and Jean Hamelin, eds. Québec and Toronto: Les Presses de l'Université Laval and the University of Toronto Press, 1988, p. 988.
Buhle, Paul. *Labor's Joke Book*. St. Louis (Missouri): WD Press, 1985.
Buker, Margaret. "The Irish in Lewiston, Maine: A Search for Security on the Urban Frontier, 1850–1880." *Maine Historical Society Quarterly* 13, no. 1A, (1973), pp. 3–25.
Burnap, Courtney. "Canadian Background of the Franco-Americans of Lewiston." B.A. Thesis, Bates College, 1938.
Burnham, John. "The Military Road." N.p., n.d. Aroostook County History and Art Museum, Houlton, Maine.
Byrne, William and others. *History of the Catholic Church in the New England States*. 2 vols. Boston: Hurd and Everts, 1899.
Callnan, Sister Miriam Therese. *Aroostook Architect: The Life and Times of the Reverend Joseph S. Marcoux*. Brunswick (Maine): Harpswell Press, 1977.
Calloway, Colin. *The Western Abenakis of Vermont, 1600–1800: War, Migration, and the Survival of an Indian People*. Norman: University of Oklahoma Press, 1990.
Calvert, Mary. *Black Robe on the Kennebec*. Monmouth (Maine): Monmouth Press, 1991.
Cameron, Ardis. *Radicals of the Worst Sort: Laboring Women in Lawrence, Massachusetts, 1860–1912*. Chicago: University of Illinois Press, 1993.
Campbell, Franklin. "Industrial Survey of Waterville, Maine: Prepared for the Waterville-Winslow Chamber of Commerce." 1935. Copy held at the Miller Library, Colby College, Waterville, Maine.
Canada, Public Archives. *Collection de documents relatifs à l'histoire de la Nouvelle-France*. Ottawa: Central Microfilm Unit, 1970.
_____. Archives des Colonies, correspondence générale. MG1, C11A; C11B; C11C.
_____. Archives de la Marine. B4.
_____. *Censuses of Canada, 1665 to 1871—Recensements du Canada—Statistiques du Canada*, IV. Ottawa: L. B. Taylor, 1876, pp. 64–80.
"Canada Road," *Maine's French Communities*. Internet site: FrancoMaine.org/Français/Histo/Canada_corridor.html/.
Carleton, Guy. Letters to Lt. Col. Anstruther or Officer Commanding the 62nd Regiment, 15 November 1776, p. 63; 21 January 1777, pp. 82–83. *Haldimand Papers*, Ms. No. 21699.

_____. Letter to the Commanding Officer at Nouvelle Beauce, 22 July 1777. *Haldimand Papers*, Ms. No. 21699, p. 149.
_____. Letter to Hector Cramahé, 28 October 1776. *Haldimand Papers*, Ms. No. 21699, p. 58.
_____. Letter to the Officer Commanding upon the Chaudiere, 8 December 1776. *Haldimand Papers*, Ms. No. 21699, p. 72.
_____. Letter to Brigadier General Powell, 28 October 1776. *Haldimand Papers*, Ms. No. 21699, p. 58.
_____. Letter to Friedrich Adolph von Riedesel, 20 December 1776. *Haldimand Papers*, Ms. No. 21699, p. 76.
Caron, Adrien, Yves Hébert, and Nelson Michaud. *De Canada en Acadie: Le Grand-Portage*. La Pocatière (Québec): Société historique de la Côte-du-Sud, 1980.
Carpenter, N. *Immigrants and Their Children, 1920*. United States Census Monographs VII. Washington (D.C.): United States Government Printing Office, 1927.
Carrier, P. "Lafayette, Where Are You?" In *Le FAROG Forum* (March/April/May 1993). Originally printed in the *Portland Press Herald*, 9 February 1993.
Cassidy, F. and J. H. Hall, eds. *Dictionary of American Regional English*. Cambridge (Massachusetts): Harvard University Press, 1991.
Chamber of Commerce, Maine (Portland). "Progressive and Enterprising Dexter, Maine," *Chamber of Commerce Journal of Maine* 29, no. 9, 1917.
Chaput, Donald. "Some Repatriement Dilemmas." *Canadian Historical Review* 49 (December 1968), pp. 400–12.
Chartier, Armand. *The Franco-Americans of New England: A History*. Manchester (New Hampshire) and Worcester (Massachusetts): ACA Assurance and the Institut français, Assumption College, 1999.
_____. *Histoire des Franco-Américains de la Nouvelle-Angleterre, 1775–1990*. Sillery (Québec): Septentrion, 1991.
Chaudière-Kennebec Corridor. Internet site: www.chaudiere-kennebec.com/.
Chenard, Robert. Letter. *Bangor Daily News*, 26 August 1994, p. 1.
_____. *Marriages of St. Joseph's Catholic Church, Old Town,* Maine. Waterville (Maine): Published by the author, c. 1992.
_____. *St. Francis de Sales Catholic Church, Waterville, Maine*. Vol. 1. Waterville (Maine): Published by the author, 1994.
_____. Letter to Barry Rodrigue, 4 August 1995.
_____. comp. *Margaret Chase Smith's Franco-American Heritage*. Franco-American Women's Institute, 25 December 2006. Internet site: http://members.aol.com/FAWIDIR/SmithgoesFranco.html.
Choquette, Leslie. *Frenchmen into Peasants: Modernity and Tradition in the Peopling of French Canada*. Cambridge (Massachusetts): Harvard University Press, 1997.
Chute, Robert. *Thirteen Moons / Treize lunes*. Moonbeam (Ontario): Penumbra Press, 1982.
Cinquantième anniversaire de l'Association Saint-Dominique, Lewiston, Maine 1886–1936. Lewiston: n.p., n.d. Copy held by Yves Frenette.
Clark, Christopher. "Household Economy, Market Exchange and the Rise of Capitalism in the Connecticut Valley, 1800–1860." *Journal of Social History* XII (1979), pp. 169–89.
Clukey, Clatus and Jeanette Chabot Clukey. Interview by Dorothy Blanchard. Tape recording, 30 October 1991. Tapes held by Dorothy Blanchard, Newcastle, Maine.
Clukey, James. Interviewed by Dorothy Blanchard. Tape recording. Dexter, Maine, 30

October 1991. Tapes held by Dorothy Blanchard, Newcastle, Maine.
Coburn, Louise. *The Passage of the Arnold Expedition through Skowhegan*. Skowhegan (Maine): Louise Coburn, 1912, 1922.
Codman II, John. *Arnold's Expedition to Quebec*. New York: The MacMillan Company, 1901.
Cole, Susan. "Missing Alice: In Search of a Mother's Voice." *Figuring Age: Women, Bodies, Generations*, Kathleen Woodard, ed. Bloomington: Indiana University Press, 1999, pp. 336–39.
Coleman, Emma Lewis. *New England Captives Carried to Canada*. 2 vols. Portland (Maine): Southworth Press, 1925.
Collins, Charles, "The Acadians of Madawaska." *New England Catholic Historical Society's Publication 3*. Boston: Press of Thomas A. Whalen, 1902.
Collins, F. "Way Down East with the K.K.K." *Collier's* (15 December 1923).
Committee of American Citizens of Madawaska. Letter to Enoch Lincoln, Governor of the State of Maine, 9 January 1827. *Documentary History of the North Eastern Boundary Controversy,* John Sprague, ed., p. 351.
Connolly, Michael. *They Change Their Sky: The Irish in Maine*. Orono: University of Maine Press, 2004.
Cook, Cora. "Women Who Work for Wages." *American Federationist* 33, no. 4 (April 1926), pp. 454–59.
Copper, Babba. *Over The Hill: Reflections on Ageism between Women*. Freedom (California): Crossing Press, 1988.
Côté-Robbins, Rhéa. *Wednesday's Child*. Brunswick: Maine Writers & Publishers Alliance, 1997.
Côté-Robbins, Rhéa, Lanette Landry Petrie, Kristin Langellier, and Kathyrn Slott, eds. *I Am Franco-American and Proud of It: An Anthology of Writings of Franco-American Women / Je suis franco américaine et fière de l'être*. Fogler Library, Special Collections, University of Maine at Orono, 1995. Manuscript.
Courville, Serge. "La crise agricole du Bas Canada, éléments d'une réflection géographique." *Cahiers de Géographie du Québec* 24; Part 1 in no. 62 (September 1980), pp. 193–224; Part 2 in no. 63 (December 1980), pp. 385–428.
_____. *Entre ville et campagne: l'essor du village dans les seigneuries du Bas-Canada,* Sainte-Foy (Québec): Presse de l'université Laval, 1990.
_____. *Immigration, colonisation et propagande: du rêve américain au rêve colonial*. Sainte-Foy (Québec): Éditions MultiMondes, 2002.
_____. Personal communication with Barry Rodrigue, c. 1997.
Cox, Harold. "The French-Canadian Ethnic Factor in Maine Politics." M.A. Thesis, University of Maine at Orono, 1972.
Craig, Béatrice. "Acadian village." *Encyclopedia of New England Culture*. New Haven (Connecticut): Yale University Press, 2005.
_____. "Agricultural Settlements, 1750–1850." *Encyclopedia of New England Culture*. New Haven (Connecticut): Yale University Press, 2005.
_____. "Agriculture and the Lumberman's Frontier: The Madawaska Settlement, 1800–-1870." *Journal of Forest History* 12 (July 1988), pp. 125–37. Reprinted as "Occupational Pluralism in British North America," in *Interpreting Canada's Past*, vol. 1, Pre-Confederation, J. M. Bumsted, ed. Toronto: University of Toronto Press, 1993, pp. 366–94.

_____. "Agriculture et marché au Madawaska, 1799–1850." *The River Review/La Revue Rivière* 1 (1995), pp. 13–38. This is a journal published by the University of Maine at Fort Kent.

_____. "Agriculture in a Pioneer Region: The Upper St. John Valley in the First Half of the Nineteenth Century." *Farm, Factory, and Fortune, New Studies in the Economic History of the Maritime Provinces*, Kris Inwood, ed. Fredericton: Acadiensis Press, 1993, pp. 17–36.

_____. *Backwood Consumers and Homsepun Capitalists: The Rise of a Market Culture in Eastern Canada*. Toronto: University of Toronto Press, c. 2008.

_____. "Before Borderlands: Yankees, British, and the St. John Valley French." *New England and the Maritime Provinces: Connections and Comparisons,* Stephen Hornsby and John Reid, eds. Montréal and Kingston: McGill–Queen's University Press, 2005, pp. 74–93.

_____. "Cultural Face-Off: Yankees, British and the St John Valley French." *The River Review / La Revue Rivière* 3 (1997). This is a journal published by the University of Maine at Fort Kent.

_____. "Le développement agricole dans la haute vallée du St Jean en 1860." *Revue de la Société historique du Canada* 3 (1993), pp. 13–26.

_____. "Early French Migrations to Northern Maine, 1785–1850." *Maine Historical Society Quarterly* 25, (spring 1986), pp. 230–47.

_____. "Economie, société et migrations: le cas de la vallée du St Jean au XIXe siècle." *L'émigrant acadien vers les États Unis*, Claire Quintal, ed. Worcester (Massachusetts): Assumption College and the Council of French Life in America, 1984, pp. 120–33.

_____. "Entrepôt de l'Empire: Le magasin général rural au milieu du XIXe siècle." *Familles, terre et marchés, logiques économiques et stratégies dans les milieux ruraux (XVIIe–XXe)*, G. Beaur, Christian Dessureault, and Joseph Goy, eds. Rennes: Presses Universitaires de Rennes, 2004, pp. 33–46.

_____. "L'étude des mouvements migratoires en Amérique du Nord: sources et méthodes." *Les chemins de la migration en Belgique et au Québec*, J. Dickinson, Y. Landry, Suzy Pasleau, and Claude Desama, dirs. Montréal and Louvain: MNH/Academia, 1995, pp. 20–31.

_____. "Family, Kinship, and Community Formation on the Canadian-American Border, Madawaska, 1785–1942." Ph.D. Dissertation, University of Maine at Orono, 1983.

_____. "Farm Transmission and the Commercialization of Agriculture in Northern Maine in the Second Half of the Nineteenth Century." *History of the Family, an International Quarterly* 10 (2005), pp. 327–44.

_____. "La femme face à la transmission des patrimoines au XIXe siècle: Droit, coutume et pratiques." *Transmettre, hériter, succéder: La reproduction familiale en milieu rural, France–Québec, XVIII–XX siècles*, R. Bonnain, G. Bouchard, and J. Goy, eds. Lyons/Paris/Villeurbane: Presses Universitaires de Lyons/L'école des hautes études en sciences sociales/Programme pluriannuel en sciences humaines Rhones-Alpes, 1992, pp. 231–42.

_____. "Les francophones du Madawaska." *Par delà le Rideau, Bulletin de la Société d'histoire et de généalogie d'Ottawa* (October–November 1990), pp. 82–87.

_____. "The Homespun Paradox: Market-Oriented Production of Cloth in Eastern Canada in the Nineteenth Century." *Agricultural History* 76 (winter 2002), pp. 28–57.

_____. "Inheritance and Property Transmission in Rural Canada in the Nineteenth and Twentieth Centuries." *Family Matters: Papers in Post-Confederation Canadian Family History*, Edgar-André Montigny and Lori Chambers, eds. Toronto: Canadian Scholars Press, Inc., 1998, pp. 159–76.

_____. "Un journal frontalier et ses lecteurs américains pendant la Grande Dépression: Le Madawaska." *Le journalisme de langue française aux Etats Unis*, Claire Quintal, ed. Worcester (Massachusetts): Assumption College and the Council of French Life in America, 1983.

_____. "Kinship and Migration to the Upper St. John Valley, 1785–1842." *Quebec Studies* 1, (spring 1983), pp. 151–64.

_____. "Land Transmission Practices among Northern Maine French Canadians in the Nineteenth Century." *New England—New France, 1600–1850*, Peter Benes, ed. Boston: Boston University, 1992, pp. 68–80.

_____. "Madawaska Ancestors, Sources on Madawaska." *The Genealogist* 16, no. 4 (fall 1990), pp. 156–57.

_____. "Marchés et transmission des patrimoines fonciers au XIXe siècle." *Nécéssités économiques et pratiques juridiques: Problèmes de la transmission des exploitations agricoles (XVIIIe–XIXe siècles)*, Actes de la session C–33 du XI Congrès International d'histoire économique, G. Bouchard, J. Goy and A. Head-König, eds. Rome: École française de Rome, 1998.

_____. "Migrant Integration in a Frontier Society: The Madawaska Settlement, 1800–1850." *Histoire sociale/Social History* 38 (November 1986), pp. 277–98.

_____. "New England Acadians." *Encyclopedia of New England Culture*. New Haven (Connecticut): Yale University Press, 2005.

_____. "Pour une approche comparative de l'étude des sociétés rurales nord-américaines." *Histoire sociale—Social History* XXIII, no. 46 (November 1990), pp. 249–70. Reprinted in *New England–New France, 1600–1850*, Peter Benes, ed. Boston: Boston University, 1992, pp. 134–48.

_____. Review of *Quiet Presence* by Dyke Hendrickson. *Maine Historical Society Quarterly* 21, no. 2 (fall 1981), pp. 99–100.

_____. Rodrigue, Barry. Telephone conversation, 29 August 1995.

_____. "Solder les comptes: les sources de crédits dans les magasins généraux ruraux de l'est canadien au milieu du XIXe siècle." *Journal of the Canadian Historical Association* 13 (2003), pp. 23–48.

_____. "La transmission des patrimoines fonciers dans le Haut St-Jean au XIXe siècle." *Revue d'histoire de l'Amérique française* 45 (December 1991), pp. 207–28.

_____. "Women, Children, and the Calculation of Labour Productivity in Europe and North America." *Histoire et Mesure* (France), vol. XV, nos. 3/4 (2000), pp. 271–88.

_____. "Y-eut-il une 'révolution industrieuse' en Amérique du nord?" *Famille et marché, XVIe–XXe siècles*, Christian Dessureault, John Dickinson, and Joseph Goy, eds. Montréal: Septentrion, 2003, pp. 33–48.

Craig, Béatarice and Judith Rygiel. "Femmes, marchés et production textile domestique au Nouveau Brunswick au XIXe siècle." *Histoire et Mesure* XV, nos. 1–2 (2000), pp. 83–112.

Craig, Béatrice and Judith Rygiel and Elizabeth Turcotte. "Survival or Adaptation? Domestic Rural Textile Production in Eastern Canada in the Nineteenth Century." *Agricultural History* 49, Part II (fall 2001), pp. 140–71.

Craig, Béatrice and M. H. Sorg. "Patterns of Infant Mortality in the Upper St. John Valley French Population, 1791–1838." *Human Biology* 55 (February 1983), pp. 100–13.

Cramahé, Hector. Letters to Frederick Haldimand, 17 August 1778, pp. 9–10; 17 September 1778, pp. 41–42; 21 September 1778, p. 45. *Haldimand Papers*, Ms. No 21755.

Crane, Pamela. "Historical Archeology of Norridgewock Mission." M.A. Thesis, University of Maine at Orono, 1997.
Crane, Pamela and Peter Morrison. "Archaeological Study, Waterville Waterfront Revitalization Project, Waterville, Maine." Unpublished report. Maine Historic Preservation Commission, Augusta, Maine, 2004.
Cunningham, Robert. Personal communications with Barry Rodrigue. Telephone, 20 November 2000; letter, 28 November 2000.
Curtis, Grace Pedneault. Interview by Céleste DeRoche. Tape recording. Westbrook, Maine, 8 August 1993. Tape held by Céleste DeRoche.
Cyr, Leo. *Bicentennial Edition of Madawaska Heritage*. Bethesada (Maryland): Published by the author, 1985.
Dahlberg, Kristine. Letter to Yvon Labbé, January 1972. Franco-American Centre, University of Maine, Orono.
Daigle, Jean. "Nos amis, les ennemis: relations commerciales de l'Acadie avec le Massachusetts, 1670–1711." Ph.D. Dissertation, University of Maine at Orono, 1975.
Dana, Marian. Interview by Vaun Born. Tape recording. Westbrook, Maine, 15 June 1976. Tape held by Céleste DeRoche.
D'Arce, Baron de Lahontan, Louis-Armand de Lom. Letter, 2 May 1684. *Œuvres complètes*, vol. I. Montréal: University of Montreal Press, 1990, pp. 263–267.
Davenport, John. Letter to, 5 July 1662. *Davenport Letters*, pp. 201–202; quoted in *The New England Merchants in the Seventeenth Century* by Bernard Bailyn. Cambridge (Masssachusetts): Harvard University Press, 1979, p. 110.
Daviault, Pierre. *Le baron de Saint-Castin: chef Abénaquis*. Montréal: Éditions de l'ACF, 1939.
Davis, Dwight. U.S. Secretary of War. Letter to Henry Dunnack, Maine state librarian, 6 October 1927. Maine State Library, Augusta, Maine.
Dawson, Joan. "The Governor's Goods: The Inventories of the Personal Property of Isaac de Razilly." *Nova Scotia Historical Review* 5, no. 1 (1985), pp. 99–112.
Deane, John and Edward Kavanagh. "Report of John G. Deane and Edward Kavanagh to Samuel E. Smith, Governor of the State of Maine." *State of the Madawaska and Aroostook Settlements in 1831,* W. O. Raymond, ed. New Brunswick Historical Society, *Collection*, III, 1907. Transcription. Maine State Archives, Augusta, Maine.
Delaney, Frank. *Ireland*. New York: Harper Collins Publishers, 2005.
Denys, Nicolas. *Description and Natural History of the Coasts of North America (Acadia),* William Ganong, trans. New York: Greenwood Press, 1968, pp. 154–55.
DeRoche, Céleste. "'I Learned Things Today That I Never Knew Before:' Oral History at the Kitchen Table." *Oral History Review* 23, no. 2 (winter 1996), pp. 45–61.
_____. "How Wide the Circle of We: Cultural Pluralism and American Identity, 1910–1954." Ph.D. Dissertation, University of Maine at Orono, 2000.
_____. "These Lines of My Life: Franco-American Women in Westbrook, Maine, the Intersection of Ethnicity and Gender, 1884–1984." M.A. Thesis, University of Maine at Orono, 1994.
_____. "Walking toward the Red Sky: Franco-American Women in Maine." *Of Place and Gender: Women in Maine History*, Marli Weiner, ed. Orono: University of Maine Press, 2005.
Desjardins, P. E., comp. Case of Sacred Heart Parish. Roman Catholic Church, Diocese of Portland (Maine), Library, Documents Folio #6.

Dexter, R. "The French Canadian Invasion." *The Alien in Our Midst*, M. Grant and C. Davison, eds. New York: Galton Publishing Company, 1930.

Dexter, Town of. *Seventy-Fifth Annual Report of the Municipal Offices of the Town of Dexter, 1890*.

Di Leonardo, Michaela. *The Varieties of Ethnic Experience: Kinship, Class, and Gender among California Italian Americans*. Ithaca: Cornell University, 1984.

Diner, Hasia. *Erin's Daughters in America: Irish Immigrant Women in the Nineteenth Century*. Baltimore: Johns Hopkins University Press, 1983.

Dingley, Nelson, Jr., *Historical Sketch of Lewiston*. *Lewiston Journal*, 1871.

Donovan, Josephine. *Feminist Theory*. New York: Continuum Publishing Company, 1985.

Doty, C. Stewart. *Acadian Hard Times: The Farm Security, Administration in Maine's St. John Valley, 1940–1943*. Orono: University of Maine Press, 1991.

_____. "The American Identity of Louis Dantin, More Francophone American than Franco-American." *Revue canadienne d'études américaines* 24, no. 3 (1994), pp. 103–19.

_____. "Fill the Steins to Dear Old Rudy." *Down East* (November 1988), pp. 68–71, 94–95.

_____. *The First Franco-Americans: New England Life Stories from the Federal Writers' Project, 1938–1939*. Orono: University of Maine Press, 1985.

_____. "Franco-American History Projects in the State of Maine: Oral History, Historic Photographs, and Archival Surprises." *Le Québec et les francophones de la Nouvelle-Angleterre*, vol I: *Culture française d'Amérique*, Dean Louder, dir. Sainte-Foy (Québec): Presse de l'université Laval, 1991, pp. 165–73.

_____. "The Future of the Franco-American Past." *American Review of Canadian Studies* 10, no. 1 (spring 2000), pp. 7–17.

_____. "How Many Frenchmen Does It Take to...?" *Thought and Action* 11, no. 2 (fall 1995), pp. 85–104.

_____. "The Intellectual of the Québec Diaspora: The Case of Henri d'Arles." *Journal of Canadian Studies/Revue d'etudes canadiennes* 24, no. 4 (winter 1989–90), pp. 61–71.

_____. "'M. Maurras est ici,' French Fascism in Franco-American New England." *Journal of Contemporary History* 32, no. 4 (October, 1997), pp. 527–38.

_____. "Perspectives sur Old Town, Maine, dans les années 30: Témoignagnes tirés des récits de vie d'Acadiens et de Franco-Américains, recueillis dans le cadre du *Federal Writers' Project*." *Vie Francaise: l'Émigrant acadien vers les États-unis 1842–1950*. Québec: Le Conseil de la Vie française en Amérique, 1984, pp. 148–58.

_____. "Rudy Vallée: Franco-American and Man from Maine." *Maine Historical Society Quarterly* 33, no. 1 (summer 1993), pp. 2–19.

Downs, Jacques. *The Cities on the Saco: A Pictorial History*. Norfolk (Virginia): Doning Company, 1985.

Doyle, James. *North of America; Images of Canada in the Literature of the United States 1775–1900*. Toronto: ECW Press, 1983.

Drachsler, J. *Democracy and Assimilation*. New York: Macmillan, 1920.

Drouin, Gabriel. *Dictionnaire national des Canadiens Français, 1608–1760*. 3 vols. Montréal: Institut généalogique Drouin, 1965.

Dubé, Normand. *La broderie inachevée*. Cambridge (Massachusetts): National Assessment and Dissemination Center for Bilingual/Bicultural Education, 1979.

_____. *Au cœur du vent*. Fall River (Massachusetts): National Assessment and Dissemination Center for Bilingual/Bicultural Education, 1978.

_____. "Guidelines for the Teaching of French to Franco-Americans." Ph.D. Dissertation, Ohio State University, 1971.

_____. *Un mot de chez nous*. Fall River (Massachusetts): National Assessment and Dissemination Center for Bilingual/Bicultural Education, 1977.

_____. *Le nuage de* ma *pensée*. Bedford (New Hampshire): National Materials Development Centre, 1981.

Dublin, Thomas. *Farm to Factory: Women's Letters, 1830–1860*. New York: Columbia University Press, 1993.

_____. *Transforming Women's Work: New England Lives in the Industrial Revolution*. Ithaca: Cornell University Press, 1994.

_____. *Women at Work: The Transformation of Work and Community in Lowell, Massachusetts, 1826–1860*. New York: Columbia University Press, 1979.

Dubois, Arthur. "Respectueusement avec les Hommages de l'Auteur J. Armand LeMay," *Historique de Jackman, Maine: 1892-1975*. Québec: 8 September 1975. Archives of the Sisters of St. Joseph of Lyons (CSJ), France, Provincialate and Christian Life Center, Winslow, Maine.

Dubois, Émile. *Chez nos frères les Acadiens*. Montréal: L'Action française, 1920.

Ducharme, Jacques. *The Shadows of the Trees: The Story of French-Canadians in New England.* New York, London: Harper & Brothers, 1943.

Dugas, Don. "Normand Dubé—Lone Rider." In *Le Forum* 24, no. 4 (1998), pp. 7, 31; previously published in *Le FAROG. Forum* in 1988.

Duplessis, Stephan. *Duplessis v. Training and Development Corporation, et al.*, Civil Action No. 92–0096–B, United States District Court, District of Maine.

Early, Francis. Introduction to *Immigrant Odyssey: A French Canadian Habitant in New England,* by Félix Albert. Orono: University of Maine Press, 1991, pp. 1-24.

_____. "Mobility Potential and the Quality of Life in Working-Class Lowell, Massachusetts: The French Canadians, c. 1870." *Labour—Le Travailleur* 2 (1977), pp. 214–28.

_____. "The Settling-In Process: The Beginnings of Little Canada in Lowell, Massachusetts, in the Late Nineteenth Century." *The Little Canadas of New England*, Claire Quintal, ed. Worcester (Massachusetts): The French Institute, Assumption College, 1983, pp. 23–44.

Eaton, Cyrus. *Annals of the Town of Warren*. Hallowell, Maine: Masters, Smith and Co., 1851.

Eccles, William. *The French in North America: 1500–1783*. Markham (Ontario): Fitzhenry and Whiteside, 1998.

Eelking, Max von and J. G. Rosengarten. *The German Allied Troops in the North American War of Independence, 1776–1783*. Albany: Joel Munsell's Sons, 1893.

Elgersman Lee, Maureen. *Black Bangor: African Americans in a Maine Community 1880–1950*. Durham: University of New Hampshire Press, 2005.

_____. "What They Lack in Numbers: Locating Black Portland, 1870–1930." *Creating Portland: History and Place in Northern New England*. Joseph Conforti, ed. Hanover (New Hampshire): University Press of New England, 2005, pp. 219–46

Ellis, John. *The Life of James Cardinal Gibbons: Archbishop of Baltimore, 1834–1921*. Vols. 1 and 2. Milwaukee: Bruce Publishing, 1952; reprint, Westminster (Maryland), 1987.

Ellison, Ralph. *Invisible Man*. New York: Random House, 1952.

Ernaux, Annie. *Shame*. T. Leslie, trans. New York: Seven Stories Press, 1997.

Evans, Sara. *Personal Politics*. New York: Vintage Books, 1979.

Everest, Allan. "Hazen, Moses." *Dictionary of Canadian Biography*, vol. 5, Francess Halpenny and Jean Hamelin, eds. Québec and Toronto: Laval University Press and the University of Toronto Press, 1983, pp. 414.

Eves, Jamie. Yankee Immigrants: Ecological Crisis and the Settlement of Maine, 1763–1825. M.A. Thesis, University of Maine, 1988.

Expense Book of John Halsted, Commissary under Benedict Arnold, Before Quebec, 1776. Montréal: C. A. Marchand, 1913. Although the account book is attributed to John Halsted, the identity of the person who actually kept it is unknown, as stated by W. Patterson in a note at the back of the book.

Ezhaya, Joseph, comp. "Lebanese-American Oral History—Waterville, Maine," 1976. Waterville Public Library, Waterville, Maine.

FAROG Forum, Le, October–December, 1991; January–February, 1993.

Faulkner, Alaric. "Acadian Settlement: 1607–1700." *Maine: The Pine Tree State from Prehistory to the Present.* Richard Judd, Edwin Churchill, and Joel Eastman, eds. Orono: University of Maine Press, 1995, pp. 76–96.

_____. "Gentility on the Frontiers of Acadia, 1635–1674: An Archaeological Perspective." *New England/New France, 1600–1850,* Peter Benes, ed., *Annual Proceedings of the Dublin Seminar for New England Folklife* 14 (1989). Boston: Boston University Press, 1992, pp. 82–100.

_____. "Integrating Historical Data with Modern Cartography." Paper presented at the Seventh Workshops in Archaeometry Conference, Buffalo, New York (February 1996).

Faulkner, Alaric and Gretchen Fearon-Faulkner. *The French at Pentagoet,* 1635–1674, Augusta: Maine Historic Preservation Commission, 1987.

Faulkner, Alaric and Barry Rodrigue. *Canada Road Archaeological Survey, Misery Gore to the Frontier at Sandy Bay Township, on the Québec-Maine Frontier.* Unpublished report. Augusta: Maine Historic Preservation Commission, 1994–95.

Fecteau, Albert. "The French Canadian Community of Waterville, Maine." M.A. Thesis, University of Maine at, Orono, 1952.

Ferland, Jacques. Personal communication with Barry Rodrigue, c. 1998.

Ferron, Madeleine and Robert Cliche, *Les Beaucerons ces insoumis.* Québec: Hurtubise, 1972, 1974.

Finlay, Hugh. *Journal from the Last Settlements on the Chaudière to the First Inhabitants on the Kennebec River.* 1773. Public Archives of Canada (Ottawa), MG 21. Add. mss., vol. 21686, file folios 48–55, (reel A–615).

Fischer, Jeff. *Maine Speaks: An Anthology of Maine Literature.* Brunswick: Maine Writers and Publishers Alliance, 1989.

Fisher, Peter. *History of New Brunswick; As Originally Published in 1825, with a Few Explanatory Notes by W. O. Raymond.* St. John: New Brunswick Historical Society, 1921.

Foley, Albert. *Bishop Healy: Beloved Outcast—The Story of a Great Priest Whose Life Has Become a Legend.* New York: Farrar, Straus and Young, 1954.

Forest, Joseph. La Visite 1930, handwritten. Archives of the Roman Catholic Parish of St. Antonie de Padoue, Jackman, Maine.

Forget, U. "Onomastique franco-américaine: Étude sur la transformation des noms franco-américains." *Textes de l'exode: Recueil des textes sur l'émigration des québécois aux États-Unis (XIXe et Xxe siécles),* M. Poteet, ed. Montréal: Guérin littérature, 1987. Originally published in *L'Indépendant de Fall River* 5 and 20 (April 1949).

Forgue, Gérard. "Maine Woods Petit Canada: Jackman's Paroisse St. Antoine de Padoue,

1880–1930." M.A. Thesis, University of Maine at Orono, 1994.
_____. Telephone conversation with Barry Rodrigue, 16 September 2000.
Foster, Irene. Interview by Barry Rodrigue, 10 August 1995.
Franklin Company. Letterbooks. Letterbooks were held by the company in Lewiston, Maine, in the 1980s.
_____. Papers, "Shanties Accounts." Held by the company in Lewiston, Maine, in the 1980s.
Frenette, Yves. *Brève histoire des Canadiens français*. Montréal: Boréal, 1998. Published in France, online, by Les Éditions 00H00.
_____. "Franco-American Literature." *The Encyclopedia of New England*, Burt Feintuch and David Watters, eds. New Haven (Connecticut): Yale University Press, 2005, pp. 985–86.
_____. *Francophonies d'Amérique: les francophones de la Nouvelle-Angleterre, 1524–2000*. Sainte-Foy (Québec): Consortium des producteurs francophones et l'Institut national de la recherche scientifique Urbanisation, Culture et Société, 2001.
_____. "French Canadians." *Encyclopedia of Canada's Peoples*, Paul Magosci, ed. Toronto: University of Toronto Press, 1999, pp. 538–86.
_____. "Les fréquentations dans les communautés franco-américaines de la Nouvelle-Angleterre." Interview in *Cap-aux-Diamants: la revue d'histoire du Québec* 55 (autumn 1998), pp. 30–33.
_____. "La genèse d'une communauté canadienne-française en Nouvelle-Angleterre: Lewiston, Maine, 1800–1880." Ph.D. Dissertation, Laval University. 1988.
_____. "La grande mutation identitaire des Franco-Américains." *Cap-aux-Diamants: la revue d'histoire du Québec* 61 (spring 2000), pp. 10–13.
_____. "Lewiston's Ethnic Majority: The Francos." *Bates College: The Alumni Magazine* 86, no. 4 (May 1988), pp. 2–9.
_____. "La Louisiane et la Nouvelle-Angleterre francophones, 1865–1914: une comparaison." *Francophonies d'Amérique* 8 (1998), pp. 143–51.
_____. "Macroscopie et microscopie d'un mouvement migratoire: les Canadiens français à Lewiston au XIXe siècle." *Les chemins de la migration en Belgique et au Québec XVIIe–XXe siècles*, Yves Landry and others, eds. Louvain-la-Neuve (France): Éditions Académia—Publications MNH, 1995, pp. 221–32.
_____. "Une réalité multiple: les communautés franco-américaines." *Le congrès mondial acadien. L'Acadie en 2004: actes des conférences et des tables rondes*. Moncton (New Brunswick): Éditions d'Acadie, 1996, pp. 334–40.
_____. "Les réseaux au Canada français, 1660–1960." *Francophonie en Amérique: quatre siècles d'échanges Europe–Afrique–Amérique*, Michel Tétu, ed. Québec City, CIDEF–AFI, 2005, pp. 199–206.
_____. "Understanding the French Canadians of Lewiston, 1860–1900: An Alternate Framework." *Maine Historical Society Quarterly* 25, no. 4 (spring 1986), pp. 198–229. James Phinney Baxter Award for the best article published in the *Maine Historical Society Quarterly* in 1985–86.
_____. "Vie paroissiale et antagonismes culturels: les dominicains à Lewiston (1881–1906)." *Religion catholique et appartenance franco-américaine/Franco-Americans and Religion: Impact and Influence*, Claire Quintal, dir. Worcester (Massachusetts): The French Institute, Assumption College, 1993, pp. 25–35.
_____. Personal data bank on Lewiston's French Canadians, 1860–1900. In possession of Yves Frenette.

Frenette, Yves and Mary Aubé. "Le difficile accommodement: culture paysanne et changement socioculturel dans *Papa Martel*." *Francophonies d'Amérique* 2 (1992), pp. 201–08.
Frenette, Yves and Robert Babcock, Charles Scontras, and Eileen Eagan. "Work and Workers in the Industrial Age, 1865–1930." *Maine: The Pine Tree State from Prehistory to the Present*, Richard Judd and others, eds. Orono: University of Maine Press, 1995, pp. 448–79.
Frenette, Yves and Sylvie Beaudreau. "Les stratégies familiales des francophones de la Nouvelle-Angleterre: perspective diachronique." *Sociologie et sociétés* 26, no. 1 (spring 1994), pp. 167–78.
Frenette, Yves and Martin Pâquet and Jean Lamarre. *Les parcours de l'histoire: hommage à Yves Roby*. Sainte-Foy (Québec): Laval University, 2002.
Frenette, Yves and Yves Roby. "Guide du chercheur en études franco-américaines: un projet." *Le Québec et les francophones de la Nouvelle-Angleterre*. Vol. I: *Culture française d'Amérique*. Dean Louder, ed. Québec: Laval, University Press, 1991, pp. 129–64.
Gabaccia, Donna. *From the Other Side: Women, Gender, and Immigrant Life in the U.S., 1820–1990*. Bloomington: Indiana University Press, 1994.
_____. *From Sicily to Elizabeth Street: Housing and Social Change among Italian Immigrants*. Ithaca: Cornell University Press, 1984.
Gagnon, Ferdinand and others. *Ferdinand Gagnon: Biographie, éloge funèbre, pages choisies*. Manchester (New Hampshire): Malvina Martineau, 1940.
Gagnon, Janet. "How Sisters of St. Joseph Were Founded." *Church World* (April 1980), pp. 14–15.
Ganong, William. "Monograph of the Evolution of the Boundaries of the Province of New Brunswick." *Proceedings and Transactions*, 2D series, no. 7 (1901), Royal Society of Canada, pp. 137–49.
Garant, André. "Saint-Georges." *La Beauce et les Beaucerons: Portraits d'une région, 1737–1987*, France Bélanger and others, eds. St-Joseph: La Société du patrimoine des Beaucerons, 1988, pp. 311–314.
Gerstle, Gary. *Working-Class Americanism*. New York: Cambridge University Press, 1988.
Ghere, David. "Abenaki Factionalism, Emigration and Social Continuity: Indian Society in Northern New England, 1725 TO 1765." Ph.D. Dissertation, University of Maine, 1988.
_____. "D'abbadie, Bernard-Anselme." *American National Biography*, John Garraty and Mark Carnes, eds. 24 vols. New York: Oxford University Press, 1999, vol. 5, pp. 948–49.
_____. Diplomacy and War on the Maine Frontier, 1678–1760." *Maine: The Pine Tree State from Prehistory to the Present*, Richard Judd, Joel Eastman, and Ed Churchill, eds. Orono, Maine: University of Maine Press, 1995, pp. 120–42.
____. "The 'Disappearance' of Abenakis in Western Maine: Abenaki Factions and Euramerican Assumptions." *American Indian Quarterly*, 17 (spring 1993), pp. 193–207. Also in *After King Philip's War: Presence and Persistence in Indian New England*, Colin Calloway, ed., Hanover (New Hampshire): University Press of New England, 1997.
_____. "European Diplomacy with the Eastern Abenaki, 1725–1750." *Proceedings of the Nineteenth Meeting of the French Colonial Historical Society* (May 1993), pp. 87–100.
_____. "French Frustrations and Abenaki Autonomy, 1750–1760." *Maine History* 34 (summer 1994), pp. 2–21.
_____. "Gifts and Indian Diplomacy: The Maine Experience During the French and Indian War." *Papers of the Twenty-Fourth Algonquian Conference* 24 (1993), pp. 188–98.

_____. "Mistranslations and Misinformation: Diplomacy on the Maine Frontier, 1725 to 1755." *American Indian Culture and Research Journal* 8, no. 4 (1984), pp. 3–26.

_____. "Saint-Castin, Baron de." *American National Biography*, John Garraty and Mark Carnes, eds. 24 vols. New York: Oxford University Press, 1999, vol. 19, pp. 196–97.

_____. "Searching for Justice on the Maine Frontier: Legal Concepts, Treaties, and the 1749 Wiscasset Incident." *American Indian Quarterly* 25 (summer 2001), pp. 378–99.

_____. "Subsistence or Strategy: Cattle Killing and Abenaki Migration, 1725–1760." *Papers of the Twenty-Ninth Algonquian Conference* 29 (1998), pp. 112–27.

_____. "Treaty Mistranslations and Diplomatic Dilemmas." *Magazine of History* 9 (summer 1995), Organization of American Historians , pp. 28–31.

_____. "Venoms for Vengeance: History, Novels and Movies Surrounding Three Interrelated 'Massacres' in the Northeast, 1755–59." *Papers of the Thirtieth Algonquian Conference* 30 (1999), pp. 108–21.

Ghere, David and Alvin Morrison. "Sanctions for Slaughter: Peacetime Murders of Abenaki Indians, 1749–1768." *Papers of the Twenty-Seventh Algonquian Conference* 27 (1996), pp. 105–16.

Giguère, Madeleine. *A Franco-American Overview: New England*. Part One, vol. 3. Cambridge (Massachusetts): National Assessment and Dissemination Center for Bilingual/Bicultural Education, 1981.

_____. *A Franco-American Overview: New England*. Part Two, vol 4. Cambridge (Massachusetts): National Assessment and Dissemination Center for Bilingual/Bicultural Education, 1981.

_____. "Franco-Americans and the 1992 Elections." paper presented at the French Colonial History Society Meeting, 22 May 1993. Manuscript, held at the Franco-American Collection, University of Southern Maine, Lewiston-Auburn College, Lewiston, Maine.

_____. "Francophone Dimensions of New England." Paper presented at the eleventh conference, French Institute, Assumption College, Worcester, Massachusetts, 10 June 1994.

_____. Letter to Donald McNeil, 9 December 1971. Franco-American Centre, University of Maine, Orono.

_____. "Remarks on the Occasion of the Formal Opening of the Franco-American Reading Room." Franco-American Collection, University of Southern Maine, Lewiston-Auburn College, Lewiston, Maine, 18 April 1993.

_____. "Social and Economic Profile of French and English Mother-Tongue Persons: Maine, 1970." *A Franco-American Overview: New England.* Vol. 2, Madeleine Giguère, dir. Cambridge (Massachusetts): National Assessment and Dissemination Center for Biiingual/Bicultural Education, 1981, pp. 145–164.

Gilbert-Lewis, Paul, ed. *Traditionalism, Nationalism, and Feminism: Women Writers of Quebec*. Westport (Connecticut): Greenwood Press, 1985.

Gitlin, Todd. *The Sixties: Days of Hope, Days of Rage*. New York: Bantam Books, 1986.

Glenn, Evelyn Nakano. *Issei, Nisei, War Bride: Three Generations of Japanese American Women in Domestic Service*. Philadelphia: Temple University Press, 1986

Glenn, Susan. *Daughters of the Shtetl: Life and Labor in the Immigrant Generation.* Ithaca: Cornell University Press, 1991.

Goetz, S. "The Ku Klux Klan in New Hampshire." *Historical New Hampshire* 43, no. 4 (1988).

Gooch, Samuel and others. Letter to Samuel Ingham, Secretary of Treasury, 24 August 1829. National Archives, Washington, D.C.

Goold, William. "Fort Halifax." Maine Historical Society. *Collections I*, vol. 8 (1881), pp. 199–289.
Graham, Harry. *The Paper Rebellion*. Iowa City: University of Iowa Press, 1970.
Grant, M. *The Passing of the Great Race*. New York: C. Scribner, 1916.
Gravel-Shea, Louise. "L'influence de la frontière canado-américaine sur la population de Grande Rivière Madawaska." M.A. Thesis, Université Laval, 1999.
Greeley, Andrew. "Political Participation Among Ethnic Groups in the United States." *Ethnicity in the Unites States*, A. M. Greeley, ed. New York: John Wiley & Sons, 1974.
_____. *Why Can't They Be Like Us? America's White Ethnic Groups.* New York: E. P. Dutton, 1971.
Green, William. "Wage-Earning Women." *American Federationist* 33, no. 6 (June 1926), pp. 746–48.
Greenleaf, Moses. *Map Exhibiting the Principal Original Grants and Sales of Lands in the State of Maine,* c. 1829.
Greenspan, Arthur and the students of French 493. *Francos of Waterville—Les Francos de Waterville racontent*. Waterville (Maine): Colby College and LRC Design Studio, 2004. DVD.
Greer, Allan. *The Patriots and the People: The Rebellion of 1837 in Lower Canada*. Toronto: University of Toronto Press, 1993.
Greer, Lucille. Telephone conversation with Barry Rodrigue, 19 November 2000.
Greven, Philip. *Four Generations: Population, Land, and Family in Colonial Andover, Massachusetts.* Ithaca (New York): Cornell University Press, 1972.
Gross, James. "The Making and Shaping of Unionism in The Pulp and Paper Industry," *Labor History* (spring 1964).
Gross, Robert. *The Minutemen and Their World*. New York: Hill and Wang, 1976.
Guignard, Michael. "Ethnic Survival in a New England Milltown: The Franco-Americans of Biddeford, Maine." Ph.D. Dissertation, Syracuse University, 1976.
_____. *La Foi–La Langue–La Culture: The Franco-Americans of Biddeford, Maine*. N.p., 1982.
_____. "The Franco-Americans of Biddeford, Maine." *Steeples and Smokestacks: A Collection of Essays on the Franco-American Experience in New England*, Claire Quintal, ed. Worcester (Massachusetts): The French Institute, Assumption College, 1996, pp. 122–44.
_____. "The Franco-Americans: The Relationship Between Ethnic Identification and Political Behavior," Honors Paper, Bowdoin College, 1969.
_____. "Maine's Corporation Sole Controversy." *Maine Historical Society Newsletter* 12 (winter 1973), pp. 113–30.
Haebler, Peter. "Habitants in Holyoke: The Development of the French-Canadian Community in a Massachusetts City, 1865–1910." Ph.D. Dissertation, University of New Hampshire, 1976.
Hagel, Phyllis. *A Resource Guide for New England Libraries—Bilingual/Bicultural Education—Franco-American Studies*. Bedford (New Hampshire): U.S. National Materials Development Center for French and Portuguese, 1976.
Haldimand, Frederick. Letters to George Germain, 15 October 1778, pp. 12–16; Letter No. 23, 13 September 1779, pp. 40–41; Letter No. 32, 13 September 1779, pp. 46–48; 14 September 1779, pp. 55–57. *Haldimand Papers*, Ms. No. 21714.
_____. Letter to John Johnson, 23 May 1779. *Haldimand Papers*, Ms. No. 21819, pp. 19–20.
_____. Letter, to Daniel McAlpin, 30 August 1778. *Haldimand Papers*, Ms. No. 21722, p. 45.

_____. Letter, to Barry St. Leger, 30 August 1778. *Haldimand Papers*, Ms. No. 21722, pp. 44–45.
Haliburton, Thomas. *The Clockmaker*. Toronto: McClelland & Stewart, 1958, 1986.
Hamlin, Elijah. Bangor, Maine. Letter to Joseph Noyes, Collector of Customs, Passamaquoddy District, 14 March 1843. U.S. National Archives, Washington, D.C.
Hamon, Édouard. *Les Canadiens-Français de la Nouvelle-Angleterre*. Québec: N. S. Hardy, 1891.
Handlin, Oscar. *The Uprooted: The Epic Story of the Great Migrations that Made the American People*. Boston: Little, Brown and Company, 1951.
Hansen, Niles. *France in the Modern World*. New York: Van Nostrand Reinhold Company, 1969.
Hanson, J. W. *History of the Old Towns Norridgewock and Canaan*. Boston: J. W. Hanson, 1849.
Hardy, René and Normand Séguin. *Forêt et société: la formation de la région de Trois-Rivières, 1830–1930*. Montréal: Boréal Express, 1984.
Hareven, Tamara. *Family Time and Industrial Time: The Relationship between the Family and Work in a New England Industrial Community*. New York: Cambridge University Press, 1982.
Harris, Richard. *The Seigneurial System in Early Canada: A Geographical Study*. Montréal and Kingston: McGill–Queen's University Press, 1966, 1984.
Hartford, W. *Working People of Holyoke: Class and Ethnicity in a Massachusetts Mill Town, 1850–1960*. New Brunswick (New Jersey): Rutgers University Press, 1990.
Hartt, Rollin. "The Regeneration of Rural New England: III—Religious." *The Outlook* 64 (1900), p. 628.
Harvard Encyclopedia of American Ethnic Groups. Stephan Thernstrom, Ann Orlov, Oscar Handlin, eds. Cambridge (Massachusetts): Harvard University, 1980.
Haseltine, Kathryn. Diary, 1920–1921. Typescript by James Wintle, n.d., in the the Dexter Historical Society archives, Dexter, Maine.
Hawkes, Dorothy Harnois. Interview be Céleste DeRoche. Tape recording, 19 August 1993. Tape held by Céleste DeRoche.
Hawthorne, Nathaniel. *The American Notebooks*. New Haven (Connecticut): Yale University Press, 1932.
Haynes, Evan. *Comminique*. Sculpture. State House, underground corridor, Augusta, Maine, 2001.
Hendrickson, Dyke. *Quiet Presence: Dramatic, First-Person Accounts—The True Stories of Franco-Americans in New England*. Portland (Maine): Guy Gannett Publishing Company, 1977, 1980.
Henretta, James. "Families and Farms, *Mentalité* in Pre-Industrial America." *William and Mary Quarterly,* 3rd series, XXX (1978), pp. 3–33.
Henry, John. Journal. *March to Quebec,* Kenneth Roberts, ed. Garden City (New York): Doubleday & Company, Inc., 1946, pp. 299–430.
Henry, Louis. *Manuel de démographie historique*. Paris (France): Droz, 1970.
Herlihy, Gerald. Interview by Michael Brown. 23 January 1991. Franco-American Centre, University of Maine at Orono.
Higgins, Mary Raymond. *For Love of Mercy: Missioned in Maine and Andros Island, Bahamas, 1883–1983*. Portland (Maine): Sisters of Mercy, 1995.
Higham, J. *Strangers in the Land: Patterns of American Nativism, 1860–1925*. New Brunswick (New Jersey): Rutgers University Press, 1988.

History Committee of the Bingham Sesquicentennial. *Bingham Sesquicentennial History, 1812–1962*. Bingham (Maine): History Committee of the Bingham Sesquicentennial, 1962.
History Committee of the Jackman Bicentennial Committee. *The History of the Moose River Valley: Jackman, Moose River, Dennistown, Long Pond, Parlin Pond, Holeb, Skinner, and Lowelltown*. Augusta (Maine): Kennebec Journal Printing, 1975.
History Committee of the Solon Sesquicentennial. *Sketches from Solon's History, 1809–1959*. Skowhegan (Maine): Skowhegan Press, 1959.
Hobbs-Pruitt, Bettye. "Self-Sufficiency and the Agricultural Economy of Eighteenth-Century Massachusetts." *William and Mary Quarterly* 3, no. XLI (July 1984), pp. 333–64.
Hooglund, Eric, ed. *Crossing the Waters: Arabic-Speaking Immigrants to the United States before 1940*. Washington, D.C.: Smithsonian Institution Press, 1987.
Howard, William. Orders to James Waugh, 2 August 1777. *History of the Old Towns Norridgewock and Canaan* by J. W. Hanson. Boston: J. W. Hanson, 1849, p. 258.
Howe-Kendrick, Priscilla. "Americans in Process." Senior Thesis, Bates College, 1942.
Hoyem, Oliver. "Immigration and America's Safety." *American Federationist*, November 1922, pp. 818–27.
Hudon, Paul-Henri. "Les négociants de Kamouraska, La Madawaska et les anglophones." In the Société de généalogie de Québec, *L'ancêtre* 25, nos. 3–4 (December 1998–January 1999), pp. 77–92.
Hyman, Colette. "Labor Organizing and Female Institution-Building: The Chicago Women's Trade Union League, 1904–1924." *Women, Work and Protest: A Century of U.S. Women's Labor History*, Ruth Milkman, ed. New York: Rutledge and Kegan Paul, 1985.
Ives, Edward "Sandy." Interview by Barry Rodrigue, Orono, Maine, c. 1992.
Jabar, George. Interview by Charles O'Leary, 25 June 1969. Maine Folklife Center, University of Maine. Orono, Accession No. 574, T298.
_____. Interview conducted by Chris Lavin, 7 March 1972. Maine Folklife Center, University of Maine at Orono. Accession No. 671, T373.
Jackman Bicentennial Book Committee. *The History of the Moose River Valley*. Augusta: Kennebec Journal Printing, 1976.
Jellison, Connee. *Commemorative Markings on the Arnold Expedition Trail, 1775–1776*, Salisbury Cove (Maine): Daughters of the American Revolution, Maine State Organization, c. 1999.
_____. Letter to Barry Rodrigue, 7 March 1999.
Jock, Frank. *A History: Dexter Sports and Recreation* by James Wintle. Typescript, n.d., Dexter Historical Society archives, pp. 12, 15.
_____. Diary (World War I). Reprinted in *The Eastern Gazette,* beginning 29 April 1937.
Johnson, Roger. "French Canadian Reaction to Assimilation." School paper held by Michael Guignard, n.d.
Johnston, J. *Notes on North America: Agricultural, Economical and Social*. Edinburgh and London: W. Blackwood, 1851.
Joly, Éric. "Le milieu, l'appartenance et l'intégration à la société américaine: la littérature comme outil de connaissance des Franco-Américains." B.A. Thesis, University of Ottawa, 1999.
Judd, Richard. *Aroostook: A Century of Logging in Northern Maine*. Orono: The University of Maine Press, 1989.
Judd, Richard, Joel Eastman, and Edwin Churchill, eds. *Maine: The Pine Tree State from*

Prehistory to the Present. Orono: University of Maine Press, 1995.
Justice, La. (Journal, Biddeford, Maine).
Kelly, Richard. *Nine Lives for Labor*. New York: Frederick A. Praeger, 1956, pp. 89–98.
Kempers, Anne and Beatrice Maltais. "Name-Changing Patterns among French Canadians in Waterville, Maine." *Your Franco-American Heritage*: A series of units developed especially for the students of the Greater Waterville–Winslow Area (Title III ESEA Mini-Grant Program), pp. 4, 5; reproduced by *FAROG,* University of Maine, Orono, 1973–74.
Kenrick, John. *A History of the Musical Burlesque*, 2004, Internet site: http.//www.musicals 101.com/burlesque.htm.
Kerouac, Jack. *Visions of Gerard*. New York: Farrar, Straus, and Company, 1963.
Kessler-Harris, Alice. *Out to Work: A History of Wage-Earning Women in the United States*. Oxford: Oxford University Press, 1982.
Kessner, Thomas. *The Golden Door: Italian and Jewish Immigrant Mobility in New York City, 1880–1915*. New York: Oxford University Press, 1977.
Kiernan, Kathleen and Albert Whitaker, Jr. *Eastern Lands Papers: 1784–1868*. Boston: Massachusetts State Archives at Columbia Point, 1980.
Kirk, Geneva and Gridley Barrows. *Historic Lewiston: Its Government*. Lewiston (Maine): Lewiston Historical Commission, 1982.
Kirkpatrick, C. *Intelligence and Immigration*. Baltimore: Williams and Wilkins, 1926.
Konrad, Victor, James Herlan, and others. *The Northeastern Borderlands*. Orono (Maine) and Fredricton (New Brunswick): Canadian-American Center and Acadiensis Press, 1989.
Labbé, Lillian. Interview by Michael Brown, 19 June 1991. Franco-American Centre, University of Maine at Orono.
_____. Personal records, 1980. Cassette tape.
Labbé, Yvon. Interview by Michael Brown, 12 October 1990, 10 November 1990, 30 December 1990. Franco-American Centre, University of Maine at Orono.
_____. Interview with Dean Louder, by Barry Rodrigue, spring 2000. No transcript.
_____. Letter to Winthrop Libby, 20 December 1972. Franco-American Centre, University of Maine at Orono.
Labbé, Yvon and Kristine Dahlberg. "Franco-American Resource and Opportunity Group Description." Orono, Maine: FAROG (1972), p. 2.
Labonté, Youville. *The Necrology of St. Peter and Paul's Cemetery 1870–1976*. Auburn (Maine): n.p., n.d.
LaBrecque, Josephine DeRoche. Interview by Céleste DeRoche. Tape recording. 16 August 1993 and 30 October 1993. Tape held by Céleste DeRoche.
_____. Interview by Céleste DeRoche. Tape recording. 16 August 1993. Tape held by Céleste DeRoche.
Laflamme, Matthew. "From Colony to Class: The Changing Consciousness of Franco-American Textile Workers in Waterville, Maine, 1934–1954." M.A. Thesis, University of Maine at Orono, 1995.
Lahne, Herbert J. *The Cotton Mill Worker*. New York: Farrar and Rinehart, Inc., 1944.
Lamarre, Jean. *The French Canadians of Michigan: Their Contribution to the Development of the Saginaw Valley and the Keweenaw Peninsula, 1840–1914*. Detroit: Wayne State University Press, 2003.
Langellier, Kristin. "Passing for French." *Le FAROG Forum* (September to November 1992), p. 14. Reprinted as "Backroads: Discovering French Heritage," in *Echoes: The Northern*

Maine Journal of Rural Culture 20 (spring 1993), pp. 19–21, 47.
_____. "Performing Family Stories, Forming Cultural Identity: Franco American Mémère Stories." *Communication Studies* 53, no. 1 (spring 2002), pp. 56–73.
_____. "Responding to Ethnicity: Franco-American Studies in Maine." *Logon Didonai* by H. Barthe, ed. Munich (Germany): Ernst Reinhardt, 1996, pp. 93–100.
_____. "'Somebody's Got to Pick Eggs': Family Storytelling about Work." *Communication Monographs* 73, no. 4 (2006), pp. 468–73.
_____. *Storytelling in Daily Life: Performing Narrative*. Philadelphia: Temple University Press, 2004.
_____. "Tickling the Past," in *Le FAROG Forum* 26, no. 2 (April 1998), pp. 12, 15. Reprinted in *Echoes: The Northern Maine Journal* 45 (July–September 1999), pp. 33–37.
_____. "'Where I Come From Is Where I Want To Be:' Communicating Franco-American Ethnicity." *Communicating Ethnicitiy and Cultural Identitiy*, M. Fong and R. Chuang, eds. Lanham (Maryland): Rowman and Littlefield, 2004, pp. 297–312.
Langellier, Kristen and Eric Peterson. "Voicing Identity: The Case of Franco-American Women in Maine." *The Voice of the Voiceless*, E. Slembek, ed. St. Ingbert, (Germany): Rührig Universitätsverlag, 1999, pp. 135–45.
Langlois, Henri. *Dictionnaire généalogique du Madawaska...Répertoire des mariages du diocèse d'Edmunston, N.B,. et du comté d'Aroostook, recherches et compilations par Henri Langlois.* 8 vols. St. Basile (New Brunswick): Privately published, 1971.
Laperrière, Guy. *Les congrégations religieuses: De la France au Québec, 1880–1914*. 3 vols. Québec: Laval University Press, 1996–2005.
_____. "Persécution et Exil: La Venue au Québec des Congrégations Françaises, 1900-1914." *Revue Histoire de L'Amérique Française* 36, no. 3 (December 1982), pp. 389–411.
Lapointe, Jo Anne. "Woman Captures Mill Life of Early 1900s in *Canuck*." *Lewiston Sun Journal*, 24 January 1993.
Larkin, Mary Theresita. "The History of Catholic Education in the State of Maine from 1604 to 1933." M.A. Thesis, University of Maine at Orono, 1934.
Larock, Cindy. Personal communication with Barry Rodrigue, 28 February 2007.
Larson, Anders. "Franco-Americans and the International Paper Company Strike of 1910." *Maine Historical Society Quarterly* 33, no. 1 (summer 1993), pp. 40–60.
Lavoie, Yolande. *L'émigration des Canadiens aux États-Unis avant 1930: Mesure du phénomène*. Montréal: University of Montréal Press, 1972.
_____. *L'émigration des Québécois aux Etats-Unis de 1840 à 1930*. Québec: Éditeur officiel, 1979.
_____. "Les Mouvements migratoires des Canadiens entre leur pays et les États-Unis au XIXe siècle." *La population du Québec: Études rétrospectives*, Hubert Charbonneau, ed. Montréal: Boréal Express, 1973, pp. 73–88.
Lawrence, Benjamin. *History of Jay, Maine.* Boston: Griffith-Stillings Press, 1912.
Lawton, R. J. and others. *Franco-Americans of the State of Maine, U.S.A., and Their Achievements: Historical, Descriptive and Biographical*. Lewiston: N.p., 1915.
Leamon, James, *Historic Lewiston: A Textile City in Transition*. Auburn: Lewiston Historical Commission, 1976.
Leane, John. *A History of Rumford, Me., 1771–1971*. Rumford: Rumford Publishing Company, 1972.
LeBlanc, Robert. *Une figure légendaire de l'histoire acadienne: le baron de St-Castin*. Dax (France): Éditions P. Pradeu, 1934.

Lecker, Robert and Kathleen Brown. *An Anthology of Maine Literature*. Orono (Maine): University of Maine Press, 1982.

Ledoux, Denis, ed. *Lives in Translation: An Anthology of Contemporary Franco-American Writings*. Lisbon Falls (Maine): Soleil Press, 1991.

Lee, Robert. Letter, to Reverend Dupont. Roman Catholic Church, Diocese of Portland (Maine), Library.

LeMaistre, Francis. Letters to Daniel McAlpin, 10 January 1780, pp. 84–85; 14 November 1778, p. 30; 18 December 1778, p. 34; 2 January 1779, p. 36; 5 January 1779, p. 37. *Haldimand Papers*, Ms. No. 21740.

_____. Letter to Militia Officers at Nouvelle Beauce, 14 November 1778. *Haldimand Papers*, Ms. No. 21740, p. 30

_____. Letters to Christian Praetorius, 1 September 1781 and 3 September 1781. *Haldimand Papers*, Ms. No. 21741, p. 65.

LeMoine, James. *Album Canadien*. Québec: Le Canadien, 1870.

Lessard-Bissonnette, Camille. *Canuck*. Serialized in *Le Messager*, Lewiston, Maine, 1936. Reprinted Bedford (New Hampshire): National Materials Development Center for French, 1980.

_____. Letter to Charlotte Michaud, Lewiston, Maine, 1 September 1970. Franco-American Collection, University of Southern Maine, Lewiston-Auburn College.

Leuchtenberg, William. *Franklin D. Roosevelt and the New Deal*. New York: Harper & Row, 1963.

Levasseur, Ray. *The Trial Statements of Ray Luc Levasseur*. Montréal: Abraham Guillen Press, 2001.

_____. "Mémère." *Hauling up the Morning*, Ray LeVasseur and Tim Blunk, eds. Trenton (New Jersey): Red Sea Press, 1990, pp. 117–21.

_____. "Trouble Coming Every Day: ADX—The First Year." *The New Abolitionists*, Joy James, ed. Albany (New York): State University of New York Press, pp. 47–55.

_____. Essays. Internet site: http://home.earthlink.net/~neoludd/.

Levine, Ben. *Si je comprends bien*. Rockland (Maine): Watching Place. Film.

Lewis, Timothy. "Rooted in the Soil: Farm Family Persistence in Burton Parish, Sunbury County, New Brunswick, 1851–1901." *Acadiensis* XXXI, no. 1 (autumn 2001), pp. 35–54.

Lewiston (Maine), City of. Directory: 1890, 1900.

_____. *First Annual Report of the Receipts and Expenditures of the City Lewiston for the Fiscal Year Ending February 29, 1864....* Lewiston: George A. Callahan, 1864, p. 145

_____. Municipal Evaluation Book, 1880.

_____. Public Library. Scrapbooks on Lewiston history.

_____. Record of Streets, No. 1, November 2, 1840–August 4, 1919.

_____. *Twenty-Fifth Annual Report*. Lewiston: Journal Office, 1888.

_____. Records of the City Clerk's Office, No. 3, 27 September 1875–3 April 1879.

_____. School Committee, *Ninth Annual Report....* Lewiston: George Callahan, 1872, p. 127.

Lewiston Evening Journal (Journal, Lewiston, Maine).

Libby, Winthrop. Letter to LaGassey Montgomery, 16 November 1972, Franco-American Centre, University of Maine at Orono.

Lincoln, Charles, ed. *Correspondence of William Shirley, Governor of Massachusetts and Military Commander in America, 1731–1760*. 2 vols. New York: Macmillan, 1912.

Linteau, Paul-André. *Maisonneuve ou comment des promoteurs fabriquent une ville, 1883–1918*. Montréal: Boréal Express, 1981.

Lippard, Lucy. *Mixed Blessings: New Art in a Multicultural America*. New York: Pantheon Books, 1990.

Longfellow, Henry. *Evangeline: A Tale of Acadie*. Halifax (Nova Scotia): Nimbus Publishing, 1951.

Louder, Dean. "Américanité, Americanidad, Americanness: pourquoi pas?" *N'importe quelle route* 3, no. 2 (1989), pp. 22–23.

_____. "L'Archipel: un commentaire personnel sur deux cultures fortes mais marginales." *Géographie et cultures* 17 (1996), pp. 107–22.

_____. *Du continent perdu à l'archipel retrouvé: le Québec et l'Amérique française*. Sainte-Foy (Québec): Presses de l'Université Laval, 1983.

_____. "Le défi de la Francophonie nord-américaine." *Québec Studies* 7 (1988), pp. 28–47.

_____. "Entre progressistes et conservateurs en Franco-Américanie: Beaufrog en quête de respectabilité." *Annales d'un colloque sur la francophonie minoritaire*. Regina, Saskatchewan, 17 September 1999.

_____. *La Franco-Américanie, 1968–84*. Québec: Minister of International Relations, Division for the United States, Government of Québec, 1984.

_____. "Les Franco-Américains au carrefour de deux mutations socio-politiques." *Vie française,* hors série, 1986, pp. 7–15.

_____. *French America: Mobility, Identity and Minority Experience across the Continent*. Baton Rouge: Louisiana State University Press, 1992.

_____. "Histoire du cours le Québec et l'Amérique française." *Vie française* 37, nos. 7, 8, 9 (1983), pp. 28–31.

_____. "Introducton à l'affiche 'Population francophone aux États-Unis.'" *L'Ouest français et la francophonie nord-américaine*, G. Cesbron, ed. Angers (France): Press of the University of Angers, 1997.

_____. "L'originalité et la pertinence de la francophonie nord-américaine." *Territoires et minorités: de l'Amérique française au Lac Meech*, Notes and Documents 4. Actes de l'ACFAS, 1988, pp. 5–21.

_____. "Peut-on parler d'une Amérique française?" *Annales du 25e Congrès international de géographie,* Paris, 1984, pp. 149–52.

_____. "Picking Up the Pieces of a Broken Dream: Québec and French America." *Journal of Cultural Geography* 4, no. 1 (1984).

_____. "Québec, Canada and *la Francophonie*: Who Speaks for Canada's Francophones?" *Le Forum* 26, no. 5 (1998), pp. 14, 28–35.

_____. "Le Québec d'en haut et le Québec d'en bas: Reflections a Hundred Years After." *Journal of Cultural Geography* 8, no. 2 (1988), pp. 39–47.

_____. *Le Québec et les francophones de la Nouvelle-Angleterre*. Sainte-Foy (Québec): Laval University Press, 1991.

_____. "Le Québec et la Franco-Américanie: A Mother Country in the Making." *Four Hundred Years of Borderland Interaction in the Northeast*, Victor Konrad, James Herlan, and Stephen Hornsby, eds. Fredericton (New Brunswick): Acadiensis Press, 1989, pp. 126–39.

_____. "Ranimer la mémoire collective des Québécois: rappeler l'Amérique française aux étudiants de Laval." *L'ethnologie...en bref; bulletin des membres de la Société québécoise d'ethnologie* 2, no. 2 (2000), pp. 11–17.

_____. "3 A's for Misreading the Continent." *Le FAROG Forum* 15, no. 6 (1988).

Louder, Dean and Roland Breton. "Les aires linguistiques françaises de l'Acadiana, 1970." *Vie française* 34, nos. 7, 8, 9 (1980).

Louder, Dean and Louis Dupont. "Nouvelle sphère de sens et champ identitaire francophone et acadien." *Les Francophones sur les marges*, Carol Harvey and Alan MacDonnell, eds. Winnipeg (Manitoba): University Press of Saint-Boniface, 1997, pp. 53–66.

Louder, Dean and Barry Rodrigue. "Recherche sur les Franco-Américains du Maine, 1970–2000." *Les parcours de l'histoire*, Yves Frenette, Martin Pâquet, and Jean Lamarre, eds. Québec: Presses de l'université Laval, 2002, pp. 207–29.

Louder, Dean and Barry Rodrigue, Yves Brosseau, Sylvie St. Jacques, and Matthew Hatvany. *Maine's French Communities / Le fait Français au Maine*, Université Laval and the University of Maine (autumn 2000). Internet site: www.francomaine.org.

Louder, Dean and Cécyle Trépanier "Sur les routes de l'Amérique française: l'expérience des géographes lavallois." *Québec Studies* 33 (summer 2002), pp. 15–52.

Louder, Dean and Eric Waddell. "Du continent perdu à l'archipel retrouvé: le Québec et l'Amérique française." *Cahiers de géographie du Québec* 23, no. 48 (1979), pp. 5–13.

Louder, Dean, Eric Waddell, and Jean Morisset, eds. *Vision et* visages *de la Franco-Amérique*. Sillery (Québec): Septentrion, 2001.

Louder, Dean, Eric Waddell, and Cécyle Trépanier "La francophonie nord-américaine, mise en place et diffusion." *Langue, espace, société: les variétés du français en Amérique du nord* by Claude Poirier. Québec: Laval University Press, Collection CEFAN, 1994, pp. 187–202.

Louder, Dean, Wilbur Zelinsky, and J. Rooney. *This Remarkable Continent: An Atlas of North American Cultures and* Society. College Station: Texas A & M University Press, 1982.

Lower, Arthur. "New France in New England." *New England Quarterly* 2, April 1929.

Lucey, Anne. "Mémère: The Life of a Franco-American Woman." *"Je suis franco-américaine et fière de l'etre / I Am Franco-American and Proud of It"—An Anthology of Writings of Franco-American Women*. Rhea Côté Robbins, Lanette Landry Petrie, Kristin Langellier, Kathyrn Slot, eds. Manuscript. University of Maine at Orono, 1995.

Lucey, W. *The Catholic Church in Maine*. Francestown (New Hampshire): Marshall Jones, 1957.

Macdonald, William. "The French Canadians in New England." *The Quarterly Journal of Economics* 12 (April 1898), pp. 245–79.

MacKinnon, C. *Only Words*. Cambridge: Harvard University Press, 1993.

MacNutt, W. *New Brunswick, A History: 1784–1867*. Toronto: Macmillan of Canada, 1963, 1984.

Madawaska Historical Society, Madawaska, Maine. Ledger of the Dufour General Store, 1844–1848. Acadian Archives/Archives Acadiennes, University of Maine at Fort Kent.

Mahaffie, Charles, Jr. *A Land of Discord Always*. Camden: Down East Books, 1995.

Maine Register, 1993–1994.

Maine, State of. *Acts and Resolves as Passed by the Seventy-Ninth Legislature of the State of Maine, 1919*. Augusta, Maine: Kennebec Journal, 1919.

_____. Commission to Study the Development of Maine's Franco-American Resources. *Ici on parle français,* Report, Chapter 83, Resolves 1997. December 1997. Copy held at the Franco-American Collection, University of Southern Maine, Lewiston-Auburn College.

_____. Commissioners. *Report of the Commissioners appointed under resolve of February 21, 1843, to locate Grants and determine the extent of possessory Claims under the late treaty with Great Britain*. University of Maine at Orono, Fogler Library, Special Collections.

_____. Commissioners. *Report of the Commissioners appointed under resolve of April 12, 1854 to locate Grants and determine the extent of possessory Claims under the late treaty with Great*

Britain. University of Maine at Orono, Fogler Library, Special Collections.

_____. *Counties, Cities, Towns, and Plantations of Maine: A Handbook of Incorporations, Dissolutions, and Boundary Changes*. 1940. Maine State Archives, Maine Historical Records Survey Project, c. 1980.

_____. *Musée De L'État du Maine: Guide des galeries d'exposition*. Maine State Museum. Augusta: State of Maine, c. 2001.

"Maine's Amos Abbott Company is Still Family-Owned After 140 Years." *America's Textile Reporter* 75, no. 14 (6 April 1961), pp. 9–11.

Mallet, Edmond. *Fonds Mallet*. Correspondence between Lewiston French-Canadian leaders and Major Edmond Malle. Union Saint-Jean-Baptiste d'Amérique, Woonsocket, Rhode Island.

Map of Lewiston and Auburn, Maine, From Actual Surveys. Sanford (Maine): Everts & Company, 1873.

Map of Limestone, Maine, derived from surveys and plans by F. Rowe and N. George Colby, Philadelphia, 1877. Robert A. Frost Memorial Library, Limestone, Maine.

Marcou, Napoleon. Interview in "Franco-American Oral History–Waterville, Maine," Marilyn Mavrinac, comp., 1975–76. Waterville Public Library, Waterville, Maine.

Martin, André, comp. *A Franco-American Overview: Midwest and West*. Vol. 2. Cambridge (Massachusetts): National Assessment and Disemination Center for Bilingual/Bicultural Education, 1980.

Massachusetts, Province and State. Archives. *Conference at Falmouth in Casco-Bay* (July 1732). Boston: B. Green, 1732.

_____. *Conference Held at St. Georges* (1753). Boston: Kneeland, 1753.

_____. *Records of the Massachusetts Council, 1715–1763*. Washington, D.C.: Library of Congress, Records of the United States, microfilm edition, 1949.

_____. *Journals of the Massachusetts House of Representatives, 1715–1763*. Washington, D.C.: Library of Congress, Records of the United States, microfilm edition, 1949.

_____. *Journal of the Proceedings at Two Conferences* (1754). Boston: Draper, 1754.

_____. *Journal of the Proceedings...of the Peace...at Falmouth*. Boston: Draper, 1749.

_____. *Massachusetts Archives, 1622–1799*, 326 vols. Stoughton, Massachusetts: Graphic Microfilm, c. 1978.

_____. *Roster of the General Court, 1993–1994*.

Massé, Jean-Claude. "La guerre des fourrures au Madawaska–Témiscouata." In the Société de généalogie de Québec, *L'ancêtre* 26, nos. 3–4 (November–December 1999), pp. 89–97.

Massé, Robert. Letter to FAROG, October 1972. FACD, Franco-American Centre, University of Maine at Orono.

Mathieu, André, dir. *Saint-François-de-Beauce: je me souviens*. St-Georges-de-Beauce: Ateliers Graphiti Barbeau, c. 1985.

Matsuda, Marie and others. *Words That Wound*. Boulder: Westview, 1993.

Mattawamkeag Stage House Register, 1 January 1843 to 7 April 1845. Original held at the Sterling Inn, Caratunk, Maine; copy held by Barry Rodrigue.

Mavrinac, Marilyn, comp. "Franco-American Oral History—Waterville, Maine." 1975–1976. Waterville Public Library.

May, Herbert. "A Place to Stand: Families, Land, and Permanence in Toronto Gore Township, 1820–1890." *Historical Papers*, 1980, Canadian Historical Association, pp. 185–211.

Maynard, Theodore. *The Story of American Catholicism*. New York: Macmillan, 1941.

McAlpin, Daniel. "An Effective List of all the Loyalists in Canada receiving provisions from the King's Store," 1 July 1779. *Haldimand Papers*, Ms. No. 21826, pp. 10–14.
_____. Letters to Frederick Haldimand, 24 October 1778, *Haldimand Papers*, Ms. No. 21732, pp. 144–145; 26 July 1779, *Haldimand Papers*, Ms. No. 21821, pp. 29–30.
_____. "Monthly Return of the Corps of Loyalists Commanded by Captain Daniel McAlpin of the 60th Regt. as they are Incorporated," 1 July 1779. *Haldimand Papers*, Ms. No. 21826, p. 15.
_____. "Return of Loyalists Receiving Provisions (not paying for the same) in the District of Montreal," 25 July to 24 August 1779. *Haldimand Papers*, Ms. No. 21826, pp. 16–22.
_____. "Return of Royalists & their families who Receive Provisions," 25 September to 24 October 1779. *Haldimand Papers*, Ms. No. 21826, pp. 24–30.
_____. "The State of the Loyalists that are in pay Commanded by Capt. Danl. McAlpin," Québec, 1 November 1779. *Haldimand Papers*, Ms. No. 21826, p. 32.
McAlpin, Mary. Letter to Frederick Haldimand, 25 July 1780. *Haldimand Papers*, Ms. No. 21821, pp. 97–98.
McCalla, Douglas. "Retailing in the Countryside: Upper Canadian General Stores in the Mid-Nineteenth Century." *Business and Economic History* 26 (winter 1997), pp. 393–403.
_____. "Rural Credit and Rural Development in Upper Canada, 1790–1850." *Merchant Credit and Labour Strategies in Historical Perspective*, Rosemary Ommer, ed. Fredericton: Acadiensis Press, 1990, pp. 265–72.
McCarthy, Jeremiah. Plan and Survey of the River Chaudiere and the St. Lawrence, 1792. Québec, Ministère de Terres et Fôrets, Arpentage/Rivières, No. 59 (extrait), Archives Nationales du Québec.
McCreath, Peter and John Leefe. *History of Early Nova Scotia*. Tantallon (Nova Scotia): Four East Publications, 1982.
Mckeen, Jeff. Personal communication with Barry Rodrigue, c. 2001.
Mencken, H. L. *The American Language*. Supplement I. New York: Alfred A. Knopf, 1945.
Messager, Le. (Journal, Lewiston, Maine).
Michaud, Charlotte. "Increasing Number of Franco-Americans Interested in Bates." *Lewiston Journal Illustrated Magazine Section*, 27 May 1939.
_____. "Mother d'Youville, Founder of Gray Nuns in Lewiston." *Lewiston Journal Illustrated Magazine*, 7 January 1939.
_____. Unpublished correspondence with JoAnne Lapointe, 30 January 1976, Franco-American Collection, University of Southern Maine, Lewiston-Auburn College, Lewiston, Maine.
Michaud, Charlotte and Adelard Janelle. "Lewiston's Franco-Americans: Their Origins and Early History." *Historic Lewiston: Franco-American Origins*. Auburn: Lewiston Historical Commission, 1974, pp. 6–26.
Miller, Nancy. *Bequest and Betrayal: Memoirs of a Parent's Death*. New York: Oxford University Press, 1996.
Milton, Norma. "Mary Ann Castonguay Lebel: 'Je ne regrette rien'—'I regret nothing.'" *Old Women's Wisdom: The Women of Aroostook County, Maine*, Kathyrn Olmstead and others, eds. Presque Isle (Maine): Aroostook Area Agency on Aging, 1996.
Mitchell, George. "In Politics There are Two Maines." *Maine Sunday Telegram*, 10 January 1971, p. 10.
Montgomery, Ethelyn LaGassey. Letter to FAROG, 21 October 1972, Franco-American Centre, University of Maine at Orono.

_____. Letter to Winthrop Libby, 13 November 1972, Franco-American Centre, University of Maine at Orono.

Montmarquet, J. D. Letters to Edmond Mallet. *Fonds Mallet*. Correspondence between Lewiston French-Canadian leaders and Major Edmond Mallet. Union Saint-Jean-Baptiste d'Amérique, Woonsocket, Rhode Island.

Morrissey, Theresa. "The Irish in Lewiston, 1860–1870." Course term paper, University of Maine at Orono, 1984. Copy held by Yves Frenette.

Morawska, Ewa. *For Bread with Butter: The Life-World of East Central Europeans in Johnstown, Pennsylvania, 1890–1940*. Cambridge (England): Cambridge University Press, 1985.

Morin, Amy; Jim Bishop and others. *Nos histoires de l'Île*. Old Town (Maine): Groupe Nos histoires de l'Île, 1999. Internet site: www.old-town.lib.me.us/nos/.

Moss, Jane. "Les Théâtres francophones en Amérique du Nord." *L'Interculturalisme au sein de la communauté francophone du Canada*. Jean Morency, dir. Québec: Nota Bene, 2004, pp. 393–409.

Mulvey, Mary. *French Catholic Missionaries in the Present United States (1604–1791)*. Washington, D.C.: Catholic University, 1936.

Mundy, James. *Hard Times, Hard Men: Maine and the Irish 1830–1860*. Scarborough (Maine): Harp Publications, 1990.

Murphy, Annie. "A Brief History of St. Anne's Parish in Dexter." *The Eastern Gazette* 21 (December 1939).

Myhrman, A. and J. Rademaker. "The Second Colonization Process in an Industrial Community." Typescript. N.p., n.d. Copy held at Lewiston Public Library. The authors were instructors at Bates College between World War I and World War II.

Nadeau, Napoléon. Interview, 28 March 1972, with Michael Guignard.

Nairne, John. "General Return of Unincorporated Royalists and Families who Received their Provisions gratis from Government," 25 August to 24 September 1781. *Haldimand Papers*, Ms. No. 21826, pp. 55–61.

_____. "Return of Families of Loyalists Receiving Provisions out of the Different Magazines or Depots in the District of Montreal," 25 October to 24 November 1780. *Haldimand Papers*, Ms. No. 21826, pp. 33–39.

_____. "Return of the Loyalists who are to be struck off of the Provisions list," 1 August 1781. *Haldimand Papers*, Ms. No. 21826, p. 53–55.

Narayan, Uma. *Dislocating Cultures: Identities, Traditions, and Third World Feminism*. New York: Routledge, 1997.

New Brunswick Courier (Journal, New Brunswick, Canada).

New Brunswick, Province of. Crown Land Office. Survey Map of the Mazzerolle Grant, 1790.

_____. House of Assembly, Journal.

_____. Legislative Assembly. Papers Relating to the Settlement of Madawaska, 1834.

_____. Maps of the Madawaska Survey, conducted by Land Commissioners J. A. Maclauchlan and John C. Allen to settle the claims arising under the treaty of Washington, 1844–48.

_____. Provincial Census, 1851.

_____. Report of the Commissioner of Affairs at Madawaska, 1834. Contains Maclauchlan report: "Return showing the Number of Inhabitants in the settlement of Madawaska with their Stock," 1833.

_____. Survey Map of the Soucy Grant, 1794
_____. Victoria County, General Sessions, Minutes, 1851–56.
Newsweek, 23August 1993.
New York Times, January 1923–August 1925.
Nish, Cameron, trans. and ed. *The French Regime.* Scarborough (Ontario): Prentice-Hall of Canada, 1965.
Norridgewock, Town Meeting. Petition for Abatement of Taxes, 20 August 1788, p. 271. "Now and Then," by William Allen. *Collections of the Maine Historical Society*, vol. 7. Bath: Maine Historical Society, 1876, pp. 269–87.
Novak, Anna. Interview. *First-Person America,* Ann Banks, ed. New York: Knopf, 1980, p. 63.
Novick, P. *That Noble Dream: The "Objectivity Question" and the American Historical Profession.* New York: Cambridge University Press, 1988.
O'Brien, David. *American Catholics and Social Reform: The New Deal Years.* New York: Oxford University Press, 1968.
Observations (Journal, Lewiston, Maine).
O'Callaghan, Edmund, ed. *Documents Relative to the Colonial History of the State of New York.* 15 vols. Albany: Weed, Parsons and Company, 1853–87.
O'Connor, Richard. *The German-Americans: An Informal History.* Boston: Little, Brown and Company, 1968.
Officer of the New York troops. Letter, 9 November 1775. *Invasion du Canada,* by L'Abbé Verreau. Montréal : Eusébe Senécal, 1873, pp. 372–73.
Old Canada Road Historical Society. Internet site: www.oldcanadaroad.org.
O'Leary, Charles. "A History of Organized Labor in Maine during the New Deal." M.A. Thesis, University of Maine at Orono, 1970.
Oliphant, Patrick. *Washington Post*, 17 November 2005.
Oliver, James. "The History of Lewiston." Typescript. Bates College, 1934.
Olivier, Reginald. *Your Ancient Canadian Family Ties*. Logan (Utah): Everton Publishers, 1972.
Olmstead, Kathyrn and others, eds. *Old Women's Wisdom: The Women of Aroostook County, Maine*. Presque Isle (Maine): Aroostook Area Agency on Aging, 1996.
Ouellette, Cléo. "A New Look at French in the St. John Valley." Work Session, Department of Education, University of Maine at Fort Kent, 1993.
Ouellette, James. *Eagle Lake: The History of a Lumbering Town in Aroostook County, Maine,* Brunswick (Maine): Harpswell Press, 1980.
Oxford English Dictionary, The. Oxford: Clarendon Press, 1989.
Page, Linda. Cote Family Tree. Origin unknown, n.d., from Linda Page, Limestone, Maine.
_____Letter to Barry Rodrigue, 16 May 1995. Franco-American Collection, University of Southern Maine, Lewiston, Maine.
Paquet, Gilles. "L'émigration des Canadiens français vers la Nouvelle-Angleterre, 1870–1910: prises de vue quantitatives." *Recherches Sociographiques* 5 (September–December 1964), pp. 319–70.
Paré, Paul. *Les Trois Anges*. *À tour de rôle: neuf pièces en un acte*, Renaud Albert, ed. Bedford (New Hampshire): National Materials Development Center for French and Creole, 1980.
_____. "Les vingt premières années du *Messager* de Lewiston, Maine." In *Le journalisme de langue française aux États-Unis*, Claire Quintal, ed. Québec City: Conseil de la vie française en Amérique, 1984, pp. 81–96.

Parent, Michael. *American Storytelling, Michael Parent*. New York: Second Story Television, 1984. Cine Golden Eagle Award. Videocassette.

_____. "The Archduke and the Wizards." *Spinning Tales, Weaving Hope*, Brody, Goldspinner, Greene, Leventhal, Porcino, eds. Gabriola Island (British Columbia): New Society Publishers, 1992, pp. 102–11

_____. "Charlie Pinchhits." *American Storytelling Series*. Vol. 7. Bronx (New York): H. W. Wilson Company, 1986. Video.

_____. *Growing Up is a Fulltime Job, Stories for Young Readers*. Lewiston (Maine): Published by the author, 1998.

_____. "Olive and Bidou." *Lives in Translation*, Denis Ledoux, ed. Lisbon Falls (Maine): Soleil Press, 1991, pp. 49–54.

_____. "Panther and Rabbit." *Ready-To-Tell Tales*, David Holt and Bill Mooney, eds. Little Rock (Arkansas): August House Publishers, 1994, pp. 157–61.

_____. "The Pinch-Hitter." *Best-Loved Stories Told at the National Festival*. Jonesborough (Tennessee): National Storytelling Press, 1991, pp. 147–52. Reprinted in *On Common Ground*, Jerry George, Don Stone, Faye Ward, eds. Toronto (Ontario): Oxford University Press, 1994, pp. 38–43. Reprinted in *Heroes and Villains in American Literature*, Henry Christ, ed. New York: Amsco Publications, 1996, pp. 470–79.

_____. "Secret of the Animals." *More Ready-To-Tell Tales*, David Holt and Bill Mooney, eds. Little Rock (Arkansas): August House Publishers, 2001, pp. 172–76.

_____. *Sundays at Grandma's*. Charlottesville (Virginia): Virginia Arts Recording, 1990. Parents' Choice Magazine Gold Award. Cassette tape.

_____. *Tails and Childhood*. Weston (Connecticut): A.L.A. Notable Record, Weston Woods Studios, 1986. Cassette tape.

Parent, Michael and Greg Boardman. *Chantons, Let's Sing—in French & English: Traditional French Songs* (with sung English translations). Lewiston (Maine): LA Arts, 2000. Music C.D.

Parent, Michael and Julien Olivier. *Of Kings and Fools, Stories from the French Tradition in North America*. Little Rock (Arkansas): August House Publishers, 1996.

Park, Edwards. "Could Canada Have Ever Been Our Fourteenth Colony?" *Smithsonian Magazine*, December 1987, pp. 40–49.

Parkman, Francis. *A Half-Century Conflict: France and England in North America*. Boston: Little, Brown & Company, 1909.

_____. "1755–1763: Removal of the Acadians." *Montcalm and Wolfe,* by Francis Parkman. New York: Modern Library, 1999, pp. 120–44.

Pawling, Micah. *Wabanaki Homeland and the New State of Maine: The 1820 Journal and Plans of Survey of Joseph Treat*. Amherst: University of Massachusetts Press, 2007.

_____. "Petitions and the Reconfiguration of Homeland: Persistance and Tradition Among Wabanaki Peoples in the Nineteenth Century." Ph.D. Dissertation, University of Maine at Orono, 2007. Draft title.

Pearce, Abraham. Letter to Samuel Ingham, Secretary of the Treasury, 24 August 1829. U.S. National Archives, Washington, D.C.

Peiss, Kathy. *Cheap Amusements: Working Women and Leisure in Turn-of-the-Century New York*. Philadelphia: Temple University Press, 1986.

Pelletier, Fran. *Little Pine to King Spruce: A Franco-American Childhood*. Gardiner (Maine): Tilbury House, Publishers, 2003.

Pelletier, Martine and Monica Dionne Ferreti. *A Folkloric History of Van Buren Settlers*. Van Buren (Maine): Published by the authors, 1979.

_____. *Van Buren History*. Madawaska (Maine): St. John Valley Publishing Company, 1979.

Pelletier, Susann. *Immigrant Dream and Other Poems*. Lisbon Falls (Maine): Soleil Press, 1989; second printing, 1995; third printing 1997; fourth printing 1999.

_____. "Immigrant Dream." In *Lives in Translation: An Anthology of Contemporary Franco-American Writings*, Denis Ledoux (editor). Lisbon Falls: Soleil Press, 1991, p. 91.

_____. In *Contemporary New England Poetry: A Sampler*. Huntsville (Texas): Sam Houston University Press and The Texas Review, 1989.

_____. In *No Hay Fronteras, a bilingual poetry anthology on the Central American Experience*. New Haven (Connecticut): New Haven/Leon Sister City Project, 1990.

_____. In *Lives in Translation: An Anthology of Contemporary Franco-American Writings*. Denis Ledoux, ed. Lisbon Falls (Maine): Soleil Press, 1991.

_____. In *Live Poets' Anthology*. Rockland (Maine): Live Poets' Society Press, 1997.

_____. In *A Sense of Place: Collected Maine Poems*. Lillian Kennedy, Alice Persons, Nancy Henry, eds. Auburn (Maine): Bay River Press, 2002.

_____. In *Goose River Anthology*. Waldoboro (Maine): Goose River Press, 2003.

_____. In *Fierce with Reality: An Anthology of Literature on Aging*. Minnesota: North Star, 1995; Margaret Cruikshank, ed, Topsham (Maine): Published by the editor, 2006.

Perlmutter, P. *Divided We Fall: A History of Ethnic, Religious, and Racial Prejudice in America*. Ames: Iowa State University Press, 1992.

Peterson, Eric. "Dial 581-FROG: The Struggle Over Self-Naming by Franco-Americans in Maine." *Culture and Communication*, E. Slembek, ed. Frankfurt-am-Main: Verlag für Interculturalle Kommunikation, 1991.

____"Diversity in Franco-American Identity Politics." *Maine Historical Society* 34, no. 1 (1994).

Peterson, Lisa. "Class Dramatizes the Franco-Mainer Experience." *The Bowdoin Orient*, Brunswick, Maine, 7 May 2004. Internet site: http://orient.bowdoin.edu/orient/article.php?date=2004-05-07&section=4&id=9.

Petrin, Ronald. *French Canadians in Massachusetts Politics, 1885–1915: Ethnicity and Political Pragmatism*. Philadelphia: Balch Institute Press, 1990.

Plourde, Antonin. "Les dominicains à Lewiston." *Le Rosaire* 854–855 (August 1970), pp. 3–70.

_____. *Dominicains au Canada: Livre de documents*, 2, *Les cinq fondations avant l'autonomie (1881–1911)*. Montréal: Les Éditions du Levrier, 1975.

_____. *Qui sont-ils et d'où viennent-ils? Nécrologe dominicain, 1965–1990*. Vol. II. Montréal: The Dominicans of Canada, n.d.

Plummer, Stanley. *History of Dexter, Maine, 1801–1901*. Reprint, Dexter: Dexter Historical Society, 1976.

Poteet, M., ed. *Textes de l'exode: Recueil des textes sur l'émigration des québécois aux États-Unis (XIXe et Xxe siécles)*. Montréal: Guerin littérature, 1987.

Potholm, Christian. "A Grand Moment." *Maine: The Dynamics of Political Change,* by Christian Potholm. Washington: Lexington Books, 2006, pp. 16–18.

_____. *An Insider's Guide to Maine Politics, 1946–1996*. Lanham (Maryland): Madison Books, 1998.

_____. *This Splendid Game: Maine Politics from 1940 to 2002*. Washington: Lexington Books, 2004.

_____. "Up Ye Mighty Francos." *The Delights of Democracy,* by Christian Potholm. Washington: Cooper Square Press, 2002, pp. 173–76.

Poulain, Jean-Paul. *Le Droit d'Aimer*. Augusta (Maine): Mërilda Recordings, 1996. Music, Cassette Tape, and Music CD.

_____. Interview with Chase Hébert, 19 December 2006 in Augusta, Maine. Tape recording. University of Southern Maine's Franco-American Collection at Lewiston-Auburn College.

_____. *Jean-Paul Poulain Chante L'Amour*. Augusta (Maine): Mërilda Recordings, n.d. CD.

_____. *Jean-Paul Poulain chante pour ses petits et grands amis*. Augusta (Maine): Jean-Paul Poulain, n.d. Music CD.

Poulin, Pierre. Letter to Frederick Haldimand, 18 October 1778. *Haldimand Papers*, Ms. No. 21732, pp. 135–36.

Poulin, Pierre. "Les Beaucerons au Maine: des relations depuis longtemps établies." Manuscript, 2001.

_____. *Paysages, territorialités et représentations: à la recherche de l'identité régionale beauceronne*. Ph.D. Dissertation, Université Laval (Québec), 2000.

_____. Personal Communication, with Barry Rodrigue, c. 2002.

Pownall, Charles. *Thomas Pownall, Governor of Massachusetts Bay*. London: Henry Stevens, Son, and Stiles, 1908.

Price, Harriet and Gerald Talbot, eds. *Maine's Visible Black History: The First Chronicle of Its People*. Gardiner (Maine): Tilbury House, Publishers, 2006.

Programme-Souvenir 1872–1947: La célébration du 75e anniversaire de l'Institut Jacques-Cartier de Lewiston, Maine...Fondé le 12 janvier 1872. Lewiston: N.p., 1947.

Prosser, Albert, ed. *Sanford, Maine: A Bicentennial History.* Sanford: Sanford Historical Committee, 1968.

Provencher-Faucher, Doris. *Imperial Conflict*. Biddeford (Maine): Artenay Press, 2006.

_____. *Le Québécois: The Virgin Forest*. Biddeford (Maine): Artenay Press, 2000.

_____. *The Rapids*. Biddeford (Maine): Artenay Press, 2002

Provost, Honorius. "Un chapitre d'histoire religieuse dans le Maine." *La Revue de l'Université Laval* 2 (1940), pp. 853–60.

_____. *Sainte-Marie de la Nouvelle-Beauce: histoire civile*. Québec: Éditions de la Nouvelle-Beauce, 1970.

_____. "Taschereau, Gabriel-Elzéar." *Dictionary of Canadian Biography*, Francess Halpenny and Jean Hamelin, eds. Vol. 5. Québec and Toronto: Les Presses de l'Université Laval and the University of Toronto Press, 1983, pp. 793–95.

Québec, Ministère des terres et fôrets, Service de photogrammétrie et de la cartographie. Aerial photograph, St-François-de-Beauce, 1960, 1: 15,840, no. 1276–81.

Quintal, Claire, ed. *Les Franco-Américains et Leurs Institutions Scolaires*. Worcester (Massachusetts): The French Institute, Assumption College, 1990.

_____. *La Littérature franco-américaine: écrivains et écritures / Franco-American Literature: Writers and Their Writings*. Worcester (Massachusetts): The French Institute, Assumption College, 1992.

_____. *The Little Canadas of New England*. Worcester (Massachusetts): The French Institute, Assumption College, 1983.

_____. *Religion Catholique et Appartenance Franco-Américaine Franco-Americans and Religion: Impact and Influence*. Worcester (Massachusetts): The French Institute, Assumption College, 1993.

_____. *Steeples and Smokestacks: The Franco American Experience in New England.* Worchester (Massachusetts): The French Institute, Assumption College, 1996.
Ramirez, Bruno. "French Canadian Immigrants in the New England Cotton Industry: A Socioeconomic Profile." *Labour—Le Travailleur* 11 (spring 1983), pp. 125–42.
Rawlyk, George. "The American Revolution and Nova Scotia Reconsidered." *Dalhousie Review* 43 (autumn 1963), pp. 379–94.
Rhode Island and Providence Plantations. *Elected Officials, 1993–1994.*
Richard, Mark. "Coping before *l'État-providence:* Collective Welfare Strategies of New England's Franco-Americans." *Québec Studies* 25 (spring 1998), pp. 59–67.
_____. "The Ethnicity of Clerical Leadership: The Dominicans in Francophone Lewiston, Maine, 1881–1986." *Québec Studies* 33 (spring/summer 2002), pp. 83–101.
_____. "From Canadien to American: The Acculturation of French-Canadian Descendants in Lewiston, Maine, 1860 to the Present." Ph.D. Dissertation, Duke University, 2001.
_____. "From Franco-American to American: The Case of *Sainte-Famille*, an Assimilating Parish of Lewiston, Maine." *Histoire sociale/Social History* 31 (May 1998), pp. 71–93.
_____. *"Not Foreigners but Americans:" The Negotiation of Identity by French-Canadian Descendants, Lewiston, Maine, 1860–2002.* This is a book-length manuscript under contract to Michigan State University Press.
_____. *Out of Little Canada: The Assimilation of Sainte-Famille Parish, Lewiston, Maine, 1923–1994.* M.A. Thesis, University of Maine at Orono, 1994.
Richard, Mark and Stephen Hornsby. "French-Canadian Immigration," Plate 47. Forthcoming in the *Historical Atlas of Maine.* Orono (Maine): University of Maine Press, 2007.
Riedesel, Friedrich Adolph von. Letter to Frederick Haldimand, 19 October 1781, pp. 202–04; 19 December 1781, pp. 245–48. *Haldimand Papers*, Ms. No. 21796.
Rioux, Robert. *Enquête géolinguistique: du vocabulaire, et de la prononciation de celui-ci, employés dans l'État du Maine pour désigner tout ce qui se rapporte à l'intérieur et a l'extérieur de la maison, d'après le questionnaire de MM. Gaston Dulong et Gaston Bergeron de l'Université Laval.* Jane Smith, ed. Orono: University of Maine Press, 2006.
Roberge, Céleste. "Semester Review and Report for Fall, 1972." *Le FAROG Forum* (1972), pp. 1–2.
Robert, Jean-Claude. *Atlas historique de Montréal.* Montréal: Art Global et Libre Expression, 1994.
Roberts, Kenneth. *Arundel.* Garden City (New York): Doubleday & Company, Inc., 1933.
_____. *March to Quebec: Journals of the Members of Arnold's Expedition.* Garden City (New York): Doubleday & Company, Inc., 1953, pp. 717–24.
Robichaud, Gérard. *Papa Martel.* Orono (Maine): University of Maine Press, 2003.
Roby, Yves. "Émigrés canadiens-français, Franco-Américains de la Nouvelle-Angleterre et images de la société américaine." *Québécois et Américains: La culture québécoise aux XIXe et XXe siècles*, Yvan Lamonde and Gérard Bouchard, dirs. Saint-Laurent (Québec): Éditions Fides, 1995, pp. 131–56.
_____. *Les Franco-Américains de la Nouvelle-Angleterre: rêves et réalités.* Sillery (Québec): Septentrion, 2000.
_____. *Les Franco-Américains de la Nouvelle-Angleterre, 1776–1930.* Sillery (Québec): Septentrion, 1990.
_____. *Histoire d'un rêve brisé? Les Canadiens français aux États-Unis.* Sillery (Québec): Septentrion, 2007.

_____. "Québec in the United States: A Historiographical Survey." *Maine Historical Society Quarterly* 26, no. 3 (1987), pp. 126–159.

Rodrigue, Barry. "An Album in the Attic: The Forgotten Frontier of the Quebec–Maine Borderlands During the Revolutionary War." *The Journal of the Historical Society* 3, no. 1 (2003), pp. 45–73.

_____. *Avec tout mon cœur: Albert Béliveau, the Life of* a *Franco-American jurist,* 1887–1972. Unpublished manuscript and collection, held at the Franco-American Collection, Lewiston-Auburn College, University of Southern Maine, c. 1992–94.

_____. "The Canada Road Frontier." *Histoire Mythique et Paysage Symbolique*, Serge Courville and others, eds. Sainte-Foy (Québec): Laval University Press, 1997, pp. 59–69.

_____. "Canada Road / La route du Canada." *Maine's French Communities / Le fait Français au Maine*, 2000. Internet site: www.francomaine.org/English/Histo/Canada/Canada_intro.html.

_____. "The Cultural Trigonometry of Franco-American Stereotypes." *Maine History* (summer 1994), pp. 40–57.

_____. "Harmonizing Agendas: Public Geography, Government Policy, and Private Goals." Paper presented at the Eleventh International Conference of Historical Geographers. Québec, Québec, August 2001.

_____. "Maine's Canada Road Frontier: Settlement and Development, 1790–1860." Ph.D. Dissertation, University of Maine at Orono, 2000.

_____. "The Making of the St. Lawrence–Maine System: The Canada Road Frontier, 1790–1860." Ph.D. Dissertation, Laval University, 1999.

_____. "Migrations par la route Chaudière–Kennebec, 1810–1860." *Atlas historique du Québec: Population et territoire*. Sainte Foy (Québec): Laval University Press, 1996, pp. 134–35.

_____. "A Quebec Soldier: Overdue Commemoration for a Civil War Soldier." *Kennebec Journal* (28–29 March 1992), A–9.

_____. *Tom Plant: The Making of* a *Franco-American Entrepreneur, 1859–1941*. New York: Garland Publishing, 1994.

_____. "Tom Plant, la route du Canada et les stéréotypes sur les Franco-Américains." *Vision et visages de la Franco-Amérique*, Dean Louder, Jean Morisset, and Eric Waddell, eds. Sillery (Québec): Septentrion, 2001, pp. 113–39.

_____. "Le Voyageur." *Le Forum* (April–May 1990), p. 21.

Rodrigue, Barry, Serge Courville, and Pierre Poulin, eds. *Histoire régionale de Beauce–Etchemin–Amiante*. Québec: Institut national de la recherche scientifique, 2003.

Rodrigue, Barry, Serge Courville, Pierre Poulin, and Claude Pronovost. "La Beauce au XIXe Siècle." *Études canadiennes/Canadian Studies*, no. 50 (2001), pp. 63–86.

Rodrigue, Barry and Alaric Faulkner. *Canada Road Survey, Part 7, Final Report*. Augusta: Maine Historic Preservation Commission, 1995.

Rodrigue, Barry and Dean Louder. "Recherche sur les Franco-Américains du Maine, 1970–2000." *Les parcours de l'histoire*, Yves Frenette, Martin Pâquet, and Jean Lamarre, eds. Québec: Laval University Press, 2002, pp. 207–29.

Rodrigue, Barry, Dean Louder, Matthew Hatvany, Sylvie St. Jacques, Yves Brosseau, Yvon Labbé, Lisa Michaud, Susan Pinette, Viateur Boutot, and Laura Beaulieu Morin. *Maine's French Communities / Le fait Français au Maine*. Québec and Orono: Geography Department, Laval University, and Franco-American Centre, University of Maine, 2000. Internet site: www.francomaine.org.

Rodrigue, Barry, Dan Philbrick, and students in French North American Studies, spring 2002. University of Southern Maine, Lewiston-Auburn College, "Franco-American Resources." Internet site: www.usm.maine.edu/USM-LA/francoamericanstudies.

Rodrigue, Barry, Kenneth Plant, and others. "Plant Family History," 2004. Internet site: www. plantfamily.com/homepage.html. This website is related to Barry Rodrigue's book, *Tom Plant: The Making of a Franco-American Entrepreneur*.

Rodrigue, Barry and Andrew Redmond. *Memoires of Andrew J. Redmond, Entrepreneur*. Madison (Maine): Published by Andrew Redmond, 1995. Rodrigue was the project director, primary editor, and interviewer. The project materials are held at the Franco-American Collection, Lewiston-Auburn College, University of Southern Maine, c. 1992–94.

Rodrigue, Barry, Eric Waddell, and Dean Louder. *Manifesto of Franco-America*. 2002. Internet site: http://usm.maine.edu/lac/francoamericanstudies/cfa.html.

Roe, F. B. *Atlas of Aroostook County*. Philadelphia: N. Colby, 1877.

Rolde, Neil. *Maine: A Narrative History*. Gardiner (Maine): Harpswell Press, 1990.

_____. *Unsettled Past, Unsettled Future: The Story of Maine Indians*. Gardiner: Tilbury House, Publishers, 2004.

Rollins, Judith. *All Is Never Said: The Narrative of Odette Harper Hines*. Philadelphia: Temple University Press, 1995.

Roman Catholic Church. Archdiocese of Québec, Archives, Lettres des prêtres missionnaires du Madawaska à l'Evêque de Québec, 1785–1850.

_____. Convent of Lewiston Records, "Prônes."

_____. Correspondence File: 1892-1930. Handwritten and TL. Chancellory Archives, Diocese of Portland (Maine).

_____. Diocesan Clergy: A-M. Chancellory Archives, Diocese of Portland (Maine).

_____. Diocese of Portland (Maine). Chancellory Archives, Portland, Maine. St. Peter's Parish, Lewiston, Maine, file.

_____. *Dixmes de la paroisse St. François Nlle. Beauce pour l'année 1796*. Archives, Archdiocèse de Québec, AAQ 61 CD, Beauceville 1.

_____. Dominican Order, Montréal (Québec). La Chronique du couvent, 1881–1976. In the series for monasteries and parishes, sub-series for the monastery of Saints Peter and Paul of Lewiston, Maine.

_____. *Lewiston, Maine, 1971: Centenaire, Album Souvenir*. Lewiston: N.p., 1971.

_____. *The New Catholic Encyclopedia*. Vol. XI. New York: McGraw Hill, 1967.

_____. *The Official Catholic Directory*. New Providence (New Jersey): P. J. Kenedy & Sons, 1997, pp. 605–06.

_____. *Paroisse Canadienne-Française de Lewiston (Maine): Album historique*. Lewiston, (Maine): Les Pères Dominicains, 1899.

_____. Imprimerie du Messager, 1899.

_____. St. Basile, Parish of (New Brunswick), Register, 1792–1857; microfilm available from National Archives of Canada.

_____. St. Bruno, Parish of (Maine), Register, 1838–1855; original accessible at the parish.

_____. Ste. Luce, Parish of (Maine), Register, 1742–1858; original accessible at the parish.

_____. St. Peter and St. Paul Parish. *Album souvenir du 75e anniversaire de la paroisse Saint-Pierre et Saint-Paul de Lewiston, Maine, 1871–1946*. Lewiston, 1946.

_____. Sisters of St. Joseph of Lyons (CSJ), France. "Financial and Enrollment Ledgers:

1906–1967. Archives, Sisters of St. Joseph of Lyons (CSJ), France, Provincialate and Christian Life Center, Winslow, Maine.
_____. Sisters of St. Joseph of Lyons (CSJ), France. "Mission D'Amérique: Fondation du Canada (Ile à la Crosse)." *Le Regne de Dieu* (June and July 1907), pp. 181–221. Archives, Sisters of St. Joseph of Lyons (CSJ), France, Provincialate and Christian Life Center, Winslow, Maine.
_____. Sisters of St. Joseph of Lyons (CSJ), France. "Mission D'Amérique: Fondation de Jackman (États-Unis, province du Maine)." *Le Règne de Dieu* (October, November, December 1907), pp. 294–377. Archives, Sisters of St. Joseph of Lyons (CSJ), France, Provincialate and Christian Life Center, Winslow, Maine.
_____. Sisters of St. Joseph of Lyons (CSJ), France. "The Sisters of St. Joseph in the Diocese of Portland." *Church World* 22 (August 1951), pp. 10-11.
_____. South Berwick (Maine). *St. Michael's Parish Directory,* n.d.
Rowe, Amy. "An Exploration of Immigration, Industrialization and Ethnicity in Waterville, Maine." Senior Paper, B.A., Colby College, 1999.
Roy, Jacqueline. "Nairne, John." *Dictionary of Canadian Biography*. Vol. 5, Francess Halpenny and Jean Hamelin, eds. Québec and Toronto: Presses de l'Université Laval and the University of Toronto Press, 1983, pp. 620–21.
Roy, Pierre-Georges. *Inventaire des Concessions en Fief et Seigneurie Fois et Hommages et Aveux et Dénombrement Conservé aux Archives de la Province de Québec*. Vol. 5. Québec: Archives de la Province de Québec, 1929.
Ruiz, Vicki. *From Out of the Shadows: Mexican Women in Twentieth-Century America*. New York: Oxford University Press, 1998.
Rumilly, Robert. *Histoire des Acadiens.* 2 vols. Montréal: Fides, 1955.
_____. *Histoire des Franco-Américains*. Montréal: Published by the author, 1958.
Rutman, Darett. "Assessing the Little Communities of Early America." *William and Mary Quarterly* 3, no. 43 (April 1986), pp. 163–78.
Saint-Hilaire, Marc. *Peuplement et dynamique migratoire au Saguenay, 1840–1960*. Sainte-Foy (Québec): Presses de l'Université Laval, 1996.
St. Pierre, Lorraine. Interview by Michael Brown, 29 December 1990, Franco-American Centre, University of Maine at Orono.
Saint-Pierre, Marjolaine. *Saint-Castin: baron français, chef amérindien, 1652–1707*. Sillery (Québec): Septentrion, 1998.
Santerre, Richard. "Le Roman Franco-Américain en Nouvelle-Angleterre." Ph.D. Dissertation, Boston College, 1974.
Savage, Anita Ambrose. Interview by Dorothy Blanchard. Tape recording. 23 October 1991, Dexter, Maine. Tapes held by Dorothy Blanchard, Newcastle, Maine.
Schechter, Betty. *The Dreyfus Affair*. Boston: Houghton Mifflin, c. 1965.
Schideler, Janet. "Camille Lessard-Bissonette—à la recherche d'un féminisme franco-américain." *La Littérature franco-américaine: écrivains et écritures: Franco-American Literature: Writers and Their Writings*, Claire Quintal, ed. Worcester (Massachusetts): The French Institute, Assumption College, 1992, pp. 29–43.
Schwartz, Kraig. *Empowerment and Class Struggle: Factors Influencing Class Formation in the Asbestos Industry of Quebec, A Case Study of Thetford Mines, 1885–1925*. Ph.D. Dissertation, University of Maine at Orono, 1997.
Scontras, Charles. *Collective Efforts among Maine Workers: Beginnings and Foundations,*

1820–1880. Orono (Maine): Bureau of Labor Education, University of Maine, 1994.
Scottow, Joshua and Henry Josselyn. Letter to Governor Leverett, 15 September 1676. "New Evidence on the French Involvement in King Philip's War," by Emerson Baker, *Maine Historical Society Quarterly* 28, no. 2 (fall 1988), pp. 85–92.
Searles, James, Kent Morse, and Stephen Hinchman, eds. *Immigrants from the North: Franco-Americans Recall the Settlement of Their Canadian Families in the Mill Towns of New England*. Collected and written by the Franco-American Studies Class, Hyde School (Bath, Maine), 1982.
Séguin, Norman. *La conquête du sol au 19e*. Québec: Boréal Express, 1977.
Senécal, André. "Journalisme et création romanesque en Nouvelle-Angleterre francophone, 1875–1936." *Langue, espace, société: Les variétés du français en Amérique du Nord*, Claude Poirier and others, eds. Sainte-Foy (Québec): Les Presses de l'Université Laval, 1994.
Sepunik, Norman. "A Profile of Franco-American Political Attitudes in New England." *A Franco American Overview*. Vol. 3. Bedford (New Hampshire): National Assessment and Dissemination Center for Bilingual/Bicultural Education, 1981, pp. 213–33.
Sernoult, R. B. Letter to Christian Praetorius, 2 January 1781. *Haldimand Papers*, Ms. No. 21741, p. 38.
_____. Letter to Friedrich von Riedesel and Ernst von Speth, 12 June 1783. *Haldimand Papers*, Ms. No. 21742, p. 11.
_____. Letter to Johann von Loos, 17 June 1783. *Haldimand Papers*, Ms. No. 21742, p. 13.
Sévigny, Andre. *Les Abénaquis: habitat et migrations*. Montréal: Cahiers d'histore des Jésuites, 1976.
Shaw, Horace. *The First Maine Heavy Artillery, 1861–1865*. Portland: Charles J. House, 1903.
Shideler, Janet. *Camille Lessard-Bissonnette: The Quiet Evolution of French-Canadian Immigrants in New England*. New York: Peter Lang, 1998.
Shriver, Edward, ed. *The French in New England, Acadia and Quebec*. Orono (Maine): New England–Atlantic Provinces–Quebec Center, 1972.
Small, Isaac. *Aroostook Road to St. John's River*, Map and field notes, 1837, Nos. 5–12–21 to 23. Maine State Archives, Augusta, Maine.
Smith, D. "Virgin Timber: The Maine Woods As a Locale for Juvenile Fiction." *A Handful of Spice*, R. Sprague, ed. Orono (Maine): University of Maine Press, 1968.
Smith, Justin. *Arnold's March from Cambridge to Quebec; A Critical Study, Together with a Reprint from Arnold's Journal*. New York: G. P. Putnam's Sons, 1903.
_____. *Our Struggle for the Fourteenth Colony: Canada and the American Revolution*. New York: G. P. Putnam's Sons, 1907.
_____. "The Prologue of the American Revolution." *The Century Magazine*: "The Barriers Broken," 65 (1), November 1902, pp. 72–94; "Arnold's Battle with the Wilderness," Part 1, 65 (2), December 1902, pp. 351–69; "Arnold's Battle with the Wilderness," part 2, 65 (4), February 1903, pp. 529–44; "Montgomery's Struggle for Quebec," 65 (5), March 1903, pp. 713–33; "The Fortune of War," 65 (6), April 1903, pp. 899–916. These are illustrations.
Smith, N. "The Ku Klux Klan in Rhode Island." *Rhode Island History* 37, no. 2 (1978).
Smith, Sidonie and Julia Watson, eds. *Women, Autobiography, Theory: A Reader*. Madison: University of Wisconsin Press, 1998.
Sprague, John. "Documentary History of the North Eastern Boundary Controversy." *Collection of the Piscataquis County Historical Society*. Vol 1. Dover (Maine): Observer Press, 1910.

———. "Jackman and Moose River Region." *Sprague's Journal of Maine History* 3, no. 2 (July 1915), pp. 55-77.

Spugnardi, J. "Franco-Americans of Biddeford." Course Paper, University of Maine, 1993.

Stewart, Alice. "The Franco-Americans of Maine: A Historiographical Essay." *Maine Historical Society Quarterly* 26, no. 3 (1987), pp. 160–79.

Sullivan, J. "Rhode Island's 'Invisible Empire:' A Demographic Glimpse into the Ku Klux Klan." *Rhode Island History* 47, no. 2 (1989).

Talman, James. *Basic Documents in Canadian History*. Princeton (New Jersey): D. Van Norstrand Company, 1959.

Tanguay, Cyprien. *Dictionnaire généalogigue des familles canadiennes depuis la fondation de la colonie jusqu'à nos jours*. 7 vols. Montréal: Eusèbe Sénécal & fils, 1871–1890.

Tardivel, Émile. Letter to Edmond Mallet, 6 July 1887. *Fonds Mallet*. Correspondence between Lewiston French-Canadian leaders and Major Edmond Mallet, Union Saint-Jean-Baptiste d'Amérique, Woonsocket, Rhode Island.

Tatarczuk, Vincent. Letter to Kenneth Woodbury, 10 March 1964. In Kenneth Woodbury, Jr., "An Incident Between the French Canadians and the Irish in the Diocese of Maine in 1906," *New England Quarterly* 40, June 1967, pp. 261.

Tax, Meridith. *The Rising of the Women*. New York: Monthly Review Press, 1980.

Thayer, Henry. "A Page of Indian History." Maine Historical Society, *Collections*, Series 2, no. 10 (1899), pp. 81–103.

Theriault, George. "The Franco-Americans in Nashua, New Hampshire." Ph.D. Dissertation (History), Harvard University, 1951.

Thernstrom, Stephen. *Poverty and Progress: Social Mobility in a Nineteenth-Century City*. Cambridge (Massachusetts): Harvard University Press, 1964.

Therriault, Mary Carmel. *La Littérature française de Nouvelle-Angleterre*. Montréal: Fides, 1946.

Thibadeau, W. J. *The Irishman: A Factor in the Development of* Houlton. Augusta (Maine): Kennebec Journal, n.d.

Tourangeau, Emma. *Aunt Emma's Island Cookbook: Featuring Old French Canadian Recipes*. Iowa Falls: General Publishing and Binding, 1967.

———. "The French Canadian." Manuscript held by Albert Duclos.

———. Interview by Catherine Walker. Tape recording. 7 November 1982. Tape held by Céleste DeRoche.

Trudel, Marcel. *La Révolution Américaine: Pourquoi La France Refuse Le Canada, 1775–1783*. Sillery (Québec): Les Éditions du Boréal Express Limitée, 1976.

True, Betty. Letter to Barry Rodrigue, January 1997. Stinchfield genealogy, (published manuscript), p. 8.

True, Moses. *Military Road to the Baring and Houlton Road,* map, 1833, nos. 5–12–18 and 19. Maine State Archives, Augusta, Maine.

United States. Adjutant General's Office. *Order No. 39, Hancock Barracks,* Washington, D.C., 18 July 1828.

———. Congress. 20th Congress, Session I, *An act to provide for opening and making a military road in the state of Maine,* 24 May 1828 and Sessions II, Resolution in relation to the survey and laying out a military road, in the state of Maine, 2 March 1829.

———. Continental Congress. Letter to the Inhabitants of Quebec / Lettre Adressée Aux Habitans De La Province De Québec Ci-devant le Canada, 26 October 1774. Journals of the Continental Congress, 1774–1789, p. 104.

_____. Department of the Interior, National Park Service. *North Atlantic Region, Implementing the Maine Acadian Culture Preservation Act*. Washington, D.C.: U.S. Department of Interior, 1994.

_____. District Court, District of Maine. Complaint of *Steffan T. Duplessis v. Training and Development Corporation, et. al.,* Civil Action No. 92–0096–B.

_____. National Recovery Administration, Textile Labor Relations Board. *Record of the Inquiry into Labor Conditions at the Lockwood Manufacturing Company*. In the files for "Lockwood Manufacturing Company—Waterville, Maine," Record Group (RG) 9, Entry No. 402, National Archives, Washington, DC.

_____. *Report of Examiner*. File: "Lockwood Manufacturing Company—Waterville, Maine," Record Group (RG) 9, Entry No. 402, National Archives, Washington, DC.

_____. Treasury Department, Bureau of the Census. *Census of the United States*.

_____. War Department, Memorandum on the Attack of Canada by the U.S., April 1839.

Vassar, William. "Voting Patterns of Franco-Americans in Lewiston, Maine." Senior Seminar, University of Maine at Orono, n.d.

Verreau, L'Abbé. *Invasion du Canada*. Montréal: Eusébe Senécal, 1873.

Vézina, Robert and Phillipe Angers. *Histoire de Saint-Georges de Beauce*. St-Georges: Published by the authors, 1935.

Vicero, Ralph. "Immigration of French Canadians to New England, 1840–1900: A Geographical Analysis." Ph.D. Dissertation, University of Wisconsin, 1968.

_____. "Sources statistiques pour l'étude de l'immigration et du peuplement canadien-français en Nouvelle-Angleterre au cours du XIXe siècle." *Recherches sociographiques* 12 (1971), pp. 361–77.

View of the Rivers Kenebec and Chaudiere with Colonel Arnold's Route to Quebec. London: R. Baldwin, 1776.

Violette, Maurice. *The Franco-Americans: A Franco-American Chronicle of Historical and Cultural Environment—Augusta Revisited*. New York: Vantage Press. 1976.

Wack, Kevin. "Museum in the Streets Celebrates City History." *Portland Press Herald*, 13 November 2006.

Waddell, Eric. "French Louisiana: An Outpost of *l'Amérique Française* or Another Country and Another Culture?" *French America: Mobility, Identity, and Minority Experience Across the Continent*, Dean Louder and Eric Waddell, eds. Baton Rouge: Lousiana State University Press, 1993, pp. 229–51.

Wade, Mason. "French and French Canadians in the U.S." *New Catholic Encyclopedia,* vol. 6. New York: McGraw-Hill, 1967, pp. 143–48.

_____. "The French Parish and Survivance in Nineteenth-Century New England." *Catholic Historical Review* 36, July 1950, pp. 163–89.

Wade, Wyn. *The Fiery Cross: The Ku Klux Klan in America*. New York: Simon and Schuster, 1988.

Walker, David. "The Presidential Politics of the Franco-Americans." *Canadian Journal of Economics and Political Science,* August 1962. Reprinted in *A Franco-American Overview*, Bedford (New Hampshire): National Assessment and Dissemination Center for Bilingual/Bicultural Education, 1981, pp. 200–11.

Walsh, Louis. Diary. Roman Catholic Church, Diocese of Portland (Maine), Library.

_____. Letter, to L. Bergeron. Roman Catholic Church, Diocese of Portland (Maine), Library, Louis S. Walsh Papers.

_____.Letter, to Reverend Charland. Roman Catholic Church, Diocese of Portland (Maine), Library, Louis S. Walsh Papers.

_____.Letter, to P. E. Desjardins. Roman Catholic Church, Diocese of Portland (Maine), Library, Louis S. Walsh Papers.

_____.Letter, to Reverend Dupont. Roman Catholic Church, Diocese of Portland (Maine), Library, Louis S. Walsh Papers.

_____.Letter, to Thomas Dwight. Roman Catholic Church, Diocese of Portland (Maine), Library, Louis S. Walsh Papers.

_____.Letter, to D. Falconio. Roman Catholic Church, Diocese of Portland (Maine), Library, Louis S. Walsh Papers.

_____.Letter, to Reverend Jacques. Roman Catholic Church, Diocese of Portland (Maine), Library, Louis S. Walsh Papers.

_____.Letter, to Reverend Leguennec. Roman Catholic Church, Diocese of Portland (Maine), Library, Louis S. Walsh Papers.

_____.Letter, to J. B. Madigan. Roman Catholic Church, Diocese of Portland (Maine), Library, Louis S. Walsh Papers.

_____. Letter to Superior, Sister Marie-Philippine, Parish of St. Antoine de Padoue, Jackman, Maine, 27 March 1912. Archives, Sisters of St. Joseph of Lyons (CSJ), France, Provincialate and Christian Life Center, Winslow, Maine.

_____.Letter, to T. B. Walker. Roman Catholic Church, Diocese of Portland (Maine), Library, Louis S. Walsh Papers.

Ward, Edmund. *An Account of the St John and Its Tributary Rivers and Lakes*. Fredericton (New Brunswick): Sentinel Office, 1841.

Washington, George. Letter to the Continental Congress, 21 September 1775. Papers of the Continental Congress, M 247, Roll 186, Item 169, vol. 1, pp. 44–60.

_____. Manifesto: *Aux Peuples de Canada / To the Inhabitants of Canada*, 7 September 1775. George Washington to Canadian Citizens, September 7, 1775. George Washington Papers, Library of Congress, 1741–1799: Series 4, General Correspondence, 1697–1799, p. 8.

Waters, John. "Family, Inheritance, and Migration in Colonial New England: The Evidence from Guildford, Connecticut." *William and Mary Quarterly* 3, no. XXXXIX (January 1982), pp. 64–86.

Waterville Morning Sentinel. (Journal, Waterville, Maine).

Weber & Gilmore. *Aroostook Road from Military Road*. Maps, field notes, and instructions, 1831, nos. 5–12–24 a & b and 5–12–25. Maine State Archives, Augusta, Maine.

Weil, François. *Les Franco-Américains, 1860–1980*. Tours (France): Mame Imprimeurs, 1989; Paris: Éditions Belin, 1989.

Weinberg, Sydney. "The Treatment of Women in Immigration History: A Call For Change." *Journal of American Ethnic History* (summer 1992).

_____. *The World of Our Mothers: Lives of Jewish Immigrant Women*. Chapel Hill: North Carolina University Press, 1988.

Whitney, Richard. Interviewed by, Dorothy Blanchard, 23 November 1991, Dexter, Maine. Notes held by Dorothy Blanchard, Newcastle, Maine.

Whittemore, Edwin. *The Centennial History of Waterville, Kennebec County, Maine*. Waterville, Maine: Executive Committee of the Centennial Celebration. 1902.

Williams, Ruel and others. Letter to the Secretary of War, 11 October 1837. National Archives, Washington, D.C.

Williamson, Joseph. "The Proposed Province of New Ireland." *Collections of the Maine Historical Society*. Vol. 7. Bath: Maine Historical Society, 1876, pp. 199–206.

Williamson, William. *The History of the State of Maine*. 2 vols. Hallowell, Maine: Glazier, Masters, 1832.

Willis, William, ed. *Journal of the Rev. Thomas Smith and the Rev. Samuel Deane*. Portland: Joseph Bailey, 1849.

Winter, Florence Small. *The Kennebec–Chaudière "Arnold" Trail*. Augusta (Maine): Printed by the Kennebec Journal, 1978.

Winthrop, John. In *Winthrop's Journal*, vol. 2, James Hosmer, ed. New York: Charles Scribner's Sons, 1908.

Wolkovich-Valkavicius, W. "The Ku Klux Klan in the Nashoba Valley." *Historical Journal of Massachusetts* 18, no. 1 (1990).

Wolman, Leo. *Growth of American Trade Unions, 1888–1923*. New York: National Bureau of Economic Research, 1936.

Wood, Edward. Letter to Stephen Lee, 30 October 1902. Franklin Company Papers. The Franklin Company held these papers in Lewiston, Maine, in the 1980s.

Woodbury, Kenneth, Jr. "An Incident Between the French Canadians and the Irish in the Diocese of Maine in 1906." *New England Quarterly* 40, June 1967, pp. 260–69.

Woodward, Kathleen. "Inventing Generational Models: Psychoanalysis, Feminism, Literature." *Figuring Age: Women, Bodies, Generations*, Kathleen Woodward, ed. Bloomington: Indiana University Press, 1999, pp. 149–68.

Woodward, Kathleen. "Inventing Generational Models: Psychoanalysis, Feminism, Literature." *Figuring Age: Women, Bodies, Generations,* Kathleen Woodward, ed. Bloomington: Indiana University Press, pp. 149–68.

Wright, Carroll. *The Canadian French in New England*. Boston: Rand Avery & Company, Printers to the Commonwealth, 1882.

_____. *Uniform Hours of Labor: Twelfth Annual Report of the Massachusetts Bureau of Statistics of Labor*. Boston: Bureau of Statistics of Labor, State of Massachusetts, 1881.

Wynn, Graeme. "New Brunswick Parish Boundaries in the pre-1861 Census Years." *Acadiensis* VI (spring 1977), pp. 95–105.

_____. *Timber Colony: A Historical Geography of Early Nineteenth-Century New Brunswick*. Toronto: University of Toronto Press, 1981.

Yans-McLaughlin, Virginia. *Family and Community: Italian Immigrants in Buffalo, 1880–1930*. Ithaca: Cornell University Press, 1977.

Yetter, Luann. "Protector of the Past: Volunteer Oversees Franco-American Heritage Collection." Franco-American Collection, University of Southern Maine, Lewiston-Auburn College, Lewiston, Maine.

Young, Brian. *A Short History of Quebec*. Ontario: Copp Clark Pitman, Limited, 1988.

Yu, Eui-Young; and Earl Phillips, eds. *Korean Women in Transition: At Home and Abroad*. Los Angeles: Center for Korean-American and Korean Studies, California State University, 1987.

Yule, Patrick. *Remarks on the Disputed North-Western Boundary of New Brunswick, Bordering on the United States of North* America. London: J. Ridgeway, 1838.

INDEX

O

P

Q

R

S

V

W

X

Y